A Voice

The sequel to *If I Should Speak*

A Novel

Umm Zakiyyah

A Voice

The Sequel to *If I Should Speak*
A Novel
By Umm Zakiyyah

ISBN: 0970766726

Library of Congress Control Number:
2003115856

**Copies of this book can be ordered online at
www.al-walaa.com
or by calling Toll-Free 1(866)550-7839**

Quotations from the Qur'an are taken from
Yusuf Ali translations.

Published by:
Al-Walaa Publications College Park, MD USA
Printed in the USA

*All characters and events in this book are fictional, and any
resemblance to real persons or incidents is coincidental.*

All quotes from real people or books have been cited in the footnotes
as such.

Acknowledgements

"Those who are not grateful to people are not grateful to God."
—Prophet Muhammad, peace be upon him

First, I thank God for giving me the opportunity to write this book and touch the lives of so many. I thank my parents, Muhammad and Fareedah, for laying the foundation of my faith in God and instilling in me the determination to make a difference. Their daily lessons, advice, and guidance will always be invaluable to me.

I thank my sister Najla, my "twin," for always being there and eagerly listening to my stories, even when I didn't know what would happen next. Thanks for the late nights, the early mornings, and all the times you encouraged me and made me believe in my pen.

I thank Shakirah and Rasheed and all my brothers and sisters for their advice and support. I thank Faiza of Business Health Solutions for going over and beyond the call of duty in bringing this work to fruition. I thank my students and community members for their enthusiasm, ideas, and inspiration. I also thank Sakina Productions and all those whose prayers were with me at all times.

Last, but definitely not least, I thank my husband for being my backbone through it all. Certainly, none of this would be possible without his support, patience, and advice along the way. May God reward you all.

Dedication

For those who have submitted and those who have not, but will.

One

Euphoria. The feeling was poetic in the way it swept over her like a gentle breeze. The coolness enveloped her. Became her. Remained. This Tamika pondered as she placed a book in the cardboard box on her bed, the motion slowed as the realization came to her and gave name to what she had been unable to.

A month. It had only been a month since she recited the words that transformed her—redefined her and gave her life. She hadn't expected to feel anything but relief. Because the decision to become Muslim wasn't really a decision at all. It was the silencing of an incessant nagging that would not quiet on its own. Reciting the words was merely a formal confirmation of what she already knew—what she had somehow always known.

Surrender. That was the definition of Islam itself, she'd been told. And how well it described what converting to Islam actually was.

"Is that *you?*"

Aminah's voice startled her in its abruptness. It wasn't the first time Tamika was reminded suddenly of her roommate's presence. They spent their evenings studying in the same small university apartment and slept in the same room each night, yet, still, Tamika often forgot her roommate was there. It was a human flaw, she supposed, to adapt to routine so profoundly that one eventually grew unconscious of it.

"What?" Tamika echoed Aminah's laughter as she turned away from the box to look at her roommate.

Aminah's ash brown hair fell over her shoulder in a heap as she bent over to pick up the photograph that had fallen to the floor. Her ponytail fell back in place as she stood, and her green eyes widened. She grinned as she pulled the picture closer to get a better look.

Self-conscious, Tamika too grinned, wondering what Aminah was looking at. Holding a book, Tamika walked over to where her roommate stood and peered over her shoulder at the picture. Aminah's thin pale thumb covered most of the right side of the photograph, but Tamika immediately recognized the scene. Tamika stood in front of her old high school building with her hands on her hips, leaning forward and sticking out her tongue playfully. It wasn't a flattering photograph, and Tamika had long planned to rip it up and throw it in the trash. She had tucked it in the back of one of her albums and forgotten about it.

"Oh that?" She waved her hand dismissively and walked back to her bed, a smile still on her face as she shook her head and continued packing.

It was the first week of May, two weeks before summer vacation, and the roommates had decided to pack early in preparation to go home. Tamika could hardly believe the end of the year was actually upon them. Only a month before, time seemed to crawl. The night of the Spring Formal still taunted her, and she longed to escape it. And home would be her only refuge, or so she hoped.

Tamika should have known the year would not be an easy one. Living with Jennifer could have told her that.

It was true that Tamika and Jennifer were unlikely roommates from the start. Tamika was an African-American raised in a Milwaukee city home. Her mother was the head of household, and Tamika never knew her father. College was a word spoken on television and in movies, read about in books, but its reality didn't exist for Tamika's family. The system. Racism. Inner-city schools. There were a host of excuses why their heads hit the glass ceiling before they could enter the room. Latonya had been their first hope. She was an honor roll student and had even begun college coursework while she was still in high school. There was talk about her testing out of school and going to college full time. But Latonya had something stronger pulling her. Their mother told her to be careful. To watch herself. To not let them boys sweet-talk her.

When Latonya became pregnant and insisted on keeping the baby, even if it meant giving up college—and school, she became a nonperson in the family. Thelma's standoff with her oldest daughter culminated in Latonya being kicked out of the house. There was no empathy for a heinous crime as teenage pregnancy, even if it was the same one that had kept Thelma out of college herself.

The responsibility should have fallen on Philip's shoulders. He was Latonya's twin brother, a year older than Tamika. But he and school were always at odds, and a *C* on his report card was counted as a gift from God himself. Thelma's battle with her son was to keep him off the streets and out of jail. If she could win just that, she would be a grateful mother.

Tamika felt the weight of Thelma's expectation before it was placed on her. And she welcomed it—at least initially. When it was finally her sole responsibility to honor the family, Tamika was obliged. She had always been Thelma's favorite, the amenable child. It was a twinge of envy that Tamika felt when Latonya, with all her good grades and college classes, was getting all the attention. Tamika had good grades too and was on the honor roll, but her success was overshadowed by her sister's. With her sister estranged, Tamika had the opportunity to prove herself as Tamika Douglass the individual instead of Latonya Douglass's little sister.

Tamika's scholarship to college was the first milestone in her quest to be the first in the family to hold a college degree. It didn't hurt that Streamsdale University was respected for its high academic standards. When another less prominent college offered her a full scholarship, she turned it down, though the staff and student body were predominantly African-American and despite the fact that she had her heart set on it since most of her friends would go there. Instead, she would fulfill her mother's wishes by attending Streamsdale in a small, quiet, white suburban town named after the school.

Her only solace was that the college town was less than an hour from Atlanta, a city coined the Black Mecca, and it was this succor that gave her the strength to live so far from home.

Reality hit Tamika almost immediately after she arrived at Streamsdale. It was in the middle of Freshman Orientation when she realized that she never wanted to go to college. Her dream was to become a famous singer. It was her mother who convinced her that singing was an impossible career and that she would be nothing in this world without a college degree.

The idea of college had always frightened Tamika. Anything that represented the "real world" gave her anxiety. She excelled in high school, she reasoned, only because she was sheltered from reality. The principal of the school was black. Many of her teachers were black. And more than eighty percent of the students were black. Television and books were her only windows into the world of vices like racism and sexism. Somehow she had come to accept that those things were "the past," and any evidence of them existing today were rare, perpetrated only by an ignorant, uneducated person who would shout at the television between sips of whiskey and had little, if any, social status.

It was at work that she realized racism and sexism were bigger and uglier than she imagined. Pay differentials. Favoritism. Mistreatment. They began to define her days until she imagined that bigotry was the heartbeat of American society. The world around her became foreign. Dangerous. Trust was felt only when accompanied by apprehension. She was terrified. Of work, coworkers, and, finally, herself.

How did she fit into the perverse puzzle? Or did she fit at all? What did it take to actually make it in the world? If propriety, honesty, and hard work weren't the keys to success, what were?

Ironically, high school, which was supposed to prepare her for the real world, became a refuge from it. She was afraid to graduate though she anticipated it. She was petrified of going to college though she worked hard for it. Eventually, she was terrified of success itself. What would it mean if she actually did succeed? Perhaps Philip was right. To hell with the system. To hell with life. To hell with success. Why go to school if society gave you rules it didn't play by? Why study if success depended on who you knew and not who you were? *If you wanna make it in the world, you gotta do what they do*, was his motto—and that was whatever it took to survive.

Tamika initially counted it as luck, though she now knew better, that her roommate during freshman year was black in a predominantly white school. Similar backgrounds, fears, and reasons for coming to college made Makisha and Tamika friends from the start. They did nothing alone. They ate lunch together, studied together, went to church together, and partied together. Friday and Saturday nights were their favorite nights of the week, when they drove to Atlanta, where there was never a dearth of parties to choose from. Tamika's freshman year was so fulfilling that it was deceptive. When she returned to Streamsdale for her sophomore year, nothing had prepared her for what was to come.

It was both a sense of sadness and joy Tamika had felt when Makisha's name was randomly selected to have a single that year. Tamika was sad because they could no longer be roommates, but she was happy for her best friend. It was every college student's dream to live alone, a privilege enjoyed only by resident advisors and those wealthy enough to afford off-campus apartments. As Makisha decided how she would set up her room, Tamika grew anxious about living in hers. Who would be her roommate? Would she be black? If so, would they be friends? If not, *could* they be friends?

Her anxiety inspired an array of roommate possibilities in her mind. Korean. Indian. Spanish. West African. The possibility of living with a white student was in the back of her mind, but, for some reason, she never imagined it would actually happen. The tension between black and white roommates was so strong that she imagined the school sanctioned the arrangement only out of pure moral—or quota—obligation.

Tamika was just as taken aback as Jennifer when they met that first day. But they handled it with dutiful affability. They weren't surprised when they had their share of disagreements. All roommates did. But when their disagreements grew dangerously tense, Tamika had doubts about their ability to live together.

It was a Wednesday evening in February when their contempt for each other, which was usually displayed in verbal altercations, finally culminated in a physical fight. Jennifer's screams summoned the resident advisor to the room just as Tamika pressed Jennifer's arms against the floor. Despite the blood stained scratches on Tamika's face and protruding hair earned from Jennifer's scratching and yanking, Mandy saw Tamika as the aggressor. It was Mandy's duty to report the case, Tamika knew, but was it her duty to testify against her in a Conduct Board hearing when she hadn't even seen the fight?

Tamika was infuriated as she listened to Jennifer and Mandy's testimony the following evening. She couldn't imagine any of the board members taking this squabble seriously, let alone entertain such a ridiculous charge as physical assault. When she was informed of the board's decision the next morning, she was stunned. Guilty? Were they joking? She wanted to laugh, but the vicious irony of it numbed her in disbelief. She had only restrained Jennifer's arms and pushed her in an attempt to protect herself from attack. That Jennifer hit her head, causing the bleeding, wasn't her fault. And it definitely wasn't a case of assault. At most, it was a fight. At least, it was self-defense. Apparently, the board disagreed.

The hardest part of coming to terms with the charge was that Dr. Sanders, her religion professor, was on the board. He was the first African-American professor she had at the university, and he was also her favorite. How could he? Was he like the African-Americans she heard about, who only wanted a piece of the American pie and didn't care if they stepped on their own along the way? It was only time and necessity that allowed her to move on, even if she would never get over it. But at the time, she was hardly appreciative of being forced to move out of her room.

No one wanted to live in Streamsdale University Apartments except those who had at least three other friends they could live with. Though the idea of living in an apartment was appealing to students, privacy and peace of mind were more important. Sleeping in a room, even if a room in an apartment, with three other students wasn't a popular choice for students. Most students, if they could not afford an off-campus apartment, settled for the traditional dormitory arrangement. At least then they would live with only one other person. That way, the chances of roommate tension, if not eliminated, were lessened. As a result, the university apartments were comprised of mostly two types of students. Really good friends who handpicked each other, and unfortunate students forced to live with as many as three strangers—strangers forced to live together because of roommate fallouts.

It was a Monday, less than a week after the physical assault verdict, when Tamika met her first new roommate. The young woman emerged from the bathroom a few minutes after Tamika arrived in the apartment. The student was tall and slender and wore a black bathrobe with a matching towel neatly wrapped around her head, accenting her smooth tan complexion. When she smiled, she revealed dimples that illuminated the beauty of her face. It was then that Tamika recognized her. An inquiry confirmed that the young woman was indeed Dee, the student who was not only known for her academic prowess but who won almost every beauty contest and talent show she entered.

Dee's beauty, like her singing voice, was second to none. Tamika and nearly all Streamsdale students and residents of Atlanta and its suburbs admired her and were proud to be connected to her in some way. Tamika had met Dee in person only once, when she congratulated her after a show. She doubted that Dee would recall the encounter. Tamika was one in hundreds, if not thousands, of fans who eagerly awaited the opportunity to meet Dee personally and earn bragging rights. But unlike others, Tamika's desire to know Dee wasn't merely out of admiration. Dee was a role model for her. Dee had succeeded in the two most significant areas of Tamika's life. College and singing. Though Dee's prominence had not yet reached the level of fame, to her admirers, it made no difference. Dee was Dee. And that was more than anyone could say about herself.

As Tamika chatted with Dee the day she moved in, she realized that moving in the apartment wasn't a case of bad luck. God was giving her the opportunity of a lifetime. Finally, she didn't have to choose between her mother and herself. She could please her mother by continuing college and please herself by being a singer. And Dee was living proof.

Tamika had been so intoxicated by the friendly exchange with Dee that she momentarily forgot her circumstances. It was Dee's comment about another roommate that reminded Tamika that her dream come true wouldn't be without its thorns. Dee joked that Tamika, who had expressed that she was thinking of majoring in religion, would get along well with Aminah, her other roommate, who absolutely loved the subject. But Aminah's love of religion wasn't because she loved studying about it. She loved living it. As a Muslim.

Tamika's heart sank at the news. She wasn't expecting to live with a Muslim. She had come to accept that her roommates could be any race, and she had already mentally prepared herself for whatever that would mean. But somehow she imagined the variety of possibilities as one-dimensional. Racial. It was an epiphany she felt right then. The school wasn't full of Christians. The possibility of living with a heathen had never entered her mind. Though she knew little of Muslims and had never met one, she knew enough to know she didn't want one as a roommate.

Dee was smiling as she shared this little bit of news. But Tamika was not. And Tamika wasn't smiling when Dee told her that she and Aminah would get along fine. There were two other students who had lived with them at the beginning of the year, Dee informed Tamika, but after having "enough of Aminah," they moved out. Tamika detected a hint of sarcasm in Dee's voice as she assured her that she and Aminah would be fine. Tamika took it as Dee's way of warning her. Aminah wasn't only a Muslim, Dee told her, but a strict one. The word Muslim itself was synonymous with extremism in Tamika's mind. If a person could be a strict extremist, the results were terrifying.

That wouldn't be Tamika's last bit of news for the day. Dee went on to tell Tamika that she and Aminah not only grew up together but were actually good friends. What a talented model and singer from Cuba had in common with an extremist Muslim, likely from the deserts of Arabia, was beyond Tamika. But a moment later she knew.

"And it doesn't bother you that she's Muslim?" Tamika had asked.

The reply to Tamika's question had been a half smile and a raised eyebrow. "If Aminah was here, she'd lecture me if she heard you say that."

Tamika creased her forehead in confusion. "Why?"

"Because I'm Muslim too."

Had it been only three months? It was hard to believe. So much had happened since then that it seemed implausible that such a brief period in life could hold so much. Dee was dead. Tamika was Muslim. And she and Aminah were friends.

But the events of the month before still cast a shadow on them. There was a gaping distance between them that no amount of laughter or words could bridge. Yet there was the euphoria.

The moment it enveloped her Tamika thought it was a coping mechanism. A sense of denial. A trick of the mind. To escape grief was to escape sobriety. But she now realized she was wrong.

When Tamika learned of Dee's death, a storm of emotions exploded. Anger. Suffocation. And a sense of betrayal. She was powerless to resist how the world became surreal. Dark. Ominous. And cruel.

Finally, she understood. Before then she had only known. But knowledge and understanding were rarely one.

Tamika had sat next to Makisha and listened to Dee's eulogies in the chapel the Sunday after the car accident, but it was her own life that distressed her as she listened to the students recount Dee's. Tamika was in the passenger seat when the car rammed into the driver's side and killed Dee, yet she was home two nights later with nothing to speak of except a weak body that needed lots of rest.

Dee's beautiful voice rang throughout the chapel as her songs were played during the memorial. Tamika felt tears of shame glisten in her eyes as the enchanting, melodious songs harangued her. When grief overtook her during the eulogies, it was not Dee's death that grieved her, but her own.

From the moment Tamika first saw Dee on stage, there was a bond between them. The bond wasn't distant like admiration of one unreachable, but one felt in the soul. When they finally met, though a mere handshake and a forgotten moment for Dee, Tamika's exhilaration was overwhelming. Tamika was restless to know her better and could only dream of the honor of saying she actually did. She went to every concert she could and never tired of listening to Dee sing. Though Tamika could make an exhaustive list of famous singers she liked, none came close to evoking the fondness she felt for Dee.

The whys and hows were never asked for the emotions of the heart. Adoration and love were miracles, small gifts from God. If there was more to them, it was more principled to avoid delving into the unknown. The essence of the heart's beauty was its mystery. To uncover it was impossible, and seeking to unveil it was a crime against life itself.

But perhaps Tamika had it all wrong.

The video screen in the chapel had shown Dee laughing and joking during a beauty contest, and Tamika had caught a glimpse of Dee's eyes. It was only for a brief moment that Dee looked into the camera, yet that had been enough. The glance nearly numbed Tamika, and her heart made her body too heavy for the bench. It was pity she felt for Dee at that moment, and it was agonizing to withstand. When tears spilled from her eyes, it was a selfish grief. It was a grief of regret. A grief of submission. A grief over her own death.

Life was uncanny in its symbolism. And its effect could only be felt, never explained. There were some words the tongue could never speak and only the heart could understand. It was this Tamika realized during the memorial. It was a feeling too powerful to escape and too personal to share. Tears were the only testimony to her revelation. The tears of others only made her experience more impossible to deny. And more tangible in its embrace.

She was right when she suspected that being placed in a room with Dee was too monumental to be attributed to coincidence or luck, Tamika realized as she sat in the chapel. Coincidence had no higher plan, and luck did not exist. Dee—Durrah—had fascinated her, inspired her, because she represented Tamika herself. Dee was the part of Tamika that Tamika had yet to taste. But like any ephemeral pleasure of the world, the sweetness of fame was only tasted, never relished. Yet even the taste was unfulfilling because it didn't emanate from within. It depended solely on the eyes and tongues of others, and one no longer belonged to herself. For the famous, fame was more an appetite than anything satiating in itself. But the desire for the nonexistent drove both the famous and their wanna-bes nearly insane in the search.

That destructive desire killed Dee. And Dee's death obliterated it from Tamika's heart.

Tamika's mourning during the service was evoked by a painful realization of self. She had been born more than eighteen years ago, yet she hadn't known life until then. As a Christian, she was "born again," and for the first time, she knew what that meant. She had thought Jesus died for her, and now he really did. No longer was he her savior. No longer was he God's son. No longer was he God.

It wasn't volition that inspired the transformation. Entering Islam was merely accepting an appointment from God. That night when she returned from the chapel and found Aminah in the apartment, she knew what she had to do. Reciting the words was so monumental, so moving that her entire body felt the power of each word. With each utterance her body lightened, her heart eased, and serenity enveloped her until she felt she could float. The relief was intoxicating, and at that moment, she could only weep. The moment was one of mourning. They had lost Dee. And it was painful that Dee wasn't there to witness, to join in. Yet it was one of celebration, of exuberance, and its enjoyment was strengthened in the warm embrace of Aminah's arms.

Upon Aminah's instruction, Tamika had taken the ritual bath, *ghusl*, which Muslims performed to remove ceremonial impurities. The bath was a spiritual experience for Tamika. It was as if she were washing away her past. She was a new person. Born again.

When she stepped from the bath, she felt a cleanliness that penetrated the soul. And there was a powerful feeling that lingered and soothed. The feeling was ambiguous in its nature but acute in its effect. Tamika couldn't deny the phenomenal way it inspired her to move on. A sense of sadness lingered but never enough to weigh her down with distress. Islam had given her new life, and it was with eagerness she accepted the gift.

Yet Tamika, like Aminah, was still adjusting to life without Dee. The apartment carried an air of melancholy that seemed to hover like a dark cloud over each room. Dee's furniture sat lifeless, untouched, etched in loneliness. Neither dared to suggest it be removed. Neither dared to move it herself.

It wasn't an easy task for either of them, but they somehow moved on. They attended classes and maintained decent grades. Presently, they were embarking upon final exams, and it was only a matter of time before they would be set free.

They studied in the apartment mostly. It was difficult to study anywhere else. For students, the presence of Tamika or Aminah was taken as an opportunity to ask about Dee. The students meant no harm, this Tamika understood. But constant reminders of their loss were too much to bear, especially at the end of school.

"That was when I was like fifteen years old," Tamika said, hoping to downplay the significance of the picture. Still grinning, she lifted her gaze to her roommate as she placed more books in the box. Aminah was facing Tamika now and walking toward her, still amused by the picture. Her green eyes sparkled in laughter, reminding Tamika of the moment she met her. Pale skin and green eyes, wearing Arab dress. And Dee had told her that Aminah was black.

Aminah burst out laughing. "You look ridiculous!"

"Thanks for the compliment."

Friendly sarcasm was their way of bonding. For Tamika it was healing. Perhaps it was soothing because it assured her that there was more to Aminah than being Muslim and teaching those who were not.

"Anytime." Aminah set the photograph on Tamika's bed and paused as she noticed a stack of photo albums next to the box Tamika was packing. She started to lift one then hesitated. "You mind?"

"So long as you don't laugh at me. I was a lot different then."

"Different how?" Aminah eyed Tamika playfully as she toted the large album to her bed, where she sat down and opened it, inviting herself to indulge.

Tamika grinned. "Different different."

Placing the last book in the box, Tamika picked up the packaging tape and tore off a strip, using clinched teeth. She taped the box closed and smoothed the surface with her palm.

"Is this you?"

Tamika glanced up as Aminah held up the album for her to see. "Yeah." Tamika walked over to the dresser and pulled a drawer open. She tossed things aside as she searched for a permanent marker.

"Wow. *BarakAllaahufeek*[1]."

Unsure how to respond, Tamika smiled. She removed the marker from the drawer and shut it. She never knew how to take compliments. They always made her self-conscious. She doubted that it was correct to say thank you. It was God who created her, and she didn't think of herself as attractive. She was average. Not ugly, but nothing great. Thelma often said Tamika was the most beautiful child in the world. But mother's opinions didn't count. Yet Tamika couldn't help feeling proud whenever her mother described her. Almond brown eyes. Honey brown skin, soft to the touch. And a smile that made her face glow and brighten the whole room. It was poetic and motherly. Tamika could only laugh. She only wondered how much of it was true.

"Look at you!" As Aminah laughed, Tamika grinned from where she stood, not bothering to walk over and see the picture. Still smiling, she leaned forward and wrote "BOOKS" on the box.

It was only in the past month that Tamika saw the similarities between Aminah and Dee. Before becoming Muslim, Tamika saw Aminah and Dee as opposites, and it was difficult to imagine they had anything in common except their families' religion. Dee was funny, outgoing and down-to-earth, and Aminah was dull, self-righteous, and took life much more seriously than it deserved. Aminah intimidated Tamika with her need to always be right, even when others didn't care either way. Tamika was especially irritated with Aminah's nagging of Dee, whether to pray and cover in Islamic garb or to respect Islam. Why couldn't she just worry about herself?

It was amazing how differently things looked from the other side. No, she didn't agree with everything Aminah did or how she did it. But she did understand her better. Tamika could only wonder how she would have dealt with Dee had she been in Aminah's shoes.

The room was silent, and for several minutes the only sounds that could be heard were Aminah turning the pages of Tamika's photo album and Tamika packing another box.

"Is this your mom?"

Aminah's voice interrupted Tamika's thoughts, and she glanced up from the box.

"Who?"

Aminah lifted the album so Tamika could see, but the photograph was too small. Tamika placed the stack of CDs in the box and walked over to her roommate before standing at Aminah's shoulder to get a better look.

"Yeah."

"She looks like she's really nice."

Tamika smiled, resisting the urge to roll her eyes. She decided against being harsh in her honesty. "She is sometimes."

---

[1] Literally, "May God bless you," often said when giving a compliment or when praising someone.

"Sometimes? I'm sure she's a sweetheart."

Tamika sat next to Aminah on the bed, rewarding herself with a break from packing. "Yeah, she is. I guess it's just that I know my mother."

"Oh, don't we all."

Aminah studied the rest of the pictures on the page in silence, and Tamika became lost in her thoughts. There was so much more she could have said, but she withheld. Her gaze was on the photograph of her mother, but her mind was elsewhere.

How would it be when she went home? Would her mother accept her? Would they get along? The questions exhausted her, and she wished she could skip summer break.

Tamika had talked to her mother several times since Dee's death and sought comfort in Thelma's voice. It was soothing to listen to someone who loved her giving advice in hard times. She shared with her mother how difficult it was without Dee, how she had not sung a single song since the accident. It was as if she lost her voice and felt no inclination to find it. Her mother listened patiently to her struggles, and Tamika didn't hold back. She told her mother of her ups and downs, her good days and bad days, and how everything in life looked different. But she had yet to tell her mother of her conversion to Islam.

There were moments when Tamika felt she should tell her, especially when they had conversations about how Dee's death affected her life. But when she imagined how it would break her mother's heart, her spirit weakened her into silence.

Tamika was her mother's pride and joy. In many ways, she was her only child. Latonya and Philip made it clear that their relationship with Thelma was nothing more than blood and circumstance. No other familial rights would be enjoyed. They viewed their mother as selfish, heartless, and domineering, and they were not shy to express it, even to her. They resented that she turned her back on Latonya in her most difficult time, and it pained them more that her selfishness didn't break enough to be a part of her grandchild's life. They blamed Thelma for their father's absence although this was never expressed in words. That would cut too deep, even for them. It was easier to live without uttering his name, even if only to place blame where blame was due. Tamika knew what they felt. She could see it in their eyes, catch hints in their words, and sense it in their ways.

Tamika felt caught in the crossfire. She saw what they saw, but she had another perspective. Thelma's selfishness was her strong love for her children. She wanted them to do their best without making the mistakes she made. Her heartlessness was her determination to stand up for right and not be swayed by emotions. And her domineeringness was her violent love for her children, pushing her to protect them from life's painful falls. But her siblings disagreed.

To them, Tamika was siding with their mother against them. To Tamika, there were no sides. Each of them—Latonya, Philip, and her mother—represented a part of her. Her mother was her heart and her siblings her self. One without the other bore no use in life. How could she give up her heart and be left with mere flesh and blood? And how could she choose a beating heart with no body to enclose it and give it life? What they perceived as warring sides, she perceived as the tearing apart of herself. There were no winners in the fight. The fight itself doomed them all to loss before any blows were felt.

Aminah turned the page. "Who are they?"

Tamika's eyes followed Aminah's gaze. "Latonya and Philip."

"Your sister and brother?"

"Yeah."

There was a brief silence. "When was this?"

"A couple of years ago, after my graduation."

"Who's the little girl?"

"Nikki, my niece. Well, her real name's Nicole."

Aminah giggled. "She's cute."

Tamika forced a smile.

"How old is she?"

"She must be about four now."

"You don't know?" Aminah eyed her teasingly.

"I only saw her at my graduation." Tamika forced laughter, concealing her hurt. "I was lucky to even see her then."

Aminah turned the page silently, avoiding eye contact with her roommate. She didn't want Tamika to feel obligated to explain.

"I mean," Tamika's voice interrupted the silence as she sought answers more for herself than her roommate, "sometimes I wanna know where Tonya is 'cause I worry about her a lot. I feel really bad about everything."

"Why's that?" Aminah sensed Tamika needed to talk.

"It's only because of my mom that I don't talk to her anymore." She forced laughter. "It doesn't make any sense."

"What about Philip?"

"I haven't talked to him since my graduation either, but not because of my mom. He's just doing his own thing. I really think he just resents how our mother did Tonya when she got pregnant. And so he kind of just split, if you know what I mean."

"Does he call you?"

Tamika shook her head. "He doesn't know my number or anything. Once I went to college, that was pretty much the end of keepin' in touch. Unless he called home to get my information." She forced laughter. "And I'm pretty sure he ain't tryin' to do that."

Aminah stared at the album thoughtfully. "But you should try and keep in touch with them."

Tamika sucked her teeth. "I know, but that's pretty much impossible now."

"Maybe it's not. If you look 'em up, you'll probably find them. Maybe not as soon as you like, but they have to be somewhere."

"I suppose." Tamika reached forward and turned the page. "I guess I pretty much figured if they wanna talk, they know where I am."

"I thought they didn't know."

"They don't know my number, but they know I go to Streamsdale. I told 'em at graduation."

"Maybe they don't know."

"They know. It's not like my family's got money to send me anywhere else."

"But Streamsdale's expensive."

"I have a scholarship."

Aminah nodded. "Still, you never know."

"Maybe not. But if they weren't sure, they could call the school."

"Yeah, but you know how that goes. Most schools don't give out your information to anyone, even if they claim to be family. It's standard policy." She studied the pictures on the page. "You could just call them."

Tamika stood and headed toward her bed. "Maybe you're right. But I'll worry about that when I'm graduating from college, you know, for some major event." She laughed as she sorted through the books and CDs stacked on her bed. "Otherwise, they'd be like, 'What are you callin' me for?'"

There was a long pause, and Aminah closed the photo album. "What makes you think they don't wanna talk to you?"

Tamika was silent as she picked up a stack of books and placed them in a box. "Honestly, I don't know. I guess it's just that since everything happened, I could tell Tonya resented that my mom favored me, telling me don't be like her and stuff like that. So I guess Tonya was like, whatever, to both of us."

"What about Philip?"

"He's just siding with Tonya and decided to leave Mom and 'Momma's girl' alone, if you now what I mean."

Aminah nodded, a reflective expression on her face.

"But I don't get that," Tamika said, shaking her head and forcing laughter. "I didn't do anything. The whole time everything happened, I didn't say a word. So I don't know how I got branded a nonperson in their lives. But if they wanna be left alone, fine with me."

It was a half-hour later that Tamika sat on the couch and opened a book to study for her exams.

"Tamika?"

Tamika looked up to find Aminah approaching her, carrying a chemistry book in her hand. Aminah appeared reluctant to go on, and Tamika cringed. She hoped it was nothing serious.

"You know, about your brother and sister."

"Mm, hm." Tamika nodded as her gaze fell back to her book.

"You should try to get in touch with them."

"I'll think about it."

"No, I mean, for real."

Sensing this was important to Aminah, Tamika met her gaze.

Aminah sighed, apparently unsure how to explain. "You have to keep ties with your family."

"They should keep ties with me."

"No, I mean, because you're Muslim."

Tamika gathered her eyebrows and waited for an explanation.

"Keeping ties with family is one of the most important things in Islam." Aminah's voice was gentle, and Tamika could tell she was trying to be nice.

"Is it like a sin or something if you don't?"

Aminah nodded regretfully. "Yeah, it is."

Tamika let out a long sigh. Momentarily, she forgot about her exams. Her gaze lifted to the vertical blinds, whose slight openings gave a sketchy view of the trees and grass. The view was normally soothing, intoxicating in the calm it evoked. But right then Tamika felt detached and found herself reflecting on the euphoria that was fading inside.

It was the dread of facing her mother that made her realize something had changed. When she first became Muslim, nothing mattered but Islam itself. She felt as if she could conquer the world. Perhaps it was the same feeling she had felt in high school when the prospect of college was far away. But now college was her refuge and home the real world.

The euphoria was replaced by a sense of self-determination, and for that she couldn't complain. But the self-determination was just that, a determination experienced alone. How could she make her mother understand or, at the very least, accept her change? How could she convince her mother that this was something she wanted, needed, for herself? How could she tell her mother that Islam, not Christianity, was what she wanted in life?

Fear. That was what now swept over her. And it wasn't like a gentle breeze. The feeling was burdensome, nearly tortuous in its effect. She hated the idea of hurting her mother, but she couldn't help what her heart believed. Facing her mother was inevitable, yet she feared she was unable to.

And now her brother and sister. Did she have to face them too?

For more than two years, Tamika had tried to shut the thought of her brother and sister out of her mind. She contented herself with life without them. She put a mental barrier between her and them, and it was this that allowed her to move on. Whenever thoughts of them entered her mind, she pushed them away. But still, her love for them lingered in her heart. There was no barrier strong enough to block what she felt.

But she didn't want to think of her brother and sister right then. It was too much to bear. Aminah was right, that much she knew. She needed to get back in touch. But her mind was consumed with the approaching summer vacation. Facing her mother was enough to think about. She didn't need the added stress.

Aminah started to say more but decided against it and a moment later walked away. Tamika watched her roommate enter the bedroom. Even if she wanted to, she couldn't be angry with Aminah. She admired her a great deal. Aminah lost her childhood friend, and still she was strong. Dee's death couldn't have hurt Tamika more than it hurt her. Aminah and Dee grew up together and were best friends. They shared memories that Tamika would never know. That Aminah was able to keep going was amazing, and Tamika could only pray she could do the same.

There were times when Tamika didn't feel like hearing Aminah, but it was her own fear that inspired this reaction. What Aminah said about Islam always made sense, and Tamika didn't always want to make sense. Aminah wasn't perfect, but there was a glow about her, a glow that seemed to emanate from the heart. Tamika recognized it as Aminah's sincere commitment to Islam.

There was something about all Muslims that distinguished them from other people. Tamika had noticed this before she was Muslim herself. It was as if Muslims carried with them the essence of spirituality, and others could only hope for a glimmer of it. Tamika had heard that Muslims sought to be godlike in their striving against sin. People were born in sin, she was told, and it was futile for Muslims to deny this basic truth. But she now knew better because she was seeing for herself. Muslims viewed sin more as an inclination than a curse from birth. Human action, both good and bad, was a matter of choice. Prophet Muhammad, peace be upon him, taught that all of the children of Adam erred. But the best were those who repented. Sincere repentance, Tamika reflected. That was Muslims' distinguishing trait.

TWO

The last weeks of school passed too quickly. Tamika and Aminah had anticipated school ending, but when it did, they felt as if it had gone too fast. Even the dreaded final exams were over, and there was nothing left to do but face summer head-on.

It was a Wednesday afternoon in mid-May, and the campus was filling with moving trucks and students' families coming to take them home for the summer. Tamika's mother was unable to drive down to pick her up this year as she had done the year before. Things at work were tight, and Thelma felt it unwise to take off if it wasn't an emergency. People were being laid off, and although she had accrued both sick days and vacation leave, she would wait and use the hours when things loosened up a bit. Tamika told her mother not to worry. She would take a flight home and put her belongings in storage. She would offset the storage cost by finding a student to share the space. But school was over, and she had found no one. Normally, she would ask Makisha, but now that was impossible because Makisha rarely spoke to her after she accepted Islam. Tamika had asked Aminah what she thought she should do.

"You can just load your stuff into our moving truck."

Tamika laughed. "And then what? I still need somewhere to put it."

"We can just take it home with us."

Tamika stood in the center of the living room and placed her hands on her hips. The room still bore the attractive set up that it had when she first moved in and met Dee for the first time. But the once cozy atmosphere was gone. The dark gray couch with a black floral design still sat near the vertical blinds that overlooked the balcony. The jet-black coffee table with a glass top still sat in front of it, but the books and magazines had been removed and packed away in boxes. The tall shiny black vase with gold trim at the mouth still adorned the large peacock feathers that it held. The black and gray pillows that had once aligned the wall in a cozy design now sat in a pile next to the couch. The gold-trimmed black frames that enclosed poetry and famous quotes were now hidden in a cardboard box labeled "Wall Hangings" in the fading ink of a black permanent marker. The three-unit black shelves that had stored the books that led Tamika to Islam were now empty. As it had been when she first moved in, her stacks of boxes created an eye sore in the room.

Tamika bit her lower lip as her eyes traced the boxes stacked in front of the empty shelves that had once belonged to Dee. Her shoulder-length hair was pulled back in a bun, partially hidden under the navy blue and white bandana she had tied on her head before helping Aminah clean. Her pale yellow T-shirt was dingy from dusting and scrubbing floors. The lower front of it was damp with dishwater and was now tied in a heavy knot that hung at her waist. Her faded blue jeans clung to her hips, accenting her slim figure, and bore a ragged hole that exposed her left knee. But she was too tired and too sweaty to care. She considered the suggestion then shook her head. "I can't let you do that."

Aminah too surveyed the boxes, standing a few feet from Tamika. "We have space." One hand was on her hip, and the other moved when she spoke. Her hair was damp from the day's chores and was in a thick braid that hung a few inches down her back. The moisture gave her hair a dark rust color that seemed to fade into ash brown as it dried. She too wore a T-shirt, its faded black concealing evidence of the day's work. But her once-white sweatpants were proof enough.

"But—."

"What other choice do you have?" Aminah was unable to keep from smiling as she met her roommate's gaze.

"But I've been so much of a burden already."

"That's not true."

"I'll just pay for storage."

"You still need a moving truck."

"Then I can just, uh." Tamika's voice trailed off as she realized she barely had enough money for storage—even if she found someone to share the cost, let alone extra to rent a moving truck.

"Anyway, Sulayman'll kill me if I told him I let you go broke when he could've just put the stuff with mine."

Tamika grew silent at the mention of his name. There was still that awkwardness she felt about him, kindled by the contempt she had felt for him after reading his controversial articles in the school's paper *A Voice*. She had never hated a name in print as much as she did his. She saw him as a self-righteous, arrogant student who had nothing better to do than judge others. She spent much of her freshman year venting to Makisha and her mother about him. Both agreed that he had a lot of gall to write unapologetically about issues like fornication and drinking. Who did he think he was? God's messenger? Did he expect everyone to be perfect—like him? Never tempted to sin? Everyone wasn't so righteous as to resist the temptations of sex and alcohol. Tamika imagined that he and his sister were the only ones.

She had been Muslim for a month, and still there was a part of her that resented him. Tamika knew her feelings were unjustly critical, but his words had opened up wounds that she had hoped to heal. She had made many mistakes before coming to college and had sought redemption through Christ. She dedicated herself to the church and finally became saved. With a new spiritual awareness, she preferred to forget about who she used to be and define herself by who she was. But his words were vivid reminders of what she had left behind.

Caught up in the social life of high school, she hadn't seen herself drowning. Parties and clubs were regular scenes for her, and they were always filled with alcohol, marijuana, and good-looking men. She dressed the part, played the part, and eventually became the part. She partied, drank, and did whatever everyone else did. And finally, as a cruel climax to her degenerate life, she became involved with a young man who was known for crushing hearts. It was a harsh introduction to the world of men. He would be the first and last boyfriend she had. Scarred by the experience, she turned to the church and vowed to give her life to God. When she came to college, she wanted to forget about her past sins. She attended church regularly, gave up drinking, and lived a celibate life. She had continued to go to parties, but nothing more.

"If it's not a problem." Tamika no longer cared either way. If Sulayman was going to be the subject of the discussion, she couldn't participate. She wasn't in the mood.

Aminah sucked her teeth and waved her hand. "Girl, it's not a problem."

"Thanks." Tamika didn't know what else to say.

"He'll be here tonight to pick up the couches and shelves."

Most of the furniture had belonged to Dee, and Aminah thought it best to take those things out first. They were taking up the most space in the apartment—and their hearts.

"Maybe we can fit some of your stuff in there tonight."

Tamika nodded, glancing around the living room to survey what little things she still needed pack, only half-listening to Aminah talk.

Aminah started to return to the bedroom when she thought of something. She turned around to face Tamika. "When's your flight?"

"Friday morning."

"What time?"

"Seven."

"How are you getting there?"

Tamika was shy to respond. She knew what would come next. At times like this, she felt guilty. What had Tamika done to deserve all of the generosity Aminah displayed? Just months before, Tamika could barely stand her, and, surely, Aminah must have known. But now, it was as if they had always been friends. Tamika knew it was both her conversion to Islam and Dee's death that increased Aminah's concern and love for her. But still, it took some getting used to.

"I have a ride." She averted her gaze, pretending to look for something in the living room.

"Really?" Aminah creased her forehead as she searched her mind for who would have offered to give her a ride. Then it occurred to her what Tamika might have meant. "A taxi?"

Tamika groaned. Could Aminah see right through her? "Yeah, but it's not a big deal."

"We can take you."

There Aminah was again, bringing Sulayman into everything. Tamika couldn't help wondering if Sulayman was aware that his sister volunteered him so much. She felt sorry for him. He probably felt obligated when his sister nagged him about her roommate. Suddenly, a thought occurred to her. What if he thought it was Tamika asking for his help? She hoped not!

"The taxi is fine, really."

Aminah laughed. "I know that. And we'll take you still." Without waiting for a response, she disappeared into the bedroom to finish packing.

Tamika took a deep breath and sighed. What could she say?

That night Tamika was seated on the couch in the living room reading a book. She was dressed in a long sleeved white silk blouse and a navy blue rayon floral skirt that she had picked out a couple of hours before. She had rewarded herself with a long hot shower after a day's work and chose a comfortable outfit to celebrate the occasion.

Aminah was taking a nap and had told Tamika that Sulayman should be at the apartment by 9:00 to pick up the furniture and whatever boxes could fit in the moving truck. Tamika knew the information was a heads-up. Aminah didn't want Tamika to be caught off guard when her brother arrived. Tamika was still growing accustomed to the idea of covering herself when men were present. She had taken the hint and decided to get fully dressed before sitting down to finish the novel she had started after finishing her finals. Her navy blue *khimaar*[2]was lying on an arm of the couch. She would put it on once Sulayman arrived. She had grown used to covering her hair outside of the apartment, but it was difficult to get used to covering it inside.

A knock at the door startled her. She had been so engrossed in the book that she momentarily forgot where she was. Instinctively, she glanced at the clock. She remembered just then that Sulayman was due at nine. It was almost 10:00. Tamika stood. Her thoughts still lingered in the events of the story as she quickly placed the book face down on the couch.

"Who is it?" She picked up the *khimaar* and placed it on her head. Attempting to fasten the cloth under her chin, she realized she had forgotten the pin.

"Sulayman."

The voice was deep and unfamiliar, and Tamika's heart began to pound in nervousness. "Uh, just a minute!"

She hurried to the bathroom, where she found some scarf pins lying on the sink counter. Holding the cloth in place with one hand, she picked up a pin with the other and quickly fastened it on the cloth under her chin. Before leaving the bathroom, she glanced at her reflection in the mirror. She smiled beside herself, pleased with how the head cover complimented her features.

A second later, she was across the hall flicking on the bedroom light. "Aminah." Her voice was a loud whisper. "Aminah," she said a bit louder

---

[2] A *khimaar* is a head covering worn by a Muslim woman and covers her entire head and neck. It is drawn over her bosom area, exposing only her face.

when her roommate didn't budge. "Aminah!" Tamika hated shouting in such close proximity, but she didn't want to keep Sulayman waiting.

Aminah sat up quickly. "Sulayman's here?" She climbed out of bed.

"Yeah." Tamika relaxed a bit, but her heart was still racing. Why was she so nervous?

"Has he been waiting long?" Aminah headed for the living room, and Tamika followed.

"Maybe a couple of minutes."

Aminah paused before opening the door, checking her appearance. She was wearing a large white T-shirt that hung to her knees and baggy blue jeans. For a moment, she considered covering herself more but decided against it since it was only her brother. Hiding herself behind the door, she opened it slowly and greeted her brother to let him know it was she. "*As-salaamu-'alaikum*[3]."

Sulayman hesitated.

"It's okay. You can come in."

His hesitation was out of respect for Tamika, this Tamika knew. She had grown accustomed to this aspect of Muslim etiquette. Muslim men customarily waited until women had time to cover themselves before entering a room.

Sulayman returned the Islamic greeting then stepped in cautiously. His eyes searched for his sister behind the door. He didn't seem to notice Tamika standing near the couch.

He was dressed more casually than his usual slacks and button up shirt. He wore dark blue jeans and a T-shirt with "Islam" written on it in the shape of the United States. "Reach each and teach," read the inscription under the design. Immediately, Tamika saw the resemblance.

Tamika had seen Sulayman on several occasions since she began attending Streamsdale University, but it wasn't until she lived with Dee and Aminah that she discovered that he was Aminah's brother. When she learned of their relationship, she didn't think much of it, aside from her shock that the author of the infamous editorials was the brother of one of her roommates. But now, she saw that they favored each other.

Aminah was extremely fair with green eyes and could easily pass for being white, except that her wavy hair texture hinted to her father being bi-racial. Sulayman was also fair, but his complexion held a hint of brown, and anyone who saw him knew that he was at least partly African-American. Otherwise, he and Aminah's features were the same. He had Aminah's eyes and nose, and even their facial expressions were the same.

Normally, Tamika would notice sibling resemblance when she saw both of them for the first time, but Sulayman's features were somewhat hidden behind his beard. He stood almost a foot taller than his sister, who was a few

---

[3] "Peace be upon you," the standard Muslim greeting

inches shorter than Tamika herself, making his height just over six feet. He was thin, like his sister, but his build revealed athleticism, and Tamika guessed that he probably lifted weights. His demeanor was like Aminah's, calm, confident, and soft-spoken. But, like his sister, he wasn't shy when it came to Islam. His articles in the paper were proof of that. When it came to religion, both could easily be community activists although they would otherwise be considered laid back, and they both carried an air of spiritualism that was difficult not to respect.

He glanced up to greet Tamika and smiled politely before returning his gaze back to his sister. *"As-salaamu-'alaikum."*

"Wa-'alaiku-mus-salaam." Tamika too wore a polite smile and returned the greeting with ease, surprising herself. It had taken lots of practice before she was able to say it right. But Sulayman didn't seem to notice her achievement. He was talking to his sister a second later.

"You'll need to get dressed. I brought Omar with me to help carry some things."

"Oh." Aminah ran a palm over her hair. "Where is he?"

"Waiting in the hall."

"Give me a few minutes." Without thinking, she hurried from the living room and headed for the bedroom to get dressed, leaving Sulayman with Tamika in the living room.

"I'll wait in the hall," he called to his sister, who had already disappeared into her room. Without waiting for a reply, Sulayman left and let the door shut behind him.

The apartment became silent. Tamika's face grew hot in embarrassment, and she became upset. What was wrong with her? She scolded herself for being overly sensitive. It wasn't appropriate for men to be alone with women who were not family. She knew that.

But still. She felt as if she'd been slapped in the face. Couldn't he have at least addressed her before leaving? Yelling to Aminah, who wasn't even in the room, was rude.

"Are you alright?" Aminah appeared in the living room suddenly, fully dressed in a white *khimaar* and a charcoal colored *abiya*[4].

Embarrassed that her feelings showed on her face, Tamika forced a smile and waved her hand. "Yeah. It's nothing."

"Where's Sulayman?"

"He wanted to wait in the hall."

Just then Aminah realized what she had done. She cupped her hand over her mouth. "I'm sorry. I shouldn't have left like that."

"Don't worry about it. It's okay."

---

[4] An *abiya* is a large, loose outer garment similar to a dress and is worn over the Muslim women's clothes.

"*Astaghfirullaah*[5]." The words were more for self-reproach than seeking forgiveness as she headed for the front door and opened it to let the men inside.

"You can come in now."

A second later, Sulayman and a young man Tamika assumed was Omar stepped in. Omar was about two inches shorter than Sulayman and was noticeably stocky in his build, which his white football jersey did not conceal. Tamika imagined he could be on the football team at his school. He wore a thin beard that was like a shadow on his dark brown face. When he greeted the roommates, Tamika could tell his personality was easy going and that laughing came easy for him.

"What do you need me to do?" Omar clasped his hands together, a wide smile developing on his face.

"Aminah?" Sulayman turned to his sister.

"You can take all the boxes and furniture in here." She pointed her finger toward the couch and shelves. "Then, if anything else can fit, you can take the other boxes out of our room."

"Alright." Omar headed to the couch that Tamika had been sitting on when Sulayman arrived.

Sulayman followed him, and Omar started to crouch to lift the couch when he noticed a book on a cushion. His expression grew curious, and he walked around the couch to pick it up. As he studied the cover, a grin developed on his face.

Tamika's heart raced nervously, and she mentally kicked herself for leaving the book in full view.

"Hmm." He nodding approvingly, and Tamika's cheeks grew hot. "Whose is this?" Still grinning, he held up the book.

Embarrassed for the roommates, Sulayman walked over and took the book from Omar and handed it to Aminah. "Let's just get moving. It's already late."

"That's my sister's favorite author." Omar was lifting one side of the couch as he spoke, oblivious to everyone's discomfort in the room. Sulayman knelt to pick up the other side, and they began carrying the couch toward the door.

"Can you get the door?" Sulayman nodded his head toward the door as he spoke.

"Sure." Aminah tucked the book under an arm and hurried to the door. She opened it wide and stood behind it to make sure she wasn't in their way.

"We might have to tilt the couch a bit so it can fit through the door." Sulayman's voice was strained from the lifting.

---

[5] An Arabic phrase meaning "I seek God's forgiveness," often said by a Muslim after making a mistake.

"Got it." Omar's response was cheerful, and if he was straining, he was hiding it well. They tilted the couch, and after some maneuvering, they pushed the couch through the door.

Tamika was relieved when Aminah shut the door behind the men.

"I'm sorry." Aminah handed Tamika her book and shook her head.

"That's okay," Tamika lied, smiling uncomfortably as she accepted the book.

"You'll have to excuse Omar." Aminah started to say that Omar had only been Muslim for a year, but she realized the statement might offend Tamika. "He's just, uh, really friendly. So don't mind him."

"It's okay, really."

There was an awkward silence.

"I guess I'll just pack this up." Tamika forced laughter, glancing at the book in her hand as she headed for the bedroom without waiting for a response.

Inside the room, Tamika studied her novel before putting it in her shoulder bag. Her desire to read left her suddenly. She flipped through the pages and ran her hand across the cover. Maybe she would finish when she was on the plane. She found the page where she had stopped reading and folded the top corner to mark her place. She then slipped the book in her bag and zipped it shut.

Tamika's body weakened in exhaustion. She needed to sleep. She decided to pray the night prayer alone so she could go to bed. She doubted she could face the men again that night.

Three

Tamika woke to the alarm for *Fajr*, the first prayer of the day that was prayed at dawn. She sat up in the dark room. As usual, Aminah was already awake, and Tamika could hear the water running in the bathroom across the hall as her roommate performed ablution for prayer. Tamika glanced at the clock and realized that the alarm had been sounding for more than twenty minutes. She stood, turned off the alarm then flicked on the room light. She rubbed her eyes as they adjusted.

The room's bareness was depressing, and she found herself dreading going home. Most of the boxes were gone, and the tops of the dresser and desks were empty.

"*As-salaamu-'alaikum.*" Aminah appeared in the doorway and smiled.

"*Wa-'alaiku-mus-salaam.*"

"I'll just pray my *Sunnah* prayers and wait for you in the living room," Aminah said, referring to the voluntary prayer that was customary for the Prophet to pray before the obligatory dawn prayer.

"Okay."

In the bathroom, Tamika performed ablution at the bathroom sink. She slowly performed the motions she had learned from Aminah. It was only in the past two weeks that she was able to complete the task without Aminah's supervision. It seemed that the only thing that came naturally to her was learning the Qur'an, perhaps because it was similar to singing. The recitation was poetic and melodious, yet more powerful and moving than music.

Her mind drifted to all she had to do today as she washed her arms and wiped her head and ears. This was her last day on campus before her flight in the morning, and she hadn't spoken to Makisha in weeks. After Tamika had begun to dress in Islamic garb, Makisha kept her distance. Tamika knew her friend disapproved of her decision to become Muslim. Makisha had warned her on several occasions against turning away from Christ. But what should it matter to her what Tamika believed? Or had their friendship been conditional—that Tamika believed as she did?

Tamika felt herself growing upset. Part of her couldn't wait to see Makisha to confront her. But she knew she shouldn't, especially when they wouldn't see each other again for months. Besides, what impression would Makisha have of Muslims if the first thing Tamika did was argue with her?

Tamika turned off the water and opened the bathroom door to leave. After covering in an *abiya* and *khimaar*, she joined her roommate in the living room. Aminah had finished praying her *Sunnah* and was reading the Qur'an while she waited for Tamika.

"You ready?"

Tamika nodded, noticing the bareness of the living room. Aminah stood to put the Qur'an on its stand. The small X-shaped stand sat lonely on the floor near the blinds, and Tamika's gaze lingered there as she thought of her return home.

Tamika folded her hands on her chest as she stood next to Aminah in prayer. She listened to Aminah recite the Qur'anic verses with ease, and she found herself wondering at her roommate's songlike tone. Tamika had never thought of Aminah as inclined to sing. But she could never ask her about it. It would only open up wounds that had been unable to heal. Singing was Dee's trademark—her victory and defeat.

Tamika quivered at the thought of Dee and was immediately reminded of her own soul. She had admired Dee only months before and had striven to be like her. But now the thought scared her.

Suddenly, Tamika felt sorry for Dee. Why did she have to die so soon? She loved Islam. Why had God taken her soul before she had a chance to start practicing the religion again?

A frightening realization came to her. Perhaps Dee would've never returned to Islam—even if she lived on. Maybe she was never going to change, even after marriage, as she had planned to. Maybe letting go of her faith and planning to return to it later was indicative of her succumbing to one of the oldest tricks of Satan. Lure them away with the promise that someday they'll do what's right, and once they submit, steer them away from the right path so that "someday" never came. Tamika could only pray she wouldn't too succumb.

The roommates finished prayer and sat in silent reflection. Tamika pondered the mercies of their Lord and the poverty of their souls. Without the guidance of God, their souls were doomed to a never-ending darkness in this world and the next. Confusion would define their lives. What was evil they would think righteous, and what was righteous they would think vile. They would indulge in idolatry and think it piety and view piety as going astray. They would be on a path to eternal damnation and think it salvation. They would turn away from God as their savior and worship His creation instead. Perhaps in their confusion they would label creation as God, assigning the Most High sons and daughters whom they would purport share His Divine attributes that belong solely to Him. Tamika knew she could never show enough gratitude to her Lord for guiding her away from that.

"Do you need to go to the store before you leave?"

Tamika considered Aminah's question for a moment. She shook her head. "I don't think so. If I need anything, I can buy it when I get to Milwaukee."

Aminah nodded. "Just let me know if you think of anything. Sulayman and I may be going to the mall to pick up some things before Saturday."

There was a brief pause. "What's happening Saturday?"

"Graduation."

Oh. Tamika had forgotten Sulayman was a senior. She smiled. "Tell him I said congratulations."

Aminah smiled and nodded. She paused as she remembered something. "I told him about tomorrow, and he said it's no problem if we take you to the airport and that if you need anything else, just let me know."

Tamika didn't know how to respond. She was unaccustomed to such kindness coming from someone she barely knew. "I don't wanna be a burden."

Aminah laughed and shook her head. "Stop saying that."

Tamika forced laughter. "But I'm sure he'll get sick of running me all over the place."

"He's happy to do it."

Tamika couldn't help feeling flattered. She chuckled uncomfortably. "Why?"

"That's just how he is. He takes his role serious as a Muslim man, you know, looking out for the sisters. Besides," she said with a grin, "you're giving him an opportunity to earn a lot of blessings."

Tamika smiled, impressed that there were actually men who respected women that much. Before becoming Muslim, she was cautious of men who were extremely kind to women because they always expected something in return. In the world, nothing was free. A man's generosity came with a high price, and a wise woman never accepted a man's gifts—tangible or intangible—unless she was prepared to pay a hefty cost. That it was possible for a man to take care of women because he respected them and loved God was a concept difficult to comprehend, but it was one she couldn't help admiring.

Aminah stood. "*InshaAllaah*[6], I'm gonna take a nap for a few hours before Sulayman comes to pick me up."

Tamika nodded and stood too. "I think I'll just sleep until my body wakes me up." She chuckled as she unpinned the cloth and pulled it from her head. "I'm exhausted."

Aminah smiled and started for the room, where she removed her outer garment and *khimaar* before climbing into bed. Tamika followed suit, hanging her head cover and *abiya* on the footboard of her bed before lying down and going to sleep.

The sun's brightness illuminated the room, telling Tamika that she had slept past noon. She sat up and stretched before getting out of bed. The apartment was quiet, and she assumed Aminah had already gone to the store with her brother. She glanced at the clock, which read 12:56. She didn't have long before the next prayer, so she decided to shower, fix herself some breakfast, and pray before going anywhere.

---

[6] God-willing

In the kitchen, she poured herself some cereal after she showered and dressed for the day, wearing a cream-colored long sleeved blouse and a long, loose fitting jean skirt. She sat down at the table and began eating her cereal, mindlessly flipping through the school's newspaper that lay on the table. It was the latest issue and was filled with articles about summer vacation. Curiously, she turned to the editorial section, and before she had to look for it, the name "Sulayman Ali" stood out on the page.

"Getting Ready for Summer, A Little Advice," the article was titled. Tamika groaned and roll her eyes.

She reminded herself that she was Muslim now. She shouldn't dread his articles as much. But even as a Muslim, she doubted she would agree with his harsh tone. She skimmed the article, and a passage caught her eye.

"...and before doing it, ask yourself three questions. 1. Is it beneficial to me? 2. Is it beneficial to others? 3. Is it truly 'harmless fun'? If you can't answer yes to all three, think of something else to do to pass time..."

Tamika closed the paper, fearing she would be too cynical about whatever else he had to say. But she had to admit there was nothing wrong with what he suggested. In fact, it was good advice. Students often indulged in mindless activities that weren't beneficial to themselves or others and certainly couldn't count as harmless. If they heeded his advice, perhaps some lives would be saved. Even Dee had died because of a drunk driver. Perhaps if the student hadn't been drinking that day and had asked himself those three questions, her friend would still be alive...

Tamika stopped herself. *If* was a dangerous word. Nothing could erase what had happened. It was decreed long before the student or Dee ever walked the earth.

Tamika stood after finishing her food and carried her bowl to the sink, where she washed it and placed it in the dish drainer. She glanced at the clock on the stove. It was three minutes after 2:00. She went to the room to retrieve her head covering and prayed in the living room.

After praying, she pondered what she would do today, her last day on campus. She knew she would visit Makisha. She was both dreading and looking forward to the visit. But she wouldn't make Makisha's room her first stop. She considered visiting some of her professors to find out her grade on the final exam. She thought of Dr. Sanders. She would have to visit him. Although she had seen him only days before at the exam, she hadn't had the opportunity to talk to him personally. It was his term paper and presentation that prompted her study of and subsequent conversion to Islam. She knew he had a lot of questions about her journey, and he was the only non-Muslim who she felt would support her decision. She would visit him first, she decided. He would most likely be in his office. Most professors were on campus for several days after exams to grade papers and submit students' final grades.

Dr. Sanders's office door was propped open, but he didn't notice Tamika standing in the doorway. He was marking a paper, peering intently through his reading glasses at a test sheet that sat between two stacks of papers on either side of his desk. Tamika strolled in and glanced around his office. She studied the books on his shelves while she waited for permission to sit down.

"Oh." He laughed at himself and stood as he removed his glasses. He gestured for her to sit down. "Miss Douglass. What a pleasant surprise. Please have a seat."

She smiled, taking one of the seats opposite his desk. "Thank you."

"I was afraid I wouldn't get a chance to talk to you before the break." He leaned back in his seat and began rubbing his beard that was a shadow of gray and black on his face. He smiled at his favorite student. "Did you want to know your final grade?"

"Uh." An uncertain grin grew on her face. She chuckled self-consciously and shrugged. "Sure." Her response was tentative and revealed that she hadn't come to learn her grade.

He grinned, pretending not to notice her disinterest. "Well, you did quite well. As you know, your presentation was superb, and aside from some minor errors, your term paper was equally impressive. You passed."

"Passed?"

"With an *A*." His smile was wide and proud. He was always happy to see African-Americans doing well, especially at a school where they were the minority.

She nodded, unable to hide her pleasure. She had hoped she had done well in his class, but she didn't hope for more than a *B*.

There was a long pause, and an awkward silence grew in the room. Neither knew what else to say.

"So," Dr. Sanders drew in a deep breath, sparing Tamika the pressure of breaking the silence, "how does it feel?"

She knew he was referring to being a Muslim woman. "Good." She gave a thoughtful nod. "Different, but overall, I like it."

"What do you mean?" His eyes displayed the deep admiration he felt for her having the courage to take such a huge step.

"Like a big burden has been lifted from me."

He raised his eyebrows. "Really? How so?"

She shrugged, struggling to find the right words. "I don't know." She smiled to make up for the long pause. "It's like I was walking around with my eyes shut and feeling this deep pain inside. Then I woke up one day with my eyes wide open and the pain all gone."

There was a reflective silence in the room.

He nodded. "So I guess this is it for you, huh?"

"What do you mean?"

"You found your calling."

"Yeah," she said hesitantly. "But I don't think of it as my calling."

"Really? Why not?"

"Because a calling depends on the individual. But to me, it's like my," she searched for the right word, "duty."

There was a long pause. This time Tamika broke the silence.

"Remember you mentioned that you studied Islam once?"

He nodded and chuckled. "I studied almost every religion. I'm a religion professor."

She smiled reluctantly, slightly offended by his response. "Yeah, but I thought you said that you, uh," she didn't want to sound too personal, "were thinking about joining it at one point."

He nodded. He had shared that with her earlier in the semester. She had come to talk about the paper she was doing on Islam. "Yeah, but I considered joining a lot of religions. That's what happens when you study so many."

Tamika could tell he didn't want to discuss Islam, at least not as it related to him. Perhaps he thought she was trying to convert him. She grew silent, unaccustomed to him putting up a guard between them. She had admired his frankness and honesty as a professor. It was as if he viewed her more as a comrade than a student. She looked up to him as she would a father. And Dr. Sanders had welcomed it, but now she felt like he was pushing her away.

"But yes," he said, sensing he had offended her by his evasive response, "Islam is a religion I considered for quite some time."

She nodded, afraid to respond. She knew his statement was more out of politeness than any desire to discuss the issue of religion. She glanced at her wristwatch to appear as if she had somewhere to go. She stood and forced a smile. "Well, I won't take too much of your time. I know you have a lot of work to do. I just wanted to stop by and say hi before I left."

"I appreciate it."

She turned to go, avoiding eye contact. "No problem."

"Tamika."

She stopped in the doorway, and turned to him. "Yes?" .

His face was warm, and Tamika could see a tinge of admiration in his eyes. His smile apologized for not being more open. "Congratulations."

The words were soft and sincere, and Tamika knew he was referring more to her choice in religion than her *A* in his class. "Thanks." She turned to go.

"And don't worry too much about what people say."

She paused at the door without turning to meet his gaze. The office fell silent momentarily.

"Have a good summer."

"You too," she called back then disappeared down the hall.

Dr. Sanders stared at the empty doorway for sometime after Tamika had gone, his mind still on the student who reminded him so much of his own daughter who was now almost thirty years old. Felicia was reflective, kind, and studious, and she had struggled a lot with spiritual issues as a child. She had many questions for him and her mother about Jesus and the Trinity, and they were unable to answer them. They told her the only thing they could—to just believe.

Although he had let go of his belief in Jesus' divinity years ago, he never revealed this to Felicia, who had become a detached Christian, attending church only on Easter and Christmas or when someone died. Felicia rarely discussed what was on her mind in the religious realm. Their conversations usually centered around her job as an accountant in Chicago or the possibility of marrying her boyfriend of three years. Dr. Sanders often wanted to know how she was doing spiritually, but since religion had been a source of confusion for her, he decided against discussing it. The subject would cause too much discomfort—for them both. In some ways, he already knew where his daughter stood. He sensed that she was merely a reflection of himself. Like he, she believed in God, but it was difficult for her to formulate into words exactly what that meant. She likely believed that each religion had wisdom and truth, and no matter what label a religion had, doing good was the central message. It didn't matter what religion a person chose, he imagined she believed, the ultimate goal was the same.

This was the view he had held for sometime, but witnessing Tamika's search for answers and subsequent conversion to Islam rekindled unanswered questions he had pushed to the back of his mind. The likelihood of there being an absolute truth in religion always pricked at his conscience. The idea of there being no religion that was completely true or false didn't stand up to logic, at least not where belief in God was concerned. If one believed that God placed humans on the earth with guidance and purpose, then he necessarily had to believe that God taught only truth. And if so, the truth was one.

Islam had interested Dr. Sanders more than he had revealed. The religion had caused him internal turmoil and doubt about what he believed. It was Islam that solidified for him the fact that Jesus wasn't God. As he studied the religion, he was drawn to how it offered a logical explanation for the existence of so many different views of the Creator. Islam explained the varying views by simply stating that Adam was taught pure belief in and submission to God, which he taught to his descendents. As time passed, humans drifted away from the original teachings and introduced foreign concepts into the pure religion, often with good intent. Ultimately, people introduced new concepts of God himself. When paganism and sin began to define entire societies, God sent prophets and messengers to call people back to the truth. After each prophet, people strayed, whereupon God would send another prophet to clarify the truth. This was God's way until He sent His last prophet and messenger with the Qur'an, the final revelation that humans would receive until the Last Day.

When Jesus was sent, it was for the same mission as the prophets that preceded him. After he was gone, people began to stray, as the people had before him. However, their straying culminated in a blasphemous irony—the prophet, who was sent for the purpose of calling people to worship God alone, became the object of worship himself.   Meanwhile, the Day of Judgment drew nearer, and humans' time on the earth atrophied by the day. But there was to be one more prophet God would send. He would be the seal of the prophets, and his mission would be like those before him. Except for one fine point. Other prophets were sent to people of a specified time and place. But the prophet Muhammad would be God's messenger to the world until the end of time.

Why had Dr. Sanders never accepted the religion for himself? This was a question that befuddled even him. There was a time when he was tormented by his reluctance to submit, but he had long since abandoned pondering religious truths. He had resigned himself to being merely a specialist in religion. However, hearing Tamika's presentation on Islam awakened a part of him that he thought had died. It was as if he was hearing Islam for the first time.

He found himself captivated by the logic and simplicity of the religion, and the self-torment was ignited once again. Instinctively, he fought it. He would not go there. Yet, there was no resisting this religion, and it was impossible to attack it head-on. Even critics of Islam were forced to focus on extremists who practiced an Islam alien to the religion. Or they focused on particular details of its view on women and jihad, criticism which amounted more to personal opinions than any fallacy in the view itself. Other religions could be attacked at the base, Dr. Sanders couldn't help thinking as Tamika did her report. But no one, even the most scholarly of Islam's enemies, had been able to attack the foundation of the religion—the pure worship of God.

Dr. Sanders hadn't intended to offend Tamika with his evasiveness, but she was embarking upon rather sensitive ground. How could he offer simple answers to complex questions that he hadn't even addressed himself? He had lots of questions for Tamika, but he knew she wanted to talk about him. He sensed that it was perplexing to her how he could come across a religion as compelling as Islam and become content without accepting it formally. That was a question for which even he had no satisfactory response, except to say that, perhaps, Islam wasn't for him.

Outside Tamika reflected on the brief meeting with Dr. Sanders. He was indeed an interesting man. She could tell by his advice that he supported her decision. Then why the abruptness? The short answers? She pushed the questions out of her mind. She didn't want to think about that right then. She had a more pressing issue before her.

Tamika's heart pounded as she opened the door to Makisha's dormitory building. She had no idea what she would say, but she needed some closure. She couldn't go home without speaking to her best friend of two years. They couldn't go on avoiding each other. If they couldn't be friends, that was understandable. But the friendship should end with an explanation.

Tamika drew in a deep breath and exhaled before knocking on the door. She was almost certain Makisha would be in her room because most students were still packing and cleaning for the summer.

The door opened too suddenly for Tamika. A second after knocking, she stood face-to-face with Makisha, who wore a shocked expression on her face. She had expected Makisha to ask who it was.

"Oh, hi." Makisha forced a smile and opened the door to allow Tamika to enter.

"What's up?"

"Just packing." Makisha busied herself with placing books in a box that sat on top of her bed. "You?"

"I finished yesterday."

"When do you leave?"

"Tomorrow morning. You?"

"Sunday morning." Makisha's tone was without emotion, and her gaze was still on her box. "I wanted to stay to see Dante walk."

Dante was a good friend of Makisha's she had met their freshman year. Tamika often suspected the relationship was deeper than mere friendship, but since Makisha never mentioned it, Tamika hadn't either. "That's good."

"Why aren't you staying for graduation?"

"I guess I kind of forgot about it. Anyway, I don't know any seniors really well."

"Sulayman's graduating this year."

Makisha's tone was nonchalant, but her sarcasm was visceral. Tamika swallowed as anger boiled inside her. She glared at her friend, but Makisha wouldn't meet her gaze. Tamika stopped herself from uttering an evenly cruel remark, reminding herself that she was Muslim now.

She laughed, concealing her offense. "Sulayman?"

"Yeah, Aminah's brother."

"I don't know him that well."

"Really? I hear he hangs around the apartment a lot more now. You know, ever since you converted to his religion."

"I didn't covert to his religion." It was an unsuccessful attempt to conceal that she was upset.

Makisha forced laughter. "Well, you certainly look like you have."

Tamika rolled her eyes. "I converted to Islam, the religion of Jesus."

Makisha stiffened, and Tamika smelt victory.

There was a cold silence in the room.

"Is that what you came here for? To throw your so-called religion in my face?"

Tamika was silent, pleased that Makisha had tasted a bit of her own medicine.

"What is wrong with you, girl?" Makisha stared at her friend for a moment then shook her head. "How could you give up your soul for some stupid research paper?"

"I didn't give up my soul."

"Girl, you know as well as I do, there ain't no way to heaven except through Christ."

"I know that."

Makisha was taken aback momentarily, and she met Tamika's gaze as she gathered her eyebrows. "What's that supposed to mean?"

"I'm following Christ."

"Get the hell out of my room."

"Is that a teaching of Christ?" Tamika knew it was a low blow, but Makisha had gone too far.

Makisha glared at Tamika. She started to say something but was unsure how to respond. Unexpectedly, tears glistened in her eyes, and Tamika immediately regretted what she said.

"Just get out of here."

"I'm not going anywhere."

"Is that a teaching of Islam?" A tear slid down her face as she stared at Tamika coldly.

Tamika didn't respond. It was obvious that Makisha was groping for a counterattack.

"Why don't you just go?" Makisha turned her back to Tamika.

"Not until you're okay."

Several minutes passed before Makisha pulled herself together. She wiped her eyes and sat on the edge of her bed with her back to Tamika. Feeling sorry for her friend, Tamika walked around the bed and sat next to Makisha. She decided against embracing her, fearing it was too much compassion to show at the moment.

Makisha stared at the wall in deep thought. "Maybe you should just go."

"That's not how I want to end the year."

She sighed. "There's nothing you can do about that now."

Tamika considered apologizing but decided against it. She didn't want to open herself up to attack, especially if Makisha mistook the apology as Tamika taking blame for what had happened.

"Well, I just stopped by to say goodbye and—." Tamika paused as she gazed sympathetically at her friend, who wouldn't look at her. "To say thank you."

Makisha glanced over at Tamika with her forehead creased. "For what?"

"Being a friend."

She forced laughter. "If that's what you call it."

Tamika looked at her watch, as she normally did when she saw no other way out of an awkward situation. "I have a lot to do before my flight tomorrow morning. But I didn't wanna go without saying goodbye."

Makisha turned to Tamika and smiled politely, but it was clear that she was still a bit shaken. "Thanks."

Tamika considered giving her friend a hug but decided against it when Makisha didn't stand when she headed for the door. "No problem." She opened the door. "Tell Dante I said congratulations, and uh, have a nice summer."

"You too."

Tamika let the door close behind her. For a second, she paused next to the door, contemplating what had just happened. She was unsure how to take Makisha's behavior, and she was even less sure how to interpret the meeting. If nothing else, it confirmed that their friendship had ended.

Tamika spent the rest of the day browsing through books at the school library and returned to her room shortly before sunset. As she unlocked the door and pushed it open, she felt someone pulling the door from the opposite side.

Sulayman nearly ran into Tamika before he realized she was trying to come in. "Oh, I'm sorry."

She smiled self-consciously. "It's no problem."

He cast his eyes down and stepped back inside the apartment, still holding the door handle so she could enter. "*As-salaamu-'alaikum.*"

"*Wa-'alaiku-mus-salaam.*"

He shut the door behind him.

Aminah greeted her roommate from the floor in the living room, where she sat reading a book. Her hair was loosely bound in a pink ponytail holder, leaving the semblance of bangs around her face. "How was your day?"

Tamika shrugged, walking into the kitchen. "Pretty okay. You?"

"*Alhamdulillaah[7].*"

"You find everything you need?" Tamika raised her voice so that her roommate could hear her from the kitchen. She removed a carton of juice from the refrigerator and poured herself a glass, using one of the few dishes that were left in the kitchen.

"Yes, *alhamdulillaah.*" Aminah laughed. "Just pray for him."

Tamika wrinkled her forehead as she carried her juice to the living room and took a sip. "Why?"

"He's nervous."

"About graduating?" She laughed as she sat down on the floor across from her roommate. Nervousness was a strange emotion to have at graduation.

Aminah laughed again and shook her head. "No, his speech."

Tamika took another sip from her cup and set it down next to her. "Speech?"

"He's speaking at graduation."

---

[7] "All praises are due to God."

She raised her eyebrows and nodded in approval. She lifted her cup and took another sip before setting it back down. "How'd he get to do that?"

"They asked him to."

"Really? Is he the top student or something?"

Aminah shrugged. "I don't know, but he did maintain a four-point-oh GPA since his freshman year. Maybe that's why."

Tamika's eyes widened. "Are you serious?"

Aminah chuckled, suddenly self-conscious of Tamika's amazement. "Yeah."

"What's his major?"

"He double majored in biology and chemistry."

Tamika was speechless.

"He only did that because he's going to medical school, *inshaAllaah*," Aminah explained to downplay the significance of his major.

Tamika nodded dumbly, drinking the rest of her juice in a daze. Was it possible for someone to be that intelligent?

Aminah stood and stretched. "I'm gonna go ahead and get ready for prayer, *inshaAllaah*."

Tamika nodded. "I'm in *wudoo*[8]."

After Aminah performed ablution, the roommates prayed *Maghrib*, the sunset prayer, and sat quietly reflecting after they had finished. A few minutes later, Aminah stood and prayed the two-unit voluntary prayer that was customary for the Prophet to pray after *Maghrib*. Tamika watched her and began to feel guilty before finally praying herself.

"Tamika?" Aminah said shortly after they finished the voluntary prayer. Both were still seated on the floor.

"Mm, hm."

"Do you remember the brother who came over here with Sulayman last night?"

Inside Tamika groaned, remembering how he had humiliated her about her book. How could she forget him? "Uh, yeah. Omar?"

"Yeah." Aminah wore an uncomfortable smile. "What do you think of him?"

Tamika stared at Aminah with a confused expression on her face. "What do I think of him?"

Aminah chuckled. "Yeah, you know."

Tamika hoped her roommate wasn't saying what she thought. "He seems nice. Why?"

Aminah chuckled again. "Well, he asked if you were available."

Tamika laughed. "What! Are you serious?"

"Yeah. Sulayman told me today."

---

[8] *Wudoo'* is the state of ceremonial purity necessary for formal prayer, achieved by performing ablution.

"He talked about me to Sulayman?" Tamika was mortified.

"Well, he wouldn't have talked to me."

They both laughed, and Tamika nodded. "I suppose that's true." There was a brief pause. "So, what did Sulayman say?"

"To Omar?"

"No. What Omar said."

"Oh." Aminah's expression revealed the humor she found in what she was about to reveal. "Just that he thought you looked kind of good and was wondering if you were already taken."

Tamika burst out laughing, and Aminah did too, unable to contain herself. Now that she repeated it, it did sound ridiculous.

"How long has he been Muslim?" The comment struck Tamika as too worldly to come from someone raised Muslim.

"A year."

She nodded. She wasn't surprised.

"So he doesn't seem like someone you'd be interested in marrying?"

"Marrying?" Tamika was unable to keep from laughing. "I don't even know who he is." A thought came to her suddenly, and her eyes widened in fear. "Did he ask to marry me?"

"No. But he did express interest in marrying you."

"He's out of his mind."

"What makes you say that?"

Tamika shook her head. It was hard to believe they were actually discussing this. "Marriage is serious. I'd never marry some strange man I met one time and don't love."

Aminah was silent as her expression grew intent.

"And anyway, he doesn't even know me. How's he know I'm not some maniac?"

"He didn't propose, Tamika. He just expressed interest."

"That's still insane."

"What's insane about it?"

"Come on, Aminah. Shouldn't he get to know me better before saying something like that?"

A half smile formed on Aminah's face. "So you think a person has to know you really well before he says he might want to marry you?"

"Of course. Don't you?"

"No."

Tamika stared at her roommate in disbelief. "You'd marry a man you don't even know or love?"

"I didn't say that."

"But—."

"What I'm saying is, marriage is the only lawful relationship between a man and woman, and—."

"And?" Tamika rolled her eyes as she unfastened the pin under her chin and removed the head cover from her head before folding it neatly on her lap. She pulled the rubber band from her hair and ran her fingers through it, shaking it loose with her hand.

"Whenever a Muslim man is attracted to a woman," Aminah said, "he thinks of it only in terms of marriage. It's similar to how a man sees a good-looking woman and approaches her. But for most non-Muslim men, he approaches her because he hopes she'll be his girlfriend one day. Or he may just want her for one night. So when he starts chatting with her at a club or in the mall, this is his frame of mind." She paused then added, "And hers too."

Tamika nodded reluctantly. "That's true."

"So they talk to see what they have in common. If they get along pretty well, they date until they're officially a couple. If not, they go their separate ways. But the thought of her being a possible girlfriend or him a boyfriend isn't thought of as insane, even though they probably didn't even know each other's names when he first approached her."

Tamika wrinkled her nose. "So, in Islam marriage is like that?"

"Yes, in the sense that the initial attraction is thought of in terms of the goal. Of course, in this society, the goal is sin, while in Islam the goal is marriage."

"So, basically, you're saying that the word marriage is used loosely."

Aminah laughed. "I wouldn't put it like that. But, yes, I suppose you can say that because whenever marriage is brought up, it doesn't mean that he definitely wants to marry her or vice versa. It's just that they're interested in seeing if the relationship can grow to that point."

"I see." Tamika toyed with the rubber band in her hand. "But how do they go about it? Do they date, go through a friend, what?"

Aminah twisted some strands of hair around a finger then held them in front of her face to look at them. "Well, that depends on if things are done according to Islam. If they are, the man first approaches the woman's father. If the father approves of the brother, he may allow them to talk in his presence to see if they're compatible. And if they like each other, they get married."

"But what happens if a woman doesn't live with her dad?"

"The closest male Muslim relative takes the responsibility."

"Like her uncle or brother?"

"Yeah."

Tamika bound the rubber band around three forefingers until she felt it pinching her skin. She scratched at the red rubber as she considered what Aminah said. It was a strange concept, but it made sense. She admired the way Muslim men took care of their women. She wondered if she would ever know how it felt to be taken care of.

Aminah smiled as she ran her palm over her hair then let her hand fall to her lap, where she turned a page of her book and glanced at it. "So should Sulayman just tell him to forget about it?"

Tamika chuckled. "I wouldn't put it like that. But I think marriage, even if only a possibility, is a bit too much for me to digest right now. I don't think I'll get married for another ten years at least."

Aminah laughed. "Ten years! You can't be serious."

"I need to finish my degree and establish my career first."

"But then you'd be almost thirty!"

"Actually, I was thinking I'd probably wait until I'm thirty five."

Aminah's eyes widened. "Do you want children?"

"Maybe one or two."

"Well, I suppose Omar should look elsewhere, huh?"

"If he's willing to wait, he can."

Aminah forced laughter. "I think we'll just tell him you're not interested."

Tamika stood and chuckled, easing the band off her fingers with her thumb. "Anyway, I don't think he's my type."

"Who is your type?" Aminah teased as she stood to join her friend, holding the book at her side.

Tamika pulled her hair back and bound it with the rubber band until it hung in a pony tail. She hadn't really thought about it before. She was fifteen when she had her only boyfriend, and he definitely wasn't the type of man she'd marry. "I don't know."

Aminah made her way to the kitchen, setting the book on a counter. "I guess you certainly have time to figure it out."

Tamika laughed in agreement as she stood in the living room, still thinking about Omar. She wondered what he saw in her. Was he really attracted to her, or was he the type who wanted to talk to every woman he saw?

"Sulayman should get here between five and five thirty to go to the airport," Aminah said to Tamika a few minutes later, standing in the doorway of the kitchen. "So, *inshaAllaah*, we'll get you to the airport no later that six o'clock."

"He doesn't mind waking up that early?"

"He has to get up for prayer anyway."

"You know, I can take a taxi if—."

"Forget it. Sulayman'll never forgive me if I let you take a taxi, especially for that distance."

"Why?"

Aminah grinned. "Well, let's just say, the best scenario is that you avoid riding alone in a car with a strange man, especially if he isn't Muslim."

"Is he overprotective or something?"

"No, just protective. Actually, I'm not that comfortable with the idea myself, especially in this crazy country."

Tamika nodded. America definitely wasn't the safest place in the world for women, but she was reluctant to hold fast to a rule that would restrict her ability to go where she pleased.

Four

Tamika blinked in the darkness at the sound of the alarm and glanced at the clock. It was 4:00 the next morning. She sat up in the stillness of the apartment, realizing that this was the first time in weeks that she was awake before Aminah. She quietly climbed out of bed and felt her way through the darkness. In the hall, she turned on the light, hoping the brightness spilling into the room wouldn't disturb her roommate.

After using the bathroom, Tamika moved her luggage from the bedroom to the living room and pulled her blanket, sheet, and pillow from the bed. She carried the linen to where she had placed her bags and knelt down to roll the blanket and sheet so they would fit in her large bag. She opened the bag, startling herself with how loud the zipper was. Forcing the sheet and blanket in the bag, she wondered when Aminah would get up. She carefully picked up the pillow and quietly placed it on top of the sheet and blanket, accepting that it would cause the bag to bulge at one side.

After zipping the bag closed, she returned to the bathroom and pulled open the shower curtains after closing the door. She turned on the water and let it run until it was tolerably hot against her palm. A minute later, she stepped into the tub and turned on the showerhead after pulling the curtain closed. The heat of the water warmed her, and she relaxed, enjoying the tickling massage of the shower. She shut her eyes as steam rose around her, and she reflected on the significance of the shower, which would be her last in the apartment. Time had passed so quickly it was amazing. It was difficult to believe that she had experienced all that she had in only her second year in college.

Her fight with Jennifer crossed her mind, and she frowned. Tamika hated thinking anything that could be construed as racist, but living with Jennifer led her to believe that interracial roommate arrangements on a college campus weren't always a good idea. Initially, it was hard to figure out exactly why she felt this way. But she later realized that it was because society's racial barriers were so thick that they prevented people from really getting to know each other.

African Americans and Caucasians often saw each other everyday, she reflected, but there was still that barrier, as if they had come from different parts of the world. Since age earned a person the maturity and experience necessary to meet racial challenges, college students were ill-equipped for the struggle, especially if they had little interracial interaction before school. Their lack of maturity was only compounded when coupled with the fact that students had lots of stereotypes borrowed from their parents and friends at home, making it nearly impossible for any genuine understanding to take place. Perhaps that was the problem with her and Jennifer.

It must have been a tremendous disappointment for Jennifer when she walked in her dorm room and found a black student staring back at her,

Tamika imagined. What was that like for her? How would Tamika herself have felt if she were Jennifer, who came from an affluent family and grew up in a wealthy suburb where people of color rarely lived?

Jennifer had always been surrounded by her own race. She attended predominately white Catholic schools all of her life. She had never had a black friend and could only recall seeing a total of two or three black students in all of her schools from kindergarten to twelfth grade. She was raised to believe people got what they earned and earned what they got. Poor people remained poor because they didn't have the will to get out of the situation. Rich people were rich because they had the guts to do what it took to get, and stay, rich. People on welfare were lazy beggars who would rather steal from the rich than get up and work for their own bread. In Jennifer's world, there was no inequality. Slavery and racism were things of the past, and it was black people who refused to move on and quit waiting for—and taking—hand-outs while preventing qualified whites from getting what they worked hard for and rightly deserved.

In retrospect, Tamika respected Jennifer. If nothing else, Jennifer had tried. When she saw her roommate, Jennifer didn't run the other way and demand a new roommate as other students had. She extended her kindness and was open with Tamika about who she was and where she came from. She shared some laughs with Tamika and even came to appreciate some of the song artists and authors Tamika loved. She would pick up some things Tamika needed from the store if she was running to buy groceries with a friend. She had even reevaluated some of her political views on inequality and Affirmative Action after hearing Tamika's perspective.

Then what had gone wrong? What had been the last straw for her—for Tamika? Perhaps it was Tamika's insistence that Jennifer be tidier that put the rocks in the road. Tamika had come from a household where the motto was "cleanliness is next to godliness," and Jennifer had grown up with a housekeeper. Maybe Tamika could have been more understanding.

At the time, Tamika interpreted Jennifer's untidiness as a personal problem. But it must have been difficult for Jennifer to come from a home where she never even had to make her bed, to living in a room where she had to vacuum and wash her own clothes. Tamika thought Jennifer was lazy, and Jennifer thought Tamika was a nag. The tension built until it reached its climax, at which both had had enough. Tamika was sick of Jennifer's "good intentions," and Jennifer was tired of Tamika's irksome complaints. Tamika had worn her mask of diplomacy too long, and so had Jennifer. In an inevitable crescendo, the façade broke, and each exploded with what they had held in for so long.

Tamika had no socio-political objectivity when the word *nigger* stung her ears, and Jennifer forgot her willingness to make it work when Tamika angrily confronted her. The final altercation solidified for the roommates that they had been right all along. Jennifer was indeed a spoiled, racist brat who knew nothing of basic human decency, and Tamika was an angry black woman who grew dangerously violent when things didn't go her way.

Perhaps Jennifer wasn't lying when she said she lived in fear of her roommate everyday, not knowing if at any moment Tamika would become violent. It sounded like mere mendacity at the time, but Tamika now understood how Jennifer's lack of experience with African Americans might have led her to actually live in fear. Misinformation and stereotyping were powerful. They could right a wrong, wrong a right, and cloud the reality of an otherwise normal situation.

Being charged with physical assault was a smack in the face for Tamika. She couldn't imagine any other college experience being worse. When she packed her things and moved to the university apartments, it was anger she felt, and she expected nothing from the move except bitterness and disappointment as she was forced to move on. But God had another plan.

God had a blessing in what Tamika saw as a disaster. Tamika was now grateful to God for putting Aminah in her life. What would she have done without Aminah's deft explanations of Islam? How would she have come to understand her purpose in life? Even Dee, who was often irritated by Aminah, didn't have one bad thing to say about her childhood friend. Aminah had represented to Dee what she would later represent to Tamika. An often unwelcome presence but a much needed one.

Dee.

Oh, how Tamika wished Dee were alive to see her as a Muslim. Maybe she would see that practicing Islam wasn't that bad. Maybe she would think, *If Tamika can do it, why can't I?* They could weather the storm together, arm in arm, singing and praising Islam—even in the most tumultuous of storms.

Tamika stopped herself. When was she going to accept that Dee could never have lived to see her religious growth? When was she going to accept that nothing—absolutely nothing—could bring Dee back?

Even so, Tamika couldn't let go of her love for Dee. Whatever Dee's faults were spiritually, she would always have a place in Tamika's heart.

Tamika blinked, feeling tears well in her eyes as she remembered the night of the Spring Formal. Dee was so beautiful that night, so breathtaking to all who had been graced by her presence. When she began to sing, her enchanting voice soothed hearts. Everyone was speechless. Even Tamika, who stood next to Dee singing the song she herself had written, was awestruck.

Tamika swallowed as a lump developed in her throat, and she felt the tears escaping from her eyes. In a tearful blur, she could still see Dee's dimpled smile. Her excitement after their stage success glowed on her soft tan skin. Tamika could see her friend jumping up and down after the producer handed them his card. She could still feel her warmth and could almost taste the sweet scent of Dee's perfume when they embraced that night. Tears of joy filled their eyes, and they knew this was the first step to insurmountable success. Their hearts and minds were intoxicated with a happiness they had never known.

On their way from the Spring Formal, they celebrated by singing every song they could remember. Dee had thought of a famous duet between a man and woman and had sung both parts herself, deepening her voice for the man's and sweetening it for the woman's, while Tamika hummed and rocked to the sweet melody of the song and the night.

Tamika shuddered. The hot water felt cold momentarily as the dreadful sound of Dee's piercing scream echoed in her mind. Dee had been singing the duet when bright headlights poured into their car, shocking them both and transforming Dee's peaceful singing into a blood-curdling cry of panic.

Presently, tears gushed from Tamika's eyes. Surrendering to the aching of her heart, she let the tears fall as she recovered from the flashback. Tamika remembered nothing after Dee's scream except waking in the hospital, learning of the car accident from hospital workers. She had learned the painful news about Dee after her discharge.

"How," Dee's soothing voice sang that night at the formal. "How can I find the words to describe, to tell? To tell of my lessons, how I stood how I fell?"

Tamika covered her eyes and cried uncontrollably as the words she had written haunted her. It was eerie how they reflected Dee's climactic life. But Tamika had written the words about herself.

"How," Dee's voice rose that night, repeating the powerful words, "How can I find the words? How can I find the words? Tell me, how can I find the words to tell? Tell of my lessons, how I stood, how I fell?"

Minutes later, the painful thoughts halted. The sound of the shower's water was the only sound Tamika could hear at the moment. She lifted her face to the showerhead and let the water wash away her tears. She opened her eyes and felt the emptiness in her heart and throat. She hadn't sung since the night of the formal, and she stood in the moist warmth of the shower wondering if she could ever sing again.

Tamika reached down to turn off the water and dried herself before stepping out of the tub and putting on her bathrobe. The cool air of the apartment shocked Tamika's body, and she mentally scolded herself for forgetting to turn off the air conditioner before showering.

In the room she dressed in the dimly lit area near her bed using the light from the hall. The clock read 4:34 after she finished changing into the outfit she had set aside the night before. She had chosen the outfit carefully, knowing her mother would pick her up at the airport. She had wrestled with her thoughts for some time. She couldn't decide whether or not she should cover her hair in front of her mother. She wanted to wear the *khimaar* since she had grown accustomed to the head cover and felt naked without it. But wearing such an open symbol of Islam would both shock and upset her mother and give little opportunity to break the news gently. And what if she ran into old friends from high school or, worse, from church? How would she face former youth group members or children she had mentored, whom she had encouraged to "walk with Christ"? And her aunt Jackie, who was a regular at their church, still lived in the city. This was much more than she wanted to endure upon her arrival. The mere thought of everyone staring at her overwhelmed her with dread.

Perhaps she shouldn't wear it, at least not on the first day. That would give her the opportunity to see everyone before breaking the news. She didn't want to ruin their excitement about her return for the summer. In any case, she decided she would at least wear it to the airport. On the plane, she would decide whether or not to keep it on before landing in Milwaukee.

Tamika had chosen a long rayon dress of cream, one of her favorite colors. It had pearl-like buttons running along the front with a string tie in the back. She selected a lightweight navy blue blazer to wear over it since the dress was short sleeved. At first, she had worried about how she would look wearing a blazer with the dress, but when she found a cream-colored scarf with blue flower imprints, she was relieved. It matched perfectly and made the blazer-dress combination appear almost elegant. She tied the scarf around the front of her head in a small head wrap with her hair falling neatly out the back, its tips curling at the nape of her neck. She put her navy blue *khimaar* on top with the floral scarf showing in the front, making the outfit look classy.

Aminah's alarm sounded at 4:55, and she sat up in the dimly lit room and stretched. When she squinted and saw Tamika standing several feet away, she greeted her with the Islamic greeting, and Tamika replied in kind. After Aminah climbed out of bed and turned off the alarm, Tamika flicked on the room light, and Aminah blinked as her eyes adjusted.

Tamika walked over to the full-length mirror attached to one of the closet doors and surveyed her appearance. She smiled. Not bad. The combination complimented her honey brown skin and accented its smooth appearance. Her eyes had a slight slant to them, likely the result of the head wrap, and the deep brown of her eyes was enhanced by the ensemble. She hadn't expected the outfit to compliment her so well, but she wasn't complaining. Maybe she would wear the head cover when her mother picked her up. It looked beautiful.

"I guess you're ready to go," Aminah teased in her sleepy voice.

Tamika smiled, slightly embarrassed to have Aminah see what she was wearing. She knew it was a bit too decorative to count as Islamic *hijaab*[9]. "Yeah," she said, "I got up around four."

"I guess it was worth it, huh?" Aminah grinned as she headed for the bathroom to prepare for prayer.

---

[9] Literally, it means any veil or covering. In this context, it refers to the specific requirement of Muslim women to avoid displaying their beauty in public.

The corners of Tamika's mouth turned up in a smile as she shook her head at Aminah's sense of humor.

"*InshaAllaah*," Aminah raised her voice from the doorway of the bathroom across the hall, "I'll give Sulayman a call after prayer to make sure he's up."

"You don't think he left yet?" A trace of panic was in Tamika's voice.

"He stayed on campus last night," Aminah said as she realized that Tamika assumed he was coming from their home in suburban Atlanta nearly forty minutes away. "He won't go home until after graduation."

"Oh." Tamika exhaled in relief.

"Don't worry. His building isn't far from here."

After Aminah closed the door to the bathroom, Tamika walked into the living room and glanced at her luggage. She mentally reviewed what she was supposed to do before she left, and her mind drifted to her family.

Tamika missed her mother and aunt and wanted very much to see them, but she felt as if she had lost them already. It was a sense of mourning she felt as she stood there staring distantly at her bag. The euphoria she had felt upon accepting Islam was slipping from her, and reality was setting in. Fear engulfed her, and she felt a sense of sadness as she realized the sacrifice she might have to make for her soul. She couldn't give up Islam, this much she knew. But could she give up her family? She sighed, hoping she would never be faced with the decision. Perhaps her mother would accept her new identity. Tamika's heart sank. It was a hopeless desire, and she shouldn't think of it.

Tamika walked over to the patio window and stared beyond the blinds. Outside was still dark. There was no hint of blue to announce the approaching morning. Half of the world was sleeping. But Muslims were waking for prayer. Tamika felt a spiritual tranquility as she realized the powerful camaraderie of Muslims praying to their Lord at the same time. All in the universe humbled themselves and submitted to God's laws, and it was empowering to be among them. How could she ever show enough thanks to her Lord for guiding her to the religion of her inborn nature, the religion of truth? How could she show her gratitude for being chosen to be among His righteous servants? The appointment wasn't only a generous gift, but a duty placed upon her shoulders. Would she fulfill the covenant and share the mission with others?

A loud knock at the door startled Tamika. She left the window and headed for the door, walking quickly as her heart began to race. Sulayman was here. It was time for her to leave for the airport—to go home.

"Just a minute," she called a few feet from the door. She didn't bother asking who it was. She already knew. She flicked on the overhead light in the living room to give the room more brightness. Then she walked over to the bathroom, where she could hear the sound of water running as Aminah performed ablution for prayer. She tapped on the door with the back of her knuckles. She hoped she wasn't rushing her roommate.

"Yes?"

"Sulayman's here."

"Oh." There was a brief pause as Aminah gathered her thoughts. "Uh, tell him I'll be right there." She quickened her ablution as she spoke.

Tamika groaned. She didn't want to deliver the message to Sulayman. She had already told him to hold on. "Okay," she called back to the bathroom door before heading for the living room. She decided she would wait it out instead of telling him what his sister had said. Aminah would be done shortly. He can wait, she thought.

After a minute passed, Tamika felt bad that he was still standing outside the door. She drew in a deep breath as she neared the door. "Uh, Sulayman?" She leaned toward the closed door and couldn't shake the feeling of awkwardness in saying his name.

"Uh, yes?"

She could tell by his hesitance that he wasn't comfortable with the exchange either. "Aminah's in the bathroom, but she said she'll be right out."

"Okay," he said and added for Tamika's benefit, "I'm fine."

"Uh, okay." She walked away from the door and found herself pacing the floor. Why was she always nervous around him?

A second later the bathroom door opened, and Aminah emerged. She hurried into the living room, still wearing her pajama shirt and pants. She glanced over her shoulder at Tamika with her hand on the door handle.

"Is it okay if he waits inside?" Aminah asked in a loud whisper in an apparent effort to keep Sulayman from hearing.

Tamika shrugged, concealing her nervousness. "That's fine."

"*As-salaamu-'alaikum*," Aminah greeted as she opened the door.

"*Wa-'alaiku-mus-salaam.*"

After Aminah closed the door, Sulayman glanced up and saw his sister's roommate standing several feet from him. He gave a polite nod and smiled at Tamika before saying the Arabic greeting again.

Tamika smiled in return and mumbled her reply inaudibly. He looked away from her a second later and fixed his gaze on his sister. For a moment, Tamika studied him curiously. She was a bit taken aback by his new look. His hair was freshly cut and was little more than a shadow on his head, making his beard appear larger than usual. But it complimented his features. He wore a dark green *thobe*[10] that extended a couple of inches above his bare ankles, and he wore brown buckled sandals on his feet. The sweet scent of an exotic fragrance filled the room and reminded Tamika of the scented oils that were sold in Muslim-owned stores. The new look suited him and gave him a

---

[10] A large gown-like shirt that extends past the knees, often worn by Arab and Muslim men.

distinguished appearance. He could easily pass for a religious scholar or imam. Remembering the Islamic injunction, Tamika lowered her gaze and busied herself with studying her feet, which were covered in sheer knee-high stockings.

"Did you pray?" Sulayman asked Aminah.

"Not yet. Did you?"

"No, it just came in."

"Oh, well then," she hesitated, glancing at Tamika who was still studying her feet, "I guess we can all pray together and then go." She waited for Tamika to meet her gaze to approve.

Sensing Aminah waiting for her, Tamika glanced up and gave a nod and shrug, indicating that it was fine with her. She then resumed staring toward the floor. It had taken her some time to get used to keeping her gaze lowered in front of men. Growing up, people looked at the ground only if they were humiliated or embarrassed. If a person wanted to be taken seriously, she made eye contact, and held it, with women and men. But as she stood there practicing the Islamic injunction, she felt surprisingly dignified.

"I'm ready," Aminah said to her brother.

"You don't look ready." A grin formed on his face as he eyed his sister's pajamas.

Surprised at his sense of humor, Tamika glanced up to witness the exchange.

Aminah laughed. "Maybe because I'm not," she said with a playful roll of her eyes. "What I meant is I'm in *wudoo'*. All I have to do is put on some clothes."

"You better hurry," he said more seriously.

Aminah turned to go to the back room.

"Should I wait in the hall?" He didn't want to be left alone with Tamika again.

"We'll just go to the room."

Taking the hint, Tamika followed her roommate to the bedroom. In the room, Aminah put on an *abiya* and *khimaar* over her pajamas. After quickly pulling on some socks, she smiled at Tamika. "Don't worry, no one'll know what's under here."

Tamika chuckled and followed Aminah out of the room.

"That was fast," Sulayman said with a laugh.

"Well, you said hurry."

He grinned and shook his head in amazement. "Yes, I did. I guess I should say hurry more often."

Aminah rolled her eyes as they both laughed, and Tamika couldn't help grinning.

Seconds later, Sulayman took his place in front of the room in preparation to lead the prayer. Tamika waited for Aminah to line up behind him before she followed suit and stood shoulder-to-shoulder with her roommate.

Sulayman glanced behind him to make sure the women were ready before turning back to face the direction of prayer. He stood quietly looking toward the floor before beginning.

"*Allaahuakbar[11]*," he said too suddenly for Tamika, who was still mentally preparing for the prayer.

"*Alhamdulillaa-hi-rabbil-'aalameen,*" he recited praises to the Lord of all creation. His deep voice became a spiritual melody enrapturing the room in submission to God. "*Ar-Rahmaanir-raheem,*" he announced God's divine attributes of bestowing grace and mercy to the world. "*Maaliki-yawmid-deen,*" he recited, proclaiming God as the sole Master and Owner of the Day of Judgment, a day when all humans would be gathered before Him to answer for their sins. The Last Day would be a terrifying moment full of heart-wrenching trepidation, and each person would become agonizingly self-absorbed. A man would flee from his own brother, friend, mother, and father, and a mother would forget her child. The enormity of the day would be too tremendous to allow a single soul to care for another. "*Eeyaaka-na'budu, wa iyaaka nasta'een,*" he testified to their worship of God alone and proclaimed that it is only His aid that the believers seek, that all help ultimately comes from God alone.

As Sulayman continued to recite the first chapter of the Qur'an, Tamika felt the weighty meaning of God's words pierce her heart, and the beautiful recital poured forth the meaning of the divine words. She humbled herself in prayer, and her heart submitted to whatever her Lord wanted as she was captivated by the power and beauty of the words. Inside, her faith grew until she felt the love of God swell in her chest. How could anything other than God's pleasure have ever mattered to her? How could life have had even a hint of meaning before she knew her Creator, the one worthy of all praise, the Most Gracious, Most Merciful. God, the All-Powerful, owned the fate of humans and would give them their records in their hands on the Last Day. Tears welled in Tamika's eyes, and she fought them, blinking repeatedly.

"*Wal-'Asr,*" Sulayman continued, reciting another chapter from the Qur'an, the meaning taking hold of Tamika as she recalled what she had read in a translation. It was one of the first chapters Tamika memorized, and she knew she would never forget the powerful words. "*Innal insaana lafee khusr…*" Tamika could feel the words enveloping the room. *By the time, verily man is in loss, except those who believe and do righteous good deeds and join together in the mutual teaching of truth, patience, and constancy.*

Tamika had read that a Muslim scholar once said, if people followed only this verse, that would be sufficient for them. In this brief recital lay the keys

---

[11] Literally, "God is Greater (than anything)." Here, it is said to signify the beginning of formal prayer.

to salvation and the explanation of all human victory and loss. If they would only take heed.

God began the verse by swearing by the time, significant in its implication that nothing had changed. Time after time, humans remained the same. They were all in loss, in a pitiful state, chasing the world and whatever mirages it offered while leaving behind eternal life, the thirst of their souls, never knowing the pleasure of truly knowing their Lord. The lost, they were the people of the world, chasing everything the world offered and abandoning anything of benefit to their souls. Aminah told her that a scholar once reflected on their sad state and said, "The people of the world left it without ever tasting the sweetness of it." When he was asked what that sweetness was, he said, "It is to know Allah."[12]

But there was hope for those who sought knowledge of their Lord, Tamika reflected. Not everyone was doomed to a pitiful end. Those who believed in God and worshipped none but Him would be met with good at death, when others were met with the evil they earned. For the believers dedicated their lives to doing good for His pleasure alone and joined together to call people to truth. They bore with patience whatever hardships befell them on the path, and it was this calm determination that would lead them to reap the rewards of the Hereafter and quench the thirst of their souls.

As Tamika recalled her own loss before being guided, she shuddered at the thought of where she might be without Islam. What had she been before Islam but a mere feather blowing in the wind? A lump developed in her throat as she recalled what had led her to Islam. Feeling the tears threaten to escape from her eyes, she lost the will to fight them any longer. The salty moisture rushed down her cheeks and dripped from her chin, soiling her *khimaar*. But they soothed her soul. She cried in silence as they bowed and prostrated, completing the first unit of prayer before standing again.

As Sulayman began the recital again, Tamika's tears were uncontrollable. The words pierced her heart as the divine words gave her no opportunity to resist their powerful effect. She felt her nostrils moisten inside, and she sniffed quietly, hoping no one could hear her over Sulayman's recitation. When he finished reciting the first chapter of Qur'an and went on to recite another, her shoulders shook as the power of God's words overtook her entire body. She felt a weakness that she had never felt before, one that took away all energy to chase the glitter of the world. It empowered her with faithful determination to fulfill the purpose for which she was created. She felt her poverty before God and hoped that He would enrich her with strength to go all the way. She wanted to live everyday as if it were her last, until her soul was taken in submission to Him.

At that moment, Tamika didn't care what her mother, aunt, or friends thought. She would stand tall as a Muslim, not caring about anyone or

---

[12] Malik ibn Dinar

anything but God and her soul. She would live the legacy of truth, the life of a believer, and she would never give up, not for any worldly desire nor family or friend.

When they finished praying, the reality of the day came back suddenly, and Tamika wished they could have prayed longer. She lowered her head to hide the tears that she was trying to wipe away. She hoped Aminah hadn't heard her sniffles or noticed her tears. She wanted her feeling of nearness to God to be a private one.

Sulayman turned around and leaned against the wall to face them, and Tamika glanced up nervously in hopes that he hadn't seen her. To her relief, he was looking at his fingers, where he was numerating the perfection, blessings, and greatness of God.

Tamika was trying to pull herself together before they left. They would have to get in the car soon, but she needed some tissue to clean her nose. She covered her nose with one hand in an effort to prevent it from dripping on her clothes. There was no tissue in the living room, she realized in disappointment. She would have to escape to the bathroom. She started to stand, but Aminah stood before her. Discouraged, Tamika sat back down as her eyes followed her roommate, hoping Aminah wasn't heading for the bathroom. When Aminah opened the front closet, Tamika stood and started for the bathroom, hoping to make it there before anyone noticed her state. But before she could start down the hall, Aminah called her back.

Tamika turned around as Aminah walked toward her. "Here," Aminah said quietly, handing Tamika a small box of tissues from the closet. It was the complimentary box that the school kept in every room for its residents. Since neither had ever needed it, the roommates had left it in the closet for whoever would live there after them.

Tamika's heart sank, and instinctively, she glanced to where Sulayman sat, fearing he may know too. But his gaze was fixed on the floor, reciting Qur'an quietly to himself. "Thanks," she whispered before disappearing down the hall and entering the bathroom before he had a chance to see what was going on.

In the living room, Sulayman stood in preparation to go. "Is this everything?" He pointed to the two large pieces of luggage sitting on the floor.

"Yeah, I think so. She has a small bag in the room, but I'm pretty sure that's her carry-on."

He gathered his eyebrows in concern and nodded toward the hall. "Is she okay?"

Aminah glanced in the direction of the bathroom and placed her hands on her hips. "Yeah, I think it was just the prayer."

His eyebrows rose, and he held his gaze toward the hall a moment more, and Aminah thought she saw a tinge of admiration in his eyes.

"Well, I'll go ahead and take these to the car," Sulayman said. He picked up the handle of the bags with each hand and started for the door. "Just meet me at the car."

"Where are you parked?"

"Out front. It's near the front door, a few spaces to the right."

"Okay."

"Can you get the door?"

Aminah opened the door wide and stood behind it to give him room to pass.

"Oh yeah." Sulayman was outside the door when he turned slightly toward his sister before heading for the steps. "What'd she say?"

She wrinkled her forehead. "About what?"

"Omar."

"Oh." Aminah laughed and waved her hand. "She's not interested."

Sulayman forced laughter and shrugged. "*Alhamdulillaah,*" he remarked in disappointment, remembering to praise God even when receiving bad news.

"Yeah, *alhamdulillaah,*" she echoed her brother's sentiments, shrugging with a smile on her face that seemed to say, *Don't ask me.*

"*InshaAllaah,* I'll see you in a few minutes," he said as he started down the hall.

"*InshaAllaah,*" she agreed, closing the door.

Aminah was waiting in the living room when Tamika came out of the bathroom.

"He left?" Tamika asked, concern in her eyes.

"No. He's waiting for us in the car."

Sensing that they were running late, Tamika glanced around the room looking for her bags.

"He took them downstairs."

"Oh. Do I have time to call my mother?"

"Uh." Aminah glanced at her wristwatch with uncertainty. "You'll wanna make it quick."

"Forget it," Tamika said before walking to the room to grab her bag and purse. "She has my flight information anyway," she said in the living room a minute later with the straps of her carry-on bag and purse over a shoulder.

"I'm ready," she said to Aminah after slipping on her shoes.

"He's out front." Aminah started out the door, and Tamika followed.

They walked in silence until they reached the steps. "Do you need anything before we go?" Aminah asked.

Tamika shook her head. "I'm fine."

"You have a ride from the airport?"

"My mom told me she'll pick me up."

Aminah nodded then reached in her pocket and pulled out a card-size envelope. She handed it to Tamika, whose eyes widened in surprise. "Just a little card from my family."

Tamika eyed the envelope that had her name written neatly on it. "Should I open it now?"

Aminah shook her head as a half smile formed on her face. "After you're on the plane. It feels weird when people read my cards in front of me."

Tamika chuckled in agreement and pushed the card into her book bag. "Thanks."

"You're welcome."

The two descended the rest of the steps in silence and exited the building. A minute later Aminah climbed in the passenger's seat and Tamika in the seat behind her.

Sulayman turned off the Qur'an tape he was listening to as they sat down. "All set?"

"Yep," Aminah replied as they closed their doors then buckled their seatbelts.

Sulayman drove out of the parking lot in silence as his sister murmured the supplication for boarding transport. A few minutes later, he resumed listening to his tape, and Qur'anic recitation filled the car.

Tamika relaxed and stared out the window, watching the trees and buildings pass them. It was difficult to believe she had completed two years of college already. It seemed like only yesterday that she was stressing over how she would do on the SAT. She had feared that her score would be too low to permit her acceptance to any respected school. When she received her score in the mail, she was pleased to discover she had scored a 1250. It wasn't an extraordinary accomplishment, but it enabled her to take advantage of some minority scholarships that required a minimum score of 1200. Tamika smiled, remembering how proud her mother had been the day she showed her the score.

"You're truly special," her mother had said as she embraced Tamika in her large arms. "I knew that the day you were born."

Presently, Tamika wondered how her mother would take her conversion to Islam. She knew it would upset her, but it was difficult to gauge just how much. Growing up, whenever any of them didn't feel like going to church, her mother would tell them that, when they turned eighteen, they had a right to do as they pleased. "But as long as you're with me, this is a Christian house, and Christians go to church." Tamika could only hope her mother meant it.

"What airline is she flying?" Sulayman asked, glancing at his sister after pausing the Qur'anic recitation. Aminah turned to Tamika.

"Northwest," Tamika said before Aminah could repeat the question. Tamika was still getting used to how Sulayman addressed Aminah instead of her whenever he wanted to ask her something. She knew it wasn't an Islamic rule, but Tamika suspected Sulayman felt that it was more appropriate to have his sister address her if Aminah was present. Either way, it made her feel awkward.

A second later the Qur'anic recitation was playing, and they grew silent again. After some time Tamika resumed looking out the window and noticed from the interstate signs that they were about ten miles from the airport. She felt herself grow nervous as she imagined how the airport workers would react to her Islamic dress. What if they demanded that she uncover her head?

Her heart began to pound in her chest. She should've taken a taxi. Then she could take off her head cover without making a scene. If she took it off now, surely Aminah and her brother would think she had lost her mind.

She felt her palms moisten with perspiration as the signs on the interstate indicated that the airport was one exit away. When the car veered off the highway and started toward the airport, she felt as if her heart were in her throat, and her head began to ache. Would they search her bags, thinking she was a terrorist hiding an explosive? What if they didn't allow her to board the plane?

The car slowed to a stop behind other cars whose passengers were unloading their luggage and heading for the line at the curbside check-in. The airport was crowded, Tamika noticed. The noise level from outside seemed to rise as Sulayman put the car in park. Tamika stared in trepidation as other passengers lined up with ease next to their friends and families. Why couldn't it be that simple for her? She noticed a woman in a business suit jacket and short skirt glancing impatiently at her watch, a large bag with wheels in front of her. A scarf was tied around her neck and her reddish blond hair was pulled back in a ponytail. Her face was tense, as her frustration showed on her face. Tamika envied her. What she would give to have to worry only about getting to the gate on time.

Sulayman opened his door after pulling the lever for the trunk, which popped open in the back. Tamika drew in a deep breath and began opening her door, as did Aminah.

"You want to check in here or inside?" Aminah asked once they had gotten out of the car, oblivious to Tamika's nervousness.

Tamika glanced about her in uncertainty, trying to determine which would be the safest for someone dressed like she was. "I'll check in out here." She feared that too many normal families would be waiting inside, perhaps with children who would stare, wondering why she wore a cloth on her head.

Sulayman pulled the bags from the trunk one at a time and placed them on the curb. "Should we go inside?" he asked after shutting the trunk and reaching in the car to turn on the emergency lights.

"She'll check in out here." Aminah had to raise her voice over the airport commotion.

He nodded as he picked up the bags and carried them to the back of the line.

"You have everything?" Aminah asked Tamika a second later.

Tamika nodded as her eyes traced all the people who were there. She guessed they were, probably suspicious of the group of Muslims in strange clothes. "Yeah. I'm gonna take this bag with me on the plane."

"Okay." Aminah moved to stand behind her brother in line.

Tamika looked about her. Were there any other Muslims here? When a woman who appeared to be of Indian origin passed, wearing a traditional sari and a red dot in the middle of her forehead, Tamika relaxed a bit. Perhaps it was okay to be different.

When it was finally her turn to check in, Tamika kept her eyes cast down as she showed the worker her itinerary and photo identification card. *He's probably going to want to know why my hair isn't covered in the picture.*

"How many bags are you checking on?" he asked as he compared the name on her ID card to the name on the itinerary. He then glanced at her to make sure she was the woman in the picture.

"Uh, two."

"Is anyone else traveling with you?"

"No." She couldn't look at him, answering the remainder of the standard questions fiddling with her purse.

He handed the ID and paper back to her and proceeded to tag her luggage. "You Muslim?"

The question startled her. She could hardly believe what was happening. Her worst fears were unfolding before her. She avoided his gaze and felt her hands shaking as she put her ID and ticket back in her purse. She wanted to say no. She could only imagine the consequences for telling the truth. But Aminah and Sulayman stood next to her. She couldn't lie. O Lord! All she wanted to do was go home. Why this? Why now? "Uh, yeah," she said quickly, hoping to downplay the significance of her answer.

"*As-salaamu-'alaikum,*" he said with a smile, picking up her bags and placing them on the conveyer belt.

"*Wa-'alaiku-mus-salaam,*" she mumbled, too stunned to think straight. She studied him for a moment, noticing his nametag for the first time. "Ahmed Sabir." Initially, he looked African-American, but now she could tell he was probably from Africa.

"Are you all set?" Sulayman asked before returning to the car.

"Uh, yeah." She was still recovering from her shock that the worker was Muslim.

"Call us when you get there," Aminah said.

"Okay."

She approached Tamika and embraced her. "Have a safe trip."

"Thanks," Tamika said, pleasantly surprised by the show of affection.

"You have my phone number at home?"

"Yeah, in my phone book." She patted her purse. "But I thought you were gonna be at the apartment."

"I'll sleep there. But we have to go to *Jumuah*[13] today, so we'll be home all day."

Tamika nodded.

"*As-salaamu-'alaikum*," Aminah greeted her roommate before heading to the car, where her brother waited.

"*As-salaamu-'alaikum*," Sulayman called to Tamika with a wave of his hand.

"*Wa-'alaiku-mus-salaam*," Tamika replied. A second later, she disappeared into the airport.

Tamika wanted to find the nearest bathroom to remove her *khimaar*, but there wasn't enough time. She had to walk a distance to the gate, and she didn't want to miss the flight. She decided against taking it off while she walked. It would draw too much attention. Besides, it wasn't so bad looking like a Muslim in the airport. If airport employees were Muslim, why should she feel ashamed to be a Muslim passenger?

When she reached the gate, she waited for twenty minutes before the passengers began to board the flight, and she lined up behind them. The boarding process went smoothly. No one seemed to notice, or care, that she was Muslim. She found her window seat with ease and had even exchanged a few pleasant smiles with some of the other passengers. She fastened her seatbelt comfortably around her waist and glanced at her watch. It was 6:46. She still had about fifteen minutes before the scheduled departure.

She pulled the book from her bag before putting the bag under the seat in front of her. She opened the book to where she left off and began reading. A few minutes later, she sensed someone near, and she looked up to find a man wearing a business suit putting a bag in the overhead compartment. When he took the seat next to her, she forced a smile and resumed reading.

"Hi, how are you?" He adjusted his seatbelt and smiled.

"I'm fine, and you?"

"What are you reading?" he asked after a nod.

Tamika showed him, but she wasn't comfortable. She doubted that African-American authors, especially women, were respected among Caucasian men, especially those more than forty years old.

He nodded in approval. "She's a very talented writer."

Was he just trying to be polite?

"I read a lot," he said with a chuckle, noticing Tamika's surprised expression.

She nodded, unsure what to say.

---

[13] Congregational prayer for which Muslims gather on Fridays.

"I used to work for an African-American publication here in Atlanta." He smiled, the creases around his pale blue eyes deepening. "I did several book reviews and interviewed a lot of black authors."

Tamika hesitated before asking, "Did you ever interview her?"

He shook his head and ran a hand over his freckled bald spot, covering the thinning with his graying brown strands. "No, but I reviewed several of her books."

She creased her forehead as her eyes momentarily rested on the gold band on the ring finger of his left hand before meeting his gaze again. "What made you interested in African-American literature?"

He winked playfully then adjusted the silver buckle of his Rolex watch. "It's a long story. But I was always pretty open-minded about things."

She nodded, unsure how to take his openness.

"I did a lot of research on black Muslims too."

"Really?" She remembered her headdress just then.

He nodded. "When I worked for a local paper back in the seventies." He breathed, obviously pleased with himself. "I met Farrakhan a few times."

She gathered her eyebrows, trying to conceal her offense. "I'm not in the Nation of Islam."

He raised his eyebrows in surprise, adjusting his business jacket with both hands. "Then you're orthodox?"

She shrugged, unaccustomed to categorizing herself. "Just Muslim."

He nodded, seeming to understand. "Did you choose the religion?"

"Yes."

"What were you before?"

"Christian."

The pilot announced preparation for take off.

"A lot of African-American Christians are accepting Islam," he reflected aloud. "Some researchers say it's discontentment with the racial overtones of the church." He paused to hear Tamika's perspective on the speculation.

The comment seemed to reduce a person's conscious choice to a statistic, and she felt herself growing defensive. But she shouldn't be so sensitive, she told herself. He was just trying to be nice. "I don't think so."

"Really? So you don't think the racial divide of churches has anything to do with it?"

"No." She chuckled, beginning to feel more comfortable talking to the stranger. "Because that implies that Christianity is the standard religion for African-Americans."

"Hm," he thought aloud and nodded with interest. "Why do you think so?"

"Because many people simply don't believe what Christianity teaches." As the plane pulled away from the gate, she felt empowered by her statement and hoped she was making a difference in his life.

He nodded. "So you think it's the religious concept of Christianity as opposed to racial or social discontentment?"

"Of course." She almost laughed as she replied. The voice of the flight attendant giving safety instructions seemed to fade in the background as she spoke. "Perhaps social and racial factors contributed a lot to African-Americans' attraction to the Nation of Islam," she said, "but that doesn't explain why African-Americans are leaving Christianity in the first place. But there are a lot of racial issues in the Christian church," she admitted, "like the voluntary segregation and the portrayal of Jesus as Caucasian."

"Yes, but a lot of that is changing now. You have more integrated churches, and more churches are portraying Jesus to reflect the race of the congregation."

She smiled knowingly. "But those changes only attract people who believe in Christianity. But if I don't believe God is a man, why would it matter to me the race he's portrayed?"

He nodded, apparently intrigued by her point of view.

"African-Americans are becoming Muslim because they see Islam as true," she continued. "It has nothing to do with the racial or social problems in the church. Racism is everywhere, even among Muslims, I'm sure. But if I believe Islam is true, that's not going to change my belief."

"So you would stay in a Muslim church even if you experienced racism?"

"If you mean would I stay Muslim, then yes, because the truth of Islam doesn't change because of someone's personal struggle. But if you mean would I stay in that particular church, then no, maybe I wouldn't."

He nodded again. "That's a really interesting perspective."

Tamika forced a smile, wondering if he viewed any point of view outside of a social scientific perspective. Did it ever occur to him that perhaps he should be Muslim too? Part of her wanted to ask him. But she wouldn't. She reminded herself that the euphoria she was experiencing as a new Muslim must be tempered at times. He was engaging her in conversation more to make up for the awkwardness of being forced to sit next to a stranger than any genuine interest in what they were talking about. Then again, she could be wrong. It was possible that his views were deeper than he displayed. She shouldn't dismiss his sincerity any more than he should dismiss hers.

He took a deep breath and relaxed, leaning his head on the headrest of his seat as the plane took off. "I'm exhausted." He chuckled self-consciously before shutting his eyes.

She forced a smile and turned her attention back to her book, not wanting to disturb him. A moment later she was engrossed in her story again, and her mind was enveloped by the created reality on the pages, giving her a much-needed break from the reality of her own.

"Would you like something to drink?"

Startled, Tamika looked up and saw a flight attendant leaning toward her. Next to her, the man was sleeping. His head faced her slightly, and he looked as if he would fall on her any moment. "Yes, some ginger ale please."

The flight attendant prepared her drink, and Tamika glanced out the window while she waited.

"Here you go, ma'am."

Tamika accepted the drink and thanked the attendant, who studied the man for a moment then decided against disturbing him. Tamika opened her tray and placed her drink there after taking a sip. She then resumed reading.

Tamika's eyes opened to the announcement that the plane was landing, and it was then that she realized she had drifted to sleep. Immediately, she was reminded of facing her mother, and her heart sank. Then she remembered she had a stopover in Chicago before flying to Milwaukee.

Ten minutes later, the plane began to land, and she stared out the window as the houses and greenery below became more vivid. Her body jerked slightly as the wheels hit the ground, but a moment later she relaxed. As the plane slowed, she resumed reading her book. There would probably be a long wait at the gate.

The man awoke after the plane slowed in front of the gate, and a second later he remembered where he was. He smiled at Tamika and stretched a bit, exposing the cuffs of a crisp white shirt. "Short flight," he joked, and Tamika smiled.

"Still reading, huh?"

She nodded politely and smiled again, keeping her eyes on what she was reading as the plane stopped. The pilot welcomed the passengers to Chicago and thanked them for choosing Northwest. He told them that they would be unloading in a few minutes.

"Are you a student?" the man asked, apparently trying to pass time again as they waited.

She forced a smile. "Yes."

"My daughter just finished her first year of law school this year."

She nodded. "That's good."

"Where do you go, if you don't mind my asking?"

"Streamsdale."

He raised his eyebrows in approval. "I had a good friend who went there."

She smiled, hoping they could exit the plane soon. The atmosphere was becoming suffocating, especially since many passengers now stood waiting in the aisle.

"What are you studying?"

She hated when people asked that. She always felt it was asked to pass judgment. "Religion for now."

"For now?" He chuckled, but Tamika knew he meant no harm. "You think you may change your major later on?"

She lifted a shoulder in a shrug. "We'll see."

"I changed my major twice." He laughed. "I started off as pre-med, changed to education and then finally realized I wanted to be a journalist. Needless to say, I graduated a semester later than I planned." He laughed again and shook his head. "But that's life, I suppose. Everyday is different from the other."

She nodded, wondering if academic struggles prompted him to change his major. "That's true."

"But you have to follow your heart." He smiled, self-assured. "After all, that's all you got that's your own."

The pilot began allowing passengers to exit, and the crowd in the aisle slowly began to move. The man forced laughter as he unbuckled his seatbelt. "I think I'll just wait until they pass, if you don't mind."

She shrugged. Her layover was more than an hour. "That's fine."

He sighed and sat silently until the aisle had almost cleared. He then stood and removed his brown leather briefcase from the overhead bin. Tamika closed her book, unbuckled her seatbelt, and leaned forward to retrieve her bag from under the seat in front of her. After the man stepped into the aisle, she followed.

"Have a nice weekend," the pilot told them as they stepped out of the plane.

"You too," they replied in kind.

"It was nice meeting you," the man said once they entered the airport.

"You too."

As the man stood a few feet from her looking into the crowd for whoever had come to meet him, Tamika pulled her itinerary from her purse to double check what gate her next flight was leaving from. She didn't want to relax until she had found it. The airport was huge, and she needed time to walk to the terminal.

"Dad," a female voice called, and Tamika glanced up and saw a young woman who appeared to be in her early twenties approaching. Tamika glanced over her shoulder to see whom she was talking to, and the man who had sat next to her on the plane waved to the woman and embraced her. Stunned, Tamika studied the two for a moment. Maybe that was his "long story" explaining his interest in African-American studies. His daughter was bi-racial.

The walk to her terminal was a long one, and Tamika was grateful that she didn't stop to pick up a snack on the way. Once she found the gate, she purchased a bagel and an orange juice and sat down in the gate's waiting area to eat. Just then she remembered the card Aminah had given her. She set her bagel on her lap and finished the rest of her juice before opening her bag. She pulled out the card and smiled to herself as she read her name again.

A second later she tore open the paper and pulled out the lavender card which read, "For a special friend" above an artistic drawing of some flowers.

Touched, she opened the card, and the sight of a one hundred dollar bill shocked her. She glanced around to make sure no one was watching when she removed it from the card. "Just a little gift from my family for your summer vacation," the neat handwriting read. "I love you for the sake of Allah. Sincerely, Aminah." Her cheeks grew warm, and she smiled. She had never known such kindness to come from a roommate.

Five

"Tamika!" Her mother sounded pleasantly surprised to hear from her. "You doing okay, baby?"

"Yes ma'am," Tamika said, leaning against a side of the phone booth in the Milwaukee airport as she adjusted the shoulder strap of her book bag. She had called her mother at work to let her know she had arrived. "I'm just here at the airport." She glanced behind her. A man was waiting to use the phone.

"Ayanna ain't there, child?"

"Ayanna?" She ran her hand over her hair, remembering that she'd taken off her *khimaar* in the plane.

"Yeah, baby, Jackie sent Ayanna to get you."

Tamika glanced around to search for her cousin in the crowd. "I don't see her, but I can check outside."

"Alright, baby, call me back if she ain't there."

"Okay."

"Tamika!"

As she hung up the phone, Tamika turned to see a young woman coming toward her. It took a second for her to recognize Ayanna. Ayanna wasn't wearing the large bifocal glasses that had defined her as long as Tamika could remember, and Ayanna's reddish brown hair was cut short with two-inch twists about her head instead of the perm she had had since she was a girl. Her once plump build was now a shapely frame accented by her tight clothes. Ayanna gave Tamika a quick hug, and Tamika smelled traces of cigarette smoke in her cousin's clothes. Tamika didn't remember her cousin smoking, and she wondered if she had started when she turned eighteen at the beginning of the year. Or perhaps, Ayanna had been sitting with her mother.

"Girl," Ayanna said, "you betta hurry up before they tow me. I came inside 'cause I knew you ain't see me out there." Ayanna's keys jingled at her waist as she tucked a loose hem of her fitting red T-shirt into her black stonewashed jeans.

"Girl, you drivin' now?" Tamika raised her eyebrows in admiration as she walked back over to the conveyor belt where she had left her bags on the floor.

Ayanna grinned as she looked at Tamika, revealing the large gap between her front teeth. She narrowed her sandy brown eyes that were the color of the freckles sprinkled across her amber cheeks. "Girl, I been drivin' for a year. Where you been?"

Tamika stopped next to her bags and adjusted the second strap of her book bag until she wore it like a backpack. She then lifted one of her suitcases with both hands. "You're gonna wanna get the other one, 'cause I can't carry 'em both."

"What makes you think I wanna carry any 'o yo' stuff?"

Tamika rolled her eyes playfully as Ayanna lifted the bag and led the way to the car. The weight of the bags caused the cousins to galumph during the short walk to the car, which Tamika spotted with the emergency lights on. The car was the one she remembered, a charcoal gray Nissan Maxima that Jackie had bought two years ago. Tamika was never good with remembering the years of cars, but she knew the model was a 1990 because Jackie had hooted and hollered like she had lost her mind, saying "I got a nineteen *ninety* Maxima!"

Tamika grinned when they stopped at the passenger's side of her aunt's car. For a moment, she forgot her new identity as she stood there in the rushed atmosphere of the Milwaukee airport with the sun shining overhead, and even the proper English she had used at Streamsdale was shedding. At the moment, she wondered if only black people spoke two completely different variations of the same language depending on their company.

"Girl," Tamika said, setting her bag next to the car, "I 'on't know what your momma was thinkin', lettin' you drive."

Ayanna unlocked the doors after setting the bag on the curb, and it wasn't until she flipped her middle finger that Tamika was reminded of her Islam. It was a playful gesture that Tamika and her cousins had used countless times when teasing each other, but today, Tamika's cheeks grew hot at the sight of her cousin's red polished finger standing a few inches from her face. Ayanna's silver ring sparkled under the sun, and the matching bracelet slipped down her arm as she held her hand in front of Tamika a moment more.

"Anyway," Ayanna said, exaggerating the toss of her head as she rolled her eyes and made her way to the driver's side. "You can put them bags in the back by yo'self since you wanna be cute."

Tamika opened the back door, and her cheeks hurt as she struggled to maintain the smirk on her face. She lifted the bags one at a time to the back seat and shut the door before climbing in the passenger's side, slipping the straps of her bag off her shoulders. Her face was still warm from embarrassment as she buckled her seatbelt. The smell of cigarettes prompted Tamika to press the button to open the windows.

"We ain't even outta the airport, and you already startin'," Ayanna said, shaking her head as she started the car, but Tamika could tell she was enjoying the moment. Ayanna glanced sideways at her cousin and turned up her lip. "You get all e-du-ca-ted and think you all dat."

Tamika coughed, intending to laugh. Music blared in the car a second after Ayanna pulled out, and Tamika found herself repulsed by the vulgarity of the hip hop lyrics.

"You comin' over tonight?" Ayanna asked a few minutes later, reaching to turn down the music as a grin formed on one side of her mouth.

"I'm not sure. I have to see what Mom wants to do."

"She ain't tell you we hooked it up?" Ayanna's eyebrows rose as she looked at her cousin.

Tamika creased her forehead and shook her head. "Where?"

Ayanna gathered her eyebrows and lifted a shoulder in a shrug. "Oh, maybe it was supposed to be a surprise."

"A surprise?" Tamika wore a smirk. "For who?"

Grinning and shaking her head, Ayanna rolled her eyes. "Girl, you *are* stupid. 'Course I'm talkin' 'bout you!"

"Me?"

"Yeah, girl. You the college stu-*dent*." She wore a playful grimace and wiggled her shoulders to imitate the walk of an uppity girl.

Tamika shook her head. "You crazy."

"Yeah, and you got the same blood."

They laughed.

"But for real," Tamika said. "Where is it?"

"Girl, if Aunt Thelma ain't tell you, I ain't goin' to."

"Maybe she 'on't know."

Ayanna reached up to scratch her scalp with a forefinger, careful not to disturb her hairstyle. She shrugged, keeping her eyes on the road in front of them. "Probably not. I wouldn't be surprised." She shot Tamika an apologetic glance. "I ain't tryin' to be funny, though, for real."

Tamika waved her hand and shrugged.

"...Don't have to be afraid of what you aaaaare."

It took a second for Tamika to realize her cousin was singing along with Mariah Carey's popular song "Hero" that had just started playing on the radio.

"There's an aaanswer," Ayanna howled, and a second later Tamika burst into laughter. Ayanna really did sound terrible.

"Girl, I 'on't care," Ayanna said to Tamika, rolling her eyes, seeming to gather courage from her cousin's subtle insult.

"And the sorrow that you know will melt awaaay," Ayanna whined, and Tamika pondered how talent skipped over relatives.

"Help me out, girl," Ayanna said hurriedly, gesturing her hand toward Tamika.

Tamika only smiled and glanced out the window, wondering at how her desire to sing was gone. She reached forward to rearrange her backpack at her feet as her cousin whined and howled until Tamika feared she'd have a migraine before they reached the house.

"That a hero lies in," Ayanna took such a deep breath that it sounded like a sniff, "yoooouuuuuuuuuu. Mmmm," she seemed to growl more than hum. "That a hero lies in yooooouuuuuuuu."

Tamika pressed her hands over her ears and squeezed her eyelids shut as her cousin's voice squeaked and cracked.

"Man, I'm good!" Ayanna said, slapping herself on the thigh. "I know you jealous."

"Oh yeah," Tamika agreed sarcastically, opening her eyes and letting her hands fall to her lap. "I can't stand it."

"You gonna sing for us tonight, ain't you?" Ayanna asked a minute later.

Tamika wrinkled her forehead and glared at her cousin, still smiling. "Says who?"

"Says *me*." Ayanna huffed and smirked. "That's all you need to know."

"Girl, I ain't singing for nobody."

"Aw, no you ain't gonna act like you too good for the un-e-du-ca-ted."

Tamika rubbed her eyes with one hand then lifted her arm until her elbow sat at the window sill, and she tapped the back of her fingers against the glass. "I ain't say all that."

"You 'on't have to."

Tamika smiled as her gaze fell on the road ahead of them. "No, but for real."

"But for real, *what*? I know you ain't tryin' to say you gonna be a party pooper."

"Hey," Tamika cut in playfully, glancing at her cousin, "I 'on't know nothin' about a party."

"Girl, it ain't nothin' but Mom, me, and Raymond rentin' some movies and barbecuin'."

"So, my mom don't know yet?"

Ayanna shrugged. "She might. Mom told 'er when we came over a few weeks ago."

Tamika nodded. "I'll see."

"You'll see?" Ayanna laughed. "Girl, you 'on't have no choice. We bought a bunch o' food and we are ready to par-ty." She jiggled her shoulders in a dance, holding on to the steering wheel, and the car shook slightly.

"Whatever."

At the house, Ayanna helped Tamika carry her bags to the front door. "Sorry I can't help you unpack," she said, turning to go before Tamika could open the door, "but I gotta go help them get everything hooked up."

"Girl, I'm fine."

"My mom'll probably call ya'll to say what time to come."

Tamika nodded.

"Bye!" Ayanna turned to wave as she hurried back to the car.

Tamika took the house key from her purse and unlocked the door before she pushed it open. The familiar smell of potpourri filled her nostrils as she lifted the heavy bags one at a time and set them inside. Smiling, she closed the door then glanced around with her hands on her hips. She felt a peaceful relaxation as the familiar surroundings reminded her of her childhood. She took her bags to her room one at a time and stood in the middle of her bedroom. It was spotless. She guessed her mother must have cleaned it for her.

Tamika's eye caught a photograph displayed on her dresser. It was one of her senior pictures. She walked over to it and picked it up. She gazed at it momentarily. Who was she then? She studied the perfect smile outlined in glossy maroon lipstick. Her freshly permed hair fell in front of bare shoulder blades, exposed by an elegant, sleeveless black dress. A gold crucifix sparkled from her neck and complimented her chic appearance.

It had been one of Tamika's favorite pictures, perhaps because it made her look breathtaking. She had given a wallet size version to all of her friends and classmates before graduation. She wondered where everyone had gone. She had lost touch with most of them. What would they think of her now? The thought saddened her, and she frowned. She studied the picture a moment more before placing it back on the dresser and calling her mother to let her know she was home.

As Tamika hung up the phone, she felt exhausted. She would unpack later. She decided to sleep in the undershirt and skirt she was wearing under her dress. She didn't feel like going through her suitcase to find anything else. She hung her clothes on the back of the chair next to her desk. She started to get in the bed when she remembered she was supposed to call Aminah. She pulled her phonebook from her purse and dialed the number. She hoped her mother wouldn't mind the long distance call.

"Yes?" Aminah's mother answered on the third ring.

"*As-salaamu-'alaikum.*" Speaking the Arabic words at home was both soothing and encouraging for Tamika. Maybe things would work out after all.

"*Wa-'alaiku-mus-salaam,*" Sarah said cheerfully.

"Is Aminah home? This is Tamika."

"Oh, Tamika! *MashaAllaah*[14]. How are you doing?"

"Fine, *alhamdulillaah.*"

"How did school go this year?"

She chuckled self-consciously. "I pray well."

Sarah chuckled too. "Can I have Aminah call you back? I'm on long distance."

"Oh, that's okay. I was just calling to tell her I'm home. She doesn't have to call me back."

"Well, I'll give her the message, *inshaAllaah.*"

"*InshaAllaah,*" Tamika repeated, as was her habit now after becoming Muslim.

"Take care."

"You too."

After exchanging the Arabic greetings, Tamika hung up and exhaled. She could finally sleep. She walked over to her bed and lay down, pulling the covers over her head before drifting to sleep.

---

[14] Literally, "It was God's will," often said at times of happiness.

Tamika woke and glanced at the clock that sat on her dresser. It was 2:05. She sat up and looked around her room, wondering what she should do until her mother returned from work.

Just then she realized that it was time to pray. She had almost forgotten. She got out of bed and headed down the hall to the bathroom, where she prepared for prayer. It felt weird performing ablution in her home, but she imagined she would get used to it. She returned to her room a few minutes later to dress for prayer. She opened her shoulder bag and located her navy blue *khimaar*. The sight of it saddened her as she remembered taking it off in the plane. She hoped Allah would forgive her. She just needed time before she could wear it in Milwaukee.

After pinning her *khimaar,* she realized that she had no idea which direction to face for prayer. Tamika could look at the position of the sun, but in the early afternoon it was no use. She would have to wait until sunset or sunrise. That was the only way to be sure since she couldn't tell east from west until then. She sighed. God knew her intentions, and that was all that mattered. She glanced around the room for a few seconds before deciding to face away from the picture on her dresser. After praying, Tamika removed her *khimaar* and blazer and hung them on her bedpost. She would need them again for the late afternoon prayer.

Feeling hungry, Tamika went to the kitchen and surveyed the contents of the refrigerator. She picked up a pack of hotdogs and read the label. She groaned. They had pork in them. She decided to just eat some yogurt. She pulled a cup from a shelf and after getting a spoon, she sat down at the table.

As she ate, she wondered whom she should call. She thought of a few high school friends whom she had not spoken to in over a year. Maybe she would call them. But what if they invited her to hang out? What would she do? She definitely didn't want to divulge her conversion to Islam. After a few minutes, she decided that she would wait. It was more than she wanted to deal with right then.

As Tamika finished her yogurt, her mind drifted to Aminah and Sulayman. What were they doing now? They were probably at *Jumuah*. Tamika sighed. She wished she could be with them. She could use some inspiration. Maybe there were mosques in Milwaukee. She could look in the phonebook, the idea came to her suddenly. A second later she decided against it. It wasn't wise to contact any Muslims. She had to be discreet about her Islam. It was best to be patient. She had three months ahead of her. She should just focus on family for now.

After eating, Tamika strolled into the living room. Not knowing what else to do, she sat on the couch across from the television and picked up the remote control. She flipped through several channels until she found reruns of *The Cosby Show*.

Tamika laughed out loud as Vanessa and her friends, who hoped to start a professional hip hop group, danced and sang their ridiculous routine in front of Vanessa's parents. The friends sang and gyrated as Clara and Heithcliff bore the performance with as much patience as they could muster in the face of the obvious non-talent of their daughter and her friends.

When she finished watching the shows, Tamika looked at the clock hanging on the wall. It was 4:00. Remembering her book that she had been reading, she decided to read until her mother returned home from work. She brought the book back to the couch and opened it to where she had left off.

The sound of the phone ringing interrupted her thoughts. She set her book down and reached for the cordless that lay next to some magazines on the table in front of her.

"Hello?"

"Tamika?" It was Aminah.

"Yeah, *As-salaamu 'alaikum.*"

Aminah returned the greetings. "You called?"

"Yeah, but you didn't have to call me back. I didn't want you to call long distance."

"It's no problem."

"I was just calling to say I got home safely."

"*Alhamdulillaah.*"

"Oh yeah, thanks for the card and the gift."

"So you liked it?"

Tamika laughed. "Are you kidding?"

"So, how's everything going up there?"

"Well, I haven't really seen anybody yet, but it's going okay."

"*Alhamdulillaah.*"

"How's it going down there?"

"It's going well. We just got back from the *masjid*[15] a little while ago."

"I thought you might be at *Jumuah.* How was it?"

"Excellent, *mashaAllah,*" Aminah said. "I really needed it. After a year of school, spiritual inspiration is the best way to end it."

"I wish I could've been there."

"Maybe there are some *masjids* there."

"Well, we'll see," Tamika said, chuckling. "I have to get past my mother first."

There was a thoughtful pause.

"How's your brother's speech going?" Tamika asked, changing the subject.

Aminah laughed. "Just pray for him."

Tamika grinned. "You make it sound like he needs a lot of help."

"No, it's good actually, *barakAllaahufeeh*[16]. It's just that he wants everybody to make *du'aa*[17] for his speech. You know, because it's up to Allah how it goes in the end."

---

[15] mosque

"Yeah, that's true."

"Oh yeah," Aminah said, laughing as she remembered something. "Guess who we saw at *Jumuah*?"

A smile creased the corners of Tamika's mouth. "Who?"

"Omar."

She burst out laughing. "And?"

"And he asked about you again."

"Didn't you tell him I'm not interested?"

"I think Sulayman did."

"Then why's he asking about me?"

"Who knows? I think he may wait your required ten years."

They both laughed.

"I hope you're joking," Tamika said.

"Yeah, I'm kidding. But he doesn't seem to be giving up so easily. He even asked Sulayman who your *walee* is."

"My what?"

"*Walee*. The guardian who's in charge of your marriage. Remember I was saying that the man has to ask the permission of the woman's father for marriage?"

"But I don't have any Muslim family," Tamika said, remembering that the closest Muslim relative took on the role for a woman with no father.

"Well, for women without Muslim family, the imam takes on the responsibility."

"So the imam's my *walee*?" Tamika was flattered. She remembered his powerful sermon when she first visited the *masjid* for her research paper.

"Yeah." Aminah chuckled. "And that's what we told Omar."

Tamika rolled her eyes. "Gee, thanks."

Aminah laughed. "Hey, we can't get in between that. If a brother's interested, he has a right to go through the proper channels."

"But the imam doesn't know me."

"He knows of you."

Taken aback, Tamika wrinkled her forehead. "How?"

"My father told him about you after you took your *shahaadah*[18]."

"Really?"

"Yeah, so I'm sure he remembers you."

"Has he seen me before?"

"I'm not sure."

"Then what will he do when brothers ask about me?"

Aminah laughed. "Well, I guess send them away, huh? Since you wanna make them suffer for ten years!"

---

[16] "May Allah bless him," said when giving a compliment or praising someone.

[17] An informal supplication to God for what one wants.

[18] The formal testimony of faith uttered upon one's entrance into Islam.

They laughed.

"But, seriously," Tamika said a second later.

"I don't know. I guess we'll see, *inshaAllaah*, after Omar asks about you. He'll probably want your contact information and stuff."

"He'll call me here?" Tamika hoped not.

"I don't think so. I'm just guessing." There was a brief pause. "If he does want your contact information, should we give it to him?"

"To Omar?" Tamika asked in shock.

"No. To the imam."

Tamika considered it momentarily, immediately thinking of her mother. "Uh, you can," she said hesitantly, "but he'll have to pretend to be a professor or something."

"Your mother doesn't want Muslims calling?"

"She doesn't know I'm Muslim."

Aminah was silent momentarily. "Oh. Well, I'm sure he's used to this type of situation. *InshaAllaah*, he'll know what to do."

"If he asks, tell him to just try and call on the weekdays between nine and five. My mother's usually at work during that time." Tamika thought of something. "He's not going to give my number to Omar, will he?"

"No. He wouldn't do anything like that."

Aminah's response reminded Tamika of a question she had. "Is it *haraam*[19] for a brother to call me?"

"No. It's just not proper etiquette for a *walee* to just give out your number like that. If the *walee* approves of a brother, he may give out the number, but only after he gets the sister's permission and makes sure that they both understand the Islamic limits in conversation and meeting."

"I see."

"But I'm sure that's *far* in the future," Aminah teased.

Tamika laughed. "But it's still good to plan ahead."

"Yeah, I suppose."

"You think I'm crazy for waiting ten years?"

"No. It's just different, that's all."

"When do Muslims typically get married?"

"There's no typical age really. Once you're in puberty, you can get married."

"Is there an age that's best to?"

"Not really. But, on average, Muslims get married earlier than non-Muslims, especially in the West."

"How much earlier?"

"It depends. But the youngest I know of personally is sixteen—for a woman."

"Sixteen! That's young."

---

[19] Prohibited or sinful

"Yeah, I know."

"How young do men marry?"

"The youngest I've heard of is eighteen. But that's rare."

Tamika didn't know what to say.

"But you have to remember, Muslims who practice don't have relationships outside of marriage. In Western society, people have several partners before they finally get married." She chuckled. "And they start well before sixteen."

Tamika grew silent, self-conscious all of a sudden as she remembered her relationship at fifteen. Many people she knew had boyfriends and girlfriends in junior high school. "That's true."

"So, anyway, I won't hold you. I just wanted to give you a call."

"Thanks."

"No problem." There was a brief pause.

"Tamika?" There was a trace of concern in Aminah's voice.

"Yeah?"

"If you need anything, don't hesitate to call, okay?"

Tamika sensed that Aminah was concerned about her mother not knowing of her conversion to Islam. "Okay."

"And you can call collect if you need to."

She nodded more for herself than Aminah. But she doubted she would need to call for anything. She should be fine. At most, her mother would get angry. "Thanks."

"You're welcome." Aminah paused. "Take care, okay?"

"You too."

"*As-salaamu-'alaikum.*"

"*Wa-'alaiku-mus-salaam.*" Tamika hung up the phone and held it for a moment before putting it back on the table. She wondered if she would ever tell her mother.

The sound of keys turning in the door startled her. She stood and touched her head, making sure she remembered to take off her *khimaar* after praying. Her heart pounded, and she glanced around the room. There were no visible signs of her Islam. She sat back down and picked up her novel. She should appear as normal as possible.

"There you are!" her mother greeted thunderously. Wearing a large smile, she shut the door behind her and locked it. "Come and give your mother some sugar!"

Tamika smiled self-consciously and set her book down before greeting her mother at the door. They embraced and held each other for a moment more. Tamika shut her eyes and enjoyed the sweet scent of her mother's perfume emanating from her work clothes. She didn't want to let go. It felt like a goodbye hug, and she wondered when she would see her mother again. After the embrace, her mother kissed her on the cheek and stepped back to gaze at Tamika.

"How's my college graduate?"

Tamika laughed, now accustomed to the title that she had two more years to rightly earn. "Fine."

Thelma held her daughter's hand and walked with her into the kitchen. "How are your grades this semester?"

Tamika shrugged as her mother let go of her hand and opened the refrigerator. "I don't know yet."

"How you think you did?" Her mother removed the pack of hotdogs before filling a pan with water to boil.

"Okay, I suppose. I didn't ask about my grades this term."

"Oh?" She raised her eyebrows in concern and glanced at her daughter.

"But they should be okay."

Her mother nodded, putting the pan on the stove and turning it on. "What do you mean by okay?"

Tamika forced laughter. "Don't worry. I just had a lot to do before I left. I didn't have time to visit all my professors this time."

"But you must have some idea how you did."

"I got an *A* in religion," she offered with a smile, hoping that would cheer up her mother.

Thelma's face brightened as she removed her work blazer and hung it on the back of her chair. She unbuttoned the cuffs of her white blouse and pushed the sleeves up to her elbows, exposing her large forearms. She then took a seat across from Tamika. "Really?"

"Yeah."

"How do you know?"

Tamika felt like she was under interrogation, but she knew her mother only wanted to make sure she was spending her time wisely at school. There were so many minorities who never had the opportunity to go, and even those who did were not always able to finish.

"Well, I did stop by one professor's office."

Her mother smiled. "Well, I ain't surprised. I raised you Christian."

Tamika's heart pounded. She didn't know what to say. She forced a smile, hoping her mother couldn't see through her pretence.

There was a long pause as Thelma studied her daughter thoughtfully. "You still go to church with, uh, what's her name? Makisha?"

"Sometimes," Tamika said with a nod, mentally telling herself that was halfway true. She had gone to church with Makisha before she converted to Islam.

"Now, you know a Christian ain't Christian sometimes."

"I know." She nodded, lowering her eyes. How had they gotten on this subject? She should've kept her religion grade to herself. She had to take control of the conversation before it got out of hand.

"How's Aunt Jackie?"

Her mother laughed and nodded. "She's fine. You call her after you got home?"

"I figured I should wait until I was sure she was home."

Her mother glanced at the clock. "She's usually home around this time." She waved her hand. "But we can call her later." She stood and walked over to the stove to survey her hotdogs.

"You eat, child?"

"Uh, yeah," Tamika said hurriedly, sensing what was about to unfold.

"When?"

Her mother was never going to stop being a mother. She was always fretting about how poorly Tamika ate. "A few minutes ago," she exaggerated.

"What'd you eat? Don't look like much happened in here. 'Couldn't have fixed nothin' worth much."

"I had some yogurt." She feared her mother had memorized the contents of the kitchen enough to catch her in a lie.

"That's what you call eatin'?"

Tamika shrugged and forced a smile. "I'm fine."

"You need some meat on those bones. Some dogs and salad should hold you till tonight. I got some greens and pork chops I can fix if we 'on't go out." Her mother walked over to the refrigerator and opened the freezer before setting the frozen meat on the counter. She then pulled out a bag of Romaine lettuce and dressing from the refrigerator. She placed them on the counter before pulling some tomatoes from the bottom drawer. "Quit sittin' there like a guest and get up and fix yourself a salad while we wait for the dogs."

Tamika stood in obedience and mindlessly fixed herself a salad, dreading when the hotdogs would be ready. "I'm really not that hungry," she said after cutting up some tomatoes and sprinkling them on top of the lettuce.

"I'm sure you ain't." Her mother laughed, shaking her head. "You don't eat nothin'. Your stomach probably thinks a cup of yogurt is a meal."

Tamika forced a smile, unsure how she would get out of this one. She carried her plate and fork to the table with the dressing and sat down in a daze. She poured the dressing over her salad. A few seconds later, her mother sat down with hers.

"What're you waiting for, child? Eat," her mother commanded in firm love.

Tamika drew in a deep breath and exhaled before taking a bite.

"You act like you about to run a fifty-mile marathon, girl. What do you eat at school?"

She forced a smile and began eating the salad. She was careful to make it appear as if she was enjoying it. She would need to back out of the next part of the meal. "I eat whatever's there."

"Hm," her mother huffed. "When I was your age, I ate a full meal every day."

Tamika forced laughter, wanting to have a friendly exchange with her mother. "But that was a long time ago, in the South."

"Soul food is good for the soul, even if you ain't in the South. I don't forget where I come from." Thelma nodded her head toward Tamika, holding her fork still for a moment. "And don't you."

Unsure how to respond, Tamika nodded and continued eating. A few minutes later, her mother stood, and Tamika's eyes followed her to the stove. Tamika chewed the salad carefully and swallowed. She wished she could disappear. She hadn't bargained for this moment, having foolishly assumed she could avoid the issue of religion until she felt like bringing it up. She thought she could go the whole summer without dealing with it. And here she was, hadn't even been with her mother for a good hour, and she was already confronting the issue head on.

Tamika watched her mother pick up the hotdogs with a fork, lifting them one by one, the steam rising from each one and then from the pile on the plate. Her gaze followed her mother to the cabinet, where she pulled out some buns, broke off a few and placed them next to the hotdogs on the plate. Tamika's heart pounded wildly, fearing the worst. What should she do? Her mother placed the plate before them and sat down.

"Eat," her mother said stubbornly, apparently still upset about Tamika's eating habits.

Tamika stared at the hotdogs anxiously, watching the brown meat emit steam, the smell reaching her nostrils. Her stomach churned at the thought of eating swine. She hadn't eaten pork since moving in with Dee and Aminah.

"Something wrong?"

She turned to her mother too quickly, her eyes giving away her concern. "No, ma'am."

"Then why you lookin' at the dogs like somebody died?"

She didn't know what to say. "I, uh, I'm just getting stuffed."

Her mother stared at her suspiciously. "You a vegetarian or somethin'?"

A vegetarian. Why hadn't Tamika thought of that? That would definitely relieve her of having to face this dilemma each day. "Sort of." She hoped it didn't count as a lie.

Her mother wrinkled her forehead and eyed Tamika curiously. "Since when?"

Tamika shrugged. "I don't know. A month or so."

"With your size, the last thing you need to do is stop eating meat."

She nodded. "I know, but," she smiled then wrinkled her nose as her eyes fell on the hotdogs, "for some reason it makes me sick now."

"Since when?"

"Since I stopped eating it a few months ago." She hoped her mother would just leave it alone.

"Well," her mother said with such finality that Tamika feared her mother would shove it down her throat, "I don't like it, but you grown now. Do as you please."

What! Had she heard her mother correctly? This was definitely a first. Inside, she thanked God over and over. She knew this one was from Him.

"But you better finish every bit of that salad, child."

Tamika nodded and resumed eating. "Yes, ma'am."

"I guess I gotta go out and buy tofu, huh?"

She forced laughter. "Salad is fine."

"Well, you gonna need some beans or somethin'. A body can't do without protein." Her mother served herself two hotdogs and placed them in buns next to her salad. "And I certainly ain't gonna deprive this body of it."

Tamika smiled, relaxing now that the hardest part was over—at least for now. They ate the remainder of the meal with her mother occasionally asking about something related to school. When they finished, Tamika cleared the table and washed the dishes.

"I'm gonna go on and call Jackie." Her mother stood, covering her mouth as she yawned. "She should be home."

Just then Tamika remembered the late afternoon prayer. She looked at the clock. It was four minutes past 6:00. She needed to pray. She glanced over her shoulder and saw her mother entering the living room to make the phone call. This was probably the only chance she would have. After hearing her mother start dialing, she quickly dried her hands and made her way out of the kitchen and headed for the hall.

"Where you headed, child?"

"I have to get something from my room."

"Jackie!" Thelma laughed into the phone.

Tamika hurried to her room and gently closed the door before locking it. She quickly put on her *khimaar* and blazer. She pulled the head cover over her head, grateful that she hadn't bothered to remove the pin. She then faced the direction she had earlier and started the prayer. She struggled to concentrate on what she was saying and forced herself not to hurry, but it was difficult. Her mother was in the living room, and she would be off the phone any minute.

When Tamika completed half of the prayer, she was mentally counting down until she would be done. She felt guilty for not giving the prayer the attention and concentration it deserved, and she could only hope Allah would forgive her for disrespecting Him like this. She hated going through the motions and tried to put her mind on her Lord. She had one more unit of prayer left when she heard her mother calling her from the living room.

"Tamika! Your aunt wants to talk to you!"

O Lord! What now? She hurried through the prayer, barely taking time to think about what she was doing.

"Tamika!" Her mother was coming down the hall.

Tamika touched her head to the ground twice, moving more quickly than she should have. She sat down reciting the words without caring if she said them correctly. She was still new at this, and rushing through the Arabic was really a bad idea.

"Tamika!" Her mother was at her door when she quickly turned her head to the right and left, finishing the prayer.

Standing quickly, Tamika yanked the cloth from her head and threw it on the bed as her mother tried to open the door. Her heart raced as she tried to unlock it before her mother realized that it was locked. A second later her mother stood at the doorway of her room staring at Tamika in confusion, her ear to the phone and a hand covering the mouthpiece. Thelma's eyebrows gathered as she surveyed her daughter's clothes. "What the hell you wearing a jacket for?"

Tamika looked down in mortification and saw that she was still wearing the blazer she had prayed in. She forced a smile. "I was a little chilly."

Thelma studied Tamika for a moment, unsure what to think of her daughter's rushed expression and senseless explanation. She eyed her daughter suspiciously as she handed her the phone. "Your aunt wants to talk to you."

Avoiding her mother's gaze, Tamika accepted the phone and greeted her aunt with feigned excitement. But she feared her mother knew something was up. She laughed and talked with her aunt, extending the conversation more than she wanted. She dreaded facing her mother. As Tamika talked in her room, Thelma watched television in the living room, waiting for her daughter to finish.

When Tamika finally hung up, she shut her eyes and pressed the cordless against her forehead. She exhaled in mental exhaustion. What now? She stalled for a few minutes, trying to decide whether to stay in her room or join her mother and pretend nothing was wrong.

"Tamika!"

Tamika's heart pounded. She drew in a deep breath as she walked down the hall into the living room. "Ma'am?"

"Come sit next to me."

Tamika forced a smile and she sat down. "What're you watching?"

Her mother frowned and muted the television.

Tamika stiffened.

"Never mind what I'm watching. Are you sick?"

"I don't think so."

"Then why you cold and I ain't even turned on the air?"

She forced a smile. "I guess I'm not used to cool summers anymore."

Thelma studied her daughter's face in distrust. "You ain't got pneumonia, do you?"

Tamika expression grew concerned. "I hope not."

There was a long pause, and Tamika pretended to see a spot on her dress.

"Your aunt wants us to come over tonight."

"Oh, okay."

"Your cousins are renting some movies. Sounds like they 'bout to have a party." She paused and studied Tamika. "You feel well enough to go?"

Tamika considered it. Did she want to face her cousins tonight? "What time?"

"Around eight."

She tried to remember what time the sun set in Atlanta to get an idea of when it set in Milwaukee. She didn't want to go anywhere before she prayed. For the night prayer, she could just pray before bed, but if she delayed the sunset prayer, she might miss it completely. She shrugged. "I think I'll lie down for a bit to get some energy before we go." She hoped her mother would agree.

Her mother yawned and rubbed her watering eyes. "I think I need some rest myself. We'll shoot for eight. But wake me up after you rest." She clicked off the television with the remote and stood after slapping her thighs with her hands. "You know where to find me."

Tamika forced laughter. "Yes, ma'am."

She could pray in peace after all. She would simply wake her mother after she prayed. She could even go outside to see where the sun was setting. That way, she could pray in the right direction for the rest of the summer.

Tamika heard her mother's bedroom door close, and a painful realization came to her. She would have to tell her mother soon. Otherwise, all of her prayers would be an adventure. She sighed and leaned her head on the back of the couch. *O Lord, give me the strength.*

Tamika went to her room and closed the door. She decided to lock it for maximum privacy. She took off her blazer and sat at her desk. She needed to regroup. She didn't want to go to her aunt's house. They would be drinking alcohol and listening to popular hip-hop music. Then there was the dancing and R-rated movies. She would look like a party pooper if she leaned against a wall the entire time. What could she say to make them understand?

And her cousins. What would she do about them? Raymond, who was two years older, would certainly want to give her a hug, and he'd probably keep his arm around her the entire time. His affection always made her uncomfortable, but in the past she had brushed it off, telling herself they were cousins. He meant no harm. But now she understood that male cousins were like other strange men, forbidden to touch her. In retrospect, he must have viewed her as he did other women. His affection was always a bit exaggerated for mere family. She had sensed his attraction to her was deeper than he let on, but she felt bad for thinking something like that.

Inside, she cringed. She dreaded the entire scene, surprising herself with how much she had changed. Before, she saw the parties as innocent family gatherings, but now the mere thought disgusted her. Perhaps she should pretend to be ill to avoid the night entirely. It definitely wouldn't be unusual for the party to last all night. How could she pray the night prayer if it did? And if she wanted to wake at dawn to pray, she needed to go to bed at a decent hour.

She sighed. As much as she hated to admit it, this only reiterated the need to tell her mother the truth—sooner rather than later.

It was twenty minutes after 8:00 when Tamika noticed the time. She had watched television for a little while and was now sitting at her desk reading a book. She often turned on her lamplight when she read, so the growing darkness in the house hadn't alerted her to the approaching sunset. She closed her book and quietly made her way to the bathroom down the hall. She knew the sun had already set, and she needed to perform ablution for prayer.

In the bathroom she cleaned the necessary body parts for *wudoo'* then quietly headed to her room. When she passed her mother's room, which was across from hers, she noticed the darkness under the door. This was a good sign. Maybe she could make it through prayer without waking her mother. Tamika hated praying another prayer in the wrong direction, but she decided to go ahead and pray before going outside to see where the sun had set. If her mother woke up while she was outside, she would miss the prayer.

In her room, she closed the door softly and locked it before putting on her blazer and *khimaar*. She relaxed in the quiet house and tried to take her time with the prayer, reciting the Arabic in a slow, measured tone. She had to recite the Qur'an aloud for the prayer, but she was careful to recite as inaudibly as possible. She feared her mother would wake to the strange sounds.

It was refreshing to pray in peace, but Tamika knew every prayer wouldn't be like this. When she finished, she sat reflecting for a few minutes before standing to go outside. She removed her *khimaar* and kept on her blazer, fearing that outside would be cool.

She left her room nearly tiptoeing down the hall and exhaled when she passed through the living room and stood at the front door. She slipped on her shoes and quietly unlocked the door. She opened it slowly, hoping the noise wouldn't disturb her mother. She stepped out in the breezy evening and was glad she had worn her blazer. She decided against shutting the front door completely. She left it slightly ajar, not wanting to risk her mother hearing the sound of the door opening.

She walked into the middle of her yard and surveyed the horizon. She found the reddish orange of sunset at the back of her house, the direction she had been facing. She had been praying in the opposite direction. She silently sought God's forgiveness and started toward the house. She wanted to stay outside and relax in the peaceful evening, but she knew her mother would wake soon and become worried if she did.

Inside she closed the door and locked it before slipping off her shoes. She stepped into the dark living room and screamed at the sight of a silhouette standing near the couch.

"Where you been, child?" Thelma's voice rose, the scratchy tone revealing that she just woke up. She turned on the light on the nightstand and stared at her daughter with her arms folded.

Tamika's heart slowed to its normal pace as she recovered from the scare. "I was, um, just looking at the sunset."

"How long you been gone?"

Tamika's expression was of fear and uncertainty. "A few minutes."

"Don't lie to me, child. I raised three of ya'll, and I can smell trouble a mile away. You wasn't lookin' at no sunset."

Tamika didn't know what to say. She wanted to disagree, but her mother would only grow angrier.

"In fact, I don't think you slept a wink. Did you?"

She lowered her head slightly. "No ma'am, but I relaxed a little and—."

"And what?" Thelma's expression was cold, sending fear through every inch of Tamika's body. "Whatever bull you tryin' to pull," she cut in before her daughter could speak, "save it. 'Cause I want the truth. You ain't been yourself since you stepped in this house. I already know you got somethin' up your sleeve, but I ain't sure what it is. But I'll assure you, you ain't as much as steppin' out that front door for the rest of this summer till I know. And I'll let your aunt know why we couldn't make it, don't worry about that."

Tamika tried to calm herself. She felt like her head was spinning. "Yes, ma'am," she murmured, feeling her face grow hot, and her eyes burned.

Her mother huffed. "Come here and sit down on this couch, child."

Tamika obeyed and stared blankly at the dull gray screen of the television set, waiting for her next instruction. She felt the urge to cry, but she fought it. Her mother would think it was part of a game to get sympathy. The couch cushion moved as the weight of Thelma's body met it. Tamika felt her mother glaring at her, but she wouldn't meet her gaze.

"Speak." The house grew deadly silent at Thelma's command.

Tamika wanted to speak, but she couldn't. Her mother didn't say a word as she waited, and Tamika knew she wasn't getting out of this one. It was either the truth or nothing. But Tamika was afraid the truth would be more painful than the latter. So she sat in utter silence, unsure what to do. Her mother would sit there all night if she had to, and Tamika wasn't getting up until her mother knew exactly what was going on.

"Is there some boy you sneakin' off to?"

"No," Tamika mumbled loud enough for her mother to hear. The night suffocated her, and she wished she had never come home.

"Now, ain't nothin' peculiar about bein' in love." Thelma was trying to make Tamika more comfortable with talking to her, but it didn't work.

Tamika didn't speak, and the house grew silent again. She knew she should say something, but she didn't know what. In panic, words raced through her mind, but none slowed enough to reach her throat. It was her heart that held her voice, but her mother had no ears to hear it.

The living room became a blur as Tamika was consumed in her struggle to find the right words, and for a moment she felt as if she were somewhere else.

"Alright. I hate to do this."

Thelma's voice startled Tamika in its abruptness, and Tamika's surroundings came alive suddenly. The television screen reflected her mother's large body standing, and Tamika's eyes followed Thelma as she walked away from the couch. The lamp created a dark shadow on the wall that followed her out of the room.

Her mother disappeared down the hallway, and Tamika's heart went wild in her chest. A minute later Thelma returned with one of Tamika's suitcases and dropped it on the living room floor with a thud. She went to get the other one and dropped it next to the first.

Terrified, Tamika stared at her mother. She feared she was being thrown on the street. Her mother sat down and pointed to the bags.

"Open them." Thelma's tone was calm and confident. She was an expert detective, earned by years of experience with motherhood.

Tamika had no idea what was unfolding, but she knew it wasn't good.

"Now," her mother commanded too loudly for Tamika's ears, prompting Tamika to stand almost in attention and walk over to the bags. Thelma watched intently as Tamika slowly unzipped each bag and opened it so her mother could see.

"Take everything out and set it on the floor."

Her mother's voice stung her ears, and humiliation swept through her. Tamika blindly obeyed, too overwhelmed with her disgraceful state to comprehend what was going on. On her hands and knees, she did as she was told. She felt tears gather in her eyes. There was no warmth in the house at the moment, and Tamika imagined this was how Latonya and Philip had felt.

"E-ve-ry-thing." Her mother's command was thunderous as she pronounced each syllable to underscore her anger and distrust.

Tamika swallowed, feeling as if both her privacy and dignity were being snatched from her. She shivered and continued unpacking. Fear swept through her, and she could only imagine what was in store for her. Her mother watched with the eye of a hawk, and Tamika felt the assault of her glare.

When all the contents were sprawled out on the floor, her mother's voice again rose in the room. "Bring me your purse and anything else you brought with you."

In a daze, Tamika stood. The night grew ominously still as she made her way down the hall to her room. She picked up her book bag and purse and returned to the living room.

"Dump both the bags on the couch."

Emotional pain swept through her, and the tears gushed from her eyes. She coughed, almost choking, and, like a robot, she emptied her purse and bag on the couch next to her mother. Her cosmetics, keys, money, sanitary napkins, and books fell in a pitiful pile.

Ignoring her daughter's tears, Thelma stood and hovered over the contents with her hands on her wide hips. A second later she picked up Tamika's phone book and studied each page with meticulous scrutiny. "Who's Dante?"

Tears blurred Tamika's vision, and she swallowed so she could speak. "Makisha's boyfriend."

"Do I need to call him to verify that?"

"You can if you want." Tamika was too upset to care if her response counted as backtalk.

"Who's Dee?"

She clinched her teeth. She met Thelma's gaze so her mother could know her cruelty. "The girl who died in the car accident."

Thelma turned to another page. "Who's Aminah?"

"My roommate." Tamika's voice rose as she grew more confident.

Her mother eyed her suspiciously as she called off name after name until she was satisfied. Tossing the address book to the side, she picked up some of the books that had fallen. Tamika cringed as she remembered that she had put some Islamic books in her bag.

"Oh." Thelma's eyebrows rose as she picked up a small book of Muslim prayers and held it in the air. "What's this?"

Tamika looked away. Her jaw tightened in anger as the tears dripped from her chin. Did she have to treat her own daughter like this? "A book."

Her mother shook the book as she glared at Tamika. "About what?"

"What it says."

A sudden sting on her face put Tamika off balance for a second. She stumbled before standing upright again. She put a hand over the side of her face where her mother had just slapped her, feeling her cheek grow hot and swell in pain. She stared at her mother wide-eyed in disbelief.

"Watch your mouth, little girl." Her mother pointed to her daringly. A second later, a large finger pressed forcefully between her eyes. "I can break your little bones if you wanna match me."

Tamika felt her teeth chattering in fear, and fresh tears spilled from her eyes.

"I asked you a question, and I want a clear answer." Thelma raised her voice and waved the book in front of her daughter's face. "I said, what's this?"

"A b-b-b-ook of Muslim prayers."

"A book of Muslim prayers?" A thunderous laugh exploded from Thelma, and her face grew serious a second later. "What is my Christian, church-going daughter doing with a Muslim book of prayer!"

Tamika shut her eyes, feeling her mother's hot breath as she shouted in her face.

"Answer me!"

"I, I, I—."

"You what? Talk!"

Tamika felt the book being slapped against the top of her head. "I was, um, doing a research paper on Islam."

"For what?"

Her crying became uncontrollable, and she began to sob. "M-m-my, my religion course."

"Why you studying Islam when you're Christian?"

"We, um, couldn't, um, do our, uh, own religion." She tried to pull herself together, but she only sobbed more. Her response came out as a whine, "It was, um, it was, um, it was—."

"It was what!"

"It was, um, required to, uh, do another r-r-religion." Her voice cracked and she felt her body weaken. This wasn't going well at all. O Lord! What should she do?

"And when was this paper due?"

"In, uh, April."

"Did you finish it?"

She nodded as she tried to speak. "Um, yes ma'am."

"Then why you still have the book?"

"Because, um, I, um, bought it."

"And?"

"And, um, it's mine." Was she making sense? She couldn't tell. She felt faint. She was nauseated and wanted to sit down.

Her mother stared at her suspiciously then turned to go through the other contents on the couch, tossing to the floor whatever she chose. Thelma located the address book again and picked it up, this time taking a seat on the couch. Tamika watched in trepidation as her mother picked up the phone.

"We'll see if you tellin' the truth." Thelma found a name in the address book and began dialing.

"Yes, um, hello," her mother said such a sweet voice that Tamika's stomach churned. "May I speak to Makisha?"

Tamika's legs weakened and she slowly sat down on the floor. Makisha was the last person she wanted her mother to call, but her mother knew they were best friends.

"I'm Thelma, Tamika's mom." She laughed. "I'm fine, and you? How's Dante?"

Tamika glared at her, but Thelma didn't meet her gaze. Her mother could not be doing this.

Thelma laughed. "Oh, Tamika tells me everything. She says you're the best of friends." There was a long pause as her mother listened. Tamika could hear talking coming from the phone, but she couldn't make out what Makisha was saying.

"Oh, I'm sure," Thelma interjected with a laugh. "Oh, yes, she's fine. I don't want to take too much of your time, but I'm just worried about Tamika. You see, she's not been feeling well, and I was wondering if you noticed anything strange or if she had a chance to talk to you about anything." There was a long pause as Thelma listened. Seconds later, her jaw tightened in anger. "I see."

Tamika knew the truth was out, and there was nothing she could do but wait for her fate.

"An argument, you say? About what?" Thelma nodded and eyed Tamika with an icy glare, her voice still artfully sweet to Makisha. "Your religious differences? Are you Christian, sweetheart?" A laugh. "Oh you are? Then whatever could you be differing about?" Thelma nodded as she listened, her eyes on Tamika the whole time. "Mm, hm," she said sweetly into the phone. "I see." A pause. "Oh, no I understand." She laughed. "Oh yes, I knew, but it's just that I was hoping it was just a phase." A pause. "I see." A nod. "Mm, hm." Thelma listened. "Oh there's nothing to apologize about, sweetheart, nothing at all. No, no, no." She laughed. "Tamika's right here. Everything's fine." Another laugh. "She's just getting the flu, and you know, I could tell something was on her mind making her feel down." She laughed. "No problem. I sure will." A pause. "I sure will. You too. Bye, bye."

Thelma was on top of her so quickly that Tamika momentarily wondered if her mother had time to hang up the phone. Tamika felt her body being yanked forward by the front of her dress, and she stumbled to her feet with her mother's force. Her mother shoved her against the wall, still holding the dress. Thelma leaned forward, and Tamika could smell the staleness of pork hotdogs on her mother's breath.

"Why does your best friend seem to think you converted to this so-called re-li-gion you researched?"

Tamika was too frightened to speak. Everything was happening too fast. She felt her body hit the wall, and her back ached.

"Why!"

Her ears stung with the shout, and she trembled. She wanted to speak but couldn't find her voice.

Fed up, Thelma let go of her daughter's dress. Tamika could only watch in shocked disbelief as her mother rummaged through her belongings like a maniac. The scene felt surreal, and for a moment Tamika imagined herself in Atlanta with Aminah's family.

"What's this!" A book hit the wall in a loud thud, missing Tamika's face only slightly. "And this!" Another one. "And this!"

Tamika recognized this one, and she started to scream in protest. In horror, her eyes widened as she watched the scene as if in slow motion. The emerald green cover that was decorated in gold calligraphy enclosed the thickness of the Qur'an as it flew through the air and finally hit her in the stomach with so much force that she fell to her knees.

"Get the hell outta my house! Get out! Get out!"

Tamika curled up on the floor and shook in fear, afraid to stay, terrified to leave.

"I said get out! Get out! Now!"

She felt the heavy hands falling on her rapidly, and she covered her head to protect herself from the blows. The continuous shouts nearly deafened her, and for a moment she forgot where she was. She could only cry, feeling a bitter loneliness that she could not escape. Only God could save her then, and she found herself wondering if He would.

"Get out! Get the hell outta here now!"

Terrified, Tamika had no idea what to do. Her only instinct was to save her life. But how? She couldn't fight her own mother. Tamika's head jerked uncomfortably as her mother pulled her by the hair to force her from the house. Tamika stepped on the front of her dress, causing it to rip as her mother tried to yank her up. Numbed with fear, Tamika fell back to the ground in a heap. She covered her head, too frightened to move.

A second later, Thelma grabbed the back collars of Tamika's dress and blazer and dragged her daughter so violently that Tamika felt the front of the dress choking her. Gasping for air, Tamika fought herself loose and scurried to her feet. She ran into the kitchen as she struggled to catch her breath. Her mother charged after her, shouting at her to leave. Tamika ran behind the kitchen table and jumped from side to side, faking out her mother, who didn't know which way to run. Her mother stopped chasing her suddenly and contented herself with glaring at her child.

"Get out of my house before I throw you out."

Tamika backed up cautiously, as if waiting for her mother to pounce on her, but her mother didn't move. She left the kitchen walking backwards then nervously entered the living room. In panic, she rushed to her purse, stuffing her money and whatever personals she could find back into the bag. She fell to her hands and knees in tears, feeling around the floor and table for her address book, which she knew she would need. She was breathing heavily and desperately prayed she would find it before her mother went into a rage again. She found it a few feet from the cordless phone on the floor and stuffed it into her purse. She remembered her keys and glanced around for them.

"Get out!" Tamika sensed her mother coming near, and she hurried to the door, unable to grab anything else. She hugged her purse almost compulsively as she slipped on her shoes.

"And don't ever come back until you remember who you are!"

Tamika was out the door a second later, and she heard her mother shouting after her. She ran through the front yard to the sidewalk and then down the dark street. She felt tears in her eyes as she ran for her life. But she had no idea where she was heading.   Some people stopped to stare, but Tamika didn't have time to think about them right then.

Six

When Tamika tired of running, she tried to catch her breath. She leaned forward hugging her purse and breathed in and out like she had been taught when she had run track. Her breathing was painful, and she wondered if she had asthma. She noticed her torn dress and realized her tattered appearance. She would draw a lot of attention if she didn't go somewhere soon. She glanced around and guessed that she was about a mile from home. She stared ahead of her. What should she do? A phone booth stood outside of a grocery store in a plaza ahead. She immediately headed toward it.

Inside the booth, her hands shook as she dialed the operator and told her she needed to make a collect call. She hated to disturb Aminah and her family, but she didn't know what else to do. She pulled out the address book from her purse and flipped to the page that had Aminah's information on it. She then recited the number to the operator and waited to be prompted to say her name. She silently prayed they were home. When a woman's voice said, "Yes," and accepted the call, she whispered thanks to Allah. Her tears had dried, but she still felt overwhelmed and confused. The entire situation was shocking, but she shouldn't have been surprised. Her mother had a short temper when things didn't go her way. Tamika had seen Latonya treated similarly after their mother learned she was pregnant.

"Tamika?" Aminah's voice was a whisper, but her deep concern was apparent.

The soft, caring voice made Tamika weaken, and she felt a lump developing in her throat. She wished so badly that Aminah was next to her right then. She needed a hug. "Yes. It's me."

"Are you alright?" Too overcome with concern, Aminah forgot the Islamic greeting.

"I'm fine," Tamika lied, about to break down. "I'm sorry to call collect." She drew in a deep breath and exhaled, resisting the urge to cry. "I just—."

"Where are you?"

Tears welled in her eyes, and she blinked to stop them. "In a phone booth."

"You're not home?"

"My mom kicked me out." Her voice cracked and became a whine in her last breath. Unable to withhold any longer, tears spilled from her eyes, and she began to sob into the phone. She mentally kicked herself for being so weak.

"Okay," Aminah said, taking a deep breath, "tell me what's going on."

Aminah sat on her brother's bed, where she had been listening to him practice his speech. Sulayman stood a few feet from her, now distracted by the words his sister was speaking into the phone. He knew she was talking to Tamika. He had heard Aminah say her roommate's name. He watched with intent concern as Aminah lowered her head and shook it as she listened, clearly disturbed by what she was hearing. He saw her face grow pink and her eyes water, and he knew something was terribly wrong.

"Okay," Aminah said, still shaking her head in disbelief. She was silent for a few minutes then sighed and looked toward Sulayman, her eyes telling him that her friend was in trouble. "Tamika, is there a phonebook in the booth?"

Tamika glanced around the booth and spotted one attached to a thick wire. "Yes." She sniffed.

"Can you look up a hotel for me? Anything that's close to where you are now."

"I think there's a, um," she sniffed, wiping her tears with one hand, "a, um, hotel a few miles down the street."

"Is that the closest one?"

"I think so."

Aminah took a deep breath. "Okay, then, find the number."

"I, um, don't have enough money to stay there."

"Tamika, listen to me," she said as Sulayman stared at her intently. His face became flushed with worry. "Don't worry about that. Just give me the number, and do exactly what I say, okay?"

"Okay."

"After you give me the number, I want you to hang up and start walking to the hotel. Do you know where it is?"

"Yes."

"When you get to the hotel, I want you to give me a call on the nearest payphone. Try to make yourself as presentable as possible, because I don't want them to turn you away."

"But my dress is ripped," Tamika whined as tears streamed down her face.

Aminah sighed, shaking her head and trying to think what to do. "Okay, um, then can you cover it up somehow?"

Tamika tried to think as the tears flooded her vision. She wiped her face and looked down at the rip.

"Can you tie a knot to hide it?"

Tamika studied the tear and decided she could, although it would appear a bit awkward. "I think so."

"Okay, then, do that." Aminah paused to take a deep breath. "Do you have something to cover your hair?"

"No, everything's at the house."

Aminah sighed. "If you don't have a comb, just run your fingers through it until you think you look okay. But before you go in the hotel, find a restaurant bathroom or something where you can see how you look. And Tamika?"

"Yes?"

"Don't think of anything right now except that Allah is there for you, okay?"

"Okay." Tamika nodded through tears.

"It's fine to cry, but try to fight it for now, until we can get you a room." She cried more. "Okay."

"Remember, as you walk, just think about Allah and nothing else, okay?"

"Okay."

"And don't stop to talk to anyone. You can't trust anybody, especially at night. If anybody wants directions or something, play deaf, okay?"

"Okay."

"Tie your dress, and smooth down your hair so people don't call the police, okay?"

"Okay."

"Now, remember, call me before you go in the hotel, even if it's from a nearby gas station. *InshaAllaah,* I'm going to have your room number and everything then, okay?"

"Okay."

"Can you repeat what I want you to do?"

Worried, Sulayman watched his sister. He could only imagine what was going on. As the possibilities filled his head, he grew angry, fearing the worst.

"Good," Aminah said into the phone with a nod. "Yes, exactly. So I'm going to wait for your call. If I don't hear from you in an hour, I'm gonna send the police to look for you, okay?"

Tears still in her eyes, Tamika laughed beside herself. "Okay."

"I'm not playing," Aminah warned good-naturedly, but that she was serious was clear.

"I know."

"One hour, no more. Walk quickly."

"Okay."

"Now, what's the number?"

Tamika flipped to the hotel listing and found the hotel she was looking for and recited the number to Aminah, who repeated it for clarity.

"Now don't forget what to do."

"I won't."

"*InshaAllaah,*" Aminah said more for herself than Tamika.

"*InshaAllaah,*" Tamika repeated, relaxing now that she had some hope.

"*As-salaamu-'alaikum.*"

"*Wa 'alaiku-mus-salaam.*"

"What?" Sulayman demanded, dreading what he was about to hear.

Aminah rubbed her hands over her face and sighed. She shook her head as she wondered where to begin.

"What?" His voice rose in insistence.

"She's um—."

"Was it a man?" Anger swept through his body in a rage, ready to sacrifice his graduation and speech if he had to, to go break the criminal's neck.

"No, no, no." Aminah shook her head, allowing him to calm a bit. "Her mother kicked her out of the house after she found out she became Muslim."

Sulayman exhaled in relief, but he was still concerned.

"Apparently, her mother got really violent, so Tamika's on the street right now, and she called collect from a payphone." She sighed again. "She doesn't know what to do."

"What are you waiting for then? Get on the phone and reserve her room."

As his sister dialed, Sulayman folded his arms and bit his lower lip in deep thought, forgetting about his speech just then. He hoped Tamika was all right. He hated the helplessness he felt whenever something like this happened to a Muslim woman. It was frustrating. He had feared something like this would happen to Tamika. When his sister told him earlier that day that Tamika's mother didn't know that she was Muslim, he became worried. He thought of how Tamika had been moved to tears when they prayed early that morning, and he wondered at the immense faith that her mother was sure to crush. It pained him to think of a faith so pure being tainted by the selfishness of one woman. But it was possible that Tamika's mother was different, he had considered. But now he knew better.

To Aminah's relief, the hotel had several rooms available for the night. With her Visa card from her parents' account, she reserved a room for Tamika through Sunday night. After she hung up the phone, she sighed and looked to her brother, hoping Tamika would make it to the hotel safely.

"They may not let her stay because the card's not in her name," Sulayman said, voicing what they both feared.

"Well, we'll just have to pray on this one because I don't know what else to do."

"We could wire her the money."

"Yeah, but then she won't be able to get it until tomorrow," Aminah said. "And even if she could get it tonight, do you really want her roaming the city looking for the place to pick it up?"

Sulayman nodded in agreement as he tried to think of something else.

"I told them Tamika will be staying in the room, so let's just pray that the receptionist hasn't worked at the hotel long enough to know to ask for the credit card."

"We may have to go and get her."

"Go get her?" Aminah stared at her brother in amazement.

"She can't live in a hotel for the rest of the summer."

"Yeah, but how would we get her?"

"We can drive up there."

Aminah studied her brother curiously with her eyebrows gathered and felt sorry for him just then. She rarely saw him this concerned. Sulayman had a big heart, but he had never been one for a long drive. The longest distance he had ever driven was five hours, and getting him to do that was like pulling teeth. Their father and mother usually did the driving for long road trips, even if Sulayman was in the car. He was being irrational. "But your graduation is tomorrow. And then Monday, *Abee*[20] has to work."

"Maybe we should book her a flight."

"Yeah," Aminah said, doubt traceable in her voice, "but flights at such late notice are really expensive, especially from Wisconsin."

He nodded as his mind searched for alternatives. "That's true." He rubbed his forehead. "Does she have any other family in the city?"

"If she did, I'm sure she would've called them instead of us," Aminah said, scratching a spot on her arm. "Anyway, even if she did, that's probably not the wisest thing to do right now. We don't know if they would welcome her any more than her mother. I don't get the impression that her family is 'open arms' when it comes to religious differences."

"Maybe she has a friend she can stay with for a bit."

"Yeah, but they wouldn't be Muslim. The last thing she needs right now is to be taken in by someone who'll put a roof over her head but discourage her in her Islam." She chuckled and shook her head. "And I know the girl who was her best friend at Streamsdale, and if her friends are anything like that, then you can forget about her Islam."

"What happened to family values?" Sulayman's eyes narrowed as he shoved his hands into the pockets of his slacks and walked over to the window. He was growing frustrated with the same scenario each time a person became Muslim.

Aminah laughed from where she sat and smoothed a wrinkle in Sulayman's comforter. "Today, family doesn't mean much to people, especially in this country. They'd disown their children if they didn't major in what they wanted them to." She shook her head. "And that's just college. You can imagine what happens when the issue is religion."

"The Muslim community needs to set up something so new Muslims don't have to go through this each time," Sulayman said, turning away from the window and walking over to his desk, where he sat on its edge and crossed his arms.

"There are Muslim shelters," Aminah offered with a shrug.

"But we can't in good conscience put our sisters in a place we wouldn't live ourselves."

"But as the story goes, those who can help the most are the ones counting their pennies and swearing they don't have enough."

"Maybe that's the problem," Sulayman said, lifting a hand to rub his beard. "We wait for the rich Muslims to take care of all our problems. If people with even an average income worked together, we could do a lot."

---

[20] Dad

"True."

The room grew silent as Sulayman continued to rub his beard and stare distantly above his sister's head toward a framed certificate hanging on the wall next to his bed.

"So you want to go back to campus tonight?" Aminah asked a few minutes later, standing as she pulled her hair back and started to braid it with her head tilted to one side.

Sulayman shrugged as he reached to pick up a pencil that was about to fall from his desk and placed it on top of a book. "Let's just see what Dad says."

Tamika was reciting silent prayers to Allah and trying to stay focused as she walked, but her legs ached. She had made a knot at the side of her dress to make herself look presentable, but she doubted the look suited her at all. Her skirt was visible below the knot, and she had no idea how her hair looked. But she had run her fingers through it like Aminah had suggested. She walked as quickly as she could, knowing the hotel was a bit far on foot. She kept her eyes fixed ahead of her. She wouldn't even glance at anyone who passed. Alone on the street at night, she was terrified. Although she had walked at night many times before, tonight she felt helpless and wanted nothing more than shelter.

The wind ripped through her thin blazer, sending chills through her body. She slipped her hands into the jacket's pockets and began to count her steps to the hotel. She prayed that Allah would make it easy for her. She held onto the knowledge that He was there, which was all she could think of to keep her mind from drifting back to her mother and the horrible fight.

When Tamika thought she could walk no longer, she saw the sign for the hotel glowing in the distance. She whispered thanks to Allah. She kept moving, trying to quicken her steps. She wanted desperately to be in warmth. She felt her breaths becoming painful again, and her side began to cramp. But she pushed herself to keep going. She was almost there.

When the hotel was just ahead, she praised God again and again in her head. She was about to head toward the entrance when she remembered what Aminah had said. She glanced about her and saw a restaurant across the street. She looked both ways before walking quickly across the main street until she was in front of the restaurant. She took a deep breath and exhaled before entering and heading to the restroom.

She looked in the mirror and was repulsed by her appearance. Her hair was disheveled despite her attempts to smooth it down. There was a large red welt on her face, and her bottom lip was slightly swollen. She felt the urge to break down, but she held back, remembering that she had to appear respectable or the hotel may turn her away. She opened her purse and tried to find a comb, but there was none. Not knowing what else to do, she closed her purse and turned on the faucet. It wasn't the wisest thing to do on a cool night, but she had no other choice. She held her hands under the water and let it run through her fingers. With her wet hands, she wiped over her hair until it appeared neat. She found some lip-gloss and foundation in a small zipper pocket of her purse and frowned at their tattered state. She sighed and spread the gloss across her lips and used the foundation to cover the red mark. She studied her reflection. She looked a little better. But she would have to tuck her bottom lip to conceal the swelling.

She drew in a deep breath before leaving the restaurant to look for a payphone. She didn't see one, but there was a gas station next to the restaurant. She made her way there, and she saw a payphone near the bathrooms in the back. She hurried to it to make a collect call to Aminah.

"*Alhamdulillaah*," Aminah praised God for allowing Tamika to arrive safely.

"Were you able to get a room?" Tamika asked, glancing about her in the night. No one seemed to notice her.

"I reserved it and told them you would be the guest, but here's the thing," Aminah said. "If they demand to see me in person with the credit card, pretend like this was already arranged ahead of time. You can't let them turn you away."

"You think they will?" Tamika was terrified at the thought. She had nowhere else to go.

"No," Aminah assured, praying she was correct. "They shouldn't, but do that just in case, okay?"

"Okay."

"The room is three eighteen, and it's under Aminah Ali, but I told them the guest will be you, Tamika Douglass. Got it?"

"Got it."

"Call me once you get to the room, okay?"

"Okay."

"Allah's taking care of you, Tamika, so don't worry about anything."

She blinked to fight the tears. "Okay."

"I'm waiting to hear from you in the next twenty minutes."

"Okay."

"*As-salaamu-'alaikum.*"

"*Wa-'alaiku-mus-salaam.*"

Aminah hung up the phone and sighed, turning to her parents and brother, who all sat in the living room with concerned expressions on their faces. Sarah and Ismael sat next to each other on the couch under the window, and their son sat on the floor across from them, his back leaning against the wall. Aminah walked back over to the love seat where she had been sitting before Tamika called.

"I think the only thing we can do is rent a car and get the sister," Ismael said after Aminah sat down. "I just don't think it's wise for us to leave her up there."

"But you work," Sarah reminded him.

"I can drive up there with Aminah tomorrow afternoon," Sulayman offered.

Sarah looked to her husband doubtfully. "How long is the drive?"

Ismael rubbed a hand over his face as he tried to gather his thoughts. "About thirteen hours."

"Isn't that too long for you?" Sarah's expression grew concerned as she turned to her son.

"I can rest after six hours."

"I could do it," Ismael said tentatively, "but I would be cutting it close. I'd definitely need to sleep for a bit before getting back on the road."

"If you left around six o'clock in the afternoon tomorrow," Sarah estimated, "you could get there early Sunday morning, of course, assuming you take no break. But if you rest more than a few hours before coming back, you may not be able to get home by Sunday night and rest before work."

Ismael drew in a deep breath. "It would be pushing it, but I could give it a try. But tomorrow's such a full day, I doubt I'd be able to get out of here by six. And then there's rush hour, which would push us to leave seven at the earliest."

"You could skip my graduation," Sulayman said from where he sat.

"No, no, no," his father said, shaking his head. He creased his forehead as he studied his son with concern. "I'm not going to do that. I'd fly her in before I miss your speech."

"Remember, some of my family is coming in for the ceremony," Sarah reminded them, remembering herself just then. "We can't cut their visit short by jumping on the road."

Ismael frowned and nodded. "You're right." He turned to his wife. "How long are they staying?"

"There's no telling, but I'm pretty sure my mother will stay the weekend."

"Sulayman will just have to drive out Sunday or Monday after everyone leaves."

Sarah's eyes narrowed in concern as she looked at her husband, apparently taken aback by his suggestion.

"He's a man," Ismael reminded her with finality, but a trace of concern was in his voice. "He knows what to do."

"But it's such a long distance, sweetheart. We can't put him on the road alone."

"Aminah will be with him."

She almost laughed. Her husband couldn't be serious. "But she'll probably sleep."

"Sweetheart, this is a time we just have to trust in Allah."

Sarah grew silent at the reminder and stopped herself from saying more. She nodded in reluctant agreement then gazed at her son, who sat quietly listening to the exchange. His gaze was down, and his expression was hard to read. But she could tell he was determined to help in any way he could. He wanted so desperately for his parents to see him as a man, but it was difficult for Sarah to see him as anything but a child. Underneath the beard and towering height, he was still Sulayman, her baby, her firstborn. But she had to let go. It hurt to admit it, but he was a man now, and she would only handicap him by holding him back. She sighed thoughtfully and looked to her husband. "You're right."

"Everything's already paid for," Tamika told the receptionist, silently praying he wouldn't give her any trouble.

"We need to see the credit card that was used to book the room."

"Can I speak to the manager?"

"He's gone for the day."

She feigned impatience. "Sir, I traveled a long distance, and was told everything was taken care of. Do I have to take my business elsewhere?"

The receptionist looked uncertain, but Tamika's eyes told him she meant business and wasn't going to take no for an answer. Finally, he shrugged. "We usually don't do this, but," he sighed, locating the key and handing it to her, "it's room three eighteen."

She silently thanked God and tried to resist the urge to run to the room. She took the stairs two at a time, opting to avoid the elevator, fearing a delayed presence in the lobby would make the receptionist change his mind.

In the room, she called Aminah.

"*Alhamdulillaah!*" Aminah exclaimed, exhaling in relief and smiling at her family after hanging up the phone. "She checked in." She prostrated in gratefulness to her Lord then stood. "Well, at least she has a place to sleep for the weekend. But Monday morning, we'll either have to do another day or be there to pick her up."

"As long as we get there before sunset on Monday, she can go to a mall or something nearby until we arrive," Sulayman said, impressing his mother with his mature words. Maybe he could handle the drive after all.

"I don't think Grandma will stay that long," Aminah said. "She usually only stays for a few hours."

Sarah nodded. "That's true. But we should plan on her leaving late Sunday just in case."

"Who else is coming?" Ismael asked.

"Kate and Justin may come," Sarah said referring to her brother and sister, "but I'm not sure. If they do, they'll likely leave Saturday night. They don't like to hang around long."

No one responded, knowing what she meant.

Ever since Sarah became Muslim, her family had distanced themselves from her. Most times, it was a polite distance, but their displeasure with her religious choice was clear. Sarah had come from a middle class white American household, and her decision to accept Islam had come as a shock to her parents and siblings. She was the middle child, with her brother three years older and her sister two years younger. Sarah's home had been only moderately religious. As a teenager, she rejected the church completely and considered herself an atheist. Her parents were professed Christians, but they frequently made fun of organized religion, so it was difficult to tell what they really believed.

Sarah's brother was now a lawyer, and her sister was a news anchor for a local station in her city. They all thought Sarah was crazy for giving up her medical practice to stay home and raise children. Ismael was an engineer, but his salary was barely half of what hers had been as a doctor. When she married him and became Muslim, she had two things against her. She was Muslim, and she was married to a black man—it made no difference to them that Ismael's mother was white. That was the last time she knew how it felt to be a part of a family. After Sarah's parents divorced, her mother made efforts to be a part of her grandchildren's lives, but the relationship was strained. This was apparent to everyone.

Ismael, on the other hand, was an only child whose parents didn't care as much when he accepted Islam. His father and grandparents disagreed with his choice and argued with him occasionally, but their general sentiment was that Ismael had to do what he felt was right for him. Ismael's parents divorced when he was in middle school, and he was raised mostly by his paternal grandparents, who died when he was in college. He never knew his maternal grandparents because his mother had been disowned for marrying a black man. He rarely saw his mother after the divorce, and he later learned that she was trying to reestablish a relationship with her parents, who likely had no idea of his existence. His father had tried to be a part of his life, but he was on the road a lot trying to make ends meet. He died of a heart attack a few years after Ismael and Sarah married. The last thing Ismael heard about his mother was that she was in a nursing home and barely remembered her own name.

"We can just rent a car for Sulayman and Aminah," Ismael said, changing the subject. "And we can give them one of our cell phones."

Sarah nodded. The idea of them driving a reliable car and carrying a cell phone made her feel better about the journey. Part of her wanted to ride with them, but she knew Ismael would think she was being overprotective. He often told her that Sulayman needed to do things on his own and that he shouldn't depend on his mother too much.

"We'll be fine, *inshaAllaah*," Sulayman said, sensing his mother's apprehension.

She forced a smile and nodded. She could only pray he was right.

In the hotel room, Tamika sat on the bed and reflected on her predicament. She had no idea what she was going to do after tonight. But she was thankful that she had a place to sleep, even if only for a night. Aminah would probably let her stay in the room for the weekend, but where would she go after that? Her mind raced with names. Who would let her stay with them for the summer? Her flight back to Atlanta wasn't until mid-August, and she would definitely need a place until then.

She could call her aunt. It would take some convincing, but Jackie wouldn't let Tamika sleep on the street. But could Tamika live with Raymond? Maybe she could find a summer job and earn enough to pay for an apartment for a few months. She could put in an application at all the stores in the mall and pray something came through. But could a summer job pay her enough to rent an apartment? Most complexes had minimum income requirements, and even those that didn't required some sort of government voucher.

The sound of the phone ringing startled Tamika, and for a moment she considered not answering it. But it could be Aminah. She hoped the plans hadn't changed.

"Hello?"

"*As-salaamu-'alaikum.*"

"Is everything okay?" Tamika asked after returning the greetings.

"Yes, everything's fine," Aminah said. "I just wanted to call back to see if you knew anybody you could stay with for the summer."

Tamika sighed. "I'm trying to think of people right now."

"You don't have any other family in the city?"

"My aunt's here. But my cousins are there, and I don't know how that'll work out."

"There's no space?"

"There's space," Tamika said hesitantly. She didn't want to tell Aminah about Raymond. "But it'd be almost impossible to live there and be a Muslim at the same time."

"There's no one else?"

"My brother and sister, but I have no idea where they are."

There was a brief pause before Aminah said, "I see."

Tamika didn't want to stress Aminah's family. She already felt bad for all they had done. "Don't worry about it. I'll think of something before my flight back in August."

Just then an idea came to Aminah. She could have kicked herself for not thinking of it before. Why should her family drive to Milwaukee when Tamika already had a return ticket to Atlanta? "But what will you do until then?"

"I don't know." Tamika didn't want to think about it right then.

"Can't you change your flight to come back earlier?"

Hmm. She hadn't thought of that, most likely because she had no family in Atlanta. "I suppose I could, but the flight is booked on my mother's credit card."

Aminah grew silent momentarily. "But it's in your name, right?"

"The ticket is, but the credit card isn't. I think my mother has to call to change it." Tamika had bought the ticket herself with her mother's permission, but she doubted she could do that again.

"Are you sure?"

"Yeah."

"Do you think you can be your mother for a few minutes?"

At first Tamika didn't understand what Aminah meant, but a second later, she caught on. "I suppose." She paused then added skeptically, "But the university apartments are closed during the summer, at least they are for the undergraduates. So I don't know where I would stay."

"You can stay with us."

"No," Tamika said so quickly that a moment later she hoped she hadn't offended Aminah. But they had done too much already. She wouldn't dream of burdening them by living in their house. "I wouldn't feel right."

"But then where will you go?"

Tamika grew silent as her gaze fell on the keypad of the phone then on the hotel information card next to it. Where would she go?

"Tamika," Aminah said before Tamika could respond, "trust me, it's not a problem. We'd love to have you."

"But, Aminah, I wouldn't feel right. I'd feel like I'm imposing on your family."

"You are my family."

Tamika's heart drummed at the soothing words, and she felt herself getting choked up again. If only her mother felt the same.

"Just change your flight and let us know what time you'll be coming in."

Tamika picked up a blue hotel pen and toyed with it as her gaze fell on the mirror on the desk in a corner of the room. "I can't."

"Why not?"

Tamika shook her head, the capped pen's tip now in her mouth. She wished Aminah could understand. "I'm sorry, Aminah," she said, setting the pen back on the nightstand. "I just can't. I appreciate everything you're trying to do, but I really can't."

"But—."

"I wouldn't feel right," Tamika cut in, feeling the swelling on her face with her palm. It seemed to have gone down some. "And plus, it's not my money. My mom's already struggling to pay the bills, and it was really hard for her to pay for this flight."

"We can pay the difference."

Tamika sighed, her hand falling to her lap. "How Aminah?" She was trying to make her roommate understand. "My mother doesn't accept handouts, especially to make up for what she sees as stabbing her in the back. You couldn't pay her enough to use her card behind her back. Anyway, if my mother sees a charge on her card after what happened tonight, I'll probably never be able to come back home."

Aminah was silent for a moment. "I see what you're saying."

"I'm sorry," Tamika said, feeling bad for Aminah and her family. She knew they only wanted to help.

"You're sure she wouldn't just let you leave early?"

Tamika forced laughter. "Aminah, I wouldn't be surprised if she called the airline and cancelled the ticket altogether or changed her credit card number."

"You think she'd do that?"

"You don't know my mother. When she says get out, she means it. And that doesn't just mean get out of the house. It means get out of her life."

There was a brief pause. "We could buy you a bus ticket."

"No, Aminah. I'll be fine. I'll just start applying for jobs and see what happens."

"But what will you do in the meantime?"

"If nothing else comes up, I'll call my aunt."

"What if she doesn't let you stay?"

Tamika sighed. "I don't know. But I don't think she'll let me go homeless."

"Does she know you're Muslim?"

Tamika's gaze fell on the buttons of her dress, and she noticed that two were missing, exposing some of her undershirt. She put her fingers in the open space and scratched her stomach. What if Thelma hadn't told her sister? What if she had? Would Jackie turn her away too?

"I don't know," Tamika said finally, feeling the buttons under her neck to make sure they were there.

"You shouldn't stay there then."

She bit her lower lip and wrapped the phone cord around a finger. Maybe Aminah was right. "I'll be fine, *inshaAllaah*," Tamika said, betraying her true thoughts.

"Tamika, at least let us buy you a bus ticket down here."

"Aminah, no," Tamika said, releasing her finger from the cord. "I couldn't. I'd go back to my mother before I let you do that."

"Tamika, it's not a big deal. We could do it."

Tamika sighed and shook her head though she knew Aminah couldn't see her. "I know, but I just wouldn't feel right."

"But what will you do?"

"Aminah, please don't worry about it, really."

Aminah took a deep breath and exhaled. "Okay, then. I booked the room through Sunday night, so just give me a call Monday to let me know what you're going to do, okay?"

"Okay."

"Take care, Tamika. You're in our prayers."

"Tell your family thanks so much."

"I will, *inshaAllaah*."

"*As-salaamu-'alaikum*."

"*Wa-'alaiku-mus-salaam*."

"I guess this means we'll be going to get her after all," Sulayman said, rubbing a side of his face after his sister hung up. He and his parents were still in the living room and had been listening to Aminah talk to Tamika.

"I guess so." Aminah sighed and scratched her head, walking over to the love seat and standing next to it to face her family. "But we'll have to make sure we get up there before she checks out on Monday morning."

"We may have to leave Sunday morning first thing," Sulayman said, turning to his parents for approval, "even if Grandma is still here."

Ismael nodded as he listened and looked at his wife, who sat on the couch next to him with a distant look of worry on her face. He placed his hand on hers and patted it gently, and Sarah glanced at him with a forced smile. "I think that'll be fine *inshaAllaah*," he said. "Otherwise, the sister'll be roaming the streets, and we'll probably never know where she is."

"And I doubt she's gonna call again," Aminah said, sitting on an arm of the love seat and crossing her arms under her chest. "She sounds like she wants to weather this on her own."

Ismael drew in a deep breath and exhaled. "I doubt she wants to take this on alone," he said. "But she doesn't think she has a choice. Nobody wants to feel like they're disrupting someone else's life with their own."

"But I told her it's not a problem," Aminah said, shaking her head in dismay.

Ismael chuckled and squeezed the hand of his wife, who he could tell was growing more concerned about her own children's safety as the reality of everything set in. "She has no reason to believe that. That's what everyone says in situations like this."

Aminah's eyes widened as she looked at her father. "But we wouldn't *lie* to her."

He chuckled again. "Sweetheart, she doesn't think we're lying. It's just that people usually offer more than they realize they can give."

Aminah nibbled at her lower lip and scratched at a small bump on her chin with her thumb.

"But now I think you two should be heading back to the university," Ismael said, wanting to talk to his wife. "We have a big day tomorrow."

Sulayman sighed and stood. "You ready to go?" he asked Aminah as he started for the door.

Aminah forced a smile and followed suit, exhausted from the discussion. "I suppose."

"Then let's go before I get too tired to drive home."

Seven

Saturday morning was warm. At 8:00 the temperature was already seventy degrees, and there were no clouds in the sky. The sun shined high above the eastern horizon and lit the entire campus with its brightness. The dew on the grass glistened in its presence, and the artful flowers outlined the campus lawn, giving the college an atmosphere of relaxation and joy. Folding chairs were lined up in neat rows upon the grass, and in the adjacent parking lot were family and friends donning their best suits and dresses. They laughed in carefree contentment as they awaited the start of the graduation ceremony. Cameras dangled from wrists and necks, and children skipped merrily in the lot, oblivious to the monumental nature of the day. On the opposite side of the lawn, graduates wore their traditional black cap and gown, standing in alphabetical order and checking off their names on the clipboard being passed among them. Professors and honored staff stood across from them in their decorated black gowns and multicolored capes and tassels.

Sulayman stood in his assigned place among the graduates, awaiting the official start of the ceremony, when he would take his place on stage. Much of his nervousness had gone, and his mind was on the enormity of the task before him. For the past week, he had consumed himself with the particulars of his speech, and now there was nothing left to do but deliver it. He had prayed for Allah's guidance, and now he could only put his trust in his Lord. He drew in a deep breath and exhaled. He had to do well.

Aminah stood in the parking lot amidst other family and friends of graduates awaiting official permission to take a seat. She looked toward the street in the distance, hoping her parents would arrive soon. The ceremony would begin at eight thirty, and Sulayman's speech was scheduled for nine. She bit her lower lip and silently prayed they would make it in time for the speech.

"Aminah, is that you?"

Aminah turned and saw an older white woman smiling at her. The woman's face was decorated in makeup that complimented her features, making her appear younger than she was. Gray hair was pulled back into a bun under a white sun hat, and when she smiled, creases at her eyes and mouth revealed her age. She had a pleasant, fresh look about her in the white floral dress and low-heel patent leather shoes. Her white-gloved hands grasped a small two-strap shiny black purse with a gold buckle. Her green eyes sparkled in the brightness of the morning, and Aminah couldn't help but smile in return. A moment later Aminah laughed, realizing who the woman was.

"Grandma?"

"Yes, it's me, dear." The woman giggled, embracing her granddaughter as curious students studied the pair.

"I'm glad you were able to come," Aminah said as her grandmother patted her back during the hug.

Sarah's mother laughed lightly after the embrace and smoothed the front of her dress with a gloved hand. "I never miss events like these. Makes me feel young."

"Are Kate and Justin coming too?" Aminah never felt comfortable referring to them as her aunt and uncle. She was unsure if the titles would offend them, especially since they wanted to keep their distance from her family. She hadn't seen them since she graduated from high school, and even then they had only stayed until the ceremony was over.

Her grandmother laughed and nodded her head to a couple that passed. "Dear, I don't know. I'm too old to keep up with those two."

Aminah smiled, readjusting her purse strap on her shoulder, unsure how to respond. She never knew what to say around her grandmother. She rarely saw her, and when she did, she felt a sense of strangeness in her presence. Each time her grandmother visited, Aminah felt as if a stranger was in their home. Her grandmother was kind and polite and would even laugh and talk with the family. But for some reason, she never felt like family.

There was an awkward silence, and Aminah glanced toward the street to look for her parents, lifting a hand to shield her eyes from the sun spilling through the trees. A second later, she felt her grandmother's clothed hand gently holding her face. Taken aback, she looked at her grandmother with her forehead creased in confusion.

"Such a beautiful child," her grandmother marveled as her eyes traced Aminah's face. "It's a pity your mother makes you cover up with all those clothes." She dropped her hand and sighed at the thought, shaking her head.

Aminah was suddenly conscious of her white *khimaar* of georgette fabric and her aqua blue button-up *abiya* of similar material, and she felt herself grow defensive. Why must everything come back to their disagreement on religion? Couldn't her grandmother enjoy just a few minutes in their presence without casting insults? Certainly, she couldn't think her daughter forced them to dress like Muslims. Aminah had a mind of her own. If her grandmother took a moment to consider other than herself, she'd see that her grandchildren had no problem with how they were raised.

"Actually," Aminah said with a pleasant smile, "I feel more beautiful like this."

Her grandmother sucked her teeth in disapproval and shook her head. "Impossible," she seemed to say more to herself than Aminah. "Whatever has my daughter been teaching you?"

Aminah groaned. She had to excuse herself before she said something she would regret. There was no winning with Grandma. She was convinced that her daughter's children were brainwashed, and she probably didn't realize there were perspectives other than hers, or at least other legitimate ones. However distasteful it was for Aminah to accept, her grandmother was no different than other Americans who refused to respect any lifestyle but their own.

Grandma likely spent her days in front of a television set, keeping up with all the latest headlines, oblivious to the propaganda and lies amidst handfuls of truth. She was a good citizen, Aminah guessed, who saw patriotism as accepting things the way they were and not making any waves. Then how could Aminah blame her?

"I'm gonna go look for Mom and Dad," Aminah said, glancing toward the street again. "Hopefully, we'll see you a little later."

"Oh, of course!" She patted Aminah's shoulder. "And tell that mother of yours I'm looking for her."

"I sure will."

Aminah turned and started walking toward the street. Behind her, the families and friends were being told to take their seats, and Aminah prayed her parents had already arrived. She walked to the sidewalk and stood watching the passing cars. Her parents should be here any moment. Perhaps they already were and she hadn't seen them.

When ten minutes passed, Aminah sighed and made her way to where everyone was being directed to sit down. After finding a seat about three rows behind where the graduates would sit, she heard someone call her name. She looked around and spotted her mother waving to her from the end of the row behind her. Aminah waved back and joined her parents, who had saved a seat for her.

"*As-salaamu-'alaikum*," they greeted as she sat down next to her mother, who was wearing a large white peach skin *khimaar* that hung to her waist and a dark blue cotton *abiya* underneath. She wasn't wearing her face veil today. She didn't wear it to non-Muslim events. When Aminah had inquired about this once, her mother told her that she would like to wear it everywhere, but Americans had so many misunderstandings and stereotypes about the veil that she felt more comfortable without it.

"*Wa-'alaiku-mus-salaam*," Aminah said as she sat on the hot metal seat. "How long have you been here?"

"For about ten minutes," Sarah said.

"Did you see your mother?"

Sarah raised her eyebrows. "She's here?"

"I was just talking to her in the parking lot."

Sarah glanced about her and squinted her eyes in search of her mother. "Did my brother and sister come too?"

"I didn't see them."

She frowned. "Well, I suppose I can see my mother afterwards. It'll be difficult to find anyone in this crowd."

Ismael leaned forward so Aminah could see him from where he sat next to her mother. "Did you see Sulayman?"

"Not yet."

"Let me know when you spot him." He grinned and patted the camcorder that sat on his lap. One hand was in the side strap, ready to record. "I wanna get a good shot."

The music began to play, signaling the start of the ceremony, and the audience fell into an attentive silence.

"There he is," Aminah whispered a few minutes later, pointing to the aisle next to them where students were walking in. Her father lifted the camera and began recording. Some students waved as they spotted family and friends, who waved back in quiet excitement. When Sulayman saw his father and family, he waved to the camera too.

After all the students had taken their seats, the guests were welcomed to the commencement, and the introductory speeches began. Ismael looked through the camcorder at his son who sat humbly on stage listening to the welcoming address. Sulayman's black gown was donned with a gold and white cape, and a distinctive gold tassel hung from his cap. Next to her husband, Sarah beamed, proud to see her son in such a distinguished position. Maybe her mother would see her differently after today.

Their minds drifted in boredom until the dean took the podium for a second time. "It is my honor to introduce to you one of the most remarkable, intelligent students of our university." The statement prompted Ismael, Sarah, and Aminah to attention. "This young man has changed the very face of Streamsdale by his presence. He came to us as a freshman and impressed his instructors with his sharp mind, quiet nature, and uncompromising opinions. He made such an impression on them that several of them approached *A Voice*, our official school paper, and requested that the paper add him to their staff. After only two issues of printing his writing, the readership, and, of course, the advertising," he added with a grin, "increased more than double. Other schools and off-campus organizations requested copies, and on campus, we witnessed more participation from the student body than this university has ever known. Those who attend Streamsdale know why his words attracted so much attention." He chuckled. "Because they ruffled feathers, so to speak." He smiled. "But I must tell you, he has softened more hearts than he has ruffled feathers.

"Academically, his performance has been phenomenal. He is pre-med, double majoring in biology and chemistry and has maintained a four-point-oh grade point average for all four years." The audience was noticeably impressed. "Not only that, but he has been named among *Who's Who in America's Colleges and Universities* each year. He has received several rewards for his outstanding academic performance and has won three scholarships to medical school, two of them full. And I have been fortunate enough to know this young man personally." He glanced to one side and smiled at Sulayman. "This young man has received this school's President's Award, has been president of three student organizations, has received four national awards for his charity work, and has secured his place in history by being the first African-American student in Streamsdale University history to have this honor. Without further ado, ladies and gentlemen, I present to you Sulayman Mikal Ali."

The audience roared in applause, and someone shouted, "Go Sulayman!" Another called, "That's right!" Aminah and Sarah resisted the urge to stand up and shout congratulations as he took his place at the podium. He smiled politely as he situated the notes before him, where his eyes fell at the moment. After the noise subsided, he adjusted the microphone and smiled again.

"Thank you."

He continued, "I want to first start by saying, in the name of God, and may prayers and peace be upon His last messenger." The audience fell into silence as the unfamiliar words echoed through the campus. "Also, I want to thank God for blessing me to stand before you today. Because it was only by His decision and mercy that I have this opportunity, and, certainly, all praise is due to Him."

He glanced at his notes. "If it's God's will, I will not take too much of your time. I know how difficult it is to sit and listen to a long, drawn out speech from someone you don't know." Some of the audience laughed in agreement, and he smiled. "And I know it is not I whom you came so far to see. But I hope that in this brief speech I'm able to inspire you with words that will stay with you beyond today.

"As a private religious institution, Streamsdale upholds the values shared by the major religions of the world, namely that of Judaism, Christianity, and Islam. The university teaches kindness and respect to others, wise decisions in morality, and, most importantly, a consciousness of God that reaches every aspect of our lives. And this is my message to you."

He grinned. "Yes, I have been known to 'ruffle feathers.' And my message to my fellow graduates, and to family and friends, is to do just that. No," he told them as he looked out at the audience, "I don't ask you to speak for the sake of speaking, argue for the sake of arguing, and make waves wherever you find calm waters. Rather, I'm asking you to mark this occasion as one that signifies the passing of the baton of the future into your hands, a future that needs reshaping, rethinking, and open minds.

"This country has seen much progress since our forefathers first landed here. We all know of our bitter past and the sweat and blood that went into bringing it from a grim existence with hardly a glimmer of hope to a shining existence that gave hope to all, regardless of the color of one's skin or a person's nation of origin. This greatness has come about from this country only because its people have sought betterment through change and have not been afraid to speak out, even when others are silent and to be different when everyone else is conforming. This progress has not come about through complacency and contentment with the way things are. This honor has come about through hard work, sacrifice, and yes, even the loss of lives when people were courageous enough, bold enough, and determined enough to stand up and stare injustice in its face and say, 'We will not stand for it.' This honor has come about through others who have stood up and, yes, ruffled feathers.

"Why do I say all of this? You've heard it all before. It's merely the rhetoric of every American. You know what I am saying, and you all agree. But, ladies and gentlemen, agreement is not in thoughts or words. But in actions. And more than that, agreement is in the heart. If you love this country and if you believe in the equality of all, then let us all look within ourselves.

"How many of us can honestly say that our actions, our *hearts*, speak to freedom, to justice, to welcoming various cultures and faiths? Before you answer, ponder this.

"There is a woman covered head to toe and you see nothing but her eyes. Perhaps she is wearing all black, and she is shopping next to you in the grocery store." He paused to allow the scene to become vivid in their minds. "Do you laugh? Shake your head in shame? Do you feel sorry for her? Do you think she's oppressed?" He grew silent as he gazed at the crowd through narrowed eyes. "Do you wish she would dress more *American?*" He waited, blinking as the questions were pondered. "If you can answer yes to *any* of these questions, then know we do not yet believe in freedom. We do not yet believe in equality, and no, we do not yet believe in America.

"To believe in America is to believe in freedom of expression, of dress, of religion. It is to believe in free speech and to respect each individual's rights."

Aminah's gaze fell to the back of a woman's head who sat in front of her, and she could see a thin gold chain and its round clasp sparkling against the woman's tanned skin that was sprinkled with moles. The woman's brunette hair was cut in layers, and its curled tips brushed where the nape of her neck began. As Aminah reflected on her brother's words, she couldn't imagine the woman being unmoved by his message.

Next to Aminah, a gentle smile creased the corners of Sarah's mouth, and she was speechless in admiration of her son. Was this the same boy whom she had trouble convincing to clean his room? Was this the same boy who had demanded she and his father give him a little brother because he was "allergic" to sisters? Was this the same boy who refused to be the "taxi driver" for his sister after getting his license? It was hard to believe this was actually her son, the little baby she had held in her arms more than twenty years ago.

"If we take a moment and reflect on the woman in the grocery store," Sulayman was saying, "we would see that she is the embodiment of America. She is exercising her freedom of expression, her right to dress as she pleases, and her right to practice her religion in this free land." His eyes traced the entire audience, as if waiting to meet each person's gaze. "She is not anti-

American, ladies and gentlemen. But more American than we, who judged her.

"Is that too hard to believe? Too difficult to accept? Too outlandish to entertain?"

He narrowed his eyes again and tucked his bottom lip momentarily. "Then know that you, like all of us, have great strides to make in our road to true freedom. We have some battles in society and within ourselves to win before we can have a true belief in the American rhetoric we express everyday.

"And this is not an accusation. This is not pointing fingers. And this isn't even complaining of a problem." He glanced at his notes then lifted his gaze a second later. "This is simply a reminder of what it means to be American.

"To be American is to insist on change until America *is* what it stands for. And each of you, and I too, have a lot of work to do in this regard. Our progress has been tremendous, and we can only continue to progress if we constantly better ourselves and our society each day.

"Let us then take this as an incentive to make a difference, to make a change, one that shapes the future of this country. Yes, we can be like those who came before us. We can add to the already tremendous impact Streamsdale has made on our nation. Because it is only in our courage, our sacrifice, and, yes, our willingness to stand up, that we will progress and be truly American." He grinned and concluded, "Which means you have no choice *but* to ruffle feathers."

The audience roared in applause as he returned to his seat on the stage. Sarah blinked back tears, and Aminah silently thanked Allah that it had turned out well. She could only pray his words made a difference in the audience's lives.

The remainder of the ceremony was ritualistic, and time dragged before the graduates' names were finally being called. At the pronouncement of Sulayman's name, students shouted and whistled although the announcer had asked the audience to hold their applause until the end.

It felt like eternity sitting and waiting for the names to be finished, and Aminah was grateful when the closing remarks were made. When the commencement was officially over, the graduates cheered, and many threw up their hats in celebration. The music played, and the graduates exited in two single file lines on either side of the chairs, occasionally shouting in excitement if they saw a family member or friend. Cameras flashed, and Ismael followed his son with the camcorder. Sulayman left the stage and walked down the grassy aisles. He spotted his family and raised his hand in a wave toward the camcorder, a calm smile on his face. Sarah waved back and gazed at him in admiration. She was so proud of him.

Near the parking lot, Sulayman's family gathered around him, and Sarah embraced her son. "May Allah bless you," she said before kissing him on the cheek.

"You too," Sulayman said, closing his eyes and holding his mother for a moment more.

Ismael held the camcorder and captured the moment as Sarah and Sulayman held each other, each overcome with emotion.

A minute later, Ismael shook his son's hand as he continued recording. Aminah then hugged her brother and too asked that Allah bless him.

"Well, well, well," a voice cheerfully called behind them. They turned and saw Sarah's mother approaching. "I've never been so proud." She held out her arms, and Sulayman accepted the embrace. "Congratulations, son, you are certainly a special person."

Sulayman smiled uncomfortably after they hugged and glanced toward the ground before meeting his grandmother's gaze a second later. "Thanks, Grandma. I'm glad you could come."

"Mom! Sarah!"

They all turned to see where the voice was coming from.

"Kate!" Sarah's mother tossed her head back in laughter.

Kate looked only faintly familiar, but Aminah recognized her. Aminah smiled as she watched her grandmother and aunt hug and studied her mother's sister curiously. Kate's age was concealed under layers of neatly-applied foundation, and red lipstick glistened on her lips. She wore a fitting powder blue blazer and short skirt that hugged her body. Her thick blond hair fell in large curls about her head and was trimmed to shoulder length. Her powder blue heels were several inches high and accented the muscles of her legs that were covered in sheer flesh colored pantyhose. Aminah imagined that Grandma must be proud of her.

"Sulayman!" Kate rushed over to her nephew and gave him a hug before kissing him on the cheek. "You were spectacular!"

"Thanks." Pretending to smooth down a side of his beard, he wiped his cheek clear of lipstick that he imagined was on his cheek.

"I never knew!"

He forced laugher and nodded in discomfort, his gaze on his black vinyl enclosed degree in his hand.

"Is your brother here?" Sarah's mother inquired a moment later.

Kate rolled her eyes and shook her head. "No, he's swamped with some case he's working on."

"Well, it's definitely good to see you." Her mother wore a proud smile.

Kate nodded as she too smiled. "I'm glad to see you too."

A second later she turned to her sister and hugged her. "Oh, Sarah, I'm so proud of you." She held Sarah's hand for a second after the hug. "Makes me wanna get married and have kids."

Sarah echoed her sister's laughter before they released each other's hand, and Kate turned to greet Aminah. As Kate and Aminah hugged, Sarah's mouth was spread in a gentle smile, and she studied her sister, reflecting on her last comment.

Kate was forty-six and had never married. Her job demanded a lot from her, and Sarah often told her sister to take a break and settle down. But Kate didn't want to be held back. Kate wasn't happy, this much Sarah knew. Kate's success at work had once kept her going and satiated her appetite for self-satisfaction, but in the last few years, reality had begun to set in. She would likely never marry, and this saddened her. Even if she were fortunate enough to marry, Kate had told her sister once, she would probably never know motherhood. She was near menopause, and getting pregnant would be difficult.

Kate had spent many years criticizing Sarah for her "backward opinions." But recently, loneliness had taken its toll. There was always a man in her life, but for reasons Kate couldn't understand, nothing ever lasted. A couple of the relationships were serious, and talk of marriage was often brought up. But Kate's most recent relationship had fallen through when, after four years of dating, her boyfriend decided to go back to his estranged wife, for the sake of the children, Kate said. The bad news had prompted Kate to call her sister regularly, which was a rarity since Sarah accepted Islam.

Sarah didn't know what to tell her. She felt torn between wanting to comfort her sister and not wanting to condone an adulterous relationship— even if the man was separated from his wife and was in the process of filing for a divorce. When Sarah listened to the pain in her little sister's voice, her conviction in her religion grew even more. Where would she be had she chosen her family's definition of success?

"Whatever do you have planned to celebrate this occasion?" Sarah's mother asked, clasping her gloved hands together in excitement.

Sarah grinned and placed an arm around her mother. "We have a special meal at home for all of us."

"Well, I suppose that's appropriate," her mother commented with a forced smile, apparently expecting something more adventurous.

Unsure what the comment was supposed to mean, Sarah didn't respond and contented herself with patting her mother on the shoulder in affection. She had learned years ago that silence was the best defense against her mother.

Eight

"Oh, Sarah," Kate admired her sister's home upon entering, "you've set it up so well."

Sarah smiled as she closed the door. "You know, I try."

"I always thought you could be an interior decorator."

She raised her eyebrows as she locked the door, a smile still on her face. "Really?"

"I need you to come set up my house!" Kate laughed, walking into the living room.

"Don't forget about your shoes."

"Oh." Kate cupped her hand over her mouth and laughed at her forgetfulness. "I'm sorry. It's been a while." She returned to the foyer and removed her shoes.

"Now, Sarah, dear," Sarah's mother interjected from the living room where she sat on the couch, having arrived minutes earlier. "Is that really necessary?" She had taken off her shoes after complaining that her feet hurt.

Inside, Sarah groaned, but she smiled pleasantly, entering the living room. She slipped her hands into the pockets of her beige ankle-length button-up skirt that she now wore with a white blouse tucked in. Her hair was uncovered and hung at her shoulders and back. "No, I suppose not, but it's what I prefer since we pray in here."

"However do you manage with all these rules?" Her mother wrinkled her nose and shook her head, tugging gently at her clothed fingertips then pulled the gloves from her hands. Her sun hat and purse sat next to her on the couch.

"It's not a rule, Mom," Sarah said, "just a preference."

Sarah smiled at her mother and added, "Remember how you didn't allow us to wear our shoes on the carpet if it was muddy outside?"

"For heaven's sake, Sarah," her mother said with a roll of her eyes, shaking her gloves before folding them, "that was for the sake of cleanliness."

"And this is too."

"Oh, it's not a problem," Kate cut in, waving her hand as she entered the living room. "I could use a break from those heels. They're killing me!"

Their mother shrugged as she placed her gloves on her purse. "I suppose you have a right to run your house as you please."

"Why don't we all eat?" Ismael said, appearing in the entrance to the dining room, which was adjacent to the living room.

Aminah was going back and forth between the kitchen and dining room setting up the table. She had overheard the exchange, and from the kitchen, she had shaken her head to her brother, who sat at the dining room table awaiting the meal, apparently unenthusiastic about sitting in the living room with his grandmother.

"Yes, why don't we?" Kate agreed, clasping her hands together in excitement, clearly not in the mood for a disagreement today.

Everyone sat at the dining room table except Aminah and her father. They had decided to serve everyone before sitting down. Ismael preferred serving the food because he felt uncomfortable in the presence of his wife's mother and sister. Fortunately, Kate was seated on the far right side of the table, several seats from his chair at the head, and Sarah's mother sat on the opposite end of the table, across from where Ismael would sit at an angle next to his wife. Sulayman sat two seats down from Kate, an empty chair between them that belonged to Aminah. Ismael planned to keep himself busy in the kitchen until he was forced to sit down. He told his daughter to go ahead and take her seat. He would take care of everything else.

"That was a really good speech you gave," Kate said to Sulayman after they began eating.

"Thank you." He nodded, unfolding his napkin and placing it on his lap. "God is merciful."

"I honestly had no idea how intelligent you were."

He smiled uncomfortably, picking up his fork to eat his salad. He didn't like too much attention. None of his success was possible without his Lord.

"And your writing in the paper must have been something!" She laughed, picking up a forkful of salad and putting it in her mouth a second later. She chewed and swallowed before adding, "I would love to see some of those articles."

He dabbed his mouth with his napkin and took another forkful of salad before responding. "Well, as they said, it ruffled feathers."

"Oh, I don't mind." She reached for the Italian dressing and poured some over her Romaine lettuce and baby tomatoes. "You know, in the journalism industry you encounter all kinds of ideas."

"I can imagine."

She raised her eyebrows thoughtfully as she finished chewing another bite of food. "I'm actually working on some stories about some of the subcultures in our city. And it's really quite interesting."

"Subcultures?" Sulayman gathered his eyebrows as he toyed with his salad, glancing up from his plate momentarily to meet his aunt's gaze.

"Cultures that aren't very popular in mainstream American society."

"Like what?"

"Well, on one extreme, you have the Wicca movement."

"Are those the witches?" Sarah inquired, her forehead creased in concern as she served herself some more salad from the bowl.

"Yes, they are actually," Kate nodded toward her sister, gesturing with her fork as she spoke. "But they're actually quite fascinating." She took another forkful of food.

"Are you studying anyone else?" Sarah reached for the salad dressing, not wanting to discuss paganism, at least not in praiseworthy terms.

Kate nodded as she chewed. "Actually, we are," she said between bites. "There's a group of Muslim women we're researching too."

"Really?" Sarah said, her eyebrows rising in sudden interest as she poured the dressing over her salad.

"And it's funny," Kate reflected with a laugh, "because Sulayman mentioned the woman in all black in his speech. And that's the group we're looking at."

Aminah observed the conversation, eating her food in silence as she listened.

"They consider that a subculture similar to the Wicca movement?" Sarah said, returning the dressing to its place, trying to conceal her exasperation with the comparison. Her family had no idea she ever wore the face veil.

"Well, yes," Kate said, "in that it's what most Americans would consider an extreme form of self expression." She ate a few more bites of food then continued. "But, like Sulayman touched on, we're seeking answers to how this expression plays into the infrastructure of America."

Sarah nodded, narrowing her eyes in keen interest as she ate. "So the expression of, let's say, the woman in all black displaying only her eyes, you're looking at this more along the lines of a deviation from the norm than a rare variety within the norm?"

"Most definitely." Kate dabbed the corners of her mouth with her napkin then returned it to her lap. "Because the purpose of this report is to focus on the more extreme groups that many view as a threat to the fabric of our society. We analyze what they actually believe and try to determine if it's fair to view them as a part of American culture or a deviation from it."

"What's the conclusion?" Sarah lifted a forkful of lettuce to her mouth as she listened.

"Well, it's still in the research stages, but we're bringing in specialists on subcultures and exotic movements to analyze their beliefs and practices."

She nodded. "So what's the general consensus so far?"

"That these movements have to be watched closely and viewed with caution because of the harm they can cause to the more moderate subcultures."

"What moderate subcultures are you studying?" Sarah's gaze fell to her food as she gathered the rest of the salad to the middle of her plate, conscious of her mother taking in the entire conversation.

Kate's eyes widened in eagerness to discuss the project, and she pointed her fork toward her sister. "It's interesting that you asked because we're actually looking at the moderate Muslim culture, like what I'm sure you are most familiar with, compared to the more extreme expressions that aren't accepted by mainstream Muslims."

"So some of your specialists are Muslims?"

"Most definitely. We don't want a biased analysis because that wouldn't give a broad view of the problem."

Aminah listened more closely, eating her food in slow bites as she held onto every word. She wanted to interject but withheld.

"Are any of the specialists from the extreme subcultures themselves?"

Kate paused thoughtfully for a moment then shook her head. "I don't believe so."

"Don't you think it would be more unbiased to solicit specialists from the subcultures too?"

"Yes," she said slowly, the tip of her fork standing on her plate. "but I don't think that would allow us to analyze them appropriately."

"How so?"

"Well, of course, they wouldn't be objective in their conclusions, and that would impede our ability to determine if they pose a threat to our way of life."

"What about interviewing them to simply hear their analysis of the problem? Perhaps they can give more insight into the problems Americans fear."

Kate nodded, but she was reluctant to agree.

"Don't you think the person who lives it can more adequately clarify what is or isn't a danger to the society?"

"I suppose."

Aminah couldn't withhold any longer. "So, you think a person poses a danger to American society by simply dressing differently than most people?"

Kate chuckled, glancing to her niece next to her. "Of course not."

"Then why would the special study women who wear all black and cover their faces?" Aminah asked.

"Actually, we're not only looking at those who wear all black. We're also looking at the entire subculture of women who are compelled to hide their faces."

"You mean Muslim women who veil?" Aminah said, hoping her tone didn't reveal her disagreement.

"Yes, but the all-black look is the most common costume for this group."

Aminah paused and ate some food before asking, "But what is it that makes this group extreme? Their clothes?"

"No, no, no," Kate shook her head, her gaze falling to the salad that she was gathering on her fork. "Their clothes is just an expression of a deeper belief."

Aminah creased her forehead. "What deeper belief?"

"Well, of fundamentalism and anti-American sentiments."

There was a brief silence, and Aminah and her mother glanced at each other momentarily. Sulayman ate in silence, not wanting to get in the middle of it, at least not yet.

"What do you mean by fundamentalism?" Sarah asked.

Kate's eyebrows rose, unsure how to respond. "Well, for example, they have violent beliefs and tend to hate Americans."

"What makes you think that?"

"That's a constant in that extreme subculture. They believe in radical solutions to common problems."

"Radical solutions?" Aminah asked, almost laughing. "Just because they dress different?"

"Kate," Sarah said finally, setting down her fork, "I think what we're getting at is there are a lot of assumptions based on the way a Muslim dresses. I don't doubt that there are extreme subcultures, if you will, in every religion and culture, and this is true for Christians and true for any group of people. In Christianity, a classic example is that of Jim Jones."

Kate nodded in agreement, her eyebrows gathered as she tried to understand her sister's point.

"But it's a bit questionable to assume that just because a person dresses a certain way, he's a part of, let's say, Jim Jones's cult."

"I agree."

"Similarly," Sarah continued, "women who cover their faces, or who cover at all for that matter, cannot all be put in a group because of how they dress. What one person professes to believe will differ from what another person who dresses similarly will profess to believe. And I don't mean any disrespect to your television station when I say, anyone who attempts to analyze a people's beliefs by categorizing them according to dress has missed a very elementary concept in stereotyping."

Kate set down her fork and creased her forehead in interest.

"If you think back to your sociology or psychology courses in college," Sarah said, "you'll remember studying about stereotyping. And one thing that we learn is how people's brains respond when they encounter people different from them, whether in race, nationality, religion, or what have you. Our brains tend to simplify the data about an unfamiliar group, and as a result, we make gross generalizations."

Kate nodded. "I remember that."

"This is innate to humans, and you find this especially in children as they try to make sense of the world. So when a child encounters a dog for the first time, her brain processes it as a furry creature. And after that, every furry creature is a dog. What's happening is the brain focuses on the aspect that makes something different. So any peculiar attributes in behavior are attributed to that unique trait." She glanced at the napkin in her lap and folded it in half before returning her gaze to her sister. "But the fact of the matter is that, with humans, a peculiar behavior more often reflects an individual peculiarity than it does a common trait among people of that group. It is only maturity and varied experience that allows adults to realize this."

"But when a person dresses a certain way *because* of a peculiar belief, that doesn't apply."

Sarah shook her head. "The general rule still applies. It's a personal peculiarity that inspires a person to dress a certain way. If you ask another person dressed similarly, you may discover their reasons are completely different than another's."

"But these subcultures have definite deviations that make them extreme."

"And what's the deviation of the women who veil their faces?"

"Their rejection and hatred of America."

Sarah grinned. "And you think that's why they cover?"

"Well, not always," Kate said with a shrug. "In many cases, her husband is part of the extreme group and forces that upon her."

"Really?" Sarah was beginning to be amused. "And how many women-in-black have you interviewed?"

"We're interviewing three who formerly wore the costume."

"Three?" Sarah raised her eyebrows in disbelief. "And who chose them?"

Kate shook her head in uncertainty. "I'm not sure. Anchors don't always know the behind-the-scenes processes."

"Well, is it possible that a biased person purposefully selected these women *because* of their previous hatred for America? Assuming that they actually had this hatred in the first place."

Kate creased the corners of her mouth as she considered it. "Anything's possible, but I don't believe that—."

"You don't believe," Sarah repeated with a smile, "but that's not an objective analysis."

Kate picked up her fork and toyed with the food left on her plate. "I'm not sure what you're getting at, Sarah, but it's just a television special on a small local channel."

"I apologize if I sound disturbed, but I can't help feeling this way when this is the general treatment of Muslims in the media."

"We do the best we can."

Sarah started to respond but left it alone. Kate had no idea that perhaps *she* tried her best, but her superiors did not. "Why don't you tell them about me? I'd be happy to contribute to the report."

"But you're not a specialist in the area."

"I'm a Muslim."

"But we're only interviewing those who have studied this subculture and are greatly familiar with it."

"I've studied about the veil, and I'm familiar with it."

Kate raised her eyebrows in surprise. "I didn't know that," she said apologetically. "But, really, we're only interviewing those with PhD's or research in a related field."

Sarah nodded. "Well, before you do the report, just run some of your points by me, unofficially, of course. And I hope that'll give you a broader view."

"Why are you so interested in this?" Sarah's mother interjected, her forehead creased in displeasure.

Sarah lifted a shoulder in a shrug. "I suppose it's because I'm Muslim, and it's hard to watch yourself being analyzed and you have no say in it."

"But the group Kate is studying has nothing to do with you."

"I know many Muslim women who cover their faces."

The table grew silent, and Sarah knew her mother disapproved. "Dear, you need to stay away from those people."

"Why?" Sarah met her mother's gaze, unable to help feeling like a child.

"You heard what Kate said. These are maniacs."

"Maniacs?" She forced laughter. "What makes you think that?"

"These people spit on our country while they reap benefits from it."

"Mom, certainly you don't think all women who wear a veil spit on America."

"Sure they do."

Sarah grinned and shook her head. "But that's not fair. How many Muslim women do you know who veil?"

Her mother grimaced. "I don't need to know any. I know what I know."

"But where did you learn it?"

"I keep up with the news, dear, a lot more than you know. And I read a lot."

"From Muslim authors?"

Her mother huffed. "From specialists in the field."

"But what type of anti-American sentiment do these people express in what you read?"

"A lot," she said, lifting the napkin from her lap and tossing it on the table.

"Grandma." The sound of Sulayman's voice startled everyone, and they turned to him. "But don't all Americans criticize America?"

She huffed again. "Sure, but not out of hatred for it."

"But who's to say what's out of hatred and what's not?"

"I'm not in the mood for this discussion," she announced stubbornly, as she often did when she was losing an argument. "You'll stay away from those radicals, and that's that." She eyed her daughter angrily.

The table grew silent, and Ismael opted to stay busy in the kitchen. He wanted to say something, but when his mother-in-law grew angry, he decided to leave it alone. Sarah's family were not going to change what they believed about Muslim women who veiled, and there was nothing he or his wife could do about it. Perhaps leaving the issue of dress alone was the best solution. Islam was much deeper than how someone dressed, and as a general rule, the topic should be avoided when someone knew little of the religion.

"Anybody want dessert?" Ismael appeared in the doorway, grinning. They hadn't even eaten the main course yet, but he imagined everyone could use a little bit of sugar at the moment.

"I've lost my appetite." Sarah's mother glared at her daughter as she spoke. "And I think I've had enough of this Muslim stuff for one day. Ever since you joined those people, you haven't been the same. And now this!" She shook her head in contempt. "I would've never dreamed my Sarah would be friends with some deviant group of anti-Americans."

Sarah sighed and picked up her fork, playing with her food. There was no winning with her mother. Her mother had no desire to see the world any differently than she always had.

"I think I understand what she's saying," Kate said, hoping to calm the tense atmosphere.

"Kate, please," her mother cut her off. "I know you don't agree with this nonsense, and don't try to stand up for your sister. There's no excuse for this." She stood, using the table to assist her.

"I knew there was a reason I booked my flight for tonight," Sarah's mother said as she walked toward the couch. "I think I'll spend the rest of my day touring the city."

Kate looked distraught, and her gaze fell upon her sister. For the first time since Sarah became Muslim, she actually felt sorry for her. Whatever their differences, their mother shouldn't treat Sarah like this.

Their mother grabbed her purse, hat, and gloves from the couch before going to the foyer to put on her shoes. "Good day!" She left the house, slamming the door behind her.

The house grew deafly silent as the sound of the slamming door echoed throughout the room. For a few minutes, no one spoke.

Kate cleared her throat in an effort to break the tense atmosphere. "Uh, I think I'll have some dessert."

The rest of the meal was spent discussing general topics, and Kate asked Sulayman and Aminah details about Streamsdale and how they liked it. She asked Sulayman his plans for medical school and where he wanted to go. The conversation was strained, but it was pleasant nonetheless.

"How long are you staying?" Sarah asked her sister later that afternoon as they sat on the futon in the den downstairs. Kate's powder blue blazer hung across one arm of the futon, and she wore the sleeveless white blouse that had been her undershirt. Sarah wore the beige skirt and white shirt that she had earlier. Ismael had gone to the *masjid* with Sulayman, and Aminah was upstairs in her room reading. The television was on, but neither of the sisters was paying attention to it as they talked over the noise.

"Actually," Kate said, cleaning a corner of her eye with a polished fingernail, "I planned to stay the weekend. I hope you don't mind."

Sarah laughed and patted her sister on the leg. "Of course I don't mind. You're always welcome to stay."

Kate nodded, and her gaze grew distant as it fell on the television screen. She sat with one leg tucked under her, and her body faced her sister, who sat in a similar manner next to Kate. "I just needed a break from work, you know."

Sarah grew silent as her gaze followed that of her sister, who she knew had something on her mind. "Is everything alright at work?"

Kate pulled her hair away from her face with both hands and let it fall behind her back. "Work is fine."

"Then what's bothering you?"

At first Kate didn't respond, and Sarah studied her sister, whose eyes were staring beyond the television. Sarah watched as the images on the screen flickered and danced in her sister's glassy eyes, reflecting the torment that Kate must be feeling. Sarah could sense Kate's intense desire to talk, and, whatever it was that weighed on her sister, Sarah imagined that Kate hadn't been able to confide in any of her friends. It was apparent that Kate was feeling torn, and the bruises of life had brought her back to her older sister, whom she had confided in growing up. Kate had drifted from her sister after Sarah accepted Islam, leaving them hankering for the friendship they had lost.

"Kate, what is it?"

A corner of Kate's mouth creased in the hint of a hesitant smile, and her gaze fell to her fingers, where she twisted the gold band on the ring finger of her right hand. "I don't know," she said, a tinge of sadness in her voice. "A lot's been on my mind lately."

Kate forced laughter a second later. "It's men," she said finally. "Nothing ever seems to go my way."

Sarah creased her forehead in sincere concern. "What do you mean?"

Kate shook her head and grinned, as if she couldn't believe what she was about to say. "It seems like I always end up in impossible relationships." She sighed, pulling the ring to the top of her finger then pushing it back in place. "I'd give anything to know what's wrong with me."

"Is there someone now?"

Her nose flared slightly as she drew in a deep breath. "Sort of."

"Sort of?" Sarah said, chuckling. "How's that?"

Kate coughed in laughter. "Where do I begin?"

At that moment Sarah noticed the creases around her sister's eyes and gray hair strands at her temples, making Kate appear older than her years. Sarah imagined the stress of work and life were to blame. "Where did you meet him?"

"I work with him."

"So you've known him for some time?"

"Not really," Kate said with a shrug, unable to look her sister in the eye. "He's in a different department. I used to see him all the time, but now with this subculture assignment, I've been dealing with him a lot."

"So he's working on this story too?"

She nodded. "Yeah."

"How long have you been working on this story?"

"Two months."

"So this must be a pretty serious assignment."

"Well, like I was saying earlier, it's going to run as a special."

Sarah nodded, wondering at the local station's fascination with subcultures. "I see."

"So we've been working together, and we have to meet a lot."

She nodded, her gaze falling on the television as Kate spoke.

"And Sarah, I can honestly say I've never met a man like this before. He's respectful, kind, and understanding. And it's not just a façade."

Sarah smiled, glancing at her sister again.

"And he actually respects commitment," Kate added with a laugh.

Sarah chuckled, understanding that in Kate's world such a trait was rare.

"And when he talks about his life," Kate said as if breathing in the words, "I feel like there's something there, I mean really there." Her eyes stared at the screen as she reflected on him in awe. "There's something about him that makes him different from the other men I've known."

A commercial played the soft music of Stevie Wonder's "These Three Words," and for a moment the sisters sat in silence as the singer's rich voice asked, "When was the last time that they heard you say, Sister or brother, I love you. And when was the last time that they heard you say, Darling or best friend, I love you." The music faded, and Kate's nervous laughter filled the room.

"You know me," she said, meeting her sister's gaze for a second. "I'm not one for religion. But the way he talks about God makes me wonder if there really is one."

"A God you mean?"

"Yeah."

Sarah ran a finger along her ear to tuck her hair behind it. "So he's a pretty committed Christian, huh?"

A self-conscious smile formed on Kate's face, and she avoided Sarah's eyes as she scratched at a mole on her shoulder. "That's what I thought too." She looked at Sarah a moment later. "It turns out he's Syrian."

Sarah's eyebrows gathered as she held her sister's gaze, fearing what this might mean.

"You wouldn't believe the irony, but he just told me he's Muslim."

Sarah looked toward the screen, unsure how to feel. On the one hand, she was pleased that her sister was beginning to take the subject of God more seriously, but on the other, she was leery of this man. Any Muslim man who spent enough time with a woman to discuss personal matters was one who either understood little of Islam or didn't care. She didn't know what to think of him. "When did he tell you that?" she asked, looking at her sister again.

"About a week ago."

"So what does he think of you?" Sarah hated sounding as if she approved of the relationship, but their conversation would go nowhere if she didn't understand what was going on.

Kate rolled her eyes playfully. "If he'd only be more frank."

"So he's never expressed how he felt?"

She shook her head. "Not directly, but he has made general comments, hinting at what he thought." Kate couldn't keep from grinning at the memory.

"So, is that your dilemma?"

Kate's eyes saddened as the grin faded until she bit her lower lip and she toyed with her ring again. "I wish that were all." She pulled the band from her finger and put it on her pinky, where it seemed to dangle from looseness, too ashamed to look her sister in the eye. "I also discovered that he's married."

The room grew silent, and the noise of the television set rose suddenly. Sarah's eyes rested on a woman on the screen holding a dirt-stained white shirt, over which she poured blue laundry detergent to cover the muddy spot. Symphonic music blared as the woman tossed the shirt in the washer and folded her arms in determination as she waited for the cycle to finish.

This was completely unacceptable, the thought came to Sarah suddenly. She had to say something. "Kate, now you know that—."

"I know, I know." Kate raised a hand to stop her sister, her ring now back on its proper finger. "And before you judge him, Sarah, know that all of this is from me."

Sarah nibbled at her lower lip and ran a palm against her hair.

"I was just hoping all this time," Kate said, sounding frank for the first time. "In fact, he only has a vague idea what I think of him."

Sarah opened her mouth to say something, but she didn't know how to respond. What did her sister know of the ideas in this man's head? The man probably considered their relationship "professional," whatever that meant. Hearing about Muslims portraying Islam in this manner infuriated her. She met her sister's gaze in concern. "Kate, don't you think it's best just to leave this one alone?"

"I know," Kate said with a laugh as she shook her head. "I keep telling myself that everyday, but for some reason, Sarah, I just can't. I feel like this is the one."

"The one?" Sarah stared at her sister with her eyes narrowed in disbelief. "Kate, he's married."

"But that's the thing." Grinning, Kate's eyes widened as she eagerly went on, "One day I sort of asked him about it, to kind of let him know what I felt, but you know what he did?"

"What?" Sarah's tone reflected exhausted disinterest, and she felt her jaw tighten. She was unsure if she wanted to hear the rest.

"He mentioned polygamy."

Sarah's gaze returned to the television, which filled the silence between them for a few minutes. She feared she was unable to contain herself much longer. This was getting ridiculous. "What did you tell him?"

Kate laughed. "I know it sounds crazy, but I was thinking, well if that's the only way to be with him, I'd do it."

Sarah sighed and let her gaze fall to her hands that now sat linked on her lap. She didn't approve of her sister's motivations. Yes, Islam allowed a man to marry up to four wives, but it upset her when people's incentives were tainted. Besides, Kate wasn't a Christian by any stretch of the imagination, and a Muslim man could marry only a Jew or a Christian if he wasn't marrying a Muslim. And the woman had to be both religious and chaste, neither of which described her sister. Sarah couldn't help wondering if he was a Muslim by heritage or practice, but Kate wouldn't know the difference.

"So what should I do?" Kate asked, almost helplessly, and Sarah couldn't meet her gaze.

What *should* Kate do? Sarah knew the Islamic answer, but she doubted that would solve Kate's problems. Then again, perhaps, this could inspire Kate to consider the religion more seriously.

"To be honest," Sarah sighed, lifting her eyes to her sister, "it's a really difficult situation." She shut her eyes momentarily as she rubbed them. She sounded exhausted when she continued. "Yes, he can marry another woman, but, if she's not Muslim, she has to be a pretty religious Jew or Christian." She decided against mentioning chastity.

"I'm Christian," Kate said, almost pleading.

A half smile formed on Sarah's face. "Come on, Kate, you still haven't decided whether or not you believe in God."

"But we were raised Christian."

"That doesn't matter in this case."

"What if I become Christian?"

"It has to be sincere."

"I've been considering religion more lately," Kate said in a plea, as if her sister's approval would make it happen. "And I don't mind the thought of organized religion as much as I used to. In some ways having a religion makes sense." She forced laughter. "I mean, if I can put all the world's craziness off on God's plan, then I'd feel that maybe there's a method to this madness after all."

"But don't join a religion just for the sake of joining it. You should really believe it's true."

"I believe *something's* gotta be true."

"But that something has to be specific."

"I think I can deal with Christianity." Kate nodded a moment later as the idea grew on her.

"Why Christianity?"

She laughed. "Well, because I don't have to worry about drastic changes in my life."

"What about your soul?"

"Oh, you're asking too much at once, Sarah. I haven't thought about all that. I'm still trying to digest this whole idea of eternal life after I'm dust and bones." She laughed and shook her head. "Right now, I think, hell, when you die, you die. If there's anything after that, then I'll worry about that when I get there. But so far, no one can prove there's anything after this."

Sarah sighed. She decided to ignore her sister's last comment. She knew from her own experience as an atheist that people who demanded proof of God and the afterlife did so more for argument's sake than any sincere belief on their part. "Kate, I think you need to figure out who you are before you decide who you want to marry. Otherwise, you may wake up five years later and regret what you've done."

"Oh, I couldn't regret being with him."

"We never see today what's in store tomorrow."

"I know, Sarah, but to tell you the truth, I don't care. As long as I can be with him today, I don't care what happens tomorrow."

That was definitely a formula for disaster. Her sister had no clue where she was heading and didn't even care. *O Allah, protect me from misguidance!* "What if you did decide to marry him? What makes you think he'd do it?"

Kate shrugged, and her body grew limp with sadness as she twisted the ring again. "I don't know for sure, but I know he won't do it any other way."

"What makes you think that?" Sarah hoped her sister was right. The last thing she wanted to hear about was a Muslim man indulging in sin with a non-Muslim coworker, especially if the latter was her sister.

Kate grinned self-consciously. "Well, let's just say I'm getting no where."

Sarah knew what her sister meant and chose to leave that one alone. "So you think he'll ask to marry you?"

Kate shrugged. "It's difficult to determine, because he hasn't even said he would really do it. We've just kind of danced around the topic, which is why polygamy came up."

They were silent momentarily as they both gazed distantly at the television set.

Kate drew in a deep breath. "Sarah, you don't understand how much I want this to work. I've never felt like this before."

"Then just become Muslim and marry him."

Kate stared at her sister, and her eyes widened in disbelief. But she wasn't offended by the suggestion, this Sarah could tell. "Are you kidding!"

"About the first part, no, but the second, yes."

"Well, what's the point of becoming Muslim if I can't marry him?"

Sarah sighed. Her sister was really confused. "Pray on it, Kate. That's all I can tell you to do."

Kate laughed. "Pray on it?"

Sarah met her sister's gaze. "Sure, why not? I'm sure God knows what you should do."

"Then that means I'll have to leave it alone."

"Who knows?" Sarah said with a shrug. "He may have a solution you never knew possible."

"You think He would approve?" It was apparent that Kate was willing to do anything that would work in her favor.

"Under the circumstances, no. But with a little prayer, God can change things. Trust me."

Kate nodded, considering the suggestion. "But how am I supposed to pray? Should I pray to God, Jesus, Jehovah, what?"

"Just pray to God," Sarah suggested with a smile, reaching out and patting her sister on the leg. "That's the safest route. At least then you know who you're talking to."

Kate nodded again. "Is there any special prayer I can say?"

Sarah hesitated. "There is for Muslims."

"You think He can hear me if I said it?"

Sarah laughed. "Of course. It's just that, in general, it's for Muslims."

"You think it's okay if I give it a try?"

Sarah considered it. On the one hand, she didn't like teaching her sister a supplication that she would use only for personal benefit, but on the other, what if this caused her to enter Islam? Maybe she would share it with her sister. Surely, it couldn't do any harm if Kate recited the prayer. "Okay, remind me to get it when we go upstairs."

"Thanks."

"No problem."

They watched television in silence for a few minutes.

"Sarah?"

"Mm, hm."

"I'm sorry about today."

"You're sorry?" Sarah wrinkled her forehead and turned to her sister. "Why?"

"You know, how everything went with Mom."

She forced laughter. "That had nothing to do with you. Mom's just still sore about me converting."

"I know. But I guess I feel kind of responsible. None of us were really supportive, and I guess now I'm seeing that that was wrong."

Sarah nodded gratefully. "It's no problem."

"No, it is," Kate insisted. "I can't imagine how it must have felt all these years. I'd hate to be in your shoes."

"I'm doing what I believe. And that's what makes me happy."

"And that's what I admire in him," Kate said, returning to the topic of the Syrian man. "Sometimes I wish I had that faith in what I believed."

"Well, just pray to God for guidance, Kate, and He'll lead you in the right direction." She added, "For everything in your life."

"I hope so," Kate brooded.

Sarah smiled then placed a hand on her sister's. "I know so."

*****

"But don't worry about Kate," Sarah told Aminah and Sulayman that night before going to bed. They stood at the foot of their parents' bed where their mother sat with her back against a pillow next to her husband. Kate was sleeping in the guest room that they had been using as a study room. Their father had rented a car for them to drive up to Milwaukee, but they were concerned that leaving would be inconsiderate to their aunt. "Honestly, Kate wants to spend some time with me. We have a lot of catching up to do."

"If you're sure it's okay," Sulayman said.

"Trust me. Kate's fine."

Sulayman nodded and glanced at Aminah. "Then I guess we should go ahead and get some sleep."

Aminah nodded in agreement. "Yeah, I think we should."

"You printed out the directions from the Internet?" Ismael asked.

"Yes, from two different sites," Aminah said.

"And you have the cell phone?"

"Yes."

"But how do you know the address of the hotel?" Sarah said with concern.

"I have the listing Tamika gave me, and I called."

"I see," she replied with a nod.

"Don't worry," Ismael advised his wife with a smile, patting her on the leg. "Allah is in charge."

She nodded again.

"Just pray for their safety," he said with a gentle smile.

Sarah nodded, and she smiled as she gazed at her children. "You're right. It's just a new concept for me."

Her husband chuckled. "That's what happens when your children grow up. You have new concepts everyday."

She forced laughter. "I suppose that's true."

"Well, we're gonna get on to bed," Sulayman said as he turned to leave.

"Alright," Sarah said with a smile. "*As-salaamu-'alaikum.*"

"*Wa-'alaiku-mus-salaam,*" they replied in unison before leaving the room and closing the door.

In the room, Ismael brushed his wife's forehead with a kiss. "Relax, sweetheart, they'll be fine *inshaAllaah.*"

She nodded distantly and sighed. "I know." She shook her head. "But now it's Kate I'm worried about."

"Kate? Why are you worried about her?"

Sarah laughed. "She's in a sticky situation."

"What do you mean?"

"It's a man."

Ismael laughed. "When isn't it a man?"

"But this is different."

"When have I heard this before?"

"He's Muslim." Sarah met his gaze, deciding to cut to the chase.

Ismael grew silent, and his expression became serious as he narrowed his eyes. "Are you sure?"

"That's what she said."

He rubbed his hands over his face in mental exhaustion. "I pray Allah guides this brother."

She nodded. "Me too. But for now, Kate can't even think straight."

"What's wrong with this world?" Ismael shook his head in frustration. "When will Muslims stop hiding behind the name and really practice?"

"According to her, he's really religious."

His eyebrows rose, and he stared at his wife with a grin. "According to her? How can an atheist gauge what's religious? For them, a belief in God is akin to sainthood." He shook his head.

Sarah let her gaze fall to her nightgown, where she pulled a piece of lint from the fabric. "But I gave her the *Istikhaarah*[21] prayer to say."

"*Istikhaarah*?" He raised his eyebrows in surprise. "For what?"

"You think I was wrong?" Sarah gazed at her husband, a hesitant smile creasing a corner of her mouth. "I didn't know if I should, but I thought it could help her."

He lifted his shoulder in a shrug. "Allah knows best. I suppose it can't hurt. I just don't like the idea of people playing with serious prayers."

"I know," Sarah said, biting her lower lip. "But I was hoping it would help her connect with Allah more."

He frowned as he considered it. "I'm no scholar, but I can't imagine it being prohibited for her to say it if she wants to." He added, "But my only reservation is that most times, when people pray special prayers in these cases, they're in this I'll-do-anything mode. Today they're praying *Istikhaarah*, and tomorrow they're at a fortune teller, and then they're visiting a magician to 'make it happen'."

Sarah nodded with her forehead creased in concern. "That's what I was thinking."

"But don't worry about it." He gently squeezed her hand. "You did what you thought was best. Let's just pray good comes out of it."

"That's my prayer."

"Does she acknowledge there's a God now?"

"Yes," she sighed, "but I fear it's only motivated by her desire to be with this man."

"Sometimes that's what it takes for people."

"That's true."

They held each other's hand in silence for several minutes.

---

[21] A supplication to God that is made when wants to make a decision on a matter.

"But now," Ismael said, grinning and patting his wife's hand, "I think we should get some rest." He lay down and pulled the covers over himself. "Otherwise, you'll keep yourself up all night worrying."

Sarah nodded and followed suit. She would have to worry about everything tomorrow. She reached and turned off the lamp on the nightstand next to their bed and settled under the covers. Within minutes, her husband was breathing rhythmically, and she shut her eyes to try to sleep too.

After some time, she glanced at the clock and realized that more than thirty minutes had passed, and she still wasn't sleep. She shut her eyes again, trying not to think about anything, but still, she couldn't sleep. Her mind kept drifting to her sister.

Sarah felt awfully sorry for Kate, and she wished she could help her. But when a person was struck in the heart by one of Satan's poisonous arrows, getting her to think rationally was nearly impossible. Kate didn't believe in Satan or anything related to the unseen world of evil, which only complicated matters. She was in the thick of that very world and had nearly given her life to it, but she was oblivious to what she was doing, as most people were. The only things Sarah could do were pray for her sister and try to remain a part of her life on a non-intrusive level. No, she couldn't condone Kate's lifestyle or relationship with the Syrian, but she could be a source of comfort for her. Perhaps over time, Kate would begin to think straight. Who knew? Maybe Allah would bring good out of this. He could change the most shameful circumstances into praiseworthy ones. She could only pray this would be the case with Kate.

Kate was like a feather in a windstorm, Sarah reflected sadly. There was no telling where she would end up. Her choices in life might appear rational and appealing to their mother, who was easily impressed by catchy job titles and high salaries, but Sarah knew better. Kate was living a life of misery, plummeting deep into a dark hole, and she was crying for help. Kate caught only glimpses of happiness when things were going well at her job or when the man she loved loved her back. But Sarah knew all too well that that wasn't happiness. It was merely tastes of pleasure, of which every human experienced throughout life. But happiness was a matter of the soul, and only when it was content did a person know happiness in its true form.

To the outside world, Sarah was the epitome of failure, she reflected in the darkness, listening to her husband's soft breathing. She had no money except what her husband gave her, and she had no job. She stayed home all day tending to domestic concerns and had given up a golden career opportunity to stay home with her children. And after all of that, she chose not to go back to work even now. But what people didn't see was the contentment of her soul. She wasn't distracted by job titles and high salaries. She was focusing on her duty to her Lord. She loved staying home. Even in worldly terms, wasn't success doing what you loved?

But Kate didn't love what she did, this Sarah could see. Kate was reaching for the top, but as she neared it, she realized there was nothing there. Perhaps she wondered if there was any such thing as "the top." She had received endless promotions since she landed the job, and for what? She came home and sat in front of the television with a Scotch or beer only to fall asleep on the couch and wake up to the same old routine. Her spurts of excitement came only when she got a bonus at work or if there was a man in her life. What fulfillment could come from that? Sarah could see the endless rendition was running her sister dry. There had to be something more to life, Kate's heart had to be screaming—just as Sarah's had before finding Islam.

It was extremely difficult for Sarah to watch her sister spiraling down and losing all energy for anything meaningful. But talking to Kate had filled Sarah with renewed commitment to her own faith. Where would she be if she had chosen the world over her soul? Like Kate, looking to the arms of a man to fill the gaping void in her heart? Then what of her heart when things went sour with him? Where would she be? Back on the streets of loneliness and despair, searching for the next man to patch up the wound? Sarah couldn't thank her Lord enough for pulling her from that world. She had been laying the foundations for her destruction, and God pulled her back.

That she left her job to stay home with her family was only half the truth. The reality was that she had hated what she saw when she looked in the mirror. She was chasing money, status, and, yes, even men. It had become such a part of the job that when she became Muslim, she barely detected it. But when she began to look forward to going to work for reasons displeasing to God, she knew she had to take a step back and set her priorities straight. She loved practicing medicine and helping people, and that never changed. But until she could prioritize her life with her soul coming first, she decided it was time to take a break. She still saw patients from the Muslim community and did occasional consultations, but she had never returned to the office or hospital scene. Perhaps one day she would, but she had grown so attached to staying home that she doubted she would ever want to go back.

Nine

After praying *Fajr* with their parents, Sulayman and Aminah pulled out of the driveway while the sky was still dark and morning a mere hint of blue in the sky. They passed the familiar brick houses and flowerbeds sprinkled along lawns of the neighborhood they called home. It was always a sense of sadness Aminah felt watching the familiar scenery pass whenever they went on road trips, and she wondered at this feeling as they waited at a traffic light a minute before they pulled onto the interstate.

An hour into the drive, Sulayman put a lecture tape in the cassette player, and they listened to the imam remind them of their responsibilities on earth. The imam talked of how the world was an endless array of false hopes and desires and how illogical it was to fall prey. Even if one didn't believe in anything else, surely, he had to believe in death. That was the one certainty in life—that it would come to an end. Then why did so many waste their days in front of a television or with music blasting in their ears? To pass time? Was the value of life so miniscule that there was nothing more compelling than getting it over with—with as much distraction as possible? Or was life such a selfish pursuit that we should only concern ourselves with those things that brought us pleasure? To hell with starving children, to hell with people being showered with bombs, and to hell with people who believed there was actually something we could do about it. Live and let live was our motto. Or was it, live and let die?

Sulayman and Aminah listened to the imam's lecture in silence, guilt ridden by his words. Were they living their lives with purpose, or were they just waiting for time to pass? Were they, even as Muslims, allowing selfish pursuits to distract them from the higher goal? Yes, they had to make a living, and they needed something of this world. But were they prepared to take only what they needed for the Hereafter, or did their desires go beyond that?

"*SubhanAllaah*[22]," Sulayman said in deep reflection after the tape ended. "He's right."

"I know." Aminah stared out her window in contemplation.

He sighed. "Well, I pray Allah accepts this trip from us and purifies our intentions. I need all the blessings I can get."

Aminah silently agreed, reflecting on herself.

"I just hope we get there in time," she said, reminding him of their current dilemma.

"I think we will. I really don't think she'll go anywhere, at least not overnight. She may not be in her room when we get there, but I'm sure she'll come back by evening, *inshaAllaah*."

---

[22] A statement of glorification of God and admiration of how high He is above imperfection.

Sulayman began to feel tired after five hours of driving, and he caught himself dozing off at the wheel. Beside him, Aminah had fallen asleep, and her head lay against the back of the seat facing him. Her soft snores were intoxicating, and Sulayman wished he could be sleeping too. He wanted to be at least half way there before resting, which left him with only one more hour before he could stop. He felt his eyes become heavy a few minutes later, and he swerved a bit. Reluctantly, he decided to give in. He looked for rest stop signs, and fifteen minutes later, he saw one. He pulled into the rest stop and found a parking space in front of the red and brown brick building. He turned off the ignition and leaned his seat back to sleep for an hour.

The sound of the cell phone ringing woke Sulayman, and he instinctively looked at his watch. He had slept almost three hours. "Yes?" His voice was scratchy despite his attempt to conceal that he was sleeping.

"Are you on the road?" His mother's voice sounded close to panic.

"No, I'm at a rest stop."

Sarah exhaled in relief. "Well, *alhamdulillaah* you're not sleeping on the road. I was just calling to check on you."

"I think I should go ahead and get back to driving," he said with a yawn, pulling his seat into an upright position. "We're running behind."

"Well, pull over whenever you need to."

"I will, *inshaAllaah.*"

"I pray you have a safe trip."

"*Jazaakillaahukhair,*" he thanked her with what meant, "May God reward you with good."

"*Waiyyak,*" she replied, wishing him God's reward too.

After he disconnected the call, he decided they should go to the bathroom before continuing.

Aminah stretched and yawned. She wrinkled her forehead as she looked out the window. "Is this a rest stop?"

"Yep," Sulayman said with a grin as he unlocked the doors. "Let's go to the bathroom."

"Should you call her and tell her we're coming?" Sulayman asked after they returned to the car and he pulled onto the interstate. His eyebrows were gathered in concern as he glanced from the windshield to his sister.

Aminah shrugged, gazing out the window beside her before turning back to her brother. "I don't know. I was considering that, but I'm afraid she may have time to turn it down. But if we show up, she'll know we're serious."

"Don't you think she'll know we're serious if we're halfway there?"

"I suppose, but I just don't want her to get scared and leave the hotel."

He nodded, looking out at the road before them. "I see."

"I don't know, but I feel it's best to just show up. Then she'll come with us."

"*InshaAllaah.*"

"*InshaAllaah,*" Aminah repeated in agreement.

*****

"Where are Sulayman and Aminah?" Kate asked as she sat down next to her sister at the dining room table. Her hair was pulled back in a ponytail, and she wore a pale gray T-shirt with a Nike logo on the front and fitting black jeans. Ismael had gone out for the day, so the sisters had the house to themselves.

"They had to make an emergency road trip," Sarah said from her seat, where she was eating cereal and flipping through the Sunday paper. Her hair hung in a loose braid, and she wore a long sleeved white T-shirt pushed up to her elbows and a light blue jean skirt. She was eating breakfast although it was early afternoon.

"Is everything alright?"

"Yes, everything's fine."

"Oh," Kate said, her forehead creased in concern as she reached for an empty glass bowl and poured herself some cereal. "Are you sure?"

"It's just that a friend of theirs got kicked out of her house, and she has no place to stay," Sarah said, turning the page of the newspaper and meeting her sister's gaze for a second. "So they decided to drive up and get her."

"That was kind of them," Kate said with a smile, setting down the box of cereal and reaching for the milk.

Sarah read in silence, and Kate poured milk into her bowl.

"I did that prayer you told me to do," Kate said picking up a spoon with a grin.

"You did?" Sarah looked at her sister as she raised her eyebrows in pleasant surprise and folded the paper. She placed it on the table next to her.

"I was scared at first. But as I read it, it made total sense." She took a bite of cereal and chewed for a minute before continuing. "You know, I never realized how," she narrowed her eyes as she searched for a word, "peaceful prayer can be."

Sarah laughed. "So you liked it?"

"A lot." Kate took a spoonful of cereal. "I've never felt close to God before," she said after she swallowed her food. "It really made me feel like He's actually out there." She laughed self-consciously. "Somewhere."

Sarah listened with a reluctant smile. She didn't know what this all meant, but it seemed positive.

"When we were in Catholic school, I felt like I was talking to myself when I recited those prayers, and," Kate held her spoon above her bowl as she tried to think of a way to express what she felt, "now I realize it doesn't have to be like that."

"I'm happy for you."

"It's scary though," she said with a playful roll of her eyes. "I never depended on God before."

Sarah laughed. "We all depend on God. It's just that you never did it consciously."

"I suppose that's one way of looking at it."

The sisters ate in silence, and Sarah resumed flipping through the newspaper as they crunched on their food.

"It must be nice to feel like that everyday," Kate said, tilting her bowl to put the last bit of cereal and milk on her spoon.

"You mean how you felt after the prayer?"

"Yeah." Kate chuckled as she met her sister's gaze. "I envy you for that."

"God is the one who gives contentment to hearts," Sarah said, smiling gently at her sister and smoothing down the newspaper on its fold. "And it's only through obeying Him that I get that."

"But I could never be like you," Kate said with a chuckle, setting her spoon in her empty bowl. "I'm as sacrilegious as they come."

"No you're not. You just haven't found your niche in religion yet."

"But, Sarah, come on. Covering up and no dating? I'd die!"

"No you won't," Sarah grinned as she shook her head, lifting the last spoonful of cereal to her mouth. "At least not from that," she said after swallowing her food. "You'll just need time to adjust to it. Everyone does."

"But I *live* for Revlon. We have a one hour date every morning."

"Think of the bright side. You'll get an extra hour of sleep."

Kate rolled her eyes playfully. "Yeah, Lord knows I need *that*."

"Anyway, you don't have to give up your makeup and clothes love affair," Sarah said a smile. "You'll just reschedule your date for the evening right before your husband comes home."

"*You* actually dress up and put on makeup?" Kate stared at her sister in amazement.

Sarah laughed. "Of course. You think I lost my sense of style?"

"I guess I never realized Muslim women were allowed to look, uh," Kate smiled hesitantly before adding, "sophisticated."

Sarah laughed again. "For our husbands, yes."

"But isn't that boring?" Kate asked as she wrinkled her nose.

"It depends on how you define boring," Sarah said with a shrug. "If you like being available to every man who sees you, then yes, it'll be quite boring. But if you want a loving, meaningful relationship with a man committed to you, then it's as exciting as it gets."

Kate avoided her sister's gaze and looked distantly at the newspaper between them. Sarah could see in Kate's eyes that there was nothing she wanted more than a meaningful long-term relationship with a man she loved. Kate had already expressed her fear that she would never know how it felt to have a wedding.

"How does it feel to have a family?" There was a hint of sad longing in Kate's tone as she looked at her sister with a reluctant smile. "Do you ever get tired of them?"

Sarah smiled. "I love it. But there are days you think you're tired of them, but to be honest, that's just anger and frustration talking. And they disappear as quickly as they came."

"Do you ever think, there's gotta be something more to life than this?"

She shook her head. "I love what I do. This is life to me."

"Staying home, you mean?"

"No. All of it."

Kate raised her eyebrows in surprise. "So you like staying home all day?"

"It's not at all like you think. I have a zillion things to do." Sarah laughed. "I often wish there were more hours in the day."

Kate nodded and sighed, leaning back in her chair and biting her thumb nail in deep thought. "I think I might like to take a break from work one day. I used to think I just needed a vacation, but now I know I need a break."

"I know what you mean. That's how I felt as a doctor."

"But I don't see any way out. I don't have a husband to fall back on."

"Maybe you will one day."

Kate laughed. "If you have me saying this prayer, I may not have the one I want."

"You never know."

"That's the problem."

"No," Sarah said with a slight shake of the head. "That's the solution."

Kate raised an eyebrow and leaned forward. "You think it actually solves problems to live your life never knowing what tomorrow will bring?"

"That's how we all live." Sarah met her sister's gaze with a smile. "Some of us just don't like to admit it."

Kate averted her gaze, and Sarah could tell that Kate knew she was right.

"But we just have faith that it'll all be okay no matter what happens tomorrow," Sarah said.

"But you still have to work for tomorrow," Kate said, rearranging the ponytail holder at the back of her head, "even if you never see it."

"You're right. But you can't benefit from it if you don't know who's in charge of it."

Deep down inside, Kate knew her sister was right. But there was that part of her that didn't want to admit it. Sarah had everything she wanted and hadn't expended half as much energy as Kate had. It was as if fortune just fell in her lap. She had a good husband, intelligent and respectful children, and most importantly, she seemed to have internal peace. For that, Kate envied her.

Sarah decided to change the subject. She didn't want to put too many things on her sister at once. Kate already had a lot on her mind. "When will that special air?"

"On the subcultures?"

"Yeah."

"It's scheduled for mid-June."

"Oh, so you don't have much more time?"

"No, I don't actually, but," Kate sucked her teeth and shrugged, "I don't really care. It'll go how it goes."

Sarah didn't respond, and she picked up the newspaper to unfold it again.

"Do you really know people who wear all black and cover their faces?" Kate asked a minute later, her elbow propped on the table so that her chin sat on her fist as she faced her sister.

"Yes. But they wear other colors too."

"What are they like really?"

"Like me and you. They're human."

"But do they have anti-American ideas?"

"They realize the same things you realize," she said, folding the newspaper in half. "You know America isn't what it's made out to be. And, of course, you know there are a lot of improvements to be made, especially in how it deals with other nations militarily."

"So you think their view is basically the same as ours?"

"Pretty much, except they may disagree on the solution. As all Americans do."

"So what do they think is the solution?"

She grinned at her sister. "God."

Kate sat up, letting her hand fall to the table as she continued to lean on it. "That's it?"

"You think that's oversimplifying the problem?" Sarah asked with a knowing smile.

"Of course I do. Don't you?"

She shook her head. "I don't think it's oversimplifying the problem at all. It's just that people oversimplify the definition of God."

Kate raised her eyebrows. "What do you mean?"

"Well, if the solution is so simple, then why do we have such a difficult time obeying Him?"

Kate looked toward the kitchen and shook her head as her forehead creased. "But so much bloodshed has happened in the name of God. Don't you think that God's just a scapegoat for people with ulterior motives?"

"For some people, yes. But not for people who really believe in God and follow His laws."

"But the concept of God is too vague to apply to specific problems."

"In Islam, the concept of God is not vague."

Kate laughed and lifted her shoulder in a shrug. "I suppose I can't argue with that. Especially after that prayer last night."

Kate touched her neck to feel for her necklace and tugged at it a second later. "But tell me more about these women. This is a really interesting perspective."

"It's not anything to really understand, Kate, except that they're just like you. Yes, their concept of God is different, and yes, their beliefs are a little different. But what you're trying to understand is something you already do. And that's how it feels to be human and live what you believe."

"You don't think there's a radical tendency?"

Sarah laughed. "Of course not."

"But how can you be sure?"

She sighed and considered it before finally asking, "Kate, do you think of me as an anti-American fanatic?"

Kate laughed and shook her head. "Of course not."

"Then you understand them."

She creased her forehead in confusion as she looked at her sister, pulling on the gold chain with her thumb. "What do you mean?"

"I am them, Kate," Sarah said. "I wear the face veil too."

It was shortly after 9:00 that night when Sulayman and Aminah exited the interstate and entered the city of Milwaukee. Aminah silently praised God for the safe trip and studied the array of store lights and glowing windows before she began looking out for the hotel. She read the directions under the car's ceiling light as Sulayman made the necessary turns. They pulled into the parking lot of the hotel about ten minutes later.

Sulayman turned off the ignition and stretched. He turned to his sister and smiled. "I guess we should just go on in."

After calling their parents to let them know they had arrived, Sulayman and Aminah got out of the car and stretched again. "That wasn't so bad," Sulayman said with a laugh. "I still have use of most of my limbs."

Aminah laughed and nodded. "Well, I'll tell you one thing. I don't think I'll do this for leisure."

Her brother grinned. "Any leisure that requires this much energy can't be considered fun."

"Should we stop by the front desk?" Aminah asked as they approached the glass doors to the entrance.

Sulayman shook his head. "The receptionist doesn't know if we're guests or not, and either way, I don't think you need permission to visit a person."

Aminah nodded. "Yeah, it's better not to ask if someone can tell you no."

"Especially if *no* isn't an option."

"That's true," she agreed with a chuckle.

"Anyway, the room is in your name."

She laughed as they entered the lobby. "I forgot about that."

"Let's take the stairs," Sulayman said, seeing the sign pointing to an area outside the lobby.

"Okay." Aminah followed her brother around the corner and through the heavy door that led to the stairs. They walked up the stairs in silence until they reached the third floor and opened another heavy door leading to the hall. They glanced around until they saw a sign that indicated three eighteen was to the left.

"I'll just stand here," Sulayman said to Aminah once they reached the room, stopping a few feet from the door. She nodded as she approached the door and knocked.

Tamika turned down the television and listened closely. She thought she heard something outside her door, but she wasn't sure. Seconds later, she heard the knock again, but this time she was sure. Someone was at the door. For a moment, she considered ignoring it. If it was room service, they could come back later. She resumed watching television. When they knocked a third time, she grew curious and walked softly to the door. She peered through the peephole.

Her heart pounded. Was she hallucinating? There was a young woman outside the door who looked like Aminah. Perhaps she would go away. The woman knocked again, this time more forcefully, as if she knew Tamika was inside.

"Tamika?"

Tamika froze. That was Aminah's voice. She looked through the peephole again.

"Tamika? It's Aminah."

Aminah? "Hello?" Tamika called nervously through the door.

"Tamika, it's me Aminah."

Had she heard her correctly? "Aminah who?"

"Aminah Ali, your roommate."

Too stunned to respond, Tamika gathered her thoughts. What was going on? Aminah was supposed to be in Atlanta.

"We drove up to, uh, make sure you found a place to stay," Aminah called.

She couldn't be serious! They *drove* here? Hundreds of miles just to make sure she had a place to stay? A second later Tamika realized it was possible. Their family's kindness seemed to have no bounds. Slowly, she unchained the door and opened it. And sure enough, Aminah stood opposite her.

"Oh my God!" Tamika said, cupping a hand over her mouth as Aminah stepped inside and closed the door.

They hugged, and Tamika held on for a moment longer. She didn't want to let go, intoxicated by the warmth of the friendly embrace.

"I can't believe you!" Tamika stared at Aminah in disbelief. She felt her eyes water, and she stopped herself. She didn't want to break down, as she had been doing a lot lately. So many emotions were overtaking her that it was difficult to temper them. She felt like she was being pulled in a million directions, and crying was how her heart found peace. When the tug of war inside her erupted, she was so overwhelmed with sadness that crying was the only thing that both expressed and soothed her pain. When she prayed and reflected on the power of God's words and the truth of His religion, her eyes welled with tears. It was this crying that soothed her soul.

"Did everyone come?" Tamika asked.

"Just me and Sulayman."

"You drove all the way here?"

"Well," Aminah grinned, "I'd like to take the credit, but Sulayman did all the driving."

Tamika's eyes widened in disbelief. "Are you kidding?"

Aminah smiled. "If I was, I wouldn't be standing here right now."

Tamika laughed and shook her head. "You all are unbelievable."

"So are you ready to go?"

She gathered her eyebrows. "Ready to go where?"

"Home with us."

Her eyes widened in disbelief as a grin formed on her face. "What!"

"We didn't drive fifteen hours to take you around Milwaukee."

Tamika didn't know what to say. She definitely couldn't turn them down. They had gone through a lot to come here. "Right now?"

"No, maybe in the morning. We need to rest."

"Where's Sulayman?"

"In the hall."

Tamika laughed. "He seems to always be in the hall."

Aminah laughed too. "Well, you do what you have to do, I suppose."

"Where will he sleep?"

"In the car," she said, glancing around the hotel room as she walked toward the bed.

"No way." Tamika stared at her roommate, who turned to face her just then. "Can't he just sleep in here on the floor or something?"

"He wouldn't feel comfortable."

"But, Aminah," Tamika said with her eyes widening in concern, "I wouldn't get an ounce of sleep knowing he's in the car."

"He'll be fine." When she studied Tamika's shocked expression she added, "He may get a room."

Tamika exhaled. "I hope so."

Aminah forced a smile. She knew Sulayman had no intention of getting a room, but she didn't want to bother Tamika with that information. Instead, she went to the door and told her brother everything was fine and they would see him in the morning, God-willing.

Sarah embraced her sister at the front door. Kate's flight was scheduled to leave in a couple of hours, and she decided to go to the airport to get there an hour ahead of time.

"I appreciate you letting me stay with you," Kate said after the embrace.

Sarah waved a hand at her sister. "It's no problem, really. I enjoyed it."

"I did too. I'm gonna try to stay in touch more."

"Don't stress over it. I know you're really busy."

"But I don't want to let my job keep me from my family."

Sarah nodded and smiled at her sister. "You're always on my mind."

"And you're always on mine." Kate sighed. "I really feel bad for letting the years slip by. I don't know how to make up for that."

"There's no need to." Sarah placed a hand on Kate's shoulder. "We're sisters."

"But I feel so bad."

"Don't."

"No, I should." Kate shook her head. "But it's just that when you first joined this religion, I had no idea what it meant, and I guess I just made up in my mind what it was and I—."

"Kate," Sarah interrupted and squeezed her sister's shoulder gently, "you don't owe me an explanation. I understand."

Kate started to say something but stopped herself. She lowered her gaze. "I'm sorry."

"Like I said, forget it."

"I can't, Sarah." She looked up. "You know, yesterday, when Mom walked out, I realized how silly this all is. We're such hypocrites. I mean, we talk so much about treating people kindly and understanding different cultures and," she forced laughter, "we even talk about animal rights and saving rain forests. But then we can't even treat family with the same respect we treat complete strangers." She shook her head as tears welled in her eyes. "It's sad. It's so sad."

Sarah embraced Kate again, and this time she felt Kate tremble beneath her. Sarah's shirt became moist with her sister's tears, and she hugged Kate tighter. "I love you," Sarah whispered, feeling her own eyes water. The words made Kate cry more, and they held each other for a few minutes before letting go.

"Have a safe trip," she told Kate as her sister opened the door to go.

Eyes still wet with tears, Kate nodded. "Thanks."

From her front porch, Sarah watched her sister walk to the car. Once Kate was safely inside and had turned on the ignition, Sarah waved to her before coming back inside and closing the door. She sighed and wiped her eyes to prevent the tears from escaping. She then silently prayed that Allah would guide Kate to Islam.

"So you found a change of clothes?" Aminah asked as she noticed Tamika's floral skirt and long sleeved T-shirt.

"I found a store nearby and bought myself a change of clothes earlier today." She smiled. "That money your family gave me really came in handy. But I couldn't find any head scarves except really small ones."

"Don't worry. I brought an extra *abiya* and *khimaar*. They're in the car though."

Tamika laughed. "Is there anything you *didn't* think of?"

Aminah laughed too. "*Alhamdulillaah.*"

Aminah glanced toward the door. "I think I'll run to the car and get my bag now that I know you're here."

Tamika nodded. "Okay."

Aminah left the room and went back outside and found her brother praying in the dimly lit parking lot. She waited for him to finish then asked if she could get something from the car.

He took out his keys and unlocked the car. "So everything's fine?"

"*Alhamdulillaah.*"

"So she's coming with us tomorrow?"

"That's what it looks like." Aminah opened the back door on the passenger side and pulled out her backpack.

"I'll just sleep out here," Sulayman said, surveying the parking lot. "I brought a small blanket to cover me. So if I lie in the back seat, I don't think anyone'll see me."

His sister nodded. "You still have the cell phone?"

"Yeah." He patted a pocket to make sure it was still there.

"So just call upstairs if you need anything. The hotel number is written on the directions, and you already know the room number."

He nodded. "And call me if you need anything. *InshaAllaah*, I'll be out here."

"Okay." She secured a strap of the backpack over her shoulder. "*As-salaamu-'alaikum.*"

"*Wa-'alaiku-mus-salaam.*"

In the room, Aminah took the *khimaar* from her backpack and showed it to Tamika, who sat on the bed flipping through the hotel's television guide, her hair pulled neatly back in a ponytail. "Here's a scarf you can put on before we leave." Aminah placed the folded white cloth on the nightstand next to the bed.

"Thanks."

"No problem."

Tamika continued to read the thin magazine and asked a minute later, "Was Sulayman able to attend graduation?" She hoped she hadn't caused him to miss it.

"Oh yeah," Aminah said with a nod, taking a seat on the edge of the bed. "He did his speech and everything."

"Really?" The corners of Tamika's mouth turned up in a smile. She felt privileged to know the student who had given the commencement address, momentarily forgetting her previous contempt for him.

"Yes, and *alhamdulillaah*, it went really well."

"I wish I could've seen it."

"My dad has it all on video."

"Really?" She turned a page of the guide. "You think I can watch it when we get there?"

"Of course," Aminah said with a laugh. "I think we're all gonna watch it anyway."

Tamika grinned, suddenly excited about living with Aminah. Maybe her summer wouldn't be so bad after all. "It must be nice to have a Muslim family."

Aminah smiled, removing her white head cover and folding it on her lap, making her neck appear small under the collar of her black *abiya*. Her hair was braided down the nape of her neck. "*Alhamdulillaah*, it is. But not all my family is Muslim."

"Both your parents are though, right?"

"Yes, *alhamdulillaah*."

Tamika sighed longingly, and her gaze grew distant. She bit her lower lip, forgetting about the magazine for a moment. "I wish my mother was Muslim."

Aminah frowned sympathetically at her friend. "Just make *du'aa* that Allah guides her. You never know."

Tamika forced laughter, but her sadness was apparent. "That'll be the day."

"A year ago, could you have imagined you'd be here today?"

She smiled reluctantly and closed the television guide. "You're right. But I just can't see my mother being anything but Christian. It's like she lives and breathes that religion."

"You never know what can happen tomorrow. Allah is in charge of hearts."

"But isn't it true some people's hearts are sealed?"

Aminah grew silent at the reminder and ran her hand over the soft cloth of her *khimaar*, where here gaze fell. It wasn't something she liked to think about often. But there were those who heard of Islam, and after recognizing the truth, they turned away from the religion. When a person persisted upon this path, God sealed his heart, and he no longer recognized the truth. Such a person would begin to believe wholeheartedly in whatever false religion or lifestyle he ascribed to. He would view Islam as falsehood and even fight against it until he died. He would wake in the grave and face awful torment. Immense regret would nearly suffocate him, and he would beg for another chance. He would swear that if he could only go back, he would live as a Muslim. But the *barzakh*—The Barrier—would be behind him, preventing his return. Even if God allowed him to go back, he would return to his life of sin and rejection of God's religion. For in this life he chose misguidance to guidance, and as a recompense, God left him on the path he chose.

Aminah shook her head as she remembered God's words that meant, "If anyone contends with the Messenger even after guidance has been clearly conveyed to him and follows a path other than that of the believers, We shall leave him on the path he has chosen and land him in Hell—what an evil refuge!"[23]

"Yes," she replied regretfully with a sigh, "that's true."

Tamika lowered her gaze in sadness, her eyes staring beyond the movie scene on the magazine's cover as she feared the worst. Whenever she read the Qur'an, she paid close attention to the verses about the disbelievers, especially those whose hearts were sealed. The verses that pained her most were the ones in which God said what meant, "As for those who disbelieve, it is the same to them whether you warn them or do not warn them, they will not believe. God has set a seal on their hearts and on their hearing and on their eyes as a veil. Great is the penalty they incur...Deaf, dumb, and blind—they will not return to the path."[24]

O Allah! Guide my mother upon the path of truth so that she may worship You and You alone. Open her eyes to see the truth. Open her ears to hear the truth, and lift the veil from her heart so that she may heed Your warnings and be raised among the believers on the Day of Resurrection.

"But we never know whose hearts are sealed," Aminah said, unfastening the top buttons of her *abiya* until the front of her T-shirt was visible. "So we just have to keep teaching them about Islam."

Tamika nodded sadly, placing the magazine next to her on the bed. She could only pray that was the case with her mother.

"It's all still new to her," Aminah said in an effort to lighten her friend's burden. "I'm sure you know better than I do that it's not an easy thing to go to sleep believing one thing and then wake up and realize you had it all wrong. It's only natural for a person to cling to what they had believed for so long. It's human nature. No one wants to believe they're wrong." She sighed then added, "And even if they do, they definitely don't want to announce it to the world."

Tamika nodded again as she sighed and folded her arms. "You're right. I'll just make *du'aa.*"

[23] *An-Nisaa,* 4:115
[24] *Al-Baqarah,* 2:6-7, 18

The room grew silent as the roommates' minds drifted to the enormity of what they were discussing. Tamika could only pray she stayed upon the correct path. It wasn't easy to resist societal norms and be an object of ridicule, but if that was what it took to avoid God's everlasting torment in the Hell Fire, she was willing to do it.

"Aminah?" Tamika asked a few minutes later.

"Yes?"

"When a person dies, is there anything we can do for them to make their punishment lighter?"

"You mean like make *du'aa* for them?"

"Yeah or like do good deeds or something."

Aminah shrugged, standing to slip the sleeves of her *abiya* from her arms. "It depends," she said as she stepped out of the outer garment, revealing the black imprint of "Muslim by Nature" on her red shirt that complimented her black slacks. "If they died Muslim, we can pray for them and make up their fasts or do *Hajj* for them. But if they didn't die Muslim," she frowned apologetically and shook her head as she folded her *khimaar* and *abiya* over the back of a desk chair, "there's nothing we can do."

Tamika glanced toward the phone on the nightstand then blinked to shut out the incessant pounding in her head. She lifted her gaze to where Aminah undid her hair and braided it again before running her palm across it to make sure it was in place.

"What if we're not sure?"

Aminah's gaze fell to her clothes hanging on the desk chair. She couldn't look her friend in the eye, knowing that Tamika was referring to Durrah—Dee. She swallowed as she remembered her childhood friend. She could almost hear Dee's laughter in the hotel room, and her heart ached for her. She remembered how they used to walk with their arms around each other and talk about Islam and being good Muslims.

Aminah sighed, slowly sitting down on the edge of the bed. "I don't know."

The room grew still. The darkness outside seemed to envelop their presence despite the glow from the lamp on the nightstand. They thought of Dee, and Aminah could only imagine what it must be like for her in the grave. The room felt cold suddenly. The air from the vent seemed to blow more powerfully, and the curtains danced above it with each breath. Somewhere in the distance a train passed, its horn an awful cry in the night, and they couldn't help wondering if it was wailing for Dee.

Tamika woke to the chirping of birds outside the hotel window, and when she opened her eyes, she saw the glow of blue peaking through the curtains to announce the approach of sunrise. She quickly sat up, realizing they had slept longer than they had intended. She glanced at the clock. It was 6:15. If they didn't pray in the next fifteen minutes, they would miss the prayer. She climbed out of bed and found Aminah sleeping soundly on the floor, a thin off-white blanket covering up to her shoulders. She must be exhausted, Tamika thought to herself. She never knew Aminah to come this close to missing prayer.

"Aminah! We're gonna miss prayer!"

Aminah's eyes opened as she sat up and looked around her, the blanket falling to her waist. When she saw daylight illuminating the room, she threw off her cover and stood, revealing her wrinkled red shirt and black pants. "Did you pray?"

"No, I just woke up too."

"I'll hurry up and make *wudoo'*." Aminah walked quickly to the bathroom. A couple of minutes later she came out. "I'm finished. You can go ahead."

Tamika followed suit and hastened to the bathroom to perform the ablution. She finished in less than five minutes and met Aminah in the room next to the bed, where Aminah was dressed in her *abiya* and *khimaar* waiting to start the prayer. As soon as Tamika entered the room, Aminah began the prayer, and Tamika quickly put on her clothes and covered her hair before joining Aminah.

After they prayed, they exhaled in relief. They had prayed before it was too late. For a few minutes they sat in silence as they numerated their praises of God.

"You think Sulayman overslept too?" Tamika asked after they had finished.

Aminah was folding her blanket, and Tamika was collecting her belongings in preparation to leave. Aminah shrugged and shook her head. "I'm not sure. Maybe I should give him a call."

"You know what room he's in?"

Just then Aminah realized that Tamika had assumed he was sleeping in the hotel. "He has a cell phone."

Tamika nodded as Aminah picked up the hotel phone to dial her brother. But Aminah realized it would be long distance. She hesitated then hung up. It was better not to run up the room's phone bill when she could just go outside to check.

"What's wrong?"

She shook her head. "Nothing. I think I'll just wait. We're supposed to meet him at the car anyway."

Tamika nodded. "You think he's up?"

Aminah shrugged again. "I'm sure he is, *inshaAllaah*. I'm not gonna worry about it."

A minute later Aminah thought of something and turned to her roommate. "What time is check out?"

"Eleven."

Aminah nodded. They still had a while before they had to leave. "Wanna grab some breakfast?" She picked up the hotel information card and skimmed it until she found the breakfast times. "They have a free continental breakfast from seven to nine."

"That's fine with me."

"We can put our things in the car and then eat. That way we can leave right after we finish." Aminah chuckled then added, "I'm starved."

"Well," Tamika patted her purse as she forced laughter, "this is all I have. I threw away my dress, and everything else I'm wearing."

"We still have about twenty minutes before breakfast. What do you wanna do in the meantime?"

Tamika picked up the remote control and turned on the television. She stood in front of it with one hand on her hip as she flipped through the channels. "I might take a shower really quick." She grimaced and glanced away from the screen for a second. "I just feel icky."

Aminah nodded and laughed in agreement. "I do too, but I think I'll just have to wait till I get home since we're running behind. I wanna make sure Sulayman's not sleeping in." She added, "I think I'll go check on him while you shower. *InshaAllaah*, I'll be right back."

"Okay."

When Aminah reached the car, she found Sulayman still sleeping in the back seat. She knocked on the window. A moment later he sat up, and after realizing where he was, he unlocked the door. Aminah opened the back door on the passenger's side. "Did you pray?"

"What time is it?"

"About a quarter to seven."

"Really?" He threw off the blanket and started to come out of the car. Aminah stepped back to let him out. "*SubhanAllaah*." He shook his head and glanced toward the sky. "I overslept."

"You can make *wudoo'* in our room if you want." Aminah tossed her backpack in the backseat then shut the door. "We're about to eat breakfast in a minute."

He nodded. "I think I will." He surveyed his clothes. "I may need to run an iron over this."

"I'll do it."

He shook his head. "You can keep your friend company. I'll just pray and iron my clothes once you go to breakfast." He paused. "But we need to get out of here as soon as you finish because this car is due by midnight tonight."

"Yeah, I know. That's why we went ahead and got ready."

"You have the key to the room?"

"Tamika has it, but I can get it from her."

"Yeah, because I need to go on and pray."

"Okay." They started for the hotel.

Once they were upstairs, Aminah knocked on the room door and waited for Tamika to open it, but there was no answer. She waited a minute before knocking again.

"Did she leave?" Sulayman's eyebrows gathered in concern as he stood a couple of feet from the door so that he wouldn't be in view when the door opened.

Aminah shook her head. "I don't think so. She must be in the shower." She knocked again. After the third knock, Tamika opened the door. Her hair was wrapped in one of the hotel's white towels, and she was dressed in the T-shirt and skirt that she had purchased from the store. Aminah stepped inside and closed the door behind her.

"You ready to go?"

"Almost," Tamika said as she removed the towel from her head, causing her damp hair to fall to her shoulders. "I just need to put on my *khimaar*."

"Because Sulayman still needs to pray, and I told him he could pray in here."

She wrinkled her forehead in confusion as she rubbed her hair with the towel. "Why didn't he pray in his room?"

Aminah smiled self-consciously, having forgotten that Tamika thought he had a room. "It's a long story."

Tamika stared at Aminah in disbelief, stilling the towel in her hand. "Did he sleep in the car?"

Aminah smiled hesitantly and averted her gaze. "Don't worry. He's fine."

"Aminah!"

"Trust me, Tamika, he's fine."

"But I feel so bad," she shook the towel and gazed at it before tossing it on the bed.

"He's a man, Tamika. He's fine."

Tamika sighed and picked up a hotel comb from the desk before combing through her hair. "Your family is gonna be sick of me."

"You're like family to us. We won't get sick of you."

Tamika forced a smile, but she couldn't help feeling bad for being such an inconvenience. "You know," she said sadly as she picked up the head cover from the nightstand, "I don't know how I can repay your family for all you've done."

Aminah waved her hand and shook her head. "We don't do things for repayment. Allah will take care of us."

Tamika smiled as she put the *khimaar* on her head and fastened the pin Aminah had given her. The room grew silent, and Tamika's mind drifted to Sulayman. He must have a big heart, she reflected. Not many people would be willing to sleep in a car all night to help a complete stranger, even if the stranger was his sister's friend. He had no connection to Tamika except that she was a Muslim and his sister's roommate. Did she deserve all of this based on that? He had driven nearly a whole day just for her when he could have been celebrating his graduation. And he was about to drive the same distance again. His whole weekend, his whole graduation weekend, had been sacrificed for her.

She suddenly regretted all she had thought—and said—about him after reading his articles in *A Voice*. At that moment, she realized what she should have known before. You can't judge someone before you get to know him. She had no idea that behind the name "Sulayman Ali" was a caring person who loved God and was willing to sacrifice for others based on that love alone.

It was difficult to imagine that men like Sulayman existed in the world, especially ones who were barely out of their teens, Tamika thought as she put on the *abiya* Aminah was lending her. She pulled the ends of her head cover from the dress as she pondered how most men Sulayman's age were chasing the world of wealth and women. But he was chasing God's reward in the Hereafter. What purity must be in his heart, she marveled. No other man had ever done this much for her. And had any other man done it, he would have expected something in return. But Sulayman saw her as his Muslim sister, and on that account alone, he was willing to sacrifice almost anything to help her. For most people, this type of sacrifice was only for romantic love, not spiritual.

Tamika had only heard of spiritual love before Islam. But no one really felt it or knew what it meant. If you needed help, people promised to pray for you. But rarely would they do more than that—if they did that. Sadness enveloped her as her heart longed to really be a part of his family. But there was only one way that could happen, and she knew that was too much to hope for, not to mention far too much to comprehend right then.

"You have the key, right?"

Aminah's voice interrupted her thoughts. "Uh," Tamika said as she turned to glance around the room. "I think I put it in here." She lifted her purse that hung on her shoulder. "Here it is." She reached in and handed the key to Aminah.

"Thanks." Aminah pushed the card key into a pocket of her *abiya*. "We better hurry up. Sulayman's waiting in the hall."

Tamika laughed and shook her head. "Why am I not surprised?"

Aminah laughed too. "I guess he's used to it now."

The roommates left the room and saw Sulayman leaning against the wall waiting. "We're gonna grab some food and meet you at the car, *inshaAllaah*," Aminah said as she reached in her pocket and handed him the room key.

Tamika pretended to be looking in her purse for something. She couldn't look up. He would see right through her, she feared. He would see her hypocrisy and know the contempt she once felt for him. Or worse, he would see how much that had changed.

"Can you get me something too?" Sulayman asked before they walked away. "I think I'll just eat on the road."

His sister nodded. "*InshaAllaah*, we'll see you in a few minutes."

"*InshaAllaah*," he repeated before entering the room.

Tamika walked down the hall and stairs as Aminah followed. She was relieved when they were no longer in Sulayman's presence.

"You know where the breakfast is?" Aminah asked as they descended the steps.

Tamika nodded as she remembered passing the lobby before coming upstairs when she returned from the store the day before. "It's down here."

When they reached the lobby floor, they opened the heavy door and looked around before Tamika said, "I think it's this way."

Aminah followed Tamika until they saw guests standing and eating donuts and bagels, holding cups of orange juice as they chatted. The aroma of crushed coffee beans filled the air with distant politeness as Tamika and Aminah made their way to the counter and picked up their black plastic plates before selecting what they would eat.

"I think I'll take a couple of poppy seed bagels with cream cheese," Aminah said in a loud whisper as she lifted the bagels onto her plate. "I'm really hungry."

"You wanna get a plate for your brother?"

Aminah laughed. "I almost forgot." She pointed to the plates. "Can you pass me another one?"

Tamika passed her roommate the plate then selected a cream-filled donut and plain bagel for herself. "Should we take some extra for the road?"

Aminah considered it with a slight frown. "I suppose we can." She grinned. "I just hope they don't kick us out."

"Hey," Tamika joked, "you paid a lot of money to stay here. They better not say anything."

"I think I'll just take one extra."

Tamika grinned. "I'll take three donuts and bagels." She lifted another plate and served herself the food before putting a napkin over it. "And don't ask for any in the car. This is all for me."

Aminah laughed. "I suppose I can take two then."

Tamika shrugged as she put several sample-size packs of cream cheese on a plate then stacked the plates on top of each other. "Whatever you want. I'm not ashamed." She picked up two foil covered orange juice cups.

Aminah chuckled self-consciously. "I suppose I shouldn't be."

"You ready?" Tamika asked as she held her food and juice.

Aminah skimmed the rest of the food with her eyes before nodding. "Yeah, I think this is enough to at least get us started on the road."

Tamika thought of something as they walked out of the food lobby. "Is Sulayman gonna check out and everything?"

Oh. Aminah had forgotten about that. "I can check and see. I think I'll probably have to, in case they want to see the credit card."

Tamika nodded, and they walked in silence until they exited the hotel.

"Do you have the car key?" Tamika asked as they crossed the parking lot.

"*SubhanAllaah!*" Aminah laughed and shook her head. "I totally forgot. I'm not with it this morning." She shrugged a second later. "Maybe he left a door unlocked."

"I hope so." Tamika sighed playfully as she struggled to balance the stacked plates and orange juice in her hands.

"If not, he should be here in a minute."

At the car, Aminah set her plate on the roof and tried the front door on the passenger's side, but it was locked. She drew in a deep breath before trying the back door. To her relief, it was still unlocked. "We can sit back here and eat if you want." She opened the car door and removed her food from the roof.

Tamika nodded and leaned forward to set down the food. She stopped, noticing the blanket on the seat. Her heart sank as she was reminded of Sulayman sleeping in the car. It must have been a tight fit for him, she imagined, feeling bad all over again.

"Oh," Aminah laughed. "I'll get that, or you can just toss it to the side if you want."

Tamika leaned into the car and placed her food and drink in the back window. She then pushed the blanket to the side and climbed in. "You wanna sit in here too?"

"If you can unlock the doors, then I'll just come around to the other side."

Tamika nodded then reached over the seat in front of her and pressed the button to unlock the doors. A few seconds later, Aminah was opening the other back door and setting her food in the back window before sitting down. Tamika picked up a plate and sat down with a sigh, leaving the car door open to let the cool morning air drift inside. She took a bite of a donut and closed her eyes as she enjoyed the sweetness of it.

"Mmm. This is good."

Aminah took a bagel and pack of cream cheese from her plate and sat down, leaving her door open too. She spread the cream cheese with her finger and said, "*Bismillaah*" before taking a bite.

Tamika ate a few more bites then inquired, "Is that required to say before you eat?"

Aminah glanced up and put up a finger while she finished chewing. She then nodded. "It's what the Prophet, *sallaaahu'alayhi wa sallam*[25], told us to say."

"What if you forget to say it?"

---

[25] Literally, "May prayers and peace be upon him," said at each mention of his name.

"If you haven't finished eating and you remember, just say, '*Bismillaahi fee awwalihi wa aakhirih.*'"

Tamika's eyes widened, and she shook her head. "I don't know if I can remember that." She creased her forehead as she licked a finger. "What does it mean? I know *bismillaah* is 'with the name of God'."

"It means, 'In the name of God in the beginning and in the end.'"

"I guess I'll just say that then." Tamika said the English words then continued eating.

"I think I should go see if I need to be there to check out."

Tamika nodded. "I'll just wait here then, *inshaAllaah.*"

After Aminah left, Tamika sat alone in the car finishing her breakfast. She took a few more bites of her food before putting the rest on the plate in the back window. She then stood next to the car and dusted her black over garment free of powder and crumbs.

Tamika shut the car door and gazed at the morning sky. She wondered if she would ever see Milwaukee again. She had grown up in the city and considered it home. Her gaze fell upon the sun taking its place in the horizon, and she smiled at the beauty it displayed.

She strolled through the parking lot to enjoy the cool morning, which would likely be her last in the city for some time. She would miss home, she reflected. She didn't want to leave, but she was looking forward to the trip.

Just a day before, she had been praying to Allah to make it easy for her to practice Islam. The idea of sleeping on the street had terrified her, and she could only imagine what that would entail. She had considered staying with old friends, but she knew that the only ones who would be willing to take her in at a moment's notice were men. It would be better for her to lie to her mother about abandoning Islam than to sacrifice her dignity for the sake of shelter. She had spent much of the weekend agonizing over her predicament and had even doubted that things would work out. When Aminah appeared at her door, it took her some time to realize what was happening. But when she did, it was clear that Allah had answered her prayers.

Tamika wondered what it would be like at the Ali residence. She had gone there once before when she wasn't Muslim and was doing her research paper on Islam. She remembered Aminah's mother and Dee's family like it was yesterday. Even as a Christian, Tamika had been unable to deny the power of their spiritual dedication and admired it greatly. Talking to two women who converted to Islam after being raised in Christian families forced Tamika to examine her own self in relation to the religion. What had it been that made them willing to give up everything they had been taught and risk ridicule and being ostracized by family? What deep belief and dedication they must have, Tamika had pondered.

Presently, Tamika sighed as she thought of her family. What she would give to have what Aminah had. How did it feel to have Muslim family? Perhaps she would never know. Her mother would reject anything related to

Islam, Tamika thought regretfully. She had no idea where her siblings were. And the only thing she knew about her father was his name.

Her father. He seemed so distant that the name represented less a person in flesh than an ambiguous concept. Was it possible that there was a Craig Douglass who really lived and breathed? What was he like? Did he really look like her, like her aunt often said? Did he miss her? Did he even remember her—or care?

Craig's absence left Tamika feeling as if a piece of her soul was missing. It was as if only part of Tamika lived within. She went on with life, as she had to, but she never felt whole. Occasionally, she would actually forget about him. Or was it that she was so distracted by life that she forgot that she would never forget? It shouldn't have hurt so much, she often told herself, but, of course, she didn't know if that were true. Who could assess pain? Who could decide what should and should not hurt? But others moved on with their lives despite setbacks and pain. Or was it that they too wore a mask of happiness to shield the world—or themselves—from the aching reality that festered like a cancer within? Did normal people feel pain too, or was it only those without fathers?

Father. What a strange word. What did it mean? What was it supposed to mean? And what was it to Tamika? For others, the word was likely one of thousands listed in the dictionary and uttered each day. It referred to the man at home, the head of household, but beyond that, it meant nothing. When spoken, the word likely held little significance to those with a father at home. But for Tamika, the word held so much importance that when uttered, she felt as if someone had snatched a veil from her face and exposed the ugly truth in which she lived. But the irony, that she couldn't get over. One would think the word *father* would evoke emotion and significance for those who knew theirs and enjoyed his presence each day. But no, it was she, the one with no memories, no quality time, and no proof of his existence, that felt the weightiness of the word. Perhaps words like *mother* and *father* only held meaning to those with no mother and father in their lives.

Tamika was gazing toward the sky in deep thought when she heard people approaching. Startled, she turned to find Aminah and Sulayman walking toward the car, which was now about a hundred feet from her. The sight of them calmed her and convinced her that everything would be all right. But the sight of Sulayman evoked in her an aching desire for her father. Her suffering, buried for years, was now erupting, and the mere sight of a man was too much to bear. As a girl, she fought herself when such feelings overtook her, but now she felt helpless. Perhaps they would never go away.

Tamika's heart felt heavy as she walked to the car. Aminah waved to Tamika as they approached, and Tamika forced a smile.

"Everything okay?" Sulayman asked after they reached the car.

The question startled Tamika, and she felt her heart pounding in her chest. Were her feelings obvious on her face?

Aminah wore a hesitant grin and stared at Tamika curiously. "What's wrong?"

"Nothing," Tamika said as she shook her head and smiled, hoping she was doing a better job at masking her feelings.

"So are we ready to go?" Sulayman glanced at his sister, who turned to Tamika for a reply.

Tamika nodded to Aminah, now accustomed to communicating with Sulayman through Aminah. Initially, she was offended by the indirect exchange. Now she found herself admiring it for its purity. It was admirable how, even in the seemingly insignificant details of human interaction, Muslims were conscious of God. What would it be like to live like that?

She watched as Sulayman opened his door and climbed in the car, his white button-up shirt and beige slacks freshly ironed and his beard neatly brushed. Was it possible for someone like him to ever notice the beauty of a woman? She imagined his heart was so devoted to God that he had never noticed. But he was human, so certainly he wanted to marry too. But whom did he think of when he thought of a wife?

Tamika opened her door as she imagined Sulayman's wife as a phenomenal woman so enriched with beauty and righteousness that no woman could compare. She thought of a woman of Dee's beauty and Aminah's piety. The woman would cover from head to toe and be a prominent scholar of Islam. Her face would glow from the light of piety emanating from within. Tamika imagined the face as her own, but a moment later, reality set in. A man of Sulayman's nobility would never notice someone as insignificant as she.

She and Aminah closed their doors at the same time, and Sulayman recited the supplication for travel aloud as his sister recited it in a whisper to herself. Aminah didn't ask Tamika if she wanted her to sit in the back with her. Tamika imagined that Aminah already knew from past trips that Tamika preferred sitting alone if there were only three people in the car.

After buckling their seatbelts, Aminah asked Tamika to pass her a plate of food for Sulayman to eat. Tamika reached back and passed it to her then resigned herself to her thoughts. She fought against thinking of marriage and children or anything related to a happiness she would never know. If she was fortunate enough to ever marry—in her required ten years, she knew it would never be to Sulayman Ali.

Ten

The drive from Milwaukee was a mostly silent one. Most of the trip was spent listening to Qur'an and lecture tapes, but Sulayman and Aminah did exchange conversation for part of the trip. Tamika sat in the backseat and listened, too shy to join in. At moments she forgot that the trip was all for her. When she was reminded of this, she was flattered. She had managed to steal a moment's importance in their lives. She should have been bored sitting in the car for so long without talking to anyone, but she felt a sense of belonging as she watched the passing trees and hills with the calming sounds of lighthearted talk in the background. She enjoyed leaning her head back and listening to Sulayman laugh and Aminah joke. She felt as if she were part of the family, even if only for a moment. The Qur'an tapes and lectures were equally soothing, and she felt a sense of camaraderie as she reveled in her passive enjoyment. The drive offered a peaceful atmosphere, and she began to wish it would never end.

As Tamika listened to the siblings converse, she was intrigued. It was the first time she realized the power of their bond. They enjoyed each other like she never imagined a brother and sister could, and she found herself wishing she could build a similar relationship with Latonya and Phillip. But like most of her desires in life, she feared that she was living in a dream.

She relaxed to the soft humming of the car's engine and its graceful riding upon the road. Where were her brother and sister now? Did they miss her? She certainly missed them. She sighed and whispered a prayer to Allah that He would unite them soon.

Tamika had been drifting in and out of sleep when she felt the car stopping and then moving again. When she opened her eyes for a moment, she saw they were at a gas station before she drifted to sleep again. When she woke, the car wasn't moving, and she sensed a marked finality to the stop that she hadn't at the gas station. At first she thought they were in Atlanta. But when she noticed the restroom signs and formal structure of the small brick center surrounded by open grassland, she realized that they were at a rest stop.

"We're only a few hours outside of Atlanta," Tamika heard Sulayman say as she recovered from the drunkenness of sleep, "but I'm gonna take a rest. I wanted to push myself, but we have some time to get there before midnight." It was then that she realized he had turned off the ignition. The soft hum of the engine was now replaced by faint sounds of people outside the car. "We can pray *Asr* and *Thuhr* together," he continued talking to his sister. "I suppose we should just pray *Maghrib* after we get home, because I don't wanna sleep more than an hour." Tamika forced herself to open her eyes at least long enough to see the car clock. 6:08. A moment later, her eyes closed. She was too tired to calculate when they would leave.

"So I should just stay up then, huh?" Aminah's voice echoed in Tamika's head.

"If you wanna get home before tomorrow morning," Sulayman said with a chuckle. "I need you awake to wake me up." He laughed again. "I figured you'd be wide awake by now. You slept half the trip."

Aminah laughed. "I know," she apologized. "I couldn't keep my eyes open."

"*Alhamdulillaah,* Allah blessed me to keep going."

"I'm assuming you're just gonna rest right in here then."

He coughed in laughter. "I'm definitely not sleeping outside."

Aminah chuckled in agreement. "I suppose that's true. So I guess I'll just wake up Tamika so we can sit on the benches while you rest."

"Take the phone though, in case Mom or Dad calls."

She nodded as he handed her the phone. "Okay."

"But let's go ahead and pray first," Sulayman suggested as he unlocked the doors.

His sister nodded in agreement then she turned to wake Tamika.

Before Aminah could call her name, Tamika opened her eyes and sat up, sensing it was time to get out of the car. She still felt tired, but she had slept for some time. She stretched and covered her mouth as she yawned.

"You up?" Aminah smiled at Tamika.

Tamika forced a smile and nodded. "Yeah."

Fifteen minutes later, the three of them stood praying a comfortable distance from the park benches, where people sat relaxing and eating. Sulayman had spread out his blanket on the grass for when their heads would touch the ground. As they stood outside in the open area, Tamika was aware of onlookers, but she didn't care. She felt a sense of honor and pride as she stood shoulder-to-shoulder with Aminah as Sulayman led them in prayer.

The people who stared couldn't possibly comprehend the powerful significance of the prayer, Tamika imagined. They watched with interest as Sulayman proclaimed God's greatness for each change in position, and they could only wonder at the contentment the Muslims displayed as they prayed to God. The people likely had no idea what religious devotion truly meant, Tamika pondered, grateful to be among God's servants. When she had visited the mosque as part of the term paper assignment, she had been a helpless onlooker herself, only able to wish she were a part of the spiritual bond of the people who prayed. But now she was a part of the faith, and today she stood humble before God. She was Muslim, and she could only pray for the guidance of those who had no idea what the prayer could mean for them—for their souls.

When they finished praying, Sulayman shook the blanket free of grass and dirt then folded it before carrying it to the car. Tamika and Aminah stood for a moment and watched as he made his way to the car, where he became a silhouette as he prepared to sleep.

"I bet he's tired," Tamika said with a sigh.

"May Allah reward him," Aminah said, empathizing with her brother's exhaustion. She felt bad that she had been unable to stay up with him during the drive. "I know this was a difficult trip for him," she said, shaking her head in shame. She hated herself for leaving him to bear the monotony of the drive alone.

Tamika immediately felt bad, remembering that he had done all of this for her. She cast her eyes down and gently kicked at the grass. "I wish he didn't go through all of this for me. I'm really sorry."

"No, it's fine." Aminah shook her head. "I didn't mean that." She forced laughter to lighten the atmosphere. "I just meant I knew he was tired."

Tamika looked at the car in the distance, sensing the exhaustion Sulayman must be feeling as he slept. And he would sleep only an hour, certainly not long enough to recuperate from what he had already done. "Apologize to him for me," she said sadly.

"Tamika, it's okay, really."

Tamika shook her head. "No, I shouldn't have called you collect."

"It's not a problem, trust me."

But it was too late. Tamika was only half listening to her roommate. "Tell him that, okay?"

Aminah met Tamika's gaze, which was distant and sad as her eyes pleaded. She nodded in agreement. "Okay, I will *inshaAllaah*."

"You wanna go sit on a bench for a bit?" Aminah asked a minute later.

Tamika shrugged, her mind still on Sulayman as she followed Aminah through the grass that was splotched with patches of dirt. She mentally scolded herself for allowing his family to do all this for her. How could she have been so insensitive? She should have kept her fight with her mother to herself. Her aunt would have taken her in if she had only asked.

Tamika and Aminah sat on the bench in silence with their backs to the dark wood table, engrossed in their thoughts. Twenty feet away, a woman studied them curiously as her dog ran in the distance. She had been one of the onlookers when they prayed, and she continued to stare. But the roommates weren't bothered by her presence.

Tamika broke the silence. "Do you think he'll mind if I drive the rest of the way?"

For a moment Aminah didn't respond. She met Tamika's gaze and creased her forehead in confusion as she realized her roommate was serious. "Drive the rest of the way?"

A gentle wind blew a piece of Tamika's head cover in her face, and she brushed it away. "Yeah, then he can just sleep in the backseat so he can get some rest."

Aminah shook her head. "He wouldn't let you."

"Why not?"

"Tamika, he came here to help. He didn't drive all this way just to put the burden on you." She shook her head again. "He wouldn't dream of it."

Tamika didn't respond, and the two sat in silence for a few minutes. Aminah observed the scenery and studied the woman who pretended to be watching her dog. The woman turned away when their eyes met and started calling after the dog.

Tamika's gaze fell on the car where Sulayman was sleeping, and she wondered at the young man she had hated only months before.

"Is he like that all the time?" Tamika asked, still looking toward the car.

"Who, Sulayman?"

"Yeah."

"Like what all the time?"

She shrugged as she searched her mind for the right description. "So altruistic."

Aminah considered it as she stared off in the distance. The sun's glow was dimming as sunset gradually approached, giving the summer air warmth between the evening breezes. She shrugged. "It's how he was raised."

"So he is, huh?"

"I mean, like all of us, he has his days. But, yeah, that's his nature, I suppose, if that's what you mean, *barakAllaahufeeh*."

"What's it like to have a brother like that?"

Aminah considered the question, knowing her brother wouldn't approve of excessive praise. "I don't have anyone to compare him to, but he's a really good person and Allah knows best. But he's like all brothers. He gets on my nerves sometimes."

Tamika laughed, finding that hard to believe. "Really?"

Aminah grinned. "He can be annoying at times, yes."

"What does he do?"

She shrugged, unsure what was appropriate to share. "The stuff brothers do."

Tamika smiled in amusement, imagining he must have a remarkable personality. "Does he play jokes on you?"

"Not so much anymore, but he used to."

"Are you serious?" Tamika grinned and looked at her roommate. "Like what?"

Aminah laughed and shook her head as she remembered something. "He used to forbid me from coming in his room, and he'd put a sign on his door that said, 'No Girls Allowed.'" She shook her head in amusement. "But I was his only playmate at home, so you know that was short-lived. But when he really wanted me to keep out, he would crack his door just enough to tempt me to come in, and when I tried, a cup of water would fall on my head."

"What!" Tamika burst into laughter. "So he put it on top of the door?"

Aminah laughed and nodded. "But he stopped after my parents told him it wasn't Islamic to treat me like that."

"Wow," Tamika said with a shake of her head, running a finger along the splintering brown wood of the bench seat. "That must've been fun."

Aminah smiled. "It's funny now, but it wasn't at the time."

"Yeah, I can imagine." Tamika was silent, stilling her finger on a thin piece of wood that poked at her skin as she thought of something else.

"Is Omar like him?" Tamika asked, glancing at Aminah with her eyes narrowed slightly.

"Like Sulayman?"

"Yeah."

Aminah raised her eyebrows as she tried to think of the best way to respond. "I don't know him well enough to say that. But he's a really nice brother as far as I can tell, and Allah knows best."

"What do you mean?"

"Well, he's one of the few brothers Sulayman can count on when he needs help with something."

Tamika nodded as she listened, picking at the needle of wood, wondering if it was possible for Omar to compare to someone like Sulayman. "How close are they?"

"Sulayman and Omar?"

"Yeah."

Aminah shook her head. "Not that close."

Tamika wrinkled her forehead, pulling the wood splinter from the bench and letting it fall to the ground. "But I thought they were good friends."

"They're friends, but I wouldn't say 'good' friends."

"What do you mean?" She gently ran her thumb along the tip of her forefinger to make sure the wood hadn't pierced her skin.

"He hasn't known him that long."

Tamika glanced at her finger then at Aminah, sensing that her roommate was uncomfortable with the discussion. "So they're just getting to know each other?"

Aminah shrugged, her eyes looking out in the distance momentarily. "I wouldn't say that. It's just that when it comes to Muslims, we refer to them all as friends."

Tamika raised her eyebrows. "Really?"

"Yeah. The term's used loosely, and it doesn't necessarily indicate a really close bond. I guess it's just a polite way of referring to a Muslim brother or sister."

"Do you have to call them your friends?"

"No," Aminah said after a moment's consideration, "I don't think so. I think it's more out of habit. But all the believers are your friends."

"Those are the really good Muslims?"

"Yeah, I suppose you can say that. But more specifically, believers are at a higher level of faith than regular Muslims."

"But Omar's a good brother?"

Aminah turned to Tamika, a grin creasing the corners of her mouth. "Why? Are you reconsidering him?"

Tamika laughed self-consciously then shrugged. "Just curious."

Aminah nodded, still grinning a moment more before responding. "He's striving like we all are."

Tamika's smile faded, and she gathered her eyebrows. "What do you mean?"

"I mean, from what I know," Aminah said, sounding as if she were warning Tamika that the reality could be much worse, "he's a good brother, and Allah knows best. He's had his ups and downs in life, but he's getting back on track and seems to love this *deen*[26]."

"What do you mean by ups and downs?"

Aminah lifted her gaze and turned her head slightly to study the woman and her dog, but Tamika could tell her mind was on what she had asked. "He was locked up for a bit before he became Muslim."

"Locked up!" Tamika stared at her roommate in disbelief.

"But that was before he became Muslim," Aminah said again, hoping to downplay the significance of the information.

Tamika wrinkled her nose. "Why was he in jail?"

"I'm not sure exactly, but from what I understand, it had something to do with a group of friends holding up a store or something, and I guess he was there."

Tamika frowned, her interest in him suddenly dissipated. She scratched at the bench seat and felt a splinter stab her under the fingernail. She quickly pulled up her hand and observed her forefinger by pulling at the tip with her thumb to get a better look. She saw a small brown dot and picked at it until she cleared it of wood, and a second later she saw blood. She pushed at the skin until the bleeding stopped then pressed her fingertip against the cloth of her *abiya*.

"But he says he was in the car and didn't really know what they were doing."

Tamika sucked her teeth and rolled her eyes as she examined her fingertip again. "Yeah right. That's what everybody says."

Aminah's eyes widened slightly, and she started to say something in defense of the brother.

"What makes you think I'd wanna marry somebody like that?" Tamika glared at Aminah, offended that she would even mention him for her.

"I didn't *recommend* him."

"But you told me about him."

"Only because he asked about you."

"Would *you* marry him?"

"Now that's not fair."

---

[26] Religion

Tamika glanced at her roommate then rolled her eyes, her gaze falling on the car in the parking lot where Sulayman slept. "Please. That *is* fair. I mean, if that's so out of the question, why is he okay for me?"

Aminah sighed, and rubbed her eyes and forehead. Tamika could tell Aminah didn't want to argue, and she felt bad suddenly.

"Look," Aminah said more calmly, "I apologize if you were offended by us delivering his message to you, but I don't think it's my place to turn a person away when it's not me he's asking about."

Tamika rolled her eyes again as she continued to stare toward the parking lot, but she was listening.

"I'm really sorry though," Aminah said. "But my philosophy is, let the person decide. You never know."

Tamika refused to meet her roommate's gaze, but she knew Aminah could tell she was hearing her point.

"Believe me," Aminah continued, "had I known you'd be offended, I would've never told you what he said."

Tamika studied her nails and began to clean them although there was no need to.

"My brother and I are generally hands-off in situations like these," Aminah said. "But we don't feel it's right to refuse to help if someone asks." She sighed. "We've had some really bad experiences in the past with trying to help people get married, so we try to stay away from anything that resembles matchmaking if we can."

Tamika sighed too and leaned back on the bench table with her elbows, realizing Aminah had only done what she understood to be her duty.

Aminah forced laughter and shook her head as she remembered something. "I love the idea of Muslims getting married, but it's such a sensitive issue that in many cases it's better just to be happy when it happens and don't get involved." She laughed again. "We learned that the hard way."

"What happened?" Tamika asked, looking at her roommate with her forehead creased.

"All kinds of stuff," Aminah said, shaking her head. "You'd be surprised how things end up when you call yourself trying to help. But I can't get into the specifics," she apologized with a sigh, "because you'll probably meet these people one day."

"You don't have to tell me the names," Tamika offered, understanding Aminah's desire to avoid backbiting.

"But these situations are so specific that even if I kept the names anonymous, after a few weeks in the community, you'll figure it out."

"You think so?"

She laughed knowingly. "Definitely. And Allah knows best."

Tamika didn't know what to say. The sound of sudden laughter distracted her, and she turned to see a young girl and boy running in the grass near where the dog played. Their mother called after them to stay close by, but they were too engrossed in throwing sticks to the dog to hear.

"About Omar," Aminah said, prompting Tamika to meet her gaze, "I don't want you to misunderstand what I was saying about him."

Tamika forced a smile, her gaze falling to her *abiya* as she flicked away an ant making its way up her leg. "Don't worry. I'm sure he's a good Muslim, just not for me."

"I know, but I just want to say something to clarify why I said what I said. I'll feel bad if we leave here with you having a negative image of him."

Tamika nodded politely as she leaned forward and tugged at the cloth of her over garment to make sure no other creatures were lounging there, but she knew that nothing Aminah said would change her mind.

"I only said what I said so that, just in case you were considering him, you'd know a little background," Aminah said. "Islamically, if someone's considering marrying a person, that's when saying something negative is allowed—if it may affect their decision or give some information about the person's character. So I meant nothing against the brother."

"I understand," Tamika said, glancing toward the children again after she was sure her dress was free of bugs. "I didn't think you were trying to say anything bad."

"*Alhamdulillaah*. I just didn't want you to think I'm implying you shouldn't marry a brother who's been locked up before, because I don't think like that."

Tamika and Aminah watched the children play for a few minutes before Tamika turned to Aminah and asked, "So you'd marry a brother who's been to jail?"

Aminah lifted her shoulder in a shrug, her gaze still in the distance. She leaned back on the table with her elbows. "It depends on why he went to jail."

Tamika nodded as she turned her attention back to the grassy area. A child played tug of war with a stick in the dog's mouth. Her mother yelled for her to stop. The woman who owned the dog waved her hand and said something to the mother with a laugh.

"Because a person could've gone to jail for anything, especially nowadays."

"That's true," Tamika said, momentarily distracted from the conversation as she observed the scene.

"And we all make mistakes," Aminah said. "I don't feel like I'm any better than a person just because he went to jail and I didn't. For all I know, he could be innocent. It's not unusual for a person to pay for a crime he didn't commit."

As Tamika watched the children giggle running behind the dog, she thought of how her fight with Jennifer resulted in the charge of physical assault. Had the fight been settled off-campus, she could have ended up in jail.

"And then, of course, there are those who are in jail for honorable reasons, like standing up for what's right when the society was against them."

Tamika nodded, still looking at the children.

"But it's unfortunate that some people do actually commit crimes and end up in jail." Aminah shrugged. "Then again, maybe it's not so unfortunate since that's where many of them end up learning about Islam."

Tamika turned to Aminah with her eyes narrowed slightly. "What about someone like Omar? Would you overlook something like that?"

"Well," Aminah thought aloud, "I can't really say, because for one, he says he didn't know what they were doing, and then I don't really know the whole story."

"But even if he was just in the car, that still means they were 'his crowd,' if you know what I mean."

Aminah nodded. "That's probably true."

"Knowing that, would you still consider him?"

"I don't know, Tamika." Aminah sat up, removing her elbows from the table then meeting Tamika's gaze. "I just don't think it's safe to say *never* because you just don't know until you're in the situation." She shrugged. "But as a concept, it's not my preference. But I suppose I would consider it if he seems like a really special person, because some people become the best Muslims after making serious mistakes. Even at the time of the Prophet, *sallaahu'alayhi wa salaam*, some of the best Companions were the worst enemies of Islam before they converted."

Tamika nodded, but she wasn't convinced.

"But, of course, I wouldn't suggest anyone go in with their eyes closed based on how the Companions were. Because there's no denying that we're nowhere close to being like them. "

"But do you think it's wrong if someone won't consider a brother because he was in jail before?" There was an edge of defensiveness in Tamika's tone.

Aminah frowned as she considered it then shook her head. She ran a hand over her *khimaar* then touched the pin under her chin to make sure it was in place. "I wouldn't say she's wrong. Islam allows you to marry whoever you want, and if you wanna turn someone down because of whatever, that's your right. But if you mean as a general rule, I don't think that's fair. We have to separate what we prefer from what we advise others to do. Otherwise, we could be displeasing Allah."

Tamika raised an eyebrow. "You mean as long as it's just what I prefer and I don't tell other people to do the same, then it's okay?"

"In general, yeah. But more specifically, it's like a man marrying more than one wife. If a woman doesn't prefer it for herself, that's her right, but when she holds general views against polygamy itself, then she's in sin."

"So you're saying I can prefer it and even suggest that others not do it, so long as I don't believe it's wrong?"

Aminah raised her eyebrows as she drew in a deep breath. "Yes and no. Yes, in that in some cases you can suggest to others what may be your preference if you think it's best suited for them. And no, in the sense that there's a fine line between suggesting that others not do it and believing it's wrong."

Tamika wrinkled her nose and waved a bug away from her face. "What do you mean?"

"If you think about it, in most cases, you would only suggest others not do something if you see something wrong with it. But in some cases, it's okay, but you have to be careful."

"But what if I'm only telling people because I think my preference is the best thing, even though I know other opinions aren't wrong?"

"But again, the point is, why would you suggest it to others if you really think that your feeling is just a preference? And we can't say something is best unless we have proof from the Qur'an or *Sunnah*[27], and Allah knows best."

Tamika kicked at a patch of dirt on the ground, and ants scattered, fleeing for their lives.

"I guess I just get scared when people share their preferences with others," Aminah said, "especially in the form of advice. It just goes overboard most times."

Tamika lifted her foot slightly and twisted it as she observed it, making sure no ants had fled to her shoe. "How so?"

"Like many people advise others not to marry into a particular race or culture."

Tamika's eyes widened as she met Aminah's gaze. "Are you serious? Muslims do that?"

Aminah nodded regretfully, and Tamika studied the green of Aminah's eyes and the white of her skin, which appeared pale peach next to the crisp white cloth around her face. Tamika wondered what race people thought Aminah belonged to.

"If they've had a bad experience with someone from a certain race," Aminah said, "some people tell all their friends not to marry into it, and then it spreads like wildfire. You'd be surprised. People even advise against marrying their own race."

Tamika tossed her head back in laughter and shook her head as she stared at Aminah in hushed disbelief. "*No.*"

Aminah nodded, a regretful smile on her face as her eyebrows rose. "It happens a lot."

---

[27] Literally, path or way. In Islam, it refers to what God revealed to Prophet Muhammad, peace be upon him, and is not specifically mentioned in the Qur'an.

Tamika shook her head, a grin of disbelief still on her face before she turned her attention back to Aminah a second later. "Is that what you were talking about when you didn't want to tell me specifics?"

"Partly," Aminah said with a shrug. "But that was just one situation."

Tamika didn't know what to say. She stared toward the car again, wondering what experiences Sulayman and his sister had that she would never know.

"Anyway," Aminah said with a sigh, "when it's all said and done, we should just do what the Prophet, *sallaahu'alayhi wa salaam,* told us to do. Marry someone whose commitment to the religion pleases you."

Tamika nodded, Sulayman crossing her mind just then. She had no idea of Omar's commitment to Islam, but she was definitely impressed with Sulayman's. "So you think I should reconsider Omar?"

"No, not necessarily. If you don't feel comfortable with something, I'm not gonna suggest you deal with it, especially something like marriage," Aminah said, tossing an end of her *khimaar* over a shoulder. "You have to deal with that person everyday, so you should pick someone you respect and who you feel can help you please Allah. If you can't see that with Omar, then look for someone else."

The sound of a dog barking prompted Tamika to look up and find its owner approaching with her dog on a leash. A moment later she passed and headed for the parking lot. The children and their mother now walked toward the restroom area.

"But just make *Istikhaarah* for whatever you choose," Aminah said.

"Is that the prayer you make when you're trying to decide something?" Tamika remembered reading about it in a prayer book.

"Yeah."

A brisk wind blew, exposing part of Tamika's shin, and she leaned forward to hold the bottom of her dress until it passed. Aminah readjusted her *khimaar* after the wind then glanced at her watch. She bit her lower lip as a truck pulled into the parking lot and grunted as it found a parking space beyond the cars.

Tamika turned to Aminah a minute later and grinned as she sat up. "I'm surprised he didn't ask about you."

Aminah wrinkled her forehead as she met Tamika's gaze. "Who? Omar?"

"Yeah."

"What makes you say that?"

"Come on, Aminah," Tamika laughed. "You look way better than me."

Aminah stared at Tamika in confusion. "Why do you think that?"

Tamika shrugged and smiled, studying the slenderness of Aminah's face and her smooth fair skin. She imagined that the mysteriousness of Aminah's race made her beauty exotic. "I don't know. You just do."

Aminah shook her head in disagreement, and Tamika couldn't help wondering if Aminah was trying to be humble. "Beauty is in the eye of the beholder," Aminah said.

Tamika laughed out loud. "That's what they all say."

For a moment, Aminah didn't respond. Her gaze grew distant as she watched the truck driver climb from the tractor trailer and shut his door before walking toward the vending machines. "You're really pretty, Tamika," she said seriously. "May Allah bless you."

Tamika shook her head, becoming self-conscious suddenly. Her cheeks grew hot. She hadn't expected the compliment. "I don't think so."

They watched the trucker bend down to retrieve his cola then stand before putting money in the snack machine.

"What makes you think a brother would think I look better?" Aminah asked, returning her gaze to her roommate with her eyebrows gathered.

Tamika shrugged as she tried to analyze her reasoning. She had never thought about it. She had just assumed Aminah looked better. Did people actually have logical explanations why they felt someone was more attractive?

A moment later Tamika realized why she assumed Aminah was prettier, but she hesitated before responding. She glanced at Aminah to see if it was okay to share what she was thinking. A bit ashamed to admit her feelings, she forced laughter. "I guess it's just that you're always taught that people who are light-skinned with, quote, 'good hair' look better."

Aminah frowned and stared off into the distance, apparently not surprised by Tamika's answer. A moment later, she said, "Anyone who's interested in me because of that, I definitely wouldn't marry."

Tamika raised her eyebrows. "Really? But what if they think that's beautiful?"

Aminah lifted a shoulder in a shrug, unable to meet her roommate's gaze. "If he thinks that's beautiful, *alhamdulillaah*, because there's beauty in every shade Allah created. But if that's the main reason he's attracted to me, then I don't think I can handle that."

Tamika creased her forehead, still looking at Aminah. "Why not?"

"Who wants their worth measured by the color wheel?" Aminah asked, meeting Tamika's eyes with a half smile.

Tamika forced laughter and nodded. "I guess I never thought about it like that." She studied Aminah's serious expression. "But why does it bother you? Most light-skinned people are flattered that people think they're pretty."

Aminah sighed then let her gaze fall to the ground. She kicked at the dirt then gently dug into the ground with the tip of her shoe. For a moment, she didn't respond. She lifted her head and looked distantly toward the parking lot. A moment later she shook her head, a reflective frown creasing the corners of her mouth. "Growing up," she said, "that's all people seemed to care about."

Silent, Tamika studied the sadness in her roommate's eyes and could only listen.

"It was as if you were some spectacle, and no one dealt with you except to let you know you didn't belong." She sighed. "I watched how my parents struggled with the racism in their family." She shook her head at a loss for words. "I just wouldn't want to marry into it."

Tamika didn't respond, sensing the sensitive nature of the subject. She imagined it must be difficult to have people define you by the complexion of your skin.

"I remember one time," Aminah said with a forced laugh, but her displeasure with the memory was apparent, "one of my relatives on my mom's side was staring at me for a while. At first, I thought they were going to say how much I'd grown or how cute I was, like adults usually did, but instead, they frowned and said in front of everybody, and even my mother was there, 'Well, at least she doesn't look like a nigger. Nobody'll know.'"

Tamika lowered her head in sympathy, the words stinging her. She could only imagine how deeply wounded Aminah had been by them.

Aminah's eyes glistened as she shook her head. "I was only like four years old then. People just don't realize that children can hear." Her jaw tightened. "And feel."

Tamika felt helpless. She had no idea what she could say to console her friend.

Aminah sighed. "So no, I'm not interested in that type of praise. I'd feel like I was four all over again if I had to live with someone who was caught up in that."

Tamika was silent as she reflected on what Aminah said, her gaze toward the car in the parking lot. She wondered if, as a child, Sulayman had hurt like his sister. "I guess it's just that this society drills into your head, the darker, the uglier," Tamika said thoughtfully. "And it'll be hard to find someone who doesn't think like that."

"Yeah, but Allah is in charge, so I put my trust in Him."

For several minutes, neither of them spoke, and they watched as the trucker climbed back into his truck and the mother and children emerged from the restrooms and loaded their car. The truck hummed and grunted, and a beeping sound echoed in the air as he backed up. A few seconds later, he pulled away.

Aminah glanced at her wristwatch. "We better go on and wake up Sulayman," she said as she stood. "We need to get back on the road."

For the remainder of the trip, Tamika sat in the back seat reflecting on all she and Aminah had discussed, and she found herself reevaluating her opinion of Omar. No, she wasn't interested in marrying him, but after listening to Aminah's thoughts on marriage, Tamika imagined that he would probably make a pretty good husband—even if for another sister.

Tamika woke to the sound of the car door shutting, and when she opened her eyes, she saw darkness outside, realizing just then that she had drifted to sleep. She sat up and immediately realized that Sulayman was no longer in the car, and Aminah was unbuckling her seatbelt. Aminah turned in her seat to face Tamika.

"You up?" Aminah said with a smile.

Tamika nodded and stretched. "Yeah." Curious, she glanced out the window again. "Where are we?"

Aminah chuckled. "Home."

A bit surprised, Tamika looked out the window again and saw blades of grass shining under the moonlight. Her gaze fell upon a porch light glowing above the oak wood double doors that led into the Ali residence. Tamika forced laughter, slightly embarrassed for not realizing it sooner. She must have been exhausted. She reached for her purse that had fallen on the floor and smiled, pleased that they had actually arrived. In front of her, Aminah opened the door and started to get out. After glancing around the car and removing her plates from the back window, Tamika followed suit and followed Aminah into the house.

The sweet aroma of family dinner filled the air as Tamika entered the house, giving her a feeling of contentment and reminding her of home. She relaxed as she stood in the foyer, glad that she had come.

Aminah removed her shoes and placed them on a small wire shelf that stood against a wall. "You can leave your shoes here."

Glancing about her, Tamika slipped off her shoes and set them next to Aminah's. She had visited the house once before, but it was as if she were here for the first time. The atmosphere was more inviting than she remembered, and there was an air of spirituality that seemed to emanate from the walls. Why hadn't she noticed before the elegant beauty of the home?

A mirror aligned the foyer wall that opened out to the kitchen. A carpeted staircase next to the kitchen led upstairs from the foyer. Intricate, floral designs in golden bronze adorned the foyer mirror in delicate strokes. Black marbled tiles covered the foyer floor and continued into the kitchen. Opposite the mirrored wall was the entrance to the living room, covered in cream-colored carpet that complimented the cloudy design in the marble tile. A soft black couch with large cream flowers and matching throw pillows sat under a window that stretched from one end of the room to the other. A matching love seat sat at an angle to the couch on one side of a glass-topped coffee table that sat in front of the couch. Cream-colored curtains with thick black cord rope hanging at its side adorned the magnificent window. A tall glass vase with marble designs matching the foyer floor stood in a far corner of the living room with large green leaves spilling from it beautifully.

"*As-salaamu-'alaikum*," Sarah greeted the roommates, stopping to embrace her daughter and kiss her on the forehead.   Her blond hair was pulled back in a ponytail and hung longer than Tamika remembered it.   She wore a large white T-shirt and a pair of loose-fitting blue jeans, giving her a casual yet sleek look. "I'm so glad you all made it back safely," she said after the embrace. She walked over to where Tamika stood and embraced her too.

Tamika smiled shyly as she hugged Sarah, embarrassed by the show of affection.   The warmth of the embrace and the smell of food in Sarah's clothes reminded her of her own mother, and for a moment sadness swept over her.

Aminah stood a few feet from them and smiled as they hugged. "I'm gonna go shower and change real quick," Aminah said a few seconds later, starting up the steps. "I'll be back down in a minute, *inshaAllaah*."

Sarah nodded but kept her gaze on Tamika, holding her hands after the embrace. She grinned. "I hope you don't mind us stealing you away for a bit and making you part of our family."

Unsure how to respond, Tamika chuckled and averted her gaze. Sarah's brown eyes had a soft, motherly glow to them, making it difficult for Tamika to look her in the eye. "Thanks. I appreciate it."

From the living room a deep voice greeted her. She turned to see a man of light brown complexion and green eyes standing near the coffee table with his hands in his pockets. His hair and beard were dark brown with strands of gray scattered throughout.   Immediately, Tamika saw the resemblance. Aminah and Sulayman inherited much of their appearance from their father. He lowered his gaze to study something near the coffee table. "I'm Brother Ismael, Aminah and Sulayman's father. We're glad to have you with us."

Tamika smiled and nodded. "Thank you."

He waved his hand. "Don't mention it. You're welcome to stay here as long as you want."

Unsure what to say, Tamika smiled self-consciously, and the room grew silent.

"Would you like something to eat?" Sarah asked a minute later, breaking the awkward silence as she let go of Tamika's hands. "You must be hungry."

Tamika nodded, realizing just then how hungry she was. "Sure."   She followed Aminah's mother into the kitchen.

"You can sit in here if you like." Sarah gestured toward the kitchen table as she walked to the cabinets near the refrigerator and began removing dishes.

"So how was the drive?" Sarah asked, placing a glass and utensils on the table before Tamika. Picking up a plate from the table, Sarah walked to the stove and uncovered the pots, preparing to serve her guest.

"It was fine."   Tamika glanced around nervously, feeling awkward without Aminah.

"Long drive, huh?"   Sarah placed some macaroni and cheese on Tamika's plate.

Tamika chuckled in agreement. "Yeah it was."

"Ever drove that long before?"

She shook her head. "Except when my mom drove me to Freshman Orientation my first year and picked me up from school."

Sarah nodded and smiled, now placing spinach on the plate. "You like it at Streamsdale?"

Tamika shrugged and forced a smile, picking up the glass and tilting it to its side in nervousness. "It's fine, I suppose."

Sarah laughed and shot a glance at Tamika. "Tired of school already?"

Tamika laughed beside herself. "Yeah."

"I *would* say it gets easier," Sarah said as she removed some baked chicken from a pan and set in on Tamika's plate, "but it doesn't. Especially if you're continuing after your bachelor's."

Tamika nodded. "That's what I figured."

"But don't get me wrong." Sarah glanced over a shoulder. "It's not as bad as people make it out to be. It's definitely not the easiest thing in the world, but it's doable."

Tamika's eyes traced the spacious kitchen before replying. She sat at the rectangular-shaped, black-framed kitchen table in the middle of the kitchen's marbled tile floor. A small white glass vase filled with roses sat on the table's glass top a couple of feet from Tamika. The cabinets were made from rich oak and the counters a marbled glass that matched the floor. Tamika's seat faced the oak railing that overlooked the lower level like a balcony and followed a descending staircase into a large den.

"Sulayman and I are gonna run to the rental car place to return the car," Tamika heard a man say. She turned to see Ismael standing in the doorway of the kitchen adjacent to the dining room. "But they're gonna go ahead and pray first."

"Do you need to pray too?" Sarah asked Tamika after her husband disappeared into the living room.

Sarah set the plate of food before Tamika, and the sweet steam tickled Tamika's nose. Tamika's eyes fell on the enticing display of food. "Yes, but I need to make *wudoo'*."

Sarah pointed toward the den. "There's a restroom downstairs, the second door on your left."

Tamika stood, her stomach beginning to growl as the aroma of food entered her nostrils.

"You can pray after you eat if you want."

Tamika glanced at Sarah with a half smile on her face. "Is that okay?"

Sarah grinned. "Yeah, I think you better eat first."

Tamika grinned too, realizing how she must appear eyeing the plate of food. "But don't let me keep you from praying. I'll be fine."

Sarah smiled. "Don't worry. My husband and I prayed before you arrived."

Tamika smiled and nodded, picking up a fork. After pronouncing Allah's name over the food, she began eating, savoring every bite. The food seemed to melt in her mouth, and she had to force herself to eat slowly. She didn't want to appear greedy. She hoped it wouldn't be rude to ask for seconds.

"*Allaahuakbar*," Sulayman's voice rose from the living room, announcing the start of prayer.

Silently, Tamika listened as he began reciting from the Qur'an. Intrigued, she began to eat slower as she listened to the beautiful recitation of the Arabic verses. She had memorized some chapters from the last part of the Qur'an, enough to choose from in prayer, but she understood the meaning of only some of them, those that she had read in the translation of the Qur'an's meaning. She knew her recitation wasn't entirely correct, nothing like that of Sulayman's or Aminah's, but Aminah often told her she was doing well. Tamika grasped the Arabic verses quickly and was able to memorize them faster than the average new Muslim, but the Arabic language was still new to her. The rules of reciting the Qur'an were so detailed that Tamika feared she was doing it all wrong. Aminah told her that in time it would get easier. Most Muslims, even those born into Muslim families, felt overwhelmed when first learning of the rules of recitation. But the Qur'an was easy to remember, and after lots of practice, Tamika wouldn't even think about the rules, Aminah had told her. They would come naturally. Tamika could only imagine how long that would take.

After the siblings finished praying, Tamika heard Sulayman and Ismael greet Sarah from the foyer. Sarah called out to them in reply from the kitchen, and a second later, Tamika heard the front door open and close. Aminah appeared in the kitchen five minutes later and removed a plate from the cabinet to serve herself.

"So what do you two have planned for the summer?" Sarah said as she took a seat at the table across from Tamika. She had a small plate of food before her, and Tamika wondered how she could eat so little.

Tamika chuckled with a shrug, and Aminah laughed from where she stood at the stove. "We haven't really thought much about it," Aminah said. "I think Tamika'll need to get used to the idea of being here first."

"I hope we didn't inconvenience you with our offer to stay with us," Sarah apologized with her forehead creased in concern. She lifted a forkful of food to her mouth, her eyes on Tamika.

Tamika shook her head. "If you hadn't, I don't think I'd have much of a summer at all."

For a few seconds, Sarah and Tamika ate in silence as Aminah served herself some food at the stove.

"Aminah can show you around," Sarah said, not wanting Tamika to feel obliged to divulge anything personal. Before Tamika could respond, Sarah looked in the direction of her daughter.

"Does the *masjid* have any youth activities during the summer?" Sarah asked.

Aminah took her seat at the table next to Tamika. "I'm not sure. I can check though."

Sarah nodded and continued eating in silence for several minutes, as did the roommates.

Tamika cleared her throat, unable to figure out why she was nervous before asking the question. "Do they have any, uh, Arabic or Qur'an classes?"

Sarah's eyebrows rose in pleasant surprise as she put a forkful of spinach in her mouth and chewed. "I'm sure they do." She hadn't thought to ask if Tamika wanted to take classes.

"Actually," Aminah said, "they have an Arabic and Qur'an institute every summer."

"Really?" Tamika's eyebrows rose in interest. A moment later, her expression changed to one of concern. "How much does it cost?"

"Don't worry about that," Sarah said. "I'm sure it's reasonable. And if not, we'll make sure they make it reasonable."

"You'll get in," Aminah assured her. "*InshaAllaah.*"

"They have classes for beginners?" Tamika took a bite of food as she looked at her roommate.

"I'm sure they do." Aminah paused as she thought of something. "They also offer Islamic studies."

"Really?"

She nodded. "But I'll have to check to make sure they're offering it this summer."

"When will we know?"

"I can call first thing in the morning."

"Either way," Sarah said with a smile, "we'll make sure you learn everything you need to, *inshaAllaah.*" She added, "Even if it's from private classes right here in our home."

Tamika smiled gratefully and continued eating as she reflected on how fortunate she was. She had wanted to learn Arabic and Qur'an since she began researching about Islam for her term paper. She could only hope the *masjid* would be flexible regarding her financial situation.

Eleven

A week after Tamika arrived in Atlanta, she enrolled in the Qur'an and Arabic classes offered at the *masjid*, which was located in a small suburb of the city near where Aminah's family lived. The classes were held Monday through Thursday evenings from 5:30 to 9:00, Qur'an from 5:30 to 7:00 and Arabic from 7:30 to 9:00. Apparently, the late times had been chosen to accommodate the schedule of those who worked during the day or whose spouses were able to care for the children only after returning from work. Arrangements were still being made for an Islamic studies class, which the *masjid* hadn't planned to offer that summer. In the meantime, Aminah was teaching Tamika at home from some of her books.

Tamika enjoyed both classes. The small class size allowed maximum participation from the students. It also enabled her to relax and feel comfortable whenever she needed to ask a question or clarify what she needed to know. The Qur'an classes were separated by level and gender, and Tamika attended the beginning course for women. There were only five students in the class, including Tamika. Three of the women were in their mid to late forties and had been Muslim more than twenty years. Due to the demands of work and family, they had been unable to study Qur'an as much as they would have liked. The other student was a relatively new Muslim, having entered the religion two years before. Lauren was a twenty-year-old junior at a local college, where she met a Muslim student and subsequently became Muslim herself. She didn't cover in Islamic garb on campus, she had told Tamika, because she wasn't yet ready to be publicly Muslim. Her family didn't know of her conversion, and with the exception of two close friends, none of her friends knew of it either. In class Lauren wore a thin headscarf draped loosely over her red hair. Most days she rode to and from class with a young man who would wait in the prayer area until class was over. Lauren never said who he was, but Tamika assumed he was the student who had introduced Lauren to the religion.

Tamika's Arabic class was slightly larger than her Qur'an class. There were eight students, which included both males and females, and it was separated only by level. Although there was no formal requirement of gender segregation, the three male students sat in the front row each day, closest to the male teacher, while the females sat in the last two rows, apparently to have a comfortable distance from the men. Tamika soon learned that this voluntary segregation was customary for most Muslims, even for lectures and dinners.

Tamika enjoyed her Arabic class although it was a bit awkward to be in a formal class with Omar. Fortunately, he rarely spoke to her except to greet her, a gesture he extended to all of his classmates. But he often wore a smile whenever he saw her, letting her know he was pleased to see her each day.

Since she already knew he was attracted to her, she tried to avoid him whenever possible.

For the first two weeks, Aminah and her mother took turns taking Tamika to and from her classes each day, but Tamika felt this was too much trouble and insisted on taking the bus. When she found a job at a local Muslim-owned fish fry, she would take a bus to work in the morning then another bus to the *masjid* in the evening, when she would catch another one to go home. The bus ride home each night took nearly forty minutes because of all the stops along the route. Most nights Tamika didn't get in until close to 10:30 because she usually didn't leave class until 9:15, and she had a short walk from the bus stop to the house. Tamika would be only half awake when she prayed *'Ishaa* before going to bed, and she often had a difficult time waking up in the morning because of the late hours.

Ismael pulled up beside Tamika one night when he saw her dragging herself down the street. She had been particularly tired that night and it took a moment before she realized he was telling her to get in the car. She opened the back door on the passenger's side and climbed in, murmuring a reply to his greeting. She tried to keep her eyes open for the short drive, but she felt her eyelids getting heavy a moment after she climbed in the car. She leaned her head against the window and woke to the sound of Ismael saying something to her as he got out of the car. She blinked for a few seconds before realizing she should get out too.

Inside the house, Tamika lay down, still fully dressed, telling herself she would sleep for only a few minutes, after which she would pray *'Ishaa*. She woke to the sound of people talking and realized she had not only missed the night prayer but the dawn prayer too. It was 8:03, and she was due to work at nine. She hurried to the shower, dressed for work, and searched for bus fare in her room. After finding the correct change, she prayed the prayers she missed, her mind on the bus that was scheduled to arrive in less than ten minutes. She decided against grabbing the change of clothes she usually brought with her to wear after work. She would have to wear her work clothes to her classes today, she thought regretfully as she accepted that she would smell like fried fish. She hurried down the steps after prayer and yelled her greeting to whoever was in earshot. She was about to walk out the door when Sarah stopped her.

"What time are you supposed to be there?"

"Nine." Tamika started to open the door, not wanting to waste time.

Sarah glanced at her watch. "How long does it take you on the bus?"

"About forty five minutes." Tamika opened the door wider as her heart raced. The restaurant opened at 9:30, and she was supposed to unlock it for the customers and prepare some food before then.

"I'll take you."

It took a moment for Tamika to realize that Sarah was offering to give her a ride. She creased her forehead then shook her head. She hated the idea of Aminah's parents interrupting their day for her. "I'm fine. I should make it."

"It's almost eight thirty."

Worried, Tamika glanced at her watch too. The bus was scheduled to arrive at 8:25. "I have eight twenty."

"I'll take you." Sarah went back in the kitchen and emerged a second later with her *khimaar* and keys in her hand. Tamika wondered if she had planned to take her all along.

In the car, Sarah asked Tamika how she was enjoying her classes and Atlanta in general. Tamika responded in kind, feeling a bit awkward alone with Aminah's mother. She never knew what to say. When they finally pulled into the restaurant parking lot and Tamika started to get out, Sarah laid a hand on Tamika's shoulder, and Tamika turned to meet her gaze.

"We'll pick you up from class from now on."

Tamika wrinkled her forehead and started to say something. Before she could protest, Sarah went on.

"Ismael said he saw you walking home late last night." She placed her hand back on the steering wheel but continued to look at Tamika. "I never liked the idea of you taking the bus so late in the first place."

Sarah sounded so much like a mother that Tamika couldn't think of any response. She could only nod her head in humble compliance. She had to stop herself from saying, *Yes, ma'am.*

"You still get out of class at nine?"

"Yes."

"We'll be there by nine fifteen, *inshaAllaah.*" Sarah glanced at the gearshift as she put the car in drive. "*As-salaamu-'alaikum.*"

After the talk with Sarah, Tamika would sit in the front lobby of the *masjid* reading or studying after her classes until Sarah or Aminah arrived to pick her up. She normally waited no more than fifteen minutes. One Thursday night Tamika drifted to sleep in the lobby waiting for her ride. The sound of someone saying her name woke her, and instinctively, she glanced at her watch. It was 9:41.

"You need a ride?"

Tamika looked up to find Omar standing a few feet from her. She sat up, embarrassed to have fallen asleep in the lobby. She cleared her throat then averted her gaze, wondering how she had looked with her head leaning on the back of her chair. She hoped she hadn't been snoring. "No." She felt her *khimaar,* making sure everything was in place. "Aminah should be here any minute."

Omar wore an uncertain expression on his face, and a half smile creased a corner of his mouth. "Are you sure?"

Tamika looked around. The building was unusually quiet. All the students had gone home for the night, and it seemed that she and Omar were the only students still there. She heard the imam moving about in his office at the far end of the lobby. Tamika could see the blackness of the night through the windows at the lobby entrance. There were no car lights shining from the parking lot, which meant no one had arrived to pick her up. She hoped they hadn't forgotten about her.

"I can take you home if you want," Omar said.

Inside, Tamika groaned. How did she get stuck here with him? "No thanks." She lifted her purse to her lap and gathered her books. "She's just running late." Omar nodded as he took a seat next to her, a smile still on his face. Tamika turned slightly so that her knees were not directly next to his.

"Then I'll just wait with you," Omar said. "I don't think it's a good idea for you to sit here alone like this at night."

Tamika sighed, growing irritated. She wished he would just leave her alone. "I'm fine, thanks." She kept her gaze fixed ahead of her, staring into the darkness beyond the glass windows.

"I know, but I just wanna make sure you're not stranded."

"Thanks," she muttered sarcastically, stopping short of rolling her eyes.

For several minutes, they sat in silence. Tamika stared out the windows ahead, and Omar looked at his clasped hands that sat atop his books and class notebook. Outside rain began to trickle from the sky. It fell on the glass in small drops that slipped with slow hesitance like silent tears. Tamika wondered what her mother was doing right then. She imagined her standing in the kitchen fussing over her food cooking unevenly as she held the phone between her shoulder and ear, talking to Jackie. Or perhaps she sat in front of the television flipping through the channels, unable to find a show for "decent folk." Maybe Thelma stood in Tamika's bedroom gazing at the graduation picture as her eyes glistened.

Tamika's cheeks grew warm at the thought, and she suddenly became aware of how uncomfortable the temperature was in the lobby. Would every night be like this in Atlanta? The heat was already unbearable during the day. She never imagined that nights would be hot too. At home she would put a fan in the window to cool her room in the summer, but she wondered if a fan would do in Atlanta's summer heat.

Summers in Milwaukee were calmer than those in the South, and sweltering heat was a rarity. A Milwaukee summer offered a comfortable break from a long, cold winter although there were summer days in which the heat was piercing. In Atlanta the heat was oppressive, and even night offered little refuge. Often Tamika opted to stay in the air conditioned indoors than withstand the scorching heat outside. The sun, a welcomed presence back home, gave her little more than sweat-soaked clothes and headaches in Atlanta at the end of the day. Several glasses of water were like medicine for her. If she didn't drink them, she was sure to get sick. It took some time for her to realize that she had to pay close attention to the fabric of the clothes she wore. Initially, she thought it was the Islamic requirements of dress that made her gasping for air after ten minutes in the sun. But when Aminah suggested she select cooler, lighter fabric to cover her hair and body, she realized that Aminah was right. She was actually cooler covered in the sun—so long as she chose the right material.

"Why don't you like me?"

Omar's voice was a frustrating reminder that she was stuck in the *masjid* with no idea where Aminah or her mother was. Exhausted, she wasn't in the mood for conversation. For a moment, she said nothing and continued to stare ahead of her. Where was Aminah and what was taking her so long? "I never said that."

"You don't have to."

She groaned and tried to keep from rolling her eyes. She shot a glance in his direction. He sounded like a non-Muslim from high school trying to get a date. He really needed to hang around Sulayman more. "Give it a rest."

Omar laughed, stunning Tamika, who grew self-conscious all of a sudden.

"I'm sorry," he apologized without explanation. He shook his head and grinned to himself, enjoying a private joke at her expense.

She decided not to ask. She just wanted to go home. She sighed impatiently and stood, pulling her purse strap over a shoulder as she held the small plastic bag with her work clothes inside. She arranged her books in her arms before walking over to the windows and peering out. She had had enough of Omar for one night. Through the reflection on the glass, she saw Omar stand a few minutes later. Knowing he was heading toward her, she rolled her eyes and moved a few feet from where she had been standing to let him know she wasn't interested in his company. She was surprised when he disappeared into the prayer area and never returned. He hadn't even looked in her direction. Tamika's cheeks grew hot in anger, though she couldn't explain this feeling.

Tamika stood alone in the lobby as the rain pattered against the window, dull pounding in the darkness. It was then she felt her cruelty. Omar meant no harm. He obviously wasn't as knowledgeable as Sulayman about Islamic etiquette, but he was trying. He hadn't been Muslim long enough to understand when he was being too friendly.

But what made him think she'd want to ride alone with some strange man late at night? Certainly, he had to know better than that. If it wasn't an emergency, there was no excuse for him to offer her a ride.

But what image of a Muslim woman was she giving him when she treated him so coldly? Yes, he was Muslim, but he was a man, a new Muslim, who was just getting to know Muslim women. Aminah had once told her that many Muslim women were so hard on their Muslim brothers that the men often sought spouses outside the Muslim community. Who could blame them? Aminah had argued. It was as if a Muslim man was running in circles when he wanted to marry a Muslim sister. Of course, most of the blame fell on the women's guardians, who often put unrealistic, if not un-Islamic, requirements on the potential spouse. It shocked Tamika how materialism and racism had infiltrated the Muslim community. Money and race were two of the most popular reasons a Muslim man was turned down for marriage. There were those who would turn down a man based solely on his inability to give a dowry of several thousand dollars. Yet the Prophet had told the Muslims to marry, even if the dowry was no more than an iron ring.

Tamika considered apologizing to Omar. The last thing she wanted was to discourage a Muslim man from pursuing a Muslim sister he felt was striving to please Allah. She wasn't interested in Omar, but that didn't give her the right to behave as she did. If there was something he didn't understand about proper etiquette, there had to be a more civil solution than insulting him and treating him as if he were purposefully disrespecting her. God judged people based on their intentions. Who was she to do otherwise?

Tamika decided against apologizing to Omar. It would send the wrong message. She would just have to be more mindful when she was around him.

Tamika's legs began to ache from standing so long. She needed to sit down. She returned to the seats and set her purse, bag, and books on the chair Omar had sat in. She glanced at her wristwatch. It was two minutes after 10:00. The last prayer would be held at 10:30. She had never prayed *Ishaa'* in the *masjid* before, and she wondered if tonight would be her first time. Tamika yawned and stretched as she covered her mouth. She then leaned her head on the back of the chair and wondered how much longer she would wait. Staring at the ceiling, she considered taking the bus. The next one would probably be there at 10:35.

"*Allaahuakbar! Allaahuakbar!*"

Tamika was jolted awake by the sound of the call to prayer pouring through the intercom. She sat up and wiped her face, noticing that more people were in the lobby. Apparently, they had come for prayer. Looking at her watch, she became worried. It was 10:15, and Aminah still hadn't arrived. She would pray in the *masjid* after all. She could only hope she could go home after the prayer.

Tamika returned to the lobby after the prayer was finished and searched the crowd for Aminah and Sarah as people filed out of the building. As the crowd lessened to those who stood in the lobby chatting, she knew she would have to take the initiative to get home. Perhaps she should take the bus, but she first needed to make sure they weren't on their way. She headed to the imam's office to call Aminah's house. Tamika's only reservation was that she might appear demanding to them, but she couldn't stay in the *masjid* all night. Soon everyone would be gone, and the *masjid* would be locked until the morning.

The imam greeted her warmly as she walked through the door. He recognized her from when they met shortly after she arrived in Atlanta from Milwaukee. They had met when she was at the *masjid* with Aminah registering for class. Since he was her guardian for marriage, Aminah felt it was necessary that they know each other although Tamika didn't plan to marry anytime soon. The imam allowed her to use his phone while he arranged some papers on his desk in preparation to go home.

"Yes?" The sound of Aminah's voice made Tamika grow angry. How could she be home relaxing while Tamika was stranded?

Tamika greeted her and let the sound of her voice tell Aminah she was waiting for her.

"Where are you?" Aminah inquired in concern after returning the greetings.

"I'm waiting for you at the *masjid.*"

"My mother hasn't gotten there yet? *SubhaanaAllaah.*" She sounded really worried, and Tamika's heart sank in fear that something terrible had happened. She hoped everything was okay. "My parents had to go shopping, and they said they'd pick you up. And Sulayman's been gone all day, so there's no car here."

What was Tamika supposed to do now? And where were Aminah's parents? Certainly, they should be finished shopping by now.

"I can call them on their cell phone to see what's wrong." Before Tamika could respond, Aminah told her to hold on and clicked over for the three-way call.

Sarah's voice sounded far away when she answered, and Tamika guessed that she and her husband were in the car as she spoke. Aminah briefed her mother on Tamika's predicament. Sarah apologized and explained that their shopping had taken longer than expected. She had thought they would make it to the *masjid* at least in time for prayer, but they left the store almost thirty minutes ago and were now stuck in traffic. "I think there's a major accident on the interstate," Sarah guessed, concern in her voice.

Tamika groaned. Now what?

"How long do you think it'll be before you can pick her up?" Aminah said.

"Thirty minutes, at least," Sarah said regretfully. "The traffic is stop-and-go for miles." She paused as she thought of something. "Is Sulayman home yet?"

"No," Aminah apologized.

Sarah sighed, trying to figure out what to do. "Is there anyone else there who can give you a ride home?"

At first Tamika didn't reply, immediately reminded of Omar. She refused to incriminate herself. But what other choice did she have? "I can check," she offered. "If not, I can just take the bus."

"If you can't find a ride," Sarah said, "then ask the imam to wait until we can get there before he locks up so you're not waiting alone. But you shouldn't have to take the bus. We'll be there before then, *inshaAllaah*. But if you get a ride, call us, so we'll know before we swing by the *masjid*."

Tamika sighed. At least she didn't have to work in the morning. If she did, she doubted she could be patient through this. She turned to look out the open door into the lobby where people were leaving. She saw three brothers laughing and talking, Omar among them. "Okay," she nearly mumbled.

She hung up the phone and paused momentarily before dragging herself into the lobby, where she saw a total of five people. She knew none of them, not even the sister who was heading toward the door with her husband at her side. The only familiar face was that of Omar. She frowned, regretting what she would probably have to do. Instead of speaking to him, she resigned herself to standing in front of the windows and peering out next to the door. Certainly, Omar would notice that she needed a ride after all.

Outside the rain fell with more insistence. It pounded on the concrete and glass in angry thuds. A storm was brewing, and Tamika was going to be caught in the middle of it. Now she was certain Aminah's parents would never make it in time. She couldn't even wait for the bus in this weather, at least not without catching pneumonia. She didn't even have a rain jacket. But she would be here past midnight if she waited for Aminah's parents. And she definitely couldn't ask the imam to sit around until then. Maybe she could ask him to take her home.

Behind her she heard one of the brothers comment on the weather before hurrying out the door. Tamika shut her eyes and made a silent prayer to get home safely. She opened her eyes and drew in a deep breath. She wanted nothing more than the comfort of her home, or at least the home that was hers for the summer.

Tamika wished she wasn't so dependent on other people for things as basic as a ride. She needed a car. But she knew that was farfetched. The little money she earned went to restocking her wardrobe and offering Aminah's family at least something for their kindness. After that, she could barely afford the small fee required for the classes she attended, let alone a vehicle.

Tamika was an inconvenience, this much she knew. No matter how much Aminah and her mother told her they didn't mind, she wasn't convinced. It couldn't be convenient for them to rearrange schedules, drive in thunderstorms, and be at the *masjid* almost every night, all so she could attend classes she didn't have to take in the first place.

Omar and his friend passed where she stood then exited the building. Panicked, Tamika's heart pounded. What would she do now? The lobby doors closed behind them, and she was left alone in stillness of the abandoned lobby. The only sounds were the pounding rain and an occasional rustle from the imam's office. And soon even he would be leaving. He had no idea she was still there, but she desperately hoped he would either give her a ride or wait for hers to come.

Tamika blinked as she felt tears gather in her eyes. She hated her life. Why did her mother have to throw her out? Her legs weakened, and she decided to sit down. In the chair, her gaze fell to the books in her lap, her mind in a daze. Thunder exploded and nearly shook the building. Fear swept through her as her heart raced, and she lifted her gaze to the window. The wind grew fierce, and the building moaned and creaked in a pitiful cry for mercy. The atmosphere became threatening, and she wiped her face with her hands, struggling to keep from crying. She didn't want to break down right there in the lobby.

When Tamika heard the *masjid* door open and close, her heart nearly stopped. The imam was leaving! Hadn't he seen her sitting there alone? She couldn't stay here by herself! Terrified, she looked up to confirm her fears. She was ready to run after him and beg him to wait or take her home.

To her surprise, she saw Omar walking toward her. The imam was still in his office. She blinked as she stared at Omar in stunned confusion. Her lips parted to say something, but he spoke first.

"I wanted to pull the car up so you wouldn't get soaked," he apologized with a half smile. Without waiting for a reply, he turned to leave. She jumped to her feet and followed him out the door.

Tamika sat in the back seat without uttering a word as Omar pulled out of the parking lot to take her home. She stared out the window at the erupting storm while he listened to a music tape. She sighed in relief, grateful that she left when she did. The rain was tossed to and fro in the wind's fury. Tall trees bent over in trembling submission and swayed in disarray, only able to keep their feet firm as they struggled against being uprooted. Even the car wavered against the force of the wind, and Tamika silently prayed she would make it home alive.

When Omar finally pulled into the driveway of the Ali residence, Tamika couldn't have been more relieved to see the house. She slipped her books into the plastic bag that held her work clothes, hoping to protect them from the rain. She hesitated as she surveyed her path to the house before finally opening the car door.

"I'm sorry I don't have an umbrella," Omar called to her as she stepped from the car.

"I'm fine, but thanks so much, brother. *As-salaamu-'alaikum.*" She quickly shut the car door and bolted to the front door in the pouring rain.

Omar waited until he saw Tamika open the door before pulling away. She waved to him to let him know she was safely inside before shutting the door behind her. She was grateful that Sarah had given her a key to the house. She would have hated to wait until Aminah cold open the door.

Tamika leaned against the closed door and took a deep breath before exhaling a second later. She was finally home. Her clothes were soaked, but she didn't care.

"Sulayman?" Aminah called from upstairs.

"It's Tamika!" Tamika called back.

Aminah came down the stairs and met her in the foyer. "*As-salaamu-'alaikum.*" She wore a pleasant smile. "So you got a ride?"

Tamika forced laughter and sighed in relief. "Yeah. I'm sorry I forgot to call."

Aminah waved her hand. "It's no problem. I'll just call my mother to let her know you're home, *inshaAllaah.*"

Tamika nodded, and a moment later Aminah was in the kitchen dialing her mother. Tamika went upstairs to change clothes. Taking advantage of Sulayman's absence, she came back downstairs with her hair uncovered. She met Aminah in the kitchen and opened the refrigerator to see what she would eat for dinner.

"Who gave you a ride?"

Tamika laughed. "I give you one guess."

Aminah laughed knowingly, leaning her back against the sink counter and folding her arms. "Omar?"

"Yeah," Tamika said with a nod, still peering in the refrigerator. She shrugged. "I didn't know anybody else. Not that anyone else was there this late."

"I'm sorry about that."

She waved her hand. "It's no problem. It's just good to be home."

Aminah bit her lower lip as she was reminded of something. "I was thinking."

Tamika removed a pot from a shelf in the refrigerator. "Mm hm."

"Maybe we should have a dinner and invite some sisters over so you can meet other sisters in the community."

Tamika placed the pot on the stove and removed the cover to peer inside. It was beef stew. She nodded to let Aminah know she was listening. "That'd be nice, *inshaAllaah.*"

Tamika studied the stew closely. "You make this today?"

Aminah nodded. "It's still good, don't worry."

"Mind if I have some?"

"Of course not. You're welcome to anything in the house."

"Thanks." Tamika retrieved a glass bowl from a cabinet above the stove. She served herself some stew and put the bowl in the microwave.

"So what do you think?" Aminah asked a minute later.

"About what?"

"The dinner."

"I haven't tasted it yet, but it looks good."

Aminah laughed. "No, I mean having a dinner so you can meet some sisters."

"Oh," Tamika laughed then shrugged in response. "I suppose." She paused as she considered it further. "Actually, it'd be kind of nice to meet more people."

"That's what I was thinking. My mom and I were talking, and she was saying next Friday would be good."

"Whatever's best for your family."

"We just wanted to make sure you didn't mind before we set a definite date."

Tamika grinned as the hum of the microwave filled the kitchen. "Of course I don't mind. It'll probably be fun." She glanced at the microwave timer. "Will it be like a party?"

"I guess you can call it that." Aminah grinned. "But not like a Streamsdale party."

"I hope not!" Tamika peered into the microwave at her soup. A few seconds later, the timer sounded, and she opened the microwave door to remove the bowl, using the cuff of her sleeve as an oven mitt.

"So you don't have to work?"

Tamika set her bowl on the table then opened a drawer to get a spoon. She shook her head as she carried it to the table and sat down. "I usually don't work Friday through Sunday." She stirred the soup. "When they asked when I could work, I figured I may as well try and get class and work over with on the same days." She chuckled as she cut a piece of beef with the side of her spoon. "Otherwise, I won't feel like it's summer."

"Is there anyone you'd like to invite?" Aminah asked as she took a seat across from her friend.

Tamika shrugged as she took a spoonful of soup and chewed it. "I don't really know anyone."

"Didn't you meet some sisters in your classes?"

She nodded as she remembered Lauren. "One."

"You want her to come?"

She raised her eyebrows in consideration after eating another spoonful. "I can see if she doesn't have anything else to do."

Aminah tapped her fingers on the table, ideas seeming to come to her just then. She smiled, her eyes narrowing as she imagined how they would plan the day. "*InshaAllaah*, it should be fun."

Tamika smiled in return, and she ate her stew in silence as she imagined who would come next Friday.

Twelve

Sulayman put the car in park after pulling into the driveway of his home, and he sat for a moment before turning off the ignition. He lifted his hand to the cold air blowing from the vents and savored the artificial coolness that was sure to be a sharp contrast to the heat outside. He could almost feel the late afternoon sun heating his neck through the window, and he wasn't looking forward to getting out of the car.

After a minute's procrastination, he turned off the car and felt the coolness escaping like steam from a pot. The car grew uncomfortably warm, and he glanced outside before finally opening the door. No cars were parked in front of the house, at least not yet, and that was a good sign. Maybe he could steal a quick nap before the guests poured in. He had gone to sleep late the night before and was barely able to keep his eyes open during *Jumuah*. He always felt guilty when he nodded off during the Friday prayer sermon because Allah had more right to his energy than the professor he worked for. But it was hard. He could only imagine how he would continue the routine of work when he started school in the fall.

Taking a deep breath, he removed the keys from the ignition and unlocked his door before stepping out of the car. It was thoughtful of his mother and sister to host a dinner for Tamika, but he wasn't in the mood for company. The guests would be mostly women, so he didn't have too much to worry about, but his father often invited a couple of brothers when the women took over the house. Sulayman imagined it was his father's way of avoiding being confined to his room and walking on eggshells anytime he wanted a drink of water or a bite to eat. When the guests were only women, there was little, if any, opportunity to even walk down the stairs without making it a big production. Usually, Sulayman would just close his door and fire up the Internet or open a book until it was time to go to sleep. But it did get frustrating at times, especially when Aminah and his mother would encourage the guests to stay late into the night.

Today Omar would probably be there, Sulayman imagined, so he couldn't resign himself to his room the entire time. But if his mother didn't need him to do anything, he planned to escape to his room before anyone arrived. He had a lot of work to do, and he would probably return to the lab in the morning to test some of his hypotheses. Sulayman didn't have to go, but the professor would be there working on the research project, and it was always a good idea to put in extra time if he wanted the job beyond the summer.

Sulayman had started working only a few weeks before as a research assistant at a local college. He had taken the job to keep himself abreast of the subjects he had studied in school and, of course, to earn extra money. He planned to attend medical school in the fall, and he needed funds. He was already accepted to three schools, two of which were out of state. The other was located in Decatur, a city not too far from his home and had one of the most prominent medical school programs in the nation. All three schools had offered him scholarships, two of them full, after he did well at Streamsdale and earned a high score on his MCAT. The local school was covering all but one third of his fees.

After much consideration, he had decided to attend the school closest to home. With the help of his parents and his summer job, he could pay the remainder of the tuition. To save money, he agreed to live at home in the fall although he felt a private apartment was best suited for his studying. He would have to spend most of his time in the school library and study halls since studying at home would be nearly impossible.

He had discussed the particulars with his parents on many occasions, and they felt it was best if he lived at home for the first year. If he found it too difficult, they suggested that he go ahead and find an affordable apartment near campus. But it was unwise for a young, unmarried Muslim man to have an apartment all to himself, they told him. It brought with it too many temptations. His parents had legitimate concerns, Sulayman knew, but he didn't want any distractions from his studies. Medical school was hard enough without the added stress of parents and a sister in the same house. He preferred living alone to living at home. He had grown out of life with "Mom" and "Dad." He was twenty-one years old, and he needed to learn to make it on his own. He would have chosen an out-of-state school had the local school not been as prominent as it was. His parents thought it was his attachment to home that made him choose the Decatur-based school, but that was only partly true. He couldn't deny that there was a part of him that hated the idea of leaving home, where he felt most secure. But there was another part of him demanding he be a man and stand on his own.

It was with reluctance that Sulayman agreed to live at home for his first year of medical school. It was with even more reluctance that he agreed to accept his parents' financial help. He was never going to make it on his own if he continued to accept the crutches his parents handed him. He loved his parents and didn't want to hurt them, but they—and he—simply had to let go. But they weren't ready to, and part of him wondered if he was either. It was for this reason that he agreed to live at home.

But that didn't keep Sulayman from seeking alternatives. He had already contacted a few Muslim-owned financial institutions that offered interest-free loans, and he submitted the necessary applications. He hated the idea of being in debt, but in life sacrifices were a must. He was doing a lot of job hunting too, hoping to work part-time while he was in school. There was a possibility he could stay at his current job, but he still hadn't received a definite answer from the professor. It was still being determined whether or not the school needed a research assistant on the project throughout the year. His mother often warned that medical school put too many demands on students to afford them any free time, let alone time to work. But his parents were already helping him with tuition, and he certainly wasn't going to accept handouts from them for basic needs like food and books.

Sulayman was also searching for affordable apartments, in case he was able to secure a job and make enough to pay rent. If he were, he would have to convince his parents that he needed his own space. He had considered a roommate at one point, but there was no one whom he knew well enough to live with. Omar had offered for Sulayman to move in with him, but Sulayman had declined. He feared that he and Omar wouldn't fare too well as roommates. They were too different. So, as it stood, Sulayman would have to live alone if he opted to not live at home.

But Sulayman wasn't naïve. He knew it wouldn't be easy. There were benefits to living at home, and financial security was only one of them. His parents' concerns about him being single and living alone in an apartment were not unfounded. After all, he was a human being—a man.

He had toyed with the idea of marriage for some time, and in many ways, marrying now would bring a lot of benefits. But he decided against it. It simply wasn't plausible, and he had to be realistic. Medical school was difficult enough, and any added responsibility could mean disaster for his grades, if not his entire career. Of course, the strong possibility that he wouldn't be able to afford it as a student had crossed his mind many times. And what would he do if his wife became pregnant? How would they survive? It would be a miracle if he were able to afford the basic needs of just him and his spouse, not to mention children. Marriage just wasn't a possibility right then.

Even if he did decide to go ahead and marry, he often thought, there was one question that always lingered in his mind. Who? There were very few women in his local community whom he would consider. He was young and had a lot to learn about women, but he was old enough to know that a pretty face wasn't enough to sustain a marriage. If it was, he had plenty of options. There were always women at school—and the *masjid*—who showed interest in him, and many were upfront about it. Most of them were very attractive, and if he hadn't known any better, he would have chosen one of them.

It went without saying that his wife would be Muslim, which eliminated many of the women who showed interest in him at school. He would have never expected non-Muslim women who were still in college to be open to marriage. When he had made it clear to them that marriage was the only relationship he would entertain, they let him know they had no problem with that. But Sulayman knew the flip side of the coin too. Had he shown no interest in marriage and desired only a physical relationship, they would have agreed to that with no less enthusiasm. Such women were not the type he wanted to marry.

There had been a few Muslim women he had seriously considered, but each time, something happened to convince him that they were not for him. But there was one woman he hadn't ruled out, at least not entirely.

Sulayman had met Aidah the summer before during an internship in Atlanta. They worked in the same lab and had the opportunity to talk a lot during the eight-week assignment. She graduated as a pre-med major this past May, as had he, and she would attend an Atlanta-based medical school in the fall, though she hadn't decided exactly which one. She was attractive, easy-going, and intelligent. She had a sense of humor and was confident in herself. But what Sulayman liked most about her was her commitment to Islam.

Aidah covered in Islamic garb, even at work and school, and wasn't afraid to tell the world she was Muslim. She had been the president of the Muslim Students Association on her campus and had spearheaded many Islamic functions at her school. She was originally from Louisville, Kentucky, and had moved to Atlanta for college. When she fell in love with the city, she decided to stay. She loved the diversity of the Muslim community and how it was customary to see Muslims in the grocery store and walking down the street. She visited home whenever she had the opportunity, but her heart remained in Atlanta. She spent her summers in the city if she was accepted in an internship or able to find work in the city during the break. This summer she was doing another Atlanta-based internship and lived near her job in a small apartment that she shared with another Muslim sister.

Sulayman communicated with Aidah mostly through e-mail and telephone, but he tried to keep the correspondence to a minimum. Although her parents liked him from the start, even before meeting him in person, he didn't feel comfortable taking advantage of that. He wanted to limit their e-mail and phone interaction to only that which was necessary to find out if they were compatible for marriage. With the approval of her father already in place, it was only a matter of deciding whether or not she was right for him.

At times, Sulayman was so convinced that he should marry Aidah that he was ready to call her father and make a formal proposal. But there was always something holding him back, something he couldn't put his finger on. Whenever doubts crept into his mind, he would contemplate what could possibly be wrong. He had asked Aminah and his parents on several occasions what they thought of Aidah, and each time they said they liked her. He almost wished his sister would find a fault in her to validate his doubts. But she never did. The only thing that was keeping him from taking the big step, he concluded, was fear.

He was scared, he couldn't deny. But who wouldn't be? The idea of marriage was undeniably exciting, but it was equally terrifying. Whenever Sulayman thought about getting married, he was reminded of the huge responsibility it entailed. And all of it would fall on him.

But it couldn't be the idea of marriage that was keeping him from marrying Aidah. And if it wasn't, then what was?

Sulayman was definitely attracted to Aidah, but he couldn't deny that he was uncomfortable with her career choice. He hated to admit it, but he just couldn't get used to the idea of being married to a doctor. Whenever he thought of a wife, he pictured a woman who spent most of her time in the home caring for him and the children. He didn't want to appear selfish, but a career woman wasn't what he had in mind when he thought of a wife. He didn't mind the idea of his wife working to earn extra income for herself if she wanted, but he did mind having a wife coming home from work every day just as tired as he. It was difficult enough for him to deal with the idea of getting up each morning to face the impersonal, fast-paced, stressful atmosphere of a hospital, let alone his wife too. He wanted to come home and relax, forget about his rough day and spend the evening laughing and joking, enjoying the company of his wife. But he feared marrying a doctor would prevent him from that.

He wasn't being fair, he thought. He could have everything he wanted in a wife, even if she were a doctor. Who knew? It could be a perfect match. They could have a medical practice together. She could see the female patients and he the male. It could work. Then why not give it a try?

Why not?

He would have given almost anything to know the answer to that question.

The beautiful array of food on the dining room table was breathtaking, and for a moment Tamika just stood there staring at it. They had worked hard—she, Aminah, and Sarah—and now they were seeing the fruit of their work. The sweet aroma of food filled the house, tempting them to eat before everyone arrived. But they would wait. Everyone should be arriving soon.

Giggling like children, Tamika and Aminah raced up the stairs as they hurried to get dressed. They were seeing who could be back downstairs first. In the guest room where she slept, Tamika slipped on a long dark green rayon dress with pearl-like matching buttons that ran up the front of the dress. She had bought it with her first paycheck and hadn't found an opportunity to wear it before then. Tamika pulled open a drawer and chose a large cream-colored silk scarf she had bought a few weeks before and worn to *Jumuah* a few times. She draped it over a dark green under-scarf that she neatly wrapped about her head. In the mirror, she studied her reflection and smiled before leaving the room.

Tamika and Aminah nearly ran into each other as they tried to be the first one downstairs. Laughing and out of breath, they reached the living room, where Aminah collapsed on the couch and Tamika stood over her, leaning forward and holding her stomach as she laughed. They called it even. It was a tie.

From the dining room, Sulayman stood nibbling on a *samosa*, and he wrinkled his forehead in confusion as he observed the giggling women, trying to keep from laughing. When she saw him, Aminah sat up and nudged

Tamika whose back was to him. Tamika glanced over her shoulder and immediately stopped laughing at the sight of Sulayman. She turned wide-eyed to Aminah, as if asking, "Where did *he* come from?" Aminah shrugged as she chuckled and shook her head. They hadn't heard him come in the house.

The doorbell rang, and Aminah hurried to the door. After looking through the peephole, she beamed with excitement and opened the door. "*As-salaamu-'alaikum!*" Aminah welcomed the veiled woman with a warm embrace. As they hugged, a young teenager who appeared to be fifteen entered with two younger girls, who appeared to be five and nine, following close behind.

Tamika's heart raced, and she did a double take. For a moment, she thought she saw Dee, but a second later she realized it was Aesha, Dee's fourteen-year-old sister. At least she was fourteen when Tamika last saw her. But she was probably fifteen by now.

After Dee's mother finished embracing Aminah, she removed her shoes, as did her daughters, and placed them on the shoe rack. "I hope I'm not too early," she apologized in her Spanish accent.

Aminah laughed and shook her head. "You're right on time."

"Maryam!" Sarah called in excitement as she entered the foyer from the kitchen. "*As-salaamu-'alaikum,*" she greeted her friend in an embrace.

Aminah drifted back to where Tamika stood, and Aesha followed her, trailed by her younger sisters. When Tamika studied the face of the youngest, she recognized her as Naimah, Dee's four-year-old sister. During Tamika's visit to Aminah's house, Dee's family had visited, and Naimah had shown great confusion and concern as to how Tamika could choose Hell over Heaven by not being Muslim. The innocent child's embarrassing questions prompted Maryam to apologize and remove her daughter from the room.

Tamika smiled as Aminah reintroduced her to Dee's sisters, informing them that Tamika was now Muslim. The siblings smiled politely, but Tamika couldn't help noticing their eyes, how disinterested and sad they appeared. And tired. They looked terribly exhausted, and for a moment Tamika wondered what could be troubling someone so young. A second later, Tamika's heart sank at the realization. Dee. She had gone too soon. The wounds were too fresh to have adequately healed. As a friend, Tamika had suffered many nights from thoughts of Dee. What must it be like for her sisters?

Aesha shook Tamika's hand and hugged her in congratulations. But she didn't ask many questions about her conversion, and Tamika knew it was her way of avoiding the subject of her sister. Instead Aesha asked general questions about how Tamika liked being Muslim and if it was hard for her in school after she accepted Islam. From the brief exchange, Tamika could tell Aesha was intelligent for her age, which she imagined made it all the more difficult for her to get over her sister's death. Certainly, she knew her sister hadn't been in the best circumstances when she died.

"Your brothers didn't come?" Aminah asked as Dee's sisters walked with her to the lower level and Tamika followed closely behind.

Aesha shook her head. "They think it's gonna be a girlish party."

Aminah laughed. "I understand."

The doorbell rang just as they sat down, but Aminah knew her mother would answer it this time. As Aminah exchanged small talk with Aesha, Tamika could hear the sound of a woman's voice coming from upstairs. A few minutes later, a young woman who appeared to be of Korean origin came downstairs. She was no more than twenty years old, Tamika guessed.

Aminah introduced her as Faatemah, and Tamika couldn't help wondering if that was her birth name. Tamika smiled as she shook the sister's hand and hugged her after the introduction, a show of affection that she learned was customary for Muslims to show to each other, even as strangers. For a moment, Tamika studied the sister. It was both strange and refreshing to see a Korean woman donned in Islamic garb. It made Tamika realize that Islam was indeed a universal religion. Tamika would have never guessed there were Muslims in Korea.

An hour later the house was filled with guests. Ismael had arrived thirty minutes before and had set up the television and VCR in the living room for his friends. He was now enjoying himself as he relaxed with the men who had come. Of course, there were not many men at the gathering since it was mainly for Tamika. The men who came were mostly friends of Ismael who had come to visit him and keep him company while the women enjoyed themselves.

It was shortly after 7:30, two hours after the party began, when the doorbell rang. There were already seventeen women there, one of whom was Lauren, and Tamika couldn't imagine there would be anyone else arriving. She was eating and chatting with the guests, trying unsuccessfully to remember everyone's name. She was engrossed in a conversation with Lauren and a sister named Rashida when Aminah interrupted them to introduce the woman who had just arrived.

Tamika sat on the futon with Lauren and Rashida on either side of her when Aminah and the woman greeted them. As Tamika's eyes met the woman's, she sensed that they wouldn't get along, but she didn't understand this feeling. Perhaps it was the way the woman studied Tamika intently, seeming to size her up—from head to toe. It was as if the sister felt an urgency to know Tamika from everything she had heard and needed to see for herself. Taken aback by the attention, Tamika too studied the woman, sensing that she too would need to know who she was.

The young woman stood about five feet seven inches, two inches taller than Tamika. She was attractively slim, which was apparent even as she wore the loose-fitting Islamic clothes. She was striking, this Tamika couldn't deny.

Her skin was a smooth chocolate brown, and her flawless complexion was accented by hazel eyes and thick eyelashes. When she smiled, her face seemed to glow as she revealed a perfect set of white teeth and a long dimple on one side of her face. Her personality seemed one of confidence, and her presence commanded respect. She was used to being in the limelight, Tamika could tell, which was confirmed by how several of the guests came to their feet to greet her with enthusiasm. The sister wore a beige colored *khimaar* with a matching button-up *abiya* and appeared sophisticated in the simple garment. Her long fingers revealed well-kept nails that, even in their natural state, appeared manicured. She laughed every few seconds it seemed, whenever someone spoke to her. It was as if her enjoyment of one's presence made all the difference in the person's worth. When Aminah introduced her as a pre-med major who would begin medical school in the fall, Tamika wasn't surprised.

Tamika smiled and shook her hand. "What's your name again?" She had missed it when Aminah said it. But Tamika was sure she wouldn't forget it this time.

The young woman laughed. "It's okay," she assured Tamika with a wave of her hand, as if Tamika's question suggested she was apologizing for forgetting her name so soon. "Aidah."

"Aidah," Tamika repeated with a nod and forced smile. "Nice to meet you."

"Nice to meet you too."

"I've heard so many good things about you," Aidah beamed, and Tamika couldn't decide how to take the compliment. "I'm so glad I got a chance to stop by and meet you in person," she said, hinting that she couldn't stay long.

Tamika grew uncomfortable and curious. Had Aminah talked about her to Aidah?

Sounds of men cheering came from upstairs, and Aminah smiled as she shook her head knowingly.

"What are they *doing*?" Aidah asked between laughs.

Aminah nudged Aidah in response and grinned as they shared a private joke. "Watching Sulayman's graduation tape." They burst into laughter, making Tamika feel like an outsider.

"Oh that," Aidah replied with a playful roll of her eyes and wave of the hand.

"Were you there?" Aminah asked more seriously a second later.

Aidah frowned apologetically. "I wanted to come, but my parents insisted I come home that weekend. It was the only weekend I had before I started my job."

Aminah nodded. "I understand."

"But you *must* tell me how you learned about Islam," Aidah said, turning her attention back to Tamika, playfully slapping her on the shoulder as if

Tamika's conversion story was the one thing that she had come this far to hear.

Tamika forced a smile, still trying to determine the significance of Aidah's presence. Why did she and Aminah seem to know each other so well? Aminah had never mentioned her. And why did Aidah apologize for not making it to Sulayman's graduation? Was she a close family friend?

Tamika told Aidah about her research paper and reading about Islam, but her mind was only half there as she spoke. Even after Aidah left, less than an hour after she had come, Tamika couldn't get her out of her mind. Shortly before Aidah left, Tamika had overheard Aidah telling Aminah she would come back later that week to watch the graduation tape.

After all the guests had gone and Sulayman and Ismael went to their bedrooms, Tamika and Aminah changed clothes and helped Sarah clean the kitchen. The last guest had gone shortly after 11:00, and it wasn't until after 1:00 in the morning that the women finally finished cleaning. Sarah retired to her room to join her husband, and Aminah and Tamika ascended the steps to prepare for bed. Both were exhausted.

As she often did before going to sleep, at least whenever Tamika didn't have class or work the next day, Aminah followed Tamika to the guestroom, where they would stay up many nights talking about whatever was on their minds. Sometimes Aminah fell asleep on Tamika's floor after the late night talks. Tamika loved waking up and finding Aminah sleeping a few feet from her bed. It made her feel like she had a sister again. After Aminah had fallen asleep in Tamika's room for a third time, Tamika had suggested Aminah keep a sleeping bag and pillow in the room. Aminah liked the idea and kept her bed rolled up in the closet. Tonight Aminah closed the door behind her after entering Tamika's room, letting Tamika know they would talk for a few minutes before going to bed.

"How did you like the party?" Aminah opened the closet to retrieve her sleeping bag and pillow.

Tamika nodded as Aminah set up her bed in the middle of the floor. "It was really nice."

Aminah smiled at her, pleased that everything had gone well. "Did you meet anybody you really liked?"

Tamika shrugged and smiled from where she stood next to her bed. "A couple of people. Rashida and Faatemah seemed nice, but I can't remember everyone's name."

"Yeah, it was a nice turn out."

Tamika watched as Aminah shook her pillow to fluff it and knelt on a knee to smooth down the surface of the sleeping bag. "Thanks so much," Tamika said sincerely. "That was really nice of your family to do that for me."

Aminah glanced up and smiled before turning her attention back to her floor bed. "It's no problem. We enjoyed it."

Tamika pulled the comforter from the bed and shook it before putting it back in place. "I appreciate everything you've done." She ran her hand over the cloth then turned to face her roommate as a half smile creased a corner of her mouth. "Really."

Aminah smiled, pulling the ponytail holder from her hair and plaiting her hair in a thick braid as she sat cross-legged on the sleeping bag facing Tamika. "You're like family to us, and we love having you here." She grinned. "It's not everyday a person gets a sister overnight."

Tamika laughed and nodded as she sat down on the edge of her bed. A smile lingered on her face as her thoughts drifted to Aidah, whom she couldn't seem to get out of her mind. She watched as Aminah finished the plait and stretched in exhaustion. Yawning, Aminah covered her mouth then rubbed the moisture from her eyes.

"You're sleepy, huh?" Tamika teased, hoping her friend wouldn't fall asleep before she could ask about Aidah.

"Yeah, I am," Aminah chuckled in agreement, barely able to complete the sentence before she yawned again.

Tamika nodded as her gaze became distant. Aminah pulled the sleeping bag over her shoulders and lay on her side with her back to her roommate. Tamika decided this was her last chance to get some answers before morning. She didn't want to put off asking, fearing any delay would suggest that the woman was more significant to her than she really was. "Who's that sister named Aidah?"

There was a long pause as Aminah lay still, her braid lying limp on the pillow behind her. Aminah's sleeping bag cover moved up and down at her shoulders with each breath, and Tamika feared Aminah had fallen asleep. But seconds later, she heard Aminah sigh in response.

"Aidah," Aminah repeated as she turned to lie on her back. She folded her hands behind her head and stared toward the ceiling in deep thought. "Well," she said with another sigh, the inquiry seeming to have made Aminah forget she was sleepy, "that's hard to say." She forced a smile and glanced momentarily at Tamika. "I guess you can call her a family friend."

"You guess?" Tamika said playfully with a chuckle.

"Well, I'll put it this way," Aminah said, deciding to be blunt. "She's someone who Sulayman is considering marrying, but if you ask her, she's his fiancée."

Tamika's eyebrows rose in surprise, taken aback by the news. "Really?" She tried to sound excited for them, but disappointment and jealously nearly suffocated her. But she found no rational reason to feel this way.

Aminah shrugged. "I guess." Tamika could tell that Aminah wasn't pleased with the arrangement.

"You don't sound excited for them," Tamika said with a grin, hoping Aminah would reveal all she knew about the woman.

Aminah was silent for some time, and Tamika could tell by Aminah's thoughtful frown that her comment had touched on a sensitive subject. "I guess I'm still getting used to the idea." The statement sounded more like a confession to herself than Tamika.

"Why's that?"

"I don't know," she said, apparently trying to make sense of her mixed feelings.

"Do you know Aidah really well?"

She forced laughter and shook her head, still staring at the ceiling. "Do you know anyone really well?"

Tamika was silent, unsure how to respond, as the comment both offended and soothed her.

"I mean, I've known her for almost a year." Aminah stopped herself then corrected, "Well, I *met* her about a year ago when Sulayman invited her over to meet us."

"Oh, so he's been serious about her for some time then?"

A corner of Aminah's mouth turned up in a grin. "I wouldn't say that. When he invited her over the first time, it was only because she was excited to meet a fellow Muslim at work and insisted on meeting his mother and sister." She raised her eyebrows thoughtfully. "At the time, I don't think he thought much of her beyond the fact that she was a Muslim sister who needed to meet other sisters. And, of course, since he had a mother and sister at home, he felt obligated."

"So they worked together?"

"Yeah, last summer."

Tamika nodded as everything began to make sense. "You like her?" It was a bold question, but she felt it was relevant.

"You mean for me or Sulayman?"

She shrugged, ashamed to say for Sulayman. "Both, I suppose."

"I like her as a person," Aminah reasoned. "She's really nice and seems like a good sister, may Allah bless her. And Allah knows best."

"Then why do you have reservations about her for your brother?"

"I don't know if I'd call it reservations," she said, hoping she wasn't confusing Tamika. "It's just difficult to imagine her as his wife."

"Why?"

Aminah smiled uncomfortably and reflected on the question before responding. Tamika could tell she had a lot on her mind and needed to talk. "I don't know. She just doesn't seem like his type."

Tamika was silent, afraid to ask what she had wondered since the drive from Milwaukee. But now would probably be her only chance. "What is his type?"

Aminah smiled, and her face glowed as she gazed toward the ceiling. Tamika could tell Aminah had spent a lot of time pondering this. "When I think of a wife for my brother, I just don't picture someone like Aidah."

"Who do you picture?" Tamika felt her voice quiver, and her heartbeat quickened.

Aminah's eyes narrowed slightly as her thoughts drifted elsewhere. She continued to smile, and when she spoke, she seemed to be talking more to herself than Tamika. It was as if she were divulging a childhood dream that only she understood. "I picture someone like him," she said, "American, raised in a Muslim home, kind of reserved and laid back, and—."

Tamika's heart sank, and she grew disinterested all of a sudden. She didn't want to hear anymore. "She's not American?" Tamika asked in a pretense of surprise, trying to conceal her disappointment with Aminah's revelation. She should have known better than to think she could fit the description.

Aminah wrinkled her forehead and glanced at Tamika. "Who, Aidah?" Apparently, Tamika's question had interrupted her train of thought.

"Yeah."

"Yeah, Aidah's American."

"Are her parents Muslim?" Tamika shocked herself with the resentment she heard in her voice.

Just then Aminah realized her mistake. She should have never mentioned the woman being raised in a Muslim home. She had offended Tamika. Aminah had been so engrossed in her thoughts that she momentarily forgot whom she was talking to. Tamika probably could care less what type of woman her brother would marry, but it was insensitive to imply that an ideal Muslim wife should be born into a Muslim family. It could be taken the wrong way.

"Yes," Aminah said reluctantly, "Aidah was born Muslim." As she studied Tamika's expression, she saw that her words had cut deep. "But that's not it," she said, hoping to downplay the significance of the description. Inside, she kicked herself for being so careless. With all of Tamika's problems, she didn't need anything else to make her feel inadequate.

Tamika nodded dumbly, now pulling the covers over her as she lay down. Aminah's voice faded in the background as Tamika's thoughts consumed her. She only half heard Aminah that night as she rambled on about what were the most important traits of a good wife in her brother's eyes. Sulayman wanted his wife to stay home with the children, love him, and make family life her primary concern, and it would be difficult to have that with a doctor. Blah, blah, blah.

Tamika's heart was heavy when she woke the next morning for the dawn prayer. Aminah had tried to strike up a conversation with her after they prayed, but Tamika wasn't interested. She made up an excuse that she was still tired from last night and wanted to sleep. Aminah slept in her own room that morning, taking the hint. Tamika wanted to be left alone.

Tamika woke in the early afternoon but spent most of the day lying in her bed consumed by her thoughts. At moments, sadness enveloped her, and she lay still, letting the silent tears slip down her cheeks and soak her pillow. She was nothing, and she would amount to nothing. She had been a fool to hope for anything more.

Late that Saturday afternoon, Aminah entered the room to ask Tamika if she wanted to join her and her mother in going out to eat. Ismael and Sulayman had gone to visit a friend, Aminah told her, and her mother thought it was a good idea if the women had a "girls' day out." Tamika turned down the offer, saying that she wasn't feeling well and would rather stay home and rest. Aminah frowned, knowing there was more to the refusal than Tamika divulged. But there was nothing Aminah could do. As much as she wanted to make up for causing Tamika's pain, she couldn't control her friend's feelings. For a moment, she considered not going out at all but then decided against it. Tamika probably could use the time alone.

Tamika heard the front door open and shut an hour later, and she lay in bed listening to the car start outside her window and its sound fade as the women drove off. Shortly after they left, Tamika gathered enough energy to get out of bed. She hadn't eaten all day, and she had begun to feel hungry.

At the kitchen table, she sat eating in silence, nibbling mindlessly on the sandwich she had prepared. Thoughts of her mother drifted into her mind, and her eyes watered until her vision became blurred. The kitchen cabinets and the vase of flowers on the table were but images in a foggy mist a second before Tamika felt the wetness of her tears drop on her cheeks. The wetness rounded the curve of her face until its coldness rested in an ear.

At first the cry was faint, but a minute later it culminated into heavy sobs that made Tamika's shoulders tremble. She let her partially eaten sandwich fall to the table as she covered her face in grief, rocking back and forth as the tears spilled down her cheeks and her sobs became horrible cries in the desolate house. All the love she felt for her mother swelled in her chest and seemed to explode at that moment.

What had she done to her life? What was she thinking when she agreed to come here? She would probably never see her mother again. She was alone. She had no one. Not Latonya, not Philip, and now not even her own mother.

When her cries quieted to sniffles and the trembling of her body steadied, Tamika shut her eyes and could almost feel the warmth of her mother's dry lips stroking her forehead with a kiss. She could feel the coziness of her mother's large arms embracing her a little too tightly whenever Tamika made her proud.

"I knew the Lord was giving me a gift," her mother had once told her about her birth. "Wasn't nothin' but a feeling," her mother said. But Thelma was sure it was a sign from God.

Tamika had internalized her mother's feeling throughout her life. She was her mother's gift, and this knowledge became her lifeline. Whenever she was down or times got hard, thinking of herself as a gift from God kept her motivated—alive.

But what did she have now? How could she go on without the only person who mattered to her?

Tamika felt like a rejected orphan, a bastard child left unwanted and unclaimed. And unloved. What was she without her family—her mother? What would become of her?

Just then Tamika realized she hadn't prayed *Thuhr*, the early afternoon prayer. For a second, she thought, what's the point? She didn't feel like praying. Wasn't it Islam that had gotten her into this mess in the first place? Why should she commit to it when it hadn't committed to her? What had it done for her, anyway, but left her alienated and estranged? Anger and resentment burned inside her as she found herself wondering what she had done to deserve this. Where was God's mercy that she had read so much about? His love?

She stopped herself. She was being irrational. Nothing justified questioning God, no matter how bad things got. Ashamed of herself, she dragged herself to the bathroom, where she prepared for prayer.

Tamika stood to pray, but she was just going through the motions. Her heart wasn't in it today. She desired less what the prayer offered than what her mother's warm presence and approval would bring. Was it really worth it to sacrifice everything for this? What was she gaining anyway?

The desire for Heaven and its eternal bliss was but a dying flame flickering in the back of her mind. Today it all seemed like a fairy tale, and for the first time in her life, she wondered if it really existed. She hated herself for thinking that way, but it was difficult to spend the rest of her life an outcast—by choice. Certainly, pleasing God amounted to more than this. Wasn't pleasing God supposed to feel good? Then why was she feeling down? She felt as if her entire world was crumbling, and she was just watching it, powerless to do anything to stop it.

After she finished praying, Tamika sat on the couch and picked up the remote control to the television that Ismael had put in the living room the night before. She pressed the power button and let the scripted world of actors and entertainers distract her from her own. As she watched the beautiful and talented laugh carelessly and solve monumental problems in less than thirty minutes, she laughed out loud, a cynical reaction to the fictitious world millions idolized.

An hour later, Tamika studied the eyes of a beautiful woman on the screen. The woman sat opposite an interviewer as she lightheartedly discussed the trials of her life. She had overcome them, finally. The actress was lying more to convince herself than the viewers, that much was obvious, but the interviewer nodded politely and listened with dutiful interest. Drugs and alcohol were behind her, and she had moved on. She had found true love after an abusive relationship that destroyed much of her career. Tamika turned the channel, where a singer danced seductively on the screen as she sang about a man she loved. On another channel, a news anchor told of the body of a teenage girl that had been found by a jogger in a park.

It was then that Tamika realized the sense of her predicament. It was a test. All of it. There was nothing to this world but a distracting parade of fading pleasures, dying love, and hope for a happiness it could never bring. The famous had reached the top but somehow represented the darkest pit of lowness life could bring. Happiness was a façade they were paid to uphold, most likely to keep them sane—from taking a gun and blowing out their brains. But some couldn't do it. They simply could not withstand it all, unable to wear the mask without confusing it with their face. They found what little solace they could in drugs, alcohol, and passionate love affairs. Their marriages fell apart. Their families fell apart. Their lives fell apart.

And they fell apart.

No one was truly happy, Tamika realized just then. They were all reaching for the intangible. How pointless it was to spend life searching for something it could never offer. The happiest were those who made the best of what they had, content that this was as good as it got. Love didn't conquer all. It didn't even conquer life. It just distracted people from it. And when love died, people were forced to stare life in the face and accept its pain and ugliness like the flesh of an infected wound that wouldn't heal.

The God-fearing, those who believed in life beyond, were the most content and at peace with life, Tamika pondered. They could stare into the eye of a storm and see a flicker of light. But it wasn't that life brought any contentment or promise of peace that gave them this succor—because it brought none. It was the knowledge that there was something beyond this life that gave them the little solace they had. They didn't want death anymore than the worldly.

The irony was, no matter how painful life was, people clung to what they knew before they would face what they didn't. But it brought the soul tranquility to know that, when it met its fate, there was hope beyond. That was when all the patience and faith would finally win through. Delayed gratification, some would call it. But gratification nonetheless. It was better to take a stab at getting what would really last than to throw yourself into what could never.

No one could escape the bumps and bruises of life, Tamika realized as she sat before the television. How true was the saying, if it wasn't one thing, it was another. So pick your battles, people advised. But no, that could bring only partial relief. Life wasn't a gourmet menu. It didn't always give you a choice. So you could pick your battles, but it took more strength to accept the ones thrown your way.

Tamika wouldn't be avoiding sadness to give up what she believed. She wouldn't be winning a battle if she quit now. She would be facing yet another, one she was less equipped to win. How could there be any victories when your opponent was your soul? How could there be any solace when the One who granted it was the one you rejected?

It seemed like a simple solution to give her mother what she wanted. But if Tamika did, there was one obvious question. What of what *she* wanted? Was it fair that her mother demanded personal happiness through flesh other than her own? If Tamika were to be her mother's vehicle of life's contentment, what would be Tamika's? Yes, pleasing her mother did hold some weight, even God's laws attested to this. For obedience to parents was necessary to submission to God. But that obedience stopped short of the soul.

The soul was owned by God alone, and its authority on the earth was granted only to the one whose body enclosed it. No, she wouldn't surrender hers to one who knew little of her own. Her mother lived a life of religious tradition passed down to her from her parents, and she believed only what she had been taught. Thelma's blind obedience to her parents convinced her that all parent-child relationships were supposed to be like that. All give and no take. The role of the parent was to teach and demand, and the role of the child was to accept and obey. There was no wisdom or beneficial knowledge unless it was passed from parent to child. The child was just that, a child. Nothing good could come from her unless she accepted this fact in life. Years of experience by the child meant nothing unless it led her to what her parents taught. Years of seeing by the child's own eyes wasn't truly seeing unless it led to seeing what her parents' eyes saw. Years of learning meant nothing unless it led to revelations that were already in the parents' minds.

To Thelma, the child was a blank slate, an empty container waiting to be filled. And none could fill it except the parents. Those who disagreed with parents were akin to those who opposed God. The world was full of enemies except those who were the parents' friends. The world was full of the ignorant except those who agreed with what the parents believed. The world was full of heathens except those who saw religion as their parents did.

An attempt by the child to share what she learned was proof that the child was still a fool. If she shared something she thought could benefit them, it was an affront of vicious proportions, and it was forgiven only by the child realizing she had been a fool to attempt such an impossible task. There was nothing she could share unless it was to share what her parents had shared with her. Knowledge was only knowledge if it was what the parents already knew. Right was only right if the parents didn't see it as wrong. And living one's own life was truly life only if it was one the parents themselves would have lived. The child could love her parents with all her heart, but that love was not appreciated—or reciprocated—unless she gave up her life for theirs.

As Tamika sat on the couch staring at the television screen, her eyes fell upon the VCR that it sat on. It was then that she remembered the men's laughter from the night before. They had been watching Sulayman's graduation tape. She had often wondered how his speech had gone. Feeling slightly guilty for her curiosity, Tamika stood and walked over to the set and pressed the eject button on the VCR to see if the tape was still there. The machine spit out the tape, and the handwriting across the front label revealed that it was indeed the one. She pulled it out and held it up to see if it needed rewinding. Someone had rewound it already, and Tamika suspected this was in preparation for Aidah's viewing. Tamika gently pushed the tape back into the machine and watched as it was pulled and clicked in place. She paused before pressing play and returning to where she had been sitting. Hugging a pillow and sitting with her legs folded in front of her on the couch, Tamika's heart pounded as she watched the screen.

Tamika smiled beside herself as she saw Sulayman laughing childishly and waving his hand toward the camera. A second later her smile faded as she realized her insignificance in his life. She had once childishly wondered how it would feel to be a part of his family. But now she knew that was impossible.

With painful distance, Tamika watched him parade in with the other graduates before finally taking his seat of honor on the stage. He sat down and greeted an older white man who sat near him, and he laughed at something the man said.

Tamika realized then that there was no room for her in his life. He belonged to a world of dignity and honor that she would never know. Those like him were admired by many and envied by more. Thousands, if not millions, longed to be so significant to be noticed by people as distinguished as he. Tamika was like a fan whose highest hopes lay in taking home a signature on a scrap of paper as testimony that he had paused to sign it for her.

The night before, Aminah confirmed for Tamika what she should have already known. Sulayman and people of his nobility had an insurmountable level of piety that had graced them at birth. They were those born to the immaculately pious families, ones for whom sin and, most certainly, disbelief in God had never played a role. Tamika, on the other hand, belonged to the tainted, who had found grace only after falling from it. She could hope for only crumbs that she would be fortunate enough to catch from their royal table. She was like the beggar at the king's door, the one whom the king welcomed into his palace only to convince himself that he was a noble king.

The noble king fed the hungry and sheltered the homeless like noble men did. But when the beggar settled in the coziness of the palace and enjoyed the king's friendship for one too many nights, he mistook the kindness to mean that he was somehow the king's equal, separated only by an unfortunate financial barrier that fate had delivered. When the beggar's eyes were graced with the beauty of the king's daughter and, in his awe, announced his desire to marry her, the king and his princess could only giggle at the childish innocence of the visitor and pity him so.   The king would then rub the beggar's head to reassure him that he still loved him and would feed him yet another meal.   But a day later, the beggar would be back on the cold streets, home once again.

Through memories alone would the beggar taste royalty.   And it would be in the cold of the streets that he would stand among his kind.   Their dirty faces and ragged clothes would be their only possessions as they watched the darling princess on her wedding day.   She would be carried off by one worthy of her hand, a prince of royal blood who had grown up eating from silver spoons like she.

But then there was that sincerity and humility that Tamika thought she saw in Sulayman's eyes as she watched the tape.   As he spoke, she couldn't help but wonder if he was different, unlike the rest—royal blood with a beggar's heart.   Perhaps when he stood on his royal balcony and gazed down at the people of the world, he saw hearts and not the flesh that enclosed them—or the family in which they had been born.   Maybe he enjoyed the simplicities of life, unmoved by the parade of badges worn by those who lived like he.   Grace was no less grace if it had been preceded by a fall.   Perhaps the fall only enhanced the grace in his eyes.   He was impressed, perhaps, that one could pull herself up after falling pitifully low and stand tall with the most respectable, despite her past.   Maybe it was admirable to see one choose the path of struggle and sacrifice when the path of ease and pleasure was within her reach.

The words of his speech suggested that his nobility was more than skin deep.   His royalty was merely circumstance, and his heart was with the weak. As he talked, Tamika found herself contemplating the weight of his words. Wasn't that his message, to look beyond the obvious?   Look beyond the one cloaked in black cloth, and open your eyes to that which only the wise could see.   Those endowed with wisdom didn't see an oppressed woman hiding behind a veil.   They saw a woman who valued her liberty in self-expression and her choice to worship God.   To the wise, one whom the ignorant viewed as opposing good was in truth upholding it more than they.   If you believe in equality and freedom, then why do you deny her hers?   Were we so arrogant to think that the right to equality and freedom belonged only to those like us? Were we so ignorant to think a threat to civilized society could be detected by one's clothes?   Were we so un-American that we felt that the right to freedom of expression belonged only to those we chose?

Thirteen

The week came with the same slowness that the weekend had dragged on. Continuing her excuse that she wasn't feeling well, Tamika avoided facing anyone except when she had to go the bathroom or eat. She didn't go to any of her Qur'an or Arabic classes that week, and she called in sick at work. She wasn't in the mood to see anyone and wear a mask of happiness when she was drowning within.

Aidah stopped by Wednesday evening to pick up the tape, which she decided to watch at home. The sight of her only worsened Tamika's already gloomy state. Aidah had tried to strike up a conversation when Tamika happened to pass her and Aminah in the living room. Fortunately, Aminah explained to her friend that Tamika wasn't feeling well, relieving Tamika of the awkwardness of having to talk to the last person she needed to right then.

When Tamika's menses came early Thursday morning, her pretence of not feeling well finally met reality. Her abdominal cramps were more painful than usual, and she felt more nauseated than she remembered ever feeling during this time of month. To make matters worse, all of this was accompanied by a migraine headache that didn't break until late that night. She had taken medicine all day, and it finally paid off after 11:00 that night. Feeling well all of a sudden gave her renewed energy, and she didn't know what to do with herself. She no longer wanted to stay in her room, feeling suffocated by the four walls. She heard Aminah talking to someone downstairs, and she wondered if a friend was visiting.

The sound of the phone ringing shrilled throughout the house, and Tamika wondered if it was Aidah for Sulayman. Tamika didn't know whether or not it was a coincidence, but Aidah called the house frequently since they met. Apparently, Aidah viewed her as competition. Tamika wanted to laugh out loud at the ridiculous perception. The thought of her actually being a threat to Aidah's marriage to Sulayman was painfully amusing. *Don't worry*, Tamika assured Aidah in her mind. *I'm no competition next to the likes of you.* A soft knock at the door interrupted her thoughts as she slipped her arms into the *abiya* she planned to wear downstairs.

"It's Aminah," Tamika heard before she could ask who it was.

"Come in," Tamika called as she pushed the top buttons through their holes, no longer upset with Aminah.

"The phone." Aminah stepped inside and handed Tamika the cordless telephone.

Tamika creased her forehead. Who could possibly be calling her at this hour? But Aminah's expression was without emotion. She wore only a forced smile, the signs of emotional stress detectable behind her dutiful politeness. It was then that Tamika realized she wasn't the only one who was hurting. Apparently, Aminah had been deeply affected by Tamika's withdrawal and likely blamed herself. Tamika wanted to hug her and say she wasn't upset. But she wasn't ready to admit why she had taken the comment so hard. She imagined that if she avoided facing her feelings, they would eventually go away.

Tamika accepted the phone and started to say something to her friend. But Aminah disappeared from the room and closed the door before Tamika had a chance to speak. Tamika frowned, feeling bad all of sudden. She shouldn't have treated Aminah like she had.

Tamika's mind was still on Aminah when she put the phone to her ear. "Hello?"

"*As-salaamu-'alaikum*," a deep voice greeted her, and Tamika's heart skipped a beat.

"*Wa-'alaiku-mus-salaam*," she said in cautious curiosity, her mind racing as she tried to figure out who this was and why he was calling.

"I'm sorry to call so late," he said, as if they knew each other, "but when you weren't in class for the past few days, I got worried and wanted to make sure you were alright."

She calmed a bit as she realized it was just Omar. "I'm fine, *alhamdulillaah*," she said as she ran her hand across her hair and glanced around the room for her *khimaar*. "I wasn't feeling well, but I started feeling better tonight."

"I'm glad to hear that."

It was nice of him to call, Tamika thought as she saw her *khimaar* lying on her dresser and walked over to it. For the first time since she met him, she was happy to hear his voice. She picked up the white cloth and searched her mind for a response but couldn't decide what to say.

"Are you coming back next week?" he asked.

"Yes, *inshaAllaah*."

"Then I'll make a copy of the notes and drop 'em off for you tomorrow after *Jumuah*, *inshaAllaah*." He paused. "Or I'll just give the notes to Sulayman if he doesn't go anywhere else for prayer."

"I appreciate it. May Allah reward you."

"May He reward you too."

There was an awkward silence. "Well, I'm not gonna keep you," he said. "I just wanted to make sure you were okay. *InshaAllaah*, I'll see you on Monday."

Before Tamika could reply, he gave her the Islamic greetings and hung up. For a second she listened to the dial tone buzzing in her ear, still getting over what had just happened. She then pressed the button to hang up the phone. Maybe Omar wasn't so bad after all.

Tamika was still reflecting on the conversation as she held up the *khimaar* to survey it for wrinkles when the phone rang in her other hand. Expecting it to be Omar calling back, Tamika answered on the first ring. "Hello?" she said calmly, trying to conceal her excitement as a smile creased a corner of her mouth. When a woman's voice greeted her, her heart sank, and she mumbled a reply.

"Is this Tamika?" the woman said, her voice rising in pleasure to hear Tamika's voice.

"Yes," Tamika said tentatively, searching her mind for who it could be. The voice sounded familiar, but she couldn't put a face with the name.

"Are you feeling better?"

Tamika groaned, realizing just then who it was. "Yes," she said, growing impatient with the exchange. She rolled her eyes in relief when Aidah finally asked to speak to whom she had called for in the first place.

"Hold on please," Tamika said with feigned politeness. She rolled her eyes again as she removed the phone from her ear and held it in a hand at her side. She drew in a deep breath and exhaled and felt her nostrils flare in irritation before setting the phone on top of her dresser. She placed the cloth over her head and pinned it under her chin. She picked up the phone again and left the room to go downstairs.

Aminah was in the kitchen cleaning as Sulayman sat at the table when Tamika appeared in the doorway. Upon seeing her, Aminah walked toward her roommate to see what she wanted.

"The phone's for Sulayman." She handed the phone to Aminah. If Tamika hadn't been hungry, she would have gone upstairs right then. But instead, she walked over to the refrigerator to survey its contents for something to eat.

"Find out who it is," Sulayman said to his sister, glancing at his watch. He obviously wasn't in the mood to talk to anyone this late.

Tamika pulled some Kosher hotdogs from the refrigerator and proceeded to prepare her small meal.

"It's Aidah," Aminah said after asking who it was.

Instinctively, Tamika glanced in his direction to see what his reaction would be. To her surprise, he appeared disappointed and shook his head.

"Take a message. It's eleven thirty at night."

Shrugging, Aminah asked if she could take a message. As she listened to what Aidah was saying, she laughed and nodded in polite response, assuring Aidah that it was okay. After she hung up the phone, she met her brother's questioning gaze and shrugged again.

"She just finished watching the tape," Aminah said with disinterest. "And she says she was really proud of you and wanted to call to say congratulations."

The siblings looked at each other for a few more seconds, wearing half smiles on their faces before shaking their heads as if neither understood the significance of the call. The three resumed their activities in silence, and when Tamika finished preparing her hotdog, she carried her plate to her room, where she planned to relax and eat. Part of her wanted to stay in the kitchen to get a break from her room, but she knew better than to invite herself to sit with Sulayman and his sister.

Late Sunday night Tamika was reviewing the Arabic notes that Omar had sent home with Sulayman on Friday when a knock at the door disrupted her concentration. Knowing it was Aminah, she called to her to come in. Aminah entered a second later and shut the door behind her before taking a seat on the edge of the bed near where Tamika sat.

"How's it going?" Aminah asked with a friendly smile.

Tamika looked up long enough to return the smile then resumed reviewing her notes. "Pretty good, you?"

"Pretty good."

There was a long pause as Tamika read the rules of writing a definite and indefinite Arabic noun, and Aminah sat silently, apparently trying to gather her thoughts.

"Tamika," Aminah said finally, her tone soft yet serious. "I really want to thank you for taking the time to talk to me last Friday."

Tamika paused from her studying and looked in Aminah's direction, but for some reason she couldn't bring herself to smile. "No problem."

"It really made me realize how much I needed to talk to someone to sort out my feelings."

Tamika nodded as she resumed reviewing the Arabic notes, afraid to meet Aminah's gaze. She didn't want to relive the week's stress.

"Talking to you gave me the courage to tell Sulayman what I was thinking." Aminah paused as Tamika met her gaze with a shocked expression. "So whatever he decides," she shrugged, "at least he knows what I really think."

Tamika forced a smile. "I'm glad I could be of help." She hoped she sounded as sincere as she wanted to be.

"It was more than help," Aminah said with a grin. "It was relief."

"So you talked to him about it?" Tamika tried to sound as if she wanted this conversation.

Aminah nodded. "Yeah."

"So what'd he say?"

She lifted a shoulder in a shrug. "He was glad I talked to him."

Tamika nodded thoughtfully. "So it's over?" Her eyes reviewed the words on the page, feigning disinterest in the inquiry.

"You mean with Aidah?"

"Yeah."

Aminah shook her head thoughtfully. "I can't say for sure." She added after a moment's consideration, "I'm not even sure I want it to be over. But after talking to him, I can tell it put some things on his mind." She shrugged again. "I guess that's all I wanted, no matter what he decides."

Tamika nodded, suddenly wondering when Aminah would leave. She wasn't in the mood to discuss someone else's happiness when she would taste none.

"And I wanted to apologize," Aminah said a few seconds later.

Knowing what she was referring to, Tamika paused what she was doing and listened in silence to what Aminah would say. She let her gaze fall on the pen that lay next to her notebook on her lap.

"When I said that about Sulayman's ideal wife being born Muslim," she said, begging forgiveness with her tone, "I wasn't thinking. I guess my mind was on how Sulayman and I grew up. And since that was our circumstance, I guess I assumed it should be the circumstance for his wife." She forced laughter. "I know it sounds funny, but the woman being born Muslim wasn't so much a requirement in my mind as it was an assumption. I never even thought much of it, until that night. When I shared what I said with Sulayman, he questioned my logic. That's when I realized that my thoughts were a baseless fairytale.

"He told me that life was much more complex than my concept allowed," Aminah shared with a reflective smile. "He said that Allah gave each person different strengths and weaknesses, different trials and struggles, so much so that one's left to wonder if there is any such thing as ideal at all."

Tamika lifted her gaze to Aminah as she listened, wondering at Sulayman's thoughts and intrigued by his point of view.

Aminah shook her head knowingly as she apparently realized that everything her brother had said made sense. "He said there are only two possibilities when it came to a mate for marriage. Either the person is right for you or they're not." She laughed at her ignorance. "And it's true. He was saying, think about it."

As Aminah went on, Tamika realized that her roommate was repeating the conversation more for her benefit than Tamika's. It was as if Aminah was still trying to make sense of it herself.

"When you say ideal," Aminah said with a grin, "what is it really but a bunch of baseless images of perfection balled up in one person? Rarely do these images of 'ideal' ever exist in reality. And even if they did, your belief that a person is ideal just makes it that much harder for you when you see their faults. So, when you think of ideal, if you make the mistake to think it should exist in real life, then you are bound to never benefit from what's truly ideal for you."

Had Sulayman said all that? It was as if he took Tamika's scattered thoughts and confused feelings and organized them neatly into words. What could she say? He was right.

"I'm not asking you to forget what I said," Aminah said finally, "and I'm not saying I don't think like that anymore. I just want you to forgive me, despite all that." She sighed. "I don't have all the answers, and I want you to know that I know I don't."

Tamika nodded, but her mind was still on the weight of Sulayman's words.

"I've been Muslim all my life," Aminah said, "but there are some basic things that I still haven't quite grasped. But that's not to say I don't think differently than I did a week ago, because I do. But I'd be fooling myself to think that just because I realize I was wrong automatically means all remnants of my feelings have been erased from my heart." She sighed again. "I just want you to forgive me, that's all. And I'm really sorry."

At first Tamika didn't respond, taking a few minutes to let the words sink in. How could she *not* forgive Aminah? Aminah had done so much for her. Tamika couldn't continue being upset with her friend. But she couldn't deny that it was much more difficult to deal with a person's actual faults than to merely know she had them. But everyone was human and thus prone to error. And, as Tamika had read once, the best humans were those who repented from their inevitable mistakes.

So no, it wasn't the absence of faults that made one human better than another, she reflected, but the constant striving to overcome them. But the best people didn't only race to seek God's forgiveness. They overlooked and forgave in others what they wanted overlooked and forgiven in themselves.

Hadn't Aminah accepted Tamika for who she was? Tamika had not been the kindest person to Aminah when they first met, but Aminah stayed by her side and was patient with her despite that. Perhaps what made it difficult to accept Aminah's faults was that Tamika had never been convinced that she had any. Of course, in theory she knew Aminah was imperfect, but she never really believed it. Tamika knew that many others thought of Aminah similarly, and she imagined it was a difficult image to uphold. Perhaps it wasn't an image Aminah even wanted to uphold. When a person was held up to a standard higher than even she could reach, it took only one small mistake to send her toppling down. Because her entire worth had been based on something she could never possess. Seeking perfection was not a goal, Tamika realized just then, but a distraction from it. Seeking such would inevitably tire the motivated and weaken the strong—because it was only a matter of time before they realized their desire could never be.

Tamika forgave Aminah and let her know she understood. Tamika had done a lot of thinking herself, she told Aminah, and realized that, although she couldn't help feeling offended, she shouldn't have allowed it to cut so deep. Perhaps it was the feeling that everything was coming down on her at once that made her so prone to hurt, she said. After losing the last of her family and leaving the only home she had known, she wasn't strong enough to bear much more.

Their talk ended with a long embrace. Tamika and Aminah held each other in silence, enjoying the comfort of a mutual love born from true friendship and strengthened because they had survived, despite the odds—and despite the loss of one beloved to them both. It was then that Tamika realized she hadn't lost her family but had merely found another.

Fourteen

One Sunday night Tamika lay awake with her hands folded behind her head reflecting on the past two months. The window that hung over the dresser was open with a fan propped in it blowing in the warm night air and circulating it throughout the room in a gentle humming that caused the papers of her notebook to rattle. Ismael had started turning off the air at night, and Tamika began sleeping under a thin sheet or no cover at all, if it got hot enough. Tonight she lay in a thin cotton pink T-shirt and faded black shorts she found tucked away in one of the drawers. They would be her pajamas for the night. The sound of laughter rose from Aminah's room across the hall, and she heard Sulayman say something before laughing himself.

Tamika bit her lower lip, feeling distant from the siblings right then. So much had changed in the short time that it was difficult to comprehend. At moments she was content living with Aminah's family and enjoying their generosity. At others she felt disconnected and in limbo. Certainly, she couldn't live with them forever. What would she do next summer if she were still at odds with her mother? Would she live with Aminah again? It was a comfortable situation, perhaps too comfortable, to have a roof over her head, food to eat, and a ride wherever she needed to go. It was so comfortable living with the Ali family that she often forgot it wouldn't last forever. When Tamika reminded herself of this simple fact, she realized she would have to reconcile with her mother eventually, and it was better sooner than later.

Tamika had been tempted to call her mother on several occasions, but each time she stopped herself. What would she say to her mother? What would her mother say to her? She wondered if her mother would even be happy to hear from her and if she was still upset. Would they discuss religion? Could Tamika be a part of the family again?

If anything were to happen, Tamika would have to initiate it. That much she knew. For one, her mother had no idea where she was. Even if she had, Tamika doubted her mother would call first. Her mother wasn't one to appear weak, no matter what the price. Besides, from her mother's point of view, Tamika had inflicted the wound, so why should she seek to heal it?

Why did her mother have to be so difficult? Why couldn't she be normal and accept Tamika for who she was and give her the right to believe as she chose? What ever happened to family values, respect—love? Was *this* what it meant to have a family? Certainly, all families didn't behave like this when a child made her own decisions. There had to be parents out there who valued their children more than themselves.

It would be an insane world if all parents disowned their children when they didn't live as they told them, Tamika thought. How many children *ever* lived as their parents wanted? Someone had to let go. Should it be the child?

Then what of her rights to her own soul? What of her rights to live life as she believed? What of her life itself? Was a child's life to be merely an extension of the parents'?

No, it couldn't be. God didn't create humans to serve their parents. He created them to serve Him. Honoring, respecting, and obeying parents were definitely among life's virtues. But they were not its goal. The goal of life was to leave the earth having pleased the One who put you on it. Pleasing parents was virtuous only if it didn't interfere with pleasing God. But what was to be done when parents didn't see it that way? Or worse, what should one do when parents defined God's pleasure different from their child? There had to be understanding. There had to be compromise. There had to be a solution.

But no one should have to give up her soul.

Tamika sat up and glanced at the clock. It was just after 9:30. Her mother would most likely be awake. She left the bed and dressed quickly before going downstairs to get the phone. When she returned to her room, she stripped to her T-shirt and shorts and tossed her outer garment and *khimaar* to her bed. She took a deep breath before she dialed the number to her home.

The reality of what she was doing didn't hit her until the phone began to ring in her ear. It was then that Tamika realized her mother, her *mother*, could pick up the phone any second. Her heart pounded so forcefully that it hurt. She loved her mother more than she could bear, more than she could understand. She trembled. What her mother thought *did* matter to her, and her mother's opinion of life *would* influence how she lived her own. And her mother's displeasure would indeed tear her apart.

It felt like eternity as she stood there in fear, fear that her mother would pick up and fear that she would not. When the ringing stopped abruptly, she froze. What should she do? The sound of her mother's hello both soothed and terrified her. She started to speak but could not. When her mother said hello again, Tamika felt panic in her chest. If she didn't speak now, she might never have another chance. But what would she say? What *could* she say to the woman on the other line? She could never put into words how the love burned inside her. She could never find the words to express how she appreciated the companionship over the years. Tamika wanted to scream, *I love you!* But she couldn't find her voice.

"M-m-mom," Tamika said in a horrible pleading whine that escaped her throat. The mere sound of the word *Mom* put Tamika's heart in a frenzy, and she struggled to catch her breath. She swallowed but found herself getting choked up. Tears welled in her eyes, and her body weakened. She was willing to submit to whatever her mother wanted. If she could only have her back.

Tamika stiffened. The click in her ear was like a knife being jabbed into her chest. The pain was immeasurable as she stood in silence, in utter disbelief. The dial tone was the sound of a heart gone dead. And Tamika was powerless to revive it.

She hung up the phone only seconds later and stood speechless in her shock, her hand weakly grasping the dead phone. A moment later the reality of what just happened enflamed her with anger, then regret. Her legs weakened beneath her, and she fell to her bed as tears spilled from her eyes, the phone now lying face up a few feet from her on the blanket. Each tear was blood escaping from a gaping wound in her heart. Heavy sobs overtook her and exhausted her still more.

When she was too weak to cry anymore, anger swept over her like a storm. How cruel! Was this a woman who loved her child? Never, never, *ever* would Tamika treat her child this way. Oh, how she understood Latonya and Philip right then! They had been right all along. Their mother was stubborn, selfish, and heartless. How Tamika wished she could talk to her sister or brother at that moment. They would understand her pain. Her rage. *But where were they?* If her mother had even half of a human's heart, Tamika would know at least that.

Aunt Jackie would know where they were, Tamika thought, her damp eyes falling on the phone. She wiped her face free of tears and picked up the cordless. Not knowing where else to turn, Tamika dialed her aunt.

Her aunt had always been more understanding than her mother. She was the only one who gave Tamika any clues about her father. She would be the one to talk to Tamika, to encourage her when her mother wouldn't. Aunt Jackie often voiced how she disagreed with how her sister raised her children. She felt it unfair that Latonya and Philip had been estranged from the family. Families stuck together, no matter what, her aunt contended. They didn't break apart because of problems. They grew closer together. Everybody made mistakes, she would remind her sister. Even she had made the same mistake Latonya had, so why treat her so coldly? If she were not careful, Jackie had warned once, she would wake up one day and have none of her children in her life.

When her aunt picked up the phone, Tamika's heart nearly burst with the need to let loose her anguish. Like a baby, Tamika cried fresh tears as the intense honesty of her words struck her. Between angry sobs and relentless complaints, she told her aunt of how her mother hung up on her without a word. She whined. What had she ever done to deserve this? Why was her own mother treating her this way? Did she have a heart? What was wrong with just talking to your own daughter?

Jackie listened in silence as her niece vented. The words were less a revelation than a confirmation. She had known for some time that this moment would come. Thelma always had an iron fist, and her heart was no less hard. She had to have things her way, and not even her own children could change that. Growing up with Thelma had been difficult for Jacqueline, who had put up with her younger sister's stubborn ways too long.

When Thelma got pregnant with the twins, she sucked it up and pretended to be happy. Craig tried to lend a hand, but Thelma wouldn't let him. Jackie could see right through her sister, who was as scared as hell Craig would leave her after she had the children. So Thelma braced herself for the worst, never realizing that her treatment of the children's father was no less than laying the bricks for a self-fulfilling prophecy. If he wanted to buy anything for her, she would rush to get it herself. If he wanted to drive her anywhere, she would find someone else. If he offered his advice, she took someone else's. He would leave her one day, Thelma had figured, may as well prepare now. But no matter how many walls she built around her, there was a soft spot in her heart for that man, this Jackie had seen.

So when Thelma was pregnant again less than a year after the twins were born, Jackie wasn't surprised. But then Thelma was back to her old self again, pretending like Craig didn't exist. There was an argument each time he wanted to even touch the children. Thelma had told him many times that she didn't need a man to run after her. She could stand on her own two feet. She didn't need his "hand-outs." She could manage on her own.

Jackie supposed it never occurred to her sister that Craig would one day let her do just that. He was different from most eighteen-year-olds of his time. He actually wanted to be a part of his children's lives. He even wanted to marry Thelma, at least that's what he told Jackie. He had asked her advice on how to propose. Jackie had told him to just do it. Thelma hated productions. If he was going to get her hand in marriage, he shouldn't think about it too much. He should just go for it. And go for it, he did. Jackie never knew exactly what happened after that, but shortly after the proposal, he was gone. And they never saw him again.

"I ain't gonna lie to you, child," Jackie spoke so abruptly that Tamika was taken aback by the sound of her voice. "I don't support what you done anymore than your mother. It was a childish, *foolish* thing to turn your back on the religion God gave you."

As much as Jackie hated what Thelma had done to her children, she hated Tamika more for what she had done to her mother. If there was anything Thelma couldn't handle, it was a heathen child. It was almost better for Tamika to have come home pregnant than to come home without Christ. If Tamika wasn't as young and naïve as she was, Jackie would have given her the same treatment her mother had. But Tamika didn't need to be ignored. And she didn't need to be estranged. That would only push her farther away. She needed some guidance and good, no-nonsense advice.

Tamika listened to the cold words in disbelief. She was too shocked to speak. The moisture of her tears was still on her face, but her crying had ceased.

"I pray you find Christ again in your life," Jackie said. "'Cause he's the only way you'll be able to stand again. The pain you feel right now is 'cause you turned your back on him. Ain't no sense in expectin' the Lord to deliver you when you don't want what he gives.

"Everybody ain't got a mother who cares about 'em like Thelma cares for you. She gave everything up for you so you can have an education and make somethin' of yo'self. Now, I 'on't agree wit' all she does, but that don't give you no right to do what you done. You should be ashamed of yo'self, calling here like the world done you wrong. If you want love, then you gotta show it first. And ain't no better place to start than wit' the one who died for you. Don't make no sense how you can sell yo'self out for some nonsense you read in a college class. The faithful got more sense than that.

"So if you think I'm gonna side wit' you, you wrong. You ain't the only one with feelings. Thelma's got 'em too. Naw, I don't understand 'em all the time, and I sure as hell don't agree wit' 'em all the time. But one thing I know is, that woman loves you more than she loved anybody. That's why she so upset. You think you gonna just throw away everything that shaped you and be able to call her and sweet talk?" She huffed. "Don't work like that, not in the real world. You gotta a lot o' nerve, child, a lot o' nerve."

"H-h-h-ow could you say that?" Tamika said in an angry whisper.

Jackie huffed again. "I'll let you figure that out."

There was a long pause, and the shock Tamika felt hammered an aching in her head.

"You got anything else you need to get off your chest, child?"

"Latonya and Philip were right," she hissed, hoping every word would sting her aunt's ears. She wanted someone to feel the pain she felt.

"Yeah, they were," Jackie said with a burst of cruel laughter. "*You* the one who's wrong. If you want their sympathy, call 'em and see how much you get."

"What's that supposed to mean?"

"Why don't you find out for yourself?"

Tamika gritted her teeth. "If I had a mother who gave a care about anybody but herself, maybe I would know where they were so I *could* find out."

Jackie laughed again, but it sounded like a cough. "You ever think to *ask* where they were? Ain't no secret where your sister and brother are. Your momma don't gotta report nothin' to you."

"I wouldn't waste my time asking."

"Then I guess you know why you didn't spend no time knowing."

Tamika wanted to throw the phone against the wall in her fury, wishing her aunt could feel the pain of the impact where she was. Was there *anywhere* Tamika could turn?

"Where are they?" Tamika said as if her aunt was holding them captive in her basement.

Jackie chuckled and huffed a second before she responded. "Your sister and brother are in Chicago. You can look 'em up yo'self."

A second later, Tamika heard a dial tone in her ear.

It was several days before Tamika mustered up enough courage to look up her brother and sister. She had spent so much time stressing over their feelings about her that she had almost forgotten she could find out herself. She feared her aunt was right. Maybe Latonya and Philip would turn away from her too. From the way her aunt made it sound, they already knew of her conversion. Had her aunt called to tell them? Had her mother?

Bracing herself for a long, drawn out search, Tamika sat at Aminah's computer one night after her classes and logged onto the Internet. She planned to be up half the night looking for her sister and brother's number. When she searched their names under a people search, she was surprised to find several listings for a Latonya Douglass in Chicago. Some of the listings had a man's name listed along with it carrying the same last name. Since none were Philip, she deduced that none were her sister. She wrote down the remaining five numbers and disconnected the Internet.

Tamika sat on the floor in her room calmly dialing each number, not caring how late it was. She didn't expect to reach Latonya, but she hoped she would. Two of the numbers were disconnected, and one was definitely the wrong number. An old woman had answered the phone and had no idea who Tamika was, and there was no Latonya who lived there. If the remaining two numbers were wrong too, she would have no idea what to do. She dialed one of them and sat listening to the phone ring over and over in her ear. When the ringing stopped, Tamika's heart raced. A moment later an answering machine picked up. Soft music played followed by a man's voice prompting her to leave a message. She was about to hang up when she figured, why not? If it was the wrong number, there was no harm in leaving a message. If Latonya lived there, she would call back. If she didn't, she wouldn't. Tamika kept her message brief and hung up after repeating her phone number a second time. Then she dialed the last number. After one ring, the voice mail picked up. It was the standard computerized recording that repeated the number and prompted the caller to leave a message. Figuring she may as well, Tamika left a similar message and hung up. She stood and stretched, doubtful that any of the numbers were correct.

It was late one Thursday night when she returned from her classes, nearly two weeks after she made the phone calls, that Aminah told her that someone had called for her. The woman didn't want to leave a message but said she would call back later that night. Tamika was wild with excitement. Could it have been Latonya? When it was almost 11:00, Tamika feared her sister would never call again.

Tamika went downstairs to get the cordless phone and carried it to her room. Retrieving the two numbers she had saved, she dialed the first one without taking time to consider being nervous. It was the number that had a male's voice on the answering machine. She doubted it was Latonya's home, but something told her it could be. Even in college, it wasn't uncommon for women to ask the male students to leave their voice on the answering machine. Sometimes it was a boyfriend who left the greeting. Other times, it was a friend who enjoyed the idea that his voice would pick up anytime the woman wasn't home.

After the second ring, someone answered.

"Hello?" The woman sounded irritated, and the sound of a baby crying in the background created a distant commotion that assured Tamika she had called the wrong house. She didn't recognize the woman's voice, but she was too embarrassed to hang up. What if the woman lived with her sister?

"Yes, um, hello. My name is Tamika, and I was trying to reach La—."

"Tamika, girl! Is that you?" Suddenly, the voice transformed from one of strangeness to one of vague familiarity. Latonya sounded much older than she should have.

"Latonya?" Tamika's heart raced in excitement.

"Girl, I called you at that number you left, and you wasn't even home."

"Yeah, I know," she laughed. "I was in class. I'm sorry."

"You 'on't need to be sorry 'bout nothin', girl. You takin' care o' business like you should."

There was a brief pause. "Tyrone! Tyrone!"

The sound of her sister calling for whoever Tyrone was startled Tamika and made her pull the phone away from her ear to protect it from the loudness. Latonya's voice became irritated again, and her yelling made the baby scream louder. "Ty-*rone!*"

Tamika didn't know what to do except wait patiently until Tyrone answered her sister. She felt awkward, as if she were overhearing more than she should.

"Nikki, girl, take dat baby to Tyrone and tell him to shut 'im up. And get his bottle out o' the fridge." A few seconds later, there was a loud banging sound that Tamika assumed to be a door closing. A moment later the crying became muffled in the background. After a groan, Latonya apologized. "I swear dat nigga get on my nerves."

Tamika stiffened, thinking her sister was referring to the child, but as her sister spoke, she realized she was talking about Tyrone. "He act like he ain't gotta do nothin' for his child 'cept go to da store when he feel like it." She sucked her teeth. "I'm 'bout tired o' his sh-, mess," she quickly corrected herself, apparently out of respect for Tamika.

"Girl, I'm sorry," Latonya apologized again for the interruption.

"It's okay." Tamika wished she had called at another time. "I'm sorry for calling so late."

Latonya let out such a thunderous laugh that it took a second for Tamika to realize her sister was laughing at what she said. "Don't nobody sleep 'round here. You can call whenever you want, and if we sleep, we 'on't even hear the phone."

Tamika was so taken aback by her sister's hectic life that she momentarily forgot the conversation was the first they had since she graduated from high school. Her head pounded with questions and confusion. Was the baby Latonya's? Who was Tyrone?

"I know this ain't how you wanted it to be," Latonya said apologetically, surprising Tamika with her ability to shift gears quickly and tap into the meaning of the moment as if there had been no previous distractions. "You was always the one with the high hopes. But Mom don't care nothin' 'bout nobody but herself."

Not knowing what else to do, Tamika folded a leg under her on the bed and listened, struggling to make sense of what Latonya was saying and why. Her sister didn't seem to have too many questions for her. It was as if she knew more about Tamika than Tamika knew about her, which made Tamika suspect Latonya kept in touch with her aunt and mother.

"I know they givin' you a hard time 'bout being Moslem."

"How'd you know?"

Her sister laughed. "Aunt Jackie called here actin' like she had some horrible news. But I knew it wa'n't nothin' 'cause she ain't sound like she was sad, just like she had some juicy gossip dat I needed to hear." She sucked her teeth. "I listened, and she expected me to get all mad, but I really didn't care. I acted like it was all bad though, 'cause dat's what she wanted me to do. But all I could think was how her and Mom are the biggest hypocrites I know."

The cruel words came so easy for Latonya, and it scared Tamika that they actually soothed her as she listened. In that brief moment, she realized Latonya was her ally, forever bonded by their family turning their backs on them both.

"Mom don't talk to me when I call. She just sit on the phone all cold like and don't say a word. She used to hang up on me, and for a bit, I stopped calling. But I call every now and then, mostly on a holiday or somethin' like dat. I told myself I'll beat her at her own game. If she 'on't want a family, then she gonna have to fight to lose it."

"I didn't know you talked."

"Girl, it ain't talkin'. All she do is say, 'Mm, hm,' when her pride let her, and then I make up some excuse like I gotta get the baby."

"How old is he?"

She laughed again. "I'm sorry. I forgot you 'on't know nothin' about him. He's three weeks now, and his name's Tareq."

"Tareq?" Tamika said in surprise. "That sounds like a Muslim name."

"It is," Latonya said so simply that Tamika momentarily thought her sister might be Muslim too. "We got it outta a Moslem name book."

"What made you choose a Muslim name?"

"I 'on't know. I just knew I wanted somethin' different."

"Is, uh, Tyrone the father?"

"Yeah," she said with a disappointed suck of her teeth that told Tamika that her sister would rather not talk about him right then. "I guess you can call 'im dat."

Tamika was struck speechless by the weight of her sister's words. "How's Philip?" She decided it best to change the subject.

Latonya laughed, and Tamika came to realize this was Latonya's way. "Hell if I know. He only come here when he need a place to sleep."

"So he's in Chicago too?"

"He's s'posed to be."

"He moved there with you?"

"Yeah, but I ain't seen too much of 'im." Her voice sounded sad, and Tamika immediately knew that wherever he was, he wasn't living as he should.

"What's he up to nowadays?"

Latonya forced laughter and huffed. "Now dat's a million dollar question if I heard one."

"When's the last time you talked to him?"

There was a pause as she tried to remember. "Back in May, I think."

"It's been *that* long?"

"Girl, all you can do for him is remember him in yo' prayers."

The silence that followed unearthed the love they both felt for him but couldn't express in words.

"So what you go an' convert for like dat?" Latonya teased. They needed to change the subject, so Tamika didn't resist. "Aunt Jackie said you did some research at the college and lost yo' mind."

Tamika laughed, knowing the words were meant to lighten the atmosphere. "I guess she's right."

Latonya laughed too. "Well, don't go an' forget all about your big sister when you talk to Allah."

The mention of God's name in Arabic startled Tamika.

"Yeah, I know a lil' bit myself, girl," she told Tamika, as if reading her mind. "So don't get a big head."

"You studied about it before?"

"Girl, I ain't read nothin'. I just listen to my music, and I 'on't know a black person alive who 'on't know about Malcolm X."

Tamika didn't know what to say.

"I'm proud o' you," Latonya said so sincerely that Tamika felt her cheeks grow warm. "I could never do what you done."

"Why do you say that?"

"Girl, I got enough sins to make Lucifer blush, and I 'on't need to do nothin' where it's gonna be thrown in my face."

"But it's not like that."

"I ain't say it was. I'm talkin' about me."

It took a second, but Tamika understood. "Everybody makes mistakes."

"Yeah, I know." Latonya's voice grew distant, and for a moment they didn't speak. "But I'm in too deep."

"That's what I thought too."

There was a long pause and Tamika licked her finger before rubbing at a dry spot on a side of her calf.

"Just keep prayin' for me," Latonya said.

"Have you spoken to Mom about me converting?"

"No, but if I did, I 'on't think she'll say anything." She paused before asking, "You haven't?"

Tamika grew silent. She had assumed Latonya already knew. "No, but I was home for a day in the summer before she kicked me out."

"Just like dat? And she ain't speak to you since?"

"Yeah."

Tamika heard Latonya suck her teeth as if she wasn't surprised. "I 'on't know why it gotta be all like dat. But dat's how she always been. Don't nobody matter to her 'less they kissin' her feet."

Tamika didn't say anything as she studied the exposed portion of her leg. Her skirt was gathered at her knees from bending a leg and tucking the other under her on the bed.

"Dat's how she did me when I got pregnant. She ain't care nothin' bout what I was doin' until somethin' came of it. She always up in church, but she got her own definition of sin."

Tamika had never thought about it like that. She had always thought of her mother as a woman of high religious and social standards who expected her children to be the same. It hadn't occurred to Tamika that her mother's virtue was more selfish than religious. As resentful as her sister's words were, they were true.

When Tamika was dating her boyfriend, her mother's only concern was that she would get pregnant. The little advice her mother gave hinted at Tamika's need to "be careful," which was an implicit instruction to use birth control. Although Tamika had but one serious relationship, she could have had as many as she wanted, and her mother wouldn't have cared. No, promiscuity wasn't acceptable to her mother, but fornication was.

From adolescence, the expectations of Tamika and Latonya were clear. Don't get pregnant, get a college degree, and never depend on a man. These were the keys to success in life and, most importantly, the way to gain their mother's approval. What Philip's blueprint for success had been, Tamika couldn't recall, but she did remember her mother often warning him to make something of himself.

"I think she just wanted the best for us," Tamika said finally. The words soothed her conscience and protected her from drowning in the guilt she was feeling for indulging in her sister's resentment.

"Yeah," Latonya said, unconvinced, "only if it suits her."

The conversation ended too quickly, when the crying baby somehow reentered the room. Perhaps it was Nikki who was carrying the child, but this time Latonya felt the need to go. Tamika hung up feeling as if talking hadn't been enough. There was so much catching up to do with her sister, and she hadn't a clue where to begin. Her mind drifted to Philip, and she wondered where he was. Remembering her sister's advice, she decided to pray for him right then, and she didn't forget to pray for her sister too.

Fifteen

Slowly but surely the three-month long summer break drew to a close, and the start of school was a mere two weeks away. The summer had brought with it more than a scorching heat hotter than any Tamika had experienced, and lessons learned were more than those that taught her how to bear the heat. This Tamika pondered as the smell of fried fish rose around her and its sizzling popping sound nearly drowned out her thoughts. She stared into the oil boiling around the fish in the fryer and studied how the heat changed the dark brown liquid into clear yellow bubbles as it browned the whiting. She wiped her forehead with the back of her hand and felt a lump develop in her throat. She hated this place, a cheap fish fry that could be anybody's Mom and Pop shop, but it saddened her that this would be her last week.

Tamika sighed and slipped an oven mitt on her hand as the timer sounded, and she lifted the metal crate from the oil and hooked it where the fish could drip dry. She wondered at her summer job and nearly laughed at all her lost hopes. She had planned to get an apartment to herself with the money, but she could barely afford bus fare. A second later she stopped herself from complaining. She should be grateful.

She had interviewed at six other places when she arrived in Atlanta, and none gave her even as much as a phone call back. She had feared her Islamic dress would come between her and a good job. And it had. She could have taken off the head cover if she really wanted, but she didn't. This she pondered for a moment more and wondered at who she had become. Islam had changed her in ways she couldn't understand, and she was genuinely pleased to see her new self.

As she pulled off the oven mitt, Tamika lifted her gaze to the orders that were pinned to the wall and scribbled on dull yellow paper. She then tore some aluminum foil from the white and blue economy sized box that was ruined with oil stains and greasy fingertips. She slipped her hands into the clear plastic gloves that were kept in a box next to the bags of bread then removed a stack of slices from a bag. She pondered what she would do with herself after this week as she sprinkled iceberg lettuce and sliced tomatoes on a slice of bread that she had wiped with mayonnaise. But all she could think of was everything this summer had taught her.

Sulayman's theory about the ideal spouse, she discovered, turned out to be more fact than theory. And Tamika learned that Aminah hadn't been the only person with baseless fairytales floating in her head. Tamika too was guilty of having too much idealism about life.

It had been difficult to accept, but Tamika realized that her estranged relationship with her mother was probably how it was going to be for a while. Talking to Latonya had soothed her some, but there was still an aching inside that wouldn't go away. As a child, having a family was something she took for granted, like having breakfast every morning and dinner every night. It had never occurred to her that it could, or should, be any different. Stories of starving children and quarreling families were realities suited only for those in commercials and on talk shows. Although she had grown up without her father, she had never considered her home a broken one. But she now reflected on what it meant to have a broken family.

Perhaps it was Tamika's frustration with her own family that made her dream of having her own, she considered as she pinched the foil closed around the first sandwich and immediately started the next. In her mind, ideal was all that existed, or at least all that *should* exist for a person. But she hadn't known that what she wanted was ideal. After all, what was unusual about wanting a good husband, a few children, and a stable life? It wasn't until Aminah joked about her own "crazy ideas" that Tamika realized that she had them too.

For Aminah, "crazy" was marrying the son of a prominent author and speaker whom she and her family had met after his father had done an Islamic studies seminar in the city. Aminah had laughed at her foolishness, and it was then that Tamika realized that she too had been a fool. But her cause for foolishness had been her hope to marry Sulayman. It was he who was her ideal.

In a way, it was logical that she would want to marry him. He was the first Muslim man she met, and he was her roommate's brother. Aminah was like a mentor to Tamika, and in growing to admire Aminah, she had grown to admire Sulayman too. How she had gone from complete contempt to heart-felt admiration for him was an evolution only God could explain. But the transformation had occurred, and this she could no longer deny. Sulayman was ideal for her because he represented the best of herself, and she wanted to represent the best of him.

Aminah never vocalized it, but Tamika suspected Aminah knew of her feelings for Sulayman. The signs were all too clear. Tamika was irrationally critical of Aidah, who, to Tamika's disappointment, turned out to be a nice person after all. Tamika also showed an exaggerated concern for her appearance, even when she was only going downstairs to the kitchen. But she was thankful Aminah never said anything if she did know, and it was this that allowed Tamika to heal in peace.

Ironically, Omar became an integral part of Tamika's life that summer. She spent much of her free time talking to him on the telephone, and the conversations were very enjoyable. They had even gone out together on three occasions, once to the mall and twice to the movies. But they had begun to feel guilty for going out without a chaperone and mutually agreed to stick to phone conversations and events that brought them together in the presence of others. Usually, this meant Tamika could look forward to Omar stopping in every now and then to buy a fish sandwich or talk to her on her break.

Presently, Tamika lined up small paper cartons and began to scoop French fries into each one, pondering how much she respected Omar. There was still a part of her that clung to the hope of marrying Sulayman, but it was waning as his plans to marry Aidah grew. Tamika eventually began to consider how it would be to marry Omar. Maybe he was her un-ideal ideal. Since there were only two possibilities when it came to a potential mate, Tamika deduced that Omar could be the one who was right for her. But there were still moments that Tamika wished her ideal was Sulayman. She liked Omar, but she couldn't see him as her husband.

Omar, on the other hand, was convinced that Tamika was for him, but when she kept expressing doubt, it was he who called off their correspondence. Tamika blinked back tears as she thought of how he said that it hurt too much to keep on going with hopes of something that could never be. As much as he enjoyed talking to her and looked forward to their conversations each day, he had told her, he came to realize something Sulayman had said all along. If your conversations with a woman were motivated more by how much you enjoyed her company than to learn your compatibility for marriage, you should just get married or cut off the relationship.

Since Omar realized that the possibility of marrying Tamika was slim, he decided it was better to let go before he was in too deep. He had enough experience with women to know where their relationship was heading. Tamika liked him enough to not let go, and he liked her enough to keep on going. What that added up to wasn't something he thought was good for either of them to experience as a Muslim. So their relationship ended, at least for the moment.

"Add an extra fish to that order!" the cashier yelled. "No tomatoes! Extra onions!"

Tamika groaned and swore to herself that she would never ask for anything that wasn't on the menu. She would have never imagined that a simple squeeze of ketchup or sprinkle of hot pepper could cause a person as much stress as it did her. She was counting the days when she could turn in her hat and shirt. Maybe she'd turn in the name tag too. What was the point in keeping it? She had given away more significant things in her life.

"I'm gonna keep praying about us," Omar had said in their last conversation. The words sounded so sincere and hopeful that Tamika had felt her heart drum. "If I ever get a sign from Allah that I should marry you, you won't hear from me. Expect a call from the imam. And if you call him back, please don't say anything in response to my proposal except yes. If you still won't have me when he calls, just don't return the call. I don't think I can bear the sound of the word no."

Although it was a statement of closure, Tamika was left with thoughts of a new beginning. She missed talking to Omar, but she wouldn't call him. He was trying to move on and accept whatever Allah had in store for him, and if it wasn't going to include Tamika as his wife, he didn't want the distraction. It was hurtful to think of herself as a distraction to anyone, but she understood what he meant. If he was going to move on and become stronger despite his hurt, she couldn't keep hanging on. If she ever picked up the phone to call him, he had warned her, she should know that when he answered and heard her voice, he would take it as a marriage proposal on her part.

A week later Tamika stood in front of the closet in the guest room pulling clothes from hangers and neatly folding them before placing them in the suitcase that Sarah had given to her. It was a Sunday afternoon, and she and Aminah would be going back to campus that night. The dormitories had opened a week before for Freshman Orientation, but most returning students weren't arriving for another week, when classes would start. Aminah decided to go back tonight because she needed time to set up the room. They had opted not to live in the apartments this year because they would be forced to room with two other strangers.

When she finished at the closet, she lifted the suitcase to the floor in front of the dresser, where she cleaned out the drawers without bothering to fold her socks and underclothes. She knelt to zip the bag closed, and a moment later she stood with her hands on her hips to smile momentarily at how easy that was. There was a benefit to being forced to leave all her things in Milwaukee. She didn't have much stuff.

There was a knock at the door, but before Tamika could say come in, the door opened. Aminah stepped inside, and a huge smile formed on her face as she crossed her arms and pretended to pout. "Hey, that was fast. I still have a zillion things to pack."

"Try throwing everything away and starting over. It really works."

They both laughed.

"That's cute," Aminah said a moment later.

Tamika gathered her eyebrows. "What?"

"That outfit."

Tamika looked down at herself and tugged at a pant leg. "This?" She was wearing a baggy jean jumpsuit with a yellow T-shirt covered in powder blue flowers. She had pulled her hair back in a ponytail because she didn't feel like doing her hair.

"Yeah," Aminah said with a nod. "That looks good on you."

Tamika waved a hand and shrugged. "Whatever."

"Where'd you get it?"

She laughed. "The thrift shop."

"I need to go there sometime."

Tamika nodded then glanced around the room to see if she forgot anything.

"How's everything?" Aminah asked a minute later, and the tone of her voice told Tamika that she knew something was bothering her.

"Fine, *alhamdulillaah*." She met Aminah's gaze. "Why?"

Aminah shrugged and hesitated before saying, "I just noticed you've been down a lot, and—." she paused to gather her thoughts. "And I just wanted to let you know if you wanna talk, you know, I'm here."

Tamika found a scarf lying on the floor and bent down to pick it up. She held it in her hand as she stood and began to roll it up. "Thanks."

There was an awkward silence as Aminah started to say something then decided against it. "Well, anyway, I guess I'll get back to work," she said finally. "I have a lot to do."

Tamika nodded and was silent as Aminah disappeared into the hallway and closed the door. Tamika stood a moment more with her gaze on the scarf and wondered at her peculiar emotions. She wanted to talk to Aminah, but she didn't know what to say. Aminah could never understand. Tamika didn't even understand it all herself.

That night Tamika was grateful that Aminah's parents drove them to campus instead of Sulayman. He had a lot to do, and Sarah and Ismael felt like taking the drive. So for the first time, Tamika and Aminah actually sat next to each other in the back. Fortunately, Sarah put on an Islamic song tape, sparing everyone the burden of having to fill the space with conversation.

Once school started, Tamika was able to push thoughts of Omar to the back of her mind and move on. School was a refreshing new beginning for her, and she felt like herself again. Listening to Dr. Sanders lecture about the history of world religions reminded her that she had a purpose in life. She was Tamika, and she should focus on herself. Whenever Dr. Sanders asked her a question, she answered with a confidence that she had almost forgotten she had. It took a couple of weeks for her to realize why all the other students were stunned. She now wore a cloth on her head, the symbol of a Muslim woman, and people were amazed that she could actually speak.

Living with Aminah was soothing because it gave Tamika a chance to relax and take a breath. In the small dorm room, she was reminded that being Muslim was normal, how things *should* be. The only kink in her solace was the constant reminder of Sulayman. She would have liked to get over her baseless fairytales, but how could she, with his sister as a roommate? Even if she enjoyed a moment's peace without thinking of him, he would volunteer to take her and Aminah to *Jumuah* or home for the weekend even though Aminah made it clear that his medical school schedule was much too demanding to allow him to take them regularly. Staying at Aminah's house during the visits was the most difficult for Tamika. Sulayman's presence and Aidah's occasional visits made Tamika both jealous and angry. But she was angry with herself more than anyone else. She was being irrational and didn't know how to stop.

One weekend, Aminah invited Tamika to join her family at a one-day conference given by some Muslims in the area. There was a session for the youth and another for the adults. Although Tamika considered herself more an adult than a youth, she joined Aminah at the youth session, which was for those up to age twenty-six. Aminah hadn't told her any details about the conference, so Tamika was genuinely surprised when Sulayman was introduced as the keynote speaker at one of the lectures.

Aidah hadn't attended, which Tamika found peculiar, but she sat politely and listened to the speech, feeling awkward as a member of the audience. Sitting in a room full of more than one hundred people as Sulayman's voice echoed authoritatively throughout the room made it difficult to deny his charisma, and it was even more difficult to deny what she felt. It was at that moment that Tamika gave in. This was a battle she wasn't going to win. She couldn't control her heart, and she could only pray that God would quiet its emotions.

But Tamika eventually matured enough to know that her thoughts of marrying Sulayman were like Omar's had been regarding her. She knew the lesson well, but she didn't want to face it. You can't always have who you want, and who you want is not always right for you. Or was it that you weren't always right for them?

In that painful way, Tamika and Omar had been the same. Both had convinced themselves that someone they could never have was ideal for them. Sulayman and Aidah's future plans were growing more serious by the day, and although it was off and on with them, Tamika came to realize—and accept—it was going to happen eventually. There was nothing she could do about it. Aidah was everything she was not, and she couldn't blame him for choosing her.

Despite accepting her fate in this regard, Tamika found herself thinking, why Aidah and not her? What did Aidah have that she didn't? Then she would remind herself that this wasn't something she could measure with her eyes. It was Allah's decree that brought people together. Whenever Tamika thought of this simple fact, she felt somewhat better, and it renewed her faith that Allah would bring someone for her, someone better than Sulayman—*if that were possible.* But then, just as she grew content with these thoughts, Sulayman would be their designated driver to *Jumuah*, and the mere sight of him would send her back to square one.

After a couple of months of emotional hardball with herself, Tamika grew accustomed to the routine and accepted her tearing heart as a fact of life. When she finally married whomever Allah had written for her, she would have the companionship she longed and forget about Sulayman. It was loneliness that kept her attached to him, Tamika deduced one day. A moment later, a realization came over her. She could marry Omar after all.

Tamika liked Omar a great deal, and they had a lot in common. Once they married, she could laugh at her foolishness. Wasn't moving on what allowed the heart to heal? And what better way to move on than to marry the one who was right for her? Tamika considered calling Omar right then to share her revelation, but she stopped herself. If her willingness to marry him was a sign from Allah that she actually should, Allah would put it in Omar's heart to call the imam as an answer to his prayers.

Not knowing any other way to be an active participant in her destiny, Tamika began to supplicate daily to Allah, asking Him to make Omar call the imam to propose—if He felt they should marry. She had been making this prayer for nearly two weeks when Aminah casually informed her one Wednesday afternoon that the imam had called while she was in class. The news startled Tamika, and she felt her heart drum in her chest. She knew what the call was about, but for some reason, she never thought it would come. Panic stiffened her as she stared at the number written neatly in bubble letters on the sticky note. Should she call him back?

When Aminah left the apartment for a lab she had that evening, Tamika peeled the small yellow piece of paper from the shelf that sat atop her desk. She slid into the stiff wooden chair, pushing her books aside with the back of her hand. The phone sat just above eye level near where the note had been, but Tamika wouldn't look at it. She leaned back in the chair, gazing at the sticky note that she now held with both hands. A calm came over her as she studied the strokes of Aminah's handwriting in black ink, and she wondered if she would pull the note from a drawer ten years from now when she was married to Omar and laugh at this moment. The thought creased the corners of her mouth in a smile.

She should pray, she realized just then. Nothing would make sense unless she prayed. She glanced at the clock then nibbled at her lower lip nervously. It was almost time for *Maghrib*. Her heartbeat quickened as she imagined asking Allah if Omar was right for her. What if he wasn't? *What if he was?*

Sighing, Tamika leaned forward and returned the note to its place on the small shelf, running a forefinger along the top to keep it in place. She held her gaze on the writing for a moment longer and noticed she had smeared it some. She wondered if this was a sign from God then shook her head at her irrationality. She should pray about it and leave it alone until then.

Tamika pulled the books back in place in front of her and uncapped a highlighter that lay on her desk. She opened her *World Religions* text to where she had folded the corner of the page and began reading. She reached the end of the paragraph about the Tao in sixth century B.C. China, and as she continued reading, she wondered what Taoists believed about marriage. How was it set up? Were all the marriages arranged at that time? How had the birth of Jesus six centuries later changed that? Or did they know about Jesus in China?

She stopped herself. She set her highlighter down and rubbed a hand over her face. She couldn't concentrate. She slid her chair back and walked over to the sink in her room, where she turned on the faucet and let the water run until it was warm. She pushed her sleeves up to her elbows and began to prepare for prayer.

After praying *Maghrib*, Tamika sat reflecting on whether or not she should return the imam's call. A second later, she decided to pray *Istikhaarah*. She stood and began the voluntary prayer and felt tranquility with every position. When she bowed, she thought of Allah and how He could hear her most inner thoughts as they settled in her mind. She raised her hands in praise of Him and marveled that He rewarded His servants with endless treasures for these simple motions. She touched her head to the ground in *sajdah* and felt her body relax in the position as she glorified God, the Most High. The closeness she felt to God right then was so poignant she wanted to stay there all night. She supplicated to Him in soft whispers and felt the warmth of her breath brushing against her face. Her heartbeat steadied to a calm drumming that was like a soft tapping on a door, and she imagined the treasures that awaited behind it simply because she was submitting to her Lord. She lifted her head from the ground and felt lightheaded, for a moment feeling as if she had entered another world. The room was soothingly quiet, as if hushed in awe at what had just occurred. She stood again and recited the Qur'an silently but now with more calm intent.

Tamika finished the prayer by turning her head to each side saying the Islamic greeting. She waited for a few minutes before removing her *khimaar* and *abiya*, not wanting to leave the prayer's tranquility just yet. The prayer had created a spiritual air in the room that she felt escaping the minute she turned her head at its completion. She sat as if meditating, a sadness coming over her as reality drifted back into the air and settled. Omar, the thought came suddenly, and her heart fell as if in submission.

She stood and unbuttoned the *abiya* before slipping her arms out of it. She then pulled the head cover from her head and hung the prayer clothes neatly over the footboard of her bed. She lifted her gaze to the sticky note that had already begun to peel away from the wood. She walked over to her desk and pulled the small book of prayers from the shelf and wondered what outcome Allah would decree.

Tamika sat down in the desk chair and opened to the page of the *Istikhaarah* prayer. She took one look at her options and decided to recite the supplication in English, unable to decipher even the English transliteration of the Arabic prayer on the page. The English letters seemed bunched together next to consonants with which they didn't belong, and several vowels were written in succession of each other. Apostrophes were scattered between the foreign words, seemingly with no purpose. Her eyes hurt as she tried to make sense of it, and she immediately turned the page. She relaxed as her eyes fell on familiar English words, and she took a deep breath before reciting the prayer aloud.

"O Allah, I seek Your counsel by Your knowledge and by Your power I seek strength. And I ask You from Your immense favor; for verily, You are able while I am not. And verily You know while I do not, and You are the Knower of the unseen. O Allah, if You know this affair to be good for me in relation to my religion, my life, and end, then decree and facilitate it for me, and bless me with it, and if You know this affair to be ill for me towards my religion, my life, and end, then remove it from me, and remove me from it. And decree for me what is good wherever it be and make me satisfied with such."

The words were moving, and she marveled at how beautifully they sounded, even in translation. She relaxed after she finished, feeling assured Allah would guide her to do the right thing. She closed the book and returned it to its place before drawing in a deep breath and exhaling. Reaching up to place the phone before her, she felt her lips form a half smile as she thought, *I can't believe I'm doing this.* She pulled the yellow note from its place, and her smile broadened as she imagined she would remember this day for the rest of her life. Her gaze fell to the dull, off-white colored phone that held a hint of beige, and she almost laughed. She had bought it for less than fifteen dollars, and at the moment it was the most priceless possession in her room.

Tamika reached to pick up the receiver when the phone shrilled. Her heart jumped, and her body jerked slightly, causing the chair to tilt back a bit. The phone shrilled again, but this time she relaxed. Her heart still raced, but it slowed as her mind calmed at the realization it was just the phone. The ring indicated that it was an off-campus call, and she imagined it was the imam calling again. Or maybe it was Omar. Perhaps he was growing impatient and wanted to hear her response for himself.

"Yes?"

"*As-salaamu-'alaikum,*" the familiar voice greeted, and Tamika smiled.

"*Wa-'alaiku-mus-salaam,*" she replied cheerfully, letting Omar know she was happy to hear from him.

There was a brief silence on the other line, as if he hadn't expected her to answer the phone.

"So," she said, dragging her voice playfully as she leaned back in her chair and grinned. "What's going on?"

He started to say something but stopped mid-sentence.

Tamika's smile faded, and she gathered her eyebrows. "Omar?"

"Uh," she heard him say with apologetic uncertainty. "No, uh, this is Sulayman."

Her heart dropped. Heat rushed to her face, and her eyes stung in embarrassment. She didn't know what to say.

"Is, um, my sister there?"

"Um, uh," she said as casually as she could, glancing around the room though she already knew Aminah was gone to lab. "No, uh, she's in class." She leaned forward and picked up a pencil as if her life depended on it, and she tore a scrap of paper from a notebook. "May I take a message?"

"Uh, yeah." Apparently, he was as distracted as she. "Just tell her that I, uh, can't bring the books she left here until Friday, and uh—." He lost his train of thought momentarily. "And that she can just get them when she comes home this weekend."

She scribbled the message down, listening to her heart steady to its normal pace as she nodded, now holding the phone between her shoulder and ear. "O-kay," she said, stretching out the word so that she stopped speaking just as she wrote down the last part. "Is there, um, anything else?"

He was silent momentarily, and her head started to pound as she repeated the question in her head to see if it sounded out of place. "No, um, that's pretty much it," he said, "If you can just let her know that, then, uh, that'll be fine."

"Um, okay." Now *that* sounded out of place, she thought to herself and rolled her eyes. It was as if she thought they were striking a deal or something.

"Okay, then," he said, his voice trailing. It was obvious he was searching for a logical way to end the awkward encounter. "*InshaAllaah*, I'll call back later."

"Okay," she said, hoping this time she sounded more natural, but she couldn't help wondering if he noticed that she was repeating herself. "Should I have her call you back?" Finally, a logical sentence. Her sense was coming back to her.

"No, no," he said quickly, as if he too was trying to sound sensible. "I'll just see her Friday, *inshaAllaah*."

"Oh, okay." There she was again, repeating herself. "*As-salaamu-'alaikum*." Maybe it was rude to initiate the greeting when it was he who had called, but she really didn't know what else to say.

"Uh, *wa-'alaiku-mus-salaam*." His voice told her he was thinking the same thing, but he sounded relieved that he could go.

Tamika hung up the phone and exhaled. She propped her elbows on the desk, the motion causing a thud against the wood a second before she held her face in her hands. She felt so stupid right then she could scream. The desire to call the imam left her so quickly it was as if someone snatched it from her heart. Exhausted from the phone call, she sat up and picked up the yellow note that had fallen face down on her *World Religions* book when she had torn the paper from her notebook. She had to stop herself from balling it up in her frustration. Instead, she stuck it back in place on the desk shelf, this time ripping a piece of clear tape from a dispenser to make sure the note didn't peel away from the wood.

She stood a few seconds later and yanked her *khimaar* and *abiya* from the footboard. Groaning, she got dressed as she wondered what they were serving for dinner tonight. She wasn't hungry, but she could use the fresh air the short walk to the cafeteria would offer.

Sixteen

It wasn't until Friday that Tamika got over her embarrassing talk with Sulayman. She woke that morning with thoughts of the imam and Omar clouding her mind. She imagined that both were wondering what was taking her so long to call back. Omar was probably thinking this was her way of saying no, and the imam was most likely just going to leave it alone. After all, what could he do? It was her choice.

Maybe he would call back once more, she considered as she climbed out of bed, silencing the alarm with the press of a button. The imam probably assumed she didn't get the message.

Tamika prayed the morning prayer then took her bathrobe from a closet coat hook and tucked a rolled bath towel under an arm. She then picked up her small plastic shower crate that held shampoo, conditioner, a pink bath puff, and shower gel and hauled it out the room as Aminah tossed in bed. They usually prayed together, but Aminah wasn't able to pray this week due to her monthly cycle that was oddly growing closer and closer to the time of Tamika's. People said that happened to women who lived together or who were really good friends, and Tamika wondered if there was any truth to that as she pushed the bathroom door open and walked to an empty shower, her shower flip-flops smacking the bottoms of her feet.

In the room, Tamika dressed for class and sat down at her desk to review her notes in preparation for a pop quiz that was rumored to be happening today. She reviewed the historical information about religions she had never known existed and wondered what she was thinking when she declared religion her major. Confucianism, Bahai, Jainism, Shinto, and Zoroastrianism. Who would've known? She could barely pronounce the names of these faiths, let alone become a specialist in them.

Aminah's alarm went off, and she sat up and turned it off. She greeted Tamika sleepily, and Tamika replied as she continued to review her notes. Aminah moved about the room, dragging her feet as she prepared to shower, and Tamika imagined Omar pacing the floor wondering if this was it for them. Tamika let out a deep sigh, and she heard Aminah's movement stop for a moment then start again as Tamika shut her notebook. Tamika bit her lower lip as she studied the slightly worn yellow note whose corners had started to turn in, hanging on only because of the clear tape that Tamika had attached to it.

The room door opened and shut, and silence filled the room after Aminah left. Taking advantage of the time alone, Tamika reached for the phone and placed it before her. She half-expected it to ring, and she sat looking at it for a couple of minutes before finally picking it up. She lifted her gaze to the yellow note, not bothering to move it from its place as she dialed the number slowly, looking up after each press of a key to make sure she had his office number right.

The phone rang in her ear repeatedly until she drummed her fingers on the desk, thinking it was, perhaps, too early for the imam or his secretary to be in the office. She expected to get his voice mail when he picked up on the fifth ring.

"*As-salaamu-'alaikum*," he greeted, and for a moment, she wondered how he knew who it was. But a second later, she realized that this was how he normally answered his phone.

She returned the greeting, feeling nervous suddenly, and her heart raced. What was she *doing*? "Uh, this is Tamika." She cleared her throat. "You called?"

"Oh yes." He laughed. "I was thinking to tell the brother I didn't think you were interested."

She laughed. It was the only logical response she could think to give. "No, I'm interested."

"O-kay," he said, as if searching for something on his desk as he spoke. "He wants to sit down for a formal proposal on, uh—." His voice trailed as if he was skimming a paper before him. "Oh, today," he said in surprise, his voice apologizing for not realizing it sooner. "Is today okay?"

"Today?" Tamika could hardly think straight. She hadn't expected to talk to Omar so soon. "Uh, I guess so," she said slowly as she remembered Sulayman was taking them to *Jumuah* today.

"Then, *inshaAllaah*, we'll all sit down right after *Jumuah*."

"Um, okay." Doubt was still traceable in her voice as she searched her mind for a reason to delay the meeting but found none.

"Okay, then, *inshaAllaah*, I'll see you this afternoon."

"Yes, um, *inshaAllaah*."

Tamika hung up the phone in a daze, wondering what on earth she had just done. She should have prayed *Istikhaarah* again before she called, she thought to herself, feeling as if she had made a big mistake. A second later she reminded herself that once was enough.

She thought of Sulayman, and a sense of sadness weighed on her. Now it was for sure. She could *never* marry him.

Tamika felt her eyes burning the back of her eyelids, and her body grew weak as she stood. Was she out of her mind? She didn't want to get married, she realized just then. She needed to finish school, make amends with her family, and sort things out for herself. *O Allah!*

She leaned forward on the desk with both hands, letting it hold the weight of her body as she stared at the phone, tempted to call the imam right back and say that she changed her mind. Her palms grew moist as she tried to decide what to do. She stood and walked away from her desk, chewing at a hangnail in deep thought. She paced, wondering if the imam would think she was crazy for calling him back to say, *That's okay.*

She glanced at the clock. She should be heading to class now. She sat down on the edge of her bed and slipped on her shoes. She then put on her head cover and walked back over to her desk to gather her books and notebook. Just before she turned to go, her eyes fell on the large, thick green Qur'an on Aminah's desk. The sight of it calmed her, and a voice in her mind said, *Tamika, relax. You prayed to Allah, so just trust in Him.* The words soothed her, and in that moment, her fears disappeared. As she walked to class, she wondered how Allah would allow the meeting to go.

After her classes, Tamika stood in front of her closet, shifting hangers back and forth to select an outfit to wear to the meeting with Omar. She probably should just wear what she had on, she thought after a few minutes of finding nothing that satisfied her. Soon Sulayman would be waiting for them downstairs in the lobby to take them to the prayer and home for the weekend. She studied her reflection in front of the full length mirror attached to one of the sliding doors on Aminah's closet, and she frowned. Her white cotton headscarf looked plain against her skin, and the way it lay against her forehead made her face look smaller than it really was. The *abiya* she was wearing didn't help any, as the big round buttons stood out against the fading black fabric.

Sighing, she unbuttoned the over garment and let it fall to the floor as she pulled the *khimaar* from her head. She bent down to pick up the *abiya* and tossed them both on her bed. She turned back to her closet and, for the sake of time, pulled the first *abiya* she saw from a hanger and held it up against her. She lifted her foot and extended her leg as she looked down at the outer garment to gauge whether or not it would do. It was rich black with delicate maroon trim at the end of the sleeves, a design that also ran along where it closed in the front. She lifted her gaze to the shelf above the hangers and saw a maroon head cover folded among the other scarves. She reached for it and pulled it from the stack, causing a few other scarves to fall. She picked them up and tossed them on her bed too. She then dressed in the *abiya* she had chosen and unfolded the scarf before placing it on her head.

Tamika walked over to the mirror and studied her reflection after picking up a pin to fasten her *khimaar*. As she arranged the maroon cloth, she noticed that it was odd-shaped. She creased her forehead as she pulled it from her head to study it. It was a long rectangle, she realized, not the standard square that she usually folded into a triangle. She frowned before realizing she could simply wrap it about her head and under her chin as she did when she wore a small head wrap underneath. She had seen many of the Pakistani sisters wear their *khimaar* like that and had wondered how it was done. Setting the pin on her desk, she gave it a try, and a minute later she could only smile at her reflection. *Not bad for the first try.* But she would probably never be able to get it like this again, she thought, almost laughing at the way things usually turned out. But she would wear it like this whenever she could, especially since she could just tuck the fabric instead of using a pin.

Aminah opened the door, and her eyes widened as a broad grin formed on her face when she saw Tamika. "*BarakAllaahufeek*," she marveled as she closed the door. "You look nice." She walked over to her bed, lifted her duffel bag that she would use for the weekend, and placed it on the bed. She unzipped it and peered inside, tossing clothes to the side with a hand to make sure she hadn't forgotten anything. "What's the occasion?"

"Oh, just a meeting."

Aminah looked up, her forehead creasing for a moment. "You're not coming with us?"

"No, I am," Tamika said, shaking her head. "It's at the *masjid*."

Her roommate gathered her eyebrows in concern as she zipped her bag closed and placed the strap over her shoulder. "At the *masjid*? When?"

"After *Jumuah*."

"After *Jumuah*?" Aminah said as if she couldn't believe what she was hearing. "Sulayman has class right after *Jumuah*. How are you getting home?"

Tamika hadn't thought of that. She didn't know what to say. "I didn't think it'd be a problem." She wondered if that counted as lying. The truth was that she had forgotten completely about Sulayman's class and getting home. But, come to think of it, Sulayman *did* have to rush out of the *masjid* right after the prayer whenever they rode with him. He had to hurry and drop them off at home and turn right back around so he wouldn't be late to class. He never even had time to step in the house for a bite to eat.

Aminah grimaced, and Tamika sensed the tension rising in the room. "Tamika, why would you agree to have a meeting after *Jumuah* without asking me first?"

Tamika felt herself growing defensive, and she started to say something in retort but stopped herself. Aminah had every right to be upset, not to mention this was the worst time to save face. She needed a ride to the *masjid*, and Aminah was the only way she could get there. "I'm sorry, Aminah. I just didn't think it'd be a problem."

"But Tamika, how could you think that?" Aminah shook her head, apparently to keep herself from getting angry. "I can't ask Sulayman to wait for you. There's no telling how long that meeting'll take."

Tamika didn't respond. She could only stand there, speechless, wondering if this was God's sign that it just wasn't meant to be. She should have felt relieved, but it was disappointment she felt right then.

"Why don't you just schedule it for another day?" Aminah said, her voice descending to a softer tone, letting Tamika know she was sorry that she had spoken to her like she had.

"It'll be real quick," Tamika said, surprising herself by the desperation in her voice. Why she was so insistent on having it that afternoon? She probably should postpone it, but, for some reason, she didn't want to. Maybe she wanted to get it over with.

Aminah sighed, and Tamika could tell her roommate was growing impatient again. Aminah glanced at her wristwatch and tried to resist rolling her eyes. She turned as she readjusted the duffel bag strap on her shoulder. "We have to go. I'll have to see what Sulayman says," she said as she opened the door. "But I'm sure he won't be able to wait." She started to say something else but shook her head instead.

Aminah held the door open and turned to face Tamika. "Are you ready to go?"

Tamika nodded and picked up the suitcase she had used when she moved in. She had packed her things the day before, and as she lifted the light bag, she wished she had a smaller bag to bring home for the weekend.

"If he can't do it," Tamika said, walking a pace behind Aminah in the hall. "I can catch a ride with someone else." She was sure Omar wouldn't mind dropping her off.

Aminah forced laughter. "Like he's gonna just leave you at the *masjid* like that." She shook her head as if she couldn't believe this was happening, but she didn't turn to look at Tamika.

For a minute, they walked in silence, and Tamika followed Aminah down the stairs, her heart feeling heavy, realizing then that she should give up. She had prayed on it, and this was what Allah decreed. What was the big deal in rescheduling, or even canceling it altogether?

"Look," Aminah said, pausing before she opened the door leading to the lobby. She sighed, as if sympathizing with her roommate just then. "If Sulayman can't do it, I'll just call and ask Mom to come pick us up."

"I'm sorry." Tamika stopped short of offering to change the meeting, feeling her heart flutter in excitement all over again. Maybe everything would work out with Omar after all.

Aminah shook her head and waved her hand before opening the door, as if to say, *Don't mention it.* But Tamika could tell it was really Aminah's way of saying she was tired of talking about it, so just leave it alone.

It caught Tamika off guard when she stepped into the lobby and found Sulayman leaning over the pool table moving the cue through the space between his thumb and forefinger with a precision she associated with pros. He hit the cue ball with such swiftness that the only way she knew he had was the snapping sound of the stick's chalk-dusted leather end tapping the ball. Balls flew over the table, and one by one, the remaining solids on the table fell in the holes, leaving the eight ball spinning slowly until it stopped lazily along one of the soft green walls. The cue ball bounced off a wall, and Tamika held her breath as it graced the indent of a hole. She heard Aminah exhale at the same time she did as the cue ball slowed to a stop only inches from the eight after tapping two of the three striped balls left in the game.

Sulayman let out a laugh so loud that it startled Tamika, and it was then that she realized he hadn't seen them come in. "Now," he said with playful pride, nodding toward a student who stood with his arms folded and a half grin on his face while leaning against a wall overlooking the table.

Tamika hadn't realized Sulayman was playing an actual game until she saw the student bite his lower lip and study the table, his eyebrows slightly gathered, as if worried that this might be it for him. He shifted his cue to his other hand as he waited for Sulayman's next move. Tamika wondered what the student thought of this young bearded man donned in Arab dress. Even she didn't imagine someone like Sulayman knowing a game like pool.

"Watch this." As Sulayman leaned forward again, he paused, as if doubting his angle, and for a moment, his grin faded. He stood and walked around the table, cocking his head to the side slightly to get a better look. A grin formed on his face as an idea came to him suddenly, and he leaned forward at his new spot, raising his eyes to tease his opponent with a confident smile. But he did a double take as he caught a glimpse of the women who had walked in, and his smile faded for a moment as his eyes met Aminah's then Tamika's. He stood up and held his gaze at Tamika a second more, as if it took him a moment to recognize her. His eyebrows rose a bit, and he quickly turned to Aminah.

"*As-salaamu'alaikum*. You ready to go?" he said, laying the cue on the side of the table and wiping his hands on his black *thobe*.

"Maaan," the student said, elongating the word in disappointment, now walking over to Sulayman with a playful smile on his face. "You ain't gonna diss me like that, are you?"

Sulayman smiled apologetically, shaking his head, and Tamika could tell her presence was making him uncomfortable. "Sorry, man, I'm supposed to take them somewhere."

"It's just one more shot, man."

"I know, but—."

"No, go ahead," Aminah interrupted her brother, a smile forming on her face. She folded her arms in front of her. "I'd like to see this myself."

Sulayman met his sister's gaze with a serious expression on his face. He shook his head. "We gotta go." His voice was authoritative as he reached in a pocket and pulled out his car keys.

But Aminah wasn't letting him off that easy. "No, really," she said with a smirk, and Tamika almost laughed as she remembered Aminah telling her about the cup of water falling on her head. She couldn't help wondering if this was payback. "I wanna see your skills."

"See, man," the student said, picking up Sulayman's cue and handing it back to him. "Even your sister wants to see you play."

Sulayman glared at his sister, and Aminah laughed as she nodded in agreement, wearing an expression as if saying, *We're wait-ing.* But Tamika could tell that a part of him wasn't playing when he gave her that look. He accepted the cue stick with a reluctant nod, slipping his keys back in his pocket. Instinctively, he glanced at Tamika, who hadn't expected him to see the grin she was wearing at the moment. He did a double take, and her smile quickly faded before she looked away.

She didn't see him pocket the eight ball, but hearing the student say, "Man!" prompted her to look up. Aminah wore a proud smile, and Sulayman was trying to suppress a smile that creased a side of his mouth as he put the cue stick back at the edge of the table, where the cue ball slowed to a stop.

"Good game, man," the student said, shaking Sulayman's hand then giving him a stiff hug that many African-Americans gave each other in her high school.

"You too," Sulayman said, reaching in his pocket to retrieve his keys again.

"When you comin' back up here, man?" His opponent's question told Tamika that he and Sulayman knew each other from the previous year.

Sulayman shrugged. "A few weeks, maybe. I'm not sure."

"You in med school now, huh?"

He nodded and forced laughter. "Yeah, I guess I am."

"Man, I hope I get in."

"God-willing, you will, man. Just keep the faith."

"You too."

They nodded to each other as Sulayman left the lobby, and Aminah and Tamika followed him to the car. Aminah's large grin was contagious, and Tamika found it difficult to keep from smiling.

"So I see you still have a little talent in you," Aminah said as he unlocked the car.

He looked at his sister over the roof of the car to where she stood next to Tamika waiting to get in. His eyes told Aminah that now wasn't the time, and he shook his head without responding. Aminah grew quiet, apparently catching the hint, which Tamika sensed had something to do with her presence. Her smile faded with Aminah's, and she sensed an awkward sibling tension as she climbed in the car.

"Tamika has a meeting after *Jumuah*," Aminah said before they had even finished fastening their seatbelts, and Tamika was mortified that Aminah hadn't waited until she was alone with her brother. Tamika couldn't help wondering if the statement was Aminah's way of making up with Sulayman. She probably didn't imagine it made Tamika uncomfortable.

Sulayman creased his forehead in confusion and glanced at his sister as he put the car in reverse, waiting for Aminah to explain the significance of the information.

"And she needs to know if you can wait until she's done." The statement was so matter-of-fact, so blunt, that Tamika wanted to sink behind Aminah's seat and hide her face, which was growing warmer by the second. She held her breath, dreading what would come next. The silence was suffocating, and when Sulayman turned around, putting his hand on the back of his sister's seat, Tamika's heart jumped. A second later, she realized he was just looking behind him as he backed out of the parking space.

When Sulayman still didn't respond minutes later as they exited the campus, Tamika wondered if he had heard his sister's question. Apparently, Aminah wondered the same thing because she said, "Sulayman?"

"Yeah?" It was as if this was the first time his sister had said anything to him during the trip.

Aminah stared at him in amazement and let out a frustrated sigh. "Are you *ignoring* me?"

Tamika's gaze dropped to the maroon trim curving over her knees and stopping near the car's floor, where the *abiya*'s hem gently brushed the top of her shoes. She wished she could open the door and jump out the car right then.

"No," he said, "just punishing you."

Taken aback, Tamika looked up to find Sulayman wearing a grin as he glanced sideways at his sister, who struggled to stay angry behind the smile developing on her face, realizing this was his way of getting her back for forcing him to finish the game in the lobby. Aminah rolled her eyes, unable to suppress her smile any longer, and she shook her head in amusement. Tamika lowered her head again, this time to hide her own smile at the exchange.

"As for the meeting," he said seriously a minute later, prompting Tamika to lift her gaze. He shrugged as his sister turned to look at him. "I have class," he said tentatively, "but I suppose I can wait for a few minutes." He shrugged again. "I have a few errands to run and was thinking to skip it today anyway."

Aminah shrugged as if to say, *Whatever you want*, and turned to look out her window.

Tamika was both surprised and relieved at his response, and she exhaled silently as she relaxed in her seat. She turned to stare out her window too and filled the silence of the car with her thoughts. She leaned her head back as she watched the trees and grass pass, and her eyes grew heavy, the scene hypnotizing as it coaxed her to sleep.

Tamika opened her eyes suddenly, and she sat up as her heart raced in fear of the image of Omar that had just invaded her mind. She glanced around her for a moment and realized she was still in the back of the car. Sulayman was reciting a verse along with a Qur'an tape that now played in the car, and Aminah was still staring out the window in the seat in front of Tamika.

Who is Omar anyway? The question was so pronounced and desperate in Tamika's mind that she couldn't deny the panic she felt right then. Flashes of who Omar might have been before Islam had nearly choked her a second before after drifting to sleep. Presently, she couldn't help wondering what skeletons she would be forced to gaze upon if she married him.

Fear shot through her like a bullet, and she imagined a pistol in Omar's hand. Why *had* he gone to jail? Was it really a case of bad company, or was he a criminal in denial about his real self?

Tamika's short dream had revealed Omar holding a gun as his eyes grew angry and sweat beaded on his forehead. He had raised his voice a second time, waving the gun in a taunt as he demanded money from the store clerk—and marriage from her. She had put up her hands as the store clerk suddenly became her. She tried to scream for help, but no sound escaped her throat. Finally, with tears in her eyes, she asked him what he wanted, begging for her life. A wicked grin had formed on his face as he laid down the gun, its hollow mouth facing her, and demanded that she empty the cash register. She did as she was told, and a second later, she was in their apartment as his wife fixing dinner for him as the gun lay in the center of the table. In the dream, she was terrified and kept saying to herself as she stirred the soup, "It was God's will. It was God's will."

Tamika stared out the window beside her and sighed as the realization came to her so definitely that she felt she could reach out and stroke it with her hand. She couldn't marry a stranger, especially one with a criminal record. Exhausted, she leaned her head back on the seat again and wondered what she would do about the meeting. Would it be wrong to cancel it now? As the answer settled over her, she realized the answer was yes. She should go to the meeting like she planned and see what happened after that. Besides, could she base everything on a dream that was most likely from her subconscious anyway? What happened to faith in Allah? She had prayed on this, she reminded herself and mentally submitted to her obligation to at least go to the meeting. Perhaps a clearer sign would come then.

The Qur'anic recitation stopped suddenly, and Sulayman reached forward to rewind the tape. As he did, his voice was a melodic hum as he recited the verses as he waited for the tape to finish rewinding.

Tamika sighed, feeling that this ride was a farewell. It was as if Sulayman was driving her to the airport for a flight from which she would never return. Sadness enveloped her as she realized she could never be a part of his family. Her relationship with them would be forever deemed "like family," the words Aminah and Sarah used so often to describe her. The words, once so fulfilling and heart-warming, were now like the dreaded term *almost*, as if there was something within her reach, but she had missed it just as she could almost feel it in her hand.

Sulayman turned off the car and opened the door to get out, and Tamika was overwhelmed with sorrow. She watched him climb from the car as he told his sister where to meet him after the prayer. When she and Aminah climbed from their seats and shut their doors, Tamika caught a glimpse of

Sulayman disappearing into the building, and she realized then that he was disappearing from her life.

It was with a marked sense of obligation that Tamika sat through the sermon. When the imam talked of submitting to Allah, she humbled herself and accepted that she should too. God had guided her to Omar, and there was nothing left for her to do but submit. After all, didn't God know better what was good for her? Marriage wasn't about love of anyone but God, she had heard someone say once. And now she understood—or, at least, she would try to understand.

After the prayer, Tamika's heart pounded so forcefully that she found it difficult to think straight. She had to take a seat in the lobby to catch her breath before getting up the nerve to go to the imam's office. She needed time to gather her thoughts—and strength. She sat reflecting as the crowd slowly drifted outside to get in their cars and return home. She felt guilty for making Sulayman and his sister wait, but she needed to clear her head.

As she thought about everything, she came to terms with what she was feeling. It was marriage that scared her more than whom she was marrying. She had been raised to believe that being single was freedom and marriage bondage. It was the subconscious fear of letting go of her autonomy that made her feel as if she were being held hostage to her decision to marry Omar. The flood of fears that portrayed Omar as a criminal was no more than a personification of her own fear of facing up to who she had been before Islam. The gun in his hand symbolized what the agreement to marry represented to her past life. It would all be blown away in a single shot. Who held the gun was less significant than the gun itself. Had she married whom she thought she should, nothing would have been different except the one holding the pistol.

Tamika had been reared to never depend on a man, and she was terrified of the prospect of doing just that. But she couldn't continue to run from destiny. No one could live without companionship, no matter how hard she tried. And companionship without commitment was like intimacy without love—a berry with the sweetest of smells and bitterest of tastes. If she didn't marry, how could she ever have them both? Yes, she could live like most other women her age did, tasting the sweetness of companionship and living under only the guise of commitment. But she didn't want that for herself. She didn't want to make the same mistake of her sister—of her mother.

Tamika got up and drew in a deep breath and exhaled slowly before walking over to the imam's door. She hesitated for a second before she lifted her hand and knocked. She wasn't sure if he was in his office yet, but it had been more than fifteen minutes since the prayer ended. The door opened too suddenly for Tamika, and she found herself facing the imam. He greeted her with a smile and asked her to please come in. For a second, Tamika's eyes rested on his dark brown face and large graying beard, and she began to wonder who Imam Abdul-Quddus really was. She had assumed he was

African-American, but now he looked like he could be Sudanese or perhaps even Egyptian.

"Just make yourself at home." Leaving the door open, he returned to the seat behind his desk and resumed typing something at his computer. Taking one of the seats near the door, Tamika frowned in disappointment to find that he was in his office alone, and she began to wonder if Omar had changed his mind. As the imam tapped away at his keyboard, Tamika felt her insignificance.

She was one in tens of women for whom he acted as guardian or, more technically, trustee. With all his responsibilities, could he possibly have the time and dedication to each of them that such a role required? Was he really able to sift through droves of men with varying resumes of relationships and pre-Islam sins, and pair the women under his trust with only ones fit for them? Was it even *possible*? Tamika found herself wondering what her situation would be like had her father been able to fulfill this role.

"The brother will be here in just a moment, *inshaAllaah*," he told Tamika.

Tamika smiled politely, but he didn't see her. He hadn't looked up from the screen since he sat down. "Is he here?"

The imam laughed. "Yes, he's here. I spoke to him briefly after the prayer." He laughed again as he met her gaze. "He looks about as nervous as you."

Tamika chuckled, becoming self-conscious all of a sudden. *Was* she nervous? Did it show on her face?

"If I didn't know any better, I'd think you two didn't know each other." This time, he glanced up at Tamika when he spoke, and a broad smile appeared on his face. From the look in his eyes, you'd think it was his son he was talking about, and she wondered if he was the imam at the prison where Omar learned about Islam.

The sound of a tap on the open door relieved Tamika from speaking. She turned expecting to see Omar, but instead she saw Sulayman standing in the doorway, wondering if she was ready to go. She quickly stood and apologized to him before he could say anything. "I'm sorry. *InshaAllaah*, we'll be done in a minute."

Sulayman nodded, as if unsure how to respond. He looked to the imam, who stood and walked over to the door. Imam Abdul-Quddus laughed at something, and Sulayman chuckled too, as if they were sharing a private joke. Sulayman stepped inside, and the imam closed the door.

Sulayman sat down two seats from her, which was when Tamika realized something was terribly wrong. Why would he wait *in* the room during her meeting?

When the imam began to talk to them, it took her a few minutes to comprehend what was going on. As she put the pieces together, she was afraid to interpret what they meant. She must have glanced from the imam to

Sulayman and from Sulayman to the imam three times before she finally understood. But there was still a shred of doubt, which was probably why she asked, "Where's Omar?"

The question didn't seem to come as a surprise to either of the men. It was as if they were waiting for her to ask. Sulayman bowed his head and linked his hands on his lap. He appeared the most nervous Tamika had ever seen him. The imam wore a half smile and looked at Sulayman for any indication that he was prepared to give an explanation.

A moment later Sulayman lifted his head but kept his gaze averted from Tamika. "Tamika," he said, drawing in a breath then exhaling, "it's me."

The words both shocked and soothed her at once. She couldn't remember him ever addressing her by name, and she was struck speechless at the sound of it in his voice. Tamika had no idea what expression her face held at the moment, but inside she was both flattered and confused. It was her confusion that made her ask the next question. Had her head been clearer, she would have realized the senselessness of it. "What happened to Aidah?"

Sulayman started to say something, and for a moment his lips remained parted as he tried to think of the best answer. "I prayed on it," he said calmly, "and Allah guided me elsewhere." He surprised himself with the simplicity of his answer, which veiled the truth behind what had led him to where he sat right then. Whatever word described it best, *simple* was not it.

He looked to where Tamika sat and met her gaze, struggling in that moment to read what was beyond her eyes. She quickly looked away from him and he from her, but they had seen what they were looking for and assessed in silence what they could not in words.

Sulayman had seen confusion, relief, and what he thought was fear. It would take time for her to sort out her feelings, he supposed, but he would be patient until she did, even if it took longer than his heart would like.

Tamika saw sincerity and vulnerability when she looked at him, and it only increased her respect for him. She also saw a reflection of herself, the need for contentment and the willingness to love for the sake of Allah. She saw a future that promised happiness despite what pain life would bring.

The two were rendered speechless by the weightiness of it all. The sound of the imam's voice interrupted their thoughts and reminded them so abruptly where they were that it felt like an intrusion. It took some time for Tamika to pay full attention to the man who was entrusted with her guardianship. As his words gradually took meaning, she understood that he was asking if she was interesting in marrying Sulayman.

The question confused Tamika, as she momentarily forgot that her feelings for Sulayman had been known only to her. "I don't know," she said, betraying what she felt, but the words were strangely true.

Sulayman took a deep breath to ease the pain of her words. He had expected this answer but hadn't realized how much it would hurt. He became aware of his smallness all of a sudden and hoped that she didn't see him as such. He didn't have much to offer her beyond his faith and determination to make it work.

"Do you need time to think about it?" Imam Abdul-Quddus asked.

The imam's presence filled the room with an awkwardness that Tamika couldn't explain. His question was too formal, and she felt as if she were in a doctor's office forced to articulate something too private to divulge. But she knew the information was essential, so she sat trying to find the best answer. It would have been sufficient to say yes, but that was only partly true.

Tamika's heart fluttered as she realized who sat beside her and what he wanted from her. Part of her didn't want to delay her answer, fearing that a moment's hesitation would remove him from her reach. Another part of her needed to think about it, the significance of the moment too much to permit her to decide right then. She wanted to learn more about him and wanted him to do the same for her.

Just then Tamika remembered when Aminah had told her that a man being interested in marrying someone didn't necessarily mean he actually wanted to. Marriage was the only context Muslims thought in. Perhaps Sulayman wasn't asking to marry her but her permission to get to know her better in case he did later on.

The possibility terrified Tamika, and she feared she would never be good enough for him. How could she satisfy a man as remarkable as Sulayman and make him proud? How could she give him even half of what he could give her? What could she possibly say or do to prevent him from seeing her insignificance next to him?

Did she need time to think about? She didn't know. What was there to think about? Whether or not she wanted him to consider her, or if she would consider him? She didn't understand the question, and she was too ashamed to say. If she were unable to understand a simple question as this, what of marriage itself?

"Think about what?" Perhaps Tamika had been able to ask it because she turned her attention to the imam as if Sulayman wasn't there. What gave her the nerve, she didn't know, but she was pleased the question carried a tone of confidence and demanded an explanation rather than revealed she needed one.

The pressure fell on Sulayman so heavily that he was unsure if he could withstand it. The imam looked to him, the only one who could explain. Sulayman tucked his lower lip as he sensed Tamika waiting for an answer to what she had a right to know. Up until then she had no idea what was going on in his mind and heart. He had been a person who was merely the brother of her friend. So how could he expect her to think about anything? He had given her nothing about which to think.

"Tamika," he began, surprising himself as the confidence of his voice veiled his true state, "I apologize for bringing you here like this." He paused as he tried to find the words to explain something he was just beginning to understand himself. As he gathered his thoughts, he could only pray his explanation would be as powerful and convincing as his feelings. If not, Tamika would never understand.

The sound of Sulayman's voice sent her heart racing, and she shifted positions in her chair. She felt the cloth of her *khimaar* with the palm of her hand in a gesture that concealed her nervousness, or at least that she hoped did. She couldn't get used to him saying her name. It was as if she were shocked that he had noticed her enough to recognize who she was. The flattery she felt at the moment made her cheeks grow hot. She smoothed the fabric of her dress, hoping nothing in her appearance revealed to him that she didn't deserve what he hoped to give. She hoped even more that he couldn't tell she had nothing to give in return.

Seventeen

Sunday night Sulayman hung up the phone after talking to Tamika for the first time. He had waited to call until he was sure they were home after his parents took her and Aminah back to campus. He had been nervous to call her, and he was sure she hadn't expected him to call. But they needed to talk to break the discomfited tension they had felt that weekend. Naturally, they didn't speak to each other in the house after the meeting. It was too awkward. Sulayman had opted to find errands to run and reasons to stay late at campus or in the lab. Whenever he was home, Tamika mostly stayed in her room.

The conversation had gone well, and Sulayman had felt himself relaxing, and he could tell Tamika had too. He kept the call brief and limited the discussion to her family and his. Neither wanted to hang up, but he used the excuse of school in the morning to get off the phone.

Presently, he walked downstairs to the kitchen to get something to eat before he prayed. His parents still hadn't returned from their drive to Streamsdale, and Sulayman imagined they were taking advantage of their time alone. They were probably discussing his desire to marry Tamika and trying to sort out what they thought of his news.

Sulayman opened the refrigerator and bent over to peer in, his hand still on the handle. His eyes traced the contents, and he settled on a slice of apple pie. He removed the clear glass pie pan from its shelf and set it on the counter then closed the refrigerator door. He took a glass plate from a cabinet above the counter and pulled the cold aluminum foil from the pie. The foil ripped until it was almost split in half, but he shrugged as he took a knife from the counter set before serving himself a piece.

He opened the microwave and heated the pie for one minute, folding his arms and leaning with his back against the counter as he waited. He imagined how it would be if he married Tamika, and he couldn't help smiling. A second later his smile faded as he wondered what he'd do if she turned him down. He was afraid of rejection, this he couldn't deny, but that didn't stop him from going to Imam Abdul-Quddus a week before to tell him about his intention to marry Tamika.

Sulayman had asked the imam to keep him anonymous until the meeting. He didn't plan it like that initially, but as he went over in his head how he could meet with her, he saw no other way. If she had known before then whom she was meeting, the drive from Streamsdale would have been awkward and suffocating for them both. He also didn't want to risk Tamika telling his sister what was going on. He usually talked to his sister about things like this, but this was different. The newness of his feelings, at least his admission of them, made it difficult to articulate what they meant. Of course, a part of him was afraid that his sister would know too much.

The microwave timer sounded in measured beeps, and Sulayman turned and opened its door to inspect his meal. Steam floated from the pie, and the sweet apple liquid sizzled between the crevices of crust. Sulayman pulled the plate from the tray and shut the microwave door with an elbow.

The sweet aroma of cinnamon and nutmeg rose in the kitchen, and he grinned as he thought to himself that he would make it a point to remember his mother in his prayers that night. It wasn't everyday a person could have his fruit and bread group served in a pie. After placing his plate on the table, he walked over to the freezer and opened it to look for something from the dairy group to complete his meal. When he found the ice cream, he carried it to the table with a spoon and served himself three generous dips. Smiling, he put the ice cream away and took his seat before his meal. After saying *"Bismillaah,"* he began eating as he wondered if Aminah had been truly surprised when he told her after *Jumuah* of his plans.

Aminah could probably recall the events following Tamika's arrival and pinpoint when his feelings had changed. She already knew the ups and downs of his relationship with Aidah and had given her input. But she didn't know their last parting had been a final one. And she didn't know of his admiration for Tamika.

Tamika had all the qualities Sulayman wanted in a wife and more. Although he had never talked to her himself before Friday, he already knew he and she were alike. They both viewed the life of the world with obligation and indifference, and they would treat it as such. They would take only what they had to and leave the rest.

Sulayman had spent the first few minutes after the Friday prayer talking to Imam Abdul-Quddus to confirm their meeting although he was nervous about going through with it. It wasn't convenient for Sulayman to meet on a Friday afternoon, but the imam had a business trip he was leaving for that night and wouldn't return for another two weeks. And Sulayman couldn't wait that long. He disliked the idea of missing class, but it was one he could afford to miss. The class was challenging, but most of the material from the lectures came directly from the text. Nonetheless, he had asked a classmate to make a copy of the class notes, which he planned to get from him on Monday.

Presently, Sulayman savored a bite of sweet apple chunks drenched in melted vanilla bean ice cream, and he thought of Aminah's face when he told her the news. Aminah had been waiting for him where he told her to, and before returning to the imam's office to meet Tamika, he decided to tell his sister the truth.

Sulayman had stood next to her for a few seconds before he spoke. She had assumed they were both waiting—impatiently—for Tamika's meeting to end. When he let out a knowing laugh of embarrassment, she stared at him curiously and asked him what was going on. He told her between chuckles that Tamika's meeting was with him.

Aminah's confused expression told him that she didn't understand what he meant. For a second, her eyebrows rose as she imagined he was joking with her, but a moment later she just stared at him, demanding an explanation.

He told her that Tamika and the imam were waiting for him in the office. As he spoke, he stared into the crowd of Muslims to avoid her gaze, and he finally divulged the full truth. He explained that he had decided not to marry Aidah and that he was going to ask Tamika instead.

Speechless, Aminah had stared at her brother in disbelief. She felt both shocked and betrayed, this he could tell. But she couldn't keep from smiling at how cute it all was. "Why didn't you tell me?"

He had chuckled and gave a shrug before telling her the truth. "I don't know."

Sulayman lifted another spoonful of pie to his mouth and wondered at everything that had happened with Aidah. He would have liked to explain it all to Tamika in the meeting when she asked, but there really wasn't time. Everything was so complicated, and he had a difficult time sorting it out for himself.

When Sulayman met Aidah more than a year before, he wasn't attracted to her though her attractiveness was apparent to him. She carried herself with such a distinct sense of self-assurance and sufficiency that made it difficult to imagine she needed a man to make her world complete. She was used to men being drawn to her, and even before she had confirmed it in a conversation, he knew she had had more than her share of marriage proposals in her young life. For Aidah, dealing with Muslim men had always been a three-part experience. They saw her. They wanted her. She turned them down.

Sulayman understood, though, why so many men had asked to marry Aidah. She was pretty, intelligent, and religious, three traits men found difficult to resist—most often in that order. He imagined the fact that she stood in no need of them made her all the more desirable. Her financial future looked promising, much more than that of the men who proposed, which created both a challenge and a determination to have her. Aidah was so accustomed to this scenario that she began to take it for granted, Sulayman realized before he even considered her for himself. Almost everyday that they worked together, she had a funny story about a brother who had made a proposal that she turned down.

In many ways, Aidah was like her sister Jauhara, who was six years her senior, whom Sulayman first heard about a week after he and Aidah met at work. Jauhara was the subject of almost every conversation until Sulayman felt like he knew Aidah's sister more than he did her.

Jauhara, Sulayman learned, was both Aidah's rival and mentor in life, though Aidah wouldn't describe it quite like that. Jauhara had seen the side of life no Muslim woman should have, and it showed on her face when Sulayman first saw her, despite her bubbly personality and reassuring smile. When Aidah told him that Jauhara had stopped practicing Islam for several years before she returned to the religion, he wasn't surprised. Jauhara, he noticed after meeting her, moved about the world with much more confidence and ease than the average person. She had tested the waters and had more than once drunk more than her share. Islam, which was once too confining for her, became her savior for the very reason she had once felt confined. Her taste of life's bittersweet fulfillment gave her a solid commitment to the religion that nothing else could hope to give.

Aidah often referred to her sister as "someone everyone wanted to be." Initially, Sulayman didn't understand this grand description, but as she spoke about her sister more, he understood it more than Aidah had intended. Clearly, Jauhara had made her mark in the lives and hearts of many who knew her, which in itself could explain Aidah's description. But it was clear that more than anything else, "everyone" was a synonym for Aidah herself.

Jauhara was pretty—"unbelievably beautiful" in Aidah view—, intelligent, and successful. She was a successful lawyer, making nearly six figures each year, and she had once been married to a prominent politician. That the marriage was painfully short, lasting just shy of six months, didn't diminish its significance in Aidah's eyes, and it didn't seem to disturb her that the politician was not Muslim. Both of these facts, it seemed, were peculiarly admirable to her. She would mention the marriage and the man, both of which were part of Jauhara's life before rediscovering Islam, with a tone of obligated shame, but what she really revealed was the pride she felt as she told the stories.

It was mid-summer, only months before, when Sulayman finally saw in person the woman whom he had heard so much about. When Sulayman met Jauhara for the first time, he was expecting a glamorous woman more attractive than any woman he had seen in life. Aidah and Jauhara entered the living room of his home one evening while Tamika was in class, and it was then that it hit him why he couldn't marry Aidah. It was as if the sight of Aidah's sister clarified for him what he couldn't put in words.

Jauhara was several shades lighter than Aidah, her skin a golden yellow, and her eyes a hazel brown like her sister's. She stood an inch taller than Aidah, a difference that was exaggerated by her high heels. She carried with her a confidence earned from having the world constantly tell her she was pretty—and experiencing what it meant to carry that load. Her head was covered with a small headscarf tucked in the collar of her business suit jacket, indicating both her sophistication and affiliation with Islam.

Sulayman didn't call Aidah for a week after he met her sister, and Aidah was both confused and jealous. When they finally did talk, he was surprised that Aidah wanted him to recount more than once what he thought of her sister. It was then that it occurred to him that she interpreted his evasiveness as an attraction to Jauhara. In reality, he thought Aidah was much more attractive, and despite his discomfort with such a confession, he ended up telling Aidah this. What confused him, he told her once, was that she felt so small next to her sister when there was no reason to. Sulayman suspected why this was the case, but he wanted Aidah to see it for herself. But he did ask her to think about her reasons, and it was a whole week before Aidah was finally able to admit what it was.

All her life, Aidah had told Sulayman, she had walked in the shadow of Jauhara, who, because of her fair skin, was deemed more beautiful than she. Aidah had excellent grades, earned through intelligence and her own hard work, but the highest praise she ever received was that she would one day be like Jauhara. When Aidah worked hard, it was interpreted as a desire to emulate her sister, which was supposed to be a compliment. Somewhere down the line, Aidah internalized this and accepted it as her destiny. And eventually, whatever Jauhara did, she knew she should too.

When Jauhara strayed from Islam, Aidah found herself in a position she had never assumed before. She had become an individual, and all of her parents' energies and faith, for the first time, were put in her. Although she couldn't articulate it at the time, she sensed that the sudden attention was as if they were telling her, "Well, we would have preferred to be cheering for Jauhara, but you will do." What Jauhara was going through at the time, Aidah had no idea, but for her it was as if her sister suddenly dropped off the face of the earth.

When Jauhara resurfaced, as a successful lawyer and an ex-wife to a politician, she reassumed her status as the center of her family's world. It was as if her straying had only been a crazy trip she had taken without their permission. And once again, Aidah was relegated to second-best. She reluctantly submitted to the role of observer as her sister took center stage. When it was happening, Jauhara's rebellion against Islam was treated like the worst thing in the world, so much so that it was forbidden to talk about. But when she laughed and recounted stories to her family about her husband, their parents listened with intense interest, as if they were grateful to have such an important person talking to them. It was with a noticeable sense of pride that their parents listened to Jauhara talk about the "nasty food" at high-class restaurants, the "boring conversations" over dinner with other politicians, and the "hectic lifestyle" of traveling here and there with her husband.

Long after Jauhara would leave the house after telling one of her stories, Aidah said that their parents would laugh and joke as they remembered something funny Jauhara had said. Whenever their parents visited other family members, none of whom were Muslim, Jauhara's life without Islam gave them bragging rights and a status that armed them with an importance that the non-Muslim family would envy. But it was clear to Aidah, though she wouldn't have dared to say it, that her parents' talks were less a testimony to the high status Jauhara's prominent life had earned them than it was proof that they sought through Jauhara's failures what they could never earn from their family through Islam alone. And that was respect. It was then that it was solidified for Aidah what she had to do to earn hers. Worldly success and holding on to Islam—in that order.

Initially, Sulayman thought that meeting Jauhara made him less inclined to marry Aidah because of superficial motives on his part, and he had begun to feel guilty. He had interpreted the certainty that he couldn't marry Aidah after meeting her sister to mean that he was judging their family. He thought that perhaps he was judging Jauhara because she didn't dress like his sister and mother did. But he later realized that he actually respected Jauhara a great deal.

Jauhara had seen the world, the best and the worst of it, and still she returned to Islam. The pride with which she carried herself, he observed, was more out of habit than any conceit on her part. She knew no other way to behave. The air of sophistication that engulfed her was so much a part of her that she would be unable to shake it if she tried. To many Muslims, her small scarf and fancy business suit represented a desire to compromise her Islamic identity for worldly success. But she had that before she wore a scarf or covered at all. She had been to "the top" and could have stayed there if she wanted. But she saw the top for what it was and decided it was beneath her to succumb to what it would demand.

She could have reclaimed Islam and hid it from her coworkers and clients, which would have made her walk through success easier than if she did not. But Islam was too valuable to reduce to a place of shame, a place that the ailing lives of many successful people were more fitting to be reduced. The signs of avarice, deceit, and infidelity were bold in the field in which she worked, and perhaps for her, the signs of Islam not only deserved but demanded to be bolder in her life. She changed her short skirts to longer ones and her tight pants to more loose-fitting clothes, and she even covered her head.

The scholarly interpretations of Islamic law detailing the proper way for a woman to cover, Sulayman imagined, were too varying for her to settle on any one position, so she did what felt most comfortable. She balanced the expectations of her job with the requirements of her religion, and by her own admission, as Aidah had once mentioned, she was only beginning. She didn't claim to represent who a Muslim woman should be but merely did her best to represent who she was. She was both a lawyer and a servant of God. For that, Sulayman respected her and knew she was more content in her faith than many women who appeared more religiously committed than she.

Aidah was undeniably a special person, Sulayman had come to realize, but she just wasn't for him. It took some time before he came to terms with why this was the case. If Aidah had found the contentment in life that her sister had, he could have married her right then. But there were still things Aidah was reaching for that Jauhara saw for what they were. Jauhara worked as a lawyer because she felt it was her duty to give back and represent for Islam what she had represented for the world. If she ever remarried to a Muslim and had children, she wouldn't fear whatever that demanded of her, even if she left her job to care for her children. She had seen enough of life to know that whatever it owed you wouldn't pass you by. Money came and went, and success was relative. The top was nothing more than a glass ceiling that, when reached, offered nothing more than something hard and painful on which to bump your head. Happiness was something no university or career could equip you with, if it wasn't there before. Jauhara would embrace whatever happiness God gave her, regardless of its form, Sulayman imagined, and whatever it was, it would be enveloped in Islam.

Aidah, Sulayman felt, would realize the same one day. But she hadn't learned it just yet. What made Aidah admire Jauhara had nothing to do with why Sulayman respected her. Jauhara was admirable to her sister because the world had applauded her and because her success, to her family, could be found on a resume—and in a past life. But Sulayman admired Jauhara because she didn't applaud herself and because she feared that her resume—and past life—would come back to haunt her if she didn't set things right for her soul. Had she felt it better for her religion, she would have quit her job the day she reclaimed Islam, Sulayman guessed. But she knew she had to clean up the mess she had made. If she ever left her job, she would do it with dignity. She needed to show her coworkers and clients that when you fall, you get up, dust yourself off and keep going; you don't waddle in the hole you fell in and start a new life. But most of all, she wanted to let them know she considered her past life just that—a fall.

Aidah was too committed to Islam to make the same mistakes Jauhara had, so Sulayman didn't fear she would stray from the religion. He only feared that he would get caught in the crossfire when her desire to claim the grandeur of her sister clashed with what was most valuable for the Muslim wife. Marriage put demands on the man and woman like no other institution, and after faith in God, there was nothing more essential to the success of the union than the willingness to sacrifice. Sulayman didn't think Aidah was unwilling to sacrifice. But he did fear that she was unable to.

Had Aidah thought of things like medical school and being a successful doctor as less than must-haves, she and Sulayman would have been on the same page. It wasn't her being a doctor that scared him but her inability to be anything else.

Sulayman didn't require a wife who would forsake a college education or successful career, but he did require one who saw them as a means rather than a goal. When these were a means, their value was high only in that they enabled one to reach the goal. But when they were the goal, sacrifice was defined by that which had to give in order to claim the prize.

To Sulayman, the goal in life was but one, to please Allah. If it so happened that leaving medical school would help him better achieve this, he would do it. Of course, he was human, and he knew it wouldn't be an easy decision. But deep in his heart, he understood that this was how he had to view everything in the world. Its value was only value when it helped him serve God. Aidah expressed the same sentiment, but when Sulayman met

Jauhara, he realized that Aidah didn't understand what he meant. Serving God was the same as becoming a doctor to her, and that scared him.

So it wasn't Tamika that made Sulayman realize he couldn't marry Aidah, at least not entirely. But he did find himself comparing the two women whenever he saw something he disliked in Aidah. The comparison was not a conscious one but one done out of habit without allowing himself to understand why.

When Sulayman first met Tamika as his sister's roommate, there was a dignified manner about her that made him respect her, even as a non-Muslim. Tamika was distinct from other women on campus, and she inspired in him an awareness of his Islamic identity in a way he couldn't explain.

In his classes and during campus activities, he often had to remind himself that he was Muslim in order to withstand the negative pulls of the environment. At times he would be laughing with other students and suddenly become aware that he was different. Perhaps his Islamic identity was never forgotten by those around him, but for brief moments it was forgotten by him. This concerned him and made him prefer studying alone to studying in groups and socializing at home to socializing on campus. The presence of his sister was once the only tangible reminder he had of who he was, but after meeting Tamika, she too represented this for him—even before she embraced Islam.

The effect Tamika had on him was so tremendous that Sulayman had searched for a rational explanation. Initially, he assumed it had something to do with associating her with his sister. Perhaps it was Aminah's great concern for her soul, Sulayman had imagined, that moved him too. But when he reminded himself that Durrah didn't inspire the same reaction, he didn't know what to think.

Sulayman's respect for Tamika grew each time he saw her, even from afar. She kept to herself for the most part, and she seemed to take in her surroundings without allowing them to take her in. As she strolled across campus, she didn't seem to belong to the environment she was in. The stiff buildings and restless students were like the background of a canvas painting of her. She never seemed to be in a hurry, as if she knew wherever she was headed would be there when she arrived. School to her was like a bridge she was crossing to get someplace else, it seemed, and it was as if her feet were merely touching its base but never resting there. Whatever she read in her books and learned in class didn't seem to satisfy her, this he could see on her face. Her heart longed for something less transient to sustain her craving for life.

Sulayman was a man, so Tamika's feminine beauty had not escaped his eyes. And her intangible qualities made it all the more difficult to disregard their enhancement of what he could see. He had been attracted to women on campus before, but it had been easy to discount the attraction as superficial and nothing more. Whenever he thought of the women beyond the physical sense, he could see neither future nor contentment with them. That they were not Muslim furthered his ability to move on and not look back. He had decided before going to college that his wife would be Muslim. Before meeting Tamika, that decision had been easy to uphold.

Whenever Aminah spoke of her new roommate, Sulayman's curiosity about her grew. He found himself drawn to the strange woman whom Aminah liked more than any non-Muslim student she had met before. At the time, it was mere curiosity, or so he thought, that made him inquire so often about how Tamika was doing and what Islamic books she was reading. Tamika's research paper on Islam allowed Sulayman to discuss her with Aminah whenever he got the chance, giving him an opportunity to understand Tamika more.

It was Durrah to whom Tamika was most drawn, Aminah had told him, but Aminah couldn't shake the connection she felt with her. It was as if Allah put Tamika with them for a divine purpose, one that, for some time, Aminah couldn't quite figure out. Tamika's presence in the apartment brought life to their campus home and made the roommates more aware of their Islam. Even Sulayman felt the life exude from the apartment after Tamika moved in, and he too was left wondering what this meant.

Before Tamika's arrival, the apartment carried a stiff, monotonous atmosphere, as if everything in it was done out of habit and obligation, and devoid of love. Islamic books lined the apartment walls, but whatever spirituality they contained had filled only the peripheral of the women's lives who resided within. When Tamika arrived, it was as if Islam itself was reintroduced to ones who had lived it too long to assess the value it had in their lives. Even Sulayman saw the change in his sister, as if Tamika's questions about the religion gave Aminah answers to its place in her own life.

Sulayman grew accustomed to his sister's new situation like it was his own. Hearing his sister's accounts of her daily ups and downs of living with Durrah and Tamika was as normal and welcomed as the breaking of dawn. He had assumed it was with emotional detachment that he gave advice to Aminah and saw the apartment life through her eyes. He was merely an observer, close enough to see it clearly but far enough to have no personal stakes in what went right or wrong.

Durrah's death stripped the distance from him like the destruction of a foundation he didn't know was there. As he struggled to soothe the insurmountable pain he felt at the loss of a young woman he had known since he was a child, he was sick with worry about the well being of Tamika, who lay in the hospital even after Durrah's body was underground. When Aminah told him she had come home safely, he felt as if a weighty burden was lifted from him, a relief incomplete only by the knowledge that Durrah would never come home.

Despite the aching emptiness Durrah's death left him, his concern for Tamika's emotional and physical state grew each day. When Aminah had called between sobs and tears to inform him that Tamika had embraced Islam, he felt his heart swell with both pride and relief so immense that tears filled his own eyes. The news was so triumphant and climactic that he fell down to prostrate in gratefulness to God. It was as if divine meaning had been triumphantly unveiled after a tragedy so great that its impact was immeasurable in the stake it had in others' lives.

That Tamika's conversion inspired in him more than empathy was something Sulayman didn't fully comprehend, but he knew that it ignited in him an affection for her that he interpreted as what he felt for all Muslim women. Her needs, both spiritual and material, became his concern, and he found himself calling his sister often to make sure they were met.

Aminah had recounted Tamika's presentation on Islam so vividly that Sulayman felt as if he were there. As he listened to his sister, he felt honored to share in such an exceptional victory as Tamika's. Perhaps it was then that thoughts of marrying her had settled in his mind, but the occasion was much too tremendous, by both tragedy and faith, to insult with mention of selfish desires of the heart.

The school year had drawn to a close with a sense of tense obligation, as if forcing those it wounded to heal too quickly. Driving Tamika to the airport was such a painful closure that it felt unjust. Why he was so moved by the simple drive was perplexing even to him, and naturally, he could give no reason why she should stay.

When Tamika had called Aminah at their home while he was rehearsing his speech, it was as if the reason for his difficulty in letting her go was confirmed. He shouldn't have allowed her to go where she couldn't be protected, he had thought, and he felt guilt ridden right then. The anger that swept through him when he learned she was harmed was so tumultuous that he later sat confused as to why his emotions were stirred so.

Sulayman was relieved to learn that it was her mother, and not a man, that had violated her safety and pushed her to call a friend. He volunteered so quickly to save her from homelessness that inside he questioned his motives, but he was too unaware, and perhaps too ashamed, of what he wanted to identify what it was. It was a sense of security that he enjoyed when Tamika moved in with his family, and even that feeling he hadn't quite interpreted for what it was. At the time, he and Aidah were planning to marry, and he wouldn't let himself believe that what he felt for Tamika was more than brotherly love. When Omar came into the picture, he felt wronged and jealous. It was then that he began to realize that Tamika meant more to him than he was willing to admit.

When Omar had inquired about Tamika after they helped her and Aminah move, it was with detached curiosity that he awaited her answer. He didn't think anything would come of Omar's attraction, so he felt no sense of rivalry when Omar inquired about her. And, of course, even if he did, he hadn't yet admitted what he himself felt.

During the summer, Omar suddenly became important to Tamika, and this was unsettling to Sulayman, even as his plans to marry Aidah were solidified. Omar called often and spoke to Sulayman too, so Omar's desire to marry Tamika and her growing attraction to him were not secrets to him. What he didn't know was what it was that changed Tamika's opinion of Omar. Omar was nice enough, but his qualities didn't seem like those that would be appealing to her, though Sulayman was afraid to entertain the possibility that his were. What also had confused him was that Aminah told him that Tamika didn't plan to marry until she was thirty-five, which led him to believe that Tamika wouldn't marry before she finished college.

Tamika's determination to wait several years to marry was a strange concept in the Islamic sense, but it was one that Sulayman took for granted as defining the Muslims his age. On campus, he knew of no Muslims who talked about marriage outside the context of the distant future. It was as if marriage was more off-limits than sin itself.

When Sulayman had begun to seriously consider marriage during his sophomore and junior year, it was off-campus that he turned his attention. The few Muslim women on campus with whom he had shared mutual interest ultimately shied away from serious commitment, more out of fear of disappointing their parents than belief in any Islamic integrity in waiting. More than once had a Muslim woman made it clear that she was more willing to give up her chastity than withstand the shame her family would inflict on her should she marry before finishing school. For Sulayman, it became both clearer and more disturbing each year the high value that Muslim students and their families put on the status of a college degree.

It was with expectation and disappointment that Sulayman accepted Tamika's desire to wait until she was much older to marry. If Muslims, for whom marriage was half of their faith, put such an undeserving value on a college education and viewed it both as mutually exclusive to and more urgent than marriage, what should be expected of a person who grew up in a home void of Islam? Tamika had likely been reared more rigorously than the Muslims to believe that marriage was worth less than worldly success and hindered more than it permitted. Viewing marriage as a sort of damnation instead of deliverance was difficult even for Sulayman to resist.

It was only the wisdom and guidance of his parents that saved Sulayman from viewing matrimony in such a cynical view. After all, it wasn't without reason that marriage had such a bad name. Spouse abuse, high divorce rates, and bitter custody battles were among the most popular victims of the union. But what was ignored, his parents had pointed out, was that these problems were not created by marriage. Marriage was more a victim of these problems than they were victims of it. Delaying marriage to avoid abuse, divorce, and custody battles was evading the real issue. Life was full of struggles, and no matter which way you ran, you were gonna hurt.

Marriage appeared the culprit only because it made these problems more official, Sulayman's parents believed. Girlfriends, mistresses, and anonymous partners all experienced their share of viciously violent abuse. Relationships ended, and hearts were broken, even when marriage never entered the discussion.

Parents fought over children, often before they called each other husband or wife, and it was undeniable that fatherless—and motherless—children defined a large segment of American society. Aborting and abandoning children were so common that both had a system in which one could do them legally.

The society, which was based on fulfilling individual desires, taught its members to throw away responsibility like the body rids of waste. Satiating material and carnal appetites was as innocent as satiating a desire for food. One could fulfill his desire like he filled his stomach, and whatever came of the desire was like what became of his food. Responsibility was merely a foul stench lingering in the air that would go away if you just gave it time.

Promiscuity and perversion defined the lives of the young, often before they entered puberty, and this Sarah and Ismael had seen first hand. The "innocence" of girlfriends and boyfriends was flaunted even before a child entered kindergarten. Dating defined adolescence more than the physical indication itself. "First kiss" and "my first" were among the paradoxically innocent terms to describe serious intimate encounters adolescents had. "Locker room talk," in which young men talked openly about their experiences with girls, was so ingrained in American culture that one was left feeling deprived of a memorable high school experience if he could not join in.

Sexually transmitted diseases, date rapes, and permanent emotional scars were merely nuisances and risks that "the life" brought the American teen. *Freedom* described this slavery that chained the minds of the young, and *responsibility* was a word entertained only by older adults who were ready to "settle down." The misery that such a life brought was unimaginable, Sulayman's parents recalled. Without Islam, one was left to drown in a sea of confusion and take it for granted, and even call it "fun."

But *fun* didn't describe the spiritual turmoil the fast life left the young. Fun didn't describe the emotional heartache of a woman who discovered she had given up her innocence to a man she didn't love. Fun didn't describe the fear that promiscuity brought. Fun didn't describe the hangovers and migraine headaches the morning after getting drunk. Fun didn't describe the emptiness a woman felt when she realized she was pregnant by a man who was not hers. Fun didn't describe the gaping wound in the heart of a young woman who killed her unborn child. Fun didn't describe the need to turn to drugs for a high. Fun didn't describe the reason wild parties defined so much of their lives. Rather, in reality, their *fun* was merely a host of temporary distractions from what they were too spiritually weak to face— the black hole of their souls.

No, marriage wasn't the culprit, Sulayman had come to realize for himself. It was a victim of the same insanity that defined the misery of the young as *fun*. The bad name marriage had was merely a scapegoat for those who wished to simplify the problems they themselves created. Delaying marriage was paraded as honorable and wise, when the delay was simply running from what no one could escape. It was easier to live under the cloak of wisdom than to be wise. It was easier to submit to society's definition of honor than to live it in truth. It was easier to redefine nobility than to live what it meant to be noble.

Society scoffed at the young who dared to dignify their love by getting married, Sulayman noticed even before college. It deemed them "fools in love" and made bets on how long—or short— the marriage would last. Yet it turned a blind eye to the teenager who had three girlfriends or boyfriends in a year, if not a month. It was deemed normal to have broken hearts and multiple partners throughout high school and college. This wasn't scoffed at but viewed as merely life. God, sin, and matters of the soul rarely entered the discussion. When Sulayman thought of this, he was reminded of his father's words, "It is better to marry and divorce a thousand times than to fornicate once."

Presently, Sulayman scraped the last of the crust and melted ice cream from his plate and let the sweetness linger on his tongue before he swallowed. He then leaned back in his chair for a moment and wondered if Tamika would marry him.

Eighteen

"Sulayman called!" Tamika squealed as she dropped her books on her bed and rushed to tear the yellow sticky note from her desk shelf. Giddy, Tamika's face beamed as she grinned like a little girl whose mother bought her a doll for the first time. She had just returned from the library after checking out some books she needed for a paper she had to write about world religions. She wanted to get it done over the weekend.

Aminah chuckled from where she sat at her desk and turned her body to face Tamika. Grinning, Aminah placed an arm on the back of the chair and let her hand dangle as she stared at her roommate in amusement. "Yeah," she said in playful sarcasm, "he called, just like he's done every Friday night for the past four weeks." She started to add, *And every Saturday and Sunday*, but Tamika's attention span was short at the moment.

Tamika tore off her *abiya* and *khimaar* and tossed them on the bed, not bothering to hang them on the footboard this time. Walking to her phone, she glanced at Aminah. "Did he say to call him back?"

Aminah shook her head to keep from bursting into a fit of laughter. "No," she said, as if coaching a hyper child to settle down, "he said he'll call back when he gets back home, *inshaAllaah*."

Tamika turned around, and her hands dropped as she still held the note. Her eyebrows gathered in disappointment. "He's not home?"

Still smiling, Aminah shook her head, as if apologizing to a crying child. "He'll be back late."

"Where'd he go?" Tamika asked, lifting the yellow note to read it over again.

"Somewhere with Mom and Dad. I'm not sure."

Tamika poked her lip out playfully and returned the note to its place. "I should've gone to the library in the morning."

"If it makes you feel any better," Aminah said, unable to help feeling amused by the display, "he sounded as disappointed as you."

Tamika tried to maintain her frown, but a smile broke out on her face as she meet her roommate's gaze. "Really? What'd he say?"

Aminah laughed. "I didn't say he *said* anything. I was talking about how he *sounded*."

"I told you I need a cell phone," Tamika said, returning to the subject of the missed call.

Aminah could only shake her head in response as her eyes followed Tamika, who now retrieved the clothes from her bed and folded them neatly over the footboard. As Tamika walked over to her desk to sort the library books, Aminah studied the woman who would change her family's life.

Tamika was remarkable, Aminah thought, and she could see how Sulayman had chosen her. She was beautiful, though Tamika didn't give herself due credit for her looks. Even right then, in her faded blue jeans and long sleeved turquoise cotton shirt, Tamika was striking. Small gold loop earrings sparkled from her ears, giving her smooth skin a glow. Her hair was separated in two ponytails that hung at the back of her head, giving her the look of a woman and child at once. Aminah could have giggled at how cute the style was on her roommate, but she only smiled and wondered if Tamika had any idea how exceptional she was.

Aminah had watched with pleasure as the attachment grew between her brother and Tamika. She would often tease her roommate about what this would mean. She had never considered the possibility of Sulayman liking Tamika before the meeting with the imam a month before. The logic of it was so compelling that Aminah could have laughed at herself for having not thought of it herself. Sulayman and Tamika were a perfect match, and the possibility of them marrying often made her giggle in excitement. She didn't have the reservations about Tamika that she had had about Aidah, and she could hardly wait until they made their relationship official. She hadn't been to a wedding in a long time.

Tamika smiled beside herself as she arranged the last library book on her shelf and slid into her desk chair. It had been only a little over four weeks since they first talked with the imam, and Tamika imagined that she would never see the month of October the same again. It was the month in which Sulayman said what she could never forget. "Tamika, it's me." She would replay the phrase over and over in her mind, and still she couldn't get used to the sound of it. She still remembered her shock when she learned it was Sulayman and not Omar who had called Imam Abdul-Quddus about her. She couldn't keep from grinning whenever she thought about that.

Tamika couldn't forget how flattered she felt when the imam went over in the meeting where they should go from there. Imam Abdul-Quddus's words were serious, but the moment was exciting for her. The imam advised them to talk periodically to see if they were interested in taking the big step, and Tamika imagined how it would be to actually talk to Sulayman to see if she wanted to marry him. The idea was too unreal to imagine.

Imam Abdul-Quddus had gone on to tell Tamika and Sulayman that his busy schedule and multiple obligations made it impossible for him to arrange a meeting each time they needed to talk. He told them that fathers generally chaperoned the meetings of their daughter and didn't allow any private communication between her and the man, even if it was only the phone. He explained that this approach was the safest and most correct in Islam and that he would have liked to implement it himself with all the women under his care. However, since talking on the phone and e-mail correspondence couldn't be considered prohibited in the religion, he explained that he allowed the men interested in marrying the women to use them as a means to communicate.

The imam reiterated his discomfort with the allowance of even these distant means of communication, and he emphasized more than once that their talking should be restricted to necessity. He told them that the overall goal of talking should be to decide if they wanted to marry. He reminded them that they should fear Allah and avoid meeting in person, even if other peers or adults were there. At that moment, Tamika had been reminded of Omar's visits to her job, and she felt guilty for not even imagining that it was wrong. She and Omar had foolishly assumed that this was their way of avoiding displeasing Allah. Imam Abdul-Quddus went on to say that double dates and the like were not acceptable under any circumstances, and even their phone interaction should never be for leisure. He suggested that Sulayman have his parents present if he and Tamika ever needed to talk when she visited his family.

Presently, Tamika opened a library book and began reading about the ancient religion of Taoism, and her mind drifted to how her phone conversations with Sulayman were part of the necessary steps to determine if marriage was a possibility for them. Both she and Sulayman looked forward to the weekly phone calls that brought meaning and anticipation to the end of the week. School was too demanding on them both to risk talking on days when there was class. So Friday nights and the weekends were designated for their talks.

The calls were so enjoyable that they had to remind themselves of their purpose. Tamika had lots of questions for Sulayman, as he had for her. Whenever he remembered something he wanted to ask, he would call her room. Initially, Tamika let him do the calling, but after two weeks, she began to call him if there was something she needed to discuss.

Their weekly calls often amounted to five each weekend, and still that wasn't enough. Each call was rarely less than an hour and would sometimes extend to three. It was only because they felt obligated that they would end a call. Their desire to talk was so great that they would think of reasons to "need" to call. It was difficult to keep from talking for the sake of talking because of the growing affection between them. Neither would allow himself to cross the Islamic limits in conversation, but they couldn't help longing for the time when they could relax and talk whenever they wanted.

Discussions about social, political, and Islamic issues accounted for their extended time on the phone. With each new topic, they learned something about each other that they didn't know before. It was amazing how their views on the world were the same. They would talk in length about current events, school, and the society at large. But the most intriguing discussions were those in which they shared something about themselves. Sulayman had a new question each week about Tamika's conversion to Islam, and Tamika always wanted to know more about how it felt to be raised in a Muslim home.

Talking to Sulayman came so naturally for Tamika that she often forgot her previous anxiety. She had left the meeting a month before with a mixture of excitement and stress. She feared Sulayman would discover their incompatibility and reconsider his interest in her. She also feared having high hopes for something that could never be. Then there was the fear of marriage itself. What if he *did* want to marry her? What would she do? She didn't want to give up her family entirely, and she feared getting married would force her to do just that. It was difficult enough for her family to accept her conversion to Islam. What would they do when they discovered that she intended to marry too? Despite all her fears, Tamika felt such a deep connection with Sulayman that, more often than not, she was willing to take the risk.

Naturally, Tamika wanted to know what he thought of her beyond enjoying her company on the phone, but she couldn't bring herself to ask. She imagined he wanted to know the same from her, but she wouldn't have known what to say if he asked. She liked him a great deal, but she was becoming overwhelmed with doubt. There was still a part of her that feared their relationship wouldn't last beyond the phone.

Sulayman never mentioned Aidah when they talked, but Tamika imagined his relationship with her was much like the one she now had with him. If he could decide Aidah wasn't good enough for him, how did Tamika stand a chance? It was flattering that God had guided him from Aidah to "elsewhere," but what gnawed at her was that there was once a time he had been guided to Aidah too. Tamika couldn't fight the fear that their enjoyable conversations would end as merely a token of wisdom to take with him to the one who was really for him. That they hadn't seen each other since meeting with the imam only increased her fear that they wouldn't last.

They talked on the phone with ease and comfort only because of the safe distance they felt, Tamika imagined. The true test of their compatibility would come when they were face-to-face. Tamika couldn't deny the joy she felt when she talked to Sulayman on the phone, but the joy was misleading because they never had to face reality. She feared that Sulayman wasn't offering to drive her and Aminah to Atlanta because he didn't want to see her again. Perhaps he too was afraid of what an in-person meeting would do to the relationship they had built. Maybe she wasn't the only one having doubts that it could work. Talking on the phone was a form of denying the truth, she guessed. And since seeing Tamika would force him to face it, he opted not to take the chance.

Even Aminah had begun to get antsy about being stuck at the school. She wanted to go home periodically, which was understandable, and now she couldn't. Tamika couldn't help feeling a bit guilty because, after all, wasn't she the one keeping Sulayman from taking the trip? In the past week, Aminah must have joked a dozen times when she arrived in the room after class, "If you talk to that brother of mine, tell him I wouldn't mind a ride home every now and then." But Tamika knew part of Aminah wasn't joking.

Tamika would make a mental note to mention it to Sulayman, but whenever they finally talked, Aminah ceased to exist, and Tamika would even push her own anxiety to the back of her mind. Hearing him talk on the other line told her that she wasn't the only one who wanted to get married, and she forgot about her doubts—until she hung up the phone again.

Hanging up the phone not only forced Tamika to address her doubts that they would ever marry. She also had to address doubts about herself. When she and Sulayman were talking on the phone, it was as if she were wearing a mask, pretending to be who she was not. The mask had become so much a part of her that she often forgot she had it on. It felt so natural to wear it because she never needed to take it off. Then she would hang up and realize her crime. She was betraying him. And one day he would surely know.

Tamika tried to tell herself he wouldn't hold it against her. But her sin haunted her like a bad dream. A dark cloud loomed above her and threatened to storm her sense of safety as soon as she relaxed. It had only been one person, she kept telling herself, but the dark cloud would explode with thunder at the thought. He was understanding, she would tell herself, so it wouldn't matter to him.

But this conjured consolation wouldn't give her the peace she longed. She knew he assumed she was chaste, and her acquiescence itself was a lie. But how could she uncover the truth when she herself couldn't bear what was beneath? The sinful relationship had held no more meaning to her then than it did now, which should have been a source of comfort for her. But its insignificance made the sin only that much more repulsive in her eyes. She could only imagine what aversion it would erupt in Sulayman when he learned of it himself.

Hadn't God forgiven her? This was the question she kept asking herself. Didn't becoming Muslim mean Allah forgave all her sins? Yet that didn't address the more immediate question. What if Sulayman never would?

She wanted to talk to someone—*needed* to talk to someone. But Aminah was her only confidant. And carnal sin was beyond the realm of her saintly world. Even if, as a Muslim friend, Aminah wouldn't judge her for her past, she was Sulayman's sister and couldn't help desiring better for him. What sane Muslim wouldn't contest her pious brother marrying a tainted bride?

She would have to tell him.

The painful realization came to Tamika suddenly, and she lifted her gaze from the book and let it rest on the phone. What this meant for their relationship was too weighty to face right then.

Nineteen

The dark gray sky lingered with such insistence that the brightness of early afternoon cowered in retreat as if anticipating the premature setting of the sun. The day's dim light spilled into the living room window with such hesitance that it was necessary to turn on a light. Cold air stiffened the atmosphere and seemed to slow the activities of the home. Ismael turned on the heat for the first time in months and paused to gaze out the window before settling on the couch a comfortable distance from his son.

It was late November, more than six weeks after Sulayman met with Tamika and began talking to her on the phone. Aminah hadn't been home to visit her family in more than a month, and Ismael suspected his son avoided the drive to campus for fear of facing Tamika. Of course, Ismael could have driven to Streamsdale himself to bring his daughter home, but he didn't like the idea of allowing his son to continue evading an issue he eventually had to face.

It was Sunday, and Sulayman hadn't called Tamika at all this weekend, and he didn't take his sister to *Jumuah* although she had called Thursday to let him know she wanted to come. She had no school until Wednesday due to a holiday break, and she was getting frustrated stuck in the dormitory room. She had complained to Ismael and Sarah and begged them to come get her if Sulayman wouldn't. Aminah didn't mention anything about Tamika when she called, but Ismael couldn't drive to Streamsdale for Aminah and leave Tamika on campus without even the courtesy of an invitation to join.

Ismael drew in a deep breath and exhaled. He and Sulayman had returned home from the *masjid* a few minutes before and had talked on the way home. Sulayman expressed how he had strong feelings for Tamika and wondered what their next step should be. He worried about supporting her financially and if marrying now was a good idea. He and his father continued talking in the house, and Sulayman had just asked how his father had known he should marry his mother, who was visiting her friend Maryam and would be gone most of the day.

"I didn't know," Ismael said finally. It wasn't the answer Sulayman wanted, but Ismael understood his son needed truth more than comfort. "We weren't Muslim when we met, so for the most part we handled our relationship the best we knew how. I felt like I loved her, and she felt the same about me." There was a thoughtful pause.

"You know," Ismael continued in deep thought, scratching at his chin under his beard, "after a while playing house doesn't work because life catches up to you." Sulayman sat listening with such sincere concentration that Ismael could only pray his explanation would be sufficient for his son.

There was so much Sulayman needed to know, but there was so much more that Ismael didn't know himself. Even after twenty-three years of marriage, there were no easy answers. Life happened to everyone who lived, and there was no way to escape what that meant. "Successful" was a misleading term to describe a marriage that lasted as long as his. Success implied that one worked hard to arrive at a goal that he finally achieved. A runner who crossed the finish line first tasted success. The student who scored a 1600 on the SAT tasted success. A child who learned to walk tasted success, even as he was unaware of what it meant. But marriage wasn't a race or a standardized test, and it wasn't learning to walk. There were no finish lines to cross or scores to tally, and there were no feet wandering the world for the first time.

Marriage didn't consist of working hard and arriving finally at a goal. Marriage was a means and an end at the same time, and it was work itself that made it work. Measuring success in a marriage was like measuring the essence of life itself. It was so complex that how things seemed wasn't always how they actually were. What appeared like failure could actually be success. And what appeared like success could actually be failure. It was true that reconciling differences and weathering storms were essential to a marriage that worked. But there were times when divorce was more honorable than staying married and represented more triumph than defeat. The unsuccessful marriage may itself be success for a person because of what it armed him with against the trials of life and the affairs of the soul. There was no moment of success in marriage at which a couple could look back and feel proud. Marriage was like living, and at times, all one could do was thank God he survived.

Sulayman's expression grew confused, apparently unsatisfied with his father's answer. "But isn't there a sign you get that tells you what to do?"

The urgency of Sulayman's question made Ismael aware suddenly of how far he himself had come. But a sense of pride swept over him that made him unable to measure the significance of the moment right then.

There was a time Ismael could only pray for his son. Ismael had watched Sulayman struggle through his tumultuous teens, a time when Sulayman seemed to live more inside himself than their home. The little he asked of his father was material, money for a basketball game, permission to go out, or a break from burdensome household chores.

Their father-son relationship had never been strained, at least not in the absolute sense. Sulayman rarely disrespected his father, and Ismael had never found it difficult to live with his son. But it was a difficult time for Ismael when he watched his son breeze through school and grow perplexed about life.

Sulayman was a good son, the kind that would make any father proud. But being a Muslim father was not the same as being a father in the world. Ismael had higher hopes for his son than making something of himself after high school. It wasn't worldly success that he had feared Sulayman wouldn't taste. It was the spiritual. Sulayman had given his father no tangible reason to fear for him. But Ismael knew that life might find his son before Sulayman was ready. Sulayman had all the qualities of a successful man. He was intelligent, charismatic, and handsome. But that could be the recipe for disaster if he let his talents direct him instead of the other way around.

Girls called the house often while Sulayman was in high school. They always claimed to need help with homework, and Sulayman took the claim at face value and offered his help. Ismael would watch his son patiently explain the English, math, or science assignment to the girl. Sulayman's naiveté made Ismael fear that his son's innocence would be chipped away. However, there was little he could tell Sulayman then because Sulayman was in his own world. The world presented itself as innocent and Sulayman accepted that it was. Had Ismael forbade Sulayman from receiving the calls, Sulayman might have rebelled. Patience was Ismael's only recourse at the time. He would have to leave the job of granting understanding to Allah.

Whatever Sulayman learned about life in school, Ismael was pleased it had come to this. Sulayman didn't have to choose marriage, and this Ismael knew. It was obvious even to a father's eye the way young women were drawn to his son. Ismael had enough experience with women to detect impure intentions when the clear signs were there. He couldn't imagine having the ability to resist such temptations at Sulayman's age. Islam and the purpose of life itself were foreign to him at that time. But even Islam didn't protect a person from sin. It only defined the boundaries he shouldn't cross and pointed to that which would protect him. But people were people. It wasn't without wisdom that Allah put more emphasis on turning to Him in repentance than avoiding sin itself.

Ismael didn't pretend to know the faults of his son, and he was not so naïve to think his son a saint. But he did know his son was a young man, and young men desired women. Lust drove most men's relationships with women at Sulayman's age. While most young women desired commitment, most young men desired women, and nothing more. Marriage was a noose around a man's neck, in the world's view, and a man chose survival when given the choice. That Sulayman's fear and love of God made him favor marriage over sin inspired in Ismael a deep respect for him. Ismael couldn't help but recognize God's tremendous blessings in guiding his son on this path. He was forever indebted to Allah for bestowing upon him a righteous son. Even in listening to his son's question, he couldn't help but reflect on how that moment was one even Muslim fathers would rarely have with their sons at this age.

"I can't say there is," Ismael said so reflectively that Sulayman feared he would have to find the solution in those words alone. "But I can't say there isn't, because the way of Allah in these situations isn't just one. But I *do* know that how you feel about a woman isn't always a measure of what you should do." The expression on his son's face told Ismael he should make his explanation less complex.

"Do you want to marry her?" Ismael asked, feeling Sulayman could understand him better if Sulayman found the answer himself.

"Yes," Sulayman said, the honesty of his answer both shocking and calming him at once. It wasn't the most comfortable thing to discuss with his father, but it was the most urgent. Sulayman had talked with many Muslim women, but none of the relationships terrified him as much as this did. His feelings for Tamika were so profound that he was surprised that it was possible to feel this strongly for a woman who was not already his wife. He was afraid to lose her, yet he had nothing to offer her if he were to marry her right then.

"Does she want to marry you?"

The question had been one that danced in the back of Sulayman's mind ever since he and Tamika began to talk. But he had ignored it so that he could relax as they talked. He hadn't asked her how she felt about him because he was afraid of what she might say. In the imam's office she had said she didn't know, but that was because she knew nothing about him. But now she did.

"I don't know," Sulayman said, raising his eyebrows and drawing in a deep breath. A second later his eyes grew distant as he seemed to stare beyond the wall.

The fear that engulfed his son's answer made Ismael wish he could make it better for him. But without knowing what the woman wanted, it was difficult to give his son advice on what to do himself.

"Then find out before it's too late," Ismael said, patting his son's shoulder with a gentle smile of empathy creasing a corner of his mouth.

Sulayman looked to his father so quickly that his father could only meet his gaze with a gentle nod, letting him know there was such a thing as "too late."

"Once you're sure she feels the same," Ismael said, "then you both need to take some time to think about what you're embarking on." His smile broadened. "And say lots of prayers. You'll need to find out as much as you can about her, and she'll have to do the same about you."

Late Sunday night Tamika sat on the rust colored carpet of her dorm room hugging her knees. The smallness of the room crowded her, and she longed for the spacious apartment she had shared with Dee and Aminah the year before. The headboards of their beds sat against the same wall, separated only by a small cherry wood nightstand where Aminah's phone sat next to an alarm clock bearing bright red numbers and a colon that disappeared and reappeared each second as it blinked. On either side of their beds was a desk where they studied each day. Tamika's bed was closest to the window, which hung next to her desk and overlooked the side of her bed. Across from their beds were two walk-in closets with a small sink and mirror separating them.

A series of drawers were on the right and left side of the cabinet under the sink, apparently the school's attempt at giving the students a dresser that otherwise wouldn't fit.

At one time the room might have looked exquisite, Tamika imagined, but the years had worn it down. Flaws were left exposed even after the roommates had spent an entire week decorating the room. The room wasn't easy to relax in, and one couldn't help but feel immured. Often when Aminah was there, Tamika felt suffocated in the small space, but her roommate's presence gave the room a liveliness Tamika couldn't experience alone.

Tonight the room was dimly lit by a small reading light on Tamika's desk, giving the room a gloom that reflected her mood. Outside the rain began to fall lightly in the night, tapping in hesitant rhythms against the window. Earlier that evening after hanging up the phone, Aminah asked Tamika if she wanted to join her at home for the school's Thanksgiving holiday break that stretched through Wednesday. Tamika had declined, sensing the offer was motivated more by obligation than desire. Sulayman had known about the break for a week and hadn't come to pick up his sister until that night. It didn't take much thinking to deduce that he had delayed because he didn't want Tamika to come. It would have been disrespectful if they didn't let her know she was welcome—even if she were not.

Tamika had finished praying thirty minutes before, and she should have gone to sleep. But she still sat where she had prayed, wearing the faded black *abiya* and white *khimaar* that she had worn for prayer. She glanced at the clock on the nightstand and frowned. It was 10:26. Letting out a loud sigh, she stood and took off her prayer clothes before folding them over the footboard as she usually did. She pulled open one of the drawers next to the sink cabinet and took out a knee-length pink T-shirt that she often wore to sleep. As she dressed for bed, she thought of how she had wasted the whole day.

The day had dragged on, and Tamika felt as if time had slowed for her. Studying didn't hold her attention, and she spent much of the day staring at the words on the page. There was a feeling of hollowness as she sat at her desk wondering if there would ever be an end to the emptiness she felt. Up until that moment, she wasn't aware that talking to Sulayman made her feel whole, like she had a reason to keep going, to live. Without his phone calls, she felt like a part of her had died, and she could feel the energy being drained from her.

Now dressed in her sleeping tee, Tamika dropped the jeans and T-shirt she had been wearing in the laundry basket in a corner of the room, and she wondered if Sulayman would ever call her again. Perhaps it finally occurred to him that she wasn't the righteous person she had appeared to be. She imagined that he was planning the best way to tell her that he didn't want to go on. The depressing thoughts weighed on her until her body felt heavy, and she climbed into bed. Leaving on her desk light, she pulled the soft covers over her and stared at the shadowy ceiling, wondering what Sulayman was doing right then. She shut her eyes a minute later, too exhausted to think.

The sound of the phone ringing woke her, and she opened her eyes and glanced at the clock. It was 12:06. She turned over and reached for the phone on the nightstand, fearing something was terribly wrong. "Hello?" she spoke into the phone in her scratchy voice.

"*As-salaamu-'alaikum.*"

Sulayman's voice sent her heart racing, and she sat up as she felt hope renewed. "*Wa 'alaiku-mus-salaam.*"

"I apologize for calling this late. I know you were sleeping."

"It's no problem." She cleared her throat, hoping she could find some reason to keep him on the phone.

"I'm sorry for not calling this weekend. I had a lot on my mind." His voice was as sincere as she remembered it, and this soothed her. "I know it's late, so I won't hold you."

Tamika wanted to tell him it's okay, she could talk, but she decided against it. She didn't want to seem too forward. It wasn't like Sulayman to call this late, and she didn't want him to think she felt differently about the time. "What is it?"

There was a long pause, and Tamika heard Sulayman take a deep breath. "I need to know something."

The words sent Tamika's heart pounding until she could feel it in her throat, and she shuddered, knowing what he wanted to know. He would ask about her past sins, and she had no idea what she would say. She had planned to tell him when the time was right, and she hadn't anticipated him asking before then. "Okay," she said, hoping to conceal the nervousness she felt.

"Tamika," he said, and her heart drummed with more force at the sound of her name, "I know you don't know me as well as you probably would like, but this past month has been," his voice trailed off as he searched for a word, "special for me."

Tamika's palms began to sweat as she held her breath for the big "But." She shut her eyes and rubbed the space between them hoping she could bear his next words. "Mm, hm."

"And—." Tamika heard him exhale after drawing in a breath. "I'd like to go further, but I need to know if you're willing to."

Her heart was still racing, and for a moment, she thought she misunderstood. "Willing to what?" It was probably a stupid question, but she couldn't think straight right then.

"Marry me."

She lifted a hand to her chest in surprise and felt the pulsating of her heart throbbing in her hand. The phone almost slipped from her other, and she quickly readjusted it at her ear. She felt the corners of her mouth crease into a wide grin, and she felt her eyes burn with an urge to cry. "Are you proposing?"

There was a brief silence, and for a second Tamika feared she had said the wrong thing.

"I've been doing that all along," he said.

Tamika couldn't keep from smiling. She really wished they could talk all night. "Then what are you doing *now*?"

"I'm asking you for your answer."

She parted her lips to speak, but she didn't know what to say. She couldn't decide how to express what she was feeling. Part of her wanted to tell him what he wanted to hear, what she herself wanted to say. But she knew it was best to wait, at least until he learned of her past.

"You don't have to answer now," Sulayman said, and Tamika couldn't help noticing the disappointment in his voice, "but I'd like to get an idea how you feel about it."

"I, uh," she said in an apology, "I don't know." It was a weak response, she knew, the same one she had given in the *masjid* office when they first talked. Certainly, he wanted to know more than that. Sulayman's silence made her feel guilty for not saying more. How could she expect anything to happen if she wasn't honest with him?

"I want to marry you," she said after a heavy sigh, "but there's so much we still need to know."

"Tamika," he said, as if he had already thought of that, "we'll never know each other like that until we're married."

She smiled beside herself. Sulayman was speaking as if their marriage was just a matter of time. She didn't know what to say. Her smile faded a second later as she reminded herself that he didn't understand what she meant. "But—."

"Tamika," he stopped her, as if he knew why she was holding back, but of course Tamika knew he had no idea, "let's just get married."

It sounded so simple coming from him, and she couldn't help being tickled by his words. But there was still doubt and fear in the back of her mind. He didn't know about her past.

"O-kay," she said, surprising herself by her words. Her heartbeat quickened as she tried to think of a way to take it back. But she said nothing, afraid if she did, she would never have this chance again.

There was silence. Neither knew exactly what to say. They wanted to talk longer, but it was late.

"Tamika, are you in contact with your mother?"

The question threw her off guard. It took some time for her to register what he was asking. "Why?"

"I want to talk to her."

Tamika's heart nearly stopped. She wanted to forget about her mother and move on with her life. She should have known it wouldn't be that easy. Of course, Sulayman knew that her mother had thrown her out of the house after she became Muslim, but he didn't know much beyond that. When she talked to him about her family on the phone, she had mostly discussed how she was raised and her life before Islam. She had told him that she and her mother weren't speaking, but of course that was being vague.

"I don't think that's possible." Her voice was apologetic, but inside she was scared. She didn't want her mother to know anything about her decision to get married. Matters would only get worse when she discovered it was Sulayman, the author of the infamous "self-righteous" editorials she had complained so much about, whom she wanted to marry.

"Is there anyone else I can talk to?"

"Not really." Her reply was too quick, she knew. She sounded as if she were hiding something. Maybe she was.

"You don't have any uncles you keep in touch with?"

"Why?" She sounded defensive. She should really calm down.

"Tamika," he said as if apologizing, "I can't disrespect your family by marrying you without them knowing my intention."

"But they wouldn't understand either way."

"I didn't think they would."

"Then what's the point?"

He paused for a few seconds. "Marriage isn't only between a man and a woman. Our families are marrying too. I'll be your parents' son-in-law, and you'll be a daughter to my parents."

It was flattering to imagine herself as the daughter-in-law to Ismael and Sarah. But it was only dread she felt when she thought of her own family's role in Sulayman's life.

"I know," she said, although she had never thought of it quite like that before. "But my family is different. They would never agree to it."

"I don't expect them to *agree* with what we're doing, but I do want them to know."

"My mother doesn't even speak to me now," she reminded.

"What about your other family?"

He already knew that she didn't know her father. "I have other family," she said tentatively, trying to find a way to keep him from contacting them too, "but nobody who'd be willing to listen to what you have to say."

"There's gotta be somebody, Tamika. Don't you have any uncles?"

"Yes, but I have no idea where they are right now." That was only partly true. Jackie's ex-husband came to Milwaukee regularly to visit his children, and he stayed in touch with Tamika's mother too. And her mother had a half brother who lived in Cincinnati, and Tamika could call Latonya for his number.

After a few minutes more of discussion, Tamika realized there was no way around it. Sulayman wanted to talk to her family, and their marriage depended on it. He explained that he understood that she was at odds with her family because of her conversion, but he felt the problem would only worsen if she married without their knowledge. Good family relations were essential to Islam, even when the family were not Muslim.

Tamika thought of how her family would react when Sulayman called, and she imagined that any hopes she had of building understanding with them would be crushed when she gave the relationship this final blow. Then again, how could her family respect her again and see the beauty of her new faith if it represented only betrayal to them? Maybe Sulayman was right. She shouldn't marry behind their backs.

She listened as Sulayman explained that he wasn't so naïve as to believe that his talking to them would solve her family problems. But if any healing were to take place, a new wound couldn't be inflicted by her marrying without their knowledge. Let them talk, he told her. Let them disagree. Let them shake their heads in shame. But don't give them reason to. Besides, talking to her family was a step he needed to make for himself. She herself had said they needed to learn more about each other, but how could he if he never even spoke with her family?

Finally, Tamika decided that if he wished to talk to anyone, he should call her aunt Jackie. Tamika hung up the phone feeling both relief and trepidation. She was relieved that their relationship wasn't ending and that they were going to take the big step. But she feared what that would mean. She didn't want to upset her family, but, more importantly, how could she continue to hide behind a mask of righteousness after he learned where she had come from?

Tamika lay awake in the night and felt suffocated in its silence. For some reason, the room felt darker after she hung up the phone. She pulled the covers to her shoulders and felt angry with herself for refusing Aminah's invitation home. Anything was better than sleeping in a cramped dorm room alone. The rain had stopped, and there was no rhythmic tapping except that in her head. The thoughts rushed in a second later, and she found herself pondering her life in the middle of the night.

In the months since she became Muslim, Tamika had created an artificial world for herself. She lived cushioned by piety and faith, and these things enabled her to give herself to the future, and escape her past. It had been easier that way. She could focus on school and come to terms with her heart and soul. Her mother waned in importance, and so did the rest of what reminded her from where she had come.

Talking to Latonya only emboldened this feeling, though it should have destroyed it. After all, Latonya was a piece of her past, and talking to her bounded Tamika forever to what she no longer wanted part of. But Latonya didn't represent the past to Tamika. She represented her future. Latonya had let go of what Tamika had held on to, and she turned her back on what Tamika never could. In that way, Tamika needed her sister—to continue living in the world she created. She needed someone to let her know she could do it too.

Talking to Sulayman stripped all of that from Tamika, and she was forced to face the reality of her home, where her mother disowned her and her father walked out. She was forced to see herself, and the woman who stared back at her was more terrified than hopeful.

Tamika couldn't sleep. She shut her eyes to drown out her thoughts. But they disrupted her slumber as if her mother's rough hand jolting her awake. Tamika realized it was probably her desk light that made it difficult for her to rest. She sat up and turned it off in hopes of falling asleep.

In the darkness, her body relaxed and, for a brief moment, she felt herself drifting to sleep. But it was only a taunting. Her mind wouldn't submit to the rest for which her body longed. Thoughts slipped through her mind with the steadiness of water trickling down a windshield after a rain. Turning off the light did nothing to extinguish her thoughts. It had only slowed them—and made them more pronounced. The darkness made it impossible to focus on anything other than what consumed her mind.

She had given Sulayman her aunt's telephone number, and the memory terrified her right then. She had no idea when he would call, but there was no doubt that he would. Sulayman didn't do things casually. He approached everything with a sense of purpose, and he gave his efforts nothing less than his all. He believed any task worth pursuing necessitated the diligence and perfection that reflected his faith. That much was shown in his studies, and Tamika could only imagine how it would manifest in his marriage pursuit.

The thought of Sulayman talking to her aunt made Tamika shiver with fear and shame too profound to comprehend. Under the softness of her comforter, she forced the thought from her mind. But it only moved to seize her heart, and it tightened a knot in her chest. The knot sat with stubborn insistence until it formed a lump in her throat. She felt her heart swell and then weep in silence as hearts always did. Her eyes welled under her closed lids, dam walls obstructing the release. But inside she exploded, and tears broke loose with such force that her whole body shook. She surrendered to the flooding and whimpered in the night, letting her body tremble against the bed.

Lying on her side, her body stilled a few minutes later as her crying slowed to silent tears slipping down her cheeks. She could feel the cold wetness where her crying soaked her pillow under her cheek and ear. She turned to her other side, and it was then, as she lay awake in the dark room, that she allowed herself to admit why she hurt.

Tamika had grown up in a home filled with as much innocence as love. Laughter and play filled the void her father's absence left on them all. As a child, she played make-believe with her sister, with whom she competed for the role of the most distinguished in their games. The characters in their pretend world were always astonishingly beautiful, powerful women who controlled the world with immense fortune and made men their pawns.

Philip, who was often bossed around by Latonya, might be given the title king or prince in the games, but he would be treated as a slave. When he demanded his dinner be brought to him by the queen, a role always played by his twin sister, the queen laughed a taunting laugh and threw her hand at him as if he were a fly. "Get it yourself," her Majesty would command then return to admiring her beautiful hair or skin.

"What shall we do to entertain ourselves today, my dear daughter princess?" the queen would ask, imitating a royal British accent. Tamika enjoyed giving ideas and seeing the queen eagerly approve. Her ideas usually required the expulsion of the nagging king. "Oh, my dear daughter, what a wonderful idea!"

When the royal women ignored him, King Philip took matters into his own hands and would catch the woman unprepared. Often he reemerged with his face decorated in paint and his body covered in torn sheets. As a dragon, he would frighten the women from his castle. His curdling roar and scratching claws terrified even his proud wife. The women would flee from him and scream in playful terror as he neared. Usually, it was their aunt Jackie, who was married and didn't work at the time, who babysat them when their mother wasn't there. She would look up from the television for a brief moment and smile in amusement at their games.

Working two jobs, their mother would return late at night. If her children were sleeping, she would wake them. Oftentimes she bore gifts of candy and ice cream, over which they would laugh and talk before going back to bed. She would read stories and tell them about Jesus and God. On the weekends, they went to church, parks, and, occasionally, houses of their mother's friends.

Craig was never mentioned, at least not by name. But the ghost of his existence haunted Tamika even as a child. She often wondered where her father was and why he didn't live with them. She would see other fathers and ponder what it must be like to actually have one. Her mother avoided the issue completely and made it clear to Tamika and her siblings that he had betrayed them. He was to suffer for his crime, so he was erased from their lives.

But, ironically, it was they who did the suffering.

It was understood that, whatever Tamika and her sister did in life, there were two things that must be. They would be indebted to their mother who loved them, and they would resent their father who abandoned them. They would blossom into swans, their mother promised, and he would be unable to claim that he warmed the nest. Whatever career would give them their beauty, it should be earned by their own hands. For Latonya and Tamika, this meant they were to be self-made women, without the help or presence of a man. Relationships with men should be pursued only if the women had the upper hand. They were not allowed to accept gifts from men because, as their mother explained, this was how a man marked his turf. Marriage was unthinkable unless it happened after they were established, employed and owning their own home. Their mother preferred they avoided it even then.

Tamika learned the lessons well and internalized her mother's desires as her own. Witnessing her mother suffering from working so hard pained her and increased her determination to succeed. Tamika often envisioned herself on a podium one day standing before a large audience, thanking her mother for being her inspiration in life.

As an adolescent, Tamika discovered her love for singing was coupled with a talent that drew crowds to their feet in standing ovations at church. Realizing this, she wanted nothing more than to be a famous singer. But her mother wouldn't hear of it. And it was the first time Tamika's aspirations conflicted with her mother's desires. They battled for sometime about the issue, and, in the end, her mother won. Tamika pushed herself to go the college route, although in her opinion singing success would be more monumental than whatever school could bring. But she couldn't disappoint her mother, even if it meant giving up a part of herself.

When Tamika studied about Islam, it was a painful realization that came over her when she discovered the truth of the religion. Too weak to face what this meant, she pushed it to the back of her mind. But she was never able to escape reality completely. Befriending Dee both helped and confused her spiritually. She was drawn to Dee, a Muslim who fulfilled her dreams of being a model and singer at the same time, but Tamika was confused by the apparent contradictions that this forced Dee to live.

Eventually, Tamika came to love Dee as Dee, regardless of her religious struggles that Tamika couldn't comprehend. Tamika enjoyed what the friendship brought, and it was this that she savored and admired about Dee. Dee was able to fulfill two dreams at once, school to satisfy her mother and singing to satisfy herself. But Islam threatened them both. In that way, she and Dee were the same. Tamika wanted to sing and please her mother by making it through school. But accepting Islam wouldn't allow her to do either, at least not how she wanted. She could have continued school as a Muslim, but it would have to be without her mother's support. Without that, school lost all meaning in her life.

In Islam death was often referred to as "the extinguisher of desires," which Tamika assumed to mean that the deceased finally cared about nothing but her soul. But Tamika felt the extinguishing power of death reach even her when Dee died. She became Muslim and recognized no previous desire as more important than the salvation of her soul.

But it was human nature for people to have renewed desires once the impact of tragedy subsided. So Tamika found herself still hanging on to the hope that, even as a Muslim, she could make her mother proud by achieving in school. When she was thrown out of her home, Tamika felt a pain that seemed to penetrate her very soul. The message glared at her, but she didn't want to look it in the eye. And she spent much of the summer shutting her eyes to what should have been clear all along.

Nothing she did as a Muslim would her mother accept.

Time healed wounds, Tamika had been told, but as she studied the dim strip of light glowing in the darkness under her door, she wondered if there were ever exceptions to that rule.

After becoming Muslim, Tamika shut her eyes to the painful reality of her mother's stance. She pushed forward despite the tumultuous current fighting against her every move. She continued school with more determination to succeed than she had her first two years. And it was the irony of it that Tamika found difficult to admit.

When she and her mother were the best of friends, school was a burden Tamika had to force herself to fulfill. When her mother wanted nothing to do with her, Tamika wanted to give school her all. Both times, her motivation had been the same. To please her mother, however impossible it was.

Perhaps if she worked hard enough, Tamika had thought after becoming Muslim, her mother would realize how much she loved her after all. Tamika had forced herself to push the gravity of her family problems away from her at the time. But it hovered above her like a storm cloud portending ruin.

Tamika's upbringing had made it impossible to see marriage as anything but foreign. She had often daydreamed of elegant bridal gowns, as every woman did, and was intoxicated by the romantic splendor of weddings. But she treated the thoughts as she did her daydreams of becoming a princess and living in a magnificent castle. None of it was real.

Marriage was a prison, this she had understood. The extravagant production of the day was merely to satiate the childish desires of the heart that still believed in fairy tales and happily ever after. Tamika had been determined to delay the matrimony as long as she could, if it was indeed inevitable at all.

Even after becoming Muslim, she held onto these views. Her acceptance of the Islamic marriage was only in theory. But nothing directly relating to her. Men were part of a world she was detached from, and she would focus on herself. Before Islam, whenever she saw a man she was attracted to, she admired him from afar and didn't consider him beyond that. In fact, she never wanted him for herself. This detachment most likely surfaced after her vow of celibacy as a Christian, but it had carried over into her life in Islam.

Tamika had treated her attraction to Sulayman the same way. Given her previous loathing of him, she initially didn't recognize her attraction as heartfelt, interpreting it as her merely developing a kinder opinion of him. But, stealthily, her admiration for him invaded her mind and finally her heart. Even after she realized what was happening, she sought to resolve her feelings internally. It was a matter of instinct. The prospect that anything would come of her affection was as hopeless as a child's desire to be king. So she lived inside herself and allowed herself to be tormented by her feelings until they subsided. It hadn't occurred to her that they never would. And she had never imagined that she actually wanted to marry him—until she learned that Aidah did.

When she sat in the imam's office and heard his confession, it was as if life itself opened up for her once again. She was so absorbed in her excitement of what this meant for her that her previous sentiments about marriage became obscured and foreign, unrecognizable in her new world. On the phone, she was so happily content in her newfound relationship with Sulayman that she didn't want to imagine that anything could change it.

When Sulayman mentioned talking to her family, it was as if someone ripped a veil from her eyes and opened a fresh wound in her heart. She found herself suddenly thrown back into a painful existence from which she had sought escape. Her mother and aunt didn't exist in her new world, and their invasion threatened the survival of the world itself. The thought of him talking to her aunt hurt so much because of what it meant for her fairy tale existence she had created for herself.

It would be the final latch that sealed her horrible fate as an outcast to her family. It would be the detonator of the contentment she had worked so hard to construct. The talk with her aunt would threaten both her life as a family member and the life she hoped to build with Sulayman as his wife. For her family, it would be the unequivocal confirmation that they needed to turn their backs on her—irrevocably. It was a horrible affront for her to show her allegiance to Islam, an allegiance that denied the Christian faith that was her family's heart. Should they learn that she was considering marriage, it would be the final blow to any hopes she had of fulfilling the very purpose of her mother's hard work and sacrifice in life. For that, Tamika was ashamed.

And scared.

Twenty

Tamika dragged herself out of bed when the clock read 11:50 Monday morning. After the dawn prayer, she usually slept only until 9:30 when there wasn't school. She liked to begin her studies early. But the night had been mostly sleepless for Tamika, and she needed the extra rest. She showered and dressed before leaving her dorm room to eat lunch, her first meal of the day. The sun was glowing and offering its warmth to the day, but clouds lingered, as if too tired from last night's rain to move on. The air was cool, and Tamika was grateful she had worn her knee-length navy blue sweater over her black *abiya*.

The cafeteria was mostly empty because of the holiday. Most students had gone home for Thanksgiving break, and only the unfortunate students remained, those with too little money to return home and those with little reason to want to. Tamika knew which category she fell into and felt a twinge of shame at the realization. She grabbed a tray to shut out her thoughts before positioning herself before the food station.

The aroma of steamed rice, green beans, and baked chicken filled her nostrils as she studied the food choices. She was trying to stay away from fast food, but the bleak choices before her made it difficult to resist the urge to grab a burger and French fries. Growing impatient with her indecisiveness, she walked over to the salad bar and prepared herself a turkey sandwich. Lifting a plastic cup from the station next to the bar, she slid her tray down and filled the cup with pink lemonade before going to the register to have her meal card swiped.

Tamika found a seat in the far corner of the cafeteria near the conveyer belt where trays were returned. She took a seat facing the wall and began to eat. She didn't want to spend her lunch hour next to students who could empathize with her sense of family rejection. She imagined her eyes meeting another student's, after which they would smile, thinking, *You too, huh? Join the club.* She mindlessly watched the stale orange plastic trays piled with trash and wasted food slide slowly by on the belt until they disappeared into the kitchen, waiting to be emptied into the garbage. She found herself wondering if the scene represented her life.

She had been so absorbed in self-pity that she was only vaguely aware of someone standing near her table. It wasn't until she felt a hand tap her shoulder that she realized the person wanted her attention. Startled, she turned and met the person's gaze.

"Gosh, you must have a lot on your mind."

Tamika smiled. "Sorry."

Tamika had met Zahra in September at a Muslim Student Association meeting and maintained a casual relationship with her since then. Tamika had joined the group to meet more Muslims and become involved in Islamic activities on campus. Although Aminah had been active in the organization during her first three years in school, she decided to focus on her studies for her last year. Aminah attended some activities, but she wasn't involved as much as she used to be. It was difficult for Tamika to relax in the group without her roommate, and her discomfort only grew as she realized that she was the only African-American active in the group. Tamika was one of the few Muslim women who covered their hair, and this only increased her feeling of alienation. The social climate of the MSA was influenced mostly by the culture of its members, which forced Tamika to learn more about the Pakistani majority. She had never known people from Pakistan, so the experience was enlightening and enjoyable although she couldn't quite figure out how she fit in, if she did at all.

Aside from the association's activities, it was clear that the Pakistanis had a bond she couldn't hope to penetrate, and she never tried. She couldn't help feeling slighted, but she understood it was only natural that people were drawn to those of their own race. She was herself. It wasn't ill intent that motivated bonds of intra-cultural and racial friendships that excluded others. It was circumstance. After all, people were most drawn to those to whom they could closely relate. It was no one's fault that geography, skin color, and shared struggles gave people common experiences that made it difficult to understand and befriend others. Now Muslim, Tamika wanted to challenge the barriers, which she found even in herself, and test the power that sharing a common faith had in people's hearts. But the experience of the past few months taught her more than she had bargained for and shattered much of her idealism she had as a new Muslim.

Tamika learned both the bonding and destructive nature of having a common culture. She learned that, most times, cultural influence was more powerful than religious beliefs. She had heard that Islam was more a way of life than it was a religion, but it wasn't until she was an MSA member that she understood what that meant. For many of the MSA members, Islam was *only* a religion, a belief system passed down from their parents and ancestors for generations.

Many members talked openly about their boyfriends and girlfriends and parties they attended. If she hadn't known any better, she would have thought these things were permissible in Islam. She also learned that many of them didn't pray, and others prayed only during *Jumuah*. Tamika was praised so highly for wearing a *khimaar* and praying all her prayers that she sometimes wondered if she was doing something monumental by fulfilling these basic requirements. It was flattering that she, who hadn't even been Muslim for a year, was admired by people who had been Muslim since birth.

Of course, there was the painful side of the admiration too. There were those who stayed clear of her, as if her presence was a threat. She found that people were defensive whenever she was around, and they often initiated discussions asking what she thought of Muslims who didn't cover or pray. Most times she evaded these issues and changed the subject somehow, mostly by expressing her own lack of knowledge about Islam. But the frequency of the questions made it impossible to do this each time. She often felt guilty for not saying something that could benefit them and inspire change, but she was still struggling herself and hated the idea of appearing judgmental. But despite her greatest efforts to appear diplomatic, she offended someone each time and made the students feel as if she looked down upon them.

It was then that she understood how Aminah must feel. Tamika had reacted to her the same way when Aminah was trying to help Dee. Now she was in the same predicament, and she had no idea how to get out.

At one point Tamika became so frustrated with the whole scene that she decided to stop coming. But the more she thought about it, the more she realized she should keep attending. Allah would make a way for her to benefit from participating, and eventually, her presence would inspire others. But it was one thing for people who were born Muslim to be openly Muslim in the organization—it was another matter entirely to have a person who had abandoned the very life they were chasing openly practicing Islam in their midst. As threatening and intimidating as Tamika's presence was, she realized it was needed. But Tamika couldn't deny that the MSA experience, which she had hoped would help her Islam and give her solace in the un-Islamic environment, threatened her Islamic stability more than it encouraged it, and confused her more than it consoled.

"Mind if I sit with you?" Zahra asked. She was a sophomore and was one of the few students who talked to Tamika outside of MSA activities, and she seemed to genuinely enjoy Tamika's company. Zahra didn't cover her hair, but she prayed regularly and wasn't ashamed to admit that she had a long way to go in her religious commitment. She didn't participate in the discussions that accused Tamika of being judgmental, and she had even remarked once that they should stop using Tamika as a scapegoat for their own insecurities. It was apparent that Zahra admired Tamika's commitment to Islam, but she didn't dwell on it. It made Tamika feel good that there was at least one person who wasn't intimidated by her practice of Islam.

Talking to Zahra often made Tamika better understand Islam and how balanced it was. Tamika should have been able to relate to the members who covered like she, but they shied away from her for reasons Tamika couldn't pretend to understand. Zahra often explained to Tamika the peculiarities of Pakistani culture so that she could better understand why some members were treating her in the manner they did. The explanations never eliminated the pain, but they did lessen it.

Tamika shrugged and slid her purse to the end of the table. "Sure."

Zahra set her tray on the table and removed her waist length black leather jacket and hung it on the back of her chair before sitting down. She was wearing a long sleeved white cotton shirt tucked inside of her jeans. On anyone else the pants would have been revealing, but the jeans were loose against Zahra's small frame. Her straight black hair was cropped just below her ears and curled slightly at the ends. Tamika imagined she wasn't as popular as the other Pakistani women, who were admired for the length and thickness of their hair. Though Zahra's hair was probably naturally long, it wasn't thick enough to make long hair attractive on her.

"What are you doing here?" Zahra asked as she tapped her straw on the table and slid the flimsy white wrapping off the plastic before poking the straw through the top of her cup and taking a sip. "I thought you'd be home during the holiday."

Tamika chuckled. "I don't know. I guess I enjoy college more than I realized."

Zahra laughed. "Yeah right, and I'm here to gaze at the beautiful campus once more."

They both laughed. Zahra pushed her drink to the side and unwrapped her burger, and Tamika's eyes grazed the fries on her friend's tray, wishing she had chosen them after all.

"Why are *you* here?" Tamika asked, grinning as her eyes met Zahra's.

Zahra took a bite of her burger and rolled her eyes in response. She chewed and swallowed her food before she said, "I have a zillion things to study before I take a break." She forced laughter. "Besides, I'm really not in the mood for a Paki party right now."

"A Paki party?" Tamika grinned and shook her head. She was always amused when Zahra referred to her people as "Paki," as if it referred more to an affliction than an ethnicity.

"My mom invited all my cousins over this week," Zahra said with feigned boredom, "and I'll find any excuse not to go."

"It can't be that bad."

"Oh, yes it could." She rolled her eyes and narrowed them in a way that made Tamika giggle. "You can't imagine how irritating it is. All they do is gossip in Urdu the whole time." She pulled three fries from the bag and slid them in her mouth one at a time.

"I thought you lived at home."

"I live off-campus with my sister, but my parents live in Stone Mountain."

Tamika nodded.

"But I'll go home tonight," Zahra said regretfully. "I just want to pretend this is gonna be a real break for me."

The two ate in silence for a few minutes. When Tamika finished the last of her sandwich, her eyes again fell upon Zahra's fries.

"Here." Zahra handed the small bag of remaining French fries to Tamika. "I shouldn't be eating all these anyway."

Though slightly embarrassed for being so obvious, Tamika accepted the offer without a word and began eating the fries.

"When are you going home?" Zahra asked seriously a minute later.

"I'm not." Tamika surprised herself by the blunt honesty in her words.

Zahra wrinkled her forehead. "Why not?"

Tamika had never discussed her family problems with Zahra although Zahra was aware that Tamika spent most of her weekends at Aminah's house. Naturally, Zahra assumed that Tamika and Aminah were merely good friends who enjoyed spending time together. It was common for students whose families lived far away to spend their weekends with friends who lived off-campus or had families nearby.

"It's not feasible," Tamika said, hoping the response would suffice. She was a private person and hated talking about personal issues to people she barely knew.

Zahra was silent momentarily, understanding in the response more than Tamika intended to share. "What about Aminah?"

Tamika shrugged, and she tried to resist frowning at the reminder of the weekend's drama. Despite her desire to keep her life private, she found it difficult to hide her feelings. "She offered, but I decided to stay here."

Zahra nodded, but Tamika could tell she wasn't convinced. "You're going to stay on campus until Wednesday?"

The question was one of disbelief, and Tamika had a difficult time finding a sensible explanation as to why her answer would be yes. Unsure how to respond, Tamika said nothing, which only increased Zahra's concern.

"Is everything okay?"

The softness of Zahra's voice revealed a concern that penetrated Tamika's heart. She was moved. A lump developed in her throat, and her eyes burned. Between Sulayman and her family, and not being able to talk to Aminah about her struggles, Tamika felt like she was going to explode. It had been some time since she was able to confide in someone. But as tempting as it was, she didn't want to talk to Zahra. She and Zahra lived different realities, and Tamika doubted she could relate. In Pakistani culture, Tamika imagined, children didn't get kicked out of their homes after a silly fight.

Tamika darted her eyes anywhere they would land, the tall gray garbage can with black plastic gathered around its mouth, the fork and upturned milk carton that had fallen to the floor, the empty seat next to Zahra—anything but Zahra's eyes. She was concentrating all of her energy in fighting the urge to cry. And Zahra's silence didn't help. It only magnified how much Zahra empathized with her, how much Tamika had a right to feel sad, and how it was okay if she did cry. No, silence wasn't what she needed right then. She needed Zahra to say, *Oh, give it a rest,* or *Did you ever taste the baked chicken in here? It sucks.* But nothing. Nothing. That's what Zahra said, and Tamika feared she was going to break down right there.

"Let's go," Zahra said in a whisper as she leaned forward and touched Tamika's hand.

Zahra's fingers were warm, and Tamika had to resist pulling her hand away. She couldn't take affection right then, not when her eyes burned behind her lids.

Zahra stood, and Tamika's hand felt cold suddenly as she quickly put it on her lap. Zahra stacked Tamika's tray on hers before carrying them both to the conveyor belt. She returned to the table and put on her jacket. When she turned to leave, she didn't wait to see if Tamika was behind her. Of course, Tamika was. She didn't know where else to go.

Tamika followed Zahra outside and walked a pace behind her in silence. She had no idea where they were going, but she didn't protest. The sun shined with more insistence than it had earlier, Tamika noticed, and the clouds were now soft white cotton masses cushioning the afternoon sky, no hint of last night's rain. Tamika's eyes cooled under the natural beauty, the urge to cry now gone, and she wondered if the clouds of her life would evolve so magnificently.

Zahra crossed through the grass and approached a car garage that sat on one end of the campus. Tamika followed, and after entering the garage, they stopped in front of a black four-door Honda Civic that glistened even in the shadows of the garage. Zahra unlocked the doors from her key chain.

"You need a break," Zahra said with a smile before climbing in. Tamika opened the passenger side door and waited as Zahra reached over to remove the stack of textbooks and put them in the back seat.

Tamika forced laughter as she climbed in. She nodded as she fastened her seatbelt. "How'd you know?" She hoped to veil the shame she felt for revealing her grief to Zahra, even without saying a word. Tamika disliked having her personal stress in the open, but she felt relieved to be with Zahra, even if only for a little while.

Zahra smiled as she clicked her seat belt in place. "Everybody needs a break sometimes." She started the ignition and put the car in reverse before backing out of the space. She put the car in drive and made her way out of the garage. A second later the day's light spilled into the car, and Tamika marveled at how magnificent the campus appeared after a few minutes in the dark garage.

"So what should it be?" Zahra asked. She grinned and glanced sideways at Tamika. "Miniature golf or a movie?"

Tamika couldn't help being reminded of Dee. She smiled and looked out the window to resist the memory. "They have golf in Streamsdale?"

"No, but they do near my apartment."

"You don't live in Streamsdale?" The conversation soothed Tamika, and she felt herself relaxing.

Zahra shook her head. "But it's only ten minutes from here."

Tamika nodded before deciding what she wanted to do. She wasn't in the mood for anything that required too much concentration or movement. She also feared how others would react to her presence. She still wasn't accustomed to going out for leisure dressed as a Muslim. She would rather sit in a dark room where no one could stare at her than stand in bright daylight swinging a golf club while others looked on. She imagined the small town people would find it a quite a spectacle for a woman donned in Arab dress to play miniature golf. "I guess we can watch a movie."

The last time Tamika had gone to a movie was with Omar, and she felt a bit uncomfortable with the idea. Normally, she would have been excited to sit for a couple of hours in front of a large screen, but now she wasn't sure. Even as a Christian, she was uncomfortable with some of the risqué scenes in popular movies. She could only pray that Zahra wouldn't take them to a movie like that.

Zahra nodded. "I'm in the mood for a movie too."

"Do you mind?" Zahra asked a few minutes later.

Tamika turned from where she was looking out the window to see what Zahra was asking about and found Zahra reaching for the radio. Tamika shrugged.

As music filled the car, Tamika pondered how differently people practiced the same religion. Aminah had told her Muslims weren't allowed to listen to music, unless it was voice only or accompanied by a simple drum. But most of the Muslims Tamika met, including Omar, listened to music. Tamika knew enough about Islam to know that whoever was right, the issue couldn't make or break someone's Islam. Nevertheless, she wanted to research it for herself. She wasn't sure what she thought about the issue although she couldn't deny she found it a bit awkward to see Muslims singing along to popular songs.

Late that afternoon Tamika sat at the dining room table in Zahra's apartment eating the Chinese food they had ordered. They had finished watching the movie an hour before and had dropped by Zahra's apartment to relax. Tamika was grateful that the movie had been a family one. She was never sure what moviemakers meant by "family," but she was glad to be spared the foul language and illicit scenes characteristic of most 90's movies. At times she wondered if there was a record filmmakers were trying to make for making the most obscene movie before the turn of the century.

Zahra sat opposite Tamika at the glass-topped table and was flipping through a fashion magazine that her sister had left there. Occasionally, she would make a comment about some of the styles and laugh at others. Tamika almost envied how easily Zahra enjoyed her comfortable home. The apartment complex was practically brand new, having been built a mere five years earlier. Zahra had informed Tamika of this after Tamika had commented on the immaculate appearance of the garden style buildings.

The apartment that Zahra shared with her sister was spotless. The living room was covered in soft off-white carpet that stretched throughout the home. A large, rectangular-shaped bronze trimmed mirror hung above the floral couch and brightened the room. A glass-topped coffee table sat in front of the sofa. A white glass vase with flowers spilling from it sat on the small table.

Peach-colored curtains brought out the soft peach strokes on the floral design in the couch. A tall white floor lamp stood in one corner of the room next to a framed picture of who Tamika assumed were Zahra's parents. The couple was dressed in traditional *shalwar khameez* and held pleasant expressions that exhumed wisdom of a culture Tamika would never know.

"Where's your sister?"

Zahra glanced up from her magazine to roll her eyes. "At the Paki party." She closed the magazine a few seconds later and resumed eating.

"You don't have to go?" Tamika asked. She understood very little of Pakistani culture, but she knew simple family gatherings held a monumental importance Americans could only vaguely relate to.

Zahra shrugged. "I usually do, but finals are coming up soon, and my parents want me to do well."

Tamika nodded, although she didn't understand fully. "Don't let me keep you," she said, apologizing with her voice. As much as she hated inconveniencing people, she seemed to always be doing just that.

Zahra waved her hand. "You're not keeping me. I didn't plan on going anyway."

There was a long pause as they ate in silence.

"Tamika," Zahra said, toying with her food with the chopsticks she held, "if you want to take a break, you can stay here."

Tamika's eyebrows rose, and she shook her head. "No, I couldn't do that."

"We'll be gone until Wednesday, so it doesn't matter."

She was moved by the offer, but she felt uncomfortable accepting it. "No, please. I'm fine in my dorm room."

Zahra wrinkled her nose. "No," she insisted. "You'll get claustrophobic in there."

Tamika laughed. "I'm used to it."

"At least get away for the break."

She shook her head. "I'm fine, really." She loved the spacious apartment but doubted she would be able to relax in someone else's home. "Anyway, I don't have any clothes with me."

"You can borrow mine."

She laughed. "I couldn't fit my toe in your pants."

Zahra laughed too. "I have *shalwar khameez*. They're pretty big."

Tamika shook her head.

Zahra frowned and gazed sympathetically at Tamika. Tamika couldn't tell what she was thinking, but she imagined Zahra felt sorry for her and was grateful she had a family who loved her.

"I wish I could help," Zahra said.

Tamika forced a smile. She hadn't intended to give the impression that she needed help, but she had never been good at masking her feelings. She shook her head. "It's nothing, really."

The sound of the phone ringing interrupted them and prompted Zahra to stand. She hurried to the phone, which hung in the kitchen. "Hello?" A few seconds later, Zahra began to speak in Urdu. Her speech quickened a minute into the conversation, and her voice rose. It sounded as if she were arguing with someone. The exchange lasted for several minutes, and Zahra returned to the table exhausted. She groaned as she slid into her chair. "My mom and sister are on their way here."

"What?" Tamika said, feeling as if she were intruding.

Zahra rolled her eyes. "My cousins want to see my apartment."

Tamika laughed at the irony of it. Zahra had succeeded in avoiding them, and now they were coming to her. A moment later, Zahra couldn't hold it any longer, and she too laughed at the absurdity of it all.

"You can drop me back at school," Tamika offered. She didn't want to be in the way.

Zahra shook her head. "I told my mom they couldn't come because I had someone here, but she insisted on coming anyway. Anyway, they'll probably be here in twenty minutes, so I don't want to leave."

Tamika nodded and wondered what she would do while everyone spoke in Urdu. She wished she had brought some books with her to keep her preoccupied. She would definitely need to return to campus, she realized just then. She needed to study during the break. But she didn't want to be rude, so she decided she would sit politely through the visit until she could return to school. She could only pray it didn't last long.

The phone rang thirty minutes later and Zahra pressed a button for the apartment gate to let her family in. "They're here," she said with a forced smile after hanging up.

Zahra had changed to traditional Pakistani dress, and Tamika marveled at the beautiful bright orange long shirt with gold trim and matching baggy pants. A sheer orange scarf hung around her neck so the ends dangled in the back. Tamika had never seen Zahra traditionally dressed, and she was impressed with how the *shalwaar khameez* suited Zahra.

There was a soft knock at the door several minutes later, and Zahra immediately opened it. The apartment suddenly became noisy as the family greeted Zahra. Their Urdu chatter filled the living room and gave the apartment a life of its own. Tamika remained where she was sitting in the dining room and enjoyed watching the exchange as she waited patiently for someone to acknowledge her.

Zahra moved so swiftly about the living room in excited chatter that Tamika barely recognized her. Tamika was unaccustomed to hearing Zahra speak Urdu, and she was amazed at how easily Zahra spoke the strange language with her family, as if she had lived in Pakistan all her life. The only sound Tamika could make out was "*Acha*," which seemed to always come in the form of a question. Despite her comments earlier, Zahra seemed to be enjoying her family's company immensely and found many things to say

"*Acha?*" to. She laughed and talked, and became so much a part of the scene that Tamika began to wonder if Zahra forgot she was there.

Hearing her name amongst the strange words prompted Tamika to look at the person Zahra was talking to.

"This is my mom," Zahra said, introducing the woman whom Tamika had seen in the photograph earlier.

"It's good to meet you," Zahra's mother said with a nod. The words revealed a strong Indo-Pak accent that Zahra didn't have, which made Tamika wonder how long the family had lived in the states.

Tamika stood as the woman approached. She accepted her hand and shook it. Tamika felt awkward as the woman kissed her on either cheek, but she smiled politely.

"This is my sister Rabia."

Tamika turned to see a young woman who stood a few inches taller than Zahra and bore little resemblance. Her skin was a tone darker than Zahra's pale peach complexion, revealing smooth caramel-colored skin. Her eyes were large, and dark eyelashes accented the brown pupils. Her thick hair was pulled back in a long braid that hung to her waist. She smiled pleasantly at Tamika as she shook her hand and touched her cheek to hers on either side. "Nice to meet you." Her soft voice revealed no accent.

Tamika was introduced to each person, but she couldn't retain all of their names. For the remainder of the time, Tamika sat at the dining room table, where Zahra and two of her cousins sat with Tamika out of politeness. They spoke in English for Tamika's benefit, and she was grateful. She had no idea who the people were being discussed, but she enjoyed listening nonetheless. Someone named Shazia was going to marry her cousin who was a doctor twelve years older than she, and she wasn't excited about it.

"Is it an arranged marriage?" Tamika inquired after feeling it safe to ask.

One of the women, who appeared to be seventeen or eighteen years old, laughed and shrugged. "Sort of."

At first, the response confused Tamika. How could a marriage be "sort of" arranged? Either it was arranged, or it was not. But a few minutes later she realized what the woman had meant. Although Shazia didn't want to marry him, she agreed because she knew it was what her parents wanted.

The cousins continued to chat and Tamika sat fascinated by the culture. She could not understand marrying someone she didn't love, but she couldn't help admiring the strong sense of family displayed among them. Tamika could only imagine wanting to please her parents so much as to agree to marry someone they wanted for her but she didn't want for herself. It was true that she was pushing herself through school to please her mother, but going to school was short-term. Marriage was for life—at least it was in most other countries, Pakistan amongst them.

"How old is she?" Tamika asked when they began talking about the age difference again.

"Twenty-six," Zahra replied.

"I thought Muslims married early."

One of the young women shook her head. "Not in America."

Tamika gathered her eyebrows, remembering what Aminah had told her. "What about in Pakistan?"

They looked at each other and smiled knowingly. "They marry early there, at least the girls do," Zahra's cousin said.

"A sister told me Muslims marry early here too."

"But it's rare. Most people wait until they've at least finished school."

"Undergrad, you mean?"

She shook her head emphatically. "No, all levels. You can't do anything with just a bachelor's."

Tamika was offended by the comment, but she didn't show it. She wasn't planning to go on to graduate school, and she wondered what they would think of her if they knew.

"I was considering marrying early," Tamika said, surprising herself by the confession. She had no idea why she felt comfortable sharing this bit of information except that it was logical to say right then. Perhaps the statement gave her a sense of distance from what it meant for her personally.

They were silent, and Tamika began to wonder if she had said the wrong thing. She felt awkward as they avoided her gaze and looked elsewhere. No one wanted to respond, but Zahra was the first to speak. "Why?"

Tamika shrugged. "Why not?"

"Don't you want to finish school first?"

"I'm not even sure I wanna finish school." The comment was meant as a joke, but no one laughed.

"Finish school," a voice commanded with such authority that Tamika momentarily wondered if the comment was meant for her. The person who said it was not sitting at the table, which made Tamika feel self conscious for speaking so carelessly in a gathering with so many people there. Because everyone was speaking a foreign language, which had become no more than background noise, Tamika had not even considered that someone was hearing her conversation, or understanding it.

The room grew silent, and it became clear that the woman was the elder of the group. No one dared to speak over her. Tamika's gaze met that of Zahra's mother, who sat on the couch holding a cup of tea. Tamika felt her heart pound wildly as the woman continued what seemed like a lecture.

"Marriage will come. Don't ruin your life. Finish school. Many girls don't have the chance you have to go to school. Do you know how many girls in my country want the opportunity you have?"

Tamika was speechless. Her cheeks grew warm, and she felt her palms begin to sweat. She was grateful that the question was rhetorical because she had no idea how to respond.

"You take care of yourself, then marry." Her accent was thick, but the words were as clear as if Tamika had heard them from her own mother. "I came to this country nineteen years ago to give my children the opportunity they couldn't have in Pakistan. Americans take this for granted. You are young, and you don't know life. Life is not love and all these happy things. People in my country are poor and work very hard for very little. Many can't read, and the people struggle." She threw her hand in the air as if dismissing Tamika. "Don't ruin your life," she repeated with finality then took a sip from her tea.

For a minute, no one spoke, and Tamika became acutely aware of her foreignness in the room. She sensed that her comments about marriage only increased her oddity in their eyes. Bored, she had hoped to pass time by chatting, but her seemingly harmless words disrupted the entire gathering. She sensed the guests were now thinking, if they hadn't earlier, *What is she doing here anyway?*

Mortified, Tamika averted her gaze to the table where she rubbed away fingerprints on the glass, leaving oily smudges where they had been. She felt her face grow hotter until her head itched under her *khimaar* and her eyes stung. Her heart pounded so fiercely, she could feel it in her throat. She shivered in nervous embarrassment, and she scratched at a piece of dried food on the glass until she felt a burning sensation under her fingernail. She wanted to snatch the white cloth from her head and scratch her scalp until it was sore. She nibbled at her lower lip to withstand the fire that enflamed her head, and a moment later she felt the taste of blood against her tongue. She licked her lips as her mind raced in search of a response to loosen the tight atmosphere in the room. But she found none. She sat speechless, too ashamed to even look up. Waiting to disappear.

Slowly, the guests resumed talking and drinking their tea, and the clanking of metal spoons against glass was an awful musical chatter in the room as they stirred sugar into the hot liquid in their cups. Their Urdu conversation was slow, almost hesitant, as they feigned sincere interest in their words.

Minutes later, the room bore the semblance of a real party, and Tamika was relieved, though she knew that their minds were still on her. At the dining room table, Zahra and her cousins tried to make up for the woman's comments by pretending to understand where Tamika was coming from. But Tamika's mind was elsewhere, and she wanted nothing more than to leave the apartment that very moment. If she knew her way back to campus, she would have walked out right then, even if it took her three hours to reach the school.

Somehow she mustered up the strength to mask her feelings, and she began to participate in the discussion at the table. She heard herself laughing along with the women and agreeing with positions she knew too little about to even comprehend. She felt her head nodding to what she was hearing and was amazed at how easily her smile remained on her face. She even spoke in response to some remarks, all in agreement, to ease the pain swelling inside. She used all her energy to keep the mask on her face, for fear that if she let it fall off, tears of frustration and anger would be let loose.

No one other than her mother and aunt had ever spoken to her in such a condescending tone, and Tamika fought the fire of rage that burned as the woman's words pulsated in her mind. Pride suffocated her, and it fought for release. Someone had served her a cup of tea a minute before, perhaps to make up for the elder's outburst, and she gripped the hot glass so tightly that her hand hurt. Her jaws grew sore from clenched teeth, and she soothed the aching with an occasional sip of tea and forced laughter whenever Zahra and her cousins laughed. She hid inside herself at the table, counting the seconds until she could run to her dorm room, at the moment hating everyone who was in the room, including Zahra.

How *dare* Zahra's mother talk to her like that. Who did she think she was? Tamika tightened her grip on the cup at the thoughts, resisting the urge to throw it across the room, hot tea and all, to where the woman sat in royalty dignity among the guests.

After everyone had gone home that night, Tamika convinced Zahra to drop her off at school, though Tamika sensed Zahra didn't need much convincing. Tamika imagined that Zahra herself was now as uncomfortable as Tamika with the idea of her staying there.

The drive back to Streamsdale was tensely quiet, a silence interrupted only by Zahra's occasional apologies and explanations she felt obligated to offer for her mother. As anger and frustration enjoyed their release, Tamika stared out the window the entire time only half-listening, her teeth clenched. Part of her wanted to tell Zahra that she was fine and that her mother's comments hadn't offended her, but she could not. At the moment, Zahra herself was irritating Tamika, and Tamika wished she would just shut up. Fearing that any remark she made would only make matters worse, Tamika sat next to Zahra refusing to look anywhere but out the window into the growing darkness. Tamika had worn the mask too long at the party to put it back on right then.

Tamika climbed out of the car only mumbling her greeting. She didn't mean to slam the door, but its crashing sound shook the car and flung her anger at Zahra so viciously that Tamika saw her flinch. The grass crunched under her feet as she avoided the cement pathway leading to the front lobby and instead walked around the building to the side entrance.

The side door was lit by a lone dying bulb that flickered above it as Tamika approached the door in the night. She probably should have at least turned to wave at Zahra, whose kindness filled Tamika with both gratefulness and frustration right then, making her head ache in a pounding that corresponded with her steps. But instead she felt a dry burning sensation in her throat as she unlocked the door under the dim light. Tamika grew frustrated at the stubborn door, which opened finally after her third attempt.

She yanked the heavy door open, and the bulb made a crackling noise before it went black as the door slowly closed behind her then suddenly slammed shut.

Already, as she skipped the stairs two at a time, racing against the incessant pounding in her head and chest, she felt the tears gathering in her eyes. The deserted hall was constricting in its quietness, and Tamika could hear her breathing as she neared her room. She stopped at her door and pushed the key in the lock, turning it feverishly as her hands trembled in desperation to get inside. She pushed the door open and slipped inside before she quickly closed the door.

The tears burst from her eyes before she even finished locking the door. Her hand fell to the cold brass handle as she pressed her forehead against the tarnished wood until she could almost taste its stench of sweat and age in her nose. Her hot breath brushed her face as she let out a horrible sob into the door, and the smell of cloves and shrimp escaped and hung in the air. Her weeping was muffled only slightly by the door, and she cried louder, as if announcing her agony to the abandoned dorm. She thought of home and wished she could go there right then. She wanted her mother. No one else would do.

Twenty-one

Wednesday evening Sarah sat next to her husband at the dining room table of their home. Plates of spaghetti covered in a hot, thick red sauce that slipped through the crevices of the stringed pasta sat before them. Steam rose from their plates and warmed their faces as the aroma of oregano and garlic floated in the air. Butter glazed dinner rolls sat in a large wooden bowl behind their plates, and a clear glass pitcher of honey-sweetened lemon, lime, and orange juice stood next to it as pulp and seeds floated inside the glass, gathering over the ice cubes.

Sulayman had recently gone to take his sister back to school, and his parents sat down for dinner after he left. The quiet house was sobering, and they relaxed in the calm atmosphere that they would have all to themselves for an hour.

"Did he talk to her mother?" Sarah said as she broke the roll in half that she held in her hand then dabbed the bread in the sauce before taking a bite. She was seizing the opportunity to talk to her husband about their son without fearing Sulayman would overhear.

Ismael shook his head as he poured the juice into his glass. "Tamika suggested he talk to her aunt instead."

Sarah gathered her eyebrows as she set down the remaining part of the roll to pick up her fork. The sound of metal scratching the glass plate screeched slightly as she turned the pasta around her fork. "Is it really necessary for him to go all the way to Milwaukee when he can just talk to her family on the phone?" She lifted the forkful of pasta to her mouth and gazed intently at her husband as she chewed, awaiting his response.

"I suppose it's not, but I'm not going to discourage him."

She frowned in concern as she set down her fork and picked up the torn dinner roll. She soaked it in the sauce then ate it in two bites. "I don't know," she said, her voice slightly muffled by the remaining food in her mouth. She swallowed then picked up her lap napkin and dabbed the corners of her mouth. "I just don't see the sense in it. He may not even get what he's going for."

"Allah knows best. Maybe he won't," Ismael said, taking a sip from his glass before setting it back down. "But it's something he needs to find out for himself."

She sighed as she turned her pasta around her fork again, this time out of worry, as her eyes were cast down at her plate. "I just don't think it's safe. We don't know how her family's going to react to him."

"I don't think there's anything to worry about."

"Ismael, her own mother attacked her and threw her on the street."

"I don't think they'll do that to him."

"How can you be sure?" She met his gaze, holding the fork still for a moment as she demanded an answer.

He shrugged as he picked up his own fork and turned it to its side to cut the pasta to pieces. "We can never be sure about anything in life. But in general, people are harsher to their families than they are to others."

"I hope you're right."

"Sulayman's a man. He has to do what he feels is right."

"But he doesn't need their approval to marry her."

Ismael shook his head. "He's not asking for it."

"Then what's the point in going?"

He drew in a deep breath and exhaled as he reached for a roll. "I can't answer that for you, Sarah. But we raised him to have respect for family and to never marry a woman without her family's knowledge and permission."

"Yes, but this is different."

He nodded as he tore his roll in four pieces and laid each on top of his spaghetti. "I know, but he has to feel he's doing the right thing. Right now, they're strangers. If he marries her, they'll be his family." He stabbed a piece with his fork and lifted it from the plate with spaghetti and sauce. "That's a very good reason to go talk to them," he said before the fork disappeared into his mouth.

Sarah lifted her eyebrows and nodded. "That's true."

They ate in silence for some time, and the only sounds that could be heard were forks scratching the plates, juice and ice cubes plopping into glasses, and gulps as they drank.

"So he really wants to go through with it?" Sarah asked a few minutes later after taking a sip of juice.

"Going to Milwaukee, you mean?"

She shook her head as she lifted her glass again, and she drank half of it before she said, "Marrying Tamika."

Ismael lifted a shoulder and turned down a corner of his mouth, as if to say he wasn't sure. "That's what it looks like."

Her gaze fell on the doorway leading to the kitchen as she finished her juice in silence. She could see the railing that overlooked the den, obstructed only by the vase of flowers on the kitchen table. She thought of her son as a toddler wearing fuzzy sky blue pajamas that zipped up from his ankle to his neck as he pressed his face into the railing playing peek-a-boo with her and her husband who sat talking in the den as she nursed his sister. How had he grown so fast? He was her baby, her first-born. She still remembered his shrilling cries in the middle of the night when he wanted to nurse, and how she hummed a song or recited Qur'an as she fed him, stroking his soft pink-blushed cheeks. She remembered how he would pause his feeding and gaze into her eyes then break into a grin, revealing shining toothless gums before he continued his feeding. He would kick his feet softly in contentment with each drink, and his eyes would glisten under the moonlight as he took in every bit of the dark room.

"I wish he would talk to me about what he's feeling," she said, gathering the remaining pasta strands to the middle of her plate, seeming to stare far beyond the traces of sauce on her plate.

Ismael gazed at his wife and suppressed a grin that tugged at the corners of his mouth. He often told her she was cute when she was upset, but she didn't like it when he said that, saying he wasn't taking her seriously. Instead he nodded. He could tell she had been really bothered by this. "I wish he would talk to me more too."

"But he doesn't talk to me about it at all." She looked at Ismael, her large brown eyes widening slightly until he could see his reflection in them.

He held her gaze for a moment before frowning sympathetically and looking away. "Right now, I think he's trying to understand exactly what to do." He drank the last of the juice from his glass, though he tasted nothing but melted ice with a tinge of lemon and orange tang. He chewed at a lemon seed that had slid into his mouth then lifted his hand, where he deposited it before folding it in a paper napkin. "So he wants to know a lot about how I dealt with you."

Sarah smiled beside herself. It was flattering to know she wasn't completely forgotten.

"When Aminah's ready to get married, I'm sure I'll be the one feeling left out."

She couldn't help laughing, but there was a hint of sadness even in that sound. "Maybe."

"It's only natural. Some things a father can't tell her, because I'm a man."

She sighed, understanding but wishing things were different. "I just feel like a spectator. At least I can tell him what I think of Tamika."

"He knows if we disapproved, we would say so."

She nodded, more out of sadness than agreement.

"When he was considering marrying Aidah, we asked him lots of things, even without him approaching us first."

"But I didn't *disapprove* of Aidah," she said, lifting her gaze to him just then, the sorrow gone from her voice. "I just wanted him to consider what it would mean for him."

Ismael nodded thoughtfully as he shook his glass, the melting ice cubes making a clapping sound. He lifted the glass to the light and looked at the seeds floating at the bottom before setting it back down. "I know, but from that, he knows we'll say what's on our mind." He creased his forehead as he thought of something, and he looked at his wife.

"Are you concerned about his choice now?"

Sarah was silent as she tried to gather her thoughts. She didn't want to be misunderstood. "In a way, I am."

He raised his eyebrows in surprise. "You never mentioned that before."

She shrugged. "I didn't want to seem like a party pooper."

"But, Sarah, if you have some concerns, you should voice them."

"You don't have any concerns?" she asked, her eyes settling on him, a hint of accusation in her tone.

He took another sip of the melted ice water and nibbled on the three seeds that were now in his mouth. He reached for the folded paper napkin holding the first seed and unfolded it before spitting the others in one at a time. He shrugged, balling the paper in his fist. "Not any that concern Tamika directly."

"Don't get me wrong," she said, lifting her lap napkin to wipe her hands. "Tamika is a wonderful girl, and I have no problem with her." She gently tossed the cloth on the table in front of her before she drew in a deep breath, both nervous and relieved to be putting her thoughts to words. She had waited a long time for this moment, and she wanted Ismael to understand where she was coming from. She picked up her fork and toyed with a lone spaghetti noodle that sat in a small pool of sauce. "It's just that I don't think he's ready for what marrying her means."

He rubbed the side of his glass with a thumb and shook the liquid that remained there. His eyes studied a seed that seemed to be stuck to the bottom, but his mind was on what his wife was saying. "What do you mean?"

She set her fork down and waited until he met her gaze. "Ismael, doesn't it concern you that her family is putting so much pressure on her to leave Islam?"

"I've thought about it."

"What if she gives in?"

"None of us is guaranteed to be Muslim tomorrow."

"Of course not, Ismael. But that's not what I'm talking about."

He moved his hands to his beard and scratched a side of his face until the hair stuck out on one side. He smoothed it down with the palm of his hand as he thought of what Sarah was saying.

"She seems so vulnerable," she said, gathering her eyebrows and shaking her head. "And I fear for her."

Ismael nodded thoughtfully and tugged at some hair strands under his chin.

"I'm not saying she's not sincere in her Islam," Sarah said, "because I have no right to say that. But it's apparent that she's still trying to sort out what to do about her family. Of course, only Allah knows what she'll do, but sometimes I fear she may give in, if only to gain back their acceptance."

Ismael raised his eyebrows as the weight of his wife's words settled on him. He moved his forehead, the beginning of a nod. "It's possible." He scratched his beard again. "I've had the same thought. But I can't say that to him. I want him to sort out everything for himself."

"But, Ismael." Sarah's voice rose in frustration, and she paused until he looked at her. "We're his *parents*. We have an obligation to point out things he may not see."

Ismael nodded and bit his lower lip. "You're right," he said, shaking his head a moment later. "But some things don't need to be said. How do we know marrying him won't solve that problem?"

Sarah's mouth opened until he could see the shadow of her tongue. Her eyes narrowed, and his reflection disappeared behind her eyelids. "I can't believe you're saying that. Marriage can only *exacerbate* that problem. Sure, it may seem to solve it initially, but where will she run when things get rough? Every marriage has its problems."

"But we're assuming that her Islam is fragile, and I don't feel comfortable enough with that thought to express it as a legitimate concern." He shifted in his chair until his knee touched his wife's as he turned to face her. "Some doubt is just doubt, and nothing else. No matter who he considers for marriage, we're going to fear for him. It's only natural." He lifted the hand farthest from her and tapped the side of his dinner plate, his gaze falling to the cloth napkin his wife had tossed in front of her. "But I worry about his Islam too. She may be stronger than he is. We have no way of knowing."

She breathed a long sigh and leaned back in her chair until her hair was tucked between its cherry wood and her back. "I don't know, Ismael." She rubbed her fingers on her forehead and pinched the bridge of her nose as she shut her eyes in mental exhaustion. "What about her family? Is he ready for that?"

"Were we ready for it?"

Her hand stilled and she opened her eyes, letting them fall to the cloth of her shirt as it gathered at her waist. She thought of how hard it was for her and Ismael when they first married. They didn't know how they'd make it, or if they even *wanted* to make it.

"Sarah," he said, placing his hand on her lap, "Allah is the one who gives strength to people. We were once fragile too, but time healed that, with the help of Allah. We had our private doubts, and sometimes, we wanted to give up. Perhaps we still have those doubts buried in us." He dusted a bread crumb from her leg. "But it's not as much as in the beginning. Now, that seems so far away. When I look at myself, I know Allah is the one who deserves full credit for my determination to keep going. Left to myself, I wouldn't have survived a second in this crazy world."

She shut her eyes, breathing in his words then blowing the air slowly from her mouth. She leaned forward until her arm rested on the table, and she gazed at him, a concerned frown contorting her lips. "I hope you're right."

"It's not a question about whether or not I'm right." He patted his wife's leg as his lips spread into a slight smile. "It's about having faith in Allah." His hand stilled on her lap as his eyes stared into the kitchen. "Tamika may be stronger than we were when we became Muslim. Our families disagreed and fought with us, but they never threw us on the street. That she kept going even this long makes me convinced that she's a special girl, and I'd be honored to have her marry my son."

Sarah bit her lower lip, her gaze following her husband's into the kitchen, where she stared distantly at a flower that lay limp as it hung upside down against the curved glass of the vase. Its stem was bent, as if barely hanging on to its own life. She laid her hand on top of her husband's and tucked her fingers under his palm. "May Allah help them."

He gave his wife's hand a gentle squeeze. "And all of us."

Sulayman drove back home in the darkness with the melodious recitation of Qur'an filling the car. His headlights gave the street's black pavement a dim yellow glow in front of him, only yards from where twin red lights shined on the back of the next car. His eyes rested on the Arizona license plate, and he wondered what brought its driver to Georgia. He glanced up at the large green interstate sign that told him his exit was but two miles away, and he thought about his brief trip to Streamsdale.

Sulayman had been tempted to walk his sister to her door as he put the car in park and she unbuckled her seatbelt to get out of the car. But there really was no reason to. She carried only a duffel bag that was filled with more air than clothes, and when she turned around and simply lifted it off the backseat from where she sat next to him, he knew he would have appeared desperate to offer to carry it for her.

He had sat unmoving with his hands on the steering wheel, staring ahead at the glass-enclosed lobby that reminded him of a storefront. He had studied the deserted pool table with the cues lying carelessly on it and balls strewn about, thinking that his desire to see Tamika was so strong that it was better if he stayed put. His heart had pounded as he watched his sister disappear into the building until she passed through the lobby and disappeared behind a door. He wanted to jump out right then and catch up with her. But he forced himself to stay in the car.

Presently, the Qur'anic recitation stopped abruptly and was replaced by steady humming that was barely audible over the car's engine, and the tape made a clicking noise as it changed sides. A few seconds later, the recitation blared throughout the car, and Sulayman reached to turn the volume knob until the reciter's voice was a soft melody floating in the air.

Sulayman listened to the Arabic and tried to concentrate on the meaning of Allah's words, but Tamika's voice echoed in his mind.

"I want to marry you," she had told him, and Sulayman halted his thoughts right there, wanting to hear nothing that came before or after that, for fear that the meaning of her words would slip from his grip. His patience was waning, and his chest burned with the desire to turn the car around, speed to Streamsdale, and knock on Tamika's door, saying, *Let's get married right now.* He imagined she would be shocked and confused, and the dream faded as he saw her saying no.

Most of his days were spent thinking about Tamika, even in class, and he had to force her from his head. Otherwise, patience would be impossible. There were times he wanted to pick up the phone and set the date right then. He felt she was slipping from him, and if he didn't make their marriage tangible, he would wake up one day and find her gone. He even started having dreams that she would choose her family over him, and each time he'd wake fearing it would come true. But he was being paranoid, he knew.

Tamika had given him her aunt's phone number, he pondered as he gently tapped the break to slow the car to stop at the traffic light after veering onto his exit. Why would she give the number if she wasn't serious about him?

Sulayman had called Tamika's aunt Monday night, and he was grateful that the conversation was pleasant. Jackie agreed to sit down and talk to him in person and promised to ask Tamika's mother to come as well. They set the date tentatively for mid-December, and Sulayman couldn't wait to get it over with. He knew the outcome of the meeting would influence Tamika's decision greatly, and he stressed over what he would say when he was there.

He reserved his airline ticket the night before and planned to confirm it once he got home and talked to his parents. He hoped they didn't object although he knew they probably would never understand. The meeting was important to him, and his marriage to Tamika depended on it. He couldn't allow anything to go wrong.

His nervousness about it all both shocked and scared him. He had no such fear when he was planning to marry Aidah. Part of Sulayman wondered if this meant he shouldn't go through with it. But deep inside he knew it meant that marrying Tamika meant more than he could comprehend.

What made Tamika so different was something he would probably never know, but he felt an urgency to hold on to her before she was out of his reach. He wanted to let her know what he felt, in case it would encourage her to marry him, but he didn't know how to say what he felt without crossing the boundaries they had drawn in their conversations, and those that Islam had drawn for them. There were times when they talked that he sensed the time was right, but he feared it coming out wrong, not to mention how she might react, and he was scared into silence. He wanted some advice, but he was too ashamed to admit his dilemma to his father. Was it possible that his father had felt the same about his mother?

"How was your break?" Aminah asked as she unpacked her bag onto her bed then kicked the empty duffel bag underneath. The top buttons of her black *abiya* were unfastened, revealing her slender neck and the collar of a white T-shirt she wore underneath. She had taken off her forest green *khimaar* and tossed it next to her pillow, revealing a single thick braid that sat limp along the back of her neck, loosening in its plaits. Strands of hair hung in disarray at the sides of her face and brushed against her cheeks. She smiled and glanced up as she sorted through all the clothes on her bed.

Tamika sat at her desk reading a book, and she turned to face Aminah. Her hair was in a French braid with a red plastic butterfly clip tucking in its ends right above the nape of her neck. She wore a large gray hooded sweatshirt with its sleeves pushed up to her elbows and a pair of black knit pants that hugged her knees and the tops of her calves. The lower part of her shins and calves were exposed, and she curled her toes on the red flip-flops. She forced laughter. "Dull. How was yours?"

Aminah picked up a shirt and sniffed it before frowning and tossing it to the side, making Tamika laugh. "Good, *alhamdulillaah*," she said. Aminah picked up another, and after pressing it to her nose to smell, she wrinkled her nose then picked up the entire heap of clothes. She carried them to the laundry basket in the corner of the room, where she dropped them all inside. A sock and T-shirt fell to the floor, and she bent to pick them up and toss them in the hamper too. She grinned at Tamika as she walked back to her bed and plopped down.

"What are *you* so happy about?" Tamika asked, wrapping her arm around the back of her chair.

Aminah giggled but didn't respond.

"What?" Tamika said, grinning in anticipation.

"Nothing."

"Aminah," she whined playfully. "What is it?"

Aminah laughed then gave in a moment later. "You."

"*Me?*" Tamika laughed out loud. "What did I do?"

"That's exactly what I was wondering."

She creased her forehead, a smile still creasing a corner of her mouth. "I have *no* idea what you're talking about."

Aminah shook her head as if scolding her roommate, but she was joking. "It's Sulayman."

Tamika's eyes widened in sudden interest. "What did he do?"

"Nothing really," Aminah said, lifting a shoulder. "He's just so preoccupied now."

Tamika grinned. "Preoccupied?"

"Yeah," Aminah said, a hint of playful accusation in her tone, "and I know it's all because of you."

Tamika laughed, unable to help feeling flattered. "What makes you say that?"

"All he talks about is you." Aminah shook her head. "I've never seen him like this before."

Tamika beamed. She would have never imagined she could affect Sulayman that way. "What'd he say?"

Aminah glanced at her sideways and laughed. "I'm not gonna tell you!"
"Why not?"
She shook her head and grinned. "Nothing really."
"Oh, Aminah, you are so *mean*."
They laughed.
"I'm sorry, but I don't know if he wants me to make him look weak."
"Weak?" Tamika wore a broad smile. "Why would he appear weak?"
Aminah shrugged as she sat on her hands and kicked at the rough carpet,
averting her gaze, a hesitant smile on her face. "I don't know. It's just weird
to see how weak men really are, and you know it's always a woman to
blame."
Tamika laughed. "I can imagine. But I must admit, I've never seen what
you're talking about." She slipped a flip-flop off her foot and put it back on.
"Except in movies."
"It's not anything you can put your finger on." Aminah hoped her
explanation would suffice because she didn't know exactly how to articulate
what she was saying. "It's just how they do things and how they talk. It's
just weird."
Tamika nodded, satisfied that she had caused so much trouble.
"I can't wait till you get married, *inshaAllaah*."
The statement made Tamika feel awkward, and she wore a half smile,
unsure how to respond. She wasn't sure if everything would work out. There
was so much to sort out before they could get married. Being alone in the
room during the break allowed her to think over a lot of things, and although
she wanted nothing more than to marry Sulayman, she understood why her
mother discouraged marriage.
Although she was offended by the comments made by Zahra's mother,
ironically, they clarified a lot of things for her. She spent a lot of time
reflecting on what the woman had said, and it made a lot of sense. It wasn't
that marriage was a bad thing, but it could prove to be if one rushed into it.
Women who married early often gave up opportunities they could have seized
had they been more patient. Having a college degree going into marriage
was definitely more preferable than marrying without one. Though the
woman could continue school after marriage, the likelihood that she would
finish in a reasonable amount of time was slim, particularly if she had
children. If the marriage ended in divorce, the woman would find herself in a
very difficult situation, and she would likely regret her decision to marry so
soon. No one liked to think of divorce, but the reality was, it was very
common in the states. Taking care of some basic goals before marriage could
alleviate the tragedy divorce caused, not to mention offer a more fulfilling
marriage itself.
Of course, that Sulayman still knew nothing about Tamika's past
relationship made her even more doubtful that things would work out. Part of
her wanted to tell him, but she feared the repercussions of his disapproval.

She didn't want to get hurt, and putting herself out there like that was risky. Before she divulged something like that, she wanted to be sure she was going to marry him. She still felt pressured by her family to wait although they weren't a part of her life right then. She wasn't going to sacrifice her soul for their benefit, but she was willing to sacrifice her desire to get married.

The discussion at Zahra's house made her reflect on the importance of family and how seriously others took parental desires. Tamika didn't agree with marrying someone for the parents' sake alone, but she did understand the importance of considering their feelings in the process. To completely dismiss their feelings wasn't even Islamic, and she feared that she was doing just that. What could it hurt to wait? If God willed, she had a whole life ahead of her, and, as Zahra's mother said, marriage would come. Tamika even decided that she would go on to graduate school. It only made sense. As hurtful as it was, there was little she could do with a bachelor's degree nowadays, especially in religion. The realization had rejuvenated her, and she was tempted to call her mother. But she decided to be patient. Her mother would be proud of her one day. She just needed to give it time.

Tamika smiled at her roommate and turned back to her desk to resume studying. She couldn't share her thoughts with Aminah. Aminah wouldn't understand. Tamika barely understood them herself. She didn't want to let Sulayman go, but she couldn't have it both ways. Part of her was waiting to hear about his plan to talk to her aunt, but she wasn't sure if it mattered if he talked to her at all. She and Sulayman hadn't revisited the issue since she gave him her aunt's number, but she didn't know if that meant he would go ahead and talk to her or just leave it alone. She couldn't help wondering if he would tell her if he did talk to her, and Tamika wasn't even sure she wanted to know.

Fortunately, Sulayman's parents showed no signs of disapproval when he told them he planned to book the flight that night. But they did advise him to pray on it, and he prayed *Istikhaarah* right away. He called Tamika's aunt before confirming the ticket and gave her his flight information to see how she responded. She told him that she would talk to him but was unsure if her sister would. She explained that Thelma was still getting over Tamika's conversion, and talk of marriage would only compound the issue. Sulayman stressed that he and Tamika had no definite marriage plans, and Jackie said that she understood, but it would make no difference to her sister. But she promised to keep talking to her, and, most likely, he wouldn't know what she decided until he arrived. He thanked her for her help and wrote down her address before hanging up. He then called the airline and booked the flight.

Twenty-two

Tamika finished her finals the first week of December on a Wednesday, a week before the last day of school testing, and she was ecstatic. She packed her clothes for winter break, wondering how she would like Chicago. She had kept in touch with Latonya since they first talked, and they both agreed they needed to see each other. Since winter break was the next major break, they decided it was best to meet then.

Finalizing how to pay for the ticket was the most difficult part of planning the trip, but Latonya decided to put it on her credit card and pay the balance over a period of three months. Tamika thanked her profusely, but Latonya told her not to mention it. Seeing each other again was priceless, and they were not going to let money issues stop them.

Aminah wouldn't be finished with finals until Friday, but she was happy for Tamika. She told Tamika how she knew it meant a lot to her to be with family. She had been looking forward to having Tamika stay with her, she told her, but she understood visiting Latonya took precedence.

Tamika's flight was Friday afternoon, and Dr. Sanders agreed to take her to the airport. Sulayman had offered, but she didn't want him to miss class. Besides, Aminah would be taking a final at the time, and she wouldn't be able to ride with them. Tamika didn't like the idea of riding in a car with Dr. Sanders, but she decided it was wiser than taking a taxi. She knew of no female taxi drivers and felt more comfortable with a man she knew than taking her chances with whoever pulled up.

She had considered asking Zahra, with whom she maintained a cordial relationship despite the embarrassing scene at the apartment. But Zahra had a final Friday afternoon too, and Tamika knew no one else she could ask. She had casually mentioned her dilemma to Dr. Sanders a week before when he asked what she was doing for the break. She hadn't expected him to offer her a ride, but she was grateful nonetheless. Slightly embarrassed, she thanked him and told him that he didn't have to. He assured her that he would love to be of help, and it would be no inconvenience because he was giving his last final that morning.

Tamika decided against telling Aminah what she had arranged because she didn't want her to misunderstand Dr. Sanders's generosity, or her acceptance of it. Tamika was probably being irrational, and Aminah would likely think nothing of it. But she didn't want to test the waters to find out. When Aminah had asked if she had a ride, Tamika thanked her and told her that she did, and Tamika was grateful that Aminah didn't ask any details.

Late Friday morning Tamika said her goodbyes to Aminah before Aminah left the room to prepare for her last final. As they hugged, Tamika was surprised to feel tears welling in her eyes. She was even more surprised to find Aminah's cheeks wet with tears after the embrace. Aminah wiped her eyes and told Tamika she would miss her, and, blinking back tears, Tamika told her the same. Aminah headed for the door and opened it. She turned around before leaving. A smile formed on her face before she said, "I love you for the sake of Allah." Speechless, Tamika didn't know how to respond. She felt her heart thumping in her chest. She was grateful that Aminah didn't wait for a reply. As the door shut, Tamika's cheeks grew warm, and she realized how much Aminah meant to her.

The brisk wind blew against their faces as Tamika and Dr. Sanders left the Humanities building and stepped into the cold. It was noon, and Tamika had met him in his office as planned so he could take her to the airport, and they were making their way around the building to one of the parking lots reserved for faculty and staff. He had told her he would drive her back to her room to get her bags so that she didn't have to drag them across campus to his office. He would have met her in front of her dormitory except that he had a couple of things he wanted to finish before they left. He feared that, if she didn't show up at his office door, time would slip by and she would miss her flight.

Tamika folded her open jacket closed with her hands to protect herself from the wind that had turned bitterly cold in a matter of minutes. The cold weather was nothing like it had been in Milwaukee, but she had grown so accustomed to the southern heat that it was difficult to relax as her nose and cheeks grew numb. She was grateful that she had put on the knee-length black button up sweater under her jacket, not only because it was keeping her warm, but it was also keeping her *khimaar* in place. Her white cotton head cover flapped against her head in the wind, and she could barely make out what Dr. Sanders was saying as he pointed in the direction of some cars on their right. The wind made it difficult to speak, so she decided to just follow him and not ask what he had said.

He stopped next to an emerald green Camry with a small dent on the side and pulled his keys from the pocket of his black trench coat. Tamika walked around to the passenger side as he climbed in and started the car. She opened the passenger-side door and slid in the seat next to him, buckling her seatbelt for the short trip. She tucked her hands into the sleeves of her sweater and jacket to keep warm as they waited for the car's heat to kick in.

When they pulled out of the parking lot, Tamika gave Dr. Sanders directions to her dormitory although she wasn't completely sure how to drive there since she had always walked. He was vaguely familiar with that part of campus, and Tamika was grateful when they finally pulled in front of her building.

Dr. Sanders followed her to her room to get the bags, and she stood at the door and held it open so they wouldn't be alone in the room. Weeks before, she had used some of the money she still had from her summer job to buy herself some clothes and other things she needed after having to leave all her belongings in Milwaukee the summer before. After packing, she was grateful that she had decided to buy new luggage and a backpack. She ended up needing both suitcases and the bag for her carry-on.

It was weird seeing Dr. Sanders next to her bed reaching down to pick up the suitcases. He just didn't seem to fit. Tamika associated professors with grading papers in their offices and talking to students only on the phone outside of class, their interaction with students limited to whatever was covered in the course. But Dr. Sanders was different. He was like a father to her, and she trusted no professor like she trusted him. Yet still, she would have never pictured him as he was right then, a winter hat pulled over his head, his hand grabbing the handle of one of her bags, and he standing only feet from the desk at which she sat to study for his class. His charcoal gray corduroy pants brushed the comforter of her bed as he lifted the first bag to test its weight before setting it back down.

"Woe," he said, as he lifted both bags, one in each hand, "did you pack bricks?"

Tamika chuckled as she stepped aside to allow him to pass into the hallway, his face slightly contorted because of the weight of the bags. "Sorry."

"Oh, it's no problem," he said, his voice strained as he carried the two heavy bags down the hall.

"I guess it's too much to ask to have elevators, huh?" he asked, grinning as Tamika held open the exit door to the stairs so he could walk through.

She laughed. "I guess so."

The bags dropped to the ground in loud thuds as he stopped to catch a breath before descending the steps.

"I can take one," she said, feeling guilty. The bags were heavy, but she could manage if she walked carefully down the steps.

He forced laughter and shook his head. "No, no, I'm fine." A grin broke out on his face as he leaned forward to get the bags. "I guess I can take this as payback for all the papers I assign."

She laughed as he lifted both bags, and she followed behind his slow steps. She wished she could help. He carried the bags through the lobby, and Tamika's eyes rested on the pool table a moment before she held the door open for him.

In the car, there was an awkward silence, and Tamika busied herself with staring out the passenger-side window as he drove. She wanted to talk about something—anything to break the strained air of silence that hung in the car. But she couldn't think of anything to say. She wished he would put on the radio or a tape, but he seemed content with the soft humming of his engine and whatever thoughts had settled in his mind. If it weren't for the cold weather outside, she would have cracked her window to listen to the wind escape in pattering breaths into the car.

Tamika glanced at Dr. Sanders. His eyes were slightly narrowed as he studied the road with calm intent, and his lower lip was tucked in deep thought. She imagined that he had a lot on his mind and decided it was better to let him be. She resumed staring out the window, this time more content. Dr. Sanders's silence reminded her that it wasn't always necessary to talk to pass time. "The brain needs to breathe," her mother had said once. "And ain't no better way than to just let it do its work."

Barren trees and grass of faded green rushed past the window, and Tamika wondered at how peculiar it was to have winter without snow. She imagined the ground in Milwaukee buried under layers and layers of white. She thought of people shoveling their sidewalks and driveways and warming their cars for at least twenty minutes before even getting in. She imagined that Chicago would probably be the same, and she pictured Latonya scraping ice off her car and fussing over her fingers going numb. She suppressed a giggle, which she replaced with a smile a moment later as images of her niece and nephew whom she'd never seen crossed her mind. She imagined him in a snowsuit so big she couldn't see his hands or face from the attached hat falling over his eyes.

"So you're going to Chicago?"

Dr. Sanders's question hung in the air for a few seconds before Tamika could respond. She had become so engrossed in her reflections that for a moment she wanted to remain there. "Yeah."

"You ever been there before?"

She glanced at him a moment before her gaze fell upon the road through the windshield. She touched one of her sweater buttons as she lifted a shoulder in a shrug, and she scratched at the threads looped through the button's holes. "No, but I've heard a lot about it."

He turned his head to the side and smiled at her before turning his eyes back to the road. "Hearing about it and being there are two different things."

She chuckled in agreement. "Yeah, I know."

"But it's a special city."

She nodded, unsure what to say, and she busied herself twisting the button until she thought it might fall off.

"I hope you don't see the rough side of it."

She couldn't help wondering if she would be able to avoid it. She had no idea what type of neighborhood her sister lived in, but she knew it wasn't the suburbs.

They sat in silence for some time, and Tamika stared out her window again as Dr. Sanders bit his lower lip as he drove.

"Who's in Chicago?" he asked several minutes later.

"My sister." She decided against mentioning Philip. Though he had resurfaced several weeks ago, she doubted she would see him when she came. He probably didn't even know she was coming. Latonya never knew how to reach him.

He nodded. "Is she Muslim?"

She laughed beside herself. "No."

"You never know," he said, reading more into her comment than she revealed.

She felt the sweater button coming loose in her fingers, and she tugged it gently to see if it would come off. When it didn't, she left it to dangle and flop by itself and folded her hands on her lap. "That's true," she said, breathing her words, "but I don't think she'd ever become Muslim."

He creased his forehead and glanced at her. "Why not?"

She raised her eyebrows, considering it, lifting her shoulders in a shrug at the same time. "I don't know. She just doesn't seem like the type."

He laughed and looked at her sideways, amused. "Is there a *type* of person who becomes Muslim?"

She laughed too, realizing how it sounded. "I suppose not, but I know my sister. Of course, only God knows, but I'm not counting on it.

There was a thoughtful pause. "Does she accept your decision?"

Tamika nodded. "More than anyone else actually."

Dr. Sanders was silent as he seemed to be reminded of something, and Tamika turned to see a corner of his mouth turned down and his eyes staring distantly at the road as if a buried memory had drifted there.

"It's not easy to see your children choose a life different than you chose for them," he said so seriously that Tamika couldn't help wondering what inspired the statement. She turned away from him for a moment as she reflected on what he had said. She thought of her mother and imagined that she and Dr. Sanders would probably get along.

Tamika forced laughter and looked at him. "I thought we chose our own lives."

His eyes were intent, and she studied the wisdom in his face. "We all think that at some point. But there's little in life we have a right to choose."

She wrinkled her forehead in confusion, but he kept his eyes on the road. "What do you mean?"

He smiled to himself. "It's hard to explain, but let's just say, we owe a lot more to others than we realize."

Tamika was unsure what to make of what he said, and she sat pondering it silently for a moment, trying to decide if she disagreed, or if she had a right to.

"Probably the only thing that belongs exclusively to you is your soul."

The words both soothed and disturbed her. On the one hand, she was reassured that she had a right to her soul. On the other, she was disturbed by what the statement implied she would have to sacrifice in life, if he was indeed right.

"It's not something to bother yourself with too much," he said in the way adults did whenever they said something that you had no choice but to face. "It's just something we all realize in time but are ashamed to admit." He forced laughter. "Because then it means we're admitting we lived ninety percent of our lives wrong."

She glanced at him in concern, and he met her gaze with a reassuring smile. But she was not reassured. It was depressing to think that people lived their lives as fools and realized their mistake when they were too old to correct it completely. How many people had to suffer because of one person's ignorance before he woke up? Tamika could only pray she would escape such a tragic phenomenon.

"You should be grateful though." The words broke the silence and interrupted her thoughts. As she digested them, she realized she had no idea what he meant. "You're one of the brave ones."

She gathered her eyebrows and gave him a worried look. "How so?"

"Most people sell their souls to others and give their lives to themselves."

She stared at him in confusion.

"You realized as a youth that it's supposed to be the other way around." He smiled at her, but the intense sincerity of his words moved her and made her realize he was sharing some of his own pain with her. "For that, you should be grateful."

Dr. Sanders's words haunted her during the entire flight, and the effect they had on her was tremendous. Like a revelation, they unveiled a weighty reality, but the implication was too momentous to measure. As she reflected on what they meant, she realized that life was both simple and complicated at once. Simplicity was life based on the needs of the soul, and complication was life based on the desires of the heart and body. At times, people sought both. But rarely did they truly overlap.

As Tamika compared her professor's observation to what her religion taught, the revelation was heart stopping. He was right. In addition to the monotheistic teachings about God himself, Islam was based on but one component of the human being—the soul. The most crucial decision in life revolved around one simple question. *To whom will you sell your soul?*

Those who recognized the only person to whom their soul belonged was the self chose to sell it to the One who created it and gave it to them. Others sold their souls to the desires and pressures of family, friends, and society. When they chose religion, people clung to what others wanted and expected from them, but when they decided how to live their lives, they did what they wanted for themselves.

Tamika recalled a classmate from her Arabic class expressing frustration over her sister's refusal to accept Islam although she knew it was true. Her sister had told her, "If I become Muslim, Mom'll kill me." Yet, the classmate pointed out that her sister left home against her mother's wishes to live with a boyfriend she loved. The classmate told Tamika, "I just find it puzzling that when it comes to what she wants to do with her life, she could care less what our mother thinks. But when it comes to her soul, our mother is the only one who seems to matter to her."

In Islam, Tamika reflected, it was a person's life choices, not matters of the soul, that required the consideration of what others thought or expected. A child obeyed her parents. A citizen obeyed his leader. A leader consulted his fellow people. A wife consulted her husband. A husband consulted his wife. Children had rights over their parents. A sister had rights over her brother. And a brother had rights over his sister. No one was exempt. There was but one exception—when the rights of people conflicted with the rights of the soul.

Tamika shivered at the enormity of the realization. How could Dr. Sanders have known? What experiences in life led him to this understanding? The next question loomed, and she was afraid to know the answer.

Why then had he chosen not to accept Islam?

Twenty-three

The plane halted in front of the gate at the Chicago airport, and Tamika unbuckled her seatbelt. She stood and removed her backpack from the overhead bin and pulled a strap over her shoulder. In the aisle, she and the other passengers stood awaiting the announcement that they could exit the plane. Though she had arrived at her destination, her mind was still filled with thoughts of her religion professor. She wondered about him as she walked down the aisle and left the plane to enter the airport.

Sounds of chatter and laughter filled the air as people hugged and waved to loved ones at the gate. Tamika followed the signs to baggage claim and hoped her sister was on time. She was beginning to feel exhausted and doubted she could tolerate being in the airport for long.

In the baggage claim area, Tamika waited in the crowd that had gathered around the luggage conveyor belt. A minute later, the belt began to move in preparation to produce the bags. She was staring distantly at the carousel when she heard someone call her name. She immediately turned to see where the voice was coming from. Her heart nearly skipped a beat when, a second later, she realized it was not her mother coming toward her. It was her sister.

Latonya was heavier than when Tamika last saw her. The added weight made her resemble their mother so precisely that it was unsettling. Her permed hair was pulled away from her face and hung behind her head, revealing a smooth round brown face whose features were more mature than her age. The curled ends of her jet black ponytail brushed the nape of her neck. She wore a knee-length black leather coat over a white sweater that accented her shapeliness. Dark blue jeans hugged her large figure, and black low-heel boots complimented the leather coat stylishly. Her eyes were Thelma's, and they looked at Tamika as if seeing her soul. Her smile was warm and reminded Tamika of days spent in their Milwaukee home when hearing their mother's keys turn in the door was the quintessence of life.

As Tamika studied her sister, she wondered if she would be able to look at her without seeing their mother. Latonya pulled Tamika to her in an embrace, and Tamika hugged her back earnestly. She reveled in the warmth of her sister's arms and was nearly intoxicated by the sweet smell of perfume emanating from her. When they released each other seconds later, Tamika felt as if she had given up a part of herself, and sadness swept through her.

"I can't believe it's you," Tamika whispered in amazement.

"I know," Latonya laughed. "I'm as big as a house."

Tamika shook her head and laughed. As she stood next to her sister, she realized Latonya was smaller than their mother despite the extra weight. "That's not what I meant." Her face grew serious, and she met her sister's eyes. "I thought I'd never see you again." The honesty of the words moved them both, and they averted their gazes.

"Where're Nikki and Tareq?" Tamika asked, changing the subject.

Latonya sucked her teeth and rolled her eyes. "Girl, they at home with Tyrone." There was a brief pause, and she stepped toward the conveyor belt, which began to spit out luggage just then.

"Where are your bags?"

Tamika stepped closer to study the bags that were about to pass. "They haven't come around yet."

She glanced at Latonya as she thought of something. "Do you need to move your car?"

Latonya shook her head. "I got here early, so I parked in the lot."

"Don't you have to pay for that?" Tamika already felt bad about the plane ticket.

Latonya rolled her eyes and forced laughter. "Is there somethin' you ain't gotta pay for around here?" She shrugged. "But I ain't gonna be there long, so I ain't worried about it."

Tamika nodded, and they began to watch for her bags. "There they are," she said a minute later. When they approached, she lifted one of the bags from the carousel with both hands, and her body was nearly yanked forward as she let it drop on the floor, still holding the handle. She pointed to the other one. Latonya lifted it from the belt and set it on the carpet.

"Girl, what you got in here?"

Tamika chuckled self-consciously. "Sorry about that."

"I hope you 'on't think you movin' in, 'cause I ain't got room for nobody else."

They laughed.

"But I think I'm 'o have to get a cart." Latonya left the crowd and returned a minute later with a pushcart. "Put 'em in here."

After lifting the bags to the cart, Tamika followed Latonya, who pushed the bags out the exit and headed to her parking space. The cold air shocked Tamika and ripped through her jacket.

"You in Chicago now," her sister said with a grin. "You gonna need a real coat."

Tamika pushed her hands into her jacket pockets, but she felt little relief against the bitter wind. Even her sweater didn't help. Her nose and fingertips numbed, and she quickened her steps, hoping the car was parked nearby. She started to reply to her sister, but the wind made it difficult to speak. Instead, she forced a laugh and moved her feet quickly to keep them from numbing too. Tamika was grateful when her sister stopped behind a car. Latonya removed keys from her purse and unlocked the trunk. They each lifted a bag and placed it inside, and the car shook with each one. Latonya then pushed the cart away from the car and left it near a wall.

"You gonna hafta' excuse my car," Latonya apologized as she unlocked the doors. She opened the driver's side, and Tamika opened the passenger door.

"That's okay, girl. I don't even have one." Tamika climbed in after her sister and pretended not to notice the crumbs and wrappers scattered in the backseat and in the baby's car seat. The car smelled of stale food, only slightly masked by the cherry scented air freshener dangling from the rearview mirror.

"You talk to Philip recently?" Tamika asked after Latonya paid for parking and pulled out of the airport.

Latonya turned on the radio and after finding the station she wanted, she nodded her head to a song. "Girl, I ain't thinkin' about him. He 'on't call me. But I did tell 'im you were comin' when I saw him last."

"How's he doing?"

She laughed and continued to move her head to the music. "I 'on't know. Fine I guess."

They were silent for a few minutes, and Tamika studied the passing Chicago scenery, wondering what made the city famous.

"I like that cloth on you, girl." Latonya glanced sideways at her sister and nodded approvingly. "You look all holy."

Tamika laughed, remembering her headscarf just then. She had grown so accustomed to wearing it that she often forgot that she had it on. She imagined how she must look to her sister. "Anyway," she said with a playful roll of her eyes to downplay the comment.

"You do," Latonya insisted, raising her voice as she grinned.

"I don't feel holy."

"You should."

The singer's voice filled the car and reminded Tamika of the life she had given up to be Muslim. Her once burning desire to become a singer had simmered, and her heart had found contentment in Islam. She was a normal person, she reflected, but no one would guess it by looking at her. Her Islamic dress suggested a level of piety that people associated with prophets and angels. But she was no prophet, and she definitely was no angel. She was merely a human being who had made a decision to submit to God. She still made mistakes, and she still struggled against sin. But she had the hope of God's mercy, and that was what kept her going. "No I shouldn't," she said, her voice barely audible over the music. She hoped to convince her sister that she was no different than she.

Latonya forced laughter and creased her forehead. "How *should* you feel?"

Tamika's eyes narrowed as she considered the question. "Hopeful."

Latonya laughed. "Hopeful? Everybody feels hopeful."

"Hope is more than a feeling," Tamika said in her calm tone. "If I didn't do what I did," she said in reference to her conversion, "I wouldn't have any hope."

Latonya didn't respond, and for a moment the music filled the silence between them. A few minutes later, she began to sing along with a song on the radio, and Tamika marveled at how beautifully her sister sang. She had forgotten that Latonya sang too. Growing up, it was Tamika who was the singer in the family, most likely because her love for it was stronger than her sister's. But Latonya would practice for hours with Tamika when their church choir was scheduled to perform.

They didn't speak for the rest of the ride, and Tamika sensed Latonya had a lot on her mind. She wondered if Latonya would ever realize she could be Muslim too, and that it was simpler than she thought. Tamika imagined such a decision would be difficult for her though. Tamika empathized with her sister, but she couldn't help noticing the irony.

Latonya, like most people, feared changed and preferred to continue in her life than make a decision that could change everything. Yet such a decision could be the solution to the problems she stressed about daily. No, becoming Muslim wouldn't rid life of its inevitable troubles, but it did give practical solutions on how to handle them.

Now that she was Muslim, Tamika couldn't imagine going back to a life that gave her only the semblance of a relationship with God. She reflected on her previous religiosity as a Christian, and she recalled, even at moments when her faith had been at its highest, her religious contentment didn't come close to the solace she felt during a simple Muslim prayer or as she recited the Qur'an. But someone who had never heard the beautiful Qur'anic recitation and grasped its powerful meaning, or had never bowed her head in *sajdah*[28] and felt God's presence as she supplicated to Him, wouldn't know what she was missing.

But her soul would.

The car stopped in front of an apartment building thirty minutes later, and Tamika studied her surroundings. The neighborhood was not a rich one, but the building was clean and well kept. They got out of the car, and Tamika waited for Latonya to open the trunk.

"Girl, I ain't carryin' those bags up them steps. Tyrone's gonna get 'em."

Latonya was several feet ahead of her as she spoke, and Tamika followed her sister into the building. "If he doesn't mind."

"He 'on't have no choice," Latonya shot back as if contending with Tyrone himself. "We sure ain't carrying 'em."

Tamika forced laughter, but inside she hoped he wouldn't take offense to them expecting him to carry the bags.

They walked up two flights of steps, and Latonya stopped in front of an apartment door on the third floor. She unlocked it and entered the home. Tamika followed behind her and entered cautiously. She wasn't sure how

---

[28] The Islamic prayer position in which a Muslim's head touches the ground. According to Islamic belief, a person is spiritually closest to his Lord at this time.

Tyrone would receive her, and she was uncomfortable with the idea of her sister's boyfriend staying in the house with them.

The house was mostly quiet except for the sound of a television coming from a back room. As Tamika glanced about the living room, she realized her sister spent more time in her house than her car. The room was spotless, and vacuum lines were still on the carpet.

They took off their coats, and Latonya took Tamika's and hung it on a coat rack near the door.

"Nikki! Tyrone!" A few seconds later a young girl emerged from the back room. "Where da baby?" Latonya demanded before Nikki could speak.

"Sleeping."

Tyrone appeared in the living room a moment later. He forced a polite smile in Tamika's direction, and she smiled back before turning her attention back to her sister.

"I ain't want 'im sleep," Latonya grumbled as she rolled her eyes. She sucked her teeth.

"But anyway," she continued with a sigh, "this is my sister Tamika."

He smiled again and gave her a slight nod to acknowledge her. "Nice to meet you." He pushed his hands into the pockets of his jeans, and Tamika was grateful he didn't try to shake her hand.

"Nice to meet you too."

Tyrone stood about five inches taller than Tamika and wore a gray sweatshirt with jeans that hung low at the waist. A thick gold necklace shined from his neck, reminding Tamika of a famous rapper. His head was covered in small natural twists, and his beard was cut in a goatee against his almond brown face. His demeanor was laid back and reminded her of the "cool" composure of many young African-American men, borrowed from the popular hip hop culture. His face carried a distant respect for her, and she couldn't help wondering if he would become Muslim before Latonya.

"Hi, Aunt Tamika."

Tamika's eyes fell on her niece, and she couldn't help staring in amazement. Nikki was much bigger than when she saw her last. Her chocolate brown face was smooth and round, and thick eyelashes that curled up at the edges accented her large dark brown eyes. She wore long, thin synthetic braids in her hair with colorful hair clips on the ends. Her pink sweatshirt and dark blue jeans suited her, and Tamika marveled at how cute she was. She made Tamika proud to be an aunt.

Nikki gave Tamika a hug, which Tamika accepted gratefully. "Hi to you, cutie," Tamika shot back, and Nikki giggled. "I can't believe how big you are now."

"Bring me da baby," Latonya said after they finished hugging. Nikki skipped happily into the backroom in obedience.

"Tyrone, you need to get her bags from the car," she told her boyfriend. "They too heavy for us to carry."

"You got the keys?"

She handed them to him. "Don't lock 'em in the car."

He shook his head knowingly as he accepted the keys, and a half smile developed on his face. Apparently, he was hassled by his girlfriend a lot. He went to the back room and returned a moment later wearing a coat and brown leather boots. "How many bags is it?"

"They all in the trunk. You can't miss 'em."

"Two," Tamika said to make up for her sister's obvious irritation with him.

"Thanks," he mumbled, his eyes meeting Tamika's momentarily to give her a grateful smile. He opened the door and left.

"Make yo'self at home, girl, 'cause you family. You know how black folks are," she joked. "You ain't gonna eat unless you get it yo'self. And get some for me while you at it."

They laughed.

"You're a trip," Tamika said, shaking her head, and her sister smiled, letting her know nothing had changed between them. They were still sisters. Tamika had to resist the urge to hug her again.

"You can sleep in here if you want," Latonya said, placing her hands on her wide hips as her eyes surveyed the living room. "Or you can sleep in Nikki's room. It's up to you."

Tamika nodded as her gaze fell on the futon that sat across from the television and stereo. A CD tower stood next to them, a few feet from the door to the kitchen. She imagined Tyrone getting hungry in the middle of the night. "I think I'll sleep in Nikki's room."

Latonya shrugged. "Whatever. But you gonna hafta bring the futon mattress in there 'cause it's only one bed in her room. Unless you 'on't mind sleeping on the floor."

"I'll bring the mattress in."

"A'right."

Nikki returned carrying the baby carefully, holding his head against her chest with one hand, and Tamika was impressed with her skill though it was obvious the girl was struggling a bit under the child's weight. Nikki handed the baby to her mother, who accepted the child as she sat on the futon and shook him gently. Nikki stood gazing at her mother and brother for a few seconds then returned to the back room, where the soft sounds of a television carried into the living room.

"Wake up, boy," Latonya whispered softly to her son. "Auntie's here to see you." The baby resisted for a few minutes before finally giving in. He squirmed and began to cry, apparently for being aroused. "Sh, sh, sh," she shook him. "It's only Auntie Tamika." She handed him to Tamika. "He'll settle down in a minute."

Tamika bent forward slightly from where she stood, accepting the child cautiously but finding it difficult to relax while holding him. She had little experience with babies and feared doing something wrong. Tareq blinked several times before looking at Tamika with a confused expression on his face. A moment later he seemed to relax as if realizing who she was. She sat down next to her sister and gazed at him with a smile on her face. "I can't believe you have a son now too."

Latonya laughed. "Girl, I can't believe it either."

"Is it hard?"

"Yeah, but it's worth it."

"You think so?" Tamika continued to look at her nephew, but her expression grew serious. Thoughts of marriage were still on her mind, and although she was leaning toward waiting, there was still a part of her that wanted to marry soon.

Latonya laughed. "Of course it is. Children are always worth it."

Tamika frowned thoughtfully. "You don't think it's better to wait?" She hoped her sister wasn't offended by the question.

Latonya shrugged. "I have regrets about things I did. But I 'on't regret my children."

"If you could do it again, would you have Nikki a little later?"

"Yeah, maybe. But then I 'on't know, 'cause that could change more than I want to."

Tamika nodded.

"Why you ask?" Latonya studied her curiously, and Tamika feared she could read her mind.

Tamika shrugged. "I think about having children, and sometimes I wonder if I ever will."

There was loud thump outside the front door, and a second later the door opened. Tyrone picked up the bags from where he dropped them at the entrance and set them in the living room. "You got anything else?"

Tamika looked up and shook her head. "No, thank you. I really appreciate it though."

"No prob'em." A few seconds later, he returned to the room where he had been watching television with Nikki.

"I hope you ain't got her watchin' nothin' she ain't got no business watchin'!" Latonya shouted as she heard the door close. There was no response, but she knew he had heard. She calmed a second later and turned her attention back to Tamika.

"Sorry 'bout that."

"That's okay," Tamika said. But it really wasn't. Latonya shouldn't be talking to Tyrone like that, especially in front of the children. She wondered if her sister realized how much it could harm their image of him.

"Why you think you can't have kids?" Latonya asked, her eyebrows forrowed in concern.

"It's not that I think I can't have kids," Tamika said, feeling her nephew squirm in her arms. She laid his head against her chest, and his body relaxed under her soft patting on his back. "It's just that I wonder when I will."

Latonya stroked her son's face with the back of her hand. "You ain't allowed to have boyfriends, huh?"

Tamika shook her head. "No, but I don't want a boyfriend."

"Then how you gonna have kids?"

She creased her forehead and stared at her sister. "I'd get *married.*" There was a hint of defensiveness in her tone.

"Yeah," Latonya said with a shrug. "I suppose you could. But I 'on't know how you gonna find somebody to marry in this crazy world."

There was a brief pause, and Tareq squirmed until he looked up at Tamika then smiled, revealing the beginning of two teeth that had just cut his top gums. She smiled back at him and brushed his nose with her forefinger playfully.

"I already found somebody," Tamika said, placing her finger in Tareq's hand, where he shook it contently.

Latonya stared at Tamika in shock, and a grin formed on her face. "You lyin'."

Tamika chuckled and shook her head. "No, I'm serious. There's a brother who wants to marry me."

Latonya raised her eyebrows in surprise. "I 'on't know how ya'll Moslems do it. Other folks be waitin' ten years before a nigga wanna commit like that."

Tamika laughed. "Yeah, well, there're a lot of reasons for that."

"*Tell* me. 'Cause I can't get this nigga to talk about marriage." Latonya nodded her head toward the room. "He act like it's a disease or somethin'."

Tamika forced a smile. The answer was simple, but it was something too few women were willing to sacrifice. She doubted Latonya was ready to hear her perspective on the issue, and she wanted to talk about her own situation. She needed some advice. "Girl, most people don't wanna do what we do," she joked in an effort to downplay the issue.

Latonya laughed. "You right." She paused as she gathered her eyebrows and looked at her little sister.

"So you thinkin' about get'n married?"

Tamika considered the question as a slight frown creased the corners of her mouth. "Yes."

"Then why you wonderin' when you'll have kids?"

She drew in a deep breath and turned Tareq so his back leaned against her as he sat in her lap. She exhaled. "I don't know if I wanna get married now."

"Why not?" Latonya removed something from the soft curls in Tareq's hair and let it fall to the carpet. "You 'on't love 'im?"

Tamika forced laughter. She decided to leave the subject of love alone. "It's not that. I just don't know if it's smart to sacrifice my school and everything." Tareq began to squirm and reach for his mother.

Latonya took the child from her sister, and he leaned his head against her chest. "He go to school wit' you?"

Tamika shook her head. "He used to. He's in medical school now."

"*Medical* school?" Latonya raised her eyebrows in amazement. "Girl, you betta not let him go. It ain't everyday you get a doctor wantin' to marry you."

Tamika laughed and nodded in agreement. "Yeah, I know."

"Go to school while you married."

The solution sounded so simple that it was tempting, but she still wasn't sure. "But what about Mom?"

Latonya sucked her teeth and rolled her eyes. "Girl, you betta think about yo'self. You gotta do for you. I wouldn't do nothin' for Mom, 'cause she 'on't care. If you ain't doin' it the way she want, then you may as well do what you gotta do and let her find out later."

Tamika sighed. "But I don't know if that's right."

"I 'on't know, but I know it ain't right for you to give up your man when it 'on't matter what you do. If you ain't Christian, she 'on't want nothin' to do wit' you. I 'on't think it's worth the gamble. What if you do all dat and she still diss you?"

Tamika nodded thoughtfully, her gaze falling on the CD tower, where she saw the lettering of a Tupac album. "I was thinking about that."

"Naw, girl, you need to take care o' your business," Latonya said, holding her son's hands away from his body with his back to her as she bounced him on a knee. He giggled, and Tamika's gaze fell on Tareq for a second, making her smile. Latonya stopped bouncing him and let him lean on her chest. "Let Mom do her thing, and you do what you gotta do."

"What if I can't finish school?"

"Why wouldn't you finish school?"

"If I get pregnant."

"Oh." Latonya rolled her eyes and lifted a shoulder in a shrug as she patted her son's stomach. "Then finish later."

"But what if I can't?"

She sucked her teeth. "I 'on't know, girl. But I 'on't think school is all that. I wouldn't give up my man for that. I ain't sayin' I'll give up school for him. But if you can do both, do it."

Tamika nodded. "Yeah," she said slowly as she considered everything, but doubt was still in her voice.

"If you wait, how long you gonna wait?"

She laughed self-consciously. "I guess till I finish my PhD."

"When that gonna be?"

She shrugged. "I guess when I'm around thirty."

"You ain't gonna have no man till you thirty?" Her sister stared at her in disbelief. "I couldn't do that." She shook her head. "I guess you won't be havin' no kids then. If you wait that long, girl, ain't no tellin' if you gonna find a husband before you can't have kids no more."

Tamika nodded and sighed. Her sister was right. It was taking a risk, and Tamika couldn't determine if it was worth it.

"I 'on't know what you need to do," Latonya said, "but I'll say this. When you all old, ain't no college degree gonna visit you when you sick. Ain't no college degree gonna give you grandkids either. And it ain't gonna give you a hug when you need one. But your kids can do all that and then some."

Twenty-four

Sulayman blinked and sat up in bed, surveying the unfamiliar room as the drunkenness of sleep lingered. A second later he remembered where he was. It was a Saturday morning in mid-December, and he had arrived in Milwaukee the night before. He was staying in the same hotel Tamika had stayed in earlier that year.

Seeing the hotel again evoked memories of the day he and Aminah had come to take her home. The memory gave him solace, but a moment later remorse swept through him like a fond memory suddenly overtaken by the reminder of what was no more. His heart ached as he climbed out of bed, and he wondered if his trip had been in vain.

The thought weighed on him until he sat on the edge of the bed in contemplation. He couldn't deny it any longer. He was afraid. More than anything, he wanted nothing to go wrong, but he feared that his decision to talk to Tamika's aunt in person was a mistake. He had called Jackie that night after arriving in the city. She told him that her sister finally agreed to meet with him and that the meeting would be held at Thelma's house. She gave him the address, phone number, and directions to the home, which was near the hotel where he was staying.

He should have been relieved that he would meet Tamika's mother after all, but it only increased his dismay. Thelma had no desire to talk to him. It was likely the Christmas season that softened her stance and ultimately inspired her to permit him in her presence. The season inspired kindness in people that was absent in other parts of the year. He guessed that she felt it was only proper that she offer her house for the meeting since it was her daughter being discussed. Or perhaps it was not propriety that motivated her, but desire for complete control.

Tamika's laughter echoed in his mind as he recalled their first conversation on the phone. He had been nervous to call her and didn't know what to talk about first. He wanted her to have a good impression of him, so he decided to ask a little bit about her and her family. Of course, he had known there were some rifts between them, but he didn't know how deep they were.

"How long do you think she'll need before you can reconcile with her?" he had asked her that evening.

She laughed in response, and he could only imagine the magnitude of pain masked behind her laughter. "Forever."

"You never know."

"Yeah, I suppose. But I doubt it seriously."

"I don't," he replied with optimism. "*InshaAllaah*, she'll come around."

Tamika was silent momentarily before she said, as if cautioning him, "You don't know my mom."

He didn't know how to respond. It was then that he realized there was a lot he would never understand about her family. "She's your mother," he said finally, the optimism in his voice concealing his true feelings, "and all mothers love their children. She couldn't live with herself if she lost you for something like this."

"Yes she could." The certainty in her response scared him, and he was speechless. Silence filled the line for some time.

"How was it for you growing up?" he had asked a minute later.

She paused thoughtfully. "It was nice."

"So you have a lot of good memories," he concluded, hoping to find something positive to discuss. He didn't want their first conversation to be a painful one.

"Yeah," she said tentatively.

"What is one of your best memories of your mom?"

She forced laughter and was silent before she finally divulged, "When I turned nine, I thought she forgot my birthday. But then she surprised me with a birthday party, and all my friends were there."

"So you like surprises?"

She laughed self-consciously. "Yeah, a lot." She paused then added, "So long as it's a *good* surprise."

Presently, Sulayman smiled at the memory, but a moment later he was reminded of his predicament. His chest tightened in nervousness, and he glanced at the clock. It was 10:30, and he was scheduled to be at Tamika's house in an hour. His heart began to pound as he remembered he hadn't prepared anything to say. He had decided that it was best to improvise and speak from his heart, because a prepared speech would sound cajoled. But he now wished he had something to work from because his mind was drawing a blank. His heart began to drum, and he wondered why he had decided to come all the way to Milwaukee for something he could have done on the phone.

He thought of Tamika and wished he could talk to her for reassurance. But he didn't have the phone number to her sister's house. He had asked Aminah if Tamika had given it to her, and she said that she hadn't. Sulayman began to wonder if that meant she was having second thoughts about marrying him. She hadn't actually agreed to marry him, at least not entirely, but he was hopeful that she would. Even if he could call her, he doubted she would give him any solace.

Tamika knew nothing about his trip, and now wasn't a good time to tell her. She would certainly discourage him. It was with reluctance that she had even given him her aunt's telephone number. He could only imagine what she would think about him visiting her. Tamika felt it was hopeless, if not harmful, to include her family, and she preferred to keep them out of the picture. If she and Sulayman were to marry, she wanted them to know nothing about it. Sulayman empathized with her situation and understood that she knew more about it than he, but he could not agree to secrecy.

Thelma had given birth to Tamika and undoubtedly sacrificed much to raise Tamika and her siblings. Thelma was a single mother with little formal education, who had given up her own dreams to see her children fulfill theirs. Naturally, she wanted what was best for them and expected them to want the same for themselves. The sweat and blood of her work was built upon the spirituality inspired in her by the church. Sulayman could only imagine the devastation Thelma felt when she learned that her daughter converted to Islam. All of her life's work—the sacrifice, the pain, her hopes—were being thrown in her face. In a fleeting moment, Tamika turned away from everything her mother had given her.

Of course, Tamika had no choice. She was only obeying her Lord. But Thelma didn't understand this—could not understand this. She saw Islam as the culprit in destroying her family, and Sulayman didn't want to add to that pain. Even without converting to Islam, Tamika could never marry so young, at least not with her mother's blessings. That she was considering marriage to a Muslim man only complicated the issue.

If Sulayman married Tamika without her mother's knowledge, he would be inciting deeper rifts in an already crumbling relationship. Eventually, her mother would have to know—especially if they had children. Although knowing would not inspire approval, it certainly promised a less dreadful reality than secrecy did. He couldn't live with himself knowing that he contributed to the final uprooting of any possibility for reconciliation. What was more, it could destroy the marriage itself. No, he couldn't hide their marriage from her family. To do so would be an assault, not only on her and Thelma's rights, but on the rights of marriage itself.

After showering, Sulayman ironed the pants he planned to wear. He then dressed and dabbed his neck and beard with cologne. He brushed his hair then stood in front of the hotel mirror to survey his appearance. He wore black dress pants and a green sweater with black threads throughout. His eyes betrayed him, as the fear and hope—*or was it hopelessness?*—revealed themselves in the green of his eyes. Sadness swept through him, and he looked away. He sat down on the edge of the bed and pulled on his black leather boots. Already, he felt as if he had lost Tamika. He could only hope he was wrong.

He tied his boot strings and glanced at the clock. It was 11:13. The drive was only five minutes, but he needed to leave then to give himself time to get lost. He stood and drew in a deep breath before exhaling. He supplicated to Allah that the meeting would be positive and that he and Tamika would marry. He picked up his coat from where it hung on the back of a chair and put it on, feeling as if he were about to plead for his life.

Outside, the bitter cold stung him, as the wind seemed to penetrate to the bone. His thick coat bore little protection against the harsh Wisconsin air.

He felt a cold wetness on his toes, and he realized that his boots were not meant for the snow. He walked quickly to the rented car and wished he had thought to warm up the car before leaving. The stiff cold of the car was almost unbearable as he sat in the car waiting for the vents to blow hot air. He wondered how natives of the state lived in the tortuous weather. When the car finally warmed enough for driving, it was after 11:20. He studied the directions before pulling out of the parking lot and starting toward Thelma's house.

Sulayman drove cautiously down the streets for fear of crossing an ice patch. He had never driven in the snow and wondered at the cars speeding and growing impatient behind him. He had more respect for Tamika already. She had lived here most of her life, and he was sure she could give him Wisconsin driving lessons. He chuckled at the thought. A second later he was reminded that she might not marry him. He would have to prepare himself for rejection. But he had no idea how to do that.

It was two minutes after 11:30 when Sulayman stopped in front of Tamika's home. Two cars were in the driveway, so he decided to park on the street. He sat staring at the small house that sat in the snowy landscape, and he tried to imagine Tamika playing in the yard as a little girl. He wondered if she had always lived in this house. The sound of a dog barking in the distance reminded him of what was before him, and his heart began to pound as he turned off the ignition. Disbelief swept through him, and he had to convince himself that he was really here. The cold air invaded the car again, as if reprimanding him for being apprehensive about going to the door. He finally mustered enough courage to get out of the car. He walked to the door quickly, doubting his ability to withstand the weather any longer. Before he knew it, he was ringing the doorbell.

The door opened too suddenly, and before he could prepare himself, he found himself looking into the eyes of a woman who wore a smirk on her face. She stood a few inches shorter than Sulayman, which made her unusually tall for a woman. Her permed hair was curled tightly below her ears and made her appear older than her age. Her dark brown eyes appeared black against her copper brown skin. Her solemn composure reminded him of a school cafeteria worker who labored patiently, knowing no one would appreciate the wisdom and spirituality in the hands that produced the food.

"Hello, I'm Sulayman," he heard himself say with more confidence than he felt.

"I'm Jackie." The stale smell of cigarettes came from her breath, a peculiarly just complement to the cordial response devoid of warmth.

He pushed his hands deeper into the pockets of his coat, and he hoped she would not extend her hand. He was relieved when she merely opened the door wide to allow him to enter. As he stepped inside, she returned to the house, as if dismissing him. The warmth of the home was a soothing contrast to the stinging cold, and as he took off his shoes and coat, he felt as if he were thawing.

"Thelma'll be out in a minute," she said with her back to him as she headed to the rear of the house. She motioned toward the living room. "Have a seat. You can hang your coat in the front closet."

After hanging his coat, he sat down on the couch and surveyed his surroundings. The house was cozy, and the sweet aroma of food filled the air, as if welcoming him. He wondered at this family who had caused Tamika the greatest joy and pain of her life. Nothing in the home suggested her mother was capable of the cruelty she had inflicted upon her daughter. He began to feel hopeful that her mother would forgive her. She had to. She was her mother.

The sound of footsteps interrupted his thoughts, and he looked in the direction of the sound. Two silhouettes approached from the hall, one noticeably larger than the other. When they came in full view, he realized the slimmer woman was Tamika's aunt, and he assumed the other was her mother. Jackie sat down in one of the chairs that had been set up across from the couch, and Thelma disappeared into the kitchen before Sulayman had a chance to see her clearly.

Jackie forced a smile and asked him if he wanted any tea, and it was then that he noticed the crucifix dangling from the gold chain on her neck. Disappointment filled him, and he began to feel sorry for Tamika. He could only imagine how difficult life was for her.

"If you don't mind." He hadn't eaten, and he hoped the tea would hold him.

A minute later Thelma entered carrying a tray of teacups and a kettle, and the dishes clanked as she walked. She placed the tray on a small nightstand next to them, and Jackie immediately stood to serve some tea. "How much sugar you like?"

It took a moment for him to realize she was talking to him. "Three spoonfuls. Thank you."

"What's your name?"

The question startled him, and he turned to Thelma, who was now seated in the other chair with her arms folded. Her skin was a honey brown like Tamika's, but otherwise they bore no resemblance. Thelma's eyes were large and dark like her sister's, and the softness of her face was barely traceable behind her stiff jaw. He imagined that life demanded she mature before she should. Her permed hair was pulled away from her face in a small bun, revealing the youthfulness that still lingered there. She was in her mid to late thirties, Sulayman concluded, but she could pass for forty-five.

"Sulayman," he said as Jackie handed him his tea. He took a sip and silently prayed that Allah would have mercy on him. Already, he could feel his welcome evaporating to unveil a reality he would rather not see.

"That Arabic?"

"Yes, ma'am."

"What's it mean?"

"Solomon, like the prophet in the Bible."

There was a brief silence as Thelma eyed him suspiciously, as if uncertain how to take his mention of Christian scripture. "You Moslem?"

"Yes, ma'am."

"Your parents?"

"Yes, ma'am." His eyes inadvertently fell on her large hands, and he imagined the pain they had caused Tamika when she struck her. He took another sip of tea, grateful he had something to do as she drilled him.

"Good for you."

The comment startled him, and he instinctively shot her a confused glance. He wanted to ask what she meant, but he was unsure if she were insulting him.

"'Least you got sense enough not to turn yo' back on what they taught you."

Unsure how to respond, he took another sip of tea to gather his thoughts. "I've wanted to sometimes." The confession stunned him, and he was reminded of moments as a high school teenager when he wasn't enthusiastic about being Muslim.

Apparently, the response surprised Thelma and Jackie too, because a moment later, the atmosphere loosened as they were filled with curiosity too strong to conceal. But their expressions remained as disinterested as they could manage. He could tell they wanted an explanation, but they were too proud to reveal interest in the man who threatened to invade their family.

"When I was in high school, I hated it sometimes," he said, and he noticed their eyes were intent as he spoke. "I was jealous of the other students, who didn't have to pray so much and could party when they wanted." He took another sip of tea, hoping his nervousness wasn't obvious. "I tried to come up with as many ways as I could to rebel. But whatever I did, my parents either never found out or pretended not to notice."

Thelma shifted in her chair, but it was Jackie who broke the façade of disinterest. "You on your own now?"

He shrugged. "I guess you can say that. I'm still in school and live with my parents, but I'm looking for an apartment now and should have my own place soon, God-willing."

"What you studying?"

"I'm completing my first year in medical school."

Inadvertently, their eyebrows rose in surprise. "Where?"

"Emory University."

A slight smile formed on Jackie's face, and Sulayman could tell she heard about the school, but he couldn't tell if Thelma knew anything about it. "That's a good school, young man," Jackie said.

"You've heard of it?"

"I wanted to be a nurse some years back."

He nodded. "Their nursing program is good, I hear," he said.

"Yes, it is. But their medical school is one o' the best."

He took a sip of tea.

"You went to Streamsdale?" she asked.

"Yes, ma'am. I graduated last year."

"How were your grades?"

The question was an odd one, but he imagined Jackie felt free to ask what she wanted since he wanted to be a part of their family. "Good, by the mercy of God."

"They had to be betta than good to get in a school like that."

He felt uncomfortable discussing his grades because he didn't want to appear arrogant. "Yes, ma'am. By God's mercy, I did well." He knew she expected him to be specific, but he could tell she respected him for being modest.

"What you want from us?" Thelma's voice erupted in thunderous authority, and he was reminded of her presence just then.

He took another sip of tea and prayed he would explain himself clearly. "I apologize for inconveniencing you both like this, but I wanted to express my interest in your daughter."

"You need to come all the way here for that?"

"No, ma'am, but I didn't want to disrespect you. You are her family, and I didn't want to be anonymous."

"I hope Tamika ain't send you here to butter us up."

"No, ma'am. She doesn't know I'm here."

Silence filled the room. Thelma raised her eyebrows in surprise, and Jackie wrinkled her forehead in confusion. "If you ain't here for Tamika, who you here for?" Thelma demanded.

"For myself."

She huffed and forced laughter. "What you got to do with me?"

He reached forward to place his teacup on the nightstand. "I'm interested in marrying Tamika and wanted to inform you before I proposed."

"You ain't ask her yet?" Jackie asked.

"No, ma'am." The answer wasn't completely true, but saying yes would be too complicated to explain.

There was a brief silence as they wondered about the young man before them. "Your parents know you're here?" It was Thelma's question.

"Yes, ma'am."

"Ain't you a bit young to be get'n married?"

He nodded. "I suppose I am."

"Then why you wanna go and do somethin' like that?"

"I want to do what's right before God."

For a moment, no one spoke. He was speaking their language, and it was impossible to contend with such a noble cause.

"Ma'am, I apologize for coming up here like this," he said, breaking the silence. "I know it wasn't an easy decision to agree to this meeting, and I'm grateful that God allowed you to have me. I don't want to take up too much of your time, but I wanted to express my intentions out of respect for you. I know most times when young people want to marry or have a relationship, they just elope or carry on without their family's knowledge. It's only well after the fact that the family learns of it.

"I knew that by coming here, I would be taking a risk, because I'm aware that Tamika's acceptance of Islam has been understandably difficult for you. But I couldn't live with myself if I proposed to her and we married without you ever knowing. My religion holds family relations in high regard, second only to worship of God himself. And as a Muslim, I have a duty to hold it in high regard too. I want to let you know that I wish to marry your daughter, if she will have me, but if she decides not to marry me, I won't pursue the relationship any further. In any case, I want you to be aware of my plans, in case she does agree." He nearly kicked himself. He sounded like he was giving a formal speech in school. He hoped he sounded as sincere as he was.

There was a brief silence. "And what about Tamika?" Jackie asked.

Sulayman knew what she meant. "I plan to see to it that she finishes school."

"How will you do that?"

"I plan to put in our marriage contract that this is my personal financial responsibility."

"What do she think?"

He sighed thoughtfully and forced a smile. "I don't know."

Thelma huffed and Jackie forced laughter.

"How does she know you?" Thelma demanded.

"She was my sister's roommate last year, and I met her then."

"You think a year is long enough to know somebody?"

"No, ma'am."

"Then how you ready to get married?"

He took a deep breath and exhaled as he gathered his thoughts. "I know it seems rushed, but this is how we do things. Since marriage is the only relationship for us, when we marry it appears premature."

They understood his point, but he couldn't tell if they agreed. Thelma looked bored all of a sudden and glanced at the clock. She slapped her thighs with both hands and stood. "Let's eat." Apparently, she had heard enough. The meeting was over.

Jackie stood too and headed for the kitchen. "Have a seat in the dining room," she told him, nodding her head in the direction of the table in the next room. He stood and walked over to the table. He sat down feeling a bit awkward. He hadn't expected to eat lunch with them and was unsure how he would survive at the table. He could only hope this meant they would soften their stance against Tamika.

Thelma and Jackie moved effortlessly from the kitchen to the dining room to set the table. In minutes, the table was covered with an array of delicious food that he could already taste. They took their places at the table, Thelma at the head and Jackie at the opposite end. They bowed their heads briefly and mumbled a quiet prayer before serving themselves. Sulayman followed suit. As he selected his food, he was grateful that there was no red meat being served. He served himself some baked fish, spinach, and cornbread.

"Where you from?" Jackie asked a few minutes later. She took a bite of food and eyed him while she awaited his response.

He wasn't surprised by the question. It was one people asked him almost daily. His green eyes, fair skin, and beard gave the impression that he was Arab. "From here."

She creased her forehead. "Where your parents from?"

"My mother is white, and my father is bi-racial."

"They Americans?"

"Yes, ma'am." He took a bite of his food and savored it. He didn't realize how hungry he was.

"They born Moslem?"

He shook his head. "No, ma'am. They converted."

"From what?" she nearly demanded.

"Christianity."

The table fell silent except for the sounds of forks clinking against the glass plates. "Your grandparents, they Christian?"

"Yes, ma'am."

Jackie glanced at her sister, who met her gaze for a moment, as if sharing a secret between them. "That normal?"

"I'm sorry?"

"Christians and Moslems all mixed up in families like that."

He took another forkful of food and swallowed it before he spoke. "Yes, ma'am, it's very common." He hoped the information would make them realize how normal their situation was.

They ate in silence for a few minutes.

"Your parents, what they family think about that?"

"Their conversion to Islam, you mean?"

Jackie nodded as she chewed her food. "Mm, hm."

He shrugged. "Some of them don't like it, but a lot are supportive."

Thelma huffed, and Sulayman inadvertently glanced in her direction. She was eyeing him with a curiosity that seemed to replace her previous suspicion. He averted his gaze and let it fall to his plate.

"What you think o' all that?" It was the first question Thelma asked since they began to eat, and in a way, Sulayman was relieved. He felt strange talking exclusively to Jackie, as if Tamika's mother wasn't there.

"Ma'am?"

"You think it's fine to have all those religions in one family?"

He considered it and took a bite of food as he thought. "Yes, ma'am. It's only natural."

She narrowed her eyes, and he could tell she didn't like his response. "How's that natural?"

It was a challenge more than a question, but he would pretend he didn't notice. "It's only natural that people take different paths in life." He paused to give himself time to consider how to continue. He was embarking upon sensitive territory and didn't want to offend them. He picked up his cornbread and took a bite before continuing. "Religion is one of those unpredictable paths. It's such a personal experience that it's expected that any family will have a variety of them."

"Religion ain't so personal," she said with authority, and Sulayman began to understand this was her way. She probably talked to everyone in the same manner. He glanced at her and for a moment saw a flash of kindness in her eyes. "You ain't got no personal right to choose what you wanna believe."

He nodded and continued to eat before responding. "That's true," he said. "But only from God's perspective."

She gathered her eyebrows, and he felt both women staring at him waiting for an explanation.

"I think most people agree that you can't just *choose* what you believe, but they accept that each person has to conclude that on his own."

There was a long pause. Thelma set down her fork and folded her arms. "I hope you ain't intendin' to come in here and judge me for what I done with my child."

He shook his head emphatically. "No, ma'am. I understand your disappointment with Tamika."

"Do you?" She raised her eyebrows, challenging him.

"Yes, ma'am." His heart raced as he fumbled for words. "I can't imagine what I'd do if my children chose a different religion than I taught them. I'm not sure I could be too diplomatic about religion."

"Why not?"

"When you know the truth, it's hard to be diplomatic about it, especially with your children."

"You got any kids?"

"No, ma'am."

"Then you just talkin'."

He swallowed. "Yes, ma'am. But I can imagine."

"Imaginin' ain't the same as doin'."

"Yes, ma'am," he agreed humbly, lowering his head slightly.

She unfolded her arms and resumed eating. For a few minutes no one spoke.

"What's it that make you think you got somethin' worth believin'?" Thelma asked.

"Ma'am?"

"That religion. What make you think it's worth all this trouble?"

It was a challenge, a dare, but it was the opportunity he thought he would never have. He could only pray his explanation did justice to the religion. "It's the religion of God's prophets, like Adam, Abraham, Moses, and Jesus."

"What you say?"

It sounded like another challenge, but he knew she was unsure if she heard him correctly. He cleared his throat and repeated what he had said.

"What you know about Jesus?"

"I know his mother was the Virgin Mary, and God decreed he be born without a father."

Her expression told Sulayman that she had never heard anything like this before. Whatever concept she had of Islam, this was not it.

"What's that you say?" Jackie interjected.

"We believe God created Jesus without a father."

The sisters glanced at one another in surprise then turned their attention back to Sulayman. "That what Tamika believe now?" Thelma asked, as if hopeful that her daughter wasn't too far-gone.

"Yes, ma'am."

She frowned and ate in silence as she decided what to make of this information. "Then what make you so different from us?"

"We don't believe he's God's son."

She raised her eyebrows in surprise. "Why not?"

"We believe that God created Jesus by simply saying 'Be'. We don't believe he fathered him per se."

Thelma nodded and ate. Her eyes grew distant for a short while, and he searched her face for what she was thinking. "Why your women wear all them clothes?"

"They're covering their bodies in obedience to God. It's the dress of righteous women of earlier times."

"What else you believe?"

"That there's only one God, whom we've never seen and who deserves our sole worship and unconditional obedience."

"Who's this Muhammad person?"

He took a bite of food before answering. "The last prophet of God."

"He like your savior or somethin'?"

"No, ma'am. We believe God is our savior."

"Why you believe in Jesus then?"

"We can't be Muslim unless we believe in him."

Thelma's eyes narrowed in sudden curiosity. "Why?"

"We have to believe in all of God's prophets. Jesus in particular has a special status."

"Why?"

"He was raised up to God and will return before the Day of Judgment."

She huffed, but Sulayman could tell it was more out of interest than anger. "Where you learn all this?"

"It's in the Qur'an."

She cut a piece of fish with her fork and stabbed it before bringing it to her mouth. She chewed for a moment before looking in his direction, and Sulayman could tell it was the first time she realized that the Qur'an had any connection to what she believed.

"What you believe about the Bible?" she asked.

"We believe that the scriptures, like the Torah and Gospel, were revealed by God, but that today's Bible is not a completely accurate account of them."

She was silent, and no one spoke. They ate in silence, as the women pondered everything he said. Normally, he would have been uncomfortable sitting quietly at the table, but he felt more relaxed as he finished his meal. No one met the other's gaze, as they became engrossed in their personal thoughts.

Twenty-five

Monday night Tamika sat on the futon in her sister's living room watching television after she prayed. She had spent much of the day thinking about Sulayman. She missed talking to him and was often tempted to pick up the phone and call. But she resisted. She didn't want to appear desperate. She had decided to use the winter break as time for herself. She intentionally left Atlanta without leaving any contact information to assure herself that she would stick to her plan. It had been easy during the first week in Chicago, but the following week had been especially difficult for her, and she was surprised at how accustomed she had grown to him. She wondered how she would handle it if she decided not to marry him. Could she even survive?

The phone rang, but Tamika didn't answer it. Latonya was in the bedroom trying to put Tareq to sleep. Tyrone wasn't home yet, and Tamika was taking advantage of the opportunity to uncover her hair and relax. He would probably be home shortly, so she had her *khimaar* lying next to her on the futon. The phone rang again and stopped mid-ring. A second later she heard the muffled sound of Latonya's voice in the back room.

On the television, the local news told of a homicide, and Tamika was appalled by the report. A woman had been beaten to death in her home, and her boyfriend was the suspected assailant. She shivered in horror at the thought of someone inflicting harm upon a loved one. The world gave people ample precautions against criminal attacks by strangers, but were times so bad that those closest to them were more dangerous? This possibility lingered in her mind, and she only half-listened to the rest of the news report. They were talking about football, and a woman had been murdered. How could an anchor switch gears so easily? Tamika imagined she could never be a reporter. She doubted she could inform viewers of a horrific crime then joke about Super Bowl predictions a second later. Was everything a game in this world?

"Tamika."

Startled, Tamika looked up to find her sister standing a few feet from her with a concerned expression on her face. "Is everything okay?" Tamika asked.

Latonya shrugged. "I'm not sure. That was Aunt Jackie on the phone, and she was asking how to get in touch with you."

Her heart nearly skipped a beat, and the television noise faded in the background. "Why?" She couldn't imagine why her aunt would want to talk to her. Ever since her conversion, there was a mutual standoff between her and her family.

"She was asking if I knew somebody named Solomon, or some'n like that."

"Sulayman?"

"Yeah, I think so."

Tamika's heart pounded wildly in her chest, and her eyes widened. "Why?"

"Is that the person you were tellin' me about?"

She nodded slowly, terrified of what could be going on. "What happened?"

"She said her and Mom talked to him a couple o' days ago."

She stared at her sister in disbelief. "He called there?"

Latonya shook her head. "He came over our house."

Tamika's jaw dropped. She didn't know what to say. There had to be some mistake.

"And Aunt Jackie wanna talk to you."

"W-what'd you tell her?"

"I almost told her you were here, but I told 'er I'll try an' call you."

"Are you sure you heard her right?" Tamika leaned forward and narrowed her eyes.

Latonya nodded. "Yeah, she even asked me if I saw 'im before."

"Did she say how he looked?" Tamika wondered if her aunt was confusing him with someone else.

"Tall, light-skin wit' green eyes."

Tamika's heart sank.

"That him?"

She nodded slowly, and her gaze grew distant. She was too shocked to think straight. "Did she sound upset?"

Latonya shrugged. "I 'on't know. Just worried."

Tamika shook her head. She couldn't believe what she was hearing. "Why'd she call you?"

Latonya shrugged again. "Guess she figured I knew about 'im."

"Did you say you did?"

"I told 'er I ain't know nothin'."

Tamika nodded and bit her lip. "Is he still there?"

"Girl, I 'on't know. It ain't sound like it." Latonya creased her forehead. "He ain't tell you he was goin' up there?"

Tamika shook her head. "I didn't know anything about that."

"How he know where you live?"

"I don't know." She was as confounded as her sister. Then she remembered something. "I gave him Aunt Jackie's phone number a while ago."

"Why you do that?" Latonya wrinkled her nose and stared at her sister in disbelief.

Tamika shrugged. "He wanted to talk to someone in my family."

"Why?"

"I guess to, um, let them know we were gonna get married."

Latonya rolled her eyes then glared at her little sister. She didn't understand Tamika's logic. "Girl, are you crazy? You know Mom don't wanna hear nothin' bout that."

"I know," Tamika brooded and sank into the futon. She leaned her head back and stared at the ceiling. How did she get herself into such a mess?

"*Girl*," Latonya said, elongating the word, as if warning her of a dreadful fate. "I 'on't know what you was thinkin'."

Tamika didn't respond. She continued to stare at the ceiling, feeling too weak to face up to what this meant. She would have to call her aunt, but she needed to wait. She didn't have the strength to talk right then.

Late that night Tamika lay on the futon mattress next to where Nikki was sleeping in her bed. The house was dark and quiet as everyone slept. It was three minutes after midnight, and Tamika couldn't sleep. She lay on her side still pondering her unfortunate situation. Tears slid down her face and moistened the pillow. Her sadness was mixed with anger, as she grew upset with Sulayman the more she thought about what he had done. It was almost 12:30 when she threw the blanket from her in frustration and decided to call Sulayman. She had had enough time to herself, and she wanted to give him a piece of her mind.

She could hear her angry breaths as she dressed in her *abiya* and threw on a scarf, mumbling to herself. She felt her way through the dark house until she was in the living room. She turned on the kitchen light to illuminate the room. Her tears were dry from anger when she picked up the phone and dialed his home, not caring whether or not it was too late to call. Sarah answered the phone after three rings, and her voice sounded sleepy.

Tamika held her composure as she greeted her and apologized for calling so late. When Sarah realized it was Tamika, her voice sounded delighted, and she asked how she was doing. Tamika lied and forced laughter as she told her that everything was fine. She then asked to speak to Sulayman. Sarah asked her to hold, and Tamika counted the seconds until Sulayman picked up.

"Yes?" His voice sounded uncertain, as if unsure who would be calling him at this time, but Tamika could tell by his voice that he hadn't been sleeping.

"*As-salaamu-'alaikum*," Tamika said through gritted teeth, making no effort to conceal her fury.

"*Wa-'alaiku-mus-salaam*," he replied cautiously, as if unsure how to interpret her sudden call. "Is everything okay?"

"You tell me."

There was a long pause, and for a moment Tamika felt sorry for him. He was so naïve that it was sickening. He lived in utopia and couldn't imagine what it was like on the other side. He believed in fairy tales and happily ever after, families who loved unconditionally, ate dinner together, and said "I love you" everyday. He thought he could save the world, but he didn't know how to save himself.

"Tamika?"

Tears welled in her eyes at the sound of her name. He thought so highly of her that he doubted it was even Tamika on the other end of the phone. He had never seen her angry, and it hurt her that she was hurting him. But she couldn't help becoming aggravated by his naïveté.

"Are you alright?" he asked a minute later.

Tamika tried to gather her thoughts, but she couldn't. Instead, she shook her head at a loss for words and bit her lower lip, feeling the tears flood her eyes.

"Tamika?"

"Yeah," she said, finally pulling herself together. "It's me."

"What's going on?"

"Sulayman," she demanded, remembering her anger just then, "why'd you go talk to my mother without telling me?"

There was a brief silence. "I'm sorry."

"You're sorry?" Her voice rose, and her heart pounded angrily in her chest. "And what am I supposed to do now? I got my aunt on my back, calling all creation about you, and you're *sorry*?"

Tamika groaned and shook her head. She wiped the welling tears from her eyes and felt one fall on her wrist and slip down her arm. "You should've asked me first."

"Tamika, I'm sorry. I thought it was the best thing to do."

She grew livid at the thought of him going behind her back. "How could you think that? What about *me*?"

"I didn't want to marry you without talking to them first."

"Marry me?" she said, as if she had never considered such a thing.

"Yes, Tamika. You know I want to marry you."

"But I didn't know you thought you could snatch me up."

He was silent momentarily. "I'm sorry. I was hoping—."

"Hoping *what*, Sulayman?" She lowered her voice a second later when she remembered everyone was asleep. "That you could wow my family into accepting you? That you could convince them that they were wrong after all, and that their daughter had every right to turn her back on Christ for this 'insane' religion?"

Sulayman grew silent as he was filled with regret. He had tried too hard, and it had come back to haunt him. There was nothing he could say. Tamika was right. She was left to foot the cost of his arbitrary decision. He should have asked her before he called to plan the trip.

"Sulayman, what were you *thinking*?"

He felt numb at the sound of her angry voice resonating through the phone. He didn't know how to respond.

"*Sulayman*," she said, demanding an answer as she raised her voice.

"I'm sorry."

"Is there anything else you are besides sorry?" The question had a double meaning, and she let the cruelty of it linger in the air then settle on him. "I'm tired of hearing that. I want answers."

"I," he stopped himself from apologizing again, "I just wanted to respect your family and—."

"Respect my family?" She was furious in disbelief. "How could you even think it was respectful to do something like that behind my back? " She sniffed, calming herself as the anger cooled and settled in her limbs. She dropped her head and pinched the space between her eyes, feeling the wetness of fresh tears under her forefinger and thumb. "Oh, you have no *clue* what respect is."

There was a long pause.

"Tamika, I really don't know what to say except I'm sorry."

"Oh, give me a break!" Her voice echoed in the living room as she momentarily forgot that she was trying to be considerate of those who were asleep.

He hesitated before saying what he had been holding back all along. "I hope this doesn't mean it's over for us."

"Oh, it's over," she promised in a vicious whisper. "If I had any doubts before, I don't anymore."

"Tamika—."

"*As-salaamu-'alaikum.*" She slammed the receiver down. The crashing sound hung in the air for a moment more as the deafening sound of silence filled the home. She heard herself sniff, alone in the room. The kitchen's light spilled onto the CD stand and television, giving the gray screen a shining glow. It lit the futon and the coats, and Tamika herself. A spotlight, a taunting spotlight, as if it weren't enough for her to feel what she had done. Her gaze fell on her *abiya* that felt bunched up in front of her, and as she saw the uneven hems, she discovered she hadn't buttoned it properly. It was then that the realization of what she'd done collapsed on her until her body grew weak under its weight. She fell to her knees and covered her face as she cried in horrible sobs.

Sulayman listened to the dial tone for a moment before turning off the cordless that he held in his hand. He sat on the end of his bed in a daze and felt a lump develop in his throat. His chest began to hurt, and he tried to catch his breath. He had been preparing for bed when she called, but now he couldn't think of sleep. He hung his head in shame and whispered prayers to Allah to forgive him. He started to pray that Tamika would have him back, but he stopped himself. He didn't deserve her. She was right. He had a lot to learn. There was so little he knew about her and her family.

Besides, he doubted it was a good idea to hope for something that could never be. But, right then, he was too weak, too attached to accept such a fate.

He wanted to marry Tamika, and he had no idea how he could consider someone after her.

Twenty-six

Tamika sat in silence as she stared out the plane window with her head leaning back on the reclined chair, holding a book open in her lap, unable to concentrate on the words. The sky was a smooth powder blue that glowed in the sky, and the clouds were strips of strewn cotton—torn, outstretched, and fading. It was a Sunday afternoon, the last day of winter break, and Tamika was on her way back to Atlanta. She was emotionless. She neither cared that break was over nor was she enthused that classes would resume the next morning. Somehow, she had made it through the break and pushed Sulayman to the back of her mind. She was grateful that Latonya didn't revisit the subject because she wasn't prepared, or willing, to discuss it.

Tamika's gaze fell to her open book, and she ran a finger across the page, unable to determine if she felt refreshed after the break. She hadn't been able to see her brother, which was a great disappointment for her. But she was grateful to have reunited with Latonya, so she couldn't complain. She pulled her seat to an upright position, preparing to continue reading. But her eyes only fell upon the words as her thoughts drifted to her aunt and mother, and she wondered what they thought of her. She felt as if she had failed them, and she couldn't bring herself to face them. How could she when Sulayman took it upon himself to ruin her life? Tamika hadn't called her aunt yet, and she doubted that she ever would. She shut her eyes to drown out the reminder of everything she eventually had to face.

The sudden halting of the plane woke Tamika, and she realized then that she had fallen asleep. She glanced about her and saw the passengers unbuckling their seatbelts. Had they arrived already?

At baggage claim, Tamika tipped a man a few dollars to push her bags to the taxi station. She didn't want to pay for a taxi, but she knew no one she could call for a ride. She momentarily considered calling Zahra, but she didn't want to inconvenience her. Besides, she wasn't in the mood to chat and felt it best to keep to herself.

She chose the taxi closest to her, and the man lifted the bags into the trunk after the driver opened it for him. She climbed in the backseat and stared out the window. The driver returned to his seat a minute later and fastened his seatbelt. "Where to?"

"Streamsdale University."

"That'll be sixty five dollars, ma'am."

She shrugged. "That's fine."

He looked at her through the rearview mirror with his eyebrows gathered, as if surprised she didn't protest. He started the car and pulled off, and Tamika leaned her head back and shut her eyes, though she found it difficult to sleep. She was relieved when they pulled into the university, and she sat up and directed him to her dormitory. Other cars were parked throughout campus, and students unloaded their belongings and carried them to their buildings. Some had new furniture for the semester, or perhaps they were new students coming to the university for the spring.

"You need help with your bags, ma'am?" the taxi driver asked.

"Yes, please."

He carried a bag in each hand and followed her into the building. When they stopped in front of her room door, she turned to thank him. "This is fine." She reached in her purse and pulled out four of the five twenty-dollar bills she had.

The man set down the bags and frowned, unsure if he had change. He pulled a wad of cash from his pocket and flipped through the bills, licking his thumb, in search of small bills. He found a ten but could find nothing smaller.

"It's okay," she told him, doubtful that he was being honest. But she was too tired to argue.

"Thanks." He handed her the ten and turned to go. "Have a nice day, ma'am."

"You too."

She opened the door to her room and pushed in her bags one at a time. The room held a stuffy odor that she couldn't place, and it was uncomfortably cold. Apparently, she wasn't the only one counting pennies this year. She locked the door and walked over to the thermostat and turned on the heat, relieved that her roommate hadn't arrived yet. Something in the wall made a clanking noise, and a moment later she heard the hushed whisper of heat blowing through the vent. She collapsed on her bed after slipping off her shoes, still wearing her sweater, jacket, and clothes, waiting for the room to warm. She didn't feel like unpacking, and she needed to pray. But she wanted to take a moment to relax first. Lying on her back, she threw an arm over her face and felt her body growing limp in exhaustion, and she didn't protest as she felt herself drifting to sleep. Tamika woke to find the room dimly lit with the light from outside. Realizing that it was close to sunset, she sat up and hurried to prepare for the afternoon prayer before it was time to pray *Maghrib*.

As she stood in prayer, she relaxed and felt the stress of the day leaving with each movement of her limbs. She touched her head to the ground, and as she glorified her Lord, her heart ached in regret for how she had spoken to Sulayman. She would have to apologize, she realized and felt her heart grow heavy in submission. She had a right to be upset, but she could have handled the situation more civilly. She wondered if she would change her mind about marrying him. She doubted it. Tamika finished her prayer only minutes before sunset, so she remained sitting as she waited for the next prayer, her mind filled with what she would do about Sulayman.

Tamika wasn't ready for what marrying Sulayman would mean in her relationship with her family. She doubted she could take such a serious blow. She needed time to get herself together before she committed to someone. She liked Sulayman a great deal, but his trip to Milwaukee made her realize he wasn't as intelligent as she thought. There were lots of Muslim men out there, and she shouldn't restrict herself just yet. Sulayman was exceptional, no doubt, but she couldn't help wondering if his intelligence was limited to academics and Islam. As she thought of his family, she was saddened that she wouldn't be part of it. And his sincerity. She doubted she would find another man like that. Was she making a mistake by letting him go?

The sound of a key turning in the door interrupted her thoughts. Tamika immediately glanced up from where she sat on the floor dressed for prayer to see the door open. Aminah entered and smiled, her eyes a turquoise green next to the ocean blue *khimaar* she wore tucked in a beige button up sweater that hung a few inches past her waist. Aminah's wool over garment was a sandy brown with threads of blue and black grains throughout the material. She held her black coat folded over the crease in her elbow and her duffel bag over a shoulder. The sight of her moved Tamika, as if the calm normalcy of her life was settling in place, and Tamika found herself pondering the tranquility she felt.

"*As-salaamu-'alaikum,*" Aminah greeted cheerfully as she closed the door behind her. A smile spread across her face, pink-blushed from the cold, and Tamika found no indication that she knew of what had transpired between her and Sulayman.

"How was your break?" Aminah asked as she set her duffle bag and coat on her bed before she started for the door.

"Good, *alhamdulillaah,*" Tamika said, forcing a smile.

"I'll be right back, *inshaAllaah.*"

Tamika's heart raced as she realized Sulayman was probably outside helping his sister with her bags. "You need any help?"

Aminah shook her head, glancing over her shoulder a second before opening the door. "I should be fine. Sulayman's here."

Tamika nodded and watched Aminah disappear into the hall. She sat motionless, staring at the door. Should she go outside and talk to him? Her heart pounded, but she didn't move from her place. What would he say if she did? Would he ignore her?

Aminah returned a few minutes later and set her large bag on the floor next to her bed. She locked the door behind her, and Tamika's heart sank. Sulayman had gone. Chuckling, Aminah sighed and shook her head as she unzipped her duffel bag and pulled out the clothes and folded them in a stack on her bed. "I can't believe break is over."

"I know," Tamika said, echoing Aminah's carefree mood, pulling her knees up to her chest and hugging them as she laughed.

"It went by so fast. *SubhanAllaah.*"

There was a brief silence as Tamika watched Aminah fold all the clothes from her duffel bag then carry them to the drawers. The sound of drawers opening and closing filled the stillness of the room, the heat blowing from the vent a comfortable background whisper. As Aminah shut the drawers after putting the last of her clothes away, a frown formed on her face, and she lifted a hand to rub an eye as she blinked repeatedly. Apparently, something had gotten in her eye.

Tamika watched in silence and wondered what Aminah knew about her and Sulayman. Aminah leaned forward to look closely at her reflection in the mirror and rubbed her eye until she found something in its corner, cleaning it out with her pinky finger. She then reached in her sweater pocket and pulled out a stick of lip balm, which she ran across her lips before dropping it back in her pocket. She used her lips to spread the moisture and wiped the excess balm from around her mouth with a finger. She turned to go back to her bed, her lips now a glossy pink that complimented her cheeks. She knelt and opened her suitcase, the sound of the zipper an awkward moaning in the room.

"What'd you do for break?" Tamika said finally, wanting to break the tension she feared was about to build in the quiet room.

Aminah forced laughter as she stood with her hands on her hips, surveying the contents of her bag as she tried to decide if she felt like unpacking it all right then. "I can hardly remember, it went by so fast."

Tamika stood and walked over to her own bed, where she sat down on its edge and studied her roommate thoughtfully before asking, "How's your family?"

The corners of Aminah's mouth turned down slightly as she shrugged, and she knelt to take some things from the bag. When she stood again, she held a stick of deodorant, baby powder, and a bar of soap still packaged from the store. She carried them to the drawers and put them inside before walking back to the bag and zipping it closed, apparently not in the mood to put all her things away at the moment.

"*Alhamdulillaah*, they're doing well," Aminah said as she pushed the bag under her bed. A second later, she stood, and she peeled off her sweater, revealing the wrinkled ends of her blue head cover. She lifted her coat and carried it with the sweater to her closet. The sound of the closet door sliding filled the space between them for a moment. Aminah reached in and hung her sweater and coat on the same hook, sliding the door back closed a second later.

"How's your sister?" Aminah asked as she pulled the blanket and sheet from her bed and balled them up before stuffing them in the laundry basket near Tamika's bed.

"She's fine," Tamika said, studying her roommate to find the reason for changing the subject from her family. But Aminah was hard to read.

"Was she excited to see you?" Aminah asked, opening her closet again to take out a clean sheet and blanket from the top shelf. The question was cordial, but Tamika thought she detected a tone of stiff formality that suggested something else was on Aminah's mind.

Tamika chuckled and nodded. "Yeah, it was nice."

"Did you get to see your brother?"

She frowned and shook her head. "No."

Aminah smiled in sympathy as she closed the closet and carried the sheet and blanket to her bed, glancing up at Tamika for a second. "*InshaAllaah,* next time."

"Yeah, *inshaAllaah.*"

Tamika watched in silence as Aminah put the sheet on her bed, tugging at the linen's ends and lifting the edges of her mattress to fold the sheet under neatly. Aminah's face was emotionless as she shook the blanket and threw it over her bed.

"How's Sulayman?" Tamika's heart thudded with insistence as she felt her voice hanging in the air. She could hardly believe she had the nerve, but she couldn't resist the opportunity. If she had waited, the question would seem out of place. It was only natural that she wanted to know how Aminah's family was doing after being gone so long, at least she hoped so.

Aminah leaned forward and ran a hand over the soft gray cashmere blanket on her bed to smooth out any wrinkles. She sat down on its edge a second later, facing Tamika as she pulled off her shoes, revealing dark blue socks that matched the thread strokes in her *abiya.* Her eyebrows were gathered as she met Tamika's gaze, but her expression softened somewhat before she replied. "*Alhamdulillaah,*" she said, a hint of reluctance in her tone, and she lifted a shoulder in a shrug.

Tamika had thought her roommate would say more, but, instead, Aminah unbuttoned the cuffs of her over garment and pushed her sleeves up to her elbows before walking over to the sink. Tamika heard the hushed whisper of her roommate's voice saying, "*Bismillaah,*" in preparation for ablution.

The sound of water running and pounding against the metal sink was sudden, as if washing away Tamika's hope for answers. The water ran for several seconds, apparently until it was warm, before its rushing sound softened to the hum of a thin, clear stream. Tamika watched in silence as Aminah prepared for prayer, her fears confirmed. Aminah knew.

Aminah opened her closet and removed a small face cloth before closing the sliding door a second later. She dried her water-glistened arms and dripping face, and hung the mint green cloth on a small bar on the sidewall of the sink area.

"You need to pray *Maghrib?*" Aminah asked as she pulled the cuffs of her sleeves back to her wrists and buttoned them.

Tamika nodded and stood next to her roommate, who had already positioned herself in the direction of prayer. Tamika felt distant from Aminah as their shoulders and feet touched. It was the first time Tamika felt that she and Aminah were praying together out of pure obligation—because they had no other choice.

Aminah recited the Qur'an beautifully, but Tamika found it difficult to concentrate on God's words. She was distracted by thoughts of Sulayman and fears that this may be the last of her days as Aminah's friend. She wondered what Sarah thought of her, and Ismael. Surely, they knew of her argument with Sulayman. Sarah was the one who had answered the phone. What mother wouldn't ask her son what had possessed a woman to call so late, so suddenly, in the middle of her winter break?

They finished the prayer and recounted Allah's glory, praise, and greatness in voices barely audible in the otherwise quiet room. Tamika felt as if a barrier had been erected between her and Aminah, and she resigned herself to leaning her back against the side of her bed, leaving Aminah sitting where they had prayed. With her legs outstretched before her and one foot on the other, Tamika finished her recital. She sat with her hands folded on her lap and her gaze staring at the scratches on the door.

Aminah stood to pray her voluntary prayer, and Tamika didn't move from where she sat. She was still feeling tired and considered getting more rest. She was still deciding how long she should sleep when Aminah finished her prayer and stood.

Tamika's eyes followed her roommate as Aminah unbuttoned her over garment and slipped it off her arms. Aminah stepped out of the wool dress as she held it by a sleeve, revealing a pair of loose black pants of sweater material. She wore a short sleeved purple V-neck sweater with threads of black throughout. Aminah removed her *khimaar* and carried it with the *abiya* to the footboard of her bed, where she hung them before walking over to the sink and removing a large comb from the counter. She unbraided her single braid with her freehand, working her fingers in the plaits to pull them loose. Her hair fell against her neck and shoulders, and she tilted her head to the side as she lifted the comb to her hair.

Tamika bit her lower lip in contemplation, and a moment later, she stood, unbuttoning her *abiya*. After pulling the *khimaar* from her head, revealing her scarf-flattened hair that fell limp around her face and shoulders, she tossed her clothes to her bed. The room was comfortably warm now, and she walked over to her bed wearing a white turtleneck tucked in a pair of faded blue jeans. Realizing that she too should change her linen, she pulled the comforter and sheet from the bed and replaced them with clean linen from her closet.

Aminah finished combing her hair, and she walked over to the trashcan that stood at the side of her desk and pulled the hair strands from the teeth of the comb. She let the brown strands fall slowly into the trash before returning the comb back to the counter next to the sink. She moved her head to the left and right to study her appearance after grooming her hair, and Tamika's eyes fell on her roommate's back as she pulled the fresh blanket back before she climbed in the bed.

Tamika pulled the cover over her and folded her hands behind her head, staring at the ceiling. The sudden halting of the heat blowing from the vent filled the room with an abrupt silence, and each roommate became acutely aware of the other's presence in the room. For several minutes, neither spoke, and Tamika shut her eyes, less to fall asleep than to escape the suffocating awkwardness that thickened the quiet air.

"What happened?"

Aminah's voice prompted Tamika to open her eyes, and Tamika turned her head slightly to see Aminah sitting on the edge of her bed facing Tamika. Aminah sat next to a bottle of lotion that lay toppled on its side as she rubbed the moisturizer on her hands and arms. Her green eyes were a shade darker than Tamika remembered, and Tamika wondered at how Aminah's eye color changed with the color of her clothes.

Aminah's eyes were slightly narrowed with her eyebrows gathered, and her expression was one of confusion and shock. For a moment, Tamika thought she had drifted to sleep and screamed out without knowing it. She creased her forehead in concern.

"What do you mean?" Tamika asked.

"With you and Sulayman," Aminah said, as if implying, *What else?*

Tamika's heart pounded, and she turned her body to face her roommate, propping her head on her hand, hoping to sound as casual as she hoped she looked. "Why? What'd he say?"

"He didn't *say* anything." Aminah picked up the bottle of lotion and snapped it shut, avoiding Tamika's gaze with the motion. "That's why I'm concerned."

Tamika tried to appear surprised and concerned. "Is he okay?"

Aminah shrugged as she stood to place the lotion on the counter near the comb. "*Alhamdulillaah*, but he's not himself."

"He didn't say anything?"

She shook her head as she sat back on the edge of her bed near the nightstand and creased her forehead. "About what?" The question held a tone of accusation, and Tamika could tell it was rhetorical, so she decided not to respond.

"We have *no* idea what's going on," Aminah said, accusation still in her voice.

Sighing, Tamika sat up, knowing she would have to tell the truth. She rubbed her eyes, and she sensed Aminah waiting, as if demanding an explanation. "When I called," she said, figuring Aminah already knew that she had, "I was upset with him for going to my mom's house without telling me."

Aminah nodded, and a frown creased the corners of her mouth, as if she wasn't surprised. She plucked a piece of lint from her pants. "I figured it had something to do with that." She held Tamika's gaze for a few seconds before she asked, "Is that it?"

Tamika ran a hand over her hair and shrugged. "Pretty much," she said tentatively, unable to hold her roommate's gaze.

"Then what is it?"

Tamika avoided Aminah's gaze and studied a stain on the carpet. "It's over."

"*Over?*" Aminah's voice was one of disbelief, and Tamika thought she heard a tinge of disgust in her tone.

"Yeah."

"Why?"

"I just don't think he's ready to handle my family." Tamika hoped she wasn't offending his sister, but it was the truth. There was a brief pause as Tamika ran a hand across the blanket on her bed.

"What happened at the house?" Aminah asked, a hint of concern in her voice, and for a split second Tamika sensed that Aminah didn't agree with her brother's trip either.

"I'm not sure," Tamika said, meeting Aminah's gaze for a moment, "but my aunt's really upset. She called my sister's house and wanted me to call her right away."

"But why?"

Tamika shook her head. "I haven't called her yet."

"Then how do you know she's upset?" Tamika could tell that Aminah was fishing for any way to patch up the wounds and return things back to normal.

"My sister talked to her and said she sounded really worried."

Aminah bit her lip. "So you can't work it out?"

"I don't know, Aminah," Tamika said with a sigh. "It's just too much to think about right now."

"Are you sure?"

"Pretty much."

Aminah sighed in disappointment. "I'm sorry about that."

Tamika echoed her roommate's sigh. "Me too."

"I guess there's not much to say if this is what you prayed on."

Tamika couldn't tell if it was Aminah's way of reminding her that she shouldn't decide something this detrimental without praying about it first, but, in any case, Tamika doubted she needed to pray. "It's nothing to worry about though," she said, wondering if she was talking to herself or Aminah. "We'll be fine."

Aminah nodded, but she wasn't convinced. She was worried about her brother. He liked Tamika more than he had liked any woman, and Aminah was concerned about his ability to handle her rejection. She remembered his melancholy mood several days after he returned from the trip, and she had been too afraid to ask him about it. He seemed to want to be left alone, and she had given him his space. Their parents were worried about him too, but they didn't push him for an explanation. Aminah had faith that Sulayman would heal, but it pained her to know it would take some time. She hated to see him like that, and it was even more painful now that she knew why.

Three weeks passed, and Tamika didn't hear from Sulayman. She wanted to call him, but she had hoped he would call her. She was distracted in her studies, but she managed to focus on her work. Aminah was cordial and treated her well, and Tamika understood that her roommate wanted her to know that she didn't blame her for her decision.

Tamika was in her room studying one Saturday night when the phone rang. Aminah had gone home for the weekend, and Tamika had turned down an offer from Zahra to stay at her apartment. She answered the phone and was pleasantly surprised to hear Sulayman on the other end.

"*As-salaamu-'alaikum.* I hope you don't mind me calling."

"No, it's fine." She tried to conceal how elated she was to hear from him.

"Are you busy?"

"No, I'm just looking over some things for class."

"How are you doing?"

"Fine, *alhamdulillaah.* You?"

"*Alhamdulillaah.*" But his voice wasn't convincing. She could tell he was still bothered by what happened.

"How's your family?" His question held a tone of concern, and Tamika couldn't help thinking it was a bit late for him to realize the harm he caused.

"Uh, fine, *inshaAllaah.*"

"Have you spoken to your aunt yet?"

Tamika grew silent. She hadn't expected the question and was unsure how she should respond. She felt guilty for avoiding her aunt, but she couldn't bear to face her. Each time she thought of Sulayman sitting in the living room with her aunt and mother, she cringed in humiliation. She tried to forget about it, but eventually the thought would invade her mind, making it difficult for her to forgive him. "Why?"

There was a brief pause. "I'm just concerned."

Her gaze fell on her book, and she studied it for a few seconds. "There's nothing to worry about," she lied.

He paused and drew in a deep breath before exhaling. "Tamika, I talked to your family to help your relationship. I don't know if I can forgive myself if that's not what I've done."

Tamika shut her eyes and pinched the space between them, feeling exhausted just then. "Sulayman," she said before taking a deep breath, "you can't save the world." Tamika's words were calm and sincere, and she felt a sense of relief in expressing herself without getting angry. She was still upset with him, but she was over the initial fury of astonishment. "What's done is done. My family will be fine, *inshaAllaah.*"

"I'm really sorry for everything."

She drew in a deep breath. "I know."

"I understand you're upset," Sulayman said in regret, "and I don't blame you for that. I only ask that you forgive me because I don't want to be in trouble with Allah for this on the Day of Judgment."

Tamika felt sorry for him just then. He was hurting from regret, and he needed relief. She wanted to tell him what he wanted to hear, but she also wanted to be honest. As much as she wanted to forgive him, she couldn't, at least not yet. Forgiveness came from the heart, and until she felt it emanating from within, she couldn't express it. She sighed. "I need some time to think about it."

There was a long pause, and she ached as if feeling his pain. "I understand," he said, and Tamika could tell that he did.

"I'm sorry," she said, feeling her body grow heavy in sorrow for what he must be feeling at the moment.

"No, there's nothing for you to be sorry about," he said, "I'm the one who should be sorry. I know it may be years before you can forgive me, if ever." He hesitated before saying, "I just hope you're able to reconsider marrying me."

Tamika's heart pounded, and sadness overwhelmed her. Part of her wanted to marry him, but she couldn't. She had her family to think about, and she still harbored resentment for what he'd done. There was so much he didn't know about her, and she doubted he would want to marry her after he found out. Then there was school, which she wanted to continue after graduating. Marriage was something she simply could not commit to right then. She sighed. "I'm sorry, Sulayman, but I can't."

"Can't marry me, or can't reconsider?"

She paused before responding apologetically, "Both."

Tamika hung up the phone feeling as if she had given up a piece of her heart. A lump developed in her throat, and she wondered if she had made a mistake.

Twenty-seven

It was a Thursday night in late February, and Tamika lay awake, unable to sleep. In the next bed, Aminah breathed soft rhythmic breaths that incited envy in Tamika. She wished she could sleep. It was one o'clock in the morning, and all she could think about was her mother and aunt. When Tamika had begun to drift to sleep an hour before, Latonya called to tell her that their mother was in the hospital. Jackie had told Latonya a few minutes before Latonya called Tamika, and their aunt asked that Latonya come to Milwaukee right away. No one knew exactly what happened except that Thelma was having trouble breathing and said something about her heart. Of course, as far as they could guess, it was a heart attack, but the hospital wasn't sure.

When Tamika had asked Latonya if she were going to go, Latonya said that she couldn't. Her job wouldn't let her take off, so Latonya asked Tamika if she would go in her place. Latonya offered to charge the ticket to her card, and Tamika reluctantly agreed. Tamika was worried about her mother and wanted to see her, but she feared that her presence wouldn't be welcomed, especially at such a crucial time.

Tamika wondered what her aunt would say when she called to tell Jackie she was coming, not Latonya. Latonya had convinced Tamika it didn't matter who went, so long as their mother had at least one of her children by her side in this difficult time. She had told Tamika that Jackie feared that their mother's condition would only worsen if no one could make it. Thelma hadn't been herself lately, Jackie had said, and she needed comfort and support more than she did medical attention. Jackie had told Latonya that Thelma had been spending a lot of time looking through old photo albums these past few months and would often ignore her phone.

The information terrified Tamika, and she wondered how much longer her mother could continue like that. Tamika feared that her conversion was becoming more and more difficult for her mother to cope with, which was probably why she had fallen into a form of depression. Tamika imagined her mother sitting on the couch reminiscing on days too far gone to touch and too close to ignore, as the imprints were still on her heart. The albums were probably those of Tamika singing in church and of church parties and dinners. Or maybe they were pictures of Latonya, Philip, and Tamika as toddlers with baby food smeared on their mouths and hands. A smile creased the sides of Tamika's mouth as she remembered a time Latonya had styled her hair with rice cereal and vegetable oil.

Frustrated, Tamika shut her eyes and threw an arm over her face, determined to sleep. She wondered when Latonya would call to tell her she had gotten the ticket so she would know when she was leaving.

Friday evening Sulayman hung up the phone with renewed energy. He hadn't expected to hear Aidah's voice on the other end of the phone when he answered, but he was happy to hear from her. He was still hanging on to the hope that Tamika would change her mind, but he knew it was best to move on. He hadn't planned to start looking for someone else, but hearing from Aidah made him realize that now was as good time as any.

He and Aidah had a pleasant conversation, and Aidah wanted to know what had happened to make him call off their marriage. Of course, he and she had already discussed it, but she needed clarification. He was as honest as possible, and she expressed that he had misunderstood her. There was a lot she needed to work on within herself, she admitted, but she didn't want him to misjudge her. After she explained herself, he realized that the image he had of her wasn't entirely correct, and he was glad that she called. After hanging up, he was apprehensive about starting over again, but he couldn't think of a reason why he shouldn't.

Except Tamika.

He convinced himself that Tamika wasn't for him and decided to pray about reconsidering marriage to Aidah. Maybe Aidah would be better for him. He and she had been raised similarly, and he didn't have to worry about in-laws who weren't Muslim. Her parents liked him, and although her mother was a bit apprehensive about them marrying before Aidah finished medical school, her father was really hoping it would work out, regardless of when they married. Perhaps these were signs that he should reconsider her.

Aminah chuckled when Sulayman told her that Aidah had called. She shook her head and commented that Aidah was never going to give up, but she encouraged him to pursue it. She felt bad for encouraging him because she felt they weren't meant for each other, but she wanted very much to see her brother happy. The situation with Tamika had taken its toll on him, and since there was little hope that Tamika would change her mind, it was probably good for him to consider Aidah again. Inside, she feared that it was a risky move for him to make, but she prayed he wasn't making an emotional decision to make up for what had happened with Tamika. It wouldn't be fair to him or Aidah if they married half-heartedly, but she couldn't express these thoughts to her brother because his emotional state was already fragile. He needed something to hold him together, and if this would do it, even if only temporarily, she welcomed the situation.

In her bedroom at home, Aminah thought about Tamika. There were times when Aminah was upset with her for hurting her brother, but she knew it was unfair to feel that way. Tamika, like all people, had a right to decide something wasn't best for her. But why? That was what Aminah couldn't understand. Why did it have to end this way? She understood that Sulayman had made a mistake by taking a trip to her family without telling her, but was it really worth it to end the relationship because of that? She was often tempted to ask Tamika about it and encourage her to rethink her decision, but Aminah opted to keep quiet because she was too emotionally involved to give fair advice. Perhaps Sulayman wasn't good for Tamika. But Aminah couldn't pretend to understand why.

She pushed the thoughts from her head and resisted the urge to pick up the phone and call her roommate. But it was difficult, because she felt as if her own heart had been broken. She had even shed tears over the situation and wondered if *she* would heal. She loved Tamika like a sister, but she knew that a piece of that love was chipped away when Tamika decided not to marry her brother. It would have been so perfect, she thought. She had already dreamt of their children, and she had imagined visiting Tamika while she was pregnant. She thought of being married herself and their children playing together. She was being irrational, she knew, but she hoped there was room for fairytales in the harsh reality of life.

By Wednesday, a week after she was admitted to the hospital, Thelma's condition had improved, Latonya had told Tamika, but she was still in the hospital. She was expected to be released within the next two or three days. Tamika was leaving for Milwaukee Thursday evening, one week after she had spoken to Latonya.

Tamika had little money and couldn't afford to take a taxi to the airport. She considered asking Aminah for a ride, but she didn't want to see Sulayman. She was too ashamed to ask Dr. Sanders because she didn't want him to think she was taking advantage of his kindness. She hated to call Zahra on short notice, but she had no other choice. Fortunately, Zahra agreed to take her, and Tamika thanked her profusely for her kindness.

After she finished talking to Zahra, Tamika decided to call her aunt. Aminah was away at a study group meeting, and Tamika had the room to herself. She sat for a few minutes contemplating what she would say when she called. It had been nearly three months since her aunt talked to Latonya, and Tamika wondered how she would explain the delay in calling her back. Her thoughts drifted to her mother's health, and she hoped the seriousness of the situation would make her aunt forget about her not calling.

Tamika picked up the phone as she took a deep breath and exhaled. She dialed her aunt and listened to the phone ring, hoping no one would answer. When one of her cousins picked up, she asked to speak to her aunt. She was put on hold, and her heart pounded in nervousness. Her aunt was home. What would she say to her?

"Hello?" Jackie's voice sounded slightly irritated.

"Aunt Jackie, it's Tamika."

There was a brief pause. "Tamika?"

"Yes, it's me."

"You hear 'bout your mother?"

"Yes," Tamika said, regret and sadness in her voice. "That's why I called."

"Well, she a'right now. She should be home by Friday."

"Do they know what happened?"

"Not yet. But she just gotta watch 'er health, that's all."

"How's she doing?"

"She fine now, just tired. She need a lot 'o rest." She paused. "Yo' sister may be up here to check on 'er."

"Uh," Tamika searched for the words to tell her aunt about the flight. "Latonya couldn't come, so she bought me a ticket."

"What?"

She decided to cut to the chase. "I have a plane ticket for tomorrow."

There was a long pause. "You comin' *here*?"

"Yes, ma'am."

Jackie huffed. "Well, that's a surprise."

Tamika was unsure how to take the comment. "I know," she apologized. "I hope it's not a problem."

"It ain't never a problem for a child to visit 'er mother."

They were silent for some time, and Tamika toyed with the phone cord.

"Where you been?" Jackie asked.

Tamika was expecting the question, but she wasn't prepared to answer it. "Uh, what do you mean?"

"Your sister ain't tell you to call me around Christmas?"

At first, she didn't respond. She didn't want to lie, but she hadn't planned to explain herself. "Uh, yeah, I think she mentioned somethin' like that."

"You *think*? You can't remember somethin' like that?"

"Yes," she said finally, "she told me."

"Then why you ain't call?"

Her heart raced. "Latonya told me Sulayman came to talk to you and Mom, and I was upset."

"Upset?" Jackie sounded surprised.

"Yeah, because he didn't tell me he was going."

She was silent momentarily. "Yeah, but what that gotta do with callin' me?"

Tamika sighed. She decided that honesty was best. "I'm sorry for not calling, but I was angry myself and didn't know if I could take you and Mom being angry too."

"Angry fo' what, child?"

"For what he did."

Jackie paused thoughtfully. "He your fiancé?"

"No." It felt good being able to say that.

"Then who is he?"

"He wanted to marry me, but I told him no."

There was a long pause. "Why?"

"'Cause I don't think I'm ready. I have school, and I didn't wanna upset Mom anymore than I already have."

Jackie was silent for a moment. "I hope you 'on't think you doin' yo' mother a favor by not marryin' him."

Tamika sighed. "No, I don't." But she wasn't sure if that was the truth.

"'Cause yo' mom ain't got nothin' against that boy."

"I'm sorry about what he did."

Jackie forced laughter, as if Tamika still had a lot to learn. "Ain't a thing wrong with what he did. Why you sorry?"

Taken aback by the comment, Tamika was unsure how to respond.

"He's just doin' what he s'pposed to. I wish other boys had his sense. Most of 'em don't care nothin' bout no girl's parents."

She hesitated before asking, "What did Mom say about him?"

Jackie laughed again. "If you ain't marryin' 'im, why you askin'?"

Embarrassed, Tamika grew silent.

"Child, if you wanna marry the boy, marry 'im," Jackie said so simply that Tamika wondered if she had it all wrong. Maybe her family wouldn't be upset if she got married. "I 'on't know what yo' mother think of 'im, but Thelma ain't upset at you 'cause of him, so ain't no sense in you worryin' 'bout upsetting her more."

"But Mom doesn't want me to get married."

"Thelma want you to be Christian. Whatever else you do right now, I 'on't think she cares."

Tamika hung up the phone and reflected on what her aunt had said. She thought about her mother and felt her heart ache with love for her. She wanted nothing more than to make her mother love her again. Momentarily, she toyed with the thought of telling her mother she was Christian again and imagined how she would react. She wondered if her mother would believe her. She turned off the light and climbed into bed as she pondered the conversation.

In the darkness, a question loomed, and she reflected on it for a moment. What if she really did return to Christianity? She felt herself grow tired as she imagined how much easier her life would be. She imagined her mother smiling and hugging her, her aunt congratulating her, and her sister and brother laughing in enjoyment. Her eyes grew heavy as she imagined even her father coming home when he heard the good news. Her heart filled with joy as her mind held the image of everyone sitting in the living room of her home reminiscing, each person sharing a funny story about Tamika and how they always knew she'd come around. As sleep overtook her, the images became vivid as the scene transformed into a dream.

Tamika was laughing as she sat on the couch enjoying the attention for reverting back to the religion of her family. The gathering turned into a party, and her aunts, grandparents, and cousins filled the room. People from her church came through the door bearing gifts and candy. Children danced and played, elated for Tamika's happy moment. Her mother sat next to her and held her hand and squeezed it in pride. She kissed Tamika on the cheek and rubbed her head as she grinned. Then everyone hugged her and congratulated her individually.

A moment later, the people insisted she sing to them. Someone mentioned a popular gospel song, and Tamika began to sing. The beauty of her voice captivated them, and they stared at her in awe. She sang about the grace of Jesus and was moved by the power of the words. But as she sang she became less aware of them and wondered what her husband Sulayman would think of her. He was looking for her and couldn't find her, and she hadn't told him she was at her mother's home.

A second later he came through the door, but no one saw him but her. She kept singing, and he stared at her curiously with sadness on his face. Immediately, she became ashamed but kept singing for her family's sake. He frowned at her and approached, and she sang louder. When he stood before her, he asked if she had seen his wife. Confused that he didn't recognize her, she almost stopped singing to tell him it was she. But she kept singing and singing, and her family urged her on.

A second later he was gone and sadness came over her, and she cried as she sang, saddened for losing him and longing for him to return. She kept singing praises to Jesus as tears streamed down her face. But no one knew she was crying, and they clapped and whistled as she sang. They began to sing with her, and fear swept through her as she tried to stop singing but could not.

A moment later she was still singing, but her family was gone from the room. She was standing in the aisle of her childhood church singing in the empty building. She was facing a small candle burning under a painting that portrayed the crucifixion of Christ. A voice called her name, and she stopped singing to see who it was. Her pastor, who resembled Dr. Sanders, smiled at her and reached for her hands to welcome her back.

Tamika became terrified as she took his hands, and he smiled and congratulated her on her decision to return to the church. As the church light dimmed, he held her hand and walked with her through the church as he updated her on the church activities she had missed while she was gone. She felt a sudden urgency to leave but knew the church was chained from the outside. Her heart raced in fear as she tried to figure out an escape.

As if reading her mind, the pastor shook his head and told her people could enter but never leave. He then told her an old friend of hers had heard of her reversion and had traveled far to personally congratulate her. A sense of relief swept over her as she realized this was her way out. She would stay a Christian until she finished talking to her friend, and no one would suspect anything when she left. Desperately, she followed the pastor to where her friend waited in a small room.

A second later she was in the room alone and couldn't see anything in the darkness. She became terrified then relaxed when she saw Dee waving to her. Relieved to see a familiar face, Tamika sat down next to her. Dee hugged her and told her she had made the right decision and they could now be together forever. Tamika grew confused, and Dee smiled as she took her hand and led her to her home.

A second later she was in Dee's house, and they laughed and talked for some time. Then the house grew small until it was the size of a wooden box. Terrified, Tamika realized she was in a coffin and asked Dee how to get out. But Dee was in a coffin next to her and could not hear or see her anymore.

Tamika heard Dee screaming in horror, no longer aware of Tamika's presence. Tamika sensed she was about to suffer too, so she tried desperately to escape. She kicked and screamed, but the coffin only grew smaller until it squeezed her torturously. She screamed that she had only intended to be Christian for a little while and begged to go back to her husband so she could live like she was supposed to. She then heard Dee begging too, swearing that she had intended to leave Islam only for a little while.

In horror, Tamika realized her own disgraceful state. She hollered and heard the voice of Dee whisper, "At least we'll be together forever." Tamika screamed "No!" and heard her pastor's taunting laughter echo in the small space, and Dee's haranguing whisper again, "Together forever. Together forever. Together forever…"

Tamika jolted awake, and her heart pounded in fear. She sat up in bed and studied her surroundings in desperation. She was soaked in perspiration and shivering. She glanced around the dark room and saw Aminah's silhouette turn in her sleep. A sense of relief swept through her as she realized where she was.

But the relief was only partial. The ominous dream still haunted her conscience. Afraid to go back to sleep, she threw the covers from her and hurried to turn on the light. She then went to the sink and performed ablution in preparation for prayer. She dressed in her *abiya* and *khimaar* and felt calm overtake her as she recited the Qur'an in prayer. She extended her prostration longer than she usually did and supplicated to Allah to make her die as a Muslim.

Twenty-eight

Jackie met Tamika at the airport to drive her to the hospital where Thelma was staying. Tamika didn't remove her *khimaar* this time. She imagined that it didn't matter either way. Her family already knew she was Muslim, and she could do nothing to lessen the disappointment they already felt. Her aunt didn't seem to notice Tamika's new appearance, or if she did, she displayed no visible reaction to it. It was as if Jackie expected to see Tamika covered in Islamic garb. Perhaps it would have surprised her more if Tamika was not dressed like a Muslim.

It was close to 9:00 Thursday night when they pulled out of the airport parking lot. Jackie wasn't sure if the hospital would allow Tamika to visit this late, but she would try just in case.

In the car, they sat in silence. Neither knew exactly what to say to the other. The car smelled of cigarette smoke, and Tamika concentrated on breathing through her mouth. She stared out the window into the darkness and counted the minutes.

"So you still believe in Christ, huh?"

The question interrupted the still atmosphere too suddenly and startled Tamika. She turned to her aunt and wrinkled her forehead curiously, but her aunt would not meet her gaze. It took a moment before she answered. "Yes." She stared out the side window again, but her mind was on the question.

"He a prophet to you?"

She looked at her aunt, whose eyes were intent as they focused on the road ahead, but Tamika knew her aunt's mind was on their conversation. "Yes." She decided against saying more than she was asked, for fear her aunt would think she was preaching.

Jackie nodded and was silent momentarily. "Why you convert?"

Tamika reflected on what the question meant, and she wondered what inspired the sudden interest in her conversion. She had imagined that her aunt would show nothing but hostility toward her decision. But now Jackie sat next to her as if intrigued by the religion. Did she have a change of heart?

Tamika sighed to emphasize the weightiness of the answer. "It wasn't easy, but I started to realize some things I never thought about before."

"Like what?"

Her heartbeat quickened as she realized the significance of the moment. This could be a turning point for her family. Was Jackie too having doubts about the Christian faith?

"I don't know," Tamika said as she searched for words to describe what she had felt. "Just the idea of the Trinity. I guess I never understood it."

Jackie's expression was emotionless as she waited for Tamika to continue, her eyes glued to the road.

"I started to wonder if I believed in it because it was true or because it was all I knew," Tamika said. "I wondered if I really believed God could be a man and the Father, Son, and Holy Spirit at the same time. And the more I thought about it, the more I realized I never believed that, at least not completely. I just accepted it because it was wrong to question God."

Jackie didn't respond, and Tamika caught a glimpse of understanding in her aunt's eyes. Had her aunt suffered from the same doubts?

"When I studied Islam, it was just to get my term paper over with," Tamika said. "We weren't allowed to choose our own religion, so I chose the easiest thing to get me through the assignment. My roommates were Muslim, so I figured I'd do Islam." She chuckled. "And I guess the rest is history."

Jackie reflected on what Tamika had said before she spoke. "What'd you find out?"

Tamika sighed thoughtfully. "That Muslims believe like we do except they believe in the original teachings of Jesus and other prophets. They accept the Gospel and Torah as true, but only in the form of the original revelations God sent."

Jackie nodded, and Tamika could tell the information was weighing heavily on her aunt. Jackie's eyes grew distant, and she seemed afraid to look Tamika in the eye. Jackie sat in silence for a few minutes, and Tamika sensed her aunt was struggling with the same fear she had had—that Islam was true after all. "That boy, what's his name?"

"You mean Sulayman?"

Jackie nodded. "He said you 'on't believe Jesus had a father. That true?"

Tamika's heart nearly skipped a beat at the realization. It was Sulayman who had inspired the change in her aunt. She began to wonder what he had told her aunt and mother that touched Jackie in a way she herself had never been able to. Tamika realized her mistake, and fear swept through her. She shouldn't have gotten angry with him. Allah had allowed him to talk to them for a reason.

Regret nearly suffocated Tamika, and she wondered if it was too late to make amends. She wanted to marry him—needed to marry him, she realized just then. Her heart raced at the realization, and she could barely think straight as she replied to her aunt. "Uh, yes, that's true."

Her aunt was silent for the remainder of the ride, but the atmosphere was soothing. Tamika felt a bond with her aunt that she couldn't interpret fully. She sensed her aunt respected her more and that she was no longer angry. But Tamika understood that her aunt couldn't express this in words. But Jackie's eyes betrayed her, and Tamika saw in them what Jackie herself didn't know was there.

Visiting hours were over at 9:00, the hospital desk clerk informed them after they arrived. Jackie explained that Tamika had come from out of town to visit her mother, and she asked for leniency. After leaving to talk to someone, the clerk gave permission for Tamika to visit her mother but advised her to keep it brief. Jackie headed for the lobby to wait. Tamika needed time alone with Thelma, and, apparently, she didn't want to be in the way.

The clerk directed Tamika to her mother's room, and Tamika paused momentarily outside the door. Her hand rested on the handle, and her heart began to pound. She was filled with a mixture of hope and fear of what was before her. She wondered if her mother would be happy to see her. They hadn't seen each other since the fight last summer, and she could only hope time truly healed. She took a deep breath and prayed that her surprise visit would be a good one. Her palms began to sweat as she turned the handle and pushed the door open.

A lamp glowed in the dark room, and Tamika could see the shape of her mother's large body beneath a white sheet. She quietly shut the door and walked toward the bed. As she approached, she saw her mother's chest rising and falling rhythmically as she slept. Slightly relieved that she didn't have to face her mother yet, Tamika stood and studied her mother's face under the dim light. She marveled at how peaceful her mother seemed at the moment and wondered if she should wake her.

As she tried to decide, a calm came over her, and she sat in a chair next to the bed. Her heart pounded forcefully as she lifted her hand to touch her mother. She hesitated for a moment then relaxed as her palm stroked her mother's hair. Her mother didn't stir, and, gradually, Tamika's nervousness left. She paused and gently touched her mother's cheek with the back of her hand, and its warmth soothed Tamika until she felt it penetrating her heart. A lump developed in her throat, and tears welled in her eyes. She continued to stroke her mother's cheek then leaned forward to brush it with a kiss. Tears slid down her cheeks, and she wiped them away with the palm of her hand.

Tamika leaned back in the chair and relaxed as she enjoyed the moment she was stealing with her mother. She reflected on her conversation with her aunt and wondered if her mother too had been deeply affected by the talk with Sulayman. She thought of God and feared she had displeased Him by being hasty in her anger with Sulayman. Her thoughts drifted to what Dr. Sanders had told her about life and the soul, and Tamika's gaze fell on her mother as she pondered how it applied to the woman who gave birth to her. She wondered if her mother would ever rethink her religious conviction for the sake of her soul.

The recitation escaped her throat so naturally that Tamika heard the Qur'anic words filling the room before she realized she was reciting. In slow, measured tones, she pronounced the Arabic melodiously as she had learned in her class, careful to let each sound express the meaning of the miraculous words. Her heart filled with faith as she reflected on the recitation that meant:

Has the story reached you,
Of the Overwhelming Event?
Some faces that Day will be humiliated,

Laboring hard, weary—
The while they enter the Blazing Fire,
The while they are given to drink, of a boiling hot spring
No food will there be for them but a poisonous, thorny plant,
Which will neither nourish nor satisfy hunger

Other faces that Day will be joyful,
Pleased with their striving—
In a Garden on high,
Where they shall hear no word of vanity
Therein will be a bubbling spring,
Therein will be Thrones of dignity raised on high
Goblets places ready,
And cushions set in rows,
And rich carpets all spread out

Do they not look at the camels,
How they are made?
And at the sky,
How it is raised high?
And at the mountains,
How they are fixed firm?
And at the Earth,
How it is spread out?

Therefore, give admonition (O Muhammad),
For you art one to admonish
You are not one to manage their affairs
But if any turns away and rejects God—
God will punish him with a mighty Punishment
For to Us will be their Return
Then it will be for Us to call them to account.

Tamika's thoughts drifted as she pondered the meaning of the words. She had learned the verses during her summer classes and had recited them several times. The teacher had taught the class the Arabic recitation and gave thorough explanations of what the verses meant.

But it was at that moment, as Tamika sat next to her mother, that the words took on a meaning she hadn't imagined before. Her heart filled with a renewed faith, and she felt tears well in her eyes as she recited the words again. Inadvertently, her gaze fell upon her mother as she recited, and her heart nearly skipped a beat at what she saw. Her mother's eyes were now open and staring ahead distantly as she listened to the strange words, unaware that they were coming from the chair next to her. Afraid to startle her mother,

Tamika continued to recite and wondered if her mother imagined the sounds as part of a dream. Cautiously, she studied her mother's face as she continued her recitation, and she watched in amazement as her mother's eyes moistened until tears slid down her cheeks as she relaxed to the soothing words. Tamika's heart raced. She was scared her mother would glance to her left and find her there. Tamika repeated the verses, until her mother drifted back to sleep.

For a moment, Tamika sat in disbelief. Taken aback by the occurrence, Tamika decided to leave without announcing her presence. She was afraid what her mother would think if she found her there. But she couldn't help wondering what her mother was thinking when her eyes had filled with tears.

Tamika hesitated under the dim glow from the porch light of her home. Her gaze rested upon the single key in her palm, and she felt a sense of guilt sweep through her as the metal glistened in the night. Headlights shined on the front door, and like a flashlight in a search, they quickly scanned the width of the house as Jackie's car pulled out of the driveway. Jackie waited for Tamika to enter her home safely before driving away. Sensing her aunt's desire to go home, Tamika pushed the key in the doorknob and unlocked it before turning the handle to let herself in. She turned to wave to her aunt, who disappeared down the street as Tamika pushed the door open and stepped inside.

Tamika's heart raced in anticipation in the dark house, and she flicked on the light switch next to the foyer before coaxing herself to relax. Jackie had given Tamika her key to Thelma's house because Tamika didn't have one after the fight with her mother the summer before. Her aunt asked no questions when Tamika said she no longer had a key to her home. Jackie simply removed her own copy from her key ring and gave it to her niece. Tamika had wanted to say more, to explain, but Jackie's expression told her that she already understood. For a moment, Tamika had sat in the car gazing at her aunt curiously in an effort to read what was beyond Jackie's eyes. But, like most of the night, her aunt didn't meet her gaze as she offered kindness of which her niece felt undeserving.

Perhaps it was Jackie's commitment to family that inspired the turning of a new leaf. Or perhaps her sister's illness made her realize the fragility of life. Or maybe she remembered herself as a youth, when she and her own mother rarely saw eye to eye. Whatever it was that changed her aunt, Tamika was grateful. But she feared a polite distance was the closest she would ever come to being a family again.

The house carried the faint potpourri scent that had filled the house the summer before, and for a moment Tamika's heart pounded for fear her mother was coming down the hall to throw her from the home. She calmed a second later and wondered at her irrational thought. She removed her jacket and shoes and walked cautiously to the living room. She was unsure if she should sit down and relax, or if she had a right to. Her mother didn't know she was there, and she couldn't help wondering if her mother wanted her in the home.

Tamika didn't want to leave any traces of her presence, at least not yet. She wanted to wait until her mother was home and settled in before she announced herself. The sight of the couch unnerved Tamika, and the memory of her belongings scattered on it flashed through her mind. A lump gathered in her throat as she saw a weak, helpless girl crouched next to it protecting herself from her mother's violent attack. Quickly, Tamika turned away and made her way to her bedroom.

She opened the door and turned on the light. Her heart nearly stopped as she stiffened in shock. Her room was empty, as if no one had ever slept there. Her graduation picture that once sat upon her dresser was gone. In fact, nothing was on the dresser at all, or in her closet, or on her bed or walls. Her closet doors stood open, revealing a bareness that cut Tamika deep. There wasn't even a thin sheet to hide the nakedness of her worn mattress. It was as if Tamika were dead. Her face grew hot with anxiety, and she stood staring in utter disbelief at what represented her fate. She would never be Thelma's daughter again, and she would have to find the strength to accept that.

Had her aunt seen the bedroom? The question was unsettling. If her aunt had, was it possible that she wanted Tamika to see it herself? Did she *want* Tamika to hurt? Did she think she deserved it? Tamika pushed the thoughts from her mind and forced herself into the mundane preparations for sleep. She retrieved some linen from the hall closet and made her bed. What was ahead of her, she would think about later.

Tamika's night was peaceful although it had taken her some time to relax before finally drifting to sleep. She woke shortly before dawn to go to the bathroom and discovered she had begun her menses. She almost laughed at the irony. The summer before she had been afraid to reveal her conversion to her family. She had struggled with making her prayers to hide them from her mother. Now, when she had enough strength to be publicly Muslim, having even worn the *khimaar* upon her arrival, she was menstruating, so she wouldn't have to perform the formal prayers during her three-day trip. She returned to bed and decided to sleep in as long as she could. She doubted she would get much rest after her mother was released from the hospital.

Tamika woke to the sound of a phone ringing somewhere in the house. She blinked into wakefulness and realized a moment later where she was. Light filled the room, announcing more boldly the bareness of Tamika's bedroom—and life. The phone rang again, and she sat up to answer it then felt her pulse quicken as she remembered there was no phone in her bedroom, and why. She threw the cover from her and hurried to the living room before the machine could pick up. When she answered, she was relieved to hear her aunt's voice on the other line.

Jackie was about to bring Thelma home, and Tamika was unprepared. They would be on their way by noon, and, instinctively, Tamika glanced at the clock. It was a few minutes after 11:00. Tamika's heart raced as she hung up the phone. It was then that the magnitude of the situation began to sink in. Fear engulfed her, and she wondered if it was a good idea for her to come. She began to regret letting Latonya convince her. It should have been Latonya to greet their mother when she returned. Tamika would do no good. It would be a blessing if the atmosphere were even artificially cordial when her mother arrived. What if a fight ensued? What would Tamika do if her mother grew enraged at the sight of her? Was it even respectful to surprise her mother in this manner, especially in her condition?

The more Tamika thought about it, the more she realized she should leave. Her mother had no idea she had come anyway, and Tamika was sure her aunt would not tell her. It was apparent that, despite her own opinions about Tamika's decision, Jackie wasn't going to get involved in either praise or condemnation of the situation. She certainly wasn't going to play any part in worsening her sister's condition. It was doubtful that Jackie even agreed with Tamika's surprise visit, which gave Tamika all the more conviction that coming had been a mistake. If Thelma's health worsened after coming home, Tamika would be to blame. Was it worth it for her take such a risk?

Tamika glanced around the house for any signs of the intrusion. She moved swiftly down the hall and into the bathroom to remove any indication that she had come. She then moved to her bedroom and worked quickly, almost desperately, as she gathered her belongings to prepare to leave. She couldn't help wondering if her aunt's phone call was a final offering of a way out. Tamika yanked the linen from her bed in one motion and pulled too forcefully, causing her to lose balance and nearly fall backwards.

As she regained her balance, she caught her breath and suddenly became aware of the clumsiness of her thoughts. What was she running from, and where was she running to? The questions exhausted her, and she sat down on the edge of her mattress near where the sheet and blanket sat in a heap on the floor. Her heart hammered away in her chest and relaxed its pace only after her body itself relaxed.

After a few minutes, Tamika stood to remake her bed. She then went to the hallway to get a towel and washcloth to take a shower. In the bathroom, she sat on the edge of the tub and turned on the water. She let the water spill into her palm until its warmth soothed her. A second later she pulled the small metal lever, and the water rained from the showerhead.

In the shower, Tamika reflected on her decision to travel home to visit her mother. She hadn't given the decision much thought, and she wondered if having more time to consider it would have made things easier for her. Perhaps she would have talked to her mother on the phone before coming if she had thought to do it. On the other hand, maybe it was better that she had decided on a moment's notice. More time would have given her that many more reasons not to come. She made the right decision, she concluded. The last minute visit was the only way she could reunite with her mother. Under any other circumstances, her mother would not have allowed her to come home. Although her mother hadn't actually allowed her then, Thelma was in no condition to refuse her daughter. She simply did not know she was there.

Tamika let the water rinse the last of the soapsuds from her body before she reached down to turn the faucet knobs. The bathroom grew silent suddenly except for the gargling suction as the drain swallowed the water that had gathered in the tub. She drew the shower curtain open, and a cool draft swept over her. She reached to pull the towel from where it hung, and she dried herself in silence before dressing and leaving the bathroom.

In the kitchen, Tamika served herself some cold cereal and milk and sat down at the kitchen table. Her gaze grew distant as memories of the summer before invaded her mind. She chewed more slowly as she recalled her choking fear as her mother placed the hotdogs on the table. Did her mother have that much power over her? The possibility was unsettling.

Tamika glanced at the clock. It was 11:33. Her heart raced in nervousness as she realized her mother would be home soon. She ate quickly then stood to wash her dishes and place them in the drainer.

She hurried down the hall and stopped at the bathroom first. She cleaned it quickly and removed any signs that she had showered there. She then went to her room to clean. As she organized the room, she thought of her mother's arrival and how she would handle it. Would she greet her at the door? Prepare lunch for her? Offer to serve her during her stay? The questions lingered in her mind, but not long enough to mask the more important question. How would her mother react?

Tamika thought of Sulayman and tried to picture him talking to her mother, but she found it difficult to imagine. Her mother wasn't the hospitable type, and she trusted few people. Thelma rarely invited guests into her home, and except for special occasions, Tamika could only recall family coming to visit when she was a child. What was it that moved her mother enough to allow a stranger, a Muslim man, into her home? How was it that he was able to discuss religion with her? Was it because he wasn't Tamika—or was there something special about Sulayman himself?

The question troubled Tamika until her heart grew heavy. She slowed her work and sat on the edge of her bed in deep thought. Regret suffocated her, and she wondered if it was too late to make amends with Sulayman. Her face grew warm with shame as she recalled how angry she had been with him when she called him from her sister's home. She wanted to apologize to him—*needed* to apologize to him. But how? Even if she mustered up enough courage to call and apologize, how could she also tell him that she wanted to marry him too? It was humiliating to even think about. How much more would it be to actually do it? But if she didn't, what would become of them? Would Sulayman find someone else? *Would she?*

Her heart raced as she considered calling him right then, and her palms began to sweat at the thought. Did she have the nerve? What would she say? What if he didn't answer? Could she ask for him? What if he wasn't home? Would she leave a message? She stood and paced the room as she wrestled with what she should do. The possibility struck her suddenly, and she nearly panicked at the thought. What if he found someone else?

Tamika's heart sank, and the bed creaked with the weight of her body. A lump developed in her throat as she realized the likelihood of the scenario. Word likely had spread that he and Tamika were old news. And how many women would jump at the opportunity to have him for themselves? And how many of those women could he rightly refuse? They would be smart, pious, and beautiful. They would come from a host of cultures and races. He would then realize what a fool he had been to fall for someone like Tamika. And even if he would consider her again, he would quickly change his mind when he learned of her dreadful sin of the past. Grief overwhelmed her as she realized the impossibility of having him back. Tears welled in her eyes, and she blinked to hold them back. She was determined not to cry, at least not then, when she should be grateful that God had even permitted someone like Sulayman to have considered her at all.

Sulayman sighed as he started to reread the page for a third time. Halfway through the first paragraph, he shut the text in frustration, sending the sheet of loose-leaf paper scribbled with cell biology notes sailing to the floor. It was almost 11:00 Friday morning, and he had been up most of the morning preparing for his exam. He propped his elbows on his desk and supported the weight of his head with his hands that now covered his face. He had heard of mental block before, but hearing about it was nothing like experiencing it firsthand.

Perhaps he needed sleep. He had slept only three hours the night before. He had planned to study Thursday night, but he was finding it difficult to concentrate. Against his better judgment, he had called Aidah hoping that talking to her would give him a much-needed break after which he could study for the rest of the night. He knew better than calling a woman just to chat, and he should have known what the outcome would be. They ended up talking for almost four hours. He enjoyed the conversation, but when he hung up, he felt worse than he had before he called.

Quite possibly, it was the weight of the situation that made it impossible for him to resume studying that night. Their conversation was more serious than a quick study break should have allowed. He shouldn't have been surprised that the topic of marriage monopolized the conversation. After all, did he expect to dance around an issue that was so obvious to them both? Did he expect her to keep playing along as he continued to consider the *idea* of marriage to her?

Aidah was an extraordinary woman, a sought-after one at that, and she had no time for a relationship that was going nowhere. When she told him she needed to know where he stood so she could make plans for the next six months, he knew it was an ultimatum. Either they were going to keep the relationship going in preparation for marriage, or they were going to go their separate ways and discontinue talking as much as they were.

Initially, he had only agreed in theory. Yes, they should decide either to move on or let go. It was the only Islamic thing to do. They knew each other pretty well, and he was human, and so was she. Although exactly what being "human" meant was normally an unspoken understood, the night before was filled with confessions that changed that between them. They needed to get married, they concluded at the end of their conversation as they both realized their confessions of humanness had gone too far. It was a logical solution to their intensifying human emotions that would result in either blessed matrimony or carnal sin. But it wasn't until the next morning that the illogic of the solution occurred to him.

Sulayman couldn't deny that he needed to get married, and it needed to be soon. A man could survive only so long lowering his gaze and fasting regularly to cool a longing that ultimately only a woman could soothe. Patience had allowed him to survive as long as he had without a wife. As an undergraduate student living on campus, it was difficult to resist the temptations of women who didn't have the same values as he. His resistance because of religious commitment didn't deter them and, instead, intensified their determination in the games.

At times he felt like he was running a maze with only a solid wall where the final exit should be. He was active on campus, played basketball, prayed, fasted, and did everything he could think of to keep his attention diverted from what was consuming him. There were times he felt like giving up, but Allah would renew his determination to be patient upon the path by inspiring in him the faith that marriage would come soon enough. But just when Sulayman thought he had beat the pulls, another challenge, more challenging than the preceding one, would come his way.

At times like that, he envied young Muslim men who were not constantly in the limelight. Prominence on campus and in the Muslim community certainly had its advantages, but for an unmarried man, especially one in his youth, it often felt like more than he could handle. If he hadn't experienced it firsthand, he would not have imagined that the temptations of women were as far reaching as they were.

In high school, the *masjid* was a place of refuge for him, a place where he could focus on worshipping his Lord and quieting the humanness that threatened to ruin him. But after his first year in college, the *masjid* became a battleground itself. Muslim women were not ashamed to walk up to him in the *masjid* lobby and shower praises on him for all his work and express how they wished more Muslim men were like he. If the conversations ended there, it would have been easy to handle. But the women usually went on to either implicitly or explicitly inform him that they wanted him for themselves, which usually ended with the exchanging of phone numbers. If the women had come right out and said that they were interested in marriage instead of masking it behind wanting to help him with some youth group or community project he was working on, it would have been a simple matter.

But it would be three months later, after they had talked more than they needed and had one too many unnecessary "business" meetings, that it would occur to him that he was in neck deep. It was only Allah's mercy that allowed him to avoid a major pitfall as a result, but even after one situation was behind him, it was only a matter of time, perhaps only hours, before another would stare him in the face.

He was a man, so the encounters were not always one-sided. There were times when the women's intentions in assisting him in a project were pure, but he was the one who let his guard down and pursued the relationship in hopes of marriage. It was a vicious cycle, he knew, one from which he found it nearly impossible to escape. The only solution for him, he realized, was to have a woman to come home to, whom he would love and enjoy on every level he needed and desired.

What man didn't want that? But was it right for him to try to make Aidah understand what a woman never could? And was it right for Aidah to try to make him understand what a man never could? It should have been sufficient for them to know that men and women needed each other in a way that humans themselves couldn't fully explain. But it was the humanness in each of them that had been silenced too long, and they needed to find a voice for that which had no words.

It was completely logical for them to conclude they needed to get married, and soon. But what was illogical about their solution, Sulayman realized after a few hours rest, was that although it was true they both needed to get married, it didn't have to be to each other.

That would explain his mental block. How could he expect to concentrate when he had agreed to marry Aidah before he had time to think it through? Was he rushing to marry her because she happened to be on the other line when he said more than he should? Was marrying her a sort of atonement for him? It was a mistake to make the phone call. He knew that before he had called. But he ignored the pounding in his chest as he dialed the number and attributed it to nervousness. But there was no reason to be nervous. Talking to Aidah never affected him like that before. So why then?

Somewhere in the back of his mind, there was a faint whisper telling him not to make the call. If there was any genuine nervousness on his part, it was as a result of ignoring the voice that was calling him to use better judgment. The pounding was his heart portending its own suffering should he ignore that voice. It wasn't like him to call a woman to "just talk." In fact, it wasn't like him to call a woman at all.

Sulayman's one too many close calls had inspired his recent conviction to do everything by the book. He would refer all women interested in helping any community activity to his sister, who would take care of the phone calls and business meetings for him.

If he met a woman he was interested in marrying, he wouldn't express his interest to her but would instead contact her father to inform him of his intentions, unless there was a real need to talk. Casual talking, he had learned quickly, brought with it more harm than good, even when the intentions were pure, and he had decided to stay away from it as a general rule.

What possessed him to make the study break call, he would probably never know, but he feared he would regret it for life. He suspected it could have been his relationship with Tamika that made him complacent about calling Aidah to just talk.

Tamika had no Muslim father, and it was nearly impossible for the imam to be a liaison between them. He was the guardian for many Muslim women converts in the city, and he certainly couldn't play an active role in the marriage process of them all. His primary responsibility was to filter the men interested in the women, and if he approved of the man, he would allow them to communicate on their own to see if they were compatible for marriage. Certainly, this was not Aidah's situation. She had a Muslim father, and although he had given permission for them to talk, there was really no need to since they had already, and her father was readily accessible to Sulayman should he need him. How differently would Sulayman feel right then had it been Tamika he was talking to?

Tamika. The name itself flooded him with a storm of emotions that he couldn't attempt to obstruct. But the emotion that tormented him most was regret.

He lost her to a stupid decision that reeked so much of classic machismo that he grew sick with shame at the thought. That he had even imagined he was respecting her by making a trip to her home without her knowledge was arrogant and foolish indeed. Her aunt and mother were likely increasing their staunch stance against her as a result. They had probably cut her off completely after his talk with them, extinguishing any hopes of reconciliation between them. Even if he never saw Tamika again, he knew his hotheaded decision would stain her life forever. She would probably never make amends with her family.

The possibility itself caused him to lament so tremendously that he found it difficult to eat or sleep. He prayed for Tamika and her family in all of his prayers, but he feared that Allah would never forgive him for his grave error. He should have sought her advice before he had gone—even the *Istikhaarah* prayer itself enjoined him to seek advice in addition to praying for God's guidance. Perhaps it was fear of rejection that prevented him from thinking clearly. Or maybe he imagined that the trip would impress Tamika and make her admire him more.   Whatever it was that derailed him from prudent thought, he would never forget what the mistake cost him in the end.

He wanted more than anything to pick up the phone and call Tamika to beg her forgiveness for his foolish decision. But how could she forgive him when she could never rightly measure how detrimental his mistake would be to her life? Even if she wanted to forgive him, how could she? What's more, even if she *did* forgive him, it was unlikely that she would want to marry him. Why would she want an imprudent man as a husband, the father of her children—the head of her household? Certainly, she couldn't respect him after what he did, so how could he expect her to give her refusal to marry him even a second's reconsideration?

The sound of car doors closing interrupted Tamika's thoughts. She stood and hurried out of her room to peer through the living room window. A moment's glance sent her heart racing. They had arrived earlier than she expected.   Jackie stood tall, leaning forward slightly as she supported Thelma's weight by holding her sister's hand and elbow as she walked. Thin synthetic braids hung from Jackie's head, and their tips curled at the collar of her black trench coat. Thelma's expression was one of exhaustion, and she glanced about her as if she was seeing her home for the first time. Her hair was pulled neatly away from her face in a bun, and she wore a bright, floral housedress with a bulky blue coat that hugged her waistline.

Despite her refined appearance, Thelma seemed disheveled, almost distracted as she walked slowly to the house, pausing every few steps to catch her breath.   For a moment, Tamika was mesmerized by the window view, which was like an oil painting of a grassy scene with patches of melting snow scattered about the muddy ground. She recalled the scent of her mother's Sunday dress as she would bury her face in her mother's bosom during an embrace. Tamika wanted to rush outside to embrace her mother right then, but a second's thought reminded her she was no longer a child, and her mother wasn't coming home to greet her. She didn't even know she was there.

Tamika's heart sank as she realized she would never again be her mother's "special child," who had so much promise, whose adult achievements would right every wrong in her mother's life and make it all worthwhile. Her face grew warm in sadness, and as her mother neared the door, it suddenly occurred to her that she should disappear. Like a humble servant taking her place in the slave quarters after a day's work, it was with a sense of resigned obligation that Tamika retreated to her bedroom and closed the door.

The front door opened and shut, and Tamika's heart pounded anxiously. She listened to the muffled sounds of Jackie's deep voice commanding Thelma to sit and her mother's subdued tone as she struggled to convince herself more than her sister that she was capable of taking care of herself. Jackie groaned as she lead her sister down the hall, and their muffled sounds became clearer until they halted near Tamika's door.

Tamika held her breath and stared at the doorknob as she waited for the constraining silence to pass. A few seconds later, it did, and she heard her mother's room door open across the hall. She exhaled in relief as the sound of their footsteps faded until the door shut. Once again, their voices were muffled, and Tamika sat on the edge of her bed dazed, unsure what she should do. The muffled voices faded into silence, and she wondered if her mother had fallen asleep. Tamika sat still for a few minutes more and listened for any signs of movement in her mother's room, but she heard none. She stayed where she was sitting for fear her mother would hear her moving about her room and inquire about it.

It was only a matter of minutes before she grew restless sitting still with nothing to do. She glanced about the room, but its bareness stripped her of any previous motivation. She decided to lie on her side and allow her thoughts to drift until she, like a prisoner, received any word of her release.

Tamika thought of Sulayman and wondered what he was doing right then. He must be home with his family, she guessed, or perhaps, he was out with friends studying for an exam. She wondered if he ever thought of her or if his new life kept him too busy with more important things. She wondered what Aminah said about her to him or if she mentioned her at all. What did Ismael and Sarah think of her? Did they still consider her like family? Were they upset with her for getting angry with their son? Or were they relieved he was now free to entertain more distinguished, more deserving women, who were raised Muslim like he? Would she be welcome in their home again, or would they slowly erase her existence—and significance—from their minds?

Startled, Tamika opened her eyes and sat up. She had drifted to sleep, and the sound of the door handle turning woke her. Her heart pounded as she stared at the door anxiously. A second later, the door swung open, and her aunt appeared in the doorway. Jackie murmured a mechanic hello as her eyes traced the room. She showed no obvious reaction to Tamika's humble set-up, but there was a slight frown on her face as her eyes finally met her niece's.

"Come on, child," Jackie commanded as if Tamika should have known to come out and greet her mother. "Yo' mom wanna see you."

Confused, Tamika got to her feet and followed her aunt in dazed obedience. She quickly ran her hands over her hair and surveyed her clothes as she left her room. The pearl white silk blouse now had wrinkles along the left side from where she slept. Her black rayon slacks had extra creases along the left pant leg. She had chosen the outfit especially for this occasion, but she now frowned in concern that she would appear unkempt. She had never been as conscious of her appearance before her mother as she was then, and she feared nothing in her life would ever be the same.

The drumming in Tamika's chest was incessant when Jackie threw Thelma's door open too suddenly. Tamika's legs grew weak, and her chest tightened in apprehension as she crossed the threshold into her mother's room. Her eyes caught a glimpse of the queen-sized bed that appeared massive in the small room, and she averted her gaze before her eyes fell upon who lay there.

She traced the contents of the room with the interest of a child entering an entrancing museum for the first time. Her gaze halted at a framed photograph of her mother that sat atop the cherry wood dresser along the right wall. A matching wood trimmed mirror hung above it, forcing Tamika's eyes to fall upon the reflection of a large woman's body covered under a gray and red paisley print comforter. But she could not bring herself to look at her face.

Tamika turned her attention to the contents of the walk-in closet whose doors stood open across from the bed. Floral and paisley print dresses, navy blue and black business suits, and pastel colored skirts lined the closet with a sense of organization that reminded Tamika of her mother's meticulous nature that demanded a strict standard of cleanliness that Tamika could never uphold. Her eyes lingered upon the display of clothes as she was reminded of carefree time spent lying upon her mother's bed reading books and writing poetry. The precise arrangement of her mother's clothing across from her study area had been merely one of the insignificant and necessary details to a room to which she was too accustomed to fully appreciate, and now she wondered at how a routine childhood activity was now a priceless moment that had drifted too far out of reach.

"Tamika?"

She stiffened at the sound of her name. There was a hint of weakness in her mother's voice. Its tone was inquisitive, if not hopeful, in its exhaustion. The simple utterance penetrated Tamika, whose heart responded more readily than her mind and ears. Like a child responding to her name as her mother held a switch in her hands, Tamika turned too quickly to face her mother. The pounding in her chest quickened until her head throbbed, and she feared she would be unable to speak.

"Ma'am?" The sound escaped her so instinctively, so clearly, so daughter-like, that for a moment Tamika doubted that it was really she who had spoken. But it was. It could have been no one else. Jackie had retreated to the doorway and stood there with her arms folded in silence, as if unsure whether she should leave to give them privacy or stay to police the reunion in case her intervention was needed.

"Come 'ere, child." The power of her mother's command was lessened by her scratchy tone and heavy breaths that suggested that the simple utterance had deprived her of energy.

Time seemed to halt as their gazes met, and Tamika felt her heart slow its pounding, suggesting a cautiousness that reflected her state. Her mother's eyes glistened, and a slight, weary smile formed on her face. Thelma lifted her hand slowly, as if opposing a weight that was pulling it down, to reach for her child. The gesture revealed a fondness for her youngest that health had masked from her. She was too weak to show anything but gratefulness for Tamika being in her reach.

Tamika too lifted her hand as she neared her mother, and a lump developed in her throat. She felt her body grow warm, and she blinked to fight the tears that welled in her eyes. The roughness of her mother's palm grasping hers made her heart flutter as memories flooded her. In that moment, she was Tamika again, the special child with promise, Thelma's little girl. Tamika greeted her mother's firm grip with her own as she sat on the edge of her mother's bed. Thelma pulled Tamika to her in an embrace, and the tears gushed from Tamika's eyes as she buried her face in her mother's chest. Thelma's body shook, unable to hold her tears back any longer. She held her daughter tighter and sobbed as she stroked Tamika's head in affection. The faint scent of perfume on her mother's dress intoxicated her, and Tamika wished they could start over again.

"O, child," her mother choked between sobs. "The Lord is good. The Lord is good." She nestled Tamika closer and loosened her embrace slightly after they held each other in silence for several minutes. When their crying calmed, they continued to hold each other and revel in the momentousness of the occasion.

"I knew you'd come, child," Thelma said. "I knew you'd come." She stroked Tamika's head as she spoke and paused to take a deep breath before she continued.

Tamika listened to her mother's voice, enjoying the nearness of the sound more than the words themselves. She had imagined that this day would never come. She nodded slightly under her mother's large hands to let her mother know she had heard.

"O, child, the Lord told me you'd come."

Tamika shut her eyes and tried to let the moment envelop her. Then perhaps it could last forever.

"The Lord told me in a dream. It was you and your husband. What's the boy's name?"

It took a moment for Tamika to realize that her mother was asking her a question, and what she was asking about. Her mother must have sensed Tamika's confusion, because she repeated the question.

"That boy, child, what's his name?"

For a moment, Tamika was speechless. She stiffened at the realization and sat up to meet her mother's gaze, and her mother's hand fell gently upon her back, where she began to stroke. "My husband?"

"Yes, child, the boy who came here in Christmas."

Tamika started to tell her mother that she wasn't married, but remembered a second later that her mother was relating a dream. She cleared her throat and found it difficult to fight the feeling of awkwardness as she nearly stuttered her reply. "Sulayman?"

The corners of Thelma's lips turned up as a smile formed on her face in recollection. She nodded slightly. Her eyes grew distant in deep thought, and her stroking paused upon Tamika's back. "Yes, yes."

Tamika didn't know what to think of her mother's words. She could only stare in shocked disbelief as her mother went on.

"In the dream, he brought you to the hospital to visit your mother, child." Thelma started to laugh to herself, but instead it came out as a cough. A minute later she regained composure and caught her breath. "I can see you now, sittin' next to my bed and givin' me a kiss." She smiled, and tears began to slip down her cheeks. Her eyebrows gathered as if she were trying to figure out something, and a moment later it was coupled with a smile. "And child, you sang the sweetest song. Was in a language I never heard." She coughed. "But in the dream I understood every word. Was like sweet gospel from the Lord, and that's when I knew it was gonna be a'right, and my baby would come back to me."

Twenty-nine

It was Monday, the second week of May, and Tamika sat in the school library preparing for her last final. She sat at a small wooden table facing a window that stood open and allowed a gentle breeze to sweep through. The calm wind would grant Tamika only a moment's relief from the worries that enveloped her and threatened to crush her hopes of ending the semester with a peace of mind she could carry into the summer. Tamika paused from her reading and leaned back in her chair to gaze out the window that overlooked the small campus that seemed magnificent right then.

A breeze drifted through the screen and turned the pages of her Religion 350 text with its formless fingertips. There was a soft flapping of the pages as Tamika's eyes fell upon the students walking purposefully across the sidewalks and grass with their backpacks tossed over one shoulder or resting securely on their backs. She wondered at the sun's glory that created a glow on the white cottony masses that floated in the powder blue sky like a canopy. The weather was warm, and the grass seemed to sparkle like green gems under the sun, a remarkable scene that gave the students a much needed serenity at the year's end.

Celebrations were being planned, and tears were being shed as friends said their goodbyes. Tamika had reason to celebrate. Of her five classes, she had three definite *A*'s, and the other two were to be *B*'s at worst. But her grades, like the warm weather and gentle breeze, could not soothe a breaking heart. Even her renewed relationship with her mother and aunt didn't give her peace. The glory of it all felt like cruel irony, as if the world was mocking her pain. No glorious event could matter right then, when she felt as if a part of herself had been snatched away.

It was a simple white, card-sized envelope that had sat upon her bed three nights ago. Her name was written neatly on it, as if Aminah thought it would lessen the severity of the gaping wound she was to inflict by using purple ink and bubbly, calligraphic letters in each stroke of Tamika's name.

Tamika and Aminah had gradually drifted apart in the last months of school. It was as if they had somehow outgrown each other and were unsure if they could prevent it—or if they wanted to. An invisible wall was somehow erected between them and had expanded its width until neither could reach the other, even if she tried. There had been so much between them, as friends and Muslim sisters, that neither quite knew how to let go or move on, or if it was right to. Tamika had ignored the growing distance between them by convincing herself that it was their studies that kept them too busy to speak or spend time together other than sleeping in opposite beds at night. She convinced herself that the summer would be their reunion— after Tamika finished all her schoolwork, and Aminah hers.

Aminah was graduating in a week, so it should not have surprised Tamika that her roommate had packed her things and moved out so soon.

Aminah had no idea of Tamika's schedule of comings and goings, especially since Tamika had chosen to adopt the library as her study area instead of the room. It was true that Tamika sometimes wasn't in the room at all several days of the week, when Zahra would invite her to spend the night with her at her apartment. And rarely did Tamika give any indication of her whereabouts to her roommate. So it should not have hurt Tamika that Aminah's words of goodbye were in purple ink and not in real words. The bareness of Aminah's side of the room shouldn't have evoked so much emotion that Tamika found it painful to sleep at night when Tamika herself had pushed her roommate away. Perhaps that Aminah remembered her at all was cause to be grateful.

Tamika lifted the envelope from where she had tucked it in her purse and studied it for a moment. She wondered why she wouldn't just rip it to pieces and toss it in the trashcan where it belonged. But she could not bring herself to discard it, though it should have little value to her. What person kept tokens of sadness with as much attachment as those of love? Her gaze fell upon the tear through the letter *T* from where she had torn the envelope open at the top. With a gentle press of her thumb and index finger, she felt its bulkiness and could almost see its contents before her.

A card—a graduation invitation with gold embossed letters requesting Tamika's attendance at the Saturday morning commencement services at nine o'clock. Aminah's signature scribbled at the bottom under "Love always." A folded piece of notebook paper tucked behind the card written in the purple ink but apparently in more haste than Tamika's name.

As-salaamu-'alaikum, Tamika

Sorry we missed each other. I was hoping to see you before I left. As always, you're welcome to stay with us this summer. Give me a call either way. I hope to see you on Saturday.

Aminah

Oh yeah, if you can, please come to the masjid on June 8th at 12:00. Sulayman and Aidah are getting married. We hope you can make it.

Love always,
Aminah

Tamika felt a burning sensation in her chest, and she tucked the envelope back in her purse to shut out her thoughts. Sadness overwhelmed her, and she blinked back tears. She lifted her gaze to the window in hopes of catching a gentle breeze to relieve her of the suffocation she felt from regret.

She was a fool, she mentally scolded herself. She had returned from her mother's home with the intention of apologizing to Sulayman and starting off where they left off before she made the angry phone call to him. But loads of schoolwork and the approaching Spring Break distracted her, at least that was the excuse she was giving herself for not contacting him right away. She had considered the idea of writing him a letter or perhaps having the imam talk to him on her behalf. She had even thought to talk to Aminah and have her convey the message to him.

During the March break, she stayed with Zahra, whom she ended up confiding in. Zahra advised her to just call him. Otherwise, he would probably never get the message, at least not as clearly as she liked, and Tamika had agreed. She spent the entire break going over in her head what she would say. But fear of rejection prevented her from ever picking up the phone. She went back and forth between being a second away from calling to becoming paralyzed with fear—until time passed too quickly, and the semester came to an end.

Somewhere in her mind, she had foolishly believed she had the summer to sort things out. What made her forget the obvious—that she wasn't competing with only time—was beyond her. As she gazed distantly through the window, she struggled to find the logic behind her foolish thinking and became too mentally exhausted to give her studies their full due.

It had been three days since Aminah left the note on her bed, and, still, there were moments Tamika was in denial, hoping there had been some mistake. Perhaps it only made sense that the year should end like this, she thought. Hadn't last year ended with a tragedy? However different in magnitude the tragedies were, the effect of this one was no less stifling. It was a different kind of loss she felt right then, but she could not ignore that her grief was somehow the same. It was selfish of her, she knew, to compare the loss of Sulayman with Dee. But one didn't choose the parallels pain brought in life. She merely suffered in the parallels and couldn't deny them, even if logic demanded she should. Last year she lost a friend, this year she lost herself. Strangely, the only thing that made this loss less devastating was the reminder that it wasn't her first.

But why was life so unfair? The question was one she had fought fiercely for the past few days. She didn't want to doubt the fairness of God, but at the moment, she felt powerless to combat the erupting anger and confusion inside her. No, she couldn't control her thoughts. But she refused to let them find a resting place in her heart. God knew better than anyone. He was most just. He was the most merciful of the merciful, and the wisest of the wise. His knowledge was all-encompassing, and, certainly, He knew Tamika's pain more acutely than she felt it in her heart.

There was a lesson in all of this, she kept telling herself, if she only had the will to see. Don't procrastinate? Follow your heart? Speak your mind? But even so, the voice of her broken heart tugged at her thoughts. Couldn't she have learned these lessons in a less devastating way? Was a human to be condemned her entire life for a mere mortal error? Was one to live a life of sadness for one foolish mistake?

Then again, perhaps, there was a lesson for her that only patience and time could teach. What if Sulayman wasn't what he seemed to be? Was he riddled with contradictions, wearing one face for the world and another for himself? But, even so, Tamika's heart cried, who on the earth was truly free of contradictions? What person could rightly say he was without flaw? Who could claim there was never a moment that his actions betrayed his principles or beliefs? And, oh, if Sulayman had flaws, if he had faults, she only admired him more! What was nobler than a man who, despite his faults, continued to stand tall and wasn't ashamed to turn to God for strength?

Or maybe Tamika's lesson was that Sulayman, despite his nobility and piety, was not her "un-ideal ideal." Maybe the one for her was yet to come into her life. It was quite possible that she and Sulayman were not compatible at all. Could it be *that*? That her husband was to be someone else? Could the lesson be that simple? If it was, she didn't want someone else!

Tamika sensed someone standing near her, and her thoughts were interrupted as she turned to look. She found a familiar face staring at her curiously, as if he too was trying to recall how they knew each other. As she studied his face, Tamika realized a few seconds later who was standing next to her. She hadn't seen Kevin since the day of the chapel services in honor of Dee after her death. He had sat before the crowd trying to remain strong before finally breaking down in grief for the loss of his fiancée.

"Tamika?" His eyebrows rose as he recognized her at the same moment she did him.

"Kevin?" A half smile formed on her face as they both nodded in reply.

He looked different than she remembered him. A shadow of a beard was on his face, and his dark hair had grown into tight curls on his head, revealing the Egyptian heritage that was usually masked by the Caucasian in him. His skin was almost red from repeated exposure to the sun—or a tanning bed. His white Streamsdale T-shirt and red running shorts should have given him a refreshed appearance, but Tamika couldn't help sensing something tattered in his appearance that she couldn't explain. He looked tired, as if he was dragging himself through each day. His smile seemed forced, almost apologetic, if not embarrassed, upon his face. The expression puzzled Tamika until she realized a moment later how she must look to him. She wore a large ivory peach skin *khimaar* wrapped about her head, and the cloth hung in dips like drapery over the front of her long green dress of similar material that reached to her ankles. He had never seen her as a Muslim before.

Kevin started to say something but could only stare in amazed admiration at the pious woman who sat before him. He had known her as a phenomenal singer, Dee's friend. His most vivid memory of her was her singing next to Dee on stage at last year's Spring Formal. He had no idea she had become

Muslim, and he couldn't help wondering why. As he stared at her, he felt both proud and ashamed at once. "You're Muslim now?"

Tamika nodded politely before glancing away from him and reaching for her book. She didn't know what else to say. She wanted to ask him the same question, but his expression told her more than he could say.

He shook his head in amazement and continued to take in her new appearance, unaware of Tamika's growing discomfort with the excessive flattery of his gaze. "*As-salaamu-'alaikum,*" he greeted more out of congratulations than any religious conviction on his part.

She returned the greeting then leaned forward to flip through her text to find the page she was reading before she was distracted by her thoughts. She tried to concentrate on the book before her, but it was difficult with Kevin standing so close. She flashed a polite smile in his direction in hopes he would understand she was in no mood to talk.

"Kevin." He glanced over his shoulder in the direction of the female's voice, and as if realizing something suddenly, he turned to go. But the girl appeared next to the table before he could leave. "What are you *doing*?"

Tamika looked up from her book and saw a young woman staring irritably at Kevin. The woman's brunette hair was pulled back in a ponytail and hung just below the nape of her neck. She wore a pink tank top and jean shorts that exposed her tanned thighs. The spaghetti straps on her top revealed white strips of skin beneath them where bra straps most likely had been. A gold necklace with a small crucifix sparkled on her neck. Apparently, she had come with Kevin and had been looking for him. The girl groaned and inadvertently met Tamika's gaze. Her expression changed from irritation to confusion as she glanced from Tamika to Kevin, puzzled by how they knew each other. Tamika forced a smile in the woman's direction. The woman frowned and turned her attention back to Kevin. "Let's go."

"Did you find the book you needed?"

The woman slipped her hand into Kevin's, and shook her head. "No, but I'm hungry." She turned to go then glanced quickly back in Tamika's direction as if realizing something suddenly. She turned away a second later.

"See ya 'round," Kevin greeted Tamika with a wave.

"You too." Tamika smiled and nodded as the couple disappeared into the aisles of bookshelves. She resumed reading, and it was several minutes later that it occurred to her that she knew the young woman too. She almost laughed out loud at how small the world was. She had seen Christina only in passing and had known her only as Jennifer's best friend. Tamika would have never pictured Kevin with her. She chuckled to herself and shook her head. It was no wonder Kevin appeared tattered and confused. There was no way someone like Christina could replace a phenomenal woman like Dee.

"I think you should go." Zahra ran a finger along her ear to tuck her hair behind it. She then lifted a slice of pizza from the box that sat between them on her bedroom floor. She wore a plain white T-shirt tucked into her jeans and sat crossed legged with her back leaning on a side of the bed. She took a bite as Tamika nodded in response as she only half-listened to the suggestion.

Tamika had taken her last final that afternoon and accepted Zahra's invitation to spend the night at the apartment to spend time together before summer break. Zahra's sister was in the living room studying for exams, and the friends felt it best to stay in Zahra's bedroom to avoid disturbing her.

Tamika enjoyed the cozy atmosphere of Zahra's bedroom, which was a refreshing change from the dullness of her dorm. Cream-colored carpet covered the floor, and a twin size bed was neatly made with a fluffy powder blue comforter that matched the curtains that adorned the window to the left of her bed. An array of stuffed animals, some as tall as Zahra herself, aligned the wall on the other side of the room. The largest was a white teddy bear with a red and black checkered bow on his neck. Across from the bed was a five-unit white shelf that displayed Zahra's school texts and novels she read for leisure.

Tamika hugged her knees and shook her head. "I don't think it's a good idea."

Zahra set her piece of pizza on the paper plate on her lap. She sighed and gazed sympathetically at Tamika. Tamika's hair was pulled into a ponytail at the back of her head, where the rest of her neatly parted hair hung just past her shoulders. She wore the green dress she had studied in earlier, and her white *khimaar* hung over the footboard of Zahra's bed. "You'll probably regret it if you don't."

Tamika shook her head again. "I doubt it."

"But you can't avoid them forever."

She forced laughter. "I think I can."

Zahra frowned slightly as she picked up her pizza from her plate and took a bite. As she ate, she studied Tamika momentarily before returning her gaze to her plate in deep thought. She empathized with Tamika's pain and imagined it must be extremely difficult for Tamika to cope with so many issues at once. Tamika had been Muslim for only a year and had experienced more than Zahra probably ever would.

Zahra could only imagine how it felt to convert to a strange religion and change her entire life overnight. Being ostracized by family was almost unbearable to think about, let alone experience. So much of Zahra's life was centered around her family that she doubted she could survive without them. This was a strength for her, but it was also a weakness, because it was the reason she didn't wear *hijaab* though she knew she should.

How Americans were able to oppose their families, if not sacrifice them altogether, to embrace Islam and immerse themselves into Islamic culture for the sake of their souls left Zahra nearly speechless in admiration of them. To them, Islam wasn't only a way of life, but life itself. Their energy and dedication to the religion both shamed and inspired those whose families had been Muslim for generations in their countries. Observing new Muslims in America was like seeing Islam for the first time for many immigrant Muslims. For some, it made them realize they had never really known Islam.

Zahra grew up in the states, but so much of her life was based in Pakistani culture that she knew the culture of America only superficially. She had gone to public school as a child but had experienced only a taste of what it meant to be an American. Whenever she returned home after school, it was like entering a different world, and she often wouldn't hear an English word until she returned to school the next morning.

For Zahra, topics like marriage and starting a family were foreign, if not completely unheard of in her household, at least in the discussion realm. The only exception was when a family friend or cousin was getting married and her family attended the wedding. In her culture, marriage wasn't something you talked about or even chose. It was something you did. In fact, the topic of the male sex itself was off limits, and Zahra's only exposure to it was through the television and school.

In high school, many of her non-Muslim friends had boyfriends, but it wasn't something they discussed with her. It was an unspoken understood by her friends that she had no concept, or perhaps even approval, of that world, so she was shut out. Unlike her sister, Zahra wasn't popular in school and was never known for good looks, so male classmates only expressed interest in her as the butt of jokes. She had thrown herself into the world of academics and made a name for herself there. She was valedictorian of her senior class and an active member of class cabinets and honor societies. That was the closest she ever came to being a part of American culture.

Like any American, Zahra was influenced by what she saw on television and in movies, and she often imagined herself as strikingly beautiful and astonishingly intelligent. She imagined her husband as an American executive in a billion dollar corporation in which she owned millions of dollars in stock. But, of course, she never expected it to happen. In her mind, reality was getting into, then through, medical school and establishing herself as a doctor, after which her parents would find a Pakistani doctor or computer engineer for her to marry. She didn't even imagine being "happy." It wasn't a word anyone used in her world except in reference to a particular moment in the day, likely after completing an important task. In her world, happiness was neither a goal nor a means. Life was life, and you did what you had to do to avoid depending on someone else's paycheck to get by.

It was both admiration and fear Zahra felt for Tamika when Tamika told her she was thinking about getting married. Zahra could only admire the opportunity to marry whomever she wanted, when she wanted, and actually *be* happy, with no accountability to anyone except herself and her Lord. She imagined it must be exciting to be nineteen years old and getting married, and there were moments she wished she could do the same. But she couldn't help being scared for Tamika.

If she married so young, what would become of her ten years from now? Would she have no career? Would she still be happy? Or would she regret her decision and wish she'd waited until she was financially independent before taking such a huge step? Would she have no life at all, aside from husband and children?

Then there was the question a person couldn't help thinking but would never ask. *Will the marriage last?* So many American marriages ended in divorce that divorce itself had become commonplace and lost the stigma it still held in other cultures. The odds were especially against couples who came from single parent homes. Though she knew no official statistics on the subject, Zahra had heard of the divorce epidemic in the Muslim communities comprised of mostly American converts. Some marriages lasted only months, if not weeks, before the couple was in the imam's office insisting on divorce.

Perhaps it was the same television culture that inspired Zahra's own fantasy that was the culprit in this heartbreaking reality. Was it that Americans failed to realize that love wasn't a reason for marriage, but a product of it? Was the world Zahra associated with movies and romance novels an existence they thought they could really have? Did they actually think love made the world go round and that it conquered all? Whatever the reason, Zahra could ask only herself what she could never express to her friend. Could Tamika really beat the odds?

Zahra couldn't blame Tamika for thinking she would be an exception. Although Zahra didn't know Sulayman personally, she had heard nothing but good things about him. Even those who disliked him couldn't deny the charisma and intelligence he obviously possessed. He had a reputation for piety and upstanding moral character that few men his age could even comprehend. His dedication to Islam was apparent, and, unlike most charismatic people, his actions actually matched his words. There was no girlfriend on his arm after he delivered an inspirational lecture, and not a person could dispute his commitment to what he believed. If there were an exception to the general rule of failed marriages and young Muslim men being both mentally and spiritually unprepared for the union, Sulayman would be it.

Zahra had the opportunity to meet Aminah the year before when Aminah was still active in the MSA. From the little interaction she had with Sulayman's sister, it was obvious that their family had strong Islamic values and high standards for both worldly and spiritual success. So Zahra was excited for Tamika when she told her Sulayman wanted to marry her. Normally, Zahra wouldn't approve of college-aged Muslims marrying, but she encouraged Tamika to make amends with Sulayman and not let the opportunity slip through her hands. Zahra never imagined it actually would.

She was stunned and felt sad for Tamika when Tamika told her that he decided to marry someone else. Zahra hated to see Tamika hurting, and she wished there was something she could do to help. It only increased her pain to know there was none. This one Tamika would have to get through on her own.

"But why?" Zahra's question was more a plea than an inquiry. She understood Tamika's pain, but she felt it was unwise, if not ungrateful, for Tamika to cut ties with Aminah's family completely.

"I don't think they want me around anyway."

"Tamika, that's not true." She set the top crust of her pizza on her plate and frowned at Tamika.

Tamika met Zahra's gaze in a challenge. "Then why did she write me a silly 'oh yeah' at the bottom of a note instead of giving me a real wedding invitation like she did for her graduation?"

"They probably didn't send out wedding invitations."

Tamika creased her forehead in confusion. She had never considered that. "How am I supposed to believe that? They sent out invitations for the graduation."

"A lot of Muslims don't make a big deal of the wedding. Sometimes it doesn't even last more than fifteen minutes."

"Fifteen minutes?" Tamika had a difficult time believing that. She forced laughter and shook her head in disbelief.

"Yeah," her friend insisted, "it's just a contract."

Zahra's description made the whole concept seem insignificant. "They don't have a ceremony?" Tamika asked.

"No," Zahra said, shaking her head, "not an elaborate one. It's after the wedding that's a huge deal to them." She paused thoughtfully. "You ever heard of a *waleemah*?"

"A what?"

"*Waleemah*. It's like a huge party to announce the marriage. They usually have it separate from the wedding, maybe like a week or a month later."

Tamika wrinkled her forehead and shook her head. "I don't think so."

"Well, it's for the *waleemah* that a lot of Muslims send out invitations and invite a lot of people. It's like an American wedding reception, in a way." Zahra paused before she continued.

"You should probably go, because the wedding is usually kind of private, and only close relatives and friends know about it a lot of times. If Aminah even told you about it, that says a lot."

Tamika didn't know how to respond. She felt herself shrug before her gaze grew distant again. Maybe Aminah telling her in the note was her way of letting her know nothing had changed. "But she should've told me in person."

"But you're hardly ever in the room. She may have waited for you before she decided to go ahead and write you a note."

It was possible. Tamika had come home after 11:00 the night she found the envelope on her bed. Aminah probably did wait for her until she had to go, which was probably why the note seemed rushed. Tamika sighed and frowned. Did it really matter?

All of this talk about Aminah's note was exhausting. They were evading the real issue. It made no difference to Tamika if Aminah wrote the message on toilet paper. What really mattered wasn't how Aminah told her, but *what* Aminah told her. Sulayman was getting married on the eighth of June, and Aidah would be standing where Tamika should. There was but one real concern Tamika had. Did she really have the strength to be a witness to the official crushing of her heart?

"Go." Zahra's conclusion was gentle, compassionate, and final, and Tamika didn't want to hear anymore. "You really should. It would hurt them if you don't."

Tamika almost coughed as she held back laughter. Hurt *them*? Zahra couldn't be serious. Did she really think Tamika should worry about causing them pain? They had taken out her heart and cut it to pieces when they let Sulayman go through with marrying Aidah when it was Tamika who should be his wife.

The mere thought of Aminah infuriated Tamika. Aminah saw Tamika almost everyday, and they even stood shoulder-to-shoulder in prayer on occasion. They saw each other before they retired each night and even exchanged small talk. But, still, Aminah gave Tamika not even an utterance that hinted that her brother had renewed his relationship with Aidah.

Couldn't Aminah have mentioned it in passing or slipped the news in one of the rare conversations they had? Couldn't she have given Tamika a *chance* to state her case before she sent her brother off with a woman he had to convince himself was for him? Couldn't she have asked what Tamika thought, in case Tamika had good reason to object? But Aminah had chosen to throw it in her face, in a note—*after* it was decided, at that! And Tamika was now somehow, after Aminah and her family all but tore her life apart, supposed to worry about *their* feelings if she didn't attend the wedding that would be her final smack in the face?

"I know it's a hard decision, Tamika." Zahra's eyes pleaded with her to be considerate of more than herself. "But think about all they did for you. They're like a second family to you, even you said that. I know you're not meaning to seem ungrateful, but that's how it will look. Most people wouldn't have given you all they did. And it would look really bad if you don't go. For Muslims, answering a wedding invitation isn't insignificant. Some Muslim scholars even say it's obligatory to go when you're invited, unless you have a really good excuse not to."

Tamika was hearing Zahra, but she was only half listening as she grew angrier with Aminah for being a bad friend. Why should she care about all of that when no one cared about what she was feeling? It was true Aminah didn't know Tamika was reconsidering her decision, but she would have if she had taken the time to talk.

"What would they want *me* in their perfect world for anyway?" Tamika was being sarcastic. She wasn't being fair, she knew, but right then, she didn't care. "I'm just a thorn in their side when I'm around. I really don't feel like living the rest of my life as a charity case. I'd be doing them a favor by disappearing from their lives."

"Come on, Tamika. You know it's not like that. Besides, you don't want them to think you only accepted their help so you could marry Sulayman."

The words cut deep, and Tamika glared at Zahra as she clinched her teeth to calm herself. "I never said that." Her tone was accusing, and her icy stare told Zahra that she had overstepped her bounds. Tamika's face grew hot in resentment, and tears rushed to her eyes, where they gathered at the surface, insisting upon their release.

Zahra regretted the comment immediately after she said it and realized a moment too late what she had done. "No, what I meant was they'll probably never know why you didn't come, and they'll feel bad that maybe they offended you." The words were too rushed to be sincere, and Zahra stopped herself from saying more for fear she would only make matters worse.

Tamika started to say something, but her voice cracked. She blinked to fight back the tears that spilled from her eyes a second later. She folded her arms on her knees and let her head rest on them in mortification for crying in front of Zahra. Zahra saw the tears, Tamika knew, but Tamika couldn't bear to look her in the face.

Tamika cried silently for a few minutes until she felt a hand on her shoulder and Zahra's voice apologizing and telling her it would be okay. But the kind words only made it worse, and Tamika's crying became muffled sobs as her shoulders trembled with each cry. Zahra put her arm around Tamika, and there was no way Tamika could fight reality any longer. She had lost Sulayman, and there was no one she could blame but herself.

Thirty

Tamika reached forward to flush the toilet with her left hand then stood. She held onto a stall wall to support her weight as she struggled to catch her breath, which sounded like panting right then. Her body shuddered from the violent vomiting episode of seconds before. Her body relaxed a minute later as her breathing calmed and her strength returned.

She had made it through the graduation sitting three rows up from Aminah's parents. She had successfully avoided them except for the exaggerated wave in their direction when their eyes met before the ceremony began. After it was over, Sarah rushed to greet her with a warm embrace and expressed how good it was to see her there. It was at that moment Tamika realized that Zahra was right.

Their family would never want Tamika out of their lives. Sarah's pleasure in seeing Tamika was genuine, this Tamika could tell. Tamika laughed in the excitement of the moment when Sarah took her by the hand and led her to where the rest of the family stood congratulating Aminah, who had graduated with honors from the school.

Aminah was giddy in the excitement of the day. Her enthusiastic greeting shocked Tamika, who accepted the heart-felt embrace and kiss on the cheek with a sense of pleasure and relief. As they hugged, Tamika felt as if nothing had changed, and whatever gap had grown between them in the past couple of months was either quickly forgotten or too insignificant to remember. Aminah introduced Tamika to her aunt and told Kate how they were good friends. Kate seemed especially interested in Tamika's conversion to Islam and asked her several questions about it. Tamika chatted with Aminah's aunt for some time and felt grateful to Zahra for encouraging her to come.

Tamika's heart had pounded in surprise when she heard Sulayman's voice greet her. She glanced to her right and saw him smiling almost shyly at her. She turned to him and replied to his greeting with an equally shy smile. She lowered her gaze a second later but not before the sight of him evoked memories and regret for what was no more. Her heart was pattering away in her chest, and she felt flustered as she stood opposite him in search for words. From where she stood, the sweet scent of his musk entered her nostrils, and she tried to recall what prompted her foolish decision to refuse his proposal for marriage.

His gaze was toward the ground, and he kicked the ground gently with the tip of his black suede shoes as he asked how everything was going for her. She told him everything was fine, and she asked him the same. He forced a chuckle and responded similarly as he pushed his hands into the pockets of his black slacks that he wore with a green dress shirt that brought out the color of his eyes. His skin was tanned evenly and gave him a smooth golden brown complexion. She sensed Sulayman lift his gaze toward her before returning it to the ground.

She immediately grew self-conscious of her appearance and inconspicuously surveyed what she had chosen to wear. A long sleeved, cream-colored silk dress with pearl-like buttons along the front hung loosely against her and fell to her feet that were covered in brown slip-on shoes that were open in the back, revealing the cream dress socks she wore. Her *khimaar* was a large silk cloth of cream tucked neatly about her head and fell into dips of drapery like the one she had worn in the library a week before.

The sun shined brightly for the morning, and its rays fell upon her, causing her face and eyes to glow. She asked how his first year of medical school had gone, and he told her that it went quite well. The conversation was intoxicating, and she began to wonder—or rather hope—that his plans had changed for the eighth of June. She imagined how he would bring up the subject when she heard a familiar voice greeting her cheerfully from behind. Startled, she turned and was drawn quickly into an embrace with Aidah before she had time to digest why Aidah was there.

Tamika had no idea how she appeared at the moment, but she felt her body go cold in resentment as she merely accepted Aidah's gesture rather than share in it. After the hug, Aidah went on about how good it was to see her, and her voice faded into the background of Tamika's mind.

Tamika recalled nothing Aidah said after that until she heard Aidah insisting that she come to the wedding in a few weeks. Tamika's expression may have been one of disgust, or shock, perhaps. But whatever it was, it apparently prompted Aidah to stop mid-sentence to ask if she was all right. It seemed like less than a second later that Kate commented that Tamika didn't look well, which then prompted Sarah to come see if Tamika was okay. Even Aminah's smile faded in concern as she saw Tamika's face.

"You're pale," a woman's voice whispered in worry.

Someone asked if she needed water, and Tamika began to feel faint as everything around her became a blur. Someone took her hand and offered to take her to get some water, but Tamika pulled her hand away too quickly and insisted that she was fine. She murmured something about the sun making her a bit queasy.

"I'll get you some water," Aidah seemed to insist more than offer.

"Is she okay?" Sulayman asked finally, and Tamika realized then that his and Aidah's voices were the only ones she recognized when someone spoke. Tamika felt her face grow hot in embarrassment as she wondered if she was okay. She muttered an excuse about needing to go to the bathroom and turned to go before anyone could respond. She walked so quickly from them that her pace felt like a jog to the nearest building behind them.

Presently, she let herself cry silently in embarrassment for making a fool of herself. She doubted she could face them again that day. The door to the women's restroom opened, and she heard the sound of women talking. A baby started to cry a second later, and Tamika realized she didn't want to come out of the stall appearing as if something was wrong.

She pulled herself together and wiped her face with her hands. She then picked up her purse from where she dropped it on the floor and fumbled through it until she found a pack of gum. She tore the paper away from the package and unwrapped a piece before putting it in her mouth. As she chewed, she let the sweet mint juices fill her mouth. She chewed it for a minute more before discarding it in its original wrapper and putting another piece in her mouth. She hoped to conceal the smell of her breath. She pushed the wrapper and the pack of gum in a side pocket of her purse and placed its strap over a shoulder. She then smoothed her clothes with her hands and checked for any soiling of her *khimaar* or dress. When she was satisfied that she was presentable, she took a deep breath and exhaled before emerging from the stall.

A woman was changing her baby's diaper next to a sink while chatting with a friend. After cleaning the baby with a wipe, the woman removed a small container of baby powder from the diaper bag that sat next to the child and sprinkled the white powder on the baby.

"You mind if I use some of that?" Tamika was too desperate to smell and feel fresh to feel ashamed for the awkward request. She imagined it wasn't the norm for a person to ask to borrow powder reserved for use on a baby's behind.

The women stopped talking and turned to look at Tamika with puzzled expressions on their faces. "This?" The mother held the small white container with blue lettering in the air.

"Yes, thank you." Tamika accepted the powder, and the women studied Tamika curiously as she lifted the front of her head covering to expose her neck. She pulled the collar of her dress forward before giving a generous squeeze to the bottle until her chest was white.

"I appreciate it." Tamika handed the bottle back to the woman then shook her dress until white clouds puffed from her as the powder distributed itself under her dress. She then washed her hands before turning to go.

As the door swung closed behind her, she tried to decide if she would return to campus where Aminah's family was or call Zahra for a ride to the apartment, where she had stayed for the past four nights after moving out of her dormitory room. The door to the Humanities building closed behind her as the warmth of the late morning air and the rising sounds of voices reminded her of the joyous occasion. Family and friends laughed and talked in clusters, and graduates stood grinning into camera lens, wearing their caps and gowns of black polyester that was the most priceless outfit at the moment.

"Girl, what're you doin' here?"

Tamika glanced to her left and smiled in surprise at the familiar face. She hadn't expected to see Makisha there. Makisha's hair was cut low in a curly Afro that was faded at the back. She wore a double-breasted off-white floral dress that accented the curves of her body and revealed her legs that were covered in sheer pantyhose, with open-toe matching high heal shoes adorning her feet. The scent of perfume around her was strong but inoffensive as she held an expression of pleasant surprise upon seeing Tamika. She showed no signs of animosity for the friendship that had died between them, and for this Tamika was grateful. But there was a polite distance that Makisha's greeting held that told Tamika that she wasn't forgiven for betraying the church. Tamika held her smile and wondered at her almost apologetic response. "Aminah's graduating."

Before she could read Makisha's reaction, she went on, "What are you doing here?"

"A few friends are graduating this year."

"Tell 'em I said congratulations."

"I will."

"Hopefully, it'll be us next year."

Makisha nodded in agreement. "Yeah, hopefully." She smiled then waved at someone in the distance.

"It was good to see you," Makisha said as she patted Tamika on the back and turned to go.

"You too."

Makisha walked away and disappeared into a cluster of friends, and Tamika walked in the direction of Aminah's family. She decided to say her goodbyes and call Zahra to pick her up.

"Are you feeling better?" Sarah placed a hand on Tamika's shoulder and gazed at her in concern. Sulayman stood about ten feet away talking to his father and sister with Aidah standing next to him. Kate stood a few feet behind her sister and studied Tamika in curious concern.

"*Alhamdulillaah.*" Tamika forced a smile and shrugged. "I think the hot weather's a bit much for me. Where I'm from, there's probably snow on the ground now." They both laughed. "But I think I'll go home and lie down."

Sarah's eyebrows rose in surprise as she lifted her hand from Tamika. "You have an apartment now?"

Tamika forced laughter and shook her head. "No, a friend of mine has an apartment, and she's letting me stay there until her lease is up at the end of the month."

"Where are you staying for the summer?"

A half smile formed on her face, and she averted her gaze. "I don't know yet."

"We'd love to have you."

"I appreciate it, but I don't wanna be a burden. I think I'll see if my sister doesn't mind me for a while." Despite their renewed relationship, she doubted her mother was ready to have her home.

"Are you sure?"

"Allah knows best. Nothing's etched in stone."

"Will you make it to the *nikaah*?"

Tamika gathered her eyebrows. "To the what?"

"The *nikaah*, the wedding."

"Oh, yes, *inshaAllaah*. I plan to." She hoped she was masking her resentment about the ordeal.

"Then please come stay with us when you leave the apartment."

"I don't want to inconvenience you."

Sarah laughed and waved her hand. "It's never an inconvenience for you to stay with us. Besides, Aminah could use some company now that her brother's gone."

Tamika's forehead creased in sudden interest. "Where'd he go?"

Sarah laughed again and shook her head. "You know men. They want everything taken care of before the big day. He moved into an apartment at the beginning of this month."

"Oh, *mashaAllaah*. That's good." Tamika hoped her tone concealed her true feelings. Her heart sank at the realization that he was actually going to go through with it.

"So we could use the company. I'm sure Aminah will be excited to have you back."

Tamika laughed. "Well, I guess I can't refuse then."

"Of course you can't." Sarah smiled. "We look forward to having you."

"Thanks."

She reached out and gave Tamika's shoulder a gentle squeeze. "Go on and get some rest. Just give us a call whenever you're ready to come."

"Thanks. I really appreciate it." Tamika greeted Sarah before turning to go and decided against interrupting Aminah. Instead, she raised her voice from where she stood and waved to her.

"*InshaAllaah*, I'll call you later," Tamika said.

"You feel better?" Aminah asked, turning to her friend.

"A little. I'm gonna get some rest though, *inshaAllaah*."

"I hope you feel better," Aidah called out.

Tamika forced a smile and waved again. "*As-salaamu-alaikum*."

"*Wa-'alaiku-mus-salaam*," everyone replied in unison.

Tamika walked away and disappeared into the Humanities building again, this time to make a phone call.

Thirty-one

It was a Sunday night, and Tamika lay awake in the guestroom of Aminah's home, where she had slept three nights already. The light was still on as she lay in bed staring distantly at the ceiling with her hands clasped behind her head, letting herself be consumed by her thoughts. A water stain soaked a bouquet of flowers in the ceiling in one corner of the room, perhaps its own contribution for the big day.

For the past few days, the house was busy in preparation for the wedding. The ceremony would be small and attended by close friends and family. But Sarah's endless phone calls and Aminah's indecision about the menu gave Tamika the impression that their definition of "small" was different from hers.

Tamika had unpacked to keep herself busy, but now she had no idea how she should pass time. The wedding was six days away, and she suffered in silence as the date approached. Each day she woke with a determination to stay sane and look for the lesson in all of this. She had done a lot of reflecting and could only conclude that her understanding of marriage was all wrong.

Initially, she approached the issue selfishly and felt Sulayman should marry her because they were obviously attracted to each other and felt a connection between them. She wanted to marry him. He wanted to marry her. They liked each other. Therefore, they should get married. He didn't feel for Aidah what he had felt for her, Tamika concluded, so why marry Aidah? But as she thought about it, she realized that her concept of marriage was confused. A product of American society, she foolishly felt people should marry for love. But loving a person didn't make a successful marriage, she realized. Love of God did.

The night before, Tamika had entertained the same thoughts and wondered if it was Omar who was for her after all. They had a lot in common, and, perhaps, she could marry him. She had picked up the phone and dialed his number without giving it a second's thought. She wanted refuge from her grief, and he was the only person she felt could give it to her.

When the answering machine picked up, she was about to leave a message when she realized it was a woman's voice on the machine. The voice informed her that she had reached the home of Omar and Khadijah, and it was then that Tamika realized her insignificance in the world. He had moved on and married and had probably forgotten about Tamika. She hung up the phone and was stunned at the realization. The sun still rose and set each day. The rain still fell from the sky. And flowers still bloomed. The world didn't stop for Tamika.

Anger was the easiest, and most self-destructive, way to react to her predicament. It was easy to point the finger of blame at Aminah and her family, but never herself. It was easy to allow even doubts about Allah and His mercy to creep into the corners of her mind. But that was to deny faith itself. Life was full of tests, she realized, and this was just one. If she couldn't pass this, what of more trying ones that came her way? It was a simple matter really, if she thought about it. All she had to do was move on. She was Muslim, and that was the most precious gift in the world. If it was decreed for her to live to see tomorrow and have a husband, it was already written for her. She only needed patience and faith until then. The more she read and studied her religion, the more she understood this.

But part of her was still angry. Part of her still blamed Aminah. And she didn't want to be patient. Certainly, patience didn't mean she had to accept whatever people threw her way. And faith couldn't mean that she shut her eyes to everything around her. No, she would not blame herself, not when there were others to blame. She had accepted things at face value too long. There was something not right about it all. Things didn't add up. A man didn't want to marry a woman one day then choose to marry another the next, with no warning or explanation. Sulayman did not exist in a vacuum. He had a mother and a father who influenced his decisions. And a sister.

Tamika's heartbeat quickened as things began to make sense. Sulayman was the pride of the Ali household and the star of the Muslim community. He was their trophy. And no trophy could be allowed tarnish. Could it be that his attraction to Tamika was unwelcome by his family, by the community? Could it be that marriage to her would be tarnish upon their prize? The more she thought about it, the more Tamika realized that this was likely the case.

Tamika had thought little of Aminah's comment about wanting her brother to marry a woman who was born Muslim. But now it was more significant than Tamika had estimated. At the time it was merely a hurtful word to a woman who saw no possibility of being with the man she wanted. But it was more than that. Did Aminah *discourage* her brother from marrying Tamika? Did her parents?

Tamika's face grew hot in anger as she realized she had been a fool. She was a charity case for their family. She could have a warm bed, a hot meal, and a cool drink. But nothing more. She wasn't Tamika to them, but a new Muslim with personal problems so great that they left her homeless. It was their duty to help her, like it was their duty to give a penny to a panhandler. But no one expected the panhandler to have a heart. Should he dare show that he did, should he dare demand more than a penny, he would be a disgrace, an ungrateful disgrace, whose simple request for a wife would suspend all charity from him.

Betrayed. Tamika let the word soak in before she let its burning sensation envelope her completely. She wouldn't go down without a fight. She was a human being, with feelings and a heart like everyone else. And she deserved an explanation.

There was a soft tap on the door, and Tamika pretended not to hear. She had felt obligated to Aminah and her family because of their generosity, but that was no more. She refused to feel guilty for wanting some quiet time to herself. Aminah could pray by herself. She didn't always need Tamika to stand next to her. And Tamika knew the prayer times, so she didn't need the reminder that it was time to pray. There was a long pause before the tapping became a purposeful knock, and Tamika ignored it still. Perhaps Aminah would think she was sleeping and go away.

"Tamika?" Aminah's voice carried through the door and was immediately followed by a string of knocks that hoped to wake her. Tamika continued to stare at the ceiling and let her angry thoughts consume her. Aminah wasn't her friend, she realized just then. Tamika barely even knew her. They had nothing in common, and there was little Tamika could offer Aminah in any case. Friendships were mutually beneficial, and aside from good company, neither of them really benefited the other. Who was Aminah anyway? Who was the person behind the forced smiles, obligated generosity, and saintly piety?

"Tamika?" There was a hint of impatience in her raised voice that sounded as if her head was pressed against the door. The sound of the door handle turning prompted Tamika to glance in the direction of the door. She groaned and rolled her eyes. Did she have no right to privacy in this house?

"Tamika?" Aminah appeared in the doorway, her thin fingers gripping the brass handle with a concerned expression on her face, that endless concern for Tamika. Was it really necessary to have so much concern for one person? Did Aminah imagine that she had to check on Tamika regularly so she wouldn't slit her wrists?

"Are you okay?" Aminah stepped inside until she was a few feet from where Tamika lay.

Tamika held Aminah's gaze for a moment more before frowning and turning her attention back to the ceiling. Aminah's hair was pulled into a ponytail revealing the thinness of her pale face, slightly tanned from the summer heat. She wore a white T-shirt that appeared too large for her thin frame and hung almost to the knees of her jeans that clung loosely to her legs and cuffed at the heels of her bare feet. But her fragile look of innocence was irritating Tamika.

"Does it *look* like I'm okay?"

Her sarcasm stunned Aminah, whose eyes widened slightly and studied Tamika's angry expression in search for what she had done to offend her. She wondered if Sulayman's choice to marry Aidah had upset her, and she felt sorry for Tamika all of a sudden. Aminah started to say something but decided against it, realizing Tamika probably wanted to be left alone. She turned to go without responding, deciding to pray alone in her room.

"You never wanted it to work, did you?"

Aminah froze and turned around suddenly a second later as she realized the question was an accusation. "Excuse me?" Her question was defensive, almost daring in tone.

"You have what you've always wanted. You must be proud of yourself." Tamika felt Aminah's eyes on her as she wore a half smirk and continued to talk to the ceiling.

"*What?*"

"She's the perfect Muslim, complete with Muslim parents and all."

Aminah blinked repeatedly and shook her head, raising a hand as if telling Tamika to slow down. "*What* are you talking about?"

"It all makes sense now," Tamika said more to herself than Aminah and forced a laugh. "The cold shoulder, the secrets behind my back, then the note. In a way, I don't blame you. I wouldn't want to face me either after what you've done." Aminah started to say something, but Tamika continued before she could interrupt. "Did you think a note would make it all better? Did you think I would just move on and forget?"

"*You* turned Sulayman away."

"No, I got *angry* with him. *You* turned him away from me." She glanced in Aminah's direction and glared at her.

Aminah widened her eyes in disbelief and let out a laugh. "*What?*"

"Don't give me that innocent look, Aminah." Tamika sat up to face her roommate. "I'm not stupid. You expect me to believe it's just a coincidence that I'm the only one who was in the dark about all of this? You could've told me *something*, anything. But you leave me a silly note after it's all decided, like that's supposed to make up for ignoring me for two months and marrying Sulayman off to your friend."

"Oh, so *you* have feelings now. Is that what this is about?" Aminah shot back in such pronounced sarcasm that Tamika realized Aminah had a lot of attitude behind her small frame. She expected Aminah to be flustered and apologetic about her accusations, but instead, she was ready for a show down. "Never mind everyone else's. Tamika's are hurt."

Aminah narrowed her eyes and placed a hand on her hip as she shook her head in disbelief. "Do you know how much Sulayman went through to make that trip? Do you know how much he had to sacrifice to make it happen? Do you know how much he must've cared about you to even go? And after all of that, you get offended because he didn't talk to *you* before he went. And instead of thinking about what he went through, or even why he went in the first place, you stomp all over *his* feelings, and now you wanna play the victim role. And you have the nerve to blame *me* for *your* decision." She grimaced, staring at Tamika as if realizing something unbecoming about her all of a sudden. "You really *are* selfish."

Aminah's words stung, and for a moment Tamika could think of no reply. Her cheeks were hot in angry embarrassment, and her heart pounded in her chest. "If he was so hurt, why didn't you talk to me instead of setting him up with Aidah?"

Aminah forced laughter. "Setting him up with Aidah? I knew nothing about Aidah until after *he* told me she called. I had no idea about anything until *he* said he was considering marrying her again." She shook her head. "You've got it all wrong."

"Then why didn't you talk to me?"

"Talk to you about *what*?"

"About Aidah. Why was it all behind my back?" Tamika was trembling, and she struggled to keep her composure as she wondered if she was making any sense. She was angry with Aminah, and she refused to let Aminah throw the blame at her.

"I'm sorry if you thought I had to report to you everything my brother did." Aminah's face grew red as she became enraged at Tamika's accusations. "But after you made your decision, I stayed out of it and didn't even discuss it with Sulayman."

"Did it ever occur to you that I regretted my decision?"

Aminah stared at Tamika, and her nose flared. "No, it didn't. But did it occur to *you* that, even if I did, that's for *you* to sort out?"

"I thought we were friends." Tears gathered in Tamika's eyes, but she fought them. She was not going to lose control this time, at least not in front of Aminah. "Friends talk."

"Did it ever occur to you that *I* was hurt?"

Tamika didn't know how to respond.

"It was hard for me to see my brother hurt like that, and I hated you for it. I wanted more than anything to make it better for him, but I couldn't. Do you know how hard it was for me to go on living with you after what you did?"

"Then why didn't you say something? All I did for these past months was regret what I said and tried to figure out how to take it back."

"I'm not psychic, Tamika, and I have feelings too. You can't expect me to know something like that."

"But if you would've just talked to me, Aminah. Just said a *word*."

"Why didn't you call Sulayman?"

The question ripped the mask of anger from Tamika's face and replaced it with regret. Tears flooded her eyes until they sought release and spilled down her cheeks. She covered her eyes with her hands and hoped Aminah would go away. "Oh, I'm so angry with you," she heard herself saying, and she wondered if it was Aminah or herself she was talking to. "I'm so angry with you."

"Aminah?"

Aminah turned and found her mother standing at the doorway tying the waist belt of her rayon-silk robe of purple. Her hair was slightly disheveled, but she appeared as if she had been awake. Tamika kept her face covered as the sound of Sarah's sweet voice only made her cry more.

"What's all the fuss about?"

Aminah lowered her gaze and immediately felt ashamed. She shook her head in response and left the room, brushing gently past her mother, who remained in the doorway studying Tamika in concern. She started to ask if

Tamika was all right, but she realized Tamika needed some time to herself. She shut the door softly and made her way to her daughter's room, where she demanded an explanation.

From her room, Tamika heard the front door open and close Monday morning when Ismael left for work, the only sound she heard for hours in the house. The day seemed to drag on and was almost suffocating in its silence. Tamika left her room only to eat and go to the bathroom and managed a forced smile whenever she and Aminah happened to cross paths. Sarah's expression was cordial whenever her and Tamika's eyes met, and Tamika thought she saw a hint of disappointment in Sarah's gaze. She had no idea what explanation Aminah had given for the argument, but she was certain it could be from only one point of view. Tamika wanted to state her case, but what would she say to counter an accusation that was only in her mind?

That evening, after Ismael returned from work, Sarah and Aminah left with him without saying anything to Tamika except shouting their greeting up the stairs before they left. The quiet house gave Tamika her much needed space but also reminded her that she was merely a guest—an unfortunate guest—in their home. She wasn't a part of their family and should be grateful for a place to stay.

She would leave. She knew that when she woke at dawn. She had no other choice. She would stay with Latonya and find a job in Chicago until school started again. She needed to find a purpose in life until her heart healed and she could really move on. And she couldn't heal as long as she had to see Aminah and her family each day.

Tamika felt a tinge of guilt as she dialed her sister's number that evening while Aminah and her family were still gone. She should have asked permission before dialing long distance on their phone. But what other choice did she have?

Latonya answered, and they exchanged small talk before Tamika finally told her why she called. "I can't stay here," she said near desperation after briefing her sister of her unfortunate predicament, including Sulayman's marriage and the argument with Aminah. "It's too much."

"I can find a job when I get there," she offered before Latonya responded. "And I can help with the rent if you want me to, because I know two and half months is a long time."

There was a long pause. "Girl, I can't."

"I can pay you back for the ticket."

"No, it ain't that." Latonya sucked her teeth. "It's Tyrone. He ain't gonna be cool with that. He already had a hard time when you were here before. I can't ask him to leave every time you here and I ain't. This is his home."

Tamika's heart sank as she realized what she should have already known. Her Islamic lifestyle didn't permit her to be alone with a strange man. When she visited before, Tyrone would stay out until Latonya arrived, but could he continue that for more than two months straight?

Tamika hung up the phone feeling trapped. Though the idea entered her mind, she knew better than to call her aunt or mother for help. Their relationship was too fragile to test with something like this. And she could think of no one else who could give her a place to stay.

She prayed the sunset prayer alone in the living room of the still house that she had to herself. As she recited, she began to realize how ungrateful she had been. Aminah's family had extended kindness to her that no one else had. She decided then that she would be more respectful to them. It was inconsiderate of her to disrupt such a monumental event with selfish complaints. Saturday would be the marriage of their son, the first wedding in their family. The last thing they needed was Tamika spoiling it for them.

"Why are you telling me this now?" Sulayman shook his head and scratched one side of his beard as he digested the weightiness of what his sister had just shared. He sat across from Aminah at the glass topped cherry wood dining room table that his parents bought for him the week before. A worn cardboard box sat atop the glass next to stacks of school texts and papers needing organization. A few feet from the table was a workout bench that he couldn't decide where to put. Black iron weights were scattered about the carpet, and a dumbbell lay carelessly atop a pile. He wore blue jeans and a white short sleeved undershirt that clung to his muscular chest and arms, and sweat soaked his shirt at the underarms. An old fan circulated hot air behind them and hummed in the background of their conversation.

In a nervous habit, Aminah removed the ponytail holder from her hair for a third time and let her hair fall over her shoulders before pulling it back again. Her *khimaar* and *abiya* hung on the back of the chair she sat on with one leg tucked under a thigh. Her parents had dropped her off at Sulayman's so she could help him clean and decorate the apartment while they went to the store to shop for some things he still needed. "I don't know." She shrugged and shook her head. "I'd feel guilty if I didn't."

There was a long pause. Sulayman didn't know what to say. If his sister had told him this two months earlier, he would have been elated. But he had come to accept that he wouldn't marry Tamika and had even begun to realize the benefits if he did not. It was undeniable that she possessed a lot of good traits, but she was still searching for her identity as a Muslim, and he feared this could cause unnecessary difficulty in a marriage. Not only was Tamika's family non-Muslim, but they were obstinate in their disagreement with her conversion, and it was clear that her family, particularly her mother, was very influential in her life. Aidah, on the other hand, was born Muslim and comfortable with who she was. She had no pressures from family pulling her away from Islam, and she wasn't experiencing inner turmoil about being a Muslim. She was physically attractive, and this could not be trivialized. Of course, physical attraction couldn't sustain a marriage, but it definitely was necessary to a successful one.

"Did she ask you to talk to me?"

Aminah avoided her brother's gaze as she continued to toy with her hair. She shook her head. "No."

He sighed. "I don't know, Aminah. There's nothing I can really do about that now. I could talk to her, but that would only make matters worse."

"I know," she agreed apologetically. "I probably shouldn't have said anything, but I didn't want it on my conscience."

He nodded, and his eyes were distant as he became distracted by his thoughts. "*JazaakAllaahukhair.*"

"*Wa iyyak.*"

Sarah and Ismael returned from the store two hours later, and Sulayman and his sister helped them unload the van they had rented for the purpose. Sulayman and his father carried the couch up the steps as Aminah held the front door open wide for them as they struggled to fit the couch through the doorway. The family unloaded the rest of the van and then set up and cleaned the apartment until it was after 10:00. There was still a lot of work that needed to be done in the apartment, but they had made a lot of headway and could finish it before the week was out.

After everyone had gone, Sulayman stood in the living room surveying his new surroundings. The black leather couch his parents bought for him sat along a wall to the right of the front door. A large black-trimmed throw rug lay five feet in diameter in front of it and sat atop the beige colored carpet that covered the span of the apartment except the kitchen and bathroom. A cherry wood framed oil painting of a mountainous landscape hung above the couch and gave the room a relaxed atmosphere. Leaves hung a few inches from it, reaching out from the six-foot tall artificial floor plant Sarah had purchased from a clearance at a local arts and crafts store.

The only eye sore in the room was his weight lifting set. His dumbbell and weights were now piled along the wall across from the couch. The dining room was still in disarray from his papers and books from school and cardboard boxes that he hadn't unpacked. But his family had managed to give the room the semblance of organization by lining the things along a wall and clearing the dining room table. Sulayman estimated he could finish the dining room tomorrow after he returned from his summer job as a teacher's aide for a biology course at the university. He would have to make certain to come home on time to give him more time to clean and set up the apartment. His parents wouldn't be able to come each day because they still had a lot of preparations to do at home for the wedding. He could only hope he had the time and energy to make the apartment presentable before Aidah arrived Saturday.

As he made a mental schedule of all he had to do, everything felt surreal. He was actually getting married. It felt like just yesterday that marriage was only a concept for him. He would get married "one day," he would tell himself, and he somehow was remaining patient until then. When he set the date with Aidah, the day, although only a couple of months away, seemed too far from his reach to be tangible. The tangibility of the situation became apparent to him only after he moved into his apartment. That was when it hit him.

He was going to be a husband, and it would begin here. Upon realizing that marriage was in his reach, he became restless in anticipation, and the days until June eighth seemed to drag. After moving into the apartment, there was certainly a lot to do before the wedding. So even if Aidah was willing to get married sooner, he could not. There was too much to secure before the date, especially financially. He had managed to save almost $5000 in his bank account, but he knew that what was considered a lot of money for a single man living with his parents was merely pennies that would disappear quickly in the life of a married man living on his own. And of course, he had to pay Aidah her dowry, which she finally decided would be a diamond ring. He had no idea how much diamond rings cost, but after a brief Internet search at work one day, he came to realize that they cost a lot more than he could afford if he wanted anything left over for the marriage itself.

Sulayman felt inadequate for accepting his parents' offer to help him with the rent, but until he finished medical school, his finances would be tight. His parents had offered to renovate the basement of their home and convert it into an apartment for him. But when they calculated how much it would cost, they had to agree with Sulayman that it would be less expensive, at least in the short term, to help him rent an apartment of his own. Even if it was cheaper to renovate the basement, Sulayman couldn't imagine agreeing to it.

He would work two jobs and go to school at the same time if it meant he would be able to give his wife and himself an apartment of their own. The most valued thing to a newly married couple wasn't having a few extra dollars to spend, but privacy. They had waited too long to have a right to privacy to sacrifice it for financial reasons. Sulayman was already bothered by the fact that he needed his parents' help at all, but living with them would only compound the issue and make him feel less than a man.

Then, of course, there was the practical aspect of the arrangement to consider. How could he and his wife enjoy each other's company if there was the constant reminder that they were never truly alone? The thought of seeing his parents and sister each morning tainted the beauty of the relationship he would have with Aidah. Whenever his patience grew thin as he waited anxiously to get married, it was the opportunity for uninterrupted private time with his wife that inspired the anticipation.

At that moment, as he stood in the living room of the apartment that was finally his and that he would soon share with Aidah, he felt little of the restless anticipation of the weeks before. The approach of Saturday didn't inspire his feeling of waning patience and increasing desire but the feeling of anxiety and suffocation.

Part of him blamed his sister for his feelings. What had Aminah hoped to achieve by telling him about her conversation with Tamika? Did she expect him to call off the wedding and phone Tamika with a heart-felt marriage proposal? Did she think he would drop everything to live "happily ever after" with the woman he really loved? Women and their romantic notions. He had no time for it. It was no wonder that the affairs of the world were run primarily by men. Women were too idealistic and emotional. Did they think every life decision should be based on following your heart? Marriage wasn't a fairy tale. Every bride was not Cinderella, and every groom was not her prince. And every marriage wasn't the result of two people falling in love.

It would have been better for Aminah to have kept her conversation with Tamika to herself. Everything didn't need to be said, and certainly, everything did not need to be shared. Why was it that women felt the need to say whatever was on their mind, or heart, no matter how bizarre or disruptive it would be? They seemed to always feel the need to express themselves. So what, if she would feel guilty for not telling him? What of the guilt he'd feel for knowing? What was he supposed to do with the information? Be objective and move on? Or was he supposed to take some sort of action? He certainly wasn't willing to give up the opportunity to marry Aidah, not after all he had gone through to get to this point. He wasn't going to base such a crucial decision as marriage on hearing about an emotional outburst of a woman who never intended him to know what she said in the first place. He had to approach things rationally. It was the only way to survive.

But he had a heart like anyone else. How was he supposed to be rational when Aminah's revelation exposed desires and feelings that he had hoped to escape? How was he supposed to be objective toward a situation in which his heart was at stake?

It only complicated matters that Sulayman had seen Tamika at the graduation a few weeks before. For some reason, he hadn't expected to see her there. Perhaps it was his sister's silence about Tamika's existence that made him forget it himself. Or was it that it was easier to deny it? He hadn't heard even the mention of her name in the past few months, which made it deceptively easy to forget what he had lost.

The regret he felt after Tamika expressed anger over his visit to her mother was too painful to bear consciously. He had to push it out of his mind, and heart. There was a time that he thought the allusion to pain in the term *heartache* was metaphoric, but he learned that it was corporeal. The pain was suffocating in its insistence, like an ailing wound that would not heal. He could have bore it, perhaps, if it hadn't been self-inflicted.

He knew from the moment he called Imam Abdul-Quddus to arrange the surprise meeting with Tamika that there was a chance she would refuse him. But he had assumed her refusal would be based on their incompatibility, or he being unattractive to her. He had accepted that there was a possibility she wouldn't be ready to take such a big step. All of that, he had prepared himself for. But it never occurred to him that he would destroy the relationship himself with an act that should impress her.

It had been easy for Sulayman to shift his affection to Aidah, but only because he had to. It was the only way to heal, or to at least enjoy the veneer of healing. Quite possibly, it was the need for reassurance that made him accept Aidah's request for a second chance. Because he was in need of a second chance himself. He needed a sense of validity. He needed a sense of adequacy. He needed a sense of self. And he could only get it from a woman, who had taken it from him in the first place.

Seeing Tamika at the graduation evoked a flood of emotions and realizations that only her presence could bring. Her presence was a confirmation of her existence, and her existence was a confirmation of his own. He could no longer deny that he was a man with feelings that could be hurt and a heart that could be broken. Before then he had managed to live in a world separate from himself. He was Sulayman, the young Muslim medical student whose humanness was more an insignificant given than a distinct reality in itself. He was a Muslim who, of course, was human instead of a man who happened to be Muslim. Had he viewed himself as the latter, he would have been more prepared. But broken hearts and strong affection for a woman were not a part of his well-constructed world of piety and worship of God. Women had always been appealing to him, but he imagined only a wife of many years could rouse strong feelings of the heart. He imagined only after affection expressed inappropriately could an unmarried Muslim man hurt. If he lowered his gaze, was never alone with the woman, and guarded his conversations with her, he would feel nothing more than brief disappointment if she refused his offer for marriage. But he was wrong. Unless he had in fact overstepped the bounds.

Sulayman couldn't deny that it was difficult to stay within the bounds, and he would occasionally slip. At the graduation, he found it difficult to lower his gaze before Tamika. Her beauty was stunning and refreshing, as if he was seeing her for the first time. He gazed at her more than once, and it was only selfish desire that made it impossible to turn away. It was unwise to initiate a conversation, but speaking to her gave him an excuse to study her more. It wasn't Sulayman the young Muslim medical student standing opposite Tamika that day, but Sulayman the man. It was his manly instincts that made him forget who he was. He saw a beautiful woman, and he wanted her for himself. The eighth of June and Aidah herself ceased to exist at the moment, and it wasn't until Aidah interrupted them suddenly that reality fell upon him like falling rocks. It took him several days to recover from his encounter with Tamika and re-ignite the anticipation he had felt for his approaching wedding day.

It was naiveté, Sulayman concluded, that inspired Aminah to share what Tamika had divulged to her in private. Aminah had no idea the torment it would cause her brother. She was simply doing what she had always done by confiding in her brother what was on her mind. They had always talked about everything, though there were things he held back because she could never understand. There were things a sister could never know, not if she was to respect him as a brother who was different from other men.

But Aminah rarely held back anything she felt and talked to Sulayman like she would a girl friend. He had been her confidant since childhood, and nothing had changed. Whenever their parents upset or punished her, it was Sulayman who got an earful. Sulayman and Aminah knew things about each other that their parents would probably never know, and it was only natural that they grew closer as a result. He was like a best friend to her, and for a woman, nothing was too private to share with a close friend, even if it would disrupt the friend's life or involved her in some undesirable way.

Aminah was in her "best friend" mode when she revealed the frustration Tamika had expressed. And he was to play the role of the friend who was to merely listen and not react. He was to nod his head and feign interest with his emotions aside. He wasn't to allow his heart to be torn—when there was no decision to make. In less than a week, he would be a husband, and a silly emotional confession by his little sister should not change that. He wouldn't give the information a moment's consideration, he decided just then. He was rational, and it only made sense to go ahead with what was planned. And besides, he had no other choice.

Thirty-two

Tamika and Aminah laughed out loud as Sarah continued to tell the story of how she wrote a runaway letter at age thirteen then slept on the back porch of her home because she was too afraid to leave her yard. It was Friday afternoon, and hot oil sizzled and popped as Sarah stood at the stove with a spatula in hand cooking *samosa's*[29]. On top of a pair of faded blue jeans and a navy blue T-shirt damp with sweat, Sarah wore a white apron with brown oil stains on the front from wiping her hands and turning the patties. A red paisley-designed bandana was tied on her head, displaying only her ponytail at the back of her head, and she wore black flip-flops on her feet.

Tamika and Aminah stood approximately six feet from her on opposite sides of the kitchen table stuffing and rolling the *samosa* dough before placing them on a wax paper lined cookie tray that they would give to Sarah when it was full. A similar tray that was half full sat on the counter next to Sarah. Aminah wore a loose-fitting powder blue housedress with short sleeves and a string tied at the back with dingy pink house slippers on her feet. Tamika's hair was covered in a black headscarf tied back in a bun. She wore a Streamsdale University T-shirt tucked in a pair of dark blue jeans with ragged edges at her bare feet. The patio door was open and a fan stood at its screen blowing the hot air outside. They had been up since early morning preparing for Saturday.

It wasn't until late Tuesday night that Tamika managed to pull herself out of her emotional slum. She had sulked in self-pity too long, she had told herself, and it was time to move on. Initially, she resented the way Aminah's family shut her out of everything and discussed Sulayman's wedding only amongst themselves when she was out of earshot. It was as if her merely overhearing the mention of his marriage to Aidah was a threat to the union itself.

After a couple of days of feeling sorry for herself, she realized it was useless to go on like that. It was her own doing that put her in a world of her own. Instead of accepting what Allah had decreed, she had chosen to blow up at Aminah and blame her for what her own hands had done. She had felt like she was living on a deserted island in the house only because she chose to be resentful of the family's happiness instead of being happy for them. She was being irrational, and the loss of rationale knew no bounds.

Tamika had hoped that Sulayman would call and tell her that it was all a joke and that the marriage to Aidah was called off. She imagined the scenario so vividly that whenever the phone rang, her heart would drum in hopes that it was for her. When the phone rang Wednesday afternoon and Sarah told

---

[29] An Indian food consisting of dough stuffed with meat or vegetables, which is then fried.

Tamika that it was for her, her hands shook with nervousness as she picked up to say hello. She had already prepared her response to Sulayman's proposal and reviewed it in her mind. She imagined it would be like Malcolm X's proposal to Betty in the movie X. In one breath she would say yes, and he would momentarily doubt that she had heard what he asked. He would ask if she heard what he said, and she would simply ask him if he heard her reply.

It was such romanticism that intoxicated her when she picked up the phone Wednesday afternoon and felt her voice quiver. When she heard Zahra's voice on the other line, her heart dropped. Zahra asked how she was doing, and Tamika managed to pretend as if she were doing fine. Tamika did her best to sound upbeat, but she felt like she was losing her mind. She hung up the phone nearly shivering from her foolishness and sat in a daze on her bed, mentally exhausted from the futile hopes that were draining energy from her.

It was over an hour after she hung up the phone that a thought that had been tapping at the back of her mind surfaced and demanded release. God had not forgotten her, she realized, but it was she who had forgotten herself. She forgot that life was a test and rarely went the way a person chose. Allah brought the best out of the most catastrophic circumstances and put silver lining on every cloud. Wasn't that how she found Islam in the first place?

There was good to come out of this heartbreak, she was sure at that moment Wednesday evening. The sense of certainty renewed her faith and gave her strength to go on. Wednesday night Tamika turned a new leaf and asked Aminah and Sarah if they needed help with anything. Fortunately, they included her with the wedding preparations without hesitation or question. Tamika thought helping would depress her, but it proved therapeutic. She laughed and joked with Aminah and Sarah and found the hard work healing and felt more confident as a result.

But there was still that emotional suffering within that Tamika imagined would never go away. She was still fond of Sulayman, and she concluded that Allah was the only one who could relieve her of that. She talked to Zahra regularly about her struggles, sometimes several times a day, and Zahra's consistent advice was to cheer up. Zahra maintained a sense of humor through Tamika's distressful episodes and often made Tamika laugh.

Thursday night Tamika had called Zahra close to tears and expressed her doubts she would ever find anyone to replace Sulayman.

"It's not mutually exclusive, you know," Zahra had told Tamika that night.

Tamika became puzzled and asked Zahra what she meant.

"You can still marry him if you hang around a while." Zahra paused and added jokingly, "You can always be his second wife." Zahra chuckled at the thought, and Tamika laughed beside herself.

It was probably more the need to laugh than the humor in the statement itself that kept her laughing for a minute more. It was indeed comical to imagine herself hanging around hoping for the impossible. What made the thought funnier was that Tamika didn't think the idea was half bad. She was reaching, she knew, but there was little else to do when things didn't turn out how she pleased.

Talking to Zahra was healing, and fortunately, Zahra didn't complain about her frequent calls. But the relief was only temporary, and the pain would return when she hung up the phone. Her only protection against drowning again was to go downstairs and immerse herself in the mundane preparations Aminah and Sarah were making for the big day.

Tamika would exhaust herself in helping with cooking, folding streamers, and blowing balloons until she felt like she would collapse. She would ask about Sarah's childhood (never Aminah's because that would necessitate discussing Sulayman, and that she couldn't handle), and she would laugh readily and find humor in the mundane. She was able to shut out her feelings in this manner during the day, but she had no choice but to surrender at night.

Whenever her eyes grew heavy, her mind grew weak, and the feelings would pour over her and take life in the form of a vivid dream. In each dream, which had visited her nearly every night for the past few months and became more resolute in the last few weeks, she was married to Sulayman. Sometimes the scene would begin in the *masjid* with her taking her seat opposite him. Other times it would begin in their home, and they would be eating a meal together or enjoying each other's company between laughter and silent expressions of love. Her heart would be fluttering in pronounced excitement after which she would wake in a dreamy state. Sometimes the dream included Aidah, with whom she would have a heated argument about who rightly belonged to him. Each time Tamika won the argument, and often Sulayman would comfort her and tell her he would explain everything to Aidah himself.

It would take a moment for Tamika to distinguish dream from reality after she woke. When she did, a gloomy sadness made her body limp, and she would drag herself from bed to wash her face so she could face Aminah and Sarah and offer to be of help while pretending to be happy for them.

"Did your parents find you?" Tamika inquired presently as she lifted a handful of cooked ground beef from the stainless steel mixing bowl into the moist dough that was rolled out in front of her on the floured section of the kitchen table.

Sarah laughed and wiped the sweat from her forehead with the back of her hand that held the spatula over the popping oil. "After they called the police, and the whole force and neighborhood went to search for me."

Tamika chuckled. "I wasn't brave enough to do anything like that."

"Oh, I wasn't either. That's why I slept where I did."

They all laughed.

Tamika rolled the *samosa* and softly pressed it closed. "I would've been too scared to even write a runaway note, let alone leave, even if I slept on the back porch. All I'd be able to think about is my mom finding me and spanking me until I couldn't sit down."

Sarah smiled and shook her head. "I didn't have to worry about anything like that. The most my parents would do is ground me, or maybe not allow me to watch TV for the rest of the day."

"Why didn't you do that with us?" Aminah glanced over her shoulder at her mother with a grin on her face.

Sarah shook her head and chuckled as she teased the side of a patty in the pan before glancing in her daughter's direction. "Because your dad would've spanked you himself if I didn't. And I didn't want that." She paused and shook her head again as a smile formed on her face. "And I'm sure you didn't either."

Aminah laughed in agreement. "But I kind of like the idea of no spankings."

Sarah grinned. "I bet you do."

Tamika laughed at the friendly exchange and found herself momentarily intoxicated by the atmosphere. She couldn't imagine life without Sarah, even if she could never marry her son. But she couldn't help thinking it would be perfect if she could. But she would survive, she was sure. She just had to hang on until she was rescued from herself.

Tamika groaned and threw the covers from her in frustration for being unable to sleep. She squinted her eyes in the dark room and saw the red glow of digital numbers telling her it was 4:21. She sighed and sat up. In another forty minutes it would be time to pray the dawn prayer. She dragged herself from where she sat and fumbled for the light.

Part of her was tempted to go to the restroom without covering the pink teddy bear pajama T-shirt she was wearing right then. It was tedious putting on a *khimaar* and *abiya* every time she wanted to go to the bathroom or leave the room, especially at night.

She flicked on the light switch then blinked and rubbed her eyes until her sight adjusted to the sudden brightness of the room. She then walked over to the closet and pulled her covering from the hanger before lazily pulling it over her body. She didn't bother to pin the head covering and instead threw one edge over a shoulder.

As she walked down the hall to the bathroom, it was both sleeplessness and emotional dread for the day's event that exhausted her. The bathroom door stood open, and she reached in to turn on the light. She shut the door behind her mindlessly and undressed as she mentally calculated how many prayers she could make before the prayer at dawn.

It was a shame, she knew, but she didn't feel like praying right then. It was selfish to be too consumed by self-pity to have time for her Lord, but she really wasn't in the mood for a lot of prayers. After using the toilet, her body felt like a dead weight, and her eyelids grew heavy with the sleepiness she had longed for all night. She would set the alarm and sleep for an hour, she planned, as she turned on the water at the sink.

She felt a tinge of guilt as she ignored the warning in her mind that she would likely miss prayer if she went to sleep right then. She held her palm under the faucet until the water warmed to her satisfaction. She then pushed the soap dispenser until the pinkish clear liquid plopped onto her palm. She rubbed her hands together and avoided her reflection in the mirror as she rinsed the suds from her hands.

She didn't want to see herself at the moment, maybe Sunday, but not Saturday morning. She couldn't handle what the sight of herself would evoke. She had already tormented herself enough for the last week, and she was determined to make it through the eighth of June as sane as she had been on that same day a year before. She kept telling herself the date was nothing more than a number on the Gregorian calendar, and she shouldn't let it get her down too much.

But right then she couldn't help hating the number eight and the month of June, and it was difficult to keep herself from hating the entire Ali household. To hell with Sulayman and his family, she thought angrily right then, and she began to wonder about something she read about the devil toying with people at night.

Had she recited the Qur'an before she went to bed the night before? She couldn't remember. But she most likely did not. She had been too preoccupied with her own words going through her mind to remember to recite God's. Maybe that's why she was too wretched to be a member of the household of saints. How could she rightly be one of them if she couldn't even remember something as basic as reciting *Ayatul-Kursee* before she went to bed?

But so what if she forgot? Was that a reason to be considered a heathen? What made Aminah's family so special that they were treated like angels?

Tamika turned off the water, and the sudden silence halted her thoughts and reminded her to be rational. She was only going to set herself back farther if she went on like this for much longer.

She sighed and stood with her head lowered for a moment as a hand was still on the faucet handle. She then turned to pick up her head covering and outer garment from where she dropped them carelessly on the floor. She stood with them bunched under an arm, too tired to get dressed again for the brief journey to her room.

No one was awake anyway. And Ismael was the only male at home. What were the chances that he would happen to be walking down the hall right then? It was the middle of the night, and he had a bathroom in his room. She would go quickly to her room, she decided, as she placed her hand on the door handle, tossing the thought over in her head.

She started to pull the door open and step into the dark hallway illuminated by the dull glow of light coming from her room down the hall. Her heart nearly stopped as her eyes caught sight of her name upon the door, and she shut it quickly to get a better look in case she was imagining things.

Her heartbeat quickened as her eyes fell upon the large white card-sized envelope with purple ink strokes of bubbly letters across it spelling her name. For a second she thought someone had taken the envelope Aminah had given her from her purse, but a moment later she realized that that was impossible. She had ripped it open, and this one was untouched.

She couldn't help wondering if this was someone's idea of a cruel joke. But who else besides Aminah would know about the first envelope?

Curiously, Tamika yanked the envelope that was stuck to the door with clear tape and was unsure if she should be angry with Aminah for not talking to her in person about whatever it was. She ripped the envelope open and pulled out its contents, fearing the worst. There was another slightly smaller white envelope sealed with a card inside, and a folded piece of notebook paper was taped to it with the same clear tape that was used to stick the envelope inside the bathroom door.

She pulled the notebook paper from the sealed envelope and unfolded it while holding the other contents with the same hand. Nervously, she read Aminah's purple ink handwriting that appeared neater than the one she had left on Tamika's dorm bed.

As-salaamu-alaikum, Tamika

> *I apologize for leaving this for you in the bathroom, but you went to sleep early last night, and your door was locked when I tried to come in and leave it for you on your bed. And I figured the bathroom was the only place I could put it without you missing it when you woke up.*
>
> *Also, I apologize for being so insensitive last Sunday. I should've just listened and not upset you more. You made a lot of good points, and as I thought about it, I guess you're right. In a way, I did a lot of the things you said. I know it seems futile to apologize now, but I don't want to have any hard feelings between us after today.*
>
> *I felt so bad for hurting you that I asked your friend Zahra's advice one time when she called. I hope this was okay, but I just wanted to get another perspective and I figured she knew better than anyone else. She told me that my biggest mistake was leaving that note instead of formally inviting you or telling you beforehand. She told me she told you many Muslims don't do invitations for weddings, and she's right. I apologize, but I realize now how that*

must've looked. But I still didn't think it would be right unless I made up for what I did, although I don't know if that's possible.

I also talked to Sulayman for advice, and I'm not sure if that was the best thing either, but he did offer his own "token of good faith," and designed an invitation especially for you. We didn't send out invitations, so this is really especially for you. Also, a couple of particulars have changed, and you'll see them denoted on your invitation. I would've just told you in person, but I figured you'd be with us anyway, and Sulayman felt it was best to do it this way.

I love you for the sake of Allah.

Love, Aminah

Tamika smiled dryly. They were trying, and for that they couldn't be blamed. No, it wasn't okay to talk to Zahra, and definitely not Sulayman. But it did make her feel good that Sulayman hadn't forgotten her completely.

She forced laughter as she opened the bathroom door and walked to her bedroom, momentarily forgetting that she should be hurrying because she was uncovered. She closed the room door behind her without locking it and walked over to her bed, where she let her clothes fall. She was too tired to hang them up. She was going to sleep for an hour, and she didn't feel like doing much else.

She sat on the edge of her bed still holding the torn envelope, the letter, and the sealed invitation. She was too tired to read anything else. She started to lie down but realized that the time for the wedding might have changed. If they had changed the time to the morning, she might oversleep not only for prayer but for the wedding too. Part of her didn't care. She didn't want to go anyway. But she knew she should. It was only respectful. She yawned and stretched, still holding the papers in her hand. She then tore open the invitation and reviewed it mindlessly for any changes to the time.

Tamika became alert suddenly, and her heartbeat quickened as she read over the invitation for a second time. Her heart pounded with insistence, and her palms began to sweat. She stood abruptly and held the invitation closer as if that would change what it said, but she wanted to be sure it wasn't her mind but her eyes too that was seeing what she saw.

As she reviewed the wording a third time, she gasped and let the weight of her body fall back on the bed as she sat back down. She had not misread it. There was no time change, but there were certainly a "couple of particulars" that had, which were outlined on Sulayman's plain formal white card paper that he had sent through his inkjet printer for the effect.

Sarah and Ismael request your attendance at the marriage of their son, Sulayman Ali

To
Tamika Douglass,
Daughter of Thelma and Craig

Saturday, the eighth of June at
Two o'clock p.m.
At the Ali Residence

R.S.V.P. by 8:00 a.m. the eighth of June.
If you are unable to make it, please call, because we have a few family and
friends who need to know before noon, not to mention a lot of food to give
away before it goes bad.

Tears filled Tamika's eyes, and she made no effort to stop them as she covered her face until her sobbing became almost hysterical in its sound. She didn't know what to say or think as she cried, but she could only surrender to the flood of emotion that overtook her.

After she pulled herself together, she put on the clothes she had dropped on her bed and made her way to the bathroom to prepare for prayer. Before praying, she carried the invitation with her downstairs into the kitchen, where she found the cordless phone on the table and dialed the number written at the bottom of the homemade card. It was a lot earlier than 8:00, but she figured this RSVP couldn't wait. Questions flooded her mind and she needed answers, and besides, she doubted he could be sleeping on a morning like this.

Thirty-three

It was early Tuesday morning, only four days before their scheduled *nikaah*, that Sulayman and Aidah agreed to go their separate ways, and the parting, ironically, had more to do with Aidah's reservations than Sulayman's. Securing a date for the marriage contract had been a tug of war between them for months. Sulayman had chosen to limit their phone conversations until they secured a date, and Aidah felt it necessary to talk regularly to do just that. Feeling guilty for the "study break" call he had made, Sulayman was reluctant to call Aidah unless it was absolutely necessary. Sulayman suggested that his and Aidah's mother coordinate the details, but Aidah reminded him that her mother was skeptical about them marrying so soon. But Sulayman soon learned that "skeptical" was an understatement, and between talking to Aidah and her father, the reality became clear.

Although Aidah's mother approved of her daughter marrying Sulayman, she felt that he and Aidah should wait until they both finished medical school. Even Aidah felt that it was a good idea to wait at least a year. She had just begun medical school and her family was concerned about the feasibility of her marrying before she finished. Aidah's mother was firm in her belief that they should wait, but Aidah's father was unsure if waiting was a good idea. Aidah's father wanted his daughter to finish school, but he feared that, if they made her wait to marry until then, they would be pushing her in the same direction they had pushed Jauhara.

The signs that Jauhara should have married in college were clear to both her father and mother, but they pushed her to finish school and worry about marriage later. When a respected Muslim brother from their local community proposed, they refused the proposal on the grounds that their daughter was still in school. The refusal upset Jauhara, who was completing her second year of undergraduate studies at the time, and she began to slowly drift away from her family, first emotionally and then spiritually. She talked to her parents less and stayed in her dormitory room for school vacations although her campus in Lexington was less than two hours from home. She even discontinued her involvement with the MSA, apparently, to focus on her studies.

Her parents thought little of her behavior and labeled it a phase. Naturally, Jauhara was upset because of their decision, they reasoned, and she would get over it in time. They were right, at least partly. She did get over the marriage proposal being refused, but not her parents trying to control her life.

Since Jauhara was no longer active in the Muslim association, her association with Muslims themselves decreased until she had no Muslim friends at all. Her new group of friends concerned her parents, but because her relationship with them was already strained, they rarely mentioned it except to encourage her to come to more *masjid*-sponsored events. The few events to which she agreed to come, she was always accompanied by one of her close non-Muslim friends, with whom she would immediately leave when the event was over, usually to attend a party on campus or at a friend's house.

When Jauhara left Islam and disappeared from her family's life almost completely, it was then that her father realized their mistake. Although he was very committed to Islam and tried to follow the *Sunnah* as much as he could, he had paid little attention to the hadith in which the Prophet gave advice to the women's guardians. He advised them that if a man whose religious commitment and character pleases you comes with a marriage proposal for your daughter, then marry her to him, and if you do not, there will be severe trials and widespread corruption upon the earth. And Jauhara's father was seeing firsthand the truth of the Prophet's statement.

Aidah's father was no more excited than his wife when Aidah called to tell them she had met a good Muslim brother at her summer internship and wanted them to meet him. It was with a sense of obligation that he talked to Sulayman on the phone before meeting him in person. He had hoped to find some sign, any sign, that the brother wasn't committed to Islam or that his character was questionable so that he would be justified in refusing the proposal. He even called friends and acquaintances in Atlanta to find out what they knew about Sulayman and his family. But each person who knew them spoke highly of them. After praying *Istikhaarah*, Aidah's father told Sulayman of his approval and gave his permission for them to correspond to see if they wanted to marry. But his wife's sentiments were drastically different.

Aidah's mother didn't see Jauhara's situation as having any relation to Aidah's whatsoever. Jauhara's mistake had been her own, and it had little to do with their refusal to allow her to marry the brother. Jauhara was struggling spiritually before the proposal, and marrying a righteous brother wouldn't have changed anything except the context in which she struggled. If she or her husband were to blame at all for their daughter's struggles, she contended, they should look at their permitting her to live on-campus away from home before they looked at an isolated incident that had little if any relation to her downfall.

Sulayman talked to Aidah and her father for weeks before he had a clear idea what was going on. When Aidah's father finally agreed to go ahead and set a wedding date, his wife was livid. She argued with her husband and Aidah almost everyday about the decision. But Aidah resorted to avoiding her, which wasn't too difficult since they lived in different states, and she assured Sulayman that her mother would get over it in time. Sulayman had taken Aidah's word. He went on planning the details of the *nikaah* and thought little of her mother's feelings except to label them as Aidah had— skepticism. But it wasn't long before the issue of Aidah's mother came up again, and now it was Aidah who was becoming skeptical about getting married.

Aidah's first suggestion was to wait to marry until she and her father could get her mother to at least "agree to disagree" about the marriage. But Sulayman felt it was unwise to set a date then wait indefinitely to change it. So Aidah agreed to keep the date, at least tentatively, with the hope that her mother would accept the inevitable as the date neared. When her mother didn't seem to be giving in anytime soon, Aidah suggested setting the date a year from then. Initially, Sulayman agreed to the idea, and it was Aidah's father who questioned the sense in that. Her father's main concern was that they both lived in Atlanta and talked regularly, and could they really avoid— for an entire year—the natural temptation such a scenario offered?

Ironically, the day before Aminah's graduation, where Sulayman would see Tamika for the first time since they had gone their separate ways, Aidah had called Sulayman to say they should wait. Her mother was threatening to leave her father if he went through with it, and even Jauhara had told Aidah to leave the situation alone and do what her mother wanted.

It wasn't worth breaking up the family to marry someone, even if he was a good brother, Jauhara had told Aidah on the phone that day. She told Aidah that marriage was only exciting in the beginning, and after only months of being married, you realize that your family is the most important thing in your life. She told Aidah that she learned a lot from her own situation and wished she had listened to her parents before going off and doing what she felt was best. Allah showed her that it wasn't without wisdom that he gave parents the high status and authority that He did. Aidah hung up the phone and after reflecting on what her sister had said, she picked up the phone to tell Sulayman she felt they should wait.

Sulayman listened patiently as Aidah explained what she was feeling, and he told her to talk to her father before making any final decisions. Sulayman expressed the same concern her father had about waiting to get married when they lived in the same city and would inevitably see each other, and it was doubtful that they would be able to resist talking on the phone. Aidah understood what he was saying but was sure this was what she wanted to do. Nevertheless, she agreed to call her father to see what he thought.

It was Saturday night, just hours after the graduation, that he and Aidah talked again. But by then Aidah had decided on her own to go through with the original date. Sulayman didn't ask her to explain the sudden change of heart, but he knew it had a lot to do with seeing him talk to Tamika earlier that day. She realized that waiting wasn't an option if she were to marry him at all.

The decision to marry in Atlanta and not Louisville had been both Aidah's and her father's, who felt it best to have a small private ceremony away from home and have a large *waleemah* in Louisville after her mother grew to accept the marriage. It would be only Aidah's father, mother, and sister who flew in for the wedding, and other family and friends would be told of the *nikaah* at the time of the *waleemah,* with the exception of those few who already lived in Atlanta.   That way they could avoid broadcasting something that would only exacerbate the growing tension in the family.

Saturday afternoon, a week before their *nikaah,* Aidah called Sulayman close to tears. Her mother was refusing to come to the ceremony. They had bought the airline tickets and everything, and her father couldn't convince her to come. Her mother had called to let Aidah know she wasn't coming and that if she wished to base her decision to marry solely on what her father thought, she could get married with only her father there.

Sulayman didn't know what to say as he listened to Aidah break down and sob into the phone. He sat in silence saying nothing as he dreaded what this would mean. He finally told Aidah to be patient and not to worry about it. He told her that other people suffered more for the sake of Allah. He reminded her that life wasn't without tests and that everything would work out in the end, if they were only patient and had faith in Allah. Allah put the father in charge of the woman's marriage, and there was a reason for this. Sulayman's words consoled her, and she felt better, although the hurt she was experiencing was insurmountable and could only be soothed after years of patience with and commitment to her mother. But when he hung up the phone, he was unconvinced of his own words.

He spent the rest of the weekend feeling torn. Maybe they should wait after all. Or should they get married at all? But he kept his doubts to himself and pushed them to the back of his mind. He had gone through a lot to get to this point, and he wasn't going to back out now. He went on preparing for his marriage and setting up the apartment, convincing himself that everything would work out in the end.

It was this mindset Sulayman was in that Monday, only days before his scheduled *nikaah,* when Aminah shared with him what Tamika had said. He should have seen it as a sign, but at the time, he was so focused on making it to Saturday without another fallout with Aidah's family that it wasn't until late that night that he realized Allah could be telling him something. The possibility had made him sleepless, and he lay awake pondering everything that had led him to where he was then.

He thought of Tamika and allowed himself to admit that his feelings had not changed. He thought of Aidah and admitted that he and she were probably marrying only because it was the logical, Islamic thing to do. Clearly, Aidah wasn't as excited about the marriage as she had been when they first began to talk, and after Aminah's confession, he wasn't either. Were both he and Aidah trying to fight the inevitable, seeing marriage as an ends instead of the means it was? Were they both living in denial, thinking that, once the eighth of June passed, they cold relax, take a breath, and laugh at all they had gone through to get to that point? Did Aidah imagine she could live happily ever after with her prince and ignore her "evil" mother?

They couldn't be serious, Sulayman had thought to himself. What were they getting themselves into? Why should Aidah marry him when her heart wasn't in it? And why should he marry Aidah when his heart wasn't in it? What were they trying to prove, and to whom were they trying to prove it? Even Aidah's father was going along with it only because Aidah herself wanted to. He was no more excited about the marriage than his wife, but his fear of Allah made him stop short of refusing it.

Sulayman could have laughed at the ridiculousness of it all, except there was nothing funny about it. Even his own family was skeptical about his decision to marry Aidah, but like Aidah's father, they didn't want to prevent something in which Allah had, perhaps, placed blessings.

Energized by the thought, Sulayman had gotten out of bed and went to the bathroom to prepare for prayer. He would call Aidah, but before he did, he needed to consult his Lord. He stayed up most of the night praying and slept for only an hour before getting up at dawn for *Fajr*. He prayed *Istikhaarah* before he picked up the phone early Tuesday morning and talked to Aidah before either of them left for work.

It was relief Sulayman heard in Aidah's voice when he told her they should cancel their plans. She could only agree when he explained his thoughts on her parents' feelings and his own family's reservations. She told him she was thinking the same thing and wanted to call it off herself but felt bad for doing it at such a short notice. Although the ceremony was supposed to be private, attended only by close friends and family, word had spread in the city about them getting married, and of course, more people than expected would come, especially since it was being held at the *masjid*.

Sulayman told her he had thought of that too, but he felt there wasn't much to worry about since there were no public announcements about it, no invitations were sent out, and since they had told only a few people, they were obligated to call only those same few people to tell them the change in plans. Anyone else could find out from the imam when they arrived. Relieved that it was all over, he hung up the phone and took a short nap before going to work.

It was on his drive to work that Sulayman reflected on his disappointment with being unable to get married Saturday. He had looked forward to the eighth of June for weeks, and although he knew he and Aidah had made the right decision in calling it off, he couldn't help feeling a sense of sadness.

As he drove, his thoughts had drifted to Tamika, and he wondered if she would marry him. Though the argument with Aminah showed that she still had feelings for him and was upset with his family for being unmindful of them, that didn't mean she would agree to marry him. She had most likely reflected a lot on what she said to Aminah during the argument and now felt regretful. She probably realized the benefits of not marrying Sulayman— which he imagined were numerous.

It was difficult for Sulayman to focus at work with all that he had on his mind. He had to tell his parents and the imam about the change in plans, and until he did, his and Aidah's decision would be incomplete.

His parents. What would he say to them? They had spent a lot of time preparing for Saturday, and they wouldn't appreciate a seemingly arbitrary decision by two young people with "cold feet." They had run to store after store buying everything he and his wife would need in the apartment, and they purchased a lot of food for the guests.

He thought of his mother and hated to hurt her. He thought of his father and hated to disappoint him. How would they look at him? Would he lose their respect? Would his mother realize that she was right after all, that Sulayman wasn't responsible enough to be considered a man.

And his sister. What would Aminah say to him when she found out?

The thoughts made him wonder if he had made the right decision in calling Aidah. Maybe he should have gone ahead with the *nikaah*. Even he was having a hard time understanding the sense in calling everything off less than a week before the day. But a moment later he stopped himself. He had prayed *Istikhaarah*, and it was none other than Allah who made it easy for him to do what he did.

As Sulayman reflected on how much he prayed the night before he called Aidah, how he begged Allah to guide him to do the right thing, how his heart soared as he asked Him to decree what was best, how tears welled in his eyes as he called on his Lord using His most beautiful names, he realized that nothing could change what had happened. Allah Himself had guided him to make the final phone call, and for that, there should be no regrets.

It wasn't his decision to not marry Aidah that disturbed him, Sulayman realized. It was having put his family through so much for nothing. If he could somehow make up for that, his heart would be at peace.

The idea came to him so suddenly that his heart raced at the thought. What if he didn't cancel Saturday at all and married Tamika instead? The thought was childish, almost ludicrous, and it was difficult to keep from laughing at the thought. It was too idealistic, too…perfect.

And that's exactly why he was determined to do it—or at least give it a try.

His mind raced as the idea became more vivid by the second. He could surprise Tamika. She had told him she liked surprises—good surprises—when they first talked.

But how could he be sure this would count? What was more, how could he be sure she would agree to marry him at all? How could he pull off a surprise *nikaah* without her approval?

Then it occurred to him. Aminah had mentioned to him that, before she knew they had sent out none, Tamika was upset for not getting an invitation to the *nikaah*. He could surprise her by giving her an invitation. She could

RSVP to say if she could come, which would be her way of accepting—or rejecting—his marriage proposal.

And then there was the issue of practicality. Could he really give her a good surprise by marrying her in the *masjid*, where most guests would be expecting to see Aidah?

The more he thought about it, the more he realized he wouldn't be able to pull it off, at least not without some practical—and quick—solutions to the obvious.

Sulayman had gone home and talked to his parents that evening about his decision to not marry Aidah after all. In hopes they wouldn't judge him as imprudent, he explained everything that happened that led up to his decision. He told them of Aidah's mother, medical school, their indecision, his prayers, and, finally, Tamika. They were visibly disappointed and didn't know what to say. But Sulayman could tell they understood. There was nothing they could say to object—and Sulayman sensed that they didn't want to. Part of them was relieved.

But what now? That was the question both of his parents had.

Sulayman was reluctant to mention his idea for fear they would think he was crazy. But what he feared more was that this was his last chance to make amends with Tamika.

His parents were silent as they listened, and they couldn't help grinning at the ridiculous of it. Sulayman was serious, that was what made it humorous. They couldn't keep from laughing before they responded, and Sulayman too laughed.

"I don't know," Sarah had said, still grinning. She shrugged. "It could work," she reasoned, glancing at her husband with uncertainty.

He rubbed a hand over his face and chuckled. He nodded before responding. "It could work, yes, but we couldn't do it at the *masjid*. And since we don't know whether or not she'll agree, we can't make it anything big. Most likely, it'll have to be here if anywhere."

Sarah nodded, as an idea came to her suddenly. "We could talk to the imam and ask if he would be willing to come and perform the ceremony privately in our home. If he agrees, we could 'invite' Tamika." She paused. "But if it's really important for it to be a surprise, she can't know anything until Friday at the earliest."

Sulayman nodded, unable to keep from smiling. They were actually discussing his idea seriously. "I can make an invitation."

"But how do you plan for a *nikaah* that we don't even know is happening?" Ismael asked.

"We already bought a lot of food to prepare," Sarah said with a shrug. "We could just cook that and invite a few friends."

"Will you tell them why they're coming?"

She considered it and shrugged. "We could, but we can just invite them first and then tell them Friday what it's for."

Ismael nodded thoughtfully and shrugged as he chuckled. He shook his head. "If this is really what you want to do, Sulayman, pray on it, and we'll see what we can do."

Thirty-four

It was fifteen minutes past two o'clock Saturday afternoon when Tamika stood grinning at her reflection in the full-length mirror that hung on the back of the door to Aminah's bedroom. They had gone shopping that morning and returned home shortly after noon. A friend of Sarah's had come over to do Tamika's hair and finished an hour before.

Tamika's hair was tucked neatly at the back of her head except for soft spirals that dangled in front of one ear and at the nape of her neck. Diamond style rhinestones ran up the back of her head, adorning the hairstyle elegantly. Black eyeliner and mascara accented the soft almond brown of her eyes and made them appear stunningly large, almost mysterious. Mahogany lipstick complimented her smooth brown complexion with a gloss that brought out her femininity intricately, making her smile intoxicating in its beauty. A gold necklace glistened from her neck, adorning the diamond-like stone that sparkled at her throat. Her soft cream-colored satin gown hung to her ankles and gently hugged her figure. A thin slit ran up the left side of her dress, exposing her left shin covered in sheer black whenever she shifted her weight or stepped forward. Diamond earrings that Sarah lent her adorned her ears, giving her an astonishing finish to her natural beauty.

"*BarakAllaahufeek.*" Aminah crossed her arms and nodded her head approvingly, and Tamika grinned.

A knock at the door interrupted them before Tamika could respond. A moment later the door opened and Sarah stepped inside. Her eyes widened in awe as her eyes fell on Tamika.

"You look beautiful, *barakAllaahufeek.* The earrings go really well."

Tamika smiled self-consciously, unsure what to say. "*InshaAllaah,* I'll give them back as soon as I can."

Sarah laughed and waved her hand. "Don't worry about that now. You have more important things to think about."

"Is everyone here?" Aminah asked.

Her mother nodded. "Yes, they're waiting downstairs."

Aminah grinned at Tamika. "This is it."

Tamika smiled as her heart raced. She could hardly believe she was actually getting married.

"Here." Aminah handed Tamika a large black peach skin cloth.

Tamika wrinkled her forehead. "What's this?"

"It's a *jilbaab.*"

"A *jilbaab?*" She felt the soft cloth and studied it curiously.

"It's like an *abiya* except it covers you from the head all the way down."

She nodded as she remembered just then. Aminah had told her about the *jilbaab* when they had gone to *Jumuah* for Tamika's term paper. "Oh yeah." She paused as she studied it closely. "How do I put it on?"

Aminah held an end to show her. "It has wide sleeves. So just put your arms through here."

Tamika placed the cloth on her head and slipped her arms through the sleeves then studied her reflection in the mirror. She looked like she was wearing a black sheet. It was difficult to get used to the style.

"That way you don't have to worry about your hair or dress getting messed up," Aminah explained. "You may wanna wear a sheer veil over your head to cover your face."

Tamika nodded. That was a good idea. That way she wouldn't have to worry about any brothers seeing her like this. "You have one?"

Aminah thought about it then shook her head. "No," she said hesitantly, "but I have a sheer scarf that basically does the same thing."

"Then give that to her," Sarah suggested as she turned to go. "And I'll tell them you'll be downstairs in a minute, *inshaAllaah*."

Five minutes later, Aminah and Tamika emerged from the room. Tamika's heart pounded in her chest as she walked down the hall. It was awkward wearing a sheer black scarf over her face, but it calmed her nervousness somewhat, perhaps because no one would see her. She reflected on what was before her, and for a moment, she wondered if it were real. Was she *really* getting married? *To Sulayman?* She would have never imagined this day would come.

As she started down the stairs, the sheer black veil gave the home a shadowy, dream-like existence, and her mind brought her back at the Ali's residence more than a year before when she had visited the home for the first time.

At the time, Sulayman was but a despised name that appeared in *A Voice* each month, and she had been ashamed to be seen riding in the back of the car as he drove her and his sister to the Friday prayer. She only agreed to join them because of her term paper assignment in Dr. Sanders's class. She was a Christian then, and Islam was but a strange religion practiced by her roommates and was the topic of her research paper and presentation. The veracity of the religion hadn't yet touched her, at least not fully. She wasn't yet ready to submit to a regimented life that meant sacrificing her carefree one.

It was a peculiar presumption, she now reflected, to count Islam as regimented and her life carefree. Yet, as she stood on the other side, the reality was quite contrary. There was no doubt that accepting Islam came with its sacrifices and struggles. She couldn't deny she had given up things she never imagined she would. And she couldn't deny her life had not been easy since she became Muslim. But her life before Islam was by far more regimented, and her life now was, in its essence, more carefree.

Regiment, or freedom from it, wasn't of the body, but of the soul, Tamika thought. And freedom wasn't to exercise free will but to discipline it. Living carefree, in actuality, was an impossibility. For no life was free from worry, and no life was free from care. But to live carefree, in the peripheral, was to direct life's worries and cares to that which benefited the soul. A life free from responsibility and self-discipline was regiment in its ugliest form. The heart ailed and the soul ached, while the person ignored their pleas. Submission to the calls was to free them from the chains of slavery that would only tighten with time.

Marriage was a prison only to those who defined freedom as regiment and saw slavery in that which was living carefree, Tamika reflected. There was no freedom in living without a companion to call your own. Even the single saw the prison bars before them and strove to break free. Their single life was spent searching for "the one," who would represent freedom from the life they loathed. Yet for no one would marriage be the goal. The goal was but to please one's Creator, and for the pious, marriage was to walk upon that path.

Imam Abdul-Quddus stood in a corner of the living room near the vase talking to Ismael, who sat in a dining room chair in front of him. Sulayman sat on the love seat, slightly turned in his chair to face them. Three men whom Tamika didn't recognize sat on the couch, and Sarah and Kate sat in chairs near the room's entrance from the foyer. Two empty seats were to the right of Sarah, and she patted the seat next to her when she saw Tamika pause at the foyer. Aminah took the seat next to Tamika, and a moment later Maryam and her daughters emerged from the kitchen. Immediately, Aminah stood and offered Maryam her seat, and Maryam accepted with a smile and a nod of her head. Her daughters sat on the floor in front of them.

The imam turned toward the dining room and leaned forward and spoke to someone Tamika couldn't see. A moment later she saw a group of young boys move into the living room and sit on the floor near Ismael.

"*Innalhamdalillaah...*," the imam began, reminding Tamika of the first time she heard the words at *Jumuah* more than a year ago.

Tamika's heart began to pound as she realized the significance of the moment. Her palms began to sweat, and she ran her hands over the black peach skin fabric nervously. For a moment, she lifted her gaze to where Sulayman sat. He was turned toward the imam, but the love seat faced her and the other women. He wore a long sleeved *thobe*-like white shirt that hung to the knees of his black dress pants. His hair was cut low in a fading shadow on his head, and his beard was neatly trimmed and gave his face an intent, distinguished appearance. His green eyes didn't leave the imam's face, and Tamika momentarily forgot that all of this was for her.

She thought of the invitation and his request for an RSVP, and she couldn't help grinning behind the veil. Elation enveloped her, and she could have cried from happiness, but she maintained her composure. She lowered her gaze a moment later, reminding herself that they were not married yet, and she listened to the speech the imam was giving to the guests—and to her and Sulayman.

The imam was saying something about loving Allah and focusing on Him to make a marriage work. Tamika found herself reflecting on those words and feeling determined to do just that. The imam told them of Sulayman's responsibilities as a husband and Tamika's as a wife. Hearing her name in this sense was awkward but pleasant to her ears. Her mind drifted again as she anticipated being married. She smiled as she imagined how it would feel to walk hand-in-hand, taking a stroll down the street.

As a non-Muslim, Tamika didn't imagine that getting married would be like this. She had imagined her wedding as an elaborate production in an expensive hall with hundreds, if not thousands, of guests. She would wear a gown worth several thousand dollars, and she would have a white tiered cake with doves atop or perhaps miniature statues of a bride and groom. Bridesmaids would be old friends color coordinated in pink or purple gowns of satin. It would be full of entertainment and music, and it would be the talk of the town.

But as Tamika sat in a chair in the living room of Sulayman's home, the anticipation to be with him was so momentous that the elaborate details of her imagined wedding paled in comparison to what she felt right then. The thought of being with Sulayman for life sent her heart fluttering in excitement, and she couldn't imagine anything could make it more priceless than it was. Perhaps a costly and elaborate show was necessary only for those who sought to make up for the fact that the thrill was gone. They had enjoyed the intimacy of marriage before the wedding, and they needed to plan an extravagant nuptial to give them something to look forward to. Tamika thought of Latonya and wondered how differently her sister's marriage would be if she married Tyrone. Was it possible for her to feel the exhilaration Tamika felt right then?

"...hereby offer you Tamika Douglass as your wife for the *mahr*[30] and conditions you both agreed upon, according to the Book of Allah and the *Sunnah* of His Messenger, *sallaahu'alayhi-was-sallam*."

Instinctively, Tamika lifted her gaze and saw the imam saying these words while looking in the direction of Sulayman. The sight of Sulayman sent her heart racing, and her hands shook as she realized he was here for her. All of this was for her. The realization overwhelmed her.

"Repeat after me."

As Sulayman stood to repeat the imam's words, Tamika felt tears gather in her eyes. The imam's voice, though audible and clear, became background noise as she awaited Sulayman's turn to speak.

"I Sulayman Ali." His voice was deep and familiar but carried a hint of strangeness that made Tamika wonder at how remarkable he was.

---

[30] dowry

She shifted in her seat and touched her head to make sure her hair was still in place under the cloth. Her face grew warm, and the pounding in her chest became more insistent as it reached her throat.

"Accept Tamika Douglass as my wife." His voice quivered slightly, and Tamika felt herself shiver at the sound of her name. The pounding now reached her head, and it was difficult to sit still.

A second later, Sarah's warm hand squeezed hers, and Tamika relaxed and held it as she felt her throat go dry, suspending all ability to speak.

"According to the Book of Allah and the *Sunnah* of His Messenger, *sallaahu'alayhi-was-sallam*."

The noise level rose suddenly as the brothers stood and blocked Sulayman from her view. The women stood a second later and swarmed Tamika in hugs and congratulations before she could stand.

It took a moment for Tamika to realize it was over and that she was officially married right then. She stood and returned the hugs dutifully but couldn't escape the distance she felt from everyone. Her mind was on the young man in the front of the room. She couldn't see him, and he couldn't see her. But they were connected by the knowledge that they now shared a bond that no one could break. She, like he, greeted the guests with enthusiasm, but their real eagerness was to escape the regimented politeness and savor the company of each other.

Tamika was grateful when Sarah hooked her arm in hers and led her through the kitchen and down the steps to the den. The women followed as Sarah said something about food being served downstairs. Tamika took a seat in a chair designated for her and wondered how much more formality she would endure before she would see Sulayman.

Someone handed her a plate of food, and she removed the veil before she began to nibble at a chicken wing more out of gratitude for being served than any hunger on her part. She couldn't hope to eat the entire plate. She was in no mood to eat. But she managed to take small bites ever so often as she conversed cordially with the guests. Tamika grew bored of the redundancy of the conversation, and she felt her mind wandering as she spoke.

Her smile was frozen on her face, and she laughed in enjoyment at whatever was being said though she was unable to keep up. As she talked, she began to believe she would be sitting there for the rest of the afternoon.

She was relieved when, nearly thirty minutes later, Sarah leaned forward to whisper in her ear, "Sulayman's waiting for you upstairs."

The words were ones she had longed to hear since she sat down, but for some reason she couldn't move. The news came so suddenly, so unexpectedly, that she didn't know what to do. She nodded calmly in response, and like a respected diplomat being told his honored guest had arrived, she didn't lift her gaze to the messenger. She continued to raise the food to her mouth, and she ate slowly.

She entertained more questions from Kate, Maryam, or whoever wanted to talk. She made her answers more thoughtful, more elaborate than before, as if she had all the time in the world. Inside she was inflamed with nervous excitement, and like a child, she was afraid to go upstairs alone. She wanted Aminah to walk with her, but Aminah was engrossed in a conversation with one of Maryam's daughters.

Tamika glanced around in search of Sarah, and she found her upstairs in the kitchen preparing food. Tamika's legs weakened as she realized she was alone, and she feared she was unable to stand. She continued to nod her head in conversation, and she had no idea how much time had passed since she was told that Sulayman—*her husband!*—was waiting upstairs. She imagined he was wondering where she was, and her heart pace quickened at the thought. She hoped he wasn't getting impatient.

The talking quieted a moment before a hand squeezed her shoulder gently, and she turned her face expecting to see Sarah. Her heart nearly skipped a beat when her eyes met Sulayman's. He leaned forward until his face was next to hers, and as her eyes fell upon it, her heart raced as she realized how handsome he was. He smelled of the sweet musk that had always defined him, and his voice was deep and gentle despite the authoritativeness in its nature.

"Are you ready to go?"

She held his gaze for a moment then lowered her own, unable to look at him too long without imagining the moment was unreal. She nodded and began to stand, using the chair to support her weight with one hand. She felt his hand take hers, and her cheeks grew warm as she realized it was the first time they had touched. His grasp was firm and gentle, and she cradled her hand in his.

He held her hand and guided her up the stairs. She was too shy to walk directly next to him and instead stood a couple of steps back as she held his hand. They passed through the kitchen and made their way through the foyer. Someone greeted them, and Sulayman replied for them both. Sulayman paused and held the front door for her, and she let go of his hand to pass and go outside. The warm afternoon air swept over her as she slipped her hand back in his and heard him close the door behind them. He walked next to her, and she reveled in the moment as they walked to his car.

Tamika caught sight of Sulayman's car parked in front of the house, the same one she had ridden in dozens of times. She wouldn't have imagined there would come a day that she and Sulayman would ride in his car alone. She walked to the car with her husband with a sense of shyness and immense pride. She was honored to be next to Sulayman, and she wanted the whole world to see. Sulayman let go of her hand when they reached the car and unlocked it from the passenger side. He held the door handle and stepped back as he opened her door. Tamika moved her lips to say thank you, but she couldn't find her voice.

Thirty-five

Late Saturday night Sulayman sat next to Tamika on the couch in their apartment. The gold band he had given her for her dowry glistened on her right hand, and she grinned as she held up her hand admiring it. It was a simple gift, Sulayman knew, but it was all he could afford. As he gazed at his wife, her beauty was intoxicating, and he wished he could give her so much more. But she had told him he had given her more than she could ever want by giving her a home.

Sulayman hadn't thought about it before, but it had been more than a year since Tamika had a place to call her own. Embracing Islam meant sacrificing more than her lifestyle. She had to sacrifice her home. He could only imagine the faith she must have to keep going despite losing almost everything. He could only pray he made her marriage to him worthwhile.

Today had been a monumental day for him. The day before, he was a young Muslim medical student, and the next he was a young Muslim husband. Undoubtedly, there was a lot of weight upon him as the head of a household, but he couldn't think of that right then.

Enjoying Tamika's company that day and hearing her laughter as they held hands made him forget the heavy responsibility on his shoulders. They were still shy in each other's presence, but as they shared their emotional turmoil and heartache of the last few months, the walls between them were breaking down.

Sulayman expressed how he feared he had lost her after his silly mistake of going to her mother's home without her knowledge. Tamika shared how she feared she had lost him after getting angry after she found out. She was thrilled that they were finally together, and he agreed. Their elation for having each other to themselves was undeniable. Being able to talk in person, with no barriers of phone or guilt, incited them with a child-like eagerness to savor every minute. As they talked, they realized how alike they were, and they couldn't imagine how unfulfilling their lives would be had they been unable to marry.

Presently, a soft smile creased the corners of Sulayman's mouth as he reflected on this immense blessing. A second later his expression became reflective as he gazed at his wife. He studied her beauty and was in awe at what he beheld. He silently prayed that Allah would bless her. Sulayman prayed that He would bestow His mercy on them and bless him to be a righteous husband and Tamika a righteous wife. The gratefulness he felt for their monumental blessing was one words could not describe. There was no expression to capture the beauty of what they felt. He pondered this greatness, and he wished the world too could understand. There was no regret in a union blessed by God. Their affection not only drew them closer to each another but to God himself.

Next to him Tamika yawned and laid her head on his shoulder in exhaustion. Sulayman smiled, and his mind drifted to what he had wanted to ask for some time but had been afraid to. He glanced at his wife whose gaze was reflective and distant, and he couldn't help wondering if they were pondering the same thing.

"Tamika?"

"Mm, hm."

When they first began talking about marriage, Sulayman sensed her apprehension. There was something more than school, family, and natural reluctance to a life change that accounted for the hesitance she felt to marry him. He sighed thoughtfully. He could only hope now was the right time. "What were you afraid of?"

Tamika grew silent, and he felt her stiffen. Her discomfort was apparent, and he felt distant from her for a moment.

Sulayman almost regretted asking when he saw the expression on her face, which confirmed the fear he had sensed from her. A moment later, he felt her relax as if submitting to the inevitable.

Tamika was unsure how to respond. She had pushed her insecurity about her past sin to the back of her mind, and her healing was in choosing to forget. It was easier to pretend it had never happened than to risk that her confession would sour what they had found in each other. But now she felt cornered, and as her mind raced in search of a safe response, she realized honesty was her only option.

She sat up and tried to gather her thoughts. For a moment more, she was silent.

"You." Her response was clear, though slightly muffled as she lowered her head next to him.

Sulayman wrinkled his forehead in confusion, and he gently held her chin and tilted her face so she would look at him. "What do you mean?"

She met his gaze with forced confidence and let her eyes tell him what her tongue couldn't fully express. "I wasn't always Muslim, Sulayman."

Immediately, he knew what she meant. With an empathetic sigh, he put an arm around her shoulder and pulled her closer as he stared distantly toward the wall. He shook his head in self-reproach for not telling her what he should have before. "I'm no angel, Tamika, and I didn't expect you to be one."

She was silent, and Sulayman sensed the response didn't convey what he had intended.

"I was afraid you'd judge me for it," she said, her voice more relaxed than before.

"Tamika." He drew in a deep breath and exhaled slowly. He couldn't look at her. He bit his lower lip and stared distantly in deep thought. How could he tell her what she needed to hear while covering his faults at the same time?

"I *was* always Muslim," he confided finally, "so I have no excuse." A moment later, he met her gaze and confessed with his eyes.

Her expression was one of shock as she studied his expression to be sure he was saying what she thought she understood. Her eyes became inquisitive as questions flooded her mind. But she didn't give voice to her thoughts. The details were irrelevant. He had repented and mended his life, and there was no point in giving life to the skeletons of the past. But she couldn't help feeling a sense of relief. If nothing else, she was not alone.

The two sat in silence, engrossed in their thoughts as the night enveloped them. They drifted to sleep next to each other, and they didn't wake until dawn.

Sulayman asked Tamika to go for a walk with him after they prayed, and in silence, they walked hand-in-hand down the street, enjoying the cozy warmth of each other's presence. They returned home shortly before sunrise, and feeling sticky from the early morning heat, Tamika decided to take a shower.

As he waited for her to finish, Sulayman stood and gazed out the window of their room. He watched as the sun outstretched its arms of rays and embraced the horizon with its golden orange glow. He thought of Tamika and wished to share with her nature's announcement of the new day. He could hear the shower running in the bathroom across the hall, and instead he stood where he was and surrendered to the flood of memories that he had held back too long.

When he had begun high school, he was indeed his parents' child. Not only had he attained academic success, but he had become the star of the Muslim community. At fourteen, he was already the president of the *masjid* youth group with ages ranging from twelve to twenty one. He spoke at *masjid* events and organized activities, giving him the semblance of maturity beyond his years.

At school he was active in Freshman Council and began to enjoy attention from both teachers and students for his success. At the end of his freshman year, girls at school began to ask him to go on dates. Naturally, he refused, and he became known as "the cute Muslim boy who isn't allowed to date." The label was meant as a joke, and, initially, he thought of it as such. But the sudden attention from freshman cheerleaders and even upperclassmen flattered him and made him think of himself as something great. Still, he was too proud to give them any indication that he was the least bit phased by the attention.

During his sophomore year, he joined the basketball team and enjoyed a comfortable level of success in sports, though his academic and leadership achievements were far more impressive. His success on the basketball court was primarily social. A Muslim boy who made straight *A*'s and "stayed clear of girls" was indeed a sight to see as he dribbled the ball and delivered a jump shot with the same precision and fade-away sleekness as the school's most celebrated athletes.

The reputation as a strict Muslim worked in his favor for a while, and he seized the opportunity to tell people about Islam. But it was difficult to keep lowering his gaze and staying clear of girls when he faced them everyday. It became especially difficult during the middle of his sophomore year when he agreed to tutor a fellow classmate.

Lindsey was a junior Sulayman had met in his chemistry class. She had red hair that she kept cropped at shoulder length, and she wasn't especially pretty or popular. But she came from an affluent family, which earned her respect and a comfortable social status among teachers and peers. She made relatively good grades and maintained the honor roll for most quarters, but her weakness was science, which was the cause for an occasional *C* on her report card.

Because of her weakness in the subject, the teacher paired her with Sulayman, for whom science was rarely challenging. Initially, he helped her only during class and lab, but she eventually began to call him at home to ask questions about homework or to review before an exam. Though most of their conversations were related to chemistry, she often asked about his religion and was impressed by the moral discipline of his faith. She often mentioned how more men should be like him.

In the middle of the third quarter, she asked him if Muslims could date. Of course, he told her they couldn't, and the issue was left alone. But each time they talked, the subject of Islamic rules was brought up. She expressed how she felt his interpretation of his religion was unusually strict, and she questioned the sense of not being allowed to go out.

Her questions were answered with elaborate Islamic explanations he learned from his parents, who had warned him of the temptations he would encounter in public school. But he had begun to ponder these inquiries and doubt that he was doing the right thing.

"Do you really think God doesn't want you to be happy?" she had asked one day.

As a youth who was embarking upon sixteen years old and had only a rote understanding of Islam, he had no intelligent response.

The summer that followed was tortuous for him as doubts surfaced about his parents' interpretation of Islam. He reflected a lot on his conversations with Lindsey and wondered if she was right. Maybe he had it all wrong. What was wrong with going out just for fun? What was the harm?

That year, at his parents' insistence, Sulayman got his driver's license. He was growing to be a young man, his parents told him, and he needed to begin driving. He would run minor errands for his family, buying groceries, taking a letter to the post office, or driving his mother to Maryam's house.

With his license, he felt like a slave to his parents rather than a maturing young adult, and he began to resent his parents for their strict rules that prohibited him from going anywhere unless they needed something for themselves. When he complained that his license was really for them, they responded by saying that once he was more mature, he could go more places.

Sulayman's first reward for "maturity" was taking his sister over Durrah's house or taking the two friends to the store or mall. He became their personal taxi driver, and his parents actually imagined he would feel grateful for running his little sister and her friend around town.

What about *his* friends? What about the places he wanted to go? But his parents didn't approve of his "acquaintances" (they refused to call them friends because most were non-Muslims he met at school). He wasn't allowed to drive them anywhere and could meet them only at sports or extracurricular activities held at the school. Naturally, if there was a school related event, Aminah wanted to go, and she would always bring her friend along.

Initially, he was Aminah's designated driver, and Durrah was merely his sister's tagalong. But it wasn't long before Durrah herself put in requests for places that she and Aminah could go, and, of course, Sulayman would drive. At first, he refused all of Durrah's requests, protesting to his parents that it wasn't fair. Durrah wasn't even family. If she wanted to go somewhere with Aminah, she should ask her parents to take them. But his parents insisted that he take them where Durrah wanted to go. So he became the taxi driver for them both.

At the time, Sulayman was still sore about his parents' strict rules and continued to doubt their interpretation of Islam. He met other Muslims his age whose parents saw nothing wrong with girls and boys going out to the movies, so long as they went in groups.

At home Aminah talked to him about her own frustrations with their parents' strict rules. She too had met Muslims who would go out to movies in groups. He indulged her and agreed that their parents were a bit extreme in their application of Islam. Hearing his sister's feelings validated his own and convinced him that his parents had it all wrong.

Toward the end of his junior year during one of his daily talks with his sister, Aminah asked him a question that neither he nor she knew would change the course of their frustrations forever.

"What do you think of Durrah?" Aminah stood across from where he sat on the edge of his bed lifting a twenty-pound weight with one hand. He was counting his repetitions and paid little attention to the question, though he had heard what she said.

"Why?"

"Just tell me." She folded her arms in playful defiance, but her anxiousness to hear his answer was unmistakable.

Sulayman glanced at his sister with his forehead creased in a curiosity tainted by disinterest. "What do you mean, what do I think of her?" He switched hands and lifted the weight up and down with the other hand as he turned his attention to his flexing muscle.

"You *know*." She wore a hesitant grin and followed his eyes until they met hers.

He paused weight lifting momentarily as he met his sister's gaze, slightly frustrated with her for interrupting his workout. He narrowed his eyes as he stared at her, demanding an explanation with his expression before he spoke. "Why?"

Aminah sauntered across the floor with her folded arms swinging back and forth, and she kicked at the hardwood floor shyly to avoid his gaze. "Well," she sang, pretending not to know whether or not she should tell.

"Aminah." His tone was louder and more authoritative now. He had no time for girlish guessing games.

"Okay, okay," she said in surrender a moment later, halting in the middle of the floor and placing her hands on her hips. Her grin widened, and her eyes sparkled at the victory she felt for having the advantage over her brother. "But you have to promise not to tell."

He rolled his eyes and shook his head as he began lifting his weight again. Ignoring her request, he said coolly, "I'm listening."

"Durrah said she likes you."

Sulayman stopped his repetition and stared at his sister, unsure how to respond to the news that neither excited nor disturbed him. It was mere curiosity that heightened his interest and accounted for his brief speechlessness. He didn't know what to say. Perhaps there was a time he would have been flattered, but he had grown so accustomed to attention from girls at school that it was a twinge of pity he felt for Aminah's friend right then.

"Really?" His tone was aloof though he didn't intend to sound so cold in his disinterest as he resumed lifting the weight a second later.

"Yeah, can you believe it?" Her excitement was excessive, and it was obvious that she was trying to make up for her brother's lack of emotion, if not convince herself that her news was as exciting to him as it was to her.

"No, I can't." He counted his repetitions and watched his muscle flex and relax with each movement.

Aminah ignored his indifference and changed the subject to something more mentally stimulating. "What do you think of her?"

He was silent before shrugging and stating honestly, "I don't know."

There was a long pause as he continued his exercise. "Well, think about it," Aminah said finally, "and don't tell her I told you."

Sulayman set his weight on the floor to give his arms a rest. He glanced at his sister humorously, unable to resist the urge to laugh. As if he were actually going to call his little sister's friend and tell her what she said.

Aminah's news, though insignificant on the scale of flattery in his life, stayed in the back of his mind. Being Aminah and Durrah's designated driver began to take on new meaning, though he couldn't fully interpret what it was. He began to study Durrah more closely and try to transform her image from one of dull familiarity to eccentric beauty. Initially, that was difficult because he knew her too well. Having known Durrah since she was a child, she was like a sister to Sulayman, and it was difficult to change that perception. Her looks were neither off-putting nor appealing. They were merely hers.

Sulayman began to enjoy being the taxi driver for Aminah and Durrah though he was unable to explain this sudden change of heart. He became more relaxed around them and began to joke with Durrah more. Durrah enjoyed the lively drives and indulged him. She laughed at all of his jokes, and Aminah laughed because her friend did, grateful that her brother and friend were getting to know each other after all.

Aminah's dream, which she shared with her brother, was that he and Durrah would marry. It was this hope that drove her to encourage the relationship as enthusiastically as she did. She began to think of places to go with Durrah so that Sulayman could drive them. She hoped that her brother and best friend would be overcome with emotional attachment that would culminate in marriage. It was naiveté on all of their parts, Sulayman imagined in retrospect, that blinded them from the portending evil.

Their parents had no idea—and perhaps they didn't either—that the weekly excursions were no longer innocent drives that Sulayman was so unfortunate to have to endure. In Sarah and Ismael's mind, taking care of his sister and taking her where she needed, or wanted, to go was an essential part of his learning to be a man. Perhaps it was the desire for a break from their parental burdens that made Sarah and Ismael blind to what was erupting before their eyes, and by their own hands. Whatever the reason, no one saw the approaching disaster that the growing attraction between Durrah and Sulayman was to bring.

Aminah's fairy tale world of her brother prince marrying her best friend princess led her to forget basic principles of a group trip, the most significant of which was that a group stayed together at all times. Occasionally, when Durrah and Sulayman were engrossed in conversation, Aminah would find something else to do.

During such trips, Sulayman and Durrah grew to like each other, at first, as friends. As they realized how much they had in common—which was no more than mutual frustration with their parents' strict rules—they began to see each other in a new light. No longer did Sulayman have to search for physical beauty in a familiar face. Her beauty blossomed before him more definitely each day.

Aminah began to bring homework and books on each trip in case she found nothing else to pass time. Overall, she remained a good sport and even agreed to go places with them that she had no interest in. She remained silent when Durrah and Sulayman went to the movies after they told their parents that they (Aminah and Durrah) were going shopping for clothes. She remained silent when they took long walks around the school building when they were supposed to be at the game.

It wasn't long before their rebellion against parents too strict pushed them too far. Playing with fire wasn't playing at all, and it was a lesson they learned the hard way. The night Sulayman learned his unforgettable lesson, he and Durrah had walked in shameful silence back to the game. The sky, which an hour before was a magnificent canvas on a romantic night, was now ominous, and the stars were reproving eyes in the dismal darkness. The excited chatter of students and fans as the couple neared the stadium was an incessant taunting whose sudden intensity threatened to deafen them in regret. Though her outward irritation was because they were late picking her up, even Aminah's eyes seemed to scold them for their crime. Her words cut deeper than she knew, when, in a bout of frustration as she followed them to the car, she spat out, "What is *wrong* with you?"

For three weeks, Sulayman and Durrah didn't speak and saw each other only in passing at school. Sulayman became a despondent drifter during the day and was afflicted with sleepless anxiety through the nights. He continued like this for several months and when his anxiety got the better of him, he would go to the bathroom to perform *wudoo'* in preparation for a voluntary prayer, in which he would beg Allah's forgiveness over and over again. Tears would stream down his face in his prayers. It was a time he could never forget. It was the first time he had cried in his prayers.

Durrah.

The mere sound of her name, even now, made Sulayman feel the blood on his hands. He couldn't think of her too long before regret threatened to suffocate him. It was he who chipped away at Durrah's walls of spiritual strength and brought them tumbling down. It was their crime that smoothed the road of transgression for her in school.

It wasn't until two years after their horrible mistake that it occurred to Sulayman that when he had sought his own redemption, he should have sought hers too. When she removed the *hijaab*[31] at Streamsdale, guilt burned inside him. He had torn down her walls of piety, and the magnitude of their sin made her too weak to rebuild. Had she too suffered from regret, and was it complete and debilitating as his had been? Or had she merely moved on?

Sulayman could only watch her from a distance in college as he saw her continuing to tumble from where their crime had pushed her over the edge. Aminah, his parents, and Durrah's parents were dumbfounded by the "sudden" change in Durrah, and they could make no sense of the change. But for Sulayman, it wasn't confusion he felt, but shame.

---

[31] The Muslim women's covering.

It wasn't a sudden senseless change of heart that destroyed Durrah and created Dee. It was a continuation of the path they had walked in satiating the selfish desires of the heart. Dee wasn't confused about what she wanted in life, as others guessed. She was searching for an escape from the contradiction she felt she was living after the fall. Like he, Dee felt a mask being forced upon her face, and she felt smothered under the thick paint. She couldn't look in the mirror with the mask removed and resist the repulsion she felt for the hypocrite who stared her in the face. It was a search for self-honesty and contentment that made her seek the balance that she sought.

It was hard for Sulayman too to fight the self-contempt and cruel mockery he felt for going on wearing the mask of a "good Muslim." It was sickening to stare the truth in the eye and submit to what it entailed. He felt like he was living the lives of two people, the life of each depending on the vicious murder of the other. The battle for control of Sulayman's body was violent, and at times he felt powerless to resist the evil self taking control.

It was only through determination and prayer that he felt a breath of relief. At times he felt like he was drowning and being pulled back down as he groped for air. When he felt he had won, the vicious battle inside would again ensue. But with persistence, his breath of relief was gradually won. Yet the torment he felt never ended and threatened to obliterate every sign of spiritual life from him. It was this battle, this horrendous battle of the self, that enabled Sulayman to relate completely to Dee. It was this battle that Dee was unable to withstand.

Their sin stripped from her what it nearly stripped from him. But through Allah's mercy he was able to redefine—reclaim—his sense of self. Sulayman imagined it brought Dee's soul the semblance of peace to remove the *hijaab* and live the life of a model and singer. After all, it was only an expression of who she "really" was finally finding release. She didn't want to hide behind a mask of piety when reality was otherwise, or so she thought.

It was Sulayman's own contorted face reflected each time he saw the degeneration of Durrah the Muslim into the model-singer Dee. It was painful to see her losing the internal battle that he too had been threatened to lose. And he could blame only himself.

He felt a calm reassurance when he convinced himself of what Aminah, his parents, and Durrah's parents felt—that life would be Dee's teacher, and she would come around. As she fell deeper into the pit of desires, he began to pray for her deliverance. It was a way of praying for his own. It wasn't only her soul at stake, he feared, as he watched her self-destruct. Every sin of hers was a sin of his, and she needed to resist the pull of hers to spare him from continually paying for his own.

There were times in college that Sulayman wanted to walk up to Dee and tell her to let go before she was in too deep. But he resisted due to his own fear of staring his old self in the face and reliving the emotional pain from which he had desperately sought relief.

It was a distant but acute pain he felt for Dee whenever he saw her on campus. It was himself he saw in Kevin when he saw them laughing and talking, oblivious to the walls of fate closing in on them. Sulayman wanted to save Dee—Durrah. But what could he say when a mere gaze would strip him of the mask he wore? What advice could he possibly give her that couldn't be thrown back in his face?

Dee's death was a violent blow to his own life, and he felt crushed by his crime when she was killed. He may as well have been the drunk driver who struck the side of her car. He was no less responsible for her death. His selfish desires had pushed her plummeting into a black hole, one that claimed her life. He grieved a tumultuous, yet silent, grief when she died, one that he could share with no one but himself and his Lord.

The snatching of her soul that night was like a warning of his own evil end. Perhaps he was spared so that he could know the ugliness of his sin was no less hideous and that his time for punishment too was near. This possibility plagued him and inspired him to pray more intensely, beyond what was obligatory, and he would often wake in the last third of the night.

Presently, Sulayman felt undeserving of a person so pious and righteous as Tamika. Yet Allah had given her to him. Sulayman could only pray he would give such an extraordinary woman what she deserved, and more. It was shame he felt when he thought of how she had been afraid of him. How could he judge her when he had an even uglier past? She wasn't always Muslim, but what of him, who knew about his Lord and the Hereafter, even as he sinned? It was he who should have been afraid of her.

Tamika was indeed a remarkable woman, and her dedication to Islam was phenomenal in his eyes. How many people were willing to risk loss of family and close friends to live as they believed? How many fewer were strong enough to overcome the inevitable pride when faced with the decision to give up what they always thought true? How many women could be dressed like an American one day and be fully covered in Islamic garb the next? How many fewer would be willing to announce their new commitment publicly to a class full of peers who had known them as their equal only a day before?

It was Sulayman who felt overcome with gratefulness to have Tamika as a wife, and he wanted nothing more than for her to understand how much she meant to him. He didn't deserve someone as phenomenal as she, but he could only hope for Allah's mercy in embarking upon such an honorable role.

Sulayman felt his body grow weak in exhaustion. His eyes grew heavy, and he blinked repeatedly, his restlessness now gone. He turned and entered the hall to see if Tamika had finished. The house was peaceful in its quietness, and as he neared the bathroom, he slowed his steps. He thought he heard a sound coming from the door. He approached slower to listen intently as the sweetness of the soft sound seemed to grow with each step.

Light glowed in a thin slit beneath the door, and the engaging sound escaped from there and grew louder as Tamika's confidence in her words grew. Sulayman stopped next to the door and decided against knocking. He grinned as he realized the source of the sweet sound. He stood enjoying his wife's melodious singing, as she was unaware of her audience as she dressed. Sulayman stood captivated by the beautiful sound of her voice and wished she would never stop. It was the first time he heard her sing, and the meaning of the words were so moving that he imagined what they meant.

"...Each day I wake, and it's the same as before
And I can't help wondering if there is any more
Is there anything else after this, I want to know
Because if it is, Lord, I want to go
So many love life, but I can't say the same
Because it hurts too much, oh the pain
The questions I have no one can tell me for sure
So I can't help wondering if there's any more
Any more to life than this, the questions, the tears
So please, I want something else, no more fears
There must be something else, I need to know
Because if it is, Lord, please, please, I want to goooooo."

The singing stopped, and he stood mesmerized as he reflected on how the words were as if his own at seventeen years old, when he was searching for meaning as he was suffocated by life. He wondered what life experience had inspired them and what she had suffered before she wrote the words. But he would have to wait to ask. She didn't know he was outside the door. As he lifted his hand to knock, he couldn't help pondering how the words of one with such a different past could give his life a voice.

About the Author

Umm Zakiyyah was born in 1975 in Long Island, New York, to parents who converted from Christianity to Islam after they married. She graduated in 1997 with a Bachelor of Arts degree in Elementary Education from Emory University in Atlanta, Georgia, where she was a Dean's List recipient each semester and named amongst *Who's Who* for her academic and leadership achievements.

A respected and accomplished essayist and poet, her work has been featured in *Kola Magazine, The Indianapolis Recorder,* and numerous collegiate publications. She has appeared on radio shows throughout the US and Canada and has served as keynote speaker and guest lecturer throughout the United States. Currently, she is named among *Who's Who in America.*

A Voice is Umm Zakiyyah's second novel, the sequel to the internationally acclaimed *If I Should Speak.* Of the first book, she explains, "I've always loved writing, and, with this book, I wanted to take the reader into the lives of people whose struggles often go unheard. I was inspired by my own spirituality and witnessing the impact religion has in people's lives."

For information on her latest titles, visit the publisher's website at www.al-walaa.com or write to alwalaapublications@yahoo.com.

Printed in the United Kingdom
by Lightning Source UK Ltd.
106944UKS00001B/59